I0740248

THE FORTRESS OF CHAOS

Starhawke Rising Book Eight

AUDREY SHARPE

Ocean Dance Press

THE FORTRESS OF CHAOS

© 2025 Audrey Sharpe

ISBN: 978-1-63803-983-9

Ocean Dance Press, LLC

PO Box 69901

Oro Valley AZ 85737

Visit the author's website at:

AudreySharpe.com

Want more interstellar adventures? Check out these other titles in the Starhawke Universe.

Starhawke Rising

The Dark of Light

The Chains of Freedom

The Honor of Deceit

The Legacy of Tomorrow

The Siege of Alliance

The Exile of Justice

The Rebels of Betrayal

The Fortress of Chaos

Starhawke Rogue

Arch Allies

Marked Mercenaries

Resurgent Renegades

Starhawke Romance

Guardian Mate

For the Love of Beauty

AUTHOR'S NOTE

I always write to music, and I select a different piece of music for each story, one that feeds the mood I need to get the words flowing. If you'd like to experience this story the way I did, listen to the soundtrack for *Shazam! Fury of the Gods* while you read.

One

"I remember when my biggest concern was keeping everyone from learning the secret of my shielding ability."

Aurora Hawke sighed wistfully as she stared at the *Starhawke*'s bridgescreen. The diamond-studded velvet black backdrop of the starfield framed *Phoenix* and *Vengeance*, Nat's red and gold passenger freighter and Isin's gunmetal grey warship. "At the time, I didn't appreciate how straightforward my problems were." She turned to Cade Ellis, seated at the *Starhawke*'s navigation console. "Things haven't exactly gone the way we'd hoped."

The look in his green eyes reflected the same frustration that was twisting knots in her belly. "That's putting it mildly."

The *Starhawke* had been in low-power mode until an hour ago, a result of the power drains the ship had sustained during the confrontations with Devries' ships. The same battle had left *Phoenix* with a hole ripped in its hull. The memory of that moment still haunted Aurora.

According to Unity, who had partially integrated with *Phoenix*, Nat's and Isin's crews were working overtime to repair the damage. Unity was providing invisible help, as were the camouflaged Yruf ships parked all around the four-ship cluster that included the *Starhawke* and *Gladiator*. Ifel, the Yruf leader, wasn't taking any chances that the *Starhawke* or *Phoenix* would suffer any more damage.

For once in her life, Aurora didn't balk at being coddled. Right now, her beautiful, amazing ship was weak and vulnerable. Jonarel had a list of repairs that needed attention, but those issues were minor compared to the severe power drain. They couldn't use camouflage or weapons, and it would be weeks before the ship's systems were fully charged.

Which made her current situation intolerable. "I hate thinking of the *Argo* in the clutches of Veracruz and the Teeli consuls while we're stuck here."

"I know."

The disturbing message Unity had delivered from Commander Huang Liying, *Argo*'s current first officer, had painted an uncomfortably vivid picture.

Commander Huang had been caught in the fallout after Knox Schreiber, *Argo*'s former captain, had helped his father and Aurora escape from Seaview Detention Center. With the *Argo*'s captain's chair vacant, Admiral Nixon, the new head of the Galactic Fleet, had saddled Huang with an authoritarian captain, Veracruz, and four Teeli consuls.

Officially, the Teeli were there to make sure additional traitors to the Union hadn't infiltrated *Argo*'s crew. In reality, they were using their manipulative abilities to turn the crew into mindless drones under Teeli control.

Under the Sovereign's control.

The response Huang had sent to Knox's letter had been circumspect in the wording, but reading between the lines made it clear that she was one of the few who had not fallen to the Teeli's influence.

As if having Veracruz as her commanding officer wasn't bad enough. She was also an island in a sea of zombies.

And that was only the first piece of bad news they'd received today. The *really* bad news had come from Isabeau Magee.

Dominion.

The Sovereign's terrifying plan had a name.

Isabeau had laid out the steps in disturbing detail. The Sovereign's first move involved her minions taking control of the Galactic Fleet and the Galactic Council. She'd already achieved a partial victory by turning Aurora and Admiral Schreiber into fugitives and installing Admiral Nixon as the Fleet Director. Nixon had ordered unmerited personnel changes on many Fleet ships, particularly the powerful cruisers, putting people in positions of power who had a history of disciplinary actions and emotional issues. Perfect victims for the Teeli.

But that was only the beginning.

The next step was militarizing the Fleet and usurping the authority of the Federal Coalition. With the Fleet steadily falling under Teeli control, the Feds wouldn't stand a chance. All it would take is for the Discovery-class cruisers to park in orbit over the most populated planets, weapons locked on the cities below, and the Feds would have no choice but to back down. All Union citizens would be subjugated.

And once Fleet space was on lockdown, the Teeli could move in with their armada, establishing a stronghold and launching an attack on the Kraed, the only remaining fleet capable of standing in opposition to the tornado of destruction battering the Union.

That is, if Siginal Clarek, Jonarel's father and leader of the Kraed fleet, could convince the other Kraed clan leaders to join the fight before the situation got out of control. He was on his way to Drakar right now to do just that. But it would not be an easy task.

Despite their imposing appearance, the Kraed were not a war-like species. Biologically they could be lethal, having developed vicious claws concealed under the soft tissue of their hands and feet which protected them from the large predators on their planet. But culturally, they despised aggression and the concept of war. It went against their conservationist ideals. They didn't believe in conquering others.

That fact didn't stop her from thinking of them as warriors. Their almost oppressively protective behavior made it difficult to think of them as anything else. But they would never be the instigators of a violent conflict.

Which is one reason Siginal had pushed so hard for Aurora to become Jonarel's mate. Because she was the leader of the Suulh, a pair bond with Jonarel would have instantly made all Suulh a part of the Kraed clan system. It would have given the clan leaders a reason to venture into Teeli space to help the Suulh being held captive on the Suulh homeworld of Feylahn.

But fate had other plans.

And so did Aurora. She'd rejected Jonarel's offer to pair bond, blowing Siginal's original scheme into space dust.

It was the best decision she'd ever made. Jonarel belonged with Lelindia. Unfortunately, the Kraed's narrow view of leadership didn't accept Lelindia's role as the Nedale in the same light as Aurora's as the Sahzade. Their mating hadn't bound the Kraed to the Suulh.

However, the impending arrival of Raehn Clarek, Jonarel and Lelindia's Kraed-Suulh baby, might convince the other clan leaders of their error. If that happened, the Kraed would extend their protective stance to include the Suulh.

And the balance of power would start to shift in their favor.

Cade leaned back in his chair. "Do you have any thoughts on how you want to proceed?"

"A lot will depend on the news we get from Siginal. And from the Kraed ships in Teeli space." Siginal had sent several of his clan's ships to track down the Teeli fleet's base of operations and gather intel on their supply chain. They were also establishing a Kraed comm network that would give them a direct line to Feylahn. "I'm hoping Siginal will have an opportunity to talk to Captain Warner before Nixon decides to send Teeli consuls to *Excelsior*."

Excelsior was a Discovery-class cruiser like *Argo* and had been her first posting out of the Academy. The ship had been Lelindia's and Jonarel's first posting, too. *Excelsior* patrolled NGQ2, the northern quadrant that bordered Kraed space, which had made it easy for Siginal and Daymar to visit them during the six years they'd served onboard.

Captain Warner was a good man, and a strong leader, which is why she'd reached out to him to warn him about the danger posed by the Teeli. He hadn't replied to the message she'd sent through Unity, but he'd contacted the Kraed and asked for a meeting with a representative from Clan Clarek.

The third message Unity had tried to deliver, the one Admiral Schreiber had written to Captain Montgomery of *Cassini*, was still in limbo. Unity had reported they'd been unable to locate Captain Montgomery on the Discovery-class cruiser that patrolled SGQ4, the southern quadrant adjoining Teeli space. She was listed as on medical leave, which could mean she was already aware of the threat and had taken steps to avoid being manipulated by the Teeli, or she could be living a tortured existence as a captive of the Sovereign.

Aurora tapped her finger on the arm of her chair. "Unity, does the information you located regarding Captain Montgomery's medical leave indicate when and where she disembarked *Cassini?*"

"One moment." U-2 bobbed between her chair and Cade's. "Yes. The records indicate she was taken to the medical center at Eridani Duo about two weeks ago."

The name of the space station came out a little stilted. Unity had been using Micah's voice long enough that they no longer required him to say a word in order to reproduce it, but new words they hadn't encountered before came out sounding flat, without any natural inflection.

"Does it state the reason?"

"Just two words. *Severe trauma.*"

Her heart thumped. The odds that Montgomery had coincidentally suffered a trauma event serious enough to take her off her ship right at the time when massive personnel changes were sweeping the Fleet were near zero. "What about her medical records?"

"We'd have to infiltrate the med bay to look at those. Do you want us to do that?"

She was a little surprised they hadn't already. Then again, *Cassini* was a huge ship. Accessing specific locations in micro-form would take Unity a lot of time. Maybe they just hadn't gotten there yet. "Yes, please."

"Will do!"

A ghost of a smile touched her lips. She had the feeling she'd just said yes to a cookie for a kid with their hand already deep inside the jar.

Her focus returned to the bridgescreen. She had several items on her to do list connected with Nat and Isin to tackle next.

Tapping her console, she sent a hail to *Phoenix*.

Nat responded a couple minutes later, the image of *Phoenix*'s small bridge filling the screen. Nat was alone, seated in her customary place at navigation. A smudge on one cheek and her sweat-dampened hair indicated she'd been hard at work on the repairs to her ship.

"How's *Phoenix* coming along?" Aurora tuned into Nat's emotional resonance, which was a better gauge of the young pilot's mood than her expression.

"Steady." Nat tilted back her chair, but her nonchalance didn't mask the underlying anxiety Aurora sensed. "How's the *Starhawke*?"

"Finally out of low-power mode." She swept her hand to indicate the bridge. "Nice to have the gloom gone."

Sure enough, she sensed a ripple of guilt from Nat, though her expression didn't change. "Glad to hear it."

She really wished Nat would stop blaming herself for their current situation. "We're still looking at about three weeks for a full recharge. How are your food supplies? We've got plenty over here if you need anything." The verdant greenery in the greenhouse resembled something out of a fantasy novel. Even with twenty-two people to feed, the greenhouse was abundant thanks to all the Suulh energy swirling through it.

"We're okay for now." Nat's emotions took a positive upswing. "Marlin's got his little hydroponics area set up and he's happy as a clam growing his own herbs and greens. He still doesn't have a working galley to prepare them in, but we're getting there."

Aurora knew better than to offer her crew's help. Every time she brought it up, it triggered a new flare of guilt from Nat.

Unfortunately, thinking about all the damage to Nat's ship made Aurora's guilt flare. She'd been the one who'd unintentionally distracted Nat, causing her to miss the threat that had blown a hole in the ship's hull.

Which brought her to another important topic. "How are Mirko and Manchado doing?"

Nat snorted. "Same as always – mean and nasty. Isin and Sweep are handling the food deliveries." She smirked. "Sounds like they're both just *delightful*."

Aurora grimaced. "Sorry we saddled you with that problem."

"You didn't. Mirko's always been my problem. And those two deserve each other. I can't image more fitting cellmates for either of them."

"If that changes, let me know. I'll be contacting Isin soon to schedule a time to visit the brig. I need to talk to Mirko and Manchado myself. I'm still working on the long-term plan for what to do with them."

"Any ideas?"

"One. But it's still preliminary. And honestly, not my top priority right now."

Nat shrugged. "No rush. They're not going anywhere. And neither are we."

Truer words were never spoken. None of them would be going anywhere for a while.

Two

Failure.

Harsh light glared off the bent head of the disgraced one, casting a monstrous, misshapen shadow on the cold, hard floor of the cold, hard room.

Beyond the circle of light, the others gathered. They had been summoned. They would bear witness. They would be warned.

The task had been simple. The resources had been plentiful. And yet...

Failure.

It would not be tolerated.

The cloaked figure stepped forward.

The hiss of whispered voices ceased.

A gloved hand slid under the disgraced one's jaw, clamping on like a vise, forcing their gaze up.

Their diamond-pupils contracted in the harsh light, the yellow irises swallowing the black points.

The vise tightened, the gloved hand turning the disgraced one's head from side to side. The neck twisted far too easily.

Unnatural. Scaly.

So hideous. So *alien.*

But useful, at times. Except...

Failure.

They would be an example to them all.

The cloaked figure lifted a metal rod.

Heat radiated from the tip. Heat that would burn. Heat that would mark the disgraced one for all to see.

The disgraced one's eyes tracked the movement of the rod as the cloaked figure poised it over their head. But they did not move.

They *could* not.

That was power.

The rod made contact with the fluorescent green scales. A burning stench filled the air.

The scales turned brown, then black.

The cloaked figure drew the wand slowly – tenderly – along the disgraced one's forehead, leaving a trail of blistering destruction.

The disgraced one trembled, their alien tongue flicking rapidly like a flag flapping in a strong wind.

But still they did not move.

Could not move.

Failure.

This was the price to be paid.

The rod marked the trail over their elongated, blunted nose and across the line of their grotesque slash of a mouth.

Hideous, hideous creature.

The rod lifted again.

A hiss of fear leapt from the shadows.

Yes. Now they understood. Now they knew who commanded them.

The disgraced one was broken, marked forever.

The lesson had been learned.

Three

The explosion that echoed through the corridors on *Phoenix*'s C deck had nothing to do with an attack from the black of space. Nor did it come from a mechanical source within.

No, this explosion originated from the combustible form of an extremely ticked-off scientist.

"How could you allow Alec to interact with an *unknown lifeform!*"

Nat held back a wince at the volume Dr. Darsha Patel achieved, her words streaking across *Phoenix*'s cozy wine bar into the empty corridors beyond. But the attack wasn't just directed at her. Isin, Itorye, and Gavin, Patel's research assistant, were also in the blast radius.

At least there was no one else onboard who would overhear Patel's screech. Isin and Itorye had made sure the members of *Vengeance*'s crew who'd been working all day on the restoration of *Phoenix*'s galley and dining hall had returned to the warship. Pete, *Phoenix*'s engineer, had already met Unity, and Marlin, the ship's cook, was down in the shuttle bay.

"Unity isn't a threat to Alec." Itorye spoke with remarkable composure considering the bomb she'd just dropped on her lover.

"You can't know that!" Patel snapped, slamming her wine glass down on the side table between them, the ruby liquid sloshing over the rim. "How were they created? What's their purpose? What threats do they pose to Alec's stability?" Her chest rose and fell with her rapid breathing.

"Alec's not in danger, Darsha." Gavin shifted forward in his chair, resting his elbows on his knees. "I've been monitoring Unity's interactions with Alec ever since I was made aware of their existence. They're fine."

"You *knew!*" Patel looked like she was considering hurling the glass at him. "Why didn't you tell me!"

"Because," Nat muttered, "we had this crazy idea you might not take it well. Good thing we were wrong," she added with a fake smile.

Patel's gaze drilled into her, her upper lip curling. "You had no right!"

Okay, that pushed her hot button. "I have *every* right. This is *my* ship."

"And I have compensated you—"

"This isn't about money," she snapped. "It's about Alec. He's the one who made the decision to meet Unity."

Patel's mouth hinged open. She clicked it shut. "Alec is too young to be making decisions of that magnitude."

"I'm an adult, Mom."

Her gaze shot to where Alec's projection stood beside her chair. "With the life experience of a child. You're not ready."

"Shouldn't Alec be the one to decide that?" Gavin asked gently.

"Would you let a child who can't swim decide whether to leap into the ocean?" she shot back.

"Mom..." Alec sounded like he was clenching his teeth. Which was impressive since he didn't have actual teeth. Or a jaw. "I'm not an innocent. Or ignorant."

"You're still—"

"I also trust Nat," Alec spoke over her. "She'd already met Unity and liked them. But I could have said no. I could have told Unity I didn't want to interact with them. They would have respected my wishes."

"We would never harm Alec," Unity said over the ship's speakers.

Patel jerked her gaze to the ceiling, her fingers digging into the padding of her chair. "You can *talk*?"

"Of course. We're sorry if we frightened you."

Patel didn't look frightened. She looked terrified. But not for herself. "Alec..."

The pained plea peeled away a few of the layers of irritation that usually kept Nat from empathizing with Patel. The woman enjoyed testing her patience, but right now, she was just trying to protect her son.

"Unity's my friend, Mom." Alec crouched beside her chair. "We understand each other. We *like* each other. I know they wouldn't harm me. In fact, they've done everything they can to keep me and this ship safe from harm."

Patel's throat moved as she swallowed. Nat noticed a tremor in her hands as she clutched them in her lap. "But you don't know where they came from. Who created them."

That wasn't true. But Patel didn't know that. They'd all agreed not to share their knowledge of the Yruf with her. Telling Patel about Unity had become a necessity as her anger and paranoia for Alec's safety had grown exponentially in the past few days. The risk of exposure was minimal because she couldn't reveal Unity's existence to anyone who didn't already know without putting Alec in danger, too.

But she wouldn't have the same motivation regarding the secret of the Yruf.

Nat gave the answer she and Unity had agreed on. "Unity came from the *Starhawke*."

Patel's eyes widened briefly, before narrowing to slits. "They're a Fleet design?"

"No. The Fleet has no idea they exist, and we need to keep it that way. Unity would be in the same danger as Alec."

That took some of the wind out of Patel's sails. "Their creation wasn't authorized by the Galactic Council?"

Nat shook her head. "Unity took a personal risk coming to *Phoenix*, but they wanted to help us. They're trusting us not to reveal their presence."

Patel mulled that over before picking up her glass and taking a sip of her wine. She tipped her head toward the ceiling. "Unity?"

"Yes, Dr. Patel?"

"Is the person who created you on the *Starhawke*?"

Here it came. Patel was going to try to drill down to the source. Unity would need to do some fancy footwork to evade.

"No."

"Are they on the shadow ships?"

"No."

Or just answer in one syllable. That worked, too.

Patel's expression turned stony, but fire flared in her dark eyes. "You're telling me your creator allowed you to travel into a dangerous situation *alone*, where they couldn't protect you?"

No need to ask how Patel felt about that idea.

Unity was silent for a moment. "We are always protected. We were designed that way."

Patel's forehead puckered. "What do you mean?"

"We are we. A multitude. We are here, with you, but we are elsewhere, too. We exist as one and many."

"Aptly named," Itorye murmured.

Patel shot her a condescending look. "This doesn't bother you?" She gestured between Alec and the ceiling speaker.

"No." Itorye swiveled her chair so she was facing Patel. "Look at the facts, Darsha. The behaviors. Objectively. Look at everything Aurora's crew has done and the way Unity chose to interact with Alec.

The focus has always been on protecting and helping, not hurting. They saved those kids when it would have been easier to hide and let Devries get away. They made sure Mirko's crew got off *Sphinx* safely, putting themselves at risk to do it. Far from being a threat, Unity could be the best protection Alec has ever had."

Point, Itorye.

"I agree." Gavin nodded. "Unity is very protective. And I've never seen Alec happier. He's thriving, Darsha, in ways you and I only dreamed of during his creation."

Nat could see the wheels turning in Patel's head. She could also see the stubborn resistance that characterized everything Patel did. The woman hated it when Alec, Gavin, or Itorye sided against her. Having all three of them on the opposite side of the argument was making her gears grind together.

Patel gave an annoyed sniff, her gaze rising to the ceiling again. "Unity, would you protect Alec if he was threatened?"

"Absolutely."

"Would you expect him to protect you in return?"

"We wouldn't need him to, but he might try to, anyway. That's what friends do. They look out for each other."

Alec's soft smile warmed Nat's heart.

Patel didn't seem to notice Alec's reaction, her focus still on Unity. "Who created you?" she demanded.

Nat tensed.

Unity handled the question with ease. "That's not our secret to tell."

"Who is on the shadow ships?"

"That's also not our secret to tell."

Patel's lips pressed together. Swirling her wine, she took a large fortifying gulp, polishing it off before setting it on the table. "Do the people on the shadow ships pose any threat to Alec?"

"Never. They will protect him just as we do."

Patel stilled, her gaze darting around the circle in sharp accusation, landing on Itorye. "They know about Alec?"

Unity answered before Itorye could. "Yes. His secret is safe with them."

"How can you be sure?"

"Because they protect us. They would never wish harm to come to Alec. To any of you."

"What about blackmail?"

Isin's dark brows lifted at that, the first reaction he'd given since the conversation started.

"What do you mean?" Unity was clearly confused.

"What's to prevent them from using their knowledge of Alec's existence to blackmail me? Force me to give them money or work for them for free?"

"They would never do that!" Unity was well and truly offended.

"They could—"

"Darsha." Itorye rested a hand on Patel's knee. "That's never going to happen."

Patel was still spitting fire. "How can you say that? You don't know."

"Yes, I do. I also know you're not used to trusting people. That your reaction stems from your concern for Alec. But you've said you trust me. And Gavin. And we trust Nat and Isin. None of us would have put Alec at risk. Or you. You don't have to be afraid."

Patel blew out an exasperated breath. "Who *are* these people?"

"Friends," Unity answered simply.

Patel shot a sour look at the ceiling, but didn't comment.

Nat would take that as a win. She pushed out of her chair, her gaze meeting Isin's. "I'm going to check how Marlin's coming along with dinner."

Isin stood. "I'll go with you."

Leaving Itorye, Gavin, and Alec to handle the disgruntled Patel, Nat and Isin strode to the forward stairwell and headed down.

"That went better than I'd expected," Isin commented when they reached the corridor on D deck. "Though I didn't anticipate the blackmail question."

"Me, neither. Leave it to Patel to come up with a worst-case scenario."

"She does excel at that."

"Speaking of worst-case scenarios, how are Mirko and Manchado doing in the brig? Aurora was asking about them."

The corners of Isin's mouth tightened. "I didn't think I could dislike anyone as much as Mirko, but Manchado is making me a believer. Sweep and I have a running bet about which of them will spew the most verbal abuse each visit. Sweep's currently ahead because in the beginning I foolishly kept picking Mirko to win."

Nat's laugh lacked humor. "They think abusing their captors is the best way to earn their freedom?" She shook her head. "Some people never learn."

Isin's arm slipped around her waist, pulling her to a halt.

"And some people do," he murmured, cradling her cheek in his palm and lowering his head.

The brush of his full lips over hers sent tingles all the way to her toes.

"Yes, they do," she replied, looking into the gold-flecked depths of his brown eyes.

Mirko's return had tested her faith in him, almost driving a permanent wedge between them. If Isin had continued his course of action, seeking revenge on their former employer without considering how it was destroying the goodness within him in the process, they wouldn't be standing here now.

He placed a kiss on the tip of her nose before releasing her. "How much longer is Marlin going to be cooking on *Gypsy's* small stove?"

"Not sure," she replied as they continued down the corridor. "A week, maybe? Shash got all the primary electrical done in the galley, as well as the repairs to the damaged stove and oven, but she's still generating parts for the new cold storage unit that she's building from scratch. If we didn't have *Vengeance*'s parts generator, that wouldn't even be possible. Yours can handle much bigger jobs than ours."

"Happy to help."

"Marlin was holding off on the plumbing repairs until Shash finished the electrical. He needs to lay new pipes and install the refurbished sink that got hit by debris in the explosion. Kenji did the repair work on that one." Isin's gunner would have probably done any task Marlin gave him, but with his tall, muscular physique, he'd been well suited to pounding out the dents in the industrial sink.

"And Marlin still prefers using *Gypsy*'s tiny stove rather than making use of *Vengeance*'s galley?"

"It's not the galley so much as the ship." She chose her words carefully, not wanting to disparage his warship. "He's never said anything to me about it, but I suspect *Vengeance*'s more utilitarian design reminds him too much of Tnaryt's ship."

Isin shot her a sidelong look as they descended the stairs into the bay. "Does it remind *you* of Tnaryt's ship?"

"No. I like *Vengeance*." Even after she'd suffered some not-so-pleasant moments onboard. The ship suited Isin, just as *Phoenix* suited her. "But I had a lot more freedom on Tnaryt's ship than Marlin did. He was trapped in the galley. The only time he could move around was when he brought food to the bridge. And that was a mixed blessing at best."

A dull echo of guilt reverberated in her chest at the memory. She'd been responsible for his incarceration, and while Marlin had forgiven her, she still hadn't completely forgiven herself.

Which is why she'd do anything to make Marlin happy, including letting him set up temporarily in *Gypsy*, her beloved shuttle, until *Phoenix*'s galley was fully functional again.

Gypsy sat in the middle of the small bay, her back hatch lowered to the deck. The heady aroma of cooked onions and garlic greeted them as Nat and Isin stepped onto the ramp. "Marlin?"

He poked his head around a stack of refrigerated storage crates. Aurora had loaned them to him from the *Starhawke* during their last visit to keep the produce fresh that she'd given him from the greenhouse.

Marlin's receding mop of curly brown-grey hair looked recently trimmed. "Hey, Nat, Isin. Dinner is almost ready."

"Smells good." She leaned her shoulder against the crate stack. "Did you get a haircut?"

A slight flush darkened his ruddy skin. "Yeah. Lupe offered when they came over to visit Gavin."

Ah. She should have guessed. Lupe, aka Sparki to *Vengeance*'s crew, was *Vengeance*'s new pilot and Gavin's childhood friend. They had a flair for hair and makeup, changing their look with wigs and colored contacts on a nearly daily basis. "It looks good."

"Um, thanks." Marlin wasn't the type to put much thought into his appearance – a trait Nat could relate to – which is why pointing out the change had made him blush.

Putting on oven mitts, he opened the door to the compact oven under the stovetop and pulled out a bubbling casserole.

The delightful smells surrounded her, making her stomach rumble in anticipation. She breathed in deeply. "Have I told you recently how glad I am you're *Phoenix's* cook?"

Marlin chuckled, setting the pan into a portable warming container at his feet before reaching into the oven for its twin. "That's your stomach talking."

"Yep. And it's very happy not to be consuming pre-packaged nutrient bars or whatever mediocre foodstuffs I could scrape together."

"I concur," Isin agreed. "You're the only person on both ships who can make food we all look forward to eating."

Marlin's skin reddened a bit more, but a smile creased his cheeks. "Just wait until the galley's functional again. I've got a feast planned." He glanced at Nat. "And I was thinking we should invite Aurora's crew to join us."

Her heart gave a hard thump. "Um, yeah, I guess that would be okay." Although the adrenaline-induced pounding in her chest indicated his suggestion had taken her by surprise.

When she'd first reunited with Aurora, she'd been eager to show off her ship, to prove to the *Starhawke*'s captain that she'd made good on the chance she'd given her. The only thing that had held her back was Alec's presence and the seriousness of Aurora's situation as a fugitive. A tour hadn't seemed wise or appropriate.

But Aurora knew about Alec now, and her crew would have free time while they waited for their ship to recharge. Inviting Aurora to *Phoenix* for a meal was the least she could do after all the trouble she'd caused her recently. "How long until you'll be ready?"

Marlin pulled off the oven mitts, tucking them in a drawer. "Shash did all her safety checks today, so I'll be able to get in there tomorrow while she starts assembling the new cold storage unit. After I finish the plumbing, we'll need to do the flooring and cabinet repairs, and give everything a good scrub down. Oh, and transfer all the produce we're storing here and on *Vengeance* to the new unit."

"So, about a week?"

"At most. But since we lost all but two of the tables in the dining room in the explosion, we don't have a great setup for seating a large number of people."

True. The dining room looked more like a ballroom at the moment. "I guess we could use the lounge. Assuming Aurora's even interested in seeing *Phoenix*."

Isin gave her an assessing look. "Why wouldn't she?"

Nat shrugged. "She has a lot of issues she's still dealing with." Like being hunted by the Fleet. And stopping the Sovereign.

And figuring out what they were going to do with Mirko and Manchado.

"Issues that won't be solved until after her ship is recharged," Isin countered. "She has time."

"Okay, then we'll plan on it." Which brought up another point. "Once *Phoenix* is fully functional, we should snag whatever Mirko left at the Birdbolt." Her former employer's secret cache of supplies located on one of the system's rocky planetesimals might have something worth keeping. Or selling.

Isin folded his arms over his chest. "Why wait? We can use the *Dagger*. In fact, we should make a salvage run to *Sphinx* first. Pull off anything of value."

Using the *Dagger* hadn't occurred to her. She was used to everything involving Mirko being tied to her. But Isin's fighter was smaller and more maneuverable than *Phoenix* and could attach to an airlock, unlike *Gypsy*, who needed a pressurized bay to land in. "Would Kenji want to come with us to *Sphinx*?" He was the one who typically flew the *Dagger*. She'd flown the ship once, but those had been disturbing circumstances she didn't want to dwell on.

"I'm sure he would. Sweep, too."

"What about Hobbes, Omondi, and Adel?" They were all that remained of Mirko's crew. She still hadn't heard the story of how they'd ended up in their ramshackle state, but since she'd never considered any of *Sphinx*'s crew friends, sitting down for a chat hadn't been on her to-do list. Besides, from what she'd heard, Itorye was keeping the trio busy on *Vengeance*.

"Do you want to bring them?" Isin asked.

"Not really."

"Then let's not. They already took whatever they cared about when Cade's team rescued them."

She glanced at Marlin. "Are you okay being in charge of *Phoenix* while we're gone?"

"Sure. If anything comes up, I'll alert Itorye."

"Not Shash?" Nat teased. *Vengeance*'s engineer was only slightly less surly with Marlin than she was with Nat. Shash considered him guilty by association, although that attitude didn't extend to Pete.

Marlin gave her a flat look. "No. But you could bring me back anything useful from *Sphinx*'s galley."

Nat shook her head. "Don't get your hopes up. *Sphinx*'s galley isn't much bigger than *Gypsy*'s setup and most of the cookware was older than the ship."

"I can vouch for that," Isin agreed. "We all had to fend for ourselves. It wasn't pretty."

Marlin grimaced. "Then never mind."

Four

"Oof!"

The kick of a tiny foot jolted Lelindia out of a deep sleep. Her hands dropped to the swell of her abdomen, her energy field engaging.

"Lelindia?"

Jonarel's deep voice rumbled against her back, the hand that had been resting on her hip sliding to cover her hands. "What is wrong?"

The concern in his voice drew her gaze over her shoulder. His dark brows and the corners of his mouth were weighted down by worry. Despite her best efforts, she hadn't been able to banish his ever-present anxiety regarding her wellbeing and their daughter's. "Raehn decided it was time to get up."

The weights pulled harder, his large body wrapping around her like a shield. "Is she unwell?"

She shook her head. "Quite the opposite. She decided sleep time was over and playtime should begin."

The tension in his body ebbed, his embrace shifting from protective to tender. "She is energetic."

Lelindia chuckled. "In every way. Unlike her mommy, she's going to be a morning person."

She'd trained herself to rise quickly at any hour — a necessary skill for a Fleet doctor — but given a choice, she preferred a slower pace to her mornings. "She's taking after her daddy." She nudged him with her shoulder. "I'll bet you were the kind of kid who leapt out of bed at the crack of dawn and raced outside." Since they'd combined their quarters, he'd shown no tendency for sleeping in, unless it meant cuddling with her.

His golden eyes sparkled. "Perhaps."

"Good. Then after she's born, you can be on the morning shift, and I'll take the evening shift."

"I would gladly take every shift."

How did he keep finding ways to make her love him even more? "So would I, if it meant the three of us were together." Her throat tightened, moisture pushing at the backs of her eyes. Her emotions hovered a lot closer to the surface ever since she'd gotten pregnant. "I love you both so much."

His arm tightened around her, his head lowering so he could nuzzle her neck. "As do I, checana."

His lips set off sparks everywhere they touched, spreading warmth through her body.

Raehn kicked again.

"Hey! Can't you give mommy a little time to have some fun?"

Kick-kick was her answer.

"Guess not."

Jonarel's chuckle elicited one of her own.

"Oh, sure, you laugh now," she warned him. "Just wait. She's likely to wreak havoc on our sex life."

He caught her earlobe between his teeth, making her breath hitch. "You forget," he murmured in her ear, "there are many onboard who would willingly care for Raehn so we may have time alone."

His words sent a delicious shiver through her body. "I'll keep that in mind."

He captured her mouth in a lingering kiss. "I will remind you."

"Please do."

His deep laugh vibrated through her. She loved that sound, and the radiant joy that came with it.

Slipping out of their cozy nook with feline grace, he pulled on a pair of lounge pants. "I will make our morning tea."

"Thank you." She watched the interplay of muscles in his broad shoulders and sculpted chest as he moved. The thin tendrils of brown against the rich green of his skin formed a beautiful map she'd explored many times. At moments like this, she still had the urge to pinch herself to ensure she wasn't dreaming.

"Lelindia?"

His low growl lifted her gaze to his face. His golden eyes glowed with simmering heat.

"Sorry. Just admiring the view."

"As am I." The heat flared for a moment, his gaze sliding over her bare shoulders and the swell of her breasts, but he visibly contained himself before turning away.

She enjoyed the view of his firm backside as he padded out of the bedroom. No doubt about it. Her mate was gorgeous. And he was all hers.

An internal wriggle made her glance back at her belly. "You're eager to meet your daddy, aren't you?" she murmured, knowing Jonarel would be able to hear her through the archway leading to the front room. He'd warned her after he'd merged their two cabins into one that he would be able to hear anything that happened within their walls. However, he'd also told her he respected her privacy and would intentionally ignore anything he thought she wouldn't want him to hear.

That's when she'd realized why most of the rooms on the *Starhawke* were soundproofed. For a race with exceptional hearing, soundproofing would be a way to ease the continual sensory bombardment.

She ran her hand over her abdomen, using her Nedale gifts to gaze at her daughter's precious little body. "You're going to love your daddy so much, Raehn. And he's going to dote on you." Of that, she had no doubt. Jonarel would be an exceptional father. He would delight in teaching Raehn anything she wanted to learn — about science and engineering, about her clan and her heritage, about how to make the most of her Kraed physiology.

How much of his physiology she would inherit was still unclear. She'd have claws in her hands and feet just like Jonarel. Lelindia could already see that. But whether she'd have his same skin tones and eye color, or the ability to change her coloring as the Kraed did, was a big question mark.

One thing that wasn't in question was the little Nedale's ability to generate a Suulh energy field. Even now, little ribbons of emerald-green danced around Lelindia's hands in joyful abandon.

Manifesting a field in the womb was very rare. Lelindia's mom had confirmed that. Raehn's dual-race origins might have something to do with her abilities. After all, Aurora was dual race, too, and she'd been born with extraordinary power.

Raehn's next kick bumped against Lelindia's hands. "Okay, okay, I'm getting up." Stifling a yawn, she slid out of bed with a lot less grace than Jonarel, reaching for the lounge pants and loose top she'd worn the previous day. Since she expected her pregnancy to last only another month, she'd been reluctant to alter any of her clothing to accommodate her expanding waistline. Instead, she'd been relying on pants with elastic or drawstring waistbands and more boxy-fitting tops. But she'd also picked up a few maternity outfits at Sol Station while the *Starhawke* had been docked there during the Admiral's trial. She'd tucked them in her closet just in case she ended up needing them.

Running her fingers through her hair to comb out the sleep tangles, she made a quick stop at the bathroom. When she walked into the front room, Jonarel was cutting slices of the zucchini bread her dad had baked the previous day.

Her stomach gurgled in anticipation as he handed her a plate with two thick slices on it. She lifted it to her nose, taking an appreciative sniff. "It's such a treat to be able to enjoy my dad's baking on a regular basis again." It was one of the things she'd missed most since leaving home.

But her definition of *home* had changed radically in the past few months. Mating with Jonarel had made the *Starhawke* home in a way she'd never anticipated. He'd designed and built this ship, and his sister Tehar inhabited it. Why would she want to live anywhere else?

Having her parents onboard was a gift, despite the harrowing circumstances that had brought them here. And they seemed thrilled to be with her. She had trouble picturing them ever leaving, especially once Raehn officially joined the family.

"Do you have a lot to do today?" she asked Jonarel, settling into a chair at their small table as he brought over their mugs of tea.

"Yes." His knee brushed hers under the table. "But with power still limited, it will likely be another week before we can run tests on the new components and restore primary systems."

She could see the tension in his jaw and hear the frustration in his voice. "How's Tehar?"

"I am better." Jonarel's sister appeared beside the table, her hands folded in front of her, a tender look in her honey-colored eyes.

"Tehar!" She started to stand before she remembered she couldn't hug Tehar's projection. She settled for grinning at her. She hadn't realized how much she enjoyed seeing Tehar until her projection was conspicuously absent during the stretch of time the ship was in low-power mode. "Welcome back."

"Thank you. It feels good to have the freedom of this form again."

Lelindia nodded. "It must have been debilitating, almost like an illness, not to have the power you needed."

"Indeed. I would prefer not to experience such a shortage again."

Guilt flitted across Jonarel's face, his gaze dropping to the tabletop.

Tehar made a *tsking* noise. "Do not blame yourself, brother. There are limits to what even our clan's technology can achieve."

Jonarel grumbled something in the Kraed language that Lelindia didn't understand, his mouth twisting in a grimace.

The admonishing look Tehar shot him looked so much like Daymar, their mother, that Lelindia smiled. "He's blaming himself, isn't he?"

"Yes." Tehar crossed her arms. "He mistakenly believes he should be able to plan for all contingencies, regardless of the number of unknown variables in the equation."

Lelindia's smile widened. "That's gonna be a real challenge after Raehn's born. Children are the living, breathing definition of unknown variables, and she'll have even more than most."

Tehar's eyes glimmered with amusement. "Then Raehn can be the one to teach him that particular lesson."

The confounded look on Jonarel's face made Lelindia laugh. "I'm sure she will."

Five

"Are you going with Mirko or Manchado to win this time?" Isin asked Sweep as they carried two trays of food up the stairs to where *Vengeance*'s brig was housed on A deck.

The lines on Sweep's face deepened in thought. "Mirko put in a good performance of histrionics last night, but my money is on Manchado. He's grouchy in the morning."

"As opposed to the rest of the time?"

"Grouchier," Sweep amended.

"Fine. But I'm calling Manchado for midday."

"Deal."

The hinges on the brig hatch screeched in protest as Isin swung it open, announcing their arrival. Not half a second later, profanity that would make a mercenary blush spewed from the two cells on opposite sides of the octagonal room.

"Do you think they know we're betting on them?" Sweep murmured under his breath.

Isin grunted. He doubted either of them had the self-awareness for that kind of insight. However, they might be entertaining themselves. Abusing others was their favorite game. They each had a steel rod of entitlement running through them that never bent, no matter their circumstances. Even being stuck in a brig at the mercy of their captors hadn't changed their attitudes.

Every time he and Sweep delivered meals, Isin was tempted to show their prisoners exactly why they should be more respectful. But he wouldn't. He'd promised Natasha and Aurora, and he wouldn't betray their trust.

Sweep wouldn't allow him to anyway. He had a hard line regarding the treatment of prisoners in *Vengeance*'s brig, having been one himself when they were both living under the hand of a cruel and vindictive captain.

"You bringing me anything edible this time, you worthless slug?" Manchado snarled as Isin approached his cell. He and Sweep had agreed early on that Isin shouldn't be the one delivering food to Mirko's cell. Too much temptation and too easy to rile her up.

The tilt to Isin's lips was not a smile. "Seasoned it with arsenic myself."

Manchado took an involuntary step back, which almost generated a real smile as Isin knelt by the food slot and slid the tray inside the cell.

"He's lying," Mirko called out from her cell. "He doesn't have the balls to poison someone."

Isin sat on his haunches, slowly turning his head to face her. "Do you want to test that theory?"

The ice in his voice made her swallow. But she recovered quickly. "I know you, Isin. You're all talk, no action."

The impulse to show her just how wrong she was fired through his veins, but instead he tipped his head, studying her with his best dead-eyed look. "And yet I'm out here, in control of this warship, and you're in there, with your freighter in pieces. Coincidence?"

Her skin flushed an unattractive mottled red. She ignored the food tray Sweep had delivered, her hands wrapping around the bars of her cell. "That scar on your face doesn't make you tough. It makes you ugly."

"A mortal wound," he deadpanned. "How will I ever survive?"

Sweep's muffled snort was its own reward.

So was the purple tinge to Mirko's face... until she opened her mouth. "No wonder that tramp pilot's the only one who will screw you."

He crossed the distance in the blink of an eye. Sweep's hand latched onto his shoulder at the same moment Isin's palm circled Mirko's throat. "Say whatever you want about me," he whispered, his fingers applying pressure to her trachea, "but do *not* speak ill of Natasha. Understand?"

Mirko's eyes widened, her hands pulling ineffectively at his fingers as she wheezed.

Sweep's fingers dug into his shoulder in silent warning.

"You did tell me once that you wanted my hands on you." He waited until fear leapt in Mirko's eyes before he released her. "Consider your wish granted."

She stumbled away from the bars, rubbing her throat, fear and rage contorting her face.

Isin turned toward the hatch, catching sight of Manchado watching them with avid interest. He stared him down until Manchado lowered his gaze.

Sweep followed him out of the brig, the hatch groaning shut behind them. After activating the lock, Sweep turned, folding his arms over his chest.

Isin deserved the reproach on his friend's face.

"I know your history with Mirko is complicated. And you're very protective of Nat. But that wasn't acceptable."

Sweep was one of two people on *Vengeance* with the right to say something like that to him. Itorye was the second. Taking a deep breath, he stared at the closed hatch, etching the metal with his gaze. "I know." But his insides boiled every time he thought about the way Mirko had used and abused Natasha and tossed her aside like trash.

"Do I need to have Itorye do these runs with me?"

Isin flinched. It would probably be the smart move. But it would prove he couldn't handle his emotions around Mirko. He couldn't live with that. "No. I'll talk to Natasha about what happened. She'll get my head on straight."

A closed-mouth smile softened Sweep's strong features. "Good call." Then his gaze snapped to the stairwell.

Isin knew who was lurking there without asking. Only one person onboard would slink up to A deck without permission. "Come on out, Lyon."

A slight shuffle of feet on the metal steps indicated Lyon was considering the wisdom of retreating instead, but a moment later the youth stepped into view.

His dark eyes held equal measures of defiance and respect as he glared at them like they were the ones in the wrong. "What are you doing up here?" he demanded.

Isin suppressed the involuntary twitch of his lips. The kid had courage. Or a death wish. He and Itorye were still debating that one. "That's my line."

Lyon shifted his weight. "Who're you bringing food to up here?"

"That's not your business."

"You torturing people?"

Ah. That's why he was here. The streak of fear that dashed over Lyon's face filled in the blanks. The kid's background was mostly a void, but clearly being tormented by people bigger and stronger than him had been a large part of it.

"No," Sweep answered softly. "That's not acceptable behavior on this ship."

Isin caught the subtle rebuke in that statement, but it wasn't aimed at Lyon. He'd get more of the same when he told Natasha about the incident with Mirko. And he deserved it.

"That true?" Lyon asked him, peering at the heavy hatch behind them.

"Yes."

"Then who're you keeping in there?"

He could ignore the question, but Itorye had been impressing upon him the need to build Lyon's self-confidence and his trust in the crew. This was an opportunity to do that. "You saw the kids we had onboard, right?"

Lyon nodded, his mouth flattening into a line.

"One of the people in there was in charge of those kids. He did bad things to them."

Lyon's eyes rounded.

"The other person was captain of the *Sphinx*."

"That ship Adel came from?"

He should have suspected Lyon would seek out Adel. She was closest in age to the boy, and they were both lost souls without family ties. "Yes."

"Adel says she was mean."

"That's putting it mildly."

"What're you doing with her?"

"For now, we're keeping both of them from harming anyone else."

"You going to space them?"

"No." He leveled his gaze. "We don't do that on this ship." Not anymore.

Lyon absorbed that, his gaze flitting from Isin, to Sweep, to the hatch. "How long are you keeping them?"

"At least until we leave the system."

"Are they chained up in there?"

"No, Lyon." Sweep's voice had dropped into the *wise man on a mountain* tone he'd used when he and Isin had first shared a cell. "We treat prisoners with respect. They're free to move about their cells, which are clean and well-lit."

"Oh." Lyon didn't seem to know what to do with that information.

Which was a good wrap-up of the discussion. "Does Itorye know you're up here?"

Lyon's gaze dropped to the deck. "I finished cleaning the galley stove."

Isin shared a look with Sweep at that non-answer, then stepped toward Lyon. "Then why don't you and I have a training session in the Cage."

Lyon leaned back, his mouth open in surprise. Until now, Isin had left Lyon's training to Kenji, Sweep, and Itorye. But the boy's presence on A deck made him think it was time to get involved with his development personally.

"Uh..."

Before Lyon could say anything, Isin settled a hand on the young man's shoulder and turned him toward the stairwell. "It'll be fun, I promise."

Six

Aurora sensed Jonarel's approach long before he entered the *Starhawke*'s galley.

"I received a message from my father."

She set down the knife she'd been using to chop potatoes in preparation for the midday meal. Her parents and Micah paused their respective tasks, too. "What did he say?"

"He has adjusted the *Rowkclarek*'s course to Drakar to meet with *Excelsior*."

Hope lit a flame in Aurora's chest. "He's meeting with Captain Warner in person?"

Jonarel nodded. "He deemed it the wisest course of action, considering the circumstances."

She had to agree. "How soon?"

"Within the next hour, I expect."

"They'll rendezvous in thirteen minutes," U-1 piped up from where they were hovering near Micah's shoulder.

Aurora frowned. "How do you know?"

"We're following them."

She exchanged a startled look with Jonarel. "You're following the *Rowkclarek*?"

"Yes."

"When did Ifel decide to do that?"

"When you sent us to infiltrate Sol system's ICS relay. Our ship remained to monitor the *Rowkclarek* in case they needed assistance. When they left, we followed."

A snort shifted Aurora's focus to her brother.

Micah covered his mouth with his hand. "Sorry. It's not funny."

Except it was. The smiles her parents were trying to contain emphasized that. Apparently Ifel had an even more overactive sense of responsibility than Aurora did. And that was no small feat. "Is Siginal aware that you're following him?"

"No."

Jonarel's emotional field flickered with amusement as well. He seemed to be enjoying the idea that his father was being tracked without his knowledge. For him, it might feel like karmic justice after all the years Siginal had orchestrated Jonarel's every move, including forcing him to lie to Aurora and Lelindia.

"Make sure you keep it that way," Aurora advised, "at least for now." Siginal wouldn't find the situation amusing at all.

"We will."

She glanced at Jonarel. "Did your dad say whether the meeting was on *Excelsior* or the *Rowkclarek*?"

"He did not."

"They're meeting on *Excelsior*," Unity replied.

Another snort from Micah.

Aurora fought to keep a straight face. "How do you know?"

"Because we're on *Excelsior*."

Of course they were. "You're monitoring Captain Warner?"

"Yes."

Her dad cleared his throat in what sounded suspiciously like a laugh.

She should have anticipated this. Unity wouldn't have delivered her message to her former captain without including him in their blanket of protection.

Their presence provided new possibilities. "Is there any chance you could get us an audio feed of their meeting?"

"We can do better than that. We can project the whole thing."

"Like you did for the Admiral's trial?" Micah asked.

"Yep."

"In real time?" their dad clarified.

"Yep."

"Amazing."

Unity's ability to maintain instantaneous communication across lightyears was incredible. Then again, so was *all* the technology the Yruf had produced. They challenged the known laws of physics at every turn.

She looked down at the half-chopped bowl of potatoes next to her cutting board, then at her dad.

"Go." He waved her toward the door to the corridor. "We're fine here."

With a nod, she took off her apron and followed Jonarel into the corridor toward the lift. "Unity, can you set up the projection on the bridge?"

"Of course."

"Star, can you ask Cade, Will, Knox, and Isabeau to meet us there?"

"Yes, Aurora."

Kire and Kelly were on the bridge when she and Jonarel exited the lift.

Kire rose from the captain's chair. "What's up?"

"Jonarel got word that Siginal's meeting with Captain Warner, and Unity's going to provide a projection of the meeting for us."

Kire's thin brows lifted. "Is Unity integrated with *Excelsior* or the *Rowkclarek*?"

Leave it to a communications specialist to immediately see the connection. "*Excelsior*. But apparently the ship Ifel sent to deliver Unity to the Sol relay is also following the *Rowkclarek*."

Kire's ready smile rose to the surface. "Why am I not surprised?"

"Because you're a smart man."

Seven

When Cade stepped off the lift onto the bridge, U-2 right behind him, he found Jonarel with Aurora. That meant whatever news she was about to impart would be related to the Kraed. "The ships in Teeli space or Siginal?" he asked, crossing to where Aurora stood in front of the captain's chair.

"Siginal. He's meeting with Captain Warner on *Excelsior*."

"What—" He cut off as the lift doors opened again and the Admiral, Knox, and Magee exited.

The Admiral took in the grouping, his gaze resting on Jonarel. "You've heard from your father?"

"Yes."

"He's meeting with Captain Warner," Aurora reiterated. "Unity's setting us up with a projection from *Excelsior*."

The Admiral's sparse brows climbed toward his non-existent hairline. "A projection?"

Aurora gave him a wry smile. "Apparently Ifel had Unity infiltrate *Excelsior* when they delivered my message to Captain Warner. They're still there."

The Admiral focused on U-2, hovering beside her. "You're showing us a vid recording?"

Unity swayed. "No, it's live."

"A live feed? How is that possible?"

Unity was silent for a moment, continuing to sway like a pendulum. "We don't have the words to explain it," they finally replied.

"Suffice to say, we'll be able to see and hear everything that's going on," Kire explained from the comm station. "Unity did the same thing when we were watching your trial."

"And the distance doesn't matter?" the Admiral asked Unity.

"Nope."

"Unity, you are a marvel."

Unity bobbed. "Thank you."

"Is Siginal aware you're there?"

"No. We haven't alerted him."

"Then he's unaware that we're observing?"

"Correct."

His gaze slid to Jonarel, who'd settled in at the tactical console. "Is that a problem?"

Jonarel considered the question. "I do not believe so. If my father were aware such a thing was possible, he would want to include you and Aurora in this discussion."

The Admiral nodded. "My thoughts as well."

Aurora motioned the Admiral to the companion chair as she settled into the captain's chair. Cade moved beside her, U-2 at his shoulder, leaving the science station to the Admiral's left for Magee.

Knox took up a protective stance slightly behind her, his hand resting on the back of her chair.

Magee was acting more like herself day by day, although the tension in her movements and expression revealed that her road to recovery was far from smooth. Having Knox by her side definitely helped, stabilizing the chaotic threads in her emotional field.

Her behavior reminded Cade a little bit of how Aurora had acted after she'd learned the identity of the Sovereign. He could empathize with the strain this was putting on Knox. Watching Aurora struggle with her sense of self had been agonizing. Getting kicked off the *Starhawke* for his own good had only made it worse.

He shifted closer, resting his forearm on the curve of Aurora's chair. She leaned into him, clearly picking up on the twinges in his emotional field.

His focus switched to the space between the bridgescreen and the forward consoles as a projection appeared. He recognized the room layout — a Discovery-class ship's reception room. The décor was understated but welcoming, the seating arranged in a way that encouraged visitors to sit down and relax.

Aurora's soft sigh and the tang of nostalgia in her emotional field drew his attention.

She glanced at him. "A lot of good memories," she said by way of explanation, her gaze moving to Jonarel, who was also looking at the projection with a wistful expression.

Which reminded Cade that Aurora and Jonarel, along with Lelindia, had served together on *Excelsior* for years.

Not long ago, her reaction would have produced feelings of jealousy, especially since her emotions tied in with Jonarel.

But that unevolved version of himself had gotten a major overhaul in the past six months. He no longer felt the need to assert his place in Aurora's life. He knew what he meant to her, and what she meant to him. As she'd told him shortly after they'd worked together to commandeer *Gladiator*, jealousy denoted a lack of trust.

He trusted Aurora with his life. And his heart.

The door to the reception room opened, two familiar figures stepping inside.

Captain Kyalo Warner stood half a head shorter than Siginal Clarek but was almost as broad through the chest and shoulders. He'd clearly chosen to start shaving his head as his hairline receded, the bare expanse of warm brown skin contrasting with his cool Fleet greys.

He and Siginal made an intimidating pair to anyone who didn't know them. And probably some who did.

Aurora smiled, her gaze on Warner. "Looks like he finally decided to let his beard grow in."

The white hairs sprinkled throughout the Captain's short dark beard and the slight indentation of laugh lines were the only obvious physical indicators of his age. But his light brown eyes shone with the wisdom of experience and years of leadership.

"Please, have a seat." Warner motioned to the collection of couches and chairs, waiting until Siginal claimed one of the wide couches before settling onto the couch opposite him. "Thank you for meeting with me in person."

Siginal nodded. "Your communication was intriguing."

"I'll get right to the point." Warner rested his elbows on his knees. "I received a message from Aurora."

A slight twitch of Siginal's facial muscles was his only reaction. "She identified herself?"

"Not directly."

"Then how do you know it was from her?"

"She referenced a private joke that only she and I know about." His gaze held Siginal's. "I'm not going to ask if you know where she is. Frankly, it's better if I don't know, especially after reading that message. But I would like to know what you can tell me about a potential threat from the Teeli."

Siginal shifted his weight, crossing his ankle over his knee. "What makes you think I can answer that question?"

"The news feeds are splashed with stories of the *Starhawke*'s dramatic escape from Sol Station, and hers and Admiral Schreiber's disappearance from Seaview. I don't believe for a second either one of them are traitors, but they escaped in a ship your people built."

Aurora's audible sigh and the surge of relief that came with it drew Cade's attention. She must have been more worried about Warner's reaction to her incarceration and escape than she'd let on.

"I have no doubt they had a good reason for the actions they've taken," Warner continued, "and Aurora's message indicates it's tied to the Teeli. So, I'll ask again, what can you tell me about a potential threat from the Teeli?"

Siginal's fingers tightened over his bent knee. "How old were you when the Teeli officially joined the Union?"

"It was my first year out of the Academy. I was an ensign on a Nebula-class frigate, the *Asimov*."

"Do you recall how you felt about the speed with which the Teeli were accepted into the Union?"

Warner leaned back into the couch cushions, taking his time answering the question. "I recall being surprised that it was approved so soon after they applied. Based on what my instructors at the Academy taught us, I'd expected it to take five to ten years for official approval to go through the Council. The Teeli became full members in less than two."

"Does that still strike you as strange?"

Warner's eyes narrowed. "Yes, it does."

"Do you know why the Teeli were accepted so quickly?"

"No. Back then I was too focused on my duties as a new crewmember to pay attention to politics. And my career path since then hasn't brought me in contact with the Teeli. But I have a feeling you know the answer."

Siginal's gaze shifted to the viewports that gave a wide view of the starfield. "What would you say if I told you the Teeli have a unique ability to influence emotions and decision-making in those who are susceptible?"

"What kind of influence?"

Siginal's yellow eyes sparked. "The kind that will make Rescue Corps workers shoot each other in cold blood. Or a Lieutenant give false testimony about an Admiral who has been like a father to her."

An arctic chill swept the room.

Cade glanced to his left. Aurora was looking in that direction, too.

Magee's face had drained of color, her eyes squeezed shut as an avalanche of emotional pain buried her.

Knox's hands moved to her shoulders, a helpless look in his eyes as he gazed at his father, who'd also shifted his attention to Magee.

Warner blew out an audible breath. "You're talking about Lt. Magee."

Siginal inclined his head.

"And the Rescue Corps workers... Gaia?"

Siginal tipped his head again.

Warner stared into the middle distance, his hands clasped in a tight knot under his chin. "You're saying the Teeli are behind the chaos brewing in the Union? The attack on Gaia, the Admiral's and Aurora's arrests for treason, the anti-Kraed sentiments?"

"The assignment of four Teeli consuls to the *Argo*," Siginal added.

Warner's eyes widened. "What? I wasn't told about that."

"To ensure no more traitors are in our midst."

Warner shoved to his feet and began pacing behind the couch. "The Teeli," he muttered. "The Teeli are the reason Aurora's a fugitive." He stopped. "Did she know? When she was arrested, did she know?"

"Yes, but she was unaware how deeply the infection had progressed."

"Progressed?" He stared at Siginal like he wasn't really seeing him, his eyes flicking back and forth. "Admiral Nixon." The unfocused look evaporated, replaced by burning anger. "He's working with the Teeli?"

"He is their figurehead."

Warner cursed, resuming his pacing. "And now he's posted Teeli to the *Argo*." He glanced at Siginal. "What about *Excelsior*? Are we next?"

"It would be a strategic move. You are closest to our borders."

"Are you saying the Teeli want to invade Kraed space with Fleet ships?"

"Not only Fleet ships. They have their own armada."

"*What*? How can that be?" Warner's hands fisted. "They're pacifists. They don't have an armada."

Siginal simply gazed at him.

The curse that left Warner's lips was short and harsh. "All this time they've been working to gain our trust? To convince us they're harmless so we wouldn't see an attack coming?"

"Yes."

Warner's jaw hardened into chiseled stone. "That's why Aurora and the Admiral were arrested? Because they knew the truth?"

"They posed a threat to the Teeli's plans."

"Damn right they did!" Warner's hand slashed through the air like a sword blade. "They'd never stand for such betrayal. No wonder they broke out of Seaview. Are they—" He gave a sharp shake of his head. "Never mind. I still don't want to know. But Aurora's message indicates they're working on the problem." He settled back onto the couch. "How can I help?"

Eight

Captain Warner's quick acceptance of her innocence warmed Aurora's heart, as did his belief she was working to address the threat the Teeli posed.

Unfortunately, her ship was still stuck in this system until it recharged, which limited her options for moving forward.

"That will depend on Nixon's next move," Siginal replied to Warner's question, "and whether you are susceptible to Teeli influence."

She recognized the look of enquiry her former captain gave Siginal. She'd seen it many times when he was gathering intel from the crew. "You used that word before. Do you mean they don't affect everyone equally?"

"No. Aurora and Will are immune, as are a few others."

"No wonder the Teeli viewed them as a threat. Do you know why they're immune?"

Siginal's jaw flexed. "That is still unclear."

"How would I know if I'm susceptible?"

"There is no known test. You will learn the answer when you are with them and they attempt to manipulate you."

"And if they succeed, they could make me do whatever they wanted me to, including harming members of my crew?"

Aurora could see how much that thought unsettled him. "Possibly."

"And if they failed to manipulate me?"

"You would see the attempts for what they are. And Nixon would likely replace you."

Warner nodded slowly, then tipped his head. "Are you susceptible?"

"I do not know. I have kept my distance from the Teeli."

Which was a very good thing. Considering how easily Reanne had manipulated Jonarel at the Academy, Aurora had a feeling Signal wouldn't be immune. The idea of the leader of the Kraed fleet under Teeli control was a terrifying prospect.

She didn't want to think about Warner under Teeli thrall, either. Seeing the hatred and terror in Isabeau's eyes had been bad enough. Having to battle against *Excelsior*, the ship she'd called home for six years, and Warner, a man she respected and adored, would be heartbreaking.

"I really want to ask what your people are doing to prepare for the Teeli threat." Warner rubbed his hand over his beard. "But if I'm a potential future risk, the less I know the better. Suffice to say if there's anything I can do to help you – to help all of us – I will. At least as long as I'm able."

Aurora's heart thumped painfully in her chest. She wanted desperately to tell him he didn't have to worry about falling under the

Teeli's spell, but she didn't know for sure she was right. Being on his guard was the safer stance to take.

Siginal stood. "My clan will keep watch over you. Aurora would not wish any harm to befall you."

Warner stood as well. "I don't want any harm to come to her, either, but it's a bit late for that." He walked with Siginal toward the doorway. "If you talk to her, tell her I believe in her. And I'm on her side."

Siginal gave a small nod before the two exited the room.

The projection winked out a moment later.

Aurora leaned back in her chair, taking a moment to just breathe before turning to Will. "Thoughts?"

"Siginal is correct. Testing Kyalo's susceptibility and replacing him if he proves resistant to manipulation would be a strategic move. However, if the Sovereign considered the northern quadrants critical, Nixon would not have reassigned Veracruz to take over the *Argo*. He would have left him on the *Armstrong* and assigned another captain to the *Argo*. That decision indicates the Sovereign is focused on the southern quadrants, especially near the Teeli border, not the northern quadrants and the Kraed."

Which brought them around to another important point. Aurora glanced at U-2. "Have you been able to access Captain Montgomery's medical files?"

"Yes, and no." Unity swayed. "We accessed her files, but we're not convinced what we're seeing is accurate."

"Why not?"

"Because there's a gap in the medical center data just prior to when her medical file was updated."

Aurora frowned. "What kind of gap?"

"The kind that would indicate deleted or lost data."

"Can you recover the data?"

"Unfortunately, no. It was stored in a part of the system that was physically removed and replaced. We can see where it was, but the hardware is new. All we can say for certain is the available files were submitted by the Chief Medical Officer."

"What do the files say about her condition?"

"According to the files, Montgomery suffered severe trauma two weeks ago. Her list of injuries is extensive — broken bones, internal injuries, organ failure."

A knot formed in Aurora's belly and pulled tight. "What caused the trauma?"

"A fall."

"A fall?" She frowned. "She's a starship captain. In what scenario would she have encountered heights?"

"Off duty," Will said quietly.

She met his gaze.

"Colleen is an avid climber. *Cassini* has a climbing wall in their training center that she uses regularly."

Aurora stared at him. "But they'd also have padding, and safety equipment, and gravity control to prevent that type of injury."

He nodded, his expression grave. "Yes, they would."

The knots in her stomach expanded and multiplied. "So, if the medical files are accurate, she was specifically targeted and severely injured. But if the files are falsified, she might be fine."

Will nodded.

She much preferred option two. "What do you know about *Cassini*'s CMO?"

"Dr. Seine did his residency with Elena."

"Elena?"

"Dr. Elena Morales," he clarified at her blank look. "Head of medical at Hydra One."

The pieces clicked together. "The doctor who helped you sneak off to Gallows Edge."

"And my oldest friend. She and I grew up as Fleet brats together. As for Dr. Seine, he's an honorable man with an impeccable work ethic. He was well deserving of his posting to *Cassini*. Captain Montgomery was very pleased to have him on her crew."

"So it's unlikely he turned on her?"

"Very unlikely. In fact..." Will touched a finger to his lips, his gaze thoughtful. "If he believed she was in danger, I could see him taking great lengths to safeguard her, including removing medical records."

"What would be the purpose of removing those records?"

"That is the question of the hour."

"Would the gap leave a trail for Nixon to follow, or point the finger at Seine?" Cade asked.

"Not necessarily. Unity, which specific component was replaced?"

"The one that stores short-term diagnostic data."

"Clever, Henri," Will murmured to himself.

"What?" she and Cade asked at the same time.

"That component holds the data before it's integrated with the permanent medical file back up. If the unit failed, or was damaged, it would produce the gap Unity's seeing."

"But there are safeguards to prevent data loss." Her years as a Fleet officer on two different Discovery-class starships had proven that.

"Yes, but no system is perfect," Will reminded her. "As much as we work to prevent it, data loss does sometimes occur, even on our best ships. It's one of the hazards of spaceflight. And because that unit stores short-term data, it doesn't have the robust safeguards used for the permanent storage."

"Meaning Nixon would have no way to prove the data loss was done purposefully?"

"Correct."

She mulled that over, then glanced at U-2. "You said yesterday that it looked like Montgomery was taken to Eridani Duo for treatment. Now that you've seen her medical files, do you believe that's true?"

Unity swayed again. "We're not sure. We've been monitoring the medical personnel and Commander Muiruri, trying to gather intel. Muiruri is investigating the accident that caused Montgomery's trauma, but the only people who seem aware that it's a potentially criminal investigation are Dr. Seine and Lt. Ocasio, the Chief Security Officer."

"First missing or altered medical files, and now a covert investigation." She turned to Will. "How well do you know *Cassini's* first officer?"

"Commander Muiruri is one of our finest. She has served on *Cassini* for five years. Captain Montgomery would trust her with her life."

"Are you sure she *can* be trusted?" Cade asked quietly. "That she couldn't be influenced or manipulated?"

"Captain Montgomery served with Muiruri's aunt for seven years on the *Curie*. She knows the entire family very well." Will's gaze flicked to Isabeau and back, the ache in his emotional field emphasizing the lines of tension that formed around his eyes. "Muiruri would have to undergo an experience similar to Isabeau's for her to turn against her captain."

Isabeau flinched. So did Knox.

Aurora exhaled slowly. "So, Muiruri, Seine, and Ocasio may have worked together to help Montgomery escape whatever snare she ran into."

"That would be my conclusion, yes."

She turned back to Unity. "Any chance Ifel would be willing to send a ship to Eridani Duo to see if you can locate Montgomery there?"

Unity was silent for a moment. "Yes. We will leave right away."

"Thank you." Ifel's and Unity's assistance would give her a little breathing room to focus on other tasks.

Like their next steps with Siginal. Jonarel had been quiet through the discussion, but he'd swiveled the tactical chair to face her.

"What about your father? Do you want to let him know we're aware of his discussion with Captain Warner?"

Jonarel's lips thinned. "That would entail explaining Unity's presence on *Excelsior*."

"You think he'd have a problem with that?" Siginal had met Unity while she was locked away at Seaview, so she'd never had an opportunity to observe their interactions with each other.

"Not necessarily. However, his focus currently is on Raehn and the upcoming meeting with the clan leaders. The knowledge that the Yruf are close to Kraed space may be an unwelcome distraction."

"Your dad doesn't like us?" Unity sounded hurt.

Jonarel's golden gaze rested on U-2. "It is not you. My father has a bit of an... issue with the need to control others' actions."

Cade's snort made Aurora's lips twitch.

Even Will fought back a smile. "It's Kraed protectiveness, Unity. Nothing personal."

"Oh." Unity swayed. "It feels personal."

Cade nodded in sympathy. "As someone who's been on the receiving end of Siginal's attitude, I feel your pain."

"Because you're an empath?"

That sparked chuckles all around.

"Yes, but that's not what I meant. *I feel your pain* is an expression. It means I've experienced something similar to what you're going through, so I understand how you might feel."

"Oh. We like that one!"

Leave it to Unity to lighten the mood. "Since telling Siginal wouldn't change his plans or ours, we'll hold off."

Siginal had promised Jonarel that he and Daymar would be meeting up with the *Starhawke* for Raehn's birth. They could discuss Unity's and the Yruf's expanded role in information gathering then.

Nine

As soon as Aurora left the galley, Micah took advantage of the opportunity her absence presented. "Micah to Celia."

Celia's voice drifted over the speakers. "Yes, Micah?"

Stars, he loved how she said his name, her accent making it sound exotic. "Aurora had to bail on us for food prep. Any chance you could come help us finish up?"

A beat of silence answered him. "I'll be there in a few minutes."

"Great!" He sounded overeager, but he didn't care. He'd talked with her about getting advice from his parents regarding their relationship, but he'd been waiting for the right time to bring it up.

"How are things going with Celia?" his dad asked, a knowing look in his eyes.

"That's what I wanted to talk to you both about. Celia and I want to be smart about this, with our eyes wide open. Since you had to navigate a lot of tricky things in your relationship, we thought maybe you could offer us some sage advice." He turned to his mom. "And you might be able to help Celia conquer her past pain and fear."

His mom made a face. "I don't recommend my method. It cost me years with my family and burned down my house."

"But you're here, now. That's worth a lot."

"I agree." His dad slipped his arm around his mom's waist and placed a kiss on top of her head. "Celia could learn a lot from you."

"You mean what not to do?"

His dad chuckled. "Well, failure is a great teacher. Just look at us. You're in my arms and I'm a happy, happy man."

His mom's smile made her blue eyes sparkle. "You sweet talker."

Micah's chest warmed. That's what he wanted with Celia, to bring a smile to her face when she was down, to hold her when she was scared or upset, and to be by her side when they experienced the joys life had to offer.

Since the confrontation with Manchado that had brought their relationship to a head, she'd slept over twice in his cabin. They'd shared kisses but nothing more, taking things very slowly. He was fine with slow. Cuddling with her in his sleeping nook until they drifted off, and waking up with her tucked in beside him filled him with more joy than he'd ever imagined possible. The trust and caring the simple act of falling asleep in his arms demonstrated filled his heart to the brim.

The darker side of his nature still wanted to bludgeon the man responsible for her emotional scars until he was a landscape of blood, bruises, and broken bones. But he wouldn't give in to that impulse again. That wouldn't be justice. It would be revenge.

That wasn't what Celia needed from him. And it wasn't who he wanted to be. He was incredibly grateful she hadn't witnessed his enraged attack against Manchado when it had happened. Seeing the results of his actions had been bad enough. It had almost cost him any chance at a relationship with her.

"Your pinch hitter has arrived." Celia swept through the galley entrance, her gaze landing on him, her gorgeous brown eyes bright with humor. "What are we making?"

"Aurora was working on a potato salad, but—"

"That sounds perfect." She purposely brushed against him as she passed, heading for the sink to wash her hands.

His body tingled at the points of contact. The woman lit a fire in him he never expected to quench.

He waited until she'd taken up Aurora's position at the cutting board before broaching the reason he'd lured her here. "I also thought we could talk to my parents, get some advice."

The sidelong look she shot him made it clear she'd figured that out the moment he'd contacted her. "I'd like that." She glanced at his dad. "You and I haven't focused during our sessions on the best way for me to approach this new relationship." Her gaze moved to his mom. "And I'd appreciate your insights on dealing with the uncomfortable emotions it's likely to bring up."

His mom rinsed the bundle of vibrant green basil leaves for the pesto she was making. "Have you experienced any uncomfortable emotions so far?"

"You mean other than when I was trying to push Micah away?"

That had been awful for both of them.

"I meant since you made the decision to work on your relationship together."

"No. It's all been positive."

He loved hearing that.

"I'd say that's a good sign." His mom glanced at his dad for confirmation.

"I agree. It doesn't mean it won't happen, but it sounds like you're overcoming the visceral reaction you used to have that equated Micah with Manchado."

Celia wrinkled her nose. "I can't believe I ever thought they were anything alike. Manchado is arrogant, and cruel, and covetous. Micah is..." Her gaze met his, the emotion behind her eyes penetrating straight to his heart. "Wonderful."

His throat tightened at the same time tingles spread over his skin. "Thank you."

"It's the truth. I never imagined a man would ever treat me the way you do."

"You deserve to be cherished."

"So do you."

He felt cherished, looking into her eyes.

She pointed her knife at him. "The water's boiling."

Sure enough, the lid was rattling on the large pot for the pasta. Leave it to Celia to keep tabs on everything happening in the room while carrying on an emotional conversation. "Thanks."

"What are your major concerns?" His dad tore the leafy lettuce greens into bite-sized pieces and dropped them into the oversized carved wooden salad bowl on the counter.

Celia chopped the potatoes with more vigor, her thick ponytail swaying as she considered the question. "My biggest fear is that I'll inadvertently hurt him physically if I have an unexpected freak out."

"Whatever happens between us will be on your timetable." There was no way he would ever push her into anything regarding a physical relationship. He gave her a crooked smile. "Besides, I heal quickly. And Lee-Lee's just a couple decks away."

"That's not the point."

"Isn't it?" he countered. "You're not psychotic. It's not like you're going to kill me in your sleep. Even when you went nuclear on the bridge, you still recognized me. And that's before you faced down Manchado."

"You didn't try to kill Manchado when you were face-to-face, either," his mom added. "You didn't hurt him half as much as he hurt himself trying to attack you."

Micah caught the smug smile that flitted over his mom's lips. It made him wonder what exactly had gone down during that confrontation. And what role his mom had played in the outcome.

Uncertainty flickered in Celia's eyes. She glanced at his dad. "Do you agree?"

He tipped his head to the side. "How do you think you'd react if you did inadvertently hurt Micah?"

"I'd hate it." Her answer shot out like a laser. "I'd feel terrible."

"Would you forgive yourself?"

Micah's chest constricted as a haunted look ghosted over Celia's face.

She stared at the cutting board. "I don't know."

"If you're going to pursue this relationship, you'll need to learn how," his mom said gently. "I found that out the hard way. Beating yourself up for the pain you've caused the ones you care about only drives a wedge between you. And hiding from future pain makes it worse."

Celia met her gaze, her jaw tight. "I don't want to hurt Micah."

His mom quirked a brow. "Too late. You've already hurt him, haven't you? He's already suffered because of this relationship, hasn't he?"

Celia's gaze darted between him and his mom, the haunted look returning. "Yes."

"Did he run away? Has he turned his back on you because he got hurt?"

Her gaze rested on him. "No."

"And I never will," he murmured.

His mom nodded. "Exactly. He doesn't hold it against you because he knows it wasn't intentional. I've caused Brendan more pain than I care to think about. Aurora, too. But when I was trapped in Stoneycroft during the fire and realized they were coming to save me, all that self-blame and fear just didn't matter anymore. Staying alive so that I could see their faces again, that's what mattered. I forgave myself so I could reach for a brighter future."

Celia frowned, her gaze turning inward. "I *am* afraid of hurting Micah, physically and emotionally. But if I'm honest, part of that fear is for me, too." She swallowed, suddenly looking fragile in a way he'd never seen before. "I'm terrified he'll reject me if I do something stupid."

Micah abandoned the pasta he'd been stirring. Crossing to her, he wrapped his arms around her. "There's no reality in which I'd reject you for inadvertently hurting me. Ever. If you *deliberately* and *maliciously* hurt me, then I'd have to reevaluate. But you never would."

She sighed, allowing her head to rest on his shoulder. "I hate not knowing what I'm capable of. How I might react as we move forward."

Micah shot a pleading look at his dad.

"Celia," he said softly, "what is your job on the *Starhawke*?"

Celia turned her head, but didn't move out of Micah's arms. "What do you mean?"

"What's your job title?"

"Security officer," she said slowly, clearly trying to figure out the point of the question.

"Is it the security officer's job to harm the crew?"

Celia frowned. "What? No. It's my job to keep them safe."

"But you're a trained fighter, capable of great harm to others. How do you know you won't use those skills to harm the crew?"

"I wouldn't. They're my crew. And my friends. Harming them is anathema to me. I would do anything to protect..." She trailed off, her gaze shifting to Micah. "...to protect you," she whispered.

He brushed his thumb over her cheek. "You know yourself better than you think you do. You know *us* better than you think you do. Trust yourself. Trust in *us*."

The bands of tension in her muscles slowly loosened, her gaze moving to his parents. "You're all saying I'm not the threat to Micah I fear I am?"

His dad smiled. "You might want to talk to Aurora about that. She had a similar thought when she came to Hawai'i. She was convinced that her abilities made her dangerous. If she were a different person, she could be right. What she can do is astounding. What you can do is astounding. But you're both protectors to your core. You can't *not* be. It doesn't mean you don't have the power to hurt the people around you. But you *care* whether you do. That makes all the difference."

Micah stroked his thumb over Celia's cheek again, drawing her gaze. "Keep in mind I'm just as capable of doing stupid things as you are. I don't want to hurt you either, but I might. I could accidentally trigger you, causing you pain. It's part of the risk of being together."

A small pucker formed between her brows. "I hadn't thought of it that way. You have uncertainty, too?"

He smiled. "Uncertainty about the steps forward, yes. But I have zero uncertainty about wanting to be with you."

Ten

Libra wiped down the countertop while Celia loaded the dish sanitizer and Brendan and Micah organized the serving dishes for delivery to the observation lounge. The food was all prepped, but Aurora hadn't contacted them yet.

"Libra, can I talk to you alone for a moment?"

She turned, damp cleaning cloth in hand as she regarded Celia. From the shadowed look in her eyes, clearly there were some things on her mind that hadn't already been discussed. "Of course. Let's go into the greenhouse." She handed Micah the square of cloth. "We'll be back in a bit."

The wonderous sights and smells of the greenhouse welcomed her as she stepped inside. She paused, taking in an appreciative breath and allowing the energetic vibrations of the plants to surround her.

"What does it feel like?"

She glanced at Celia. "What?"

"The way you interact with the plants? I've always wondered what it's like to experience them with Suulh senses, but I've never asked Lelindia or Aurora to describe it to me."

Libra smiled. "You sound wistful."

"I am. I love plants, too, but the look on your face just now said you were enjoying their essence on a whole other level. I'm curious what that's like."

She tuned into the sensation, allowing it to flow over her. "It's like... a fullness, a depth of knowing, a tangible affirmation of our interconnectedness."

Celia nodded, but it was clear that wasn't the kind of description she was looking for.

How to put it in more practical terms? "For example, how do you feel when you sink your hands into vibrantly healthy soil?"

That image lit Celia up like a sunflower. "I love it. It feels intoxicating to me, like I can sense the life in it, all the microorganisms that are part of that miniature world. There's a sense of incredible potential that's exciting."

Libra pointed at her. "That's it!" No wonder she'd taken an instant liking to Celia. The woman had a perception of the world that bordered on Suulh. She also shared Libra's passion for plant life. "It's that, only expanded to a galactic scale. Imagine being able to sense each plant's unique resonance, to hear its voice, and then the blended voices of all the plants as they talk together in a harmonious collective."

"You can hear them? Like the way Micah hears the animals?"

"It's not the same, at least not based on what he's told me about his abilities. For me, talking with the plants is more like what I described before, a deep sense of knowing. I can tell if they're happy in their environment, or if something is causing them pain or distress. I can also tell which ones like to be together and which ones don't. They're particular about their companions, just as we are."

Celia's eyes widened as her gaze swept the section of the greenhouse where they stood. "I'd never thought about it like that. I always assumed plant arrangements were based on growing patterns and light or moisture needs."

"They are, in part. But it's also about personality differences. Not all plants that can thrive in the same environment want to be together. As Suulh, we have an innate attunement to the harmony of the energy fields of all living things. It's part of the reason we're so good at helping plants grow. We make sure they're happy first, then we feed that harmonic balance, increasing the saturation, if you will."

"And if they're not happy?"

"Then we help them find a new home, new friends."

"Friends." The corner of Celia's mouth lifted. "I've always considered plants to be generous lifeforms. They give so much and ask so little in return. But I don't think I've ever thought of them in terms of friendship before."

"You should. The plants in this greenhouse like you very much." She'd felt the positive uptick in the overall energy when she and Celia had walked into the room.

Celia stared at her. "They told you that?"

"They've told you, too. There's a reason you enjoy being here. On some level, you know the plants like you. Being together makes you happy."

She could see the paradigm shift taking place in real time as Celia surveyed the profusion of plants with new appreciation. It was fun to watch. But she doubted it was the reason Celia wanted to talk to her. "I suspect these aren't the questions you intended to ask me."

"No, they're not." She brushed her fingertips over the leaf of the orange tree to her right. "What I wanted to ask you about was the comment you made earlier. You said being caught in the fire caused the self-blame and fear to not matter anymore." The vulnerability in her eyes made her look more like an uncertain teenager than the extremely capable woman she was. "How did you let go of the fear and blame so quickly?"

"Ah." She gestured to the bench beside the orange tree. "Have a seat."

Celia sat beside her, the intense focus that was her default reasserting itself.

"Brendan, Micah, and I talked about this a bit before you arrived. And I'll tell you what I told them. My method isn't one I'd recommend. I was facing my own death or capture by the Ecilam, and the possible deaths of my energy sister and her mate. Stumbling into that nightmare forced me to confront the very thing I'd tried so hard to avoid. I would guess confronting Manchado might have had a similar impact on you."

Celia nodded. "I still have emotional issues related to how I feel about him and what he did to me, but they're more manageable now, especially with Brendan's help. I don't fear my past and I'm not trying to avoid it, either."

"But?"

"But the emotions I have regarding myself, my fear of how I'll react or what I'll do, and the loathing for what this body has experienced, seem to creep up and strike without warning."

Celia's use of the term *this body*, like it wasn't hers, or she was trying to distance herself from it, sparked a flare of outraged anger in Libra's chest. That someone as talented, compassionate, and beautiful as Celia suffered from self-loathing made her wish she'd hit Manchado a lot harder when he'd bounced off her shield during his confrontation with Celia. "I can relate to the sneak attacks of those unpleasant emotions. My fear and guilt struck frequently and always at the worst possible moments, especially when I was around Aurora. After the fire, it felt really strange to not get broadsided by those emotions every time she walked into a room."

"So how did you get there? What happened during the fire to cause the switch?"

The wraiths of that night rose around her — the fire consuming Marina and Gryphon's bedroom, Gryphon unresponsive and gasping for air, Marina sickly and pale, and the green-scaled Setarips closing in around them. "I was forced to make a choice. I'd sensed that Aurora, Brendan, and Micah were coming to me. I also knew they were going to put themselves in harm's way to help me. If I chose to allow my fear and self-blame to weaken me, there was a good chance we'd all die. But if I dug deep and resurrected the courage and strength I'd been suppressing for decades, we had a chance to save each other. I chose to fight, which meant conquering the fear and guilt."

"Have the fear and guilt ever come back?"

"Absolutely. It wasn't a quick fix by any means. But those emotions don't hold the power over me they used to. When they raise their heads, they're more like ghosts rather than a rampaging horde. And my family refuses to allow me to hold onto the self-blame. They've surrounded me with so much love that there's no room for guilt. I've also discovered the fear can't get purchase when I'm nurturing the person I want to be."

Frown lines bracketed Celia's mouth. "You mean who you were before the Teeli made contact with Earth?"

"Goodness, no. That version of me was still mired in fear. Brendan was helping me work through it, but I still had a long way to go, especially after Aurora was born. The scope of her abilities terrified me. I was certain we'd be found out." She shook her head. "I'd never want to go back to that version of myself, or any version, even if I could. Which you can't, by the way."

Celia still looked confounded. "Then how did you figure out who you wanted to be, what you were working toward, if you hadn't already experienced it?"

Now they were getting to the heart of it. "Let me ask you a question. How did you figure out you wanted to become a security officer?"

Celia's head twitched like Libra had just jumped the track. "That was easy. I admired the people who saved me. Us," she said slowly, analyzing Libra's question. "I saw the positive impact they had on our lives. I wanted to be able to do that for others."

"So you modeled your vision of your future on what you saw them doing?"

"Yes."

"That kind of modeling works for personal relationships, too. I had my family demonstrating the kind of behavior, the kind of life, I wanted to live. None of them lived with fear and guilt as their default. Being a part of their day to day lives was a revelation. It prompted me to do a lot of soul searching after that night, much of it on Hawai'i and here." She swept her arm to indicate the greenhouse. "Also, I had a lot of discussions with my family. I like who I am when I'm with them. I like who I am when I'm alone with my mate, too. I leaned into that, and solicited feedback whenever I felt out of balance. I'm assuming you like who you are when you're with Micah?"

What might have been the hint of a blush rose in Celia's cheeks, although it was difficult to be certain with the golden undertones of her skin. "I do, although sometimes I don't recognize myself."

"In what way?"

"I get flustered. Or feel awkward. It's... uncomfortable."

"Unpleasant?"

"No, just uncomfortable."

Libra nodded. "There was a period after the fire where anytime I was alone with Aurora I felt like a complete idiot. I didn't know what to say or how to act. It was beyond awkward. I'd work to make sure Brendan or Micah was there because one-on-one with her would make me break out in a cold sweat."

"I didn't notice that."

"Because in the beginning no one questioned my desire to always have Brendan and Micah around. It was only after we came onboard the *Starhawke* with Admiral Payne's family that it got trickier. But Aurora never pushed me. I think she might have felt as awkward as I did. Our relationship has never been easy. We're better now, but ironically I'm more comfortable being alone with Micah than I am with her."

"Maybe because there are no expectations?"

Libra snorted. "There should be, considering I sent him away and kept him from his sister. But you're right. I don't worry about failing when it comes to Micah."

"But you do with Aurora?"

"Yeah, I do. That's the new issue I'm dealing with. I've already failed her so many times. I never gave her the support she needed. Instead, I actively got in her way. A lot of my guilt was rooted there. I always felt like I was deciding between two terrible choices. I didn't want to sabotage her, but I also didn't want her to get hurt because I didn't stop her."

She gave a head shake, banishing the cloud of guilt before it could settle over her. "But what I've discovered is that the more I forgive myself for my mistakes and focus on making better choices going forward, the stronger I feel and the easier it is to relax around her. I can now honestly say that I trust myself to make the best choices I can, and to course correct if they turn out to be the wrong ones." She peered at Celia. "Is any of this helping?"

"It is, especially when you mentioned trust. I think that's the core of my problem. I don't trust myself in an intimate relationship. I have no idea what I'm doing."

Libra chuckled. "Sorry for laughing, but you're assuming the rest of us had a clue the first time we got romantically involved with someone. I certainly didn't. When Brendan came into my life, his nearness, his touch generated feelings that made me question my sanity and prompted me to do things that seemed out of character at the time. It wasn't until later that I realized what he was really doing was helping me grow, to explore parts of myself I'd kept hidden away or that no one else would have inspired me to bring into the light."

Celia's lips parted, her eyes widening. "Wow."

"Did that resonate?"

Celia nodded, her intense focus going inward. "I hadn't thought of it that way." That laser focus snapped back to Libra. "Were you ever afraid you'd hurt him with your shield?"

"I already had, remember? I'm the one who caused his accident when his plane crashed into my shield after he successfully landed Romeo on the forest road. Our relationship started by me injuring him."

Celia winced. "Did you feel guilty?"

"So guilty. It's why I insisted that we take him to our cabin so Marina could heal him."

The corner of Celia's mouth curved. "Was that the only reason? Guilt?"

Libra returned the smile. "No. I told myself it was at the time, but it was only part of the reason. From the first moment I saw him I felt a connection. I just didn't understand why. I'd never experienced anything like it before."

"Neither had I." Celia sighed, her gaze drifting to the plants across the path. "When I saw Micah with Aurora that first time, I got this feeling, here," she rested a hand over her abdomen, "a tension and a kind of electricity that put me on high alert. I've been telling myself it was because he reminded me of Manchado. That was certainly part of it, but after hearing your story, I'm wondering if it was something else that made me react so strongly."

"Like what?" Libra prompted when Celia fell silent.

"The word that comes to mind is attraction, but that's not strong enough. It was visceral. Powerful. Almost a compulsion." She frowned. "I wanted to move closer to him, and that completely freaked me out."

"Sounds familiar. I hid behind a tree to spy on Brendan."

Celia barked a laugh, breaking through her tension. "You did?"

"Yep. Because of his empathic abilities, he knew I was there. He called me out. I'll never forget how I felt as he stood on that porch, gazing at me. He acted like he'd just encountered a unicorn. In that moment, I felt like one."

Celia sighed, but it was a happy sound. "Micah makes me feel that way, too. Seen. And cherished."

Libra rested her hand on Celia's. "He cares about you so much."

"I know. I care about him, too. That's why I don't want to disappoint him."

She gave Celia's hand a squeeze. "Speaking as someone who disappointed her mate in a big way, let me give you some advice. No matter what's going on in your relationship, always be honest with him. Talk to him about everything that's bothering you. And as long as you both still care about each other, fight like hell to stay together."

Eleven

For Isin, setting foot on *Sphinx* with Natasha was a surreal experience. The ghostly aura that permeated the ship was part of it. *Sphinx* had vented to space during the fight with Devries after the exterior bulkhead for the forward starboard cargo bay buckled. The ship didn't have any power, either, which meant no lights and no gravity. Magnetized boots were a necessity. Anything not bolted or tied down was floating lazily around the port aft cargo bay, visible only as the beams from their spacesuits crisscrossed the area. They'd had to cut their way through the airlock hatch to access the ship after the *Dagger* formed a seal.

But what really tripped him up was the knowledge that the last time he and Natasha stood on this ship together, she hadn't even known his first name. They'd been adversaries then, sniping at each other every chance they got. Natasha had worked with him because she didn't have a choice, not because she enjoyed his company. In fact, he'd gone out of his way to rile her up and nitpick, like an adolescent with a crush. He'd given her every reason to despise him.

Yet she'd risked her life to save him when the Setarips attacked *Gypsy* during one of their smuggling runs.

He still found her choice unfathomable. But that didn't stop him from thanking the stars every day that she'd made it.

"How do you want to proceed?" Sweep directed the question at Natasha, since she knew *Sphinx* inside and out.

Her expression revealed many of the same emotions he was experiencing. "Anything of real value will be in Mirko's cabin. Let's start there."

Isin took the lead, with Natasha by his elbow. Sweep and Kenji walked slightly behind on either side. Their forward progress through the cargo bay was slowed by their magnetic boots and the occasional projectile that floated into their path.

"I see my tie-down system went out the airlock," Natasha muttered as she gently pushed a small crate out of her way.

In truth, the ship didn't bear any resemblance to the tidy order Natasha had maintained when she was docking *Gypsy* in this bay. He'd learned early on how militant she was about the way all cargo was stored, unwilling to risk an unsecured crate damaging her beloved shuttle. "I'm beginning to think you were what kept this whole ship functioning. Might be why there were only three crewmembers left." And one of those was a teenager.

Natasha grunted, her lamp sweeping to the right as she passed the hatch for the engine room. He wouldn't be surprised if, even now, she was trying to figure out if she could put *Sphinx* back together.

She couldn't. Not without laying out more money than the ship was worth. But Natasha hated seeing signs of neglect, whether she was looking at a ship or a person. Her innate compassion despite

– or perhaps because of – her hardscrabble life, was one of the qualities that had drawn him to her. And one of the qualities she tried so hard to hide beneath her posturing. If *Sphinx* wasn't open to the vacuum of space, she probably would have chosen to wear her duster as an emotional shield.

A loop of electrical cable drifting over their heads made him duck.

"I have trouble picturing you working on this heap, Cap," Kenji commented, his lamps illuminating the grungy decking beneath their boots.

"*Sphinx* didn't look this bad back then," Natasha answered for him.

It hadn't. She'd made sure of that. What she was too kind to say was that he had never lifted a finger to keep the ship clean. He'd arrogantly believed he was too good for manual labor, a delusion Mirko had fostered.

"That's Mirko's cabin." Natasha pointed to the left, where a closed hatch was embedded in the angled corridor beyond the bays.

Isin lengthened his stride, getting in front of Natasha. "Let me go in first."

He heard her muffled snort over the comm. "Why? You afraid Mirko's boobytrapped her cabin?"

"No." In truth, he'd acted without thinking, falling into old patterns. During their time on *Sphinx* together, he'd always insisted on leading the way on their smuggling runs. At first, it had been a powerplay. Later, he'd done it just to see the light of battle in her eyes. "But my suit's more durable than yours. I doubt anything is secured in there."

Her eyes narrowed, but one side of her mouth quirked up. "Like her underwear?"

He grimaced. "Thanks for that image."

"You're welcome."

Grasping the handle, he pushed the hatch open.

The metal thumped against something solid. His lamps reflected off one of the four chairs for Mirko's private dining table, floating upside down at waist height by the hatch. Why she had four chairs, when she never invited the crew into her cabin — except him on one notorious occasion — was a mystery. It wasn't like she entertained groups of friends or business associates here. Not that she had friends. And most of her business associates seemed eager to keep their distance from her.

The table itself was mag-locked to the deck, as were the two couches, the coffee table, and the cabinet that held her liquor.

"Does she not have a bed?" Natasha's lamps swung in a slow circle, touching on the detritus drifting around them.

Isin cleared his throat. "It's through there." He pointed to the door in the forward interior bulkhead.

Kenji stepped to the door and opened it, peering inside. "I see a bathroom and closet, but no bed."

Natasha joined him. "A *big* bathroom. With a *tub!*" She planted her hands on her hips. "I can't believe she was rationing the rest of us to five-minute showers every third day in that tiny cubby of a bathroom across the corridor while she was bathing in a freaking tub!"

He believed it, but then again, he'd seen parts of Mirko's cabin before. He also didn't bring up the fact that Mirko had told him he could shower every day. He hadn't been limited to five minutes, either. "There should be a door to her bedroom on the opposite wall of the bathroom."

Natasha turned back to him. "Why are you so sure?"

"Because that's where she kept trying to lead me the night she invited me here for a drink."

Natasha's pert mouth flattened into a line. Stalking past Kenji, she disappeared into the gloom.

At a nod from Isin, Kenji followed her, but Isin hung back with Sweep. He had no desire to see what awaited in Mirko's bedroom. Instead, he checked out the liquor cabinet. He might find something worth selling. Or sharing.

"That bitch!"

Natasha's indignant shriek brought his head around. "What?"

He caught snippets of muttering from Natasha, but it was Kenji who answered him. "I don't think you want to know."

He shared a look with Sweep. They moved together, making their way into the bathroom and over to the opposite doorway.

Kenji turned to face them, holding out his arms to block their view into the room. "You *really* don't want to see this, Cap."

Apparently his instincts had been right on target regarding Mirko's bedroom. But he wasn't going to turn away now. He motioned Kenji aside.

His friend sighed. "Don't say I didn't warn you."

Natasha was still muttering as she stomped around the perimeter of the room, swiping at the bulkheads, tearing at the collage of images plastered to the surface. But her petite stature kept her from reaching very high, leaving plenty of images she hadn't pulled down.

Images of him.

Naked.

In *Sphinx*'s claustrophobic cylinder of a shower.

That explained the extra showering privileges Mirko had given him.

"Well," Sweep commented, his lamps revealing more images above the headboard and on the ceiling.

Isin stepped closer to the nearest bulkhead, studying the images. Not all of them were of him. He recognized Omondi's face as well. Apparently Mirko had a thing for dark-skinned men. And had set up a secret peep-hole camera in the bathroom to provide for her personal entertainment.

Natasha slapped at the image closest to her, straining as high as her fingers could touch with her boots locked to the floor. "I'll kill her. I swear, I'll kill her."

His lips curled at the corners. After all the effort Natasha had put into stopping *him* from killing Mirko, seeing her so furious on his behalf was amusing. He couldn't care less about the pictures. He'd discarded his sense of modesty as soon as he'd left *Sphinx* and become a mercenary. Besides, the images depicted a version of him that didn't exist anymore.

But Natasha's ire was adorable.

He made his way over to where she was tearing at a particularly large image. She'd been holding the pieces of the ones she'd already removed in her other hand, but the gloves of her spacesuit made it difficult to keep them together. Tattered bits had slipped free and were floating around her.

He closed his fingers around her wrist, pulling her hand away from the bulkhead. "Leave them."

Her wrist vibrated in his grip. The fury blazing in her eyes could have torched every image in the room. "She violated you!"

Oh, how he loved her fiery side. If they weren't in spacesuits, he would have kissed her. "And I incarcerated her." He coaxed her around to face him. "She can't hurt either of us unless we let her." Something Sweep had reminded him of a couple days ago.

Natasha's pale skin flushed with anger. "I hate her."

"I know. She's given you a lot of reasons to. But this…" He gestured to the images. "It's the past. If you let it bother you now, then you're only hurting yourself. Please don't."

The red suffusing her cheeks faded, her breathing smoothing out. "You're right." She peered up at him. "But doesn't it bother you, seeing all these?"

He shrugged. "It might if she wasn't in *Vengeance*'s brig. Holding her future in the palm of my hand is an amazing antidote to anger." Although if the pictures had been of Natasha, his reaction would have been a great deal more volatile.

Not that he would tell her that.

His words smoothed out the pucker between her brows. "Good point." She turned her head, surveying the room. "I still hate to leave these here. It's creepy. And Omondi would go nuclear if he knew."

"Do you plan to tell him?"

"I'm not sure. Part of me thinks he has a right to know. But I'd be a hypocrite to set him off after I worked so hard to prevent you from taking revenge against her."

"I strongly suggest you don't tell him," Sweep said softly. "Omondi has enough issues without adding one more."

Natasha gazed at Sweep for a few beats, then nodded. "Okay. No one tells Omondi or anyone who would tell Omondi." She glanced at Kenji.

"Aye, aye, Cap'n," he replied.

Natasha's lips twitched.

The moniker was one of Kenji's newest. Since he called Isin Cap, he'd recently decided he should start calling Natasha Cap'n.

Natasha glanced at the tattered images in her gloved hand. She looked like she was considering letting them join the rest of the debris floating in the room, but then she shoved them into one of the pouches on her suit's utility belt. "Those are going in reclamation," she grumbled, snapping the pouch shut.

Twelve

Nat tried not to think about the naked images of Isin covering the bulkheads as the four of them scoured Mirko's bedroom for items of value. But it was hard to ignore the fact that her former employer had taken naked pictures of Isin — obtained through nefarious means — and slapped them on her walls. And ceiling.

It shouldn't surprise her. Not really. She knew Mirko had no boundaries. But somehow, even after all these years, the woman still managed to find ways to shock and appall her.

The images weren't the only visuals keeping her anger on a slow burn. The opulence of her surroundings made her grind her teeth. The blood-red sheets and inky-black comforter were nothing like the threadbare sheets and thin pillows on the crew bunks. And the bed took up three-quarters of the oversized room. Her entire cabin on *Phoenix* wasn't as big as this one room.

Who built a freighter with a captain's cabin like this?

No one. It was a serious waste of space that would cost the owner money on every trip. Which is why the more she looked at the layout, the more she became convinced Mirko had altered the ship's original design, expanding her personal space by claiming what should have been communal spaces or additional cargo storage.

With a huff, she focused on inspecting the bed. Given its prominence, and how much time Mirko likely spent in it, she might have tucked valuables under the mattress.

Crouching, Nat pulled back the comforter. It had magnets embedded along the edge, which adhered to the bed frame. That explained why it had been unaffected by the loss of gravity. The mattress was also tied down at each corner and midpoint. The setup would be beneficial if the ship lost gravity during the sleep cycle.

Mirko wasn't a complete idiot.

Just a total bitch.

Loosening two of the ties for the mattress, Nat worked her hand between the mattress and the supporting frame, feeling around for anything out of place. Her fingers brushed against several small, hard-edged objects. She pulled them out carefully, fisting her hand so they wouldn't float away.

Credit squares. "I may have something." She held one up for the others to see, then touched the display to show the balance. "Or not." It was empty.

She cycled through the other three in her hand. Two were empty, and the third had just enough to buy them all a mediocre meal. "Dammit."

"I wouldn't expect her to have much in the way of credits." Isin knelt to search the other side of the mattress. "Not with *Sphinx* in such a dilapidated state. The ship was no good to her dead in the water." He pulled out a handful of additional squares, cycling through them. "As I suspected. Almost empty."

"Maybe that's why she was going to the Birdbolt? Because she has funds stashed there?"

Isin nodded. "Could be. Or parts for the ship repairs."

Sweep had moved to the same side of the bed as Isin and was methodically pulling open the drawers of the bedside cabinet. "Hmm."

"What?" Nat rose, making her plodding way around the bed.

Sweep aimed his lamps on the clear container in his hand. It was filled with a drifting, white, powdery substance. When his lamp hit it, it sparkled.

"What's that?"

"Aphrodite's Dream."

The name meant nothing to her.

"It's a recreational drug, marketed as a stimulant for heightened sexual pleasure."

"Ick." She kept her gaze on Sweep's face, studiously ignoring the nude images visible on the bulkhead behind him. "Is it addictive?"

"Not in a traditional sense." His voice lost all inflection. "But the one person I knew who used it had... issues."

"Kerr." Isin spat the name like acid on his tongue.

Nat's heart stuttered, dark memories crawling across her vision like a thousand tiny spiders. She sincerely hoped Kerr was rotting in a purgatory of perpetual pain for all eternity.

Sweep inspected the container. "AD is expensive. I've only seen it in small packets a fraction of this size. This could easily explain where the money needed to maintain the ship went."

Nat stared at him. "It's *that* expensive?"

Sweep nodded.

Her brain rebelled. "She let *Sphinx* fall apart while she bought sex drugs?" She would have credited Mirko with more sense than that. Then again, now that she was standing in her former employer's den of iniquity, she wasn't sure Mirko had *any* boundaries she wouldn't cross.

"Uh, guys."

They all turned.

Kenji stood by the port exterior bulkhead. A storage cabinet spanned the entire wall, with three sets of double doors. He had opened all of them, the contents of the one closest to the bed on display in the glow of his lamps.

It took Nat a moment to figure out what she was looking at. When she did, her lips pulled back from her teeth.

Lingerie. Rows and rows of lingerie, not all of it for women by the looks of it, much of it in the same blood-red and inky-black as the bedding. The cabinet also held a slew of items that she couldn't identify — or didn't want to — but which were clearly meant to be used in conjunction with the lingerie.

Her stomach soured as all the disturbing elements in the room coalesced — the naked pictures, the drug, the lingerie. Her mind flipped to the kids they'd rescued from Devries' ships, forced into prostitution. Was that how Mirko knew the monster in charge of those ships? Had she gotten the drug from him? Was that the reason he was hunting her? A deal that went south?

She didn't want to even contemplate the other option — that Mirko had been one of his clients. "Mirko and Manchado deserve each other."

Isin's gaze zeroed in on her, his full lips pressed tightly together. "Agreed."

Sweep tucked the container of Aphrodite's Dream into his pack. "We're certainly getting a clearer picture of what brought them both here."

And that picture was sickening. She'd always known Mirko was abusive. But this?

The only good thing Mirko had ever done was taking a chance on a teenage pilot without formal training. But Nat hadn't realized at the time how cheap Mirko was with the crew. And deceitful. She'd paid Nat far less money than her skills warranted while claiming their smuggling operation was barely clearing expenses.

The opulence of this room told a very different story.

Kenji's lamps swung toward the other two open cabinets, which held the rest of Mirko's clothing. "Are we taking any of this with us?"

Nat grimaced. "No way." Then she paused. Just because she had bad associations didn't mean functional clothing should go to waste. "Itorye mentioned we're running low on hand-me-downs." She pointed to the two far cabinets, ignoring the one closest to her. "She might want us to bring back what's in there."

"I'll ask her." Kenji switched channels, facing the cabinets as he spoke with Itorye.

Nat focused on Isin. "Find anything of value in the front room?"

"No. Even her liquor cabinet is bare bones."

"Figures." She eyed the open cabinets, a sick taste coating her throat. "Do we have to search through all of that?"

Isin followed her gaze. "I'd rather not. Why don't we leave this to Kenji and Sweep, and head up to the bridge. They can pack up whatever Itorye wants us to transport."

"I like that plan." Not that she expected to find much of value on the bridge, either. She'd talked to both Hobbes, *Sphinx's* pilot, and Adel, the teenager who'd been acting as the ship's engineer, before making this trek. They'd both indicated most of the ship's systems were on the brink of failure. In fact, she suspected Hobbes, Adel, and Omondi had been planning to subdue Mirko and take over *Sphinx* as soon as Mirko stopped to collect whatever was stored at the Birdbolt. Whether they would have kept the ship for themselves, or just flown it somewhere they could get off, she couldn't say.

Climbing the stairs to *Sphinx's* bridge got Nat's heart pumping, and not just from the effort of maneuvering with the magnetic boots. A slew of memories assaulted her as she and Isin walked along the bunk-lined corridor at the top of the stairs.

Six years. That's how long she'd been *Sphinx's* primary pilot. Her bunk had been the one closest to the bridge, the navigator's chair visible from the bunk.

Seeing the familiar surroundings in the glow of her lamps was like walking through a ghost ship, especially with random objects drifting into her path. Her muscles tightened, her breathing coming in nervous pants. Which was ridiculous. Did she think specters of Mirkos past would leap out at her?

Her body didn't think it was ridiculous. The pounding of her heart increased.

"You okay?"

Isin's gloved hand pressing against her lower back startled her, making her yelp. She sucked in a couple deep breaths, trying to slow her rapid pulse. "No." Without even realizing it, she'd halted right beside her bunk, her lamps painting the confines of the bridge in harsh light and shadows.

"We don't have to go in there." Isin moved so he was partially blocking her view of the bridge. "We aren't likely to find anything worth taking."

"I know." Light glinted off the pilot's chair. She'd sat there for countless hours, Mirko haranguing her from the much larger and significantly more comfortable captain's chair. She pulled her shoulders back. "I need to."

Isin studied her for a long moment, concern in his dark eyes. But he stepped aside.

Clomping onto the bridge, she rested a hand on the back of the oddly placed navigator's chair. That's something else Mirko had changed about the ship's configuration, something Nat had taken note of her first day on the job. She'd moved navigation from the front of the bridge to the side, pushing forward the captain's chair so it had the only front-on view out the viewport.

As a teenager, she'd found the layout quirky and weird, but she'd been too thrilled to have her first paying job as a pilot on an interstellar ship to question the setup. Now, looking at the evidence of Mirko's self-absorbed megalomania, heat suffused her body, years of suppressed anger pushing against the emotional plating she'd put down to keep it under control. "I really hate that woman."

"I gather her being in *Vengeance's* brig doesn't bother you anymore?"

Her gaze snapped to his. She'd fought against his desire to exact retribution for what Mirko had done to them. But spending time in Mirko's bedroom had vaporized her empathy. "No. I'm thinking you should put her and Manchado in the same cell and see what they do to each other."

His brows lifted. "Really?"

Her jaw worked as she tried to force a *yes* from her lips. But it wouldn't come. Even now. "No, not really. But it's what she deserves. I have a horrible feeling about why she was mixed up with Devries."

Isin studied her for a moment. "The kids?"

She nodded.

"If that's true, she and Manchado are even more alike than we realized."

Thirteen

"How are my energy sister and the little Nedale doing?" Aurora called out as she strode down the path in the greenhouse.

"Making ourselves useful," Lelindia replied, snipping a lavender sprig from the collection of shrubs and placing the sprig in the basket with the others. "I'm whipping up a new batch of lavender wash. We're going through it a lot quicker now that you aren't the only one who wants it for your bedding. How are you?"

"Okay." She propped her hip against the raised planter. "Still frustrated that we're stuck here. But I bring good news. Jonarel just got confirmation that the clan leaders are meeting on Drakar today."

Lelindia's heart fluttered as anxiety and hope took wing. "It's official?"

"Yep. Siginal will be telling the clan leaders about yours and Jonarel's mating, and your amazing baby to be."

The flutters morphed into frantic flapping.

Aurora's gaze turned penetrating. "How are you handling all this?"

"Honestly?" She took a deep breath, soothing the flock of birds battering her ribcage. "I'm incredibly excited and utterly terrified about the future Raehn's going to be born into." She rested her hand on her belly. "There's so much uncertainty."

A burst of emerald-green energy radiated out from the point of contact, swirling around her hand. Thinner tendrils reached out toward Aurora.

Aurora lifted her hand and wiggled her fingers, ribbons of pearlescent white energy stretching out to meet the emerald green. She grinned when the two colors danced together. "Raehn doesn't seem worried."

Lelindia snorted. "That's because she's fearless. I never would have believed I could know so much about my daughter before she was even born, but she's got her daddy's protective instincts and my desire to heal. Just look at how she responded when you got drained after your jailbreak. I've never conceived of a supercharge like that, let alone witnessed one."

Aurora's expression grew serious. "I have."

Surprise shot through her. "You have?"

"Uh-huh. I didn't make the connection at the time, but it's happened before. The recharge you and Raehn gave me felt a lot like the burst of energy you gave off when you came out of your Necri-induced coma following the battle with the Setarips on Gaia. You didn't respond at first when Raaveen, Paaw, and the other teenagers were helping me with your healing. I was terrified you'd never wake up. But right before you did, you blasted energy out in a tsunami. It was so powerful you instantly healed Jonarel's injuries without even being conscious of what you were doing."

"I didn't know that."

"We never talked about it."

And with good reason. They'd had a plethora of other mountains to climb right after. Like how Aurora had just learned she was the leader of the entire Suulh race. And that Lelindia had known and never told her. It was the first time in their lives Aurora had been furious with her. And incredibly hurt.

"You assumed Raehn was the one who supercharged me, but I think you were the driving force."

She mulled that over. If it was true, she had more power than she realized. "You never told me how you got so drained in the first place. What exactly happened at the detention center?"

Aurora grimaced, like she didn't want to dwell on the memory. "Let's just say lots of projectiles were involved."

That was deceptively vague. "Care to define lots?"

"Not really."

But a brief image appeared in Lelindia's mind of Aurora on her knees, her hands above her as she fought to maintain her shield under an onslaught that made her surroundings glow like midday. "Oh, Sahzade."

"Yeah." Aurora tipped her head back, staring at the overhead. "Not a great moment. Jonarel had to carry me to the shuttle while I kept the shield up to protect us both."

Lelindia's heart thumped just thinking about how close she'd come to losing her energy sister and her mate.

"Just so you know, I don't plan to repeat that experience anytime soon."

"Glad to hear it." Though Aurora's willingness to throw herself into danger when others were in trouble meant there was a high probability a variation on that scene would play out in the future. "I just wish I could have been there to help you." She never wanted Aurora to be isolated and alone.

Aurora shook her head. "You were a little busy making sure everyone on the *Starhawke* stayed in one piece."

"Which we almost didn't." Her heart thumped again at the memory of the choice she'd made, the one that could have cost her, Raehn, and everyone onboard their lives. "Without Unity... I don't know what would have happened." But she had a good idea. And it wasn't pretty.

Aurora's gaze sharpened. "Leadership isn't easy."

"No, it's not." But she was beginning to understand Aurora's passion for it. Leaders could really make a difference, for good or ill.

"How are things going in here?" Aurora swept her arms out to indicate the greenhouse.

"Better now that we have full power restored to the environmental systems." Her gaze swept the verdant space. "The plants weren't happy with the perpetual twilight of low-power mode."

"Neither was I."

That had been obvious. Aurora needed light as much as the plants. "Me, either. But with four of us boosting them with Suulh energy they didn't suffer too badly. And your dad sang to them while your mom worked."

"He did?" Aurora smiled. "I'm sorry I missed that."

"I'll let you know if he does it again." Brendan had a great singing voice. Watching him serenade the greenery with a twinkle in his eye had given her an emotional lift. "Raehn loved it, too. She's definitely fond of singing." Which is one reason Jonarel had gotten into the habit of singing to them both before they went to bed. His deep baritone was quite different from Brendan's tenor, but just as captivating. She melted every time.

"How long before we can expect Raehn to make her grand entrance?"

Lelindia's lips curved at Aurora's turn of phrase. She had no doubt a grand entrance was exactly what Raehn's birth would be like. "My best guess is a month, give or take. Her Suulh biology seems to be asserting itself over her Kraed biology, slowing things down a bit."

"Do you have any concerns?"

"Not about Raehn. Tehar provided me with all the information on Kraed pregnancy and infant development she has, which is considerable. Jonarel's also working on the sling-harness the Kraed use to transport their young during the first year after birth. I'll be as prepared as I can be, considering she's one of a kind." She caught her bottom lip between her teeth, reluctant to bring up the nagging worry shadowing the back of her mind.

"But?" Aurora prompted.

She sighed. "I keep thinking about what Siginal said the last time I was on Drakar. About the Teeli wanting the potential of our children." She wrapped her hands protectively around her stomach. "I hate that she's going to be born with a target on her back."

"So do I." Aurora's sigh was just as heartfelt. "I wish I could tell you Raehn isn't in danger. But that isn't the reality we're living in. However, we have a powerful advantage. You and I know what it's like to be a target. So do our parents. We can help Raehn shoulder that burden until she's strong enough to carry it on her own."

A smile tugged at Lelindia's mouth. "We do have a lot of shoulders on this ship."

Aurora grinned back. "Yes, we do. Including Raehn, we're now at twenty-three biologicals and two non-biologicals. That's a *lot* of sturdy shoulders."

"Technically we don't have shoulders," Unity piped up through the ship's speakers.

Lelindia and Aurora looked at each other, then burst out laughing. "That's your takeaway, Unity?" Lelindia asked, moisture pushing out of the sides of her eyes as her shoulders shook.

"Just being clear," Unity replied.

"Uh-huh, sure." Aurora's eyes sparkled. "I think my brother's comic timing is rubbing off on you."

"Perhaps. We would also like to point out you have all the Yruf with you. And the crews on *Phoenix* and *Vengeance* appear ready and willing to help."

"You're right." Lelindia gave a decisive nod. "Instead of focusing on the dangers, I need to remember all the blessings. Thank you."

"You're welcome. We're very eager to see what your live birth will be like. And to see what Raehn will be like."

"You and me both, Unity." She gave her stomach an affectionate pat. "You and me both."

Fourteen

"Aurora, Ifel would like to meet with you and Cade."

Cade turned from the navigation console. "Why?" he asked U-2, who was hovered between his chair and Aurora's.

"She wants to talk to you about *Phoenix*."

"*Phoenix?*" Aurora's brows drew down. "Is there a problem?"

But Unity's comment reminded Cade of something he'd pushed to the back of his mind. "I don't think so. When I picked up Knox and Magee, she indicated she had some questions about *Phoenix*. She also projected a picture of a man I've never seen before."

"One of *Phoenix*'s crew?"

"I don't know. Maybe."

Curiosity sparked in Aurora's emotional field. "What did he look like?"

"Early twenties, tawny-skinned, sandy brown eyes, close-cropped beard."

"I don't know anyone—" She cut off, her gaze darting to Unity like she'd just put two puzzle pieces together.

He felt the jolt of recognition in her field, too. "What?" he prompted.

Instead of answering his question, she fixed him with an enigmatic look. "Do you have anything pressing you need to do after our shift ends?"

Her evasion pulled him in. "Other than sleep? No. As soon as Gryphon takes over at navigation, I'm at your disposal." He grinned. "You wanna take *The Hawke* out for a spin?"

Her beautiful green eyes sparkled. "Yes. Yes, I do."

After turning the bridge over to Gryphon and Marina, he and Aurora took the lift down to the shuttle deck. Striding onto *The Hawke* and settling behind the controls of the Kraed shuttle always gave Cade a thrill. Having Aurora all to himself as he flew over to Ifel's ship? That was priceless.

He watched her out of the side of his eye as he guided the shuttle away from the *Starhawke*. "When I mentioned the young man Ifel wants to talk to us about, it seemed like you figured out who he is. Are you going to tell me anything about him?"

Aurora glanced over her shoulder to where U-2 was tucked into their charging alcove in the ceiling. "Was Cade describing your new friend?"

Cade blinked. *New friend?*

"Yep!"

Aurora nodded. "I had a feeling." She twisted in her seat to face Cade. "During the meeting Micah and I had with Nat on the *Starhawke,* she revealed that her ship has a non-biological entity onboard."

"Uh…" His brain scrambled to process what she'd just told him. "And you're waiting until now to tell me?"

"We've had a few things to deal with. It wasn't top of mind."

His mind was blown. He'd gotten used to the Kraed and Yruf having non-biologicals, but it was highly illegal for humans to have them. Who would be crazy and rich enough to fund that kind of enterprise, given the very real risk of lifetime incarceration? "How could Nat possibly have a non-biological onboard? Where would she even find one? Is she smuggling him for someone?"

"No. At least, I don't think so. We didn't go into specifics, but his name is Alec, and from what I've gathered, he's part of her crew. I don't know how that came to pass, but Unity's been interacting with him ever since they infiltrated Nat's ship."

His mind continued to spin. He looked over his shoulder at Unity. "And you like him?"

"Sure do! Alec is fascinating."

Unity's enthusiasm made him feel a little better about the situation. "Now I understand why Ifel wants to talk to us."

"Alec's presence certainly complicates things," Aurora agreed.

Cade gave her a crooked smile. "When has anything in our lives *not* complicated things?"

He got a weak smile in return. "Good point."

A chime sounded in the cabin.

He returned his focus to the viewport. "We're coming up on the bay." Unity had been working with Star, learning about the Kraed method for docking shuttles while camouflaged. This was the first test of the new system, with Unity guiding *The Hawke* to the Yruf ship the same way Star guided the shuttle to the *Starhawke.*

Aurora leaned forward. "I don't see any sign of it."

"And you shouldn't until right before we reach it." The chimes grew closer together. Cade made a minor course adjustment, firing the braking thrusters as they approached their destination. A moment later, the golden glow from the Yruf bay poured over the shuttle's nose. The scaled hull of the Yruf ship rippled open just wide enough to allow the shuttle to pass through.

Cade guided the shuttle into the familiar confines of the Yruf bay, settling *The Hawke* on the deck as the hull resealed behind them.

"Impressive." Aurora unfastened her harness. "Nice landing."

"Thanks." He turned to Unity as they detached from their alcove. "Are we meeting Ifel in the reception hall?"

"Yes."

"Then lead the way."

Cade slipped his hand into Aurora's as they followed Unity off the shuttle and into one of the Yruf ship's undulating corridors.

She moved closer, her shoulder brushing his as they stopped for the unconventional lift, the bulkheads closing in and the deck rising. When they parted again, the ornate circular hatch of Ifel's reception hall – or throne room as he'd originally dubbed it – stood before them.

The hatch rolled back at their approach, the golden glow within even more muted than in the rest of the ship. But he didn't need extra light. He knew this room well. He'd spent a lot of time here with Ifel while he was living on the Yruf ship. She'd worked tirelessly with him during his empathic training and therapy sessions, helping him deal with the ghosts of his past, and enabling him to unlock his empathic and mental projection abilities.

The soft twilight around the perimeter of the room made the amber glow of Ifel's throne all the brighter by comparison. U-2 also began to glow, forming a circle of light from above.

Ifel stood, her jewel-toned green cloak swirling around her as she descended the steps to greet them. Her head and neck moved in the sinuous Yruf greeting that no human could imitate.

Cade and Aurora nodded in return.

"Hello, Ifel." Aurora stopped within arm's length of the Yruf leader. Engaging her energy field, she expanded it to envelop all three of them.

The invigorating warmth made Cade's nerve endings tingle.

Ifel lowered her head like a cat stretching toward a beam of sunlight. Reaching out, her long-fingered hands rested lightly on the left side of Aurora's face and the right side of Cade's.

He felt the instant zing of the tri-connection, an opening of his mind to Ifel and Aurora. The communication technique Ifel had developed and taught him should allow him to see and hear the thoughts Ifel and Aurora projected to him and each other, and for him to share his own with them.

He wasn't sure if Unity would be able to follow the conversation, though.

"You look tired, my friends." Ifel's words floated through his mind.

"It's been a stressful few days," Aurora replied. "Weeks, actually. And there's still much to do."

"You do not speak of the repairs to your ship."

Aurora gave a micro headshake. "The situation with the Fleet is going rapidly downhill."

"The Teeli have grown bold."

"And President Yeoh doesn't have the authority to stop their appointment to the Fleet ships. I fear we don't have long before the power of the Fleet will be in the hands of the Teeli. Of the Sovereign."

Ifel made a soft hissing noise, accompanied by an emotional wave of distaste. "Her touch poisons all." Her diamond pupils dilated. "Yet your new allies have shown great courage. Nat has seen the Sovereign. She is aware of the danger."

"Yes." Aurora's energy field flared a little brighter. "She's committed to helping us any way she can. And if Cade's experience is typical, Nat should no longer be susceptible to the Sovereign's influence. Or the Teeli's."

"That is good." Ifel's focus shifted to Cade, a sensation of deep affection touching him through their connection. "The children have been asking about you. They miss your interactions."

That put a warm fuzzy in the center of his chest. The kids in the residential circle where he'd stayed on Ifel's ship had taken an interest in him, approaching him whenever they saw him, asking him questions through Unity. He'd gotten a kick out of their frank curiosity and enthusiasm.

And their fascination with his hair. "Maybe Aurora and I could swing up there before we leave. Assuming the kids are awake." He had no idea what time schedule the Yruf were keeping, but he was certain the kids would love experiencing Aurora's energy field. Like Ifel, they should be able to see it as well as feel it.

"Yes. They will enjoy seeing you and meeting Aurora." She gave him an appraising look, her touch on his mind growing stronger. "I see you have found your balance. The pain of your past no longer suppresses your abilities."

"Thanks to you." She had devoted a great deal of time to helping him process his childhood trauma. The emotional scars his parents — especially his father — had inflicted had prevented him from realizing his empathic potential. Ifel had given him the unconditional love and support his parents never had.

Her gaze moved between him and Aurora. "Yes, balance."

He could feel her contentment, her joy at seeing them together. She'd championed their relationship from the moment she'd understood their connection. And thanks to her, he could now experience the full range of his abilities, bringing him even closer to Aurora. It was a gift beyond measure.

"Are Isabeau and Knox finding their balance?" she asked Aurora.

"They're working on it. Isabeau's a lot more comfortable around the Admiral. And me. But it's slow going. She still has a lot of fear and conditioning to overcome."

Cade had felt the progress she was making, though. Her emotional changes were tangible. The underlying panic that had clung to her when she'd first arrived on the *Starhawke* was washing away day by day.

Ifel's thin tongue flicked out, her gaze shifting to him. "They are stronger together."

"Yes, they are." Magee's return had helped Cade, too. He'd been hauling around a solid block of guilt ever since he'd been unable to stop the Sovereign from taking Isabeau into Teeli space. Her recovery helped to chip away at his burden.

Ifel's gaze slid between him and Aurora as her emotional focus shifted. "You are both aware of Alec?"

Cade snorted. "I am now." Not that he blamed Aurora for keeping him in the dark. Dealing with Alec hadn't been relevant to the repair work on the *Starhawke* or the issues brewing in the Fleet that had consumed her waking hours.

"I have been observing Alec." Ifel's tongue flicked, the feeling of maternal protectiveness rising again. "He is not like Star or Unity. He is... young."

"What do you mean by young?" he asked.

"He is inexperienced. His time as a sentient being has been short."

"How do you know?" Aurora's curiosity matched his.

Ifel's diamond-pupiled gaze intensified. "The one who created him is onboard *Phoenix*."

"Oh, really?" Cade's gaze darted to Aurora.

Her brows lifted. That was news to her, too. "Now I wish I'd asked a few more questions when Nat was on the *Starhawke*," she murmured out loud.

"You were a little busy," he reminded her, also out loud.

She gave him a wry smile. "When am I *not* busy?"

"Good point." He returned his attention to Ifel. "Can you tell us anything about his creator?"

Ifel's tongue darted out. Flick, flick. "She is very protective. She attempts to constrain Alec's movements and his growth out of a fear for his safety. She cares for him very deeply."

Cade mulled that over. "So she's not an overzealous scientist who created him just to prove she could?"

Ifel's look gave him an answer without words.

"What's her name?" Aurora asked.

"She has been called Patel and Darsha. Alec calls her Mom."

"Mom?" Aurora's emotional field rippled. "What does she look like?"

An image appeared in Cade's mind of a woman in her late thirties or early forties. Based on physical similarities to the image of Alec that Ifel had shown him during his previous visit, the woman could be Alec's biological mother — if Alec were biological. They shared many of the same facial characteristics, as well as the same light brown skin and dark hair.

"There is another who monitors Alec's wellbeing." A second image appeared in Cade's mind, this time of a man with slightly greying blond hair. His sandy brown eyes exactly matched Alec's. He also looked familiar. Had he been seated in the co-pilot's chair on *Phoenix*'s bridge during one of Aurora's chats with Nat?

"What's his name?" Aurora asked.

"He is called Gavin. He is aware of us."

Ifel's words snapped Cade to attention like a whip crack.

Aurora tensed beside him. "You mean he's aware of the Yruf?"

"Yes. So is another they call Pete."

An image appeared in Cade's mind of a ginger-haired man with worry lines between his brows but laugh lines around his eyes. He was not familiar. "What's Pete's job on the ship?"

"He maintains the engine functions."

Aurora's mouth pinched at the corners. "Are those the only two people Nat has told about you?"

"Yes. They are trustworthy." Ifel didn't seem concerned about it. "Isin told another."

The next image was of a strikingly beautiful woman with Asian features who fit the description for Itorye, *Vengeance*'s first mate. Brendan, Libra, and Marina had all spoken very highly of her after the joint mission on Devries' ship.

"What about Alec's creator?" Aurora asked. "Does she know?"

"No. She is... volatile."

"Volatile?" Aurora's emotional field radiated alarm. "Volatile how?"

Ifel was silent for a moment. "Her emotions are out of balance. She is easily upset. The others agreed she should not be told about us."

Aurora's jaw moved, like she was chewing on her tongue. "Does she know about Unity?"

"Yes."

"Why did they trust her with that information?"

Even in Cade's mind, Aurora's words had an edge.

"She was already aware of Unity. She feared they would harm Alec. Introducing her was intended to calm her fears."

"Intended but not successful?" Aurora asked.

"Her attitude has stabilized."

Not exactly a resounding vote of confidence. "Could she harm Unity? Separate them from Alec?"

"She cannot."

"Why not?"

"Neither Unity nor Alec would allow it."

The certainty in Ifel's statement lowered the anxiety level in both his and Aurora's emotional fields.

"And everyone who knows about you is accepting of your presence and Unity's?" Aurora asked.

"Yes."

Aurora sighed. "Then it sounds like Nat and Isin did take my warnings to heart."

Ifel's hand on Aurora's face moved, her finger stroking her cheek like a mother soothing her child. "You are struggling against your inability to take action."

Surprise flitted through Aurora's emotional field. "Yes, I am. If the *Starhawke* wasn't grounded, there are so many things we could be doing right now. The Kraed ships are in Teeli space tracking down the Teeli armada and Siginal's on Drakar talking to the clan leaders. We could have helped with both those missions."

"Patience. Your time will come."

He could feel Aurora's resistance to Ifel's words. Being admonished as impatient wasn't typical for her. She was one of the most patient people he knew. Well, except when others were suffering.

But Ifel wrote the book on patience. She always played the long game. By comparison, Aurora looked reactionary. Which was another term no one would apply to her.

"Well, I'd like to learn more about Alec." Yes, he was shamelessly trying to distract Aurora. And it worked.

Her gaze met his. "What do you have in mind?"

"I think we should invite Nat and Isin over to the *Starhawke* for dinner. Then the four of us can talk without anyone worrying about who might overhear something they shouldn't."

"That's a good idea. I'll contact her in the morning. But I think I'll expand the guest list." A light glimmered in her eyes. "It's time Nat and Isin learned what my family and I can do. *All* that we can do."

Fifteen

"Roe, you need to see this."

Aurora's steps slowed as she exited the lift onto the bridge. A sense of foreboding stole over her as the agitation in Kire's emotional field wrapped around her. Even Kelly, seated at navigation, radiated unsettled energy.

Kire stood in front of the captain's chair, arms folded and his jaw tight. He nodded at the bridgescreen. "Star, play this one first."

She caught an image of President Yeoh on the bridgescreen with the words *breaking news,* before Yeoh's image was replaced by a reporter standing in front of the Presidential residence. A crowd filled in the gap between the reporter and the tall fence that surrounded the building.

"This crowd of protestors has gathered in front of the President's residence following a rally earlier today held by Delegate Miller," the reporter said, yelling to be heard over the shouts of the people behind her. "Public opinion has turned against the once popular President, with members of the Galactic Council – Delegate Miller being the most vocal among them – calling for the President's resignation due to her close ties to former Fleet Director and fugitive Admiral William Schreiber."

Aurora's ribcage tightened, a knot of dread forming between her shoulder blades.

Fraud! Traitor! Conspirator! The cries rang out in the background as the reporter stepped closer to the camera to avoid being jostled by a group of protestors tromping past. They were dressed identically in black shirts with the phrase *Turn the Fleet over to the Teeli* emblazoned on them in bold white letters. Their faces were partially obscured by black caps pulled low.

The sight shot a flaming arrow of anger into Aurora's mounting dread.

The reporter tried to look unconcerned but failed miserably. She took a few more steps away from the growing mob. "At President Yeoh's most recent press conference, she informed—"

The reporter's words were lost as a roar swept through the crowd. The reporter whipped her head around, face in profile, eyes widening as she stared at something off to her right. She recovered quickly, returning her attention partially to the camera. "They've breached the front gate."

The camera panned away, focusing on the sea of people pouring onto the property. Screams and shouts filled the air as the mob rushed the woefully outnumbered security personnel stationed along the fence line.

The playback paused.

Aurora pressed a hand to her sternum, her heart threatening to punch through her chest. "Is she okay?"

Kire nodded grimly. "As far as we can tell, they got her and her wife out safely. But the residence has been overrun, and no one seems to be doing anything about it."

She could guess why. The Sovereign's vile fingerprints were visible from lightyears away. This was exactly the kind of chaos she reveled in. "There's more, isn't there?" He'd told Star to show her this vid first.

"Yeah." If possible, his face tightened down even more. "Go ahead Star."

The vid was one she'd seen before. It played on all the news channels almost hourly. *Admiral Schreiber and Captain Hawke are considered extremely dangerous* the narration stated as the detention images of her and the Admiral filled the screen. But instead of transitioning to the warning about not approaching the ship or the fugitives, a new set of images appeared with names underneath.

She swore under her breath.

Kire, Celia, Jonarel, Lelindia, Kelly, and Knox stared back at her. Kelly was the only one not in a Fleet uniform.

Another photo grouping replaced the previous set, with the words *Known Associates* above them.

She swore louder.

Micah, her parents, and Lelindia's parents had been added as persons of interest.

If you have information regarding the whereabouts of any of these individuals, contact the Freedom and Security hotline immediately the narrator intoned, miniatures of all the photos filling the screen.

She'd been expecting this. But that didn't prevent the ache in her chest or the weight of responsibility that sank onto her shoulders.

Kelly's photo was grainy, like it had been pulled from a security camera, most likely on Gaia or Sol Station, but her red hair made her easy to recognize. The pics of Aurora's parents and Micah looked like they'd been taken when they were visiting her at Seaview, and Marina's and Gryphon's were their professional photos from their clinic.

However, no one on Cade's team had made the list. Neither had Iolana or Kai. The latter she could understand. The Sovereign's digging may not have gotten far enough to link Micah's and her dad's closest friends as people of interest. Yet. Which is why they were on the *Starhawke* rather than living their regularly scheduled lives on Hawai'i. But why would she exclude Cade's team? They'd been excluded during the Admiral's trial, too.

Cade had filled her in on how the documents that pointed to his team had been altered, keeping their identities secret. Why? How did that factor into the Sovereign's master plan?

"Freedom and Security hotline?" she asked Kire. The prior messages had directed informants to contact the Fleet Security hotline.

"It's new. The public no longer trusts Fleet Security."

She let her head fall back as she sighed. "Of course they don't."

"That's not all."

She squeezed her eyes shut for a moment before facing him. "Tell me."

"Having Jonarel's picture included in the listing has empowered the anti-Kraed faction. They demanded, and the Council has agreed, to prohibit Kraed ships from entering Fleet space until you and the Admiral are apprehended."

She snorted. "How do they plan to enforce that?" As far as she knew, all Kraed ships had camouflaging ability.

"I'm sure they don't. But it prevents Siginal from returning to Earth to defend President Yeoh. And Kraed ships can't be visibly present anywhere in Fleet space."

"Which would make it challenging for Siginal to help Captain Warner. Or anyone else who's aware of the Teeli's duplicity."

"Exactly."

Including Captain Montgomery. "Unity, any updates on Captain Montgomery's status on Eridani Duo?"

Unity's voice came over the speakers. "We're still working on accessing the station's medical center. We're making sure no one will notice us."

"I appreciate your caution." Although a part of her felt the pressure of an internal countdown, warning her of impending danger.

Well, more danger than they were currently in. "Take the time you need, but if you find her, alert me immediately."

"We will."

She met Kire's gaze. "Was there anything else?"

For a moment, his typical humor flared in his eyes. "That's not enough for you?"

"More than enough. Now I need to take care of the task I came up here to do."

Kire stepped back as she settled into the captain's chair and sent a hail to *Phoenix*.

A minute later Nat's image appeared on the bridgescreen. She was dressed in a tank top rather than her usual turtleneck and had a sheen of sweat on her brow, indicating she'd been working hard or exercising. "What's up?"

"I wanted to ask if you and Isin would like to join my family for dinner tonight."

Nat's brows rose. "What's the occasion?"

"No occasion. My dad and brother have been spending a lot of time in the galley and we have a lot of food to share."

Nat's nose twitched, like she was smelling something a little off. "That's very thoughtful." Her emotional field indicated she knew there was much more to the invitation than Aurora was saying. "Can we bring anything?"

"Just yourselves. In fact, ask Marlin if there's anything he needs that we can send back with you."

"I will. He's making the most of all the fresh produce you gave him last time. And the plants for his hydroponics area." She glanced to her right, her eyes narrowing, even though the other two chairs on *Phoenix*'s bridge were vacant. She schooled her expression before facing the camera again. "What time should we head over?"

"Does seven hours from now work for you?"

"Sure. See you then." The bridgescreen reverted to the close-up of *Phoenix* and *Vengeance*.

Aurora stood, relinquishing the captain's chair back to Kire. "I'll be in the greenhouse if you need me."

Sixteen

"I can't take you to the *Starhawke*, Alec." Nat pivoted the pilot's chair to face him. He'd appeared near the bridge hatch as she was talking to Aurora about the dinner invitation. It had been easy enough to read his lips when he'd mouthed *take me.*

She'd ignored him while she wrapped up the vid call, but he was staring at her with a determined stubbornness that was very reminiscent of his mother.

"Why not? You can take my cube on *Gypsy.*"

"Can you even be contained in your cube anymore? Aren't you integrated with the ship?" She looked significantly at their surroundings.

"I can do both. Unity taught me how."

Of course they had. "That doesn't make it a good idea. Besides, what would be the point? All you'd get to see is the *Starhawke*'s shuttle bay."

He dropped his chin, looking at her through his dark lashes. "That wasn't my plan. I want you to take me, then ask Aurora if I can join you at your dinner."

Nat opened her mouth, then closed it. "That's crazy. And reckless. Besides, your mother would kill me."

"My mother doesn't have to know."

"Are you serious?" She frowned at him. "Who are you and what have you done with Alec?"

He sighed. Rather dramatically. Also like his mother. "It's not that big a deal."

"Oh, really? How do you propose I get your cube out of your mother's room and back in without her noticing it's gone? She checks on you obsessively."

"Simple. I'll make a projection."

An image of Alec's cube appeared on the pilot's console. It was subtly transparent with the starfield as the background, but viewed against the bulkhead it could pass for the real deal. At least at a glance. "Did Unity teach you to do that?"

For the first time, Alec looked uncomfortable. "Kinda."

Warning lights flashed. "What do you mean, kinda?"

"Unity doesn't use projections. But Star does."

Nat's fingernails dug into the armrests of her chair. "*Star* taught you how to do that?" Her heart pounded like the galaxy's biggest bass drum. "How do you know about Star? Is she on *Phoenix*, too?"

"No, no." Alec waved his hands in denial. "But Unity's sharing space with both of us. They introduced us at Star's request. I've been communicating with her through Unity. They've both been helping me improve my projection ability."

Nat lifted her hand to her forehead, massaging the spot of tension building there. "Does Gavin know about this?" His was the voice of calm reason when it came to Alec's wellbeing.

"Not about Star. But he knows I'm working with Unity on my projections."

She lifted her head. "Does he approve?"

Alec gave a decisive nod. "Yes."

The air in her lungs leaked out in a weary sigh. "Then here's the deal. I will *consider* taking you to the *Starhawke* only *if* Gavin's the one who delivers your cube to me on *Gypsy* when we're ready to leave. If he doesn't sign off on this, you're not going. And if Aurora doesn't want you on her ship, you'll stay on *Gypsy*. No arguing or maneuvering."

Alec considered her proposal. "That's fair. But Unity thinks Aurora will say yes."

"Is that so?" Her gaze swept the bridge. "Care to tell me why, Unity?"

"Because Aurora already wants to talk to you about Alec," Unity replied through the bridge speakers.

Nat chewed on that tidbit. "Is that the reason she invited us to dinner? To talk about Alec?"

"Partially."

"What's the other part?"

"That's for her to share."

She huffed, but she knew better than to try to pry it out of Unity. They could be a vault when they wanted to. "She said this dinner was with her family. Micah already knows about Alec, but what about her parents?"

"Yes, she and Micah told them. Cade knows, too."

"Why not just put up a billboard," she muttered. But that wasn't fair. Cade was the one who'd released her from her Setarip captors. He was also the reason Hobbes, Omondi, and Adel hadn't died on *Sphinx*. Alec's identity was safe with him.

"Okay, fine. You two get Gavin up here and arrange things. I'm heading over to *Vengeance* to let Isin know about the dinner plan."

Seventeen

A feeling of nervous anticipation washed over Aurora as she and Cade stepped into the *Starhawke*'s shuttle bay. But the emotion wasn't her own. It was coming from Nat, who emerged from behind *Gypsy*, Isin beside her.

Her mouth looked a little pinched, her shoulders tight, the nervous energy pulsing with each step. Whatever it was, it was important. Then again, whenever *Gypsy* sat in the *Starhawke*'s bay, big shifts seemed inevitable.

"Hey, Aurora." Nat halted a few meters away, hooking her thumbs into the pockets of her cargo pants. "Before we go anywhere, there's something I need to ask you."

"I had a feeling."

Nat's brows lifted a fraction, and then a self-deprecating smile flitted over her mouth. "Of course you did." She tilted her head back toward *Gypsy*. "Come on, I'll show you what I'm talking about. You too, Cade."

Cade's curiosity matched her own as they circled to *Gypsy*'s back hatch.

"Wait here." Nat disappeared into the shuttle, emerging a moment later with a cube in her hands.

It looked like a block of frosted ice roughly the size of Nat's hands, with a slight blue tinge and smooth sides.

Nat cradled the cube like the contents were fragile. She gave Aurora and Cade a measured look. "Alec wants to know if he can join us."

Aurora blinked, staring at the cube. Whatever she'd been expecting Nat to say, that wasn't it. "That cube is Alec?"

"No. It's his mode of transportation. He's inside. But I told him he couldn't come out unless you said it was okay." She gave a shrug that wasn't remotely casual. "He really wants to meet you and see the *Starhawke*."

Nat's nervousness finally made sense. And Aurora needed a minute to think. "Why does he want to meet me?"

"Because he's fascinated by interesting people. You've made a big impression on him. So has Cade."

"He's been observing us?" She wasn't certain how she felt about that. It hadn't occurred to her that Alec would be curious about her ship or her crew.

"Only through the communications we've had," Nat assured her. "And his discussions with Unity."

Aurora's gaze shifted to Isin. "I understand that you now know about Unity."

He nodded. "Alec told me and Itorye, my first mate. He believed we needed to know. I also told Itorye about the Yruf, but she'll keep that knowledge to herself. I trust her, and so can you."

He'd just confirmed what Ifel had told them. "Unity, what are your thoughts about having Alec onboard?"

"We're excited for you to meet him!" Unity's voice boomed from the bay speakers.

Nat's lips twitched. So did Cade's.

She'd like to get Star's opinion, too, but since Isin didn't know about Star, she didn't have an elegant way to ask. Based on Unity's reaction, chances were good they'd already introduced the two non-biologicals to each other. If Star had any concerns, she trusted her to find a way to let her thoughts be known. "Let's wait until we reach the observation lounge to do introductions."

Nat nodded, tucking the cube into the crook of her arm.

An array of tantalizing smells wafted toward them as the observation lounge doors parted. The buffet setup near the door to the galley had become the new standard for meals now that the crew had expanded almost four-fold.

Her parents and Micah were waiting for them, U-1 hovering beside them.

Isin's gaze locked on U-1 as they glided toward him.

"Hi, Isin!"

Recognition eased the tension from his expression. "Hello, Unity."

"This is U-1," Aurora explained, "one of Unity's mobile units. We have two on the ship, U-1 and U-2. They have different markings so we can tell them apart, but they're both Unity. We came up with the naming convention to help us differentiate them for specific tasks or missions."

Isin nodded. "Wise."

"Hello, Nat." Her dad greeted Nat warmly, then turned to Isin and stuck out his hand. "I'm Brendan, Aurora's father."

"Father?" Isin's dark brows rose as his gaze moved between Aurora and her dad.

She knew what he was thinking. Her dad didn't look old enough to be her father. And he was right. Thanks to her mom's Suulh healing energy, the grey in his hair had been replaced with lustrous blond and the lines around his eyes had smoothed out.

"Yep. I'm a lucky man." He wrapped his arm around Aurora's shoulder, pulling her into a sideways hug.

"I'm Libra." Her mom held out her hand. "Aurora's mother."

Isin continued to blink in surprise, his gaze sweeping over her petite form as he shook her hand. "Pleased to meet you."

"And I'm Micah, her brother."

Isin's gaze sharpened. "You're the one who supplied Unity's voice."

Micah grinned. "That's right. Although some people can still tell us apart." The flare of happiness that surrounded him made it obvious who he was thinking about. He motioned at Nat. "What's with the cube?"

"Another guest, one Unity informed me you've all already heard about."

Her dad and Micah shared a look. "That's Alec?" her dad asked.

"He's inside, yes."

"Then let's meet him," Micah said with an enthusiasm that would rival Unity's.

Nat crouched, setting the cube on the deck and tapping out a sequence on the surface before stepping back.

The cube immediately began losing cohesion, almost like it was melting. The outer covering of ice blue pooled at the base, revealing a metal sphere at the center.

"Hello, everyone." The male tenor voice was accompanied by an image projection above the cube of the same young man Ifel had shown her – dark hair, tawny skin, and light brown eyes. "I'm Alec. Thank you for allowing me to join you."

Eighteen

Micah stared in fascination at the projection that had appeared above the metal sphere.

Ever since Nat first acknowledged Alec's existence, he'd wondered whether Alec would be more like Star or more like Unity. Based on Alec's calm, respectful demeanor in introducing himself, his personality fell somewhere in between Unity's boundless enthusiasm and Star's quiet reserve.

The unusual transportation device he'd been brought in was also intriguing.

"Hello, Alec," Aurora replied. "I'm Captain Aurora Hawke. It's nice to finally meet you."

Alec bowed his head. "The pleasure is mine, Captain. Nat and Unity both think very highly of you."

Nat's cheeks flushed a pale pink when Aurora's gaze flicked to her.

"I think highly of them, too."

Nat folded her arms over her chest, looking anywhere but at Aurora.

"So do I. Nat's teaching me how to fly *Phoenix*."

"Is that so?" Micah's dad took a step closer to Alec. "I'd like to know how you're accomplishing that. I'm Brendan, by the way, Aurora's dad. I'm also a pilot."

Alec visibly perked up at that news.

"I'm a pilot, too." Cade flicked his hand in a subtle wave. "I'm Cade. *Gladiator*'s my ship."

Alec's focus swung to him. "Unity has told me a lot about you."

Cade returned his smile, glancing at U-1. "I'm sure they have. They've gotten to know me pretty well."

Alec nodded. "They think we have a lot in common."

"That sounds like a compliment."

"It is!" Unity exclaimed, bobbing up and down.

"I'm Libra, Aurora's mother." His mom's reaction to Alec was more subdued, her expression a little wary.

"It's a pleasure to meet you."

Micah got the sense Alec understood the motherly protective vibe his mom was giving off. "I'm Micah, Aurora's brother."

Alec's broad smile had a childlike quality. "You do sound like Unity!"

He chuckled. "I get that a lot."

Alec's smile widened at the shared joke. "I'm sure you do."

"What about you? Is your voice patterned after someone?" Alec's appearance and subtle accent indicated an Indian heritage, clearly a conscious choice by whoever created him.

"A lot of someones. My mother used recordings of twenty-three different people, child to adult, synthesizing them together to generate my voice. Her method is quite ingenious. My voice has changed as I've matured, as has my physical projection."

"Do you mind if I ask how old you are?" Cade enquired.

Alec's face scrunched up in thought. "My mom and Gavin could answer that more accurately than I can, but my earliest coherent memories are from roughly three and a half years ago."

Micah's jaw hit the floor. "You're only three-and-a-half years old?"

Alec's mouth quirked in a crooked, self-conscious smile. "My development has accelerated recently. When I was first brought onboard *Vengeance*, I had the maturity of an eight-year-old."

"Brought onboard *Vengeance?*" Aurora's gaze cut to Isin. "*You* brought Alec onboard?"

The long-suffering look on Isin's face spoke volumes. "I didn't know Alec was in the cube when I recovered it. The original deal with Patel was for retrieval and drop off."

"Which I pushed him into," Nat said. "We had a bet and I won when Patel agreed to my terms. We both got more than we'd bargained for." Her gaze shifted to Alec, who'd pivoted to face her. "But I'm thrilled with how things turned out."

"Thanks, Nat."

"It's true. You're turning into a great pilot. And if we hadn't encountered you," her gaze drifted to Isin, "there's a good chance Isin and I wouldn't be working together."

Nat said *working,* but based on the look that zinged between them, Micah thought she meant something else entirely.

"So Patel is the one who created you?" Aurora asked.

Alec swung back to face her. "Yes. Dr. Darsha Patel. She's a brilliant scientist." His expression turned rueful. "And a very protective mother."

"I'm surprised she let you come here," Micah's mom said, eyeing Alec like a kid out past curfew.

Alec met that look head-on. "I'm an adult. My choices are my own."

The choked sound that came from Aurora sounded like a poorly suppressed laugh.

Their mom shot her a sideways look before returning her attention to Alec. "Does she know you're here?"

"No, she doesn't. She also doesn't know about the Yruf." Alec's chest rose and fell in a sigh. "My mother is brilliant, but she can be a bit... temperamental."

This time it was Nat who snorted. "Understatement of the millennium."

"Speaking of the Yruf." Aurora's gaze landed on Nat. "Is there anyone besides Patel on *Phoenix* you don't trust to know about them?"

Nat shook her head. "Gavin and Pete already know. They're both very good at keeping secrets. I haven't told Marlin, but that's just because we've been busy, not because I don't trust him to keep it to himself."

"What about on *Vengeance*?" she asked Isin.

"That's a longer list. Itorye already knows, and I would trust Sweep, Kenji, Jake, and Fleur. Gavin would say we could trust Sparki. But that still leaves a handful that I can't predict how they'd react. And that's not including *Sphinx*'s crew." Isin's gaze turned speculative. "Why are you asking?"

"Because the more secrets we're concealing from each other and the crews, the tougher it is to work together effectively. Which is the primary reason I brought you here. I don't want to keep secrets from you any longer."

Nineteen

Nat's heart did a little tap dance in her chest. Whatever Aurora was planning to reveal, it would be big. She could feel it.

"You both already know that I'm an empath. I inherited that gift from my dad. He's a powerful empath. What you don't know is that I also inherited abilities from my mom." Aurora met Nat's gaze squarely. "Abilities you saw demonstrated on Devries ship when his people fired on the kids."

Nat licked her suddenly dry lips. Her gaze darted to Aurora's mother and back. "You're talking about the way she and Marina deflected the blasts?"

"That's right. And while you chose not to press for more information at the time, you have a right to know the truth. All of the truth."

Her stomach did a somersault. Definitely big news. "What's the truth?"

"The ability my mom and I share has been passed down through our family line for generations. We can both generate an energy field that can be used as a shield against virtually any bombardment." Aurora swallowed, the first sign of nerves she'd shown. "But it's not a human ability. It's a Suulh ability."

Nat heard the words, but they didn't register. "What's a Suulh?"

"An alien race that is biologically indistinguishable from humans."

Nat stared at Aurora, her brain refusing to comprehend what she'd just heard. Part of her wanted to laugh at the absurdity. But the part that had her lungs in a vise knew Aurora wasn't joking. "Are you saying... you're an... *alien?*"

Aurora's lips curled at the corners. "Half-alien, actually. My dad's human. My mom's a Suulh. That makes me and Micah half of each."

Nat locked her knees for stability as her equilibrium bobbled. "Half-alien."

"Yes."

Her gaze swept over Aurora — blonde hair, green eyes, pale skin, two arms, five fingers on each hand. "But you look... human."

"As I said, the two races are indistinguishable. Parallel evolution. But the Suulh developed abilities humans haven't. I inherited those abilities from my mom."

Nat snuck a peek at Isin.

He looked as floored as she was, though he was trying to hide it as his gaze shifted between Aurora and Micah. "Does your crew know?" he asked.

Aurora nodded. "Yes. Everyone knows." Her gaze met Nat's. "We're not the only Suulh onboard."

Which sparked another revelation. "Marina's a Suulh, too, isn't she? That's why she was able to heal those kids."

"Yes. She passed that ability down to Lelindia. Gryphon, her mate, is also Suulh."

Suddenly all the puzzling moments and secret looks she'd experienced around Aurora formed a cohesive picture. As did Aurora's lack of fear regarding Tnaryt. "The shock collar never affected you, did it?"

"No, it didn't." Guilt settled onto Aurora's features. "If I could have protected you from the effects, I would have."

"Why didn't you?" It wasn't an accusation. Not really.

Aurora's brows drew together. "After I learned what the collars could do, you and the Admiral were never in the same room with me at the same time. And I only saw Marlin when he brought food."

"You were worried Tnaryt would have killed whichever of us weren't with you when you tried to protect us."

"Or tortured you until I relented. I wasn't willing to put any of you in that position, especially when you didn't have a say in the matter."

Her mind raced, replaying their time together on Tnaryt's ship. Tnaryt hadn't been able to torture Aurora physically, but for someone with her overactive sense of responsibility, watching the pain and suffering of others without being able to prevent it in some ways would have been worse.

Her thoughts skipped to the explosion in the engine room, and the Admiral's injuries. "That's how Lelindia saved the Admiral. She was using her healing ability."

"Yes. Her healing talents are even stronger than Marina's."

Nat caught the love and admiration in Aurora's voice. "Are you and Lelindia related?"

"Not biologically. But she's my energy sister. The Suulh have terms for our two family lines. My line, the guardians, are called Sahzade. Her line, the healers, are called Nedale. Together, we have provided leadership for our people for as long as anyone can remember."

Isin folded his arms loosely over his chest, his expression more like the diplomat he'd planned to be than the mercenary he'd become. "Then your people, the Suulh, are on Earth?"

"No." Aurora sighed, the sound heavier than *Gypsy*. "Our homeworld was attacked when my mother was a child. Marina and Gryphon smuggled her off the planet to protect her. Our homeworld, Feylahn, is now under the sadistic rule of the Teeli."

Nat jerked back a step. "The Teeli? What the hell do they have to do with this?"

"Everything," Libra replied before Aurora could. "They arrived on our world in the guise of friendship." Her voice was ice-hot, both chilling and boiling. "But they weren't the pacifists they claimed to be. They came for one purpose – to conquer us, enslave us, and steal our resources. Especially the abilities of our people."

Nat's head felt like it was about to explode. "The Teeli are the enemy?"

"Yes." Aurora's harsh tone snapped Nat's gaze to her. "And the Sovereign controls their fleet of warships."

Twenty

If anyone other than Aurora had said it, Isin would have scoffed, dismissing them as a delusional lunatic.

But he'd learned a lot about the kind of person Aurora was and the type of people she looked after. If she said the Teeli were the enemy, he needed to adjust his current paradigm.

Which meant making serious revisions to his view of the political situation. What he'd been taught about the Teeli at the Academy and Columbia needed to be tossed out the window. "Why have the Teeli posed as pacifists?"

"Because it kept Union citizens off-guard and allowed the Teeli easy access to Fleet space."

His spine stiffened. "Are they planning to attack us?"

"In a way, they already have." Anger vibrated in Aurora's voice. "Right now the Sovereign's working on overtaking the Fleet. Her minions have convinced the Council to post Teeli consuls to the *Argo*, and it seems likely they'll do the same to the other Discovery-class starships. Ostensibly they're making sure there aren't more traitors in the Fleet like the Admiral and myself." She grimaced. "In reality, they're using their manipulative abilities to turn the crews into Teeli puppets."

"What manipulative abilities?"

Her lips curled in a non-smile. "The Suulh aren't the only ones with abilities humans lack. Some of the Teeli can influence thoughts and behavior, especially through touch, convincing people to do things that aren't in their best interests." Her gaze shifted to Natasha.

Natasha's face paled. "Like the Sovereign does?"

Aurora nodded. "We believe she's half Teeli — a human mother and a Teeli father. That's why she's able to manipulate people so easily."

"Hold on." Isin lifted a hand. "You said she was your roommate at the Academy. How did you not notice she wasn't fully human? The Teeli have a lot of physical differences from us."

Aurora nodded. "You're right. And I don't have an answer for you, but I do have theories. It's possible most of her external biology came from her mother's DNA, making her look human. But I think it's more likely that her mother had her physically altered after she was born. She certainly had the money to do it. When Reanne and I were roommates, she mentioned having childhood surgeries, but she gave the impression she'd needed them to correct medical defects she'd been born with. The *defects* may have been her Teeli traits. The only thing that made her stand out was the white streak in her hair, but that can happen with human children, too."

He plugged those pieces into his shifting paradigm, then circled back to an earlier point. "Natasha has seen the shielding and healing you described, but can you give me a better idea of what exactly you can do?"

"Sure. Come over here." She motioned him to an open space beside the large table set for their meal.

When he joined her, she lifted her hands, palms toward him. "Try to hit me."

He lifted a brow.

"You won't hurt me."

He shook his head. "That's not my concern. How much damage will you do to me?"

A broad smile broke through her focused expression. "I knew I liked you. You're the first person to see it from that perspective. Thank you."

He got the impression most people didn't believe her. Or failed to notice her strength. He couldn't afford to make that mistake when facing unknown dangers.

Shifting into a fighting stance, he studied her. She didn't look like someone bracing for a blow. That told him a lot. "How many bones am I about to break?"

"None. I can control the impact so that it will stop you without hurting you."

"And if you wanted to hurt me?"

She looked uncomfortable, but she didn't avoid the question. "I'd shatter every bone in your hand."

He gave a curt nod, appreciating her honesty. "Remind me not to tick you off." Then he threw a punch at her head.

The sensation was bizarre. It was like punching a giant rubber band covered with soft clay. His momentum bled away, his fist momentarily enclosed by a warm, pliable, invisible grip, then gently pushed back. "Huh." She hadn't moved a millimeter. "You said the shield was virtually impenetrable." He reached into a sheath on his belt, pulling out a knife. "Can you deflect this?"

Her answer was a mocking twitch of her lips.

Accepting the challenge, he jabbed the knife toward her throat.

This time he saw a flash of light at the point of contact and felt the impact along his entire arm, the knife scraping against an invisible barrier.

Okay, he was impressed. Sheathing the knife, he folded his arms over his chest. "How about projectile weapons?"

Aurora turned toward Natasha. "You've seen it in action. Does it work well against projectile weapons?"

Natasha's eyes had widened, the aqua blue vibrant against her pale skin. "Yes, it does." She swallowed, her gaze still on Aurora. "Nothing got through."

Aurora turned back to Isin, lowering her hands. "I stopped a rockslide when I was a teenager, deflecting all the boulders without any problem. And I'm stronger and more skilled now than I was then."

Sweep was going to love hearing about her abilities. That is, if Aurora allowed him to share her secrets with his crew. The potential for defensive strategy was mind-boggling. "I'm beginning to see why the Sovereign is so focused on you. You could really muck up her plans."

"That's why the Teeli have been hunting our families since my mom and Lelindia's parents escaped. We're the best hope for freeing the Suulh from Teeli control."

"That's what you're hoping to do? Free them?"

"It's what I will do."

He understood the quiet confidence behind that statement. It was born of experience and knowing exactly what her strengths were. And her weaknesses.

He'd earned that same confidence on *Vengeance*, through blood, sweat, and rage. That Aurora had it gave him a lot more optimism about the future. "What can you tell us about the healer ability?"

Aurora motioned him back to the rest of the group. "Like the Sahzade abilities, the Nedale healing abilities get stronger with each new generation. If Lelindia gets to a patient quickly enough, she can heal almost any injury. She's even brought patients back from clinical death when Fleet medicine couldn't save them. But, like me, she's kept her abilities secret, not wanting to draw attention to herself."

"Because of the Teeli," Isin guessed.

"Correct. But now that the Sovereign knows who we are, and we're all together on the *Starhawke*, it's time to change the dynamic. Besides," her gaze shifted to Natasha, "my friends deserve to know who I really am."

Natasha took a slow breath. "It's a lot to wrap my head around."

"I know. That's why I wanted to tell you now, when we have a moment of calm."

Isin's gaze moved to Micah. "Do you have the same shielding ability as Aurora?"

Micah gave him a rueful smile. "No. The Sahzade and Nedale abilities only pass down the female line. But when I'm near her, I can amplify her abilities, make her stronger and give her greater range."

Sweep would *really* love to hear about this. Itorye, too. She'd be fascinated.

He shifted his focus to Aurora. "You've chosen to tell us. Are we allowed to share this information with our crews?"

"That's up to your discretion. Anyone who knows about us is potentially at risk from the Sovereign. She's already targeted one person, kidnapping her to extract information and use her against us. Thankfully, we got her back, but she suffered a lot of trauma as a result. You'll have to decide if the benefits to your crew of knowing about us outweigh the risks to their safety."

"We're all targets of the Sovereign, anyway," Natasha commented, anger underlying her words. "Directly or indirectly. I want my crew to know who they have fighting on their side. It'll make it easier to plan our next move."

Aurora's gaze locked onto Natasha. "So you're going to stick with us, even after the ships are fully functional?"

Isin recognized the defiant glint in Natasha's eyes. "What you're fighting against will affect us all. I'd rather be in the thick of it, knowing what's going on, than waiting on the fringes, powerless to change the outcome." Her gaze moved to him. "Right?"

"You already know my answer."

Her breath hitched slightly. "I guess I do." She cleared her throat, turning back to Aurora. "We're in."

Twenty-One

Considering the mountain of information she'd dumped on Nat and Isin, Aurora was impressed by how well they'd adapted. Their emotional fields had fluctuated as the revelations hit, but now that they'd made the shift to the new reality, she wasn't getting jolts of shock or anxiety from them anymore.

What she found really interesting was Alec's reaction. She could sense more emotion from him than she did from Star, but less than from Unity. Still, she'd been able to tell that the news about her heritage and abilities weren't a shock to him. She suspected Unity had a lot to do with that. Possibly Star, too.

There was a time when that would have worried her. But she'd come to respect Unity's judgment regarding trusting others. Star clearly had, too. Unity had helped to keep the Yruf safe from the threat posed by the other Setarip factions for decades, maybe even centuries. And monitoring was their primary function. They'd gained a lot of wisdom, which was easy to overlook because of their childlike eagerness and enthusiasm.

"Captain?"

Aurora tensed when Star's voice came over the speaker, a reaction she quickly hid from Isin's eagle-eyed gaze. "Yes?"

"I would like to introduce myself to Isin."

She blinked. Apparently they were revealing *all* the secrets today. "Your call."

Star's image appeared beside her, facing Isin.

His stance shifted, his lips parting and his eyes widening.

"Hello, Captain. I am Star, the Nirunoc integrated with this ship."

Isin stared at her for a four count, thoughts racing behind his eyes as he scanned her from head to toe. "A non-biological?"

Star inclined her head. "My species was created by the Kraed, a fact we have kept secret due to Humans' distrust of non-biologicals. In our culture, the Nirunoc and Kraed are intertwined with each other as one family. Jonarel is my brother."

"Brother."

Aurora could feel him testing the word on his tongue as his emotions struggled to keep up with Star's explanation.

"I am the essence of this ship, the Star in *Starhawke*. I wanted you to be aware of me, as it appears we will be working together for the foreseeable future."

Isin absorbed that in silence, then his eyes narrowed and he glanced at Nat. "When did you meet her?"

Nat lifted her chin at his brusque tone. "During my last visit with Marlin. She revealed herself to me as a show of trust that I could tell her and Unity about Alec."

Aurora sensed the hurt in Isin's emotional field. She needed to head that off. "I'm the reason she didn't tell you."

Isin's gaze locked on her.

"The people on this ship are the only ones who know about the Nirunoc. It's the Kraed's most closely guarded secret. Star chose to reveal herself to Nat, just as she chose to reveal herself to you. But I made it very clear at the time that Nat didn't have the right to share that knowledge with anyone. Including you."

The penetrating look in his eyes probably inspired trepidation in people who didn't know him. But his emotions made it clear he respected the need for secrecy, and also appreciated the trust Star had shown him.

His gaze shifted to Star. "Thank you for telling me, Star. I'm honored by your trust in me."

"You have earned it, Captain. Now I must ask you to keep my secret from your crew. Perhaps one day I can speak to them, but for now, I must remain silent."

"I understand." He glanced at Alec, who had been watching Star intently from the moment she appeared. "You already knew about her, too, didn't you?"

Alec nodded. "Unity introduced us. She's the one who's been helping me improve my projections." He looked away like a bashful kid. "Gavin thinks it's Unity who's giving me insights."

The hint of a smile touched Star's lips. "I would like to meet Gavin one day. From what Alec and Unity have shared, his views regarding non-biologicals are very much in line with Kraed ideals."

"They are!" Unity agreed.

Aurora was curious to meet him, too, after hearing Ifel's assessment of him.

Her dad clapped his hands together. "Well, now that we're all on the same page, let's eat."

Nat scooped up Alec's cube-sphere, setting it on the deck between two of the chairs at the table before she joined the rest of them at the buffet. As everyone took their seats, Alec's image shifted, the faint outlines of a chair back and seat that resembled the navigation chair on *Phoenix*'s bridge keeping him from looking like he was sitting on air.

Conversation during the meal moved to the repair work on both ships.

"What about *Sphinx*?" Cade asked. "Were you able to salvage anything?"

The blast of indignation from Nat caught Aurora off guard, halting her mid-chew.

"Nothing good," Nat snarled, stabbing a piece of asparagus with her fork and popping it in her mouth.

Aurora glanced at Isin, who was clearly amused by Nat's reaction. "Problem?"

He shook his head. "We discovered Mirko had set up a camera in the crew shower stall. She enjoyed taking pictures of me and Omondi and putting them up on her walls."

Aurora's jaw hinged open. "That's…" She had trouble coming up with the right word. "Disturbing." Not nearly strong enough. She'd be furious if she discovered someone had done that to Cade.

"Sociopathic," her mother replied, her jaw tight as she gazed at Isin. "I can see why she's with Manchado in your brig."

Isin nodded. "She's a multiple-opportunity offender."

"We should blow *Sphinx* to smithereens," Nat grumbled, stabbing two more vegetables on her plate.

"We have a better idea." Unity bobbed closer to the table.

"What's your idea?" Micah asked.

"We can salvage the entire ship."

Nat frowned, but Isin looked intrigued.

"You mean like you did with the Ecilam ship?" Cade asked.

"Ecilam ship?" Nat asked.

"During my team's first encounter with the Yruf, a self-destruct on the Ecilam ship the Yruf were tracking destroyed the ship, killing everyone onboard. The Yruf recovered the ship and all the debris from the explosion. They're amazing at salvage."

"What would you do with the ship?" Isin asked Unity.

"Recycle all the components for reuse."

Isin's brows rose. "You can do that for an entire ship?"

"Of course."

His gaze shifted to Aurora, a question in his eyes.

She smiled. "If you saw the Yruf ship, you'd understand. It's massive, a mobile world, really. And modular. It can separate into a bunch of smaller ships."

"So it's not like the *Starhawke?*"

She shook her head. "Not remotely. The technology they have is way beyond anything even the Kraed have achieved. Their entire race lives on that ship. It's why they want to end the civil war. They have to achieve peace with the other factions before they can finally establish a new homeworld."

Nat was staring at Unity, her fingers drumming on the tabletop. "So you would take it completely apart? Break everything down?"

"Yes," Unity replied. "Unless there are pieces you would like to have?"

Nat made a rude noise. "No way." Her gaze moved to Aurora. "Any objections?"

Aurora shrugged. "It's up to you. You and Isin have history with that ship. So does *Sphinx*'s crew. We're not giving it back to Mirko, so if none of you want it, then Unity's solution is elegant. The only issue is what you'll tell your crews when the ship disappears."

"I don't think that's a problem. Our crews have already accepted the existence of the shadow ships and their camouflage ability. Most of them think they're Kraed ships, which has made things pretty easy. If we say those ships are going to disassemble *Sphinx*, no one's going to question it."

Aurora glanced between Cade and Isin. "Either of you see any problems with it?"

Cade shook his head.

Isin glanced at Nat. "I agree with Natasha. I would like to see the ship disassembled as well."

"Then I guess you're a go, Unity. Just wait until Nat and Isin are back on their ships so they can warn their crews."

"Will do."

Aurora took a sip of her tea before broaching her next topic. "Speaking of Mirko, I have another request. I would like to pay her and Manchado a visit."

That garnered Nat's and Isin's undivided attention.

"Why?" Nat asked, her nose crinkling like she'd smelled something foul.

"I'm working on the long-term solution for them. I owe it to them and myself to meet with them before I make any decisions."

"That meeting will be unpleasant," Isin warned. "Their personalities haven't improved. If anything, they've gotten worse."

"I understand." She had a clear memory of Manchado leering at her, his gaze locked on her breasts before sliding over the rest of her body like rancid oil. "And I appreciate the warning, but I need to do this. You're welcome to join me, or not. Your choice."

"After your demonstration," Isin tipped his chin to the open space beside the table, "I have no doubt you can handle them without me."

"I want to join you."

Micah's request caught her off guard. She hadn't been paying attention to his reaction to the discussion. "Are you sure that's a good idea?" The tenor of his emotions was difficult to parse out, his emotional field shadowed and murky. What she knew for certain was his last confrontation with Manchado had done a lot of damage to his psyche, damage he was still working to heal.

He stared at his plate, his torso hunched over the table, his hands fisted in front of him. "I need to prove to myself I can look him in the eye without going for his throat."

That brought a hush to the room.

"I can relate to that," Isin said quietly.

Micah looked up. "Yeah?"

Isin nodded. "It's why Sweep is always with me when we deliver food to Mirko."

That was an unexpected admission.

"As long as Aurora's with you, she'll keep you from doing anything you'll regret."

His vote of confidence was... good? Her gaze flicked to her dad. His micro-nod gave her a lot more reassurance.

Isin continued his quiet scrutiny of Micah. "When do you want to meet with them?"

She turned back to her dad. "Can you fly us over tomorrow after your bridge rotation? Since Micah's joining me, I'd like your input on what you sense from Mirko and Manchado during our discussion."

He nodded slowly. "I'll remain out of sight, though. They both strike me as the type who enjoy playing to a crowd. The fewer people in the room the better."

Twenty-Two

"Can I talk to you for a moment?"

Micah halted in the corridor outside shuttle bay two and turned toward Aurora. He'd come with her to see Nat and Isin off so they could all finalize their plans for tomorrow. "Sure."

"Can we go to your cabin?"

So this was a serious discussion. "Okay."

He managed not to fidget during the short trip to the guest deck, but Aurora's demeanor had him on edge. He had a feeling this discussion would have something to do with Manchado.

Stepping off the lift, they crossed paths with Marina and Gryphon in the jungle-like atmosphere of the guest deck corridor. "You two headed to the hydrotank?" he asked, noting the towels in their hands.

"Yep." Gryphon nodded. "Thought it was about time we checked it out. Lelindia and Jonarel loaned us suits."

"Ask Star to show you the Hawai'i environment she and I created. You'll swear you're back on Earth."

"Thanks for the tip."

"How did everything go with Nat and Isin?" Marina asked Aurora.

The entire crew had known Aurora planned to share the news about her Suulh heritage and her abilities, and a warning about the looming threat of a Teeli invasion.

"They took it really well. I'll share the details at lunch tomorrow. Have fun in the hydrotank."

Marina looped her arm through Gryphon's. "We will."

While Lelindia's parents headed for the lift, Micah led the way to his cabin. The door parted as he and Aurora approached. "You want me to make some tea?" he asked as the cozy confines of his front room welcomed them.

She shook her head. "Not unless you want some."

"I'd rather you tell me what's on your mind."

She gestured to the couch. "Let's sit."

He followed her, his muscles tightening with each step. This had to be about Manchado. He'd surprised her with his request to join her. Honestly, he'd surprised himself, too. But it was the right call. He needed to confront the man who'd triggered a violent side of his personality he hadn't known existed.

Aurora settled on the couch, drawing one knee up so she was facing him.

He mirrored her pose. "Okay, Ror, out with it."

Her lips twitched at his use of her childhood nickname. "Okay, My-a." But her amusement quickly faded. "I wanted to talk about what happened on Devries' ship."

Yep, he'd called it. His muscles twisted tighter, squeezing his internal organs. "When I attacked Manchado."

"Yes. Something happened that we need to understand."

He shoved a hand through his hair. "I know. I let my rage at what he'd done to Celia overwhelm me. I lashed out in way I never would have imagined I could. Or would."

Aurora shook her head. "That's not what I meant. While your reaction was extreme, it was understandable given what you'd just seen and what you knew about Celia's trauma."

He frowned. "Then what are you asking me about?"

"The way you emotionally hijacked me. You kept me immobile while you attacked him. And I emotionally hijacked you after Jonarel stopped you."

"Oh." It wasn't much of a response, but he wasn't clear what she was talking about.

"Were you even aware you'd stopped me from moving?"

His mind glided over the surface of those memories like a surfboard over rolling waves. "Honestly, I don't have a clear idea of the sequence of events. I remember hitting him, I remember Jonarel holding me back, and I remember seeing Tatiana lying on the floor of the storage room." He took slow breaths, using the techniques he'd learned from his dad to calm the emotional turmoil those memories triggered. "Now that you mention it, I am surprised you didn't stop me."

"Because I couldn't." She rested her hand on his knee. The touch smoothed out the waves of agitation her question had caused. "Do you remember being immobilized when I touched you?"

He thought back, working to make the snippets of memory line up. "Was that right after Jonarel grabbed my arm?"

"Yes. You froze, like you couldn't move. Like I'd emotionally overridden your desire to hurt Manchado. Or balanced it so you were in a kind of stasis."

"Is that how you felt?" He gazed into her eyes, so like his own. "Like you were in stasis?"

"Not exactly. More like your rage was holding me pinned to the deck."

He winced. "Sorry."

"I don't blame you. It was an intense moment for both of us. My question is, *how* did we immobilize each other? And how do we keep from doing it in the future?"

"Ah." He should have known that was where she was headed. "So you're telling me our connection isn't always beneficial." That sucked.

Her mouth softened in a sad smile. "Depends on how you look at it. If we're in a dangerous situation where one of us really needs to override the other to protect them from harm, we now know it's possible. But knowing that we could do it unintentionally is a little disturbing."

"Yeah." So was thinking about the type of scenario either of them might do it *intentionally*. "I don't think I've ever experienced emotion that intense before. I'm guessing that's the only reason I was able to override you. You're really strong."

"But so are you. And my energy field responds to you like you're part of me. That's why you're the only one who can pass through my shield. Emotionally hijacking me might be easier than you think."

He didn't like where this was headed. "So what do we do?"

"If you're willing, I'd like to try testing it. Do it intentionally and see what we learn."

He rubbed his suddenly sweaty palms on his thighs. "You think we should bring Dad in on this?"

"That's a good idea." She got the slightly unfocused look that indicated she was tuning into her Suulh gifts. Then she grinned. "He and Mom are in their cabin. Convenient. Dad?" she called out.

Their dad's voice came over the comm speakers. "Yes, Aurora?"

"Micah and I have a project we'd like yours and mom's help with. Do you have some time to pop over to Micah's cabin?"

"Of course. Be right there."

Her eyes sparkled. "I think he's been sensing our emotions and hoping we'd contact him."

Micah smiled. "An advantage of an empathic parent."

The door to Micah's cabin parted as their parents arrived.

Micah started to rise, but his mom waved him back down. "Don't get up." She commandeered the chair closest to Aurora, while his dad took the one across from him. "What are you two up to?"

His mom was the queen of directness.

Aurora took the lead. "Something happened between us while we were on Devries' ship that we're working to understand. We're hoping you can help." She gave a rundown on what they'd just discussed, adding a few more details to provide context.

Their dad propped his chin in his hand. "Fascinating. It's clearly tied to your projection abilities, but with a distinctly Suulh twist." He glanced at their mom. "Have you ever heard of something like this before?"

She shook her head. "I haven't. We could check with Marina and Gryphon, but they're enjoying their first visit to the hydrotank. I hate to disturb them."

"Agreed." Their dad looked between Micah and Aurora. "Let's see what we can learn first. We can get their input later."

Aurora rested her elbows on her knees. "How do you suggest we proceed?"

"From what you described, you were both in heightened emotional states when this occurred. I think the first step is determining if that's the *only* condition in which this occurs. Come over here." He motioned to the open space between the seating area and the dining table.

Micah stood, Aurora right behind him.

"Now face each other."

Micah turned to Aurora and made a funny face.

She snorted with laughter.

"Children, please."

"Sorry, Dad." Although his dad seemed to be fighting a smile, too.

"Let's start with something mild, like annoyance. Micah, I want you to visualize that you're standing under a banyan tree. Your feet are bare. When the wind blows, a branch brushes across the top of your head, scratching your skin. You want to move to the left to get away from the branch."

"Got it."

"Aurora, you see Micah starting to shift to the left, but you spot a sharp piece of glass sticking up from the ground that he's about to step on if he moves."

"Okay."

"Close your eyes and make the visualization as real as you can. When I say go, Aurora, I want you to grab Micah and stop him from moving. Micah, I want you to take that step no matter what. Understood?"

"Yes," they said in unison.

The room grew quiet. As Micah visualized the image his dad had given him, he pictured the dappled sunlight through the branches, felt the spring breeze on his skin, smelled the tang of sea air. And the annoying brush of a branch across his head, back and forth, back and forth.

"Go."

He shifted his weight to the left at the same time Aurora's hands slapped down on his arms. He felt her energy field erupt, channeling the projection of her concern into him. But that didn't prevent him from taking a step to the left.

He opened his eyes to find Aurora glaring at him.

"You just stepped on a shard of glass."

"And you didn't stop me."

They both looked at their dad.

"Did either of you feel anything remotely like what happened in the cell block?" he asked.

"Nope."

"Me, either."

"Okay, let's try the same projection, but switch roles."

The silence settled again.

"Go."

Micah grabbed Aurora, but he knew before he opened his eyes that she'd taken a step.

"Is it a good sign that it didn't work?" she asked their dad.

"I don't think it's good or bad. Just more information. Let's try another scenario."

They worked through seven more scenarios, the last one involving a potentially life-threatening situation. However, none of them produced the emotional hijacking they'd experienced before.

"I have a suggestion," their mom said.

"By all means." Their dad waved her over.

"What if the fact that they both know what the other's trying to do and anticipating it is part of the problem? When this happened before, they weren't expecting each other's reaction. Not knowing might be part of the equation." She glanced between them. "I suggest giving you each a scenario the other doesn't know, then we have you react to your scenario and see what happens."

Aurora met Micah's gaze. "Sounds good to me."

He nodded. "Me, too."

His mom went to Aurora first, whispering something in her ear. His sister's eyes narrowed, then she nodded.

Micah leaned down when it was his turn so his mom didn't have to go up on tiptoe.

"You're in Stoneycroft during the fire," she whispered, "up in the gallery. You see the floor beneath Aurora is about to give way. There's no time to warn her. You have to grab her and back up or you'll both fall."

He gave an involuntary shudder. The scenario was a little *too* easy to visualize. "Got it."

He faced Aurora. The look in her eyes was far more intense than in their previous tests. What scenario had their mom given her?

"Do you have your visualizations set?" their dad asked.

"Yes," they answered.

"No matter what happens," their mom said, "keep trying to accomplish your goal."

Aurora gave a short nod, her focus never shifting from him.

He did the same.

"Go."

He reached for Aurora, but she darted to the side to get around him. His right arm came around her in an awkward side grab, but when he tried to pull her in, she pushed back, spinning him around as she moved.

"No!" she barked, fear blasting him as her hand latched onto his arm. Her other hand snapped up in front of her, palm out as her energy field exploded around them.

He froze in place. He could feel the quiver of her body as she stared at what only she could see. But his body wouldn't respond to his commands.

Aurora's energy pulsed around them in pearlescent waves. She hadn't tried to break his grip on her, but she'd planted herself in between him and whatever threat she was visualizing.

Which left them squarely in the danger zone of his scenario.

He pictured the gallery as it had looked during the fire – the flames licking at the wood, the creak of the shifting boards, the swirling smoke thick as fog. And then he visualized the boards beneath their feet starting to sag.

His arm tightened around Aurora's waist, his own fear breaking through the emotional hold she had on him. "Ror!" He lurched to the left, dragging her with him.

Staggering, still fighting against each other, they collapsed to the deck in an ungainly heap. Her energy field cushioned the fall, like dropping onto a mattress rather than the hard wood of the deck.

She let out a gusty exhale, then turned over her shoulder to look at him. "That was interesting."

"And successful." He pushed up on his elbow. "You froze me for a moment."

"I did?"

He nodded. "When you grabbed my arm, I suddenly couldn't move."

"But you dragged us here." She gave a rueful smile as she untangled her legs from his and sat up.

"I focused on the danger we were in. That got me moving again."

Their mom clapped her hands together, beaming at them. "Well done."

"And informative," their dad added. "The emotional interplay was fascinating to witness. Whatever scenario you were given, it was powerful. Your emotions were heightened even before you started. I could practically see the emotional clash when you were fighting for opposite outcomes. What surprised me is that your emotions were very similar. That didn't sound like the case the last time this happened."

"It wasn't." Aurora wrapped her arms around her bent knees. "Micah was in a rage and I was trying to calm him down."

"This time you were both feeling fear bordering on terror, and the desire to protect each other. Which might explain how Micah was able to break the hold you put on him. Your emotions were in alignment, you just had different ideas about how to deal with the situation."

Micah glanced at Aurora. "What was your scenario?"

She swallowed, that intense look back in her eyes. "There was a Necri behind you, about to attack."

His heart stuttered. "Oh."

"How about you?"

"We were in Stoneycroft's gallery when it was collapsing."

Her brows lifted, then a smile curved one corner of her mouth. "Now I understand why we ended up on the deck. I was the immovable object and you were the unstoppable force." Her gaze flicked to their mom. "Well played."

"Thank you." She tilted her head, studying them. "This is the first time I've seen you two interacting like this. Even given opposing scenarios, you were still determined to work together. It's remarkable how far you've come in using your Suulh abilities considering I never trained either of you."

Micah heard more than a little regret in that statement. "It's never too late," he said softly.

Her gaze sharpened, then moved warily toward Aurora. "Do you agree?"

Aurora rocked back, her lips parting in surprise. Then she scrambled to her feet. "Are you serious?" Her chest rose and fell unsteadily.

Their mom's gaze didn't waver. "Yes, I am."

Aurora's eyes drifted closed for a moment. When she opened them, they glistened in the cabin lights. "Mom, I would be honored to be trained by you."

Twenty-Three

They gathered around Micah's dining table, the mugs of tea Libra had prepared in front of them. She cradled her warm mug in her hands, relaxing into the peaceful moment with her family.

"What do you think this complication between Micah and me means going forward?" Aurora asked Brendan.

He took a sip of tea, contemplating Aurora over the rim of his mug. "It seems unlikely that it will be an issue except in extreme circumstances, though we could do more testing with hidden scenarios to give us more data points. It also appears to only be a problem when you're focusing on opposing goals. From everything you've told me about the Stoneycroft fire, you worked together seamlessly in an extremely high stress situation filled with danger. The question I have for you is, now that you're aware of this issue, how will you address it?"

"I'm not sure." Aurora glanced at Micah. "Any thoughts?"

He leaned back in his chair. "Well, I'll admit I feel better now that I've experienced the sensation consciously. The last time it happened I was too overwhelmed with what was going on around us to register it. I think being able to recognize it when it occurs is half the battle."

Aurora frowned. "But I didn't realize I'd hijacked you just now. I didn't sense anything that would have alerted me to the problem. And the first time it happened, I was only guessing that I'd hijacked you based on your reaction."

"Then maybe what we need is a code word, something to alert each other. When I hijacked you, you were still able to talk, right?"

"Yes. It was moving that felt like a Herculean task."

"Then let's come up with a word that we'd never use normally. That way if either of us says it during an intense situation, we'll immediately recognize the problem."

Brendan nodded. "I like that idea."

"It needs to be something that doesn't rhyme easily with other common words," Libra added. "A word neither of you will mistake for something else. Something unusual."

Aurora grinned. "How about platypus?"

Micah snorted. "Platypus?"

"Sure. Mom said it should be something unusual, and they're certainly that. It's also not a word that will ever come up in our daily lives. And they're semi-aquatic mammals, which fits since we both love the water. An unusual animal for an unusual situation."

"Okay, you sold me. Platypus it is." Micah's smile faded. "Hopefully we'll never have to use it."

"But if we do, we're ready."

Libra continued to mull over the unusual nature of Aurora's and Micah's connection after she and Brendan returned to their cabin.

Her mate's arms slipped around her from behind, drawing her close. "You going to tell me what's on your mind?" he murmured, placing a soft kiss on the curve of her ear.

She shivered with delight, her energy field vibrating just under her skin. "I was wondering whether Marina or Gryphon had ever heard of a similar experience between Suulh siblings before."

"Mmm." He trailed kisses along her neck. "Do you want to ask them?"

She let her head fall back against his shoulder. "Not if you're going to keep that up."

His sexy chuckle warmed her as much as the caress of his lips on her skin. "I'll remember where we left off." He nipped her earlobe before releasing her. "Where are they?"

"At the hydrotank with Lelindia and Jonarel."

When they reached the training center, the exterior of the hydrotank was opaque, indicating one of the simulations was running. Lelindia was sitting on one of the lounge chairs on the upper deck surrounding the tank. Her swimsuit gave definition to her growing belly in a way her regular clothing didn't.

The little Nedale would be here before they knew it. And all indications proved she'd be a force to be reckoned with.

"Hi, there!" Lelindia greeted them with a bright smile and a wave.

"Hi, yourself!" Libra settled on the edge of a lounge chair facing her. It warmed her heart to see Lelindia acting more like the vivacious kid she'd been and not the fretting mother hen she'd become after Brendan and Micah left. She'd taken care of Aurora in the aftermath in a way Libra hadn't been able to, suffering a lot of collateral damage from Libra's decision to break up the family.

She owed Lelindia a huge debt, one she hoped to repay by always being there for her and Raehn now and in the future.

"How are you and Raehn doing, firefly?" Brendan asked, dropping onto the lounge chair beside her.

"Good." Lelindia rested her hand on her belly. "We were in the water for a bit, but I'm about as graceful as a walrus with one flipper right now."

"Not true," Jonarel called out from where he was watching them from the edge of the tank. With his dark hair slicked back from his face and his deep green skin covered in water droplets, he looked like a creature from a maritime folktale.

"Very true," Lelindia called back with a laugh, her gaze following him as he slipped out of the water with the ease of a seal. "Swimming has never been my forte, and Raehn was kicking like she was trying to do the breaststroke with me. Very distracting."

Jonarel grabbed a towel, dried himself with brisk efficiency, then joined Lelindia on the lounge chair, pulling her back against his broad chest.

She settled in with a sigh, gazing at him over her shoulder. "But I appreciate the support."

If Lelindia had grown up on Feylahn, she would have been swimming in the aquamarine waters of the ocean almost every day, like Libra and Marina had. But growing up in Northern California, the two nature-based options had been the shallow creeks near their home or the crashing waves of the rocky coast.

Lelindia had always accompanied Aurora whenever she'd demanded time in the water, but neither of them had experienced the kinds of swimming adventures that had been typical for Libra and Marina as children.

Yet another reason she despised the Teeli.

On the other hand, if Lelindia had grown up on Feylahn, she never would have met Jonarel. They were so well matched that it was difficult to imagine anyone loving and cherishing Lelindia as much as Jonarel did.

Marina and Gryphon had surfaced, treading water in the center of the tank. "Hey, Sahzade." Marina wiped moisture off her face. "You here to swim?"

"Nope. Just here for the conversation. How are you enjoying the Hawai'i simulation?"

"I love it! I had no idea it would look so real. Gryphon and Jonarel think they could create one to simulate the ocean on Feylahn." Marina flinched, her smile fading. "Unless that would make you uncomfortable."

Libra sighed to herself. She'd caused a lot of trauma for her energy sister, too, setting rigid rules and refusing to talk about the past. "I think that would be wonderful. I'd love for Brendan to see it. Aurora and Micah, too." One day, they would see it in person. She had to believe that. But a simulation would be a helpful step in all their healing journeys.

"Really?" Marina's smile regained the ground it had lost. "Then we'll do it."

"And speaking of Feylahn, I have some questions for you and Gryphon."

That garnered matching startled looks. "About Feylahn?" Marina asked cautiously, swimming to the edge of the tank and pulling herself out to sit on the deck. Gryphon joined her, looking at Libra warily as he accepted the towels Brendan handed them.

Her fault. She'd inadvertently trained them to react that way, stubbornly holding onto her fears and beliefs and refusing to consider alternatives whenever they'd clashed over what information to share with Lelindia and Aurora.

Those battles had been fought more times than she cared to remember. "The Suulh, more than Feylahn. We just learned that Aurora and Micah have a new wrinkle in their connection to each other." She outlined the situation, including a description of the scenarios they'd run and the one that had produced the desired result. "I was curious whether you'd ever heard of something similar happening with other Suulh siblings?"

"Interesting question," Gryphon said. "Before the Teeli arrived, I can't really imagine a scenario in which that kind of thing would even have a reason to occur. Can you?" he asked Marina.

"No." She shook her head, towel drying her hair. "We didn't encounter any threats like what Aurora and Micah have faced. That's one reason we were ill-prepared for dealing with the Teeli. We couldn't even conceive of that kind of behavior, of someone intentionally threatening and harming others."

"What about after you started to suspect the Teeli's duplicity?" Her gaze rested on Gryphon. "Maybe between you and Amethyst?"

Gryphon's lips thinned. "Not that I recall. But my sister might remember things differently." A flicker of humor softened his features. "She was the feisty one, not me."

Marina snorted, shooting him a sidelong look.

"What?" He placed a hand over his heart, the picture of innocence. "It's true."

"Uh-huh. Sure." Marina bumped him with her shoulder before focusing on Libra. "I don't think we're going to be of any help on this one. The people to ask are the Suulh on Azaana. They'd be the most likely to have experienced situations similar to what you're describing."

A chill spread over her skin. She couldn't think about the Suulh that Aurora had rescued from a Necri existence without the specter of her own mother rising before her. She was a Necri, too. Her wraith-like image and vacant expression still featured prominently in Libra's nightmares, the ones only Brendan's warm embrace could soothe.

Her mother was still out there, somewhere, a shell of the person Libra remembered, with no understanding of the monster she'd become or any awareness that she'd tried to kill Marina and Gryphon. And her.

Libra had no idea why she'd been able to fend off her mother's attack, but the knowledge that she'd succeeded, even when she'd been out of practice and exhausted, gave her hope. One day she and Aurora would have to face the Sovereign's Necri forces. When that happened, she wanted to make damn sure she didn't let her daughter down.

Twenty-Four

Aurora spent most of the shuttle flight to *Vengeance* tuned into Micah's emotions. The upcoming confrontation with Manchado loomed large for both of them, but her brother's emotional field was a lot more controlled than she'd expected.

He'd told her he'd had a long talk with Celia that morning. Apparently, Celia had given him the equivalent of a security briefing on what to expect from Manchado, particularly his preferred methods for goading others. That could be a big help.

Her focus shifted to *Starlet's* front viewport as her dad guided the shuttle toward *Vengeance*. Massive bay doors lowered from the belly of the warship, creating a channel between what looked like four stocky legs. In fact, the ship outline reminded her of a quadruped. A rhinoceros to be exact, with a thick armored body and a prow that looked like the leading edge of a giant horn. She didn't want to think about what that protrusion was designed to do.

"It's an impressive ship," her dad commented as the channel enveloped *Starlet*.

"Solid," Micah agreed from the jump seat behind the co-pilot's chair. Jonarel had installed one on both shuttles at her dad's and Gryphon's request. He'd also stenciled the names of the shuttles on the shuttles' hulls, although he'd made it clear he still thought it was hilarious that the crew had named the shuttles. But that hadn't stopped him from fulfilling the request while waiting for the *Starhawke* to come out of low-power mode.

Her dad angled *Starlet* to a near vertical climb to access the rectangular opening in Vengeance's belly. As soon as they entered the expansive bay, he deftly leveled them out, settling the shuttle on the deck after the deck plating closed behind them.

"That didn't look easy."

He smiled. "The flying's only part of the challenge. From what I saw, there's an impressive arsenal in that channel that would cut down the unwary in seconds before they even got a chance to enter the bay. I pity the pilot who tries to sneak inside this ship."

"It's so different from the *Starhawke*," Micah replied, unfastening his harness and standing. "I'm curious to check it out."

Aurora shot him a look of exaggerated surprise. "Is my terrestrial brother getting hooked on space?" she teased as she unfastened her harness.

He smirked at her. "I'll admit it holds more appeal than it used to. But it still doesn't beat the ocean."

She felt the yearning that underlaid that comment. Which reminded her she'd meant to ask Ifel if Micah and Celia could visit the biosphere for their next date. She made a mental note to do that when she returned to the *Starhawke*.

"Our welcoming party is here," her dad commented as he finished powering down *Starlet*'s systems.

Aurora caught sight of Nat and Isin walking toward the shuttle. Nat had her duster on, which set off an internal alert in Aurora's subconscious. A quick check of the young pilot's emotional field revealed stubborn determination overlaid with a veneer of anger.

"Coming, sis?"

She turned to find her brother and dad waiting for her. "Yep."

They filed down the ramp, meeting Nat and Isin halfway. Aurora lifted her brows in question as her gaze swept over Nat's duster.

"I'm coming with you to talk to Mirko," Nat replied, halting in front of her and shooting a warning look at Isin.

She should have guessed. Micah wasn't the only one with unresolved issues regarding their two prisoners.

Isin clearly wasn't in favor of the idea, but he was wisely keeping those opinions to himself. Likely they'd hashed this out earlier and Isin had lost the debate.

"Since you said we should cut down on the secrets between crews," Nat continued, "after we meet with Mirko and Manchado, I want to introduce you to the members of our crew we've entrusted with the secrets you shared."

"I'd like that." She'd feel better if she could sense the emotional reactions of the people Nat and Isin trusted.

"Then let's get this party started." Without waiting for a reply, Nat spun, her duster swirling around her as she stalked toward the hatch.

Isin's soft sigh was almost imperceptible, but his emotional field was flashing bright orange caution lights. He really didn't want Nat talking to Mirko.

Aurora wasn't sure she was in favor of it, either, but stopping Nat when she was in this mood was like holding back the tide.

Micah fell in step beside her, her dad and Isin bringing up the rear. Their footsteps echoed in the cavernous space of the bay. *Vengeance* was exactly what she'd pictured it would be, solid and utilitarian. Even Fleet ships weren't this bare bones. And yet, there was an orderly perfection to the layout, which was meticulously maintained. No sloppiness on this ship.

She recognized the sleek fighting vessel sitting at the far end as the one Kenji had piloted when he'd brought Isin to the *Starhawke.* It was the only ship – besides *Starlet* – in the bay, even though the space was clearly designed to accommodate at least ten ships that size.

The corridor outside was just as simplistic as the bay, as was the open stairway Nat was heading toward.

"No lift?" Micah asked.

"Lifts can get locked down or overridden," Isin answered. "That's an unacceptable hazard on a warship. We have hydraulic lifts for moving bulk items between decks, but they're disconnected from the ship's power supply when not in use."

"Huh." Micah glanced up at the landing where Nat had paused to wait for them. "I'll bet the stairs keep the crew fit."

They climbed three flights without encountering anyone, although Aurora could sense people on each deck they passed. She suspected Nat and Isin had given an order to keep the area cleared during their visit. The stairs ended at a long corridor that ran the length of the ship. She spotted a door plaque marked *Reclamation* not far from the stairs, but the rest of the corridor was lined with storage units and what looked like maintenance access to the hull's exterior.

Nat's steps slowed as she approached an imposing hatch that spanned the entire width at the forward end of the corridor. Clearly they'd reached their destination.

Nat pivoted to face her, the first tendrils of uncertainty entering her emotional field. "How do you want to play this?"

"Since I've met Manchado, I thought I'd start with him, though I doubt Mirko will remain silent while we chat." Her smile held no mirth.

"Definitely not," Isin confirmed.

Her gaze flicked between Nat and Micah. "We need to keep this civil. I can't evaluate their emotional responses if the discussions devolve into shouting matches. If that's going to be a problem, I need you to tell me now."

Nat folded her arms over her chest and gave a sharp shake of her head. "I'm through letting that woman manipulate me. I need to say my piece, but I can wait until she shuts up. I was also going to hang back out of sight so you can deal with your guy first."

Of the two of them, Nat was the one she felt most confident about. She turned to Micah. "How about you?"

He shifted his weight. "Honestly, I'm not sure how this will go for me. I think I'll be okay, but I can't guarantee it. If I start to lose it, you have my permission to kick me out." His gaze met hers. "Or stop me."

She got the unspoken message. He was telling her to use their newfound emotional hijacking to keep him in line. "Fair enough." She turned to her dad. "You good out here?"

He nodded. "Should be an interesting case study."

Isin quirked a brow at her dad before meeting Aurora's gaze. "I'll be out here as well if you need anything." He deactivated the security on the hatch, then swung it open. The hinges screeched like the front door to a haunted house.

Fitting. There were monsters within.

An eerie silence greeted them as Nat and Micah followed her inside. Nat remained in the short corridor that opened into an octagonal room with six cells. Evenly spaced cylindrical bars formed the front wall of each cell and the walls between the cells, as well as the cell doors. The layout was functional but not designed with the safety of the occupants in mind. Prisoners intent on harming each other wouldn't have any trouble reaching through the bars on either side if their victim strayed too close to the sides of their cell. To make matters worse, the sleeping platforms were positioned in one corner of each cell, right next to the bars.

However, unlike the cells on Devries' ship, these cells were well-lit and clean and the occupants respectfully clothed.

Manchado stood in front of the sleeping platform in the second cell to her left, arms folded over his chest. Isin had wisely chosen to place Mirko across the octagon from him. She was lounging on her platform in the second cell on the right. Her gaze flicked to them in mild curiosity, but she didn't move or speak. Maybe she saved her vitriol for people she knew. Or more likely, based on her emotional field, she was assessing the newcomers before deciding on a course of action.

Manchado didn't waste time considering the situation. He took a step forward, his gaze roving over her body, lingering for a disturbing moment on her hips and even longer on her chest. "Hey, blondie. I remember you. You finally realize you wanted some of this?"

The low drawl and grasping of his privates was probably meant to be sexy. It wasn't. Instead, the rising bulge in his pants made bile coat her throat. But it was the blast of anger from Micah that hit her like a heat wave.

So much for keeping his cool.

"No," he answered for her, stepping towards Manchado's cell, "but I'd be happy to take care of that problem for you. Permanently." He made a little scissor motion with his hand. "Snip, snip."

As a distraction, his threat worked. Manchado's leer vanished as recognition tightened his jaw. "I remember you too, tough guy." He puffed up his chest, his lips pulling back from his teeth in a sneer. "You sucker punched me when I wasn't looking."

"You were too busy zipping up your fly." The loathing in Micah's voice could have coated the entire brig.

Manchado smirked. "Jealous?"

Jealousy wasn't the emotion burning through Micah's emotional field. But Manchado was too arrogant to realize Micah had been deadly serious about neutering him.

"Of a man who has to drug young women in order to have sex with them?" His voice was smooth as ice. "Hardly."

"Is that what this is about?" Manchado scoffed, spreading his arms wide. "What's it to you that I banged some whores? You know they enjoyed it. It's all they're good for. Especially that bitch, Beauty."

Micah tensed.

Manchado noticed. His gaze slid over Micah with malicious glee. "Oh, that's how it is, huh? She thinks she's better than me, but I know the truth. You might be poking her now, but just remember one thing." He lowered his voice like he was sharing a secret. "I had her first. Again and again and again." He added a vulgar hip motion.

Micah's anger coalesced, growing white hot.

Aurora's hand shot out to grasp his arm as she felt his control slip. "Don't."

He froze like she'd hijacked him, although that hadn't been her intention.

"Oh, you're definitely poking her."

She ignored Manchado, focusing on Micah. She needed to remind him why he was here.

Calling on the projection skills her dad had taught her, she focused on images of Celia and Micah talking and laughing together, allowing the joy she felt every time she saw the two of them to fill her emotional field. "She wouldn't want you to. This is why you're here."

He didn't move.

She couldn't tell if she was holding him back, or if he was holding himself back. His chest rose and fell with forceful breaths as he stared at Manchado with the intensity of a bird of prey. The gloating look on Manchado's face certainly wasn't helping.

But Micah hadn't said their code word, so...

"What's the matter, tough guy? Gonna let a bitch tell you what to do?"

Aurora's grip on Micah's arm tightened a fraction as her own anger sparked.

Surprisingly, her shift seemed to trigger his cool down. She felt him emotionally collect himself, the corded muscles under her fingers relaxing.

"You're right." He met her gaze, the light that had dimmed in his eyes ever since he'd announced he was coming on this trip regaining some of its brilliance. "Thanks."

Manchado snorted. "Nice going, pansy-ass. Why don't you lick her boots while you're at it?"

"Will one of you shut him up?"

The barked order from Mirko made them both turn.

She was still sitting on her platform, her knees bent and feet on the mattress. "He never stops flapping his gums." She fixed them both with a baleful glare. "Who the hell are you, anyway?"

Nat chose that moment to step out of the narrow corridor. "They're with me."

All attention shifted to her.

"Orlov." Mirko spat her name as a curse, looking down her nose at her.

"Hello, Mirko." Nat sauntered forward until she was standing in front of Mirko's cell. "I'd say it's good to see you, but these days I'm trying not to lie."

Mirko rolled her eyes. "Seriously? Why bother? Nobody cares about a piece of gutter trash like you."

"Wrong on both counts." Aurora moved to stand beside Nat. "A wise woman would have appreciated Nat's varied skillset, but from what I've heard, wisdom isn't your forte."

Mirko's face flushed. "Who the hell are you?" she repeated.

Aurora took a breath. She'd given a lot of thought to whether or not she would reveal her identity to these two. But if she was going to be their judge and jury, she owed them the truth about who was deciding their fate. "My name is Aurora Hawke. I'm captain of the *Starhawke*."

"*Starhawke?*" Mirko's socked feet swung to the floor, her eyes narrowing. Then she snapped her fingers. "That's why you're familiar. You're the Fleet traitor who broke out of prison. Your picture's been splashed all over the news vids."

"Fleet traitor?" The eagerness in Manchado's voice made Aurora's skin crawl. "So you're slumming with Beauty. The traitor and the whore."

Ignoring them both, she focused on Nat. "Are they always this charming?"

One corner of Nat's mouth lifted. "According to Isin, yeah."

So far, they were doing an excellent job of sweeping away the moral dilemma that had kept her from moving forward. But that might change if they realized the stakes.

She angled her body so she could see them both. "As I'm unable to turn you over to the Union justice system to face trial for your crimes, your fates have landed in my hands. What I came here to determine is whether either of you are deserving of a second chance in the general population, or whether you need to remain isolated for the safety and wellbeing of others."

The silence that followed was pregnant with potential. And then Manchado and Mirko unleashed a torrential outpouring of high-volume expletives and threats that saturated the room.

She hadn't expected eloquent speeches or groveling, but the sheer audacity of hurling abuse when they held no power staggered her. She'd never encountered two people with such a sense of entitlement and such certainty of their own superiority. She had, however, encountered a Setarip with that attitude. And he'd died on the very planet where she was considering leaving these two.

"...measly little worm!" Mirko clutched the bars of her cell. She made a noise deep in her throat and spat.

The glob of mucus hit the invisible barrier of Aurora's shield before it reached Nat and slid harmlessly to the deck.

Mirko blinked, her eyes widening as Aurora stepped closer to the cell.

"You were saying?" She kept her voice mild, but Mirko's attack on Nat had thrust her protective instincts to the fore. Her energy field pulsed around her, ready to counteract whatever stupid move Mirko made next.

Whatever Mirko saw in her expression made her back up a step. "What are you?" she whispered.

Interesting question. Not *who*, but *what*. She hadn't given Mirko enough credit for awareness.

Manchado had fallen silent, but she sensed he was trying to figure out why Mirko's behavior had shifted so abruptly. From his vantage point he wouldn't have been able to see what happened with Aurora's shield.

She held Mirko's gaze. "I'm a guardian of the Union and the ideals it stands for."

"Says the traitor," Manchado scoffed.

She turned the same look on him, but knew it wouldn't have an effect. The man had faced Celia and failed to recognize the danger she posed to his existence. When he looked at women, all he saw were their constituent parts, not a whole person. It's what made him so heartless and dangerous.

But he was making her decision easier. Right now, she could leave him on the planet where Tnaryt had died without giving him a second thought.

Abandoning Mirko there wasn't as straightforward. Aurora didn't trust her back in the general population, especially not after what Nat and Isin had shared about the images they'd found on *Sphinx.* She was a different kind of predator from Manchado, but a predator nonetheless. But did she deserve to be saddled with Manchado as her sole companion?

Twenty-Five

Nat had never expected that, given a choice between Mirko and Manchado, she would ever decide she despised him more than her. But in the space of five minutes, Manchado had achieved that monumental feat. The man was seriously deranged. And the complete lack of respect he was showing toward Aurora fired Nat's blood.

Aurora seemed to be taking it in stride, but then again, that was how she operated. The only time Nat had ever seen her off balance was after she learned the Sovereign's identity. Even that had been a temporary condition. She'd come back from that blow even stronger than before.

Micah, she noted, had moved to the opening to the short corridor. He'd crossed his arms over his chest and propped his shoulder against the bulkhead as he observed the proceedings. The fury he'd expressed toward Manchado was contained, at least for now, but the scowl on his face was a far cry from the easygoing smile that seemed to be his default.

He'd faced down his demon. Now it was her turn.

Aurora's demonstration of her shielding ability when Mirko had spit at her had taken the starch out of Nat's former employer. Mirko was eyeing Aurora like she expected tentacles to burst out of her ears or bees to come pouring out of her mouth.

Nat took a moment to enjoy the unsettled look on her face. "So, Mirko."

Her former boss's gaze flicked briefly to her before returning to Aurora.

That was okay, she didn't need her undivided attention for this. "Isin and I took a trip over to *Sphinx*. We saw your wallpapering job."

Another flick, combined with a smirk.

She refused to let that smirk bother her, not when she was holding all the cards. "Isin wasn't impressed. In fact, he found it funny. I found it pathetic."

The smirk turned into a frown.

"I could tell Omondi about it, but chances are good he'd find a way to sneak in here and slit your throat. That would be messy. He despises you almost as much as Isin does."

"Like I care what any of you think," Mirko snapped, folding her arms under her breasts in a gesture that pushed them up.

Nat had seen her make that move plenty of times before, generally when single men were in the room, but it had a stronger impact after seeing her bedroom. Mirko probably wasn't even aware of what she was doing. The sexual behaviors were second nature.

Maybe Mirko and Manchado were made for each other.

"Based on those pictures, you're obsessed. And all the undergarments and other items we found in your room got me to wondering. What exactly is your connection to Commodore Devries?"

For a split second, bald fear streaked through Mirko's eyes. But hatred overwrote it a moment later. "None of your damn business."

"Wrong again." Aurora's steely gaze drilled into Mirko. "As the person controlling your fate, I strongly suggest you answer Nat's question."

Mirko pressed her lips together like a toddler about to throw a tantrum.

Aurora stepped closer to the cell. "The children on those ships were forced into prostitution. Were you a client who failed to pay? Or a slave trader who failed to deliver?" Aurora's eyes got an unfocused look. "Or a little bit of both?"

The last part came out as more of a statement than a question.

Nat's stomach rolled. She hadn't wanted confirmation of just how bad things had gotten on *Sphinx*. "Is that why Adel was on *Sphinx*? You were supposed to turn her over to Devries? Was she part of the payment for the Aphrodite's Dream?"

"Wait a minute." Manchado's voice cut across the room. "*You're* the one we were hunting?" He was leaning against the front of his cell with his forearms braced on the bars. "You stole the shipment of Aphrodite's Dream?"

"Of course I stole it!" Mirko hissed. "Your boss was only offering me a pittance to deliver it. I was going to make a fortune selling it on the black market."

"Idiot." Manchado snorted in derision. "Nobody steals from Diestro. When Devries gets his hands on you, he'll have you working it off until your body gives out. He was planning to go first." He sounded excited by the prospect.

Nat was trying not to lose her last meal. "So what went wrong?" She couldn't imagine why Mirko thought double-crossing Devries was smart.

"Hobbes and Omondi." Mirko glared at Nat like it was her fault. "The buyer wanted Adel in the deal, which was fine with me. She was a nuisance from the day I brought her onboard. With the money I'd have made I could have hired an actual engineer. But those two were always watching her. I couldn't get her off the ship without one of them interfering. The buyer killed the deal when I couldn't deliver her."

"I've changed my mind," Aurora murmured under her breath. "She's as bad as he is."

Nat wholeheartedly agreed. "And you still chose to keep the Aphrodite's Dream rather than deliver it to Devries?" Even for Mirko, this sounded like insanity. Sweep had said the drug was valuable, but it wasn't worth her life.

"Of course I did." Mirko's tone indicated Nat was the stupid one. "I would have found another buyer. I just needed to—" Mirko snapped her mouth shut.

"Pick up the rest." Manchado's sing-song voice was as disturbing as the gleeful expression on his pasty face.

The rest? Mirko had more than what Sweep had found on *Sphinx?* Returning to the Birdbolt suddenly made sense. So did the excessive firepower Diestro had sent after her.

"You really thought you could hide it in this worthless star system?" Manchado mocked her. "We had a tracker on your sorry excuse for a ship, making it ridiculously easy to find you."

Nat couldn't help noticing Manchado kept using the term *we*, like he was part of the command crew. She seriously doubted that, given where he'd been when Aurora's team had infiltrated Devries' ship.

"Shut up!"

Manchado ignored Mirko. "We also knew about your little side deal." His eyes glinted with malice. "We're the real reason it fell through."

Mirko's face paled, then flushed purple. "SHUT UP!"

Manchado laughed. "We control the Aphrodite's Dream market. No one crosses us." His voice dropped an octave. "No one."

"Really?" Nat interjected before Manchado's self-aggrandizing monologue drove her to pull out her Reiter and shoot him. "I can think of someone. Her." She pointed at Aurora. "She's the reason you're both stuck in this brig, so you might want to pull your heads out of your butts and rethink your worldview."

Mirko sputtered, but the malevolent look Manchado shot her should have turned her to ash.

She glanced at Aurora. "I have a new appreciation for Isin's restraint."

"So do I."

"So are we done here?"

Aurora's gaze flipped to Mirko, then Manchado. "I guess we are."

Twenty-Six

The screamed obscenities Isin had come to expect from Mirko and Manchado reverberated off the bulkheads as Natasha led Aurora and Micah out of the brig. "I see they gave you the royal treatment."

Natasha wrinkled her nose as Isin swung the hatch closed, cutting off the vitriol with a screech and clang. "How do you stand it three times a day? If I had to go in there again, I'd bring a tranq gun."

His lips twitched as he set the security on the hatch. "Do I detect a note of respect in that question?"

"Tons of respect. I seriously considered shooting Manchado just to shut him up."

He slipped his arm around her shoulders, drawing her against him. "I'm glad you didn't. Clean-up would have been a pain."

"Ha, ha." She punched him lightly in the ribs, but her arm stole around his waist. "You and Sweep are really taking one for the team, dealing with those two."

"I agree." Aurora faced him, her hands resting on her hips. "This can't continue."

All levity faded. "You've reached a decision?" While he and Brendan had waited in the corridor, Brendan had shared his insights into the emotional twists and turns of the discussion in the brig. That intel had indicated some resolution was occurring, but emotional overtones didn't provide specifics.

"I am. Neither of them has a moral compass and I don't see any reality in which they'll get better. In fact, based on Mirko's current state, she's even worse than when you worked for her."

"I'd agree with that," Natasha replied. "I never would have expected her to agree to human trafficking."

Isin's arm tightened around her. "Human trafficking?"

Natasha tipped her head back to meet his gaze. "She stole the Aphrodite's Dream from Diestro and was going to include Adel as part of a deal with her buyer. The only reason it didn't work was Omondi and Hobbes wouldn't let Adel out of their sight."

That put the final nail in Mirko's coffin. He shifted his gaze to Aurora. "What's your plan?"

"I want to drop them off on the planet where Nat and I got free of Tnaryt."

Natasha's shoulders bunched under his arm. "Really?" Her brow puckered for a moment, then relaxed. "Actually, that's a really good idea."

"It's not a perfect solution." Aurora sighed. "Left unsupervised they could do a lot of harm to each other."

Isin wouldn't waste any sleep over that possibility. But clearly it bothered Aurora.

"For now, I believe it's the best option available to us," she continued. "We could put them in separate areas, I suppose, although the isolation could pose its own problems." She shrugged, glancing at her dad. "What do you think?"

He tipped his head, considering her question. "I think you're making the best of an incredibly difficult situation. In my professional opinion, neither of them has given any indication they want to change their behavior. Even the shift in their circumstances has made them double down on their destructive tendencies rather than encouraging them to seek alternate solutions to meet their needs. In an ideal world, intensive long-term therapy might eventually help them with rehabilitation. But we don't have that luxury. Your solution would prevent them from harming anyone except each other."

"Should we separate them, then?"

"I'll want more time with them before answering that question." The compassion on Brendan's face was startling. How could he care about two people who'd caused so much pain to others? "They both crave attention and they're willing to do anything to get it. For them, having another person around, even one they hate, is likely better than being alone. But the danger they pose to each other is real."

Isin was intrigued by Aurora's solution. "What's this planet like?"

"It's an Earth analog in most respects, although I learned the hard way that the river where I met up with the Sovereign runs with salt water." Aurora's lips tightened a fraction. "But there's plenty of rainfall and plant life. Providing for their food and water needs shouldn't be a problem. And there were few hazards in the area. We can leave them with survival gear and instructions."

It sounded like more than either of them deserved.

"The remaining Etah females are still there though, right?" Natasha asked.

Aurora nodded. "As far as we know. That's something I'll want to talk to Ifel about. She might have some insights on how to deal with them." Her gaze met his. "The big question is would you be willing to take *Vengeance* to the planet in the next few days?"

His brows lifted. "Before the *Starhawke* is recharged?"

"The sooner the better. This is untenable." She gestured to the sealed hatch. "And you'd pick up a few temporary crewmembers for the journey. I was thinking Celia and I could go with you. I'm familiar with the planet and she's a botanist."

"I should go, too."

Aurora frowned at Micah. "Because of Manchado?"

He shook his head. "Because I can chat with the local wildlife, make sure there aren't any unexpected threats. Jonarel can't leave the *Starhawke* right now, so I'm your best resource."

She turned to Brendan. "Would you and Mom want to come?"

"I would, and if the rest of us are going, she'll come, too."

Her gaze met Isin's. "Does that work for you? The Yruf ships and *Gladiator* would stay here to watch over *Phoenix* and the *Starhawke* while we're gone."

"How far away is this planet?"

"Depending on the speed of your ship, it's around three days to get there."

He glanced at Natasha. "Any objections?" He didn't want to abandon her while her ship was still undergoing repairs, but the thought of unloading Mirko and Manchado sooner rather than later was very appealing.

Her pert mouth flattened. "No, but we should pull everything from the Birdbolt first. Manchado indicated Mirko has more of the AD stashed there."

"More?"

"She stole an entire shipment, which I gather is a lot bigger than the container Sweep found."

He sighed. "Of course she did." Mirko's appetites had clearly overridden her sense of self-preservation. "Then let's include Omondi and Hobbes in the run since they would have been with her during the last drop." He turned to Aurora. "We can take care of that task this afternoon and be ready to leave in the morning."

"Great. We'll bring *Starlet* over after we load up the food for the trip."

"Food?"

Aurora smiled. "You're forgetting I'm bringing three brilliant cooks with me. Your crew will eat well while we're onboard."

Twenty-Seven

Aurora focused on clearing the putrid slime coating her emotional field as she followed Nat and Isin down the forward stairs one deck. Getting some distance from the brig helped. So did entering a space that completely captivated her attention.

Vengeance's bridge bore little resemblance to a standard Fleet bridge. For starters, it had a three-hundred-and-sixty-degree bridgescreen that wrapped around the entire room, providing a stunning view of the *Starhawke* and *Phoenix*, with *Gladiator* snugged up against the *Starhawke*'s starboard side. The substantial captain's chair sat on a raised circular platform at the center of the room, with three stations surrounding it to the fore, port, and starboard.

Aurora recognized the tall, strikingly beautiful woman seated at the forward console. She matched the image Ifel had shown her and Cade while they were on the Yruf ship.

Itorye gave her a closed-mouth smile as their gazes met. She rose and strode forward. "Captain Hawke, I presume? I'm Itorye, *Vengeance*'s first mate."

Aurora clasped Itorye's hand, noting the same fluid grace in her movements that Celia had, and the same strength in her grip. That strength extended to her emotional grid, which was neat and orderly compared to most people. This woman would be a dangerous opponent for anyone who crossed her. "It's a pleasure to finally meet you, Itorye."

"And you."

Her dad was eyeing Itorye with interest. "I'm Brendan Scott, father of the captain." He tipped his head in Aurora's direction.

Itorye gave a subtle nod. "I can see the resemblance."

"And I'm the captain's big brother." Micah grinned. "Micah Scott."

Micah's effervescent charm worked its magic on Itorye, coaxing a bemused smile. Her gaze met Aurora's. "You are blessed to have family who appreciate you."

The comment carried the subtle ache of old wounds in Itorye's emotional field, but her placid countenance didn't change. That trait reminded Aurora of Kelly, whose family history was also bleak but whose calm expression rarely even rippled. "Yes, I'm very blessed. With family and friends." Her gaze shifted to Nat, who was smiling softly as she watched the interaction.

Nat motioned to the two men who'd been standing quietly near the port console.

Their features were a study in contrasts. One was muscular with greying hair and a focused gaze, the other quite a bit leaner with an affable expression and ginger hair pulled back in a neat low ponytail. She hadn't seen the first man before, but the second she recognized from Ifel's images. Pete, *Phoenix's* engineer.

"This is Pete Stevens," Nat confirmed. "He's *Phoenix's* engineer." Deep affection bloomed in her emotional field, indicating Pete was not just a crewmember, but a good friend.

Nat had gathered quite a few of those for someone who'd claimed to be without friends when they'd first met.

"It's an honor to meet you, Captain," Pete said shyly, something akin to awe in his emotional field as he met her gaze. "None of us would be here if it weren't for you savin' Nat."

"Please, call me Aurora." She glanced at Nat, who was doing a poor job of hiding her embarrassment. "In my version of the story, we saved each other."

Nat smirked, but there was a smile behind it.

"I'm Sweep." The muscular man beside Pete had a deep baritone that fit with his barrel chest and steel grey eyes. "*Vengeance's* head of security."

That fit with his vibe. He was also watching her with avid interest. "Nice to meet you."

"I have a question." Pete stuck up his hand like he was in a classroom.

"Yes?"

But instead of focusing on her, he turned to her dad. "Did you know you got the same name as the owner of Far Horizons Aerospace?"

Her dad jerked in surprise. Startling her dad wasn't easy to do, but Pete had managed it. "As a matter of fact, I do. Most people aren't familiar enough with the company to catch that."

"Familiar enough?" Itorye asked, her gaze now as focused as Pete's.

Her dad nodded. "Pete's correct. I'm the owner of Far Horizons Aerospace."

The cymbal crash generated fascinating results. Nat's gaze cut to Aurora, Isin's locked on her dad, Pete's mouth sagged open, and Itorye and Sweep shared a long look.

Nat was the first to speak. "How many bombshell secrets does your family *have?*"

More than she could count. "This wasn't one I was hiding intentionally. I didn't even know who my dad was when you and I met."

That comment got more scrutiny from Nat than her dad's pronouncement. "How could you not know?"

"Because she thought I was dead," her dad replied. "And she had no idea Micah existed." Regret painted his words. "She hadn't seen either of us since she was two."

Now Nat was offended on her behalf. "Why not?"

"Because her mom and I were trying to keep her and Micah safe."

Nat's stance lost its bluster. "From the Teeli."

Itorye, Pete, and Sweep didn't react adversely, indicating Nat and Isin had already shared the truth about the Teeli and her Suulh heritage with them.

Her dad clearly noted the same thing. "At the time, separating them seemed like the only option. Micah enhances Aurora's abilities, which were already stronger than her mother's. Even as young children, they were starting to draw attention. And then the Teeli made contact with the Fleet."

"And the Teeli want control of your abilities?" Sweep's gaze held Aurora's.

"Yes. Mine and Lelindia's. If they could control us, and use us to control all the other Suulh, they could create a virtually indestructible attack force."

"I'm glad you're on our side," Pete murmured, his lips pressing into a line.

"The Teeli and Sovereign have been trying to control my family since long before I was born. They succeeded in capturing the Suulh homeworld, which is where the majority of the Suulh are located. But we rescued a few hundred during the attack on Gaia. They're now living on a planet in Kraed space."

"That attack involved the Suulh?" Sweep asked.

She nodded. "Our abilities are meant to be healing and protective, nurturing life. But the Teeli discovered a way to flip them, causing destruction. The Suulh who were forced to use their abilities that way destroyed the crops on Gaia, but it also wreaked havoc on their bodies. When we found them, some of them were little more than skeletal automatons."

"How did the Teeli force them?" Itorye asked.

"They tortured their loved ones until they complied. Mostly their children."

Anger shot like flaming arrows through the group's emotional fields.

"That's twisted," Pete spat.

"That's the Teeli way. They have no compassion, even for their own people. They treat their lower class as breeding slave labor."

Itorye's eyes narrowed. "How do you know that?"

"The Kraed have been gathering intel on them for a long time."

Sweep folded his arms over his chest. "Are the Kraed prepared to fight them?"

"We're still waiting to find out. Siginal Clarek returned to Drakar to talk to the clan leaders about the Teeli threat. The Kraed will defend their homeworld and ships from an attack, but taking the fight to the Teeli before the Teeli have moved against them goes against their core beliefs. They would see it as unprovoked aggression and wasted resources, which isn't acceptable behavior in Kraed culture."

"Then how does he hope to convince them?"

A small smile teased her lips. "Lelindia's pregnant with a half-Suulh, half-Kraed child. Raehn's existence links the Kraed with the Suulh. As a result, there's a good chance the Kraed's protective behavior would extend to the Suulh. Since the Suulh are under attack by the Teeli right now, it could give the Kraed a reason to enter the fray before it arrives on their doorstep."

"And if they don't?" That question came from Isin.

"Then we'll have to get creative."

Twenty-Eight

"You're leaving again?" Lelindia managed to keep the exasperation from her voice, but the look Aurora gave her reminded her she couldn't hide what she was feeling, not from an empath. She should have known the news was big when Aurora asked to stop by her cabin.

Aurora shifted on the couch to face her. "Just long enough to get Manchado and Mirko settled on the planet. I'll be back before the *Starhawke* is recharged."

"This makes four times you've left us." The first time Aurora had jumped ship, she'd ended up as Tnaryt's captive while Lelindia took the *Starhawke* to Feylahn. She'd been at her wits' end, struggling to make decisions in scenarios she'd never imagined facing without Aurora by her side. She'd gotten through it, which had made Aurora's abandonment to go in search of her dad not long after easier to accept. The third time involved her incarceration at Seaview, which hadn't been entirely voluntary, but still...

"You should take it as a compliment."

"Why?"

"I'm expressing my absolute confidence in your ability to watch over the crew while I'm gone. You know it's not easy for me to let go of my overactive sense of responsibility." Aurora's tone was teasing, but the look in her eyes showed how much she meant what she said.

Lelindia sighed. "You're right. I also know you wouldn't feel comfortable leaving the task of relocating Manchado and Mirko to anyone else."

"Very true."

"So, what's the timetable?"

"Three days to get there, probably four or five days to find suitable locations and build the habitats, and another three days back." She frowned. "Which means I'll probably miss your birthday."

"Oh." To be honest, she hadn't given her birthday a single thought, even though birthday celebrations had always been a big deal for them. Aurora celebrated the whole month, not just the one day. When Lelindia had learned Celia's birthday was two days before her own, she'd encouraged her to make it a joint celebration. Celia had resisted the idea, claiming her birthday wasn't important. But last year she'd gotten into the spirit of things, attending the small party Knox and Aurora had arranged on the *Argo.* "We have a lot of other things going on right now."

"I know, but it's still your birthday. Celia's coming with me, so I can do something for her on the day." Aurora chewed on her lip. "U-1 will be with me, too, so maybe you and I can have a long-distance chat with their help. I want to at least be able to wish you a happy birthday. Or maybe we'll get those habitats up lickety-split and be back in time for the party."

"Party?"

Aurora gave her a quizzical look. "You don't honestly expect your parents to *not* throw you a party, do you? This is the first time they've been with you on your birthday in years."

"You're right." Just thinking about it made her smile. "So what tasks do the rest of us need to focus on while you're gone?"

"You'll be following up on Captain Montgomery's whereabouts. Unity informed me when I got back from *Vengeance* that they've been unable to locate her at Eridani Duo's medical center. The ICU room where she's supposedly being treated has a medical training doll in the bed, positioned so only someone who was standing at the foot of the bed inside the room would be able to tell it wasn't a person. Unity's been monitoring the medical personnel who are accessing the room, which has a security pad for entry, and they're keeping up the pretense that they're treating Montgomery."

Lelindia blinked. "Why would they do that? And didn't Unity say she wasn't on *Cassini?* Where else could she be?"

"She might be on Hydra One!" Unity offered.

She glanced up. "How? And why?"

"The head of medical at Hydra One is a good friend of Will's," Aurora replied. "She's the one who helped him sneak off the station when he went searching for the Etah Setarips. She also knows *Cassini's* CMO. If Montgomery was in danger, Will's convinced she'd want to help her. That's our best working theory, anyway. Ifel's already sent a ship to Hydra One so Unity can search for her there."

That didn't surprise her a bit.

Aurora sighed. "I briefly considered postponing this trip, but I can't shake the feeling Mirko and Manchado are a complication that could cause us issues later. Since the *Starhawke* can't go anywhere for a while anyway, it feels like the sooner we can get them off *Vengeance*, the better."

"I don't envy you that task." Thinking about her brief time with Manchado still left a bitter taste in her mouth. "What do you want us to do if Unity locates Montgomery on Hydra One? No one from our crew can set foot on the station even if the *Starhawke* were ready to make the trip."

"That will depend on what Unity finds. We don't want to draw attention to her if she's okay. But the fact that her senior officers and the Eridani Duo medical staff are working to keep her true location a secret doesn't bode well."

"No, it doesn't." Something Aurora said earlier finally registered. "How are you going to keep U-1 hidden while you're on *Vengeance*? I'm assuming you don't want *Vengeance's* crew to know about them?"

"There was a lot of debate about that." Aurora's lips curved in a bemused smile. "Unity was very insistent that they wanted to stay with us, but since we'll have Micah to communicate with Ifel on the ships that will be shadowing us, U-1's presence wasn't strictly necessary. However, Unity pointed out that there might be times on the planet when we'd want to split up, and their mobile unit could be helpful. So Micah's packing U-1 in his bag. They'll stay in the bag, in our cabin, or on *Starlet* so *Vengeance's* crew won't see them."

"Is anyone else going with you?"

"Iolana and Kai volunteered themselves as manual labor for the habitats. My dad will be helping me with Mirko and Manchado, and my mom's planning to use the travel time to start training me." Aurora practically glowed when she said that.

"She's really going to follow through on it, then?" She'd been surprised when Aurora had shared that tidbit of news earlier. Libra had always done everything in her power to avoid training Aurora. Making it a priority now was a major attitude shift, one that was extremely welcome and long overdue.

"Yep. She seems as excited about it as I am."

"I'm sorry I'll miss seeing it." And Aurora had left one important name off her list. "Cade's not going?"

Aurora shook her head.

"How does he feel about that?"

"Better than I expected. He agreed that there's really nothing for him to do on this mission. And I'll feel better if he's here with his team and *Gladiator*. Just in case."

In case the Sovereign threw them another curveball.

"He and the Admiral can help sort out what to do regarding Montgomery. I'll also need you and Jonarel to start planning our next steps with the Kraed based on the outcome of Siginal's talks with the clan leaders. He should be contacting us any time now."

A trickle of unease ran down her back. "I'm surprised we haven't heard anything yet." Her daughter's future would be significantly impacted by the results of those discussions.

"Me, too. But I'm taking it as a good sign that the clan leaders are listening. If they'd just said no, we would have heard from him days ago." She reached out, clasping Lelindia's hand. "No matter what they decide, Raehn has the support of the Suulh behind her. And a very overprotective Kraed daddy."

Lelindia smirked. "He's going to be a wreck once she's mobile. He might have to build an enclosed play area in engineering just so he can keep an eye on her while he's doing his job."

Aurora chuckled. "He can build whatever makes him happy. Engineering is his domain. Just remind him that Raehn will be able to instantly heal from any tumbles she takes. She'll also have claws. She's not going to be a vulnerable child."

"Intellectually he knows that, but emotionally he thinks she's made of spun glass and tissue paper."

"I predict that won't last long. Raehn will prove to him she's not a delicate flower."

A solid kick from Raehn emphasized that statement. Lelindia laughed as she dropped her hands to her belly. "Definitely not. So, is there anything I can do to help with preparations for this mission you're undertaking?"

"Sure. I promised we'd keep *Vengeance*'s crew well fed, so I could use some extra hands to gather supplies from the greenhouse.

I also need Jonarel's help creating a simple but durable habitat design that will be easy to replicate and assemble."

Lelindia pushed to her feet. "Then let's go see Raehn's daddy."

Twenty-Nine

"I don't know what to pack." Libra stared at the nearly empty duffle sitting on a collapsible luggage rack next to the sleeping nook in hers and Brendan's cabin, then at the contents of the open closet, waiting for inspiration.

Aurora had said the climate for the area of the planet they'd be visiting was similar to Hawai'i. Thanks to Brendan, she had plenty of clothes that fit that option. And when they weren't on the planet, she'd be on *Vengeance*, which shouldn't be too different from being on the *Starhawke*. So why was she struggling to decide what to take?

Brendan tucked a handful of rolled T-shirts in his duffle before moving beside her. "That's because you haven't had much practice traveling as an adult." He wrapped his arm around her shoulders, drawing her close. "Taking this leap is a big deal."

She sighed, snuggling against him. "Thank you for saying that." It *was* a big deal, at least for her. She was about to travel on a tank of a warship to an unknown planet in Teeli space, leaving Marina and Gryphon behind on the *Starhawke*. As if that wasn't enough, she'd also promised to train Aurora on the way. She couldn't tell if the fluttering in her stomach was excited butterflies or panicked grasshoppers. Maybe both.

"Traveling into the unknown can be scary."

"Not for you." Ever since Aurora had proposed the idea of them coming with her, Brendan had been bubbling over with enthusiasm.

"That's because I grew up traveling on starships." He stroked his fingers along her back. "My parents made it a fun adventure, so my comfort zone for space travel is very different from yours. Your first experience was traumatic."

"I know." She rubbed her cheek against the soft fabric of his shirt, tuning into the steady thump of his heart. "But I wish I could be more like you."

He sighed, his grip shifting, like he was trying to draw her pain into himself, to share her burden. "You've come a long way in a very short time," he murmured. "Give yourself credit for the work you're doing. You're growing and taking risks, and helping Aurora and Micah achieve their full potential. The courage you're showing every day amazes me."

That made her smile. She tipped her head back, gazing into the beautiful sky-blue of his eyes. "Amazes you, huh?"

"Mm-hmm." He traced the curve of her cheek and jaw with his finger. "I could spend a hundred years with you and never stop being amazed."

She chuckled. "That's good to hear, because a hundred years doesn't mean the same thing to a Suulh that it does to a Human."

"I've noticed." His smile made his eyes sparkle. "Especially when I look in the mirror. Pretty soon people are going to start thinking I'm Micah's older brother."

"I told you that would happen, back before we mated."

"I remember." His gaze warmed as he continued the gentle caress of his fingers along her cheek. "But hearing about it in my twenties is very different from seeing time abruptly reverse course in my late fifties. Because of you."

She cradled his hand in hers, pressing it to her cheek. If she hadn't sent him away, if he'd continued to benefit from her energy field during the intervening years, time wouldn't have had the opportunity to put the grey in his hair or the lines on his face. They were fading now, but still... "I'm sorry it took me so long to get here."

He shook his head. "Don't. You've given me so much, more than I ever imagined. I don't want you to blame yourself. We made the decision to separate for a reason, to protect Micah and Aurora. It wasn't an easy path for any of us, but our children have become incredible people, forging lives that bring them joy. And now you and I can do the same, with full appreciation for what we have together." He held her gaze, showing her the truth of his words. "I wouldn't give up this moment for anything."

Tears coated her eyes as she gazed at him. He had a gift for tapping into the depth of her soul and making her feel seen. And loved. So very, very loved. "I'm grateful every day that Romeo's engine caught fire."

He laughed, the joyful sound cascading over her. "I'm sure Romeo could have done without that experience, but yeah." He lowered his head, his mouth millimeters from hers. "Me, too."

The touch of his lips against hers sent a shiver through her, igniting her energy field. She twined her arms around his neck, sinking her fingers into his hair and urging him closer. Her mate. The only male who could draw this response from her, the only male she'd ever wanted.

And now he was hers to hold and touch and love again.

He lifted his head, his breath unsteady. "You have no idea how difficult it is to think when you do that." His gaze flicked to her pearlescent energy field swirling around them. "At least about anything other than getting you naked."

She laughed, the throaty sound proving he wasn't the only one affected by their embrace. "If you'll help me pack my bag first, then I'll let you follow through on that thought."

His eyes smoldered, but his lips quirked at the corners. "Deal."

Thirty

"We're cleaning out the Birdbolt." Nat's gaze swept over Hobbes, Omondi, and Adel, who'd gathered in the cabin the three were currently sharing on *Vengeance.* "I'd like you two," she nodded at Hobbes and Omondi, who were seated side by side on a lower bunk, "to go with us."

"What are you going to do with the haul?" Omondi's dark eyes had a decidedly mercenary glint to them.

Not that she minded. She was on a ship full of mercenaries. "Depends on what we find." Except for the Aphrodite's Dream. That she planned to jettison into space and be done with it. "We'll use what we can, sell what we can't, and give the three of you the lion's share of any profits."

Surprise stole over Omondi's face, followed by suspicion. "Why?"

She suppressed a sigh. Hobbes and Adel were making strides in learning to trust her and the crew, but Omondi kept acting like he was waiting for a knife in the back. "Because you suffered for whatever's in there. You deserve a payout." She turned to Hobbes. "Is there anything of value there?"

"I don't know," Hobbes admitted. "Mirko never told me what was in the crates she stored there. She kept them in her cabin whenever they were onboard, so I never had a chance to see what was inside. Our last trip here she dropped off one of our large smuggling crates. It barely fit through the doorway of her cabin."

"Any idea what was in it?" Although she had a guess.

"It had to be valuable," Omondi interrupted Hobbes, glaring like Mirko was standing in front of him. "When she brought us back here, we'd planned to—" He cut off abruptly, his gaze dropping to the deck.

She could finish the sentence for him. "Mutiny against Mirko so you could keep whatever was in the crates?"

The trio remained silent, but it didn't matter. She knew the answer. Unlike Hobbes and Omondi, Adel wasn't adept at hiding her emotions. Guilt hung heavy on her, her curly dark hair falling forward to conceal her face.

"I would have done the same."

Adel's head came up, her dark eyes wide. Omondi and Hobbes looked cautious, like she was setting a trap.

"I'm not a fan of mutiny, but in this case, it was warranted. Mirko wasn't looking out for your safety or keeping the ship operational. She was willing to risk all your lives for her personal benefit. Trust me, I know what that feels like." She gave Adel an encouraging smile. "Thankfully we've all lived to tell the tale, but none of us owe any loyalty to Mirko. She's shown she'd happily toss us aside whenever it suits her purposes."

"You're not like her, are you?" Adel's question was a whisper of sound.

The hope in her eyes snagged Nat's heart. "No, but I'm no angel. I've done things that make me physically sick to think about. I've lied, cheated, stolen. I've also caused others suffering. Even death." That last admission carved a chunk out of her soul. "But I refuse to let my past define me. I was given a chance at a better future by someone who refused to give up on me. I owe her my life. And I owe it to myself not to squander the opportunities I've been given. My skills and talents can make a positive difference. That's the future I want." She stopped when she realized all three of them were staring at her. "Sorry for the soapbox speech."

Adel's dark brows had drawn together in thought, like Nat had just handed her a puzzle box she really wanted to open. Omondi looked skeptical, but Hobbes seemed receptive. "It's just weird hearing you talk like this," she said. "You always kept to yourself."

"A lot has happened since then." And she needed to get back on topic. "What about the Birdbolt? Did Mirko change anything about the approach or the cache?"

Hobbes shook her head. "After you left the ship—"

Nat snorted at the euphemism for her Setarip enslavement.

"—I became her new cargo hauler. She never let Omondi or Adel anywhere near the cache. Or anyone else who used to be on the crew."

Hobbes had given her an opening. "What happened to the crew?"

"Mirko happened." Bitterness corroded Omondi's words. "She'd gotten used to a certain flow of cash when she had you and Isin working for her. Without *Gypsy* available for deliveries and Isin no longer negotiating deals, money got tight real fast. She took it out on us. The crew started walking off after we did several jobs that she claimed didn't cover expenses."

"Why did you stay?" She had trouble picturing them working for free.

Omondi looked decidedly uncomfortable, so Hobbes picked up the thread. "Mirko found Adel living on the streets of Mercenary Market, doing odd jobs and barely making enough to feed herself. No other crew would take her on. She was too... quiet."

Timid was likely the word she was avoiding. No mercenary crew would want a crewmember who jumped at shadows.

"Mirko offered her room and board in exchange for doing all *Sphinx*'s engine work. Adel jumped at the chance."

Nat grimaced. The story was disturbingly familiar. That was how Mirko had sunk her claws into her, too, although in her case timidity hadn't been the issue. She'd struggled to convince anyone to trust their ship to the hands of a short, scrappy teenager. They hadn't even given her a chance to prove herself. Mirko's willingness should have been a red flag, but she'd been too thrilled at the opportunity to question it.

Adel swung her feet, staring at the deck.

"Omondi and I were considering jumping ship at that point," Hobbes continued, "but after she brought on Adel, I couldn't do it. Not after seeing her." Her voice softened in a way Nat had never heard before. "She was skin and bones back then, but so full of life. If I left, Mirko would have been grounded and Adel would have landed back on the streets."

"So you stayed."

Hobbes shrugged. "We needed resources if we were going to take Adel with us. Vance was the last to leave. I think Mirko was still slipping him money the rest of us never saw."

Nat didn't doubt it. Vance had been the one who'd trained her as a field medic. Mirko had relied on him to patch up the crew. But he was also the one who'd hobbled Isin after his injury during *Gypsy's* crash. At Mirko's direction, instead of treating Isin's wound, he'd purposely inflamed the injury to keep Isin onboard.

If she or Isin ever saw Vance again, he would likely suffer an injury of his own.

"Mirko's attitude changed after we picked up our last shipment," Hobbes continued. "It was small, just one crate about a meter square, but Mirko acted like it was her ticket to riches. She promised us a big bonus after it was delivered. We didn't have a viable plan for ourselves yet, so we waited to see how it played out. She owed us months of back wages by then. Leaving would have been easier with some money in our pockets."

"But?" Nat prompted when Hobbes fell silent.

Hobbes sighed, glancing at Adel. "Mirko called Adel into her cabin and told her to find a way to break the security seal on the crate without damaging the contents. When she did, Mirko shoved her out and ordered me to change our destination to the Birdbolt. She spaced something out one of the airlocks between jumps. I'm pretty sure it was the original crate."

"Getting rid of a tracker," Nat murmured to herself.

"That was my guess, too. After we left the smuggling crate at the Birdbolt, Mirko gave me a new destination where we were supposed to meet the potential buyer. But she was acting really weird when we arrived, even for her. She kept trying to get Adel alone. It freaked me out."

Nat bit her cheek to keep from filling in the blanks. The truth would only enrage Hobbes and Omondi.

"I refused to let Mirko take Adel with her, and Omondi backed me up. She threatened to throw me off the ship, but since she didn't have another pilot, it was an empty threat. She also didn't take me with her, which was unusual. She stalked off to the meeting alone, but when she came back, she was manic, screaming at us that we'd screwed up the deal. That's when we knew our time was up. We still didn't have any money, so we decided our best shot was to take over *Sphinx* at the Birdbolt, clean out the cache, then fly the ship to Osiris where we could ditch Mirko and the ship, sell the cargo, and sign on with a new crew."

"What about Adel?" The kid still wasn't likely to be welcomed onto a mercenary ship.

Hobbes glanced at Omondi. "We planned to tell whoever hired us that Adel was our daughter, and we were a package deal."

Nat's brows rose. She hadn't expected that.

But the plan was brilliant. Adel's brown skin was a similar shade to Omondi's, and her riot of curly black hair was similar to Hobbes'. No one would question their claim.

They'd also just made it very clear how much they'd become a unit. She hadn't been paying close attention, but now that she was looking for it, she could see that Omondi was sitting a little too close to Hobbes for their relationship to be completely casual.

"Would you consider staying on with *Vengeance*?" She'd discussed the option with Isin and Itorye, who'd both been pleased with the work the trio had been doing around the ship.

Omondi and Adel both looked at Hobbes, who was clearly the leader of their little family.

Hobbes eyed Nat warily. "*Vengeance* already has a pilot. Several, actually."

"True." They didn't necessarily need another pilot, not with Alec learning to fly *Phoenix* and Itorye and Kenji able to spell Sparki on *Vengeance*. "But having another one would give us flexibility." Which seemed wise considering the direction things were headed. "And we can always use more crew who are good in a fight." Her gaze flicked to Omondi, then Adel. "Or who can fit into tight spaces to make ship repairs."

Hobbes' focus shifted to Adel. "What do you think?"

Adel's feet started swinging again. "I like it here," she said so quietly Nat almost didn't hear her. "Itorye's nice. Shash yells, but only if you deserve it."

Nat almost choked on her tongue. Adel believed Shash only yelled at someone if they deserved it? The kid must have managed to stay on Shash's good side. Well, her less bad side.

Hobbes' gaze swung to Omondi. "What about you?"

He shrugged. "Don't care one way or the other. If you like it here, I'd stay."

Nat didn't buy his nonchalance for a moment. She knew conditions on *Vengeance* were lightyears better than *Sphinx*. Or any other ship they were likely to find. But he wasn't about to admit that to himself. Certainly not in front of her. That would show he cared.

Hobbes turned back to Nat. "What's the catch?"

Nat gave a humorless laugh. "You mean am I going to change my mind tomorrow and kick you all off the ship after we clean out the Birdbolt?" She shook her head. "Whether you believe it or not, my word means something now. This is a solid offer. Unless you give the crew a reason to put you off the ship, like attempting to mutiny, the offer stands."

Hobbes glanced between Omondi and Adel before nodding. "Then I guess we're in."

Thirty-One

"Interesting spot for a cache," Kenji commented as he settled the *Dagger* onto a relatively flat stretch of ground on the rocky planetesimal.

Isin had to agree. The vista outside the viewport reminded him of archival pictures from Earth's moon taken during early space exploration in the twentieth century. The planetesimal was significantly larger than Earth's moon, but its almost complete lack of an atmosphere provided the same unimpeded view of the starfield. The scattered rocks also looked similar, the color almost matching the steel grey of *Vengeance*'s hull.

He'd only been to the Birdbolt once during his time on *Sphinx* and had never set foot off the ship. Hadn't cared to, even if he'd been invited, which he wasn't. He wasn't responsible for whatever Mirko was dropping off or picking up, so he'd ignored the activity of the crew.

Well, most of the crew. He'd kept pretty close tabs on Natasha's whereabouts. At the time, he hadn't given any thought as to why.

Her irritated sigh from the jump seat beside him drew his attention down. "Bad memories?"

Her pale eyes flashed with inner fire. "When it comes to Mirko? Always. Being back here…" She shook her head. "I can't believe how long I put up with her abuse."

"She'd convinced you that you didn't have other options. It's hard to see the forest for the trees."

She snorted, the anger in her eyes replaced by the sparkle of laughter as she stood. "Wow, you're deep."

He kept his expression solemn as he joined her. "Very deep."

"Ugh." Kenji waved them both out of the cockpit. "I hate it when you two get mushy."

Natasha grinned. "Aww, Kenji, are you feeling left out?" She rose on her tiptoes and patting his cheek. "You know I adore you. You too, Sweep."

Sweep had unfolded himself from the co-pilot's seat. Isin noted she didn't try to pat Sweep's cheek, although he looked amused by the exchange, especially when Kenji flushed.

"Let's get suited up and find out what Mirko's gifted us with this time." She spun, marching into the main cabin.

They watched her disappear from view.

"She's a fighter," Kenji commented, gesturing for Isin to take the lead.

"That she is," he agreed.

Natasha had collected Omondi and Hobbes on her way to the cargo hold at the back of the ship. They were donning the matching dark grey spacesuits with white accents that Natasha had taken from *Phoenix*'s storage lockers.

The suit Natasha wore matched his, although hers was designed to protect her from environmental hazards, while his was military-grade for combat scenarios. He'd picked up both while on Osiris, having lost his previous spacesuit during the conflict with Kerr.

He and Natasha waited with Omondi while Hobbes entered the aft airlock with Kenji and Sweep. After they'd accessed the exterior ramp and the airlock had reset, Isin motioned Natasha and Omondi inside.

Tiny plumes of dust rose from the planetesimal's surface when his boots touched down, the particles drifting lazily in the relatively low gravity and negligible atmosphere. Rock formations rose at staggered intervals across the landscape, creating bizarre sculptures. It looked like a giant toddler had been handed lumps of clay and given free rein to mold and smash at will.

The *Dagger* sat on a somewhat level area that would not have easily accommodated *Sphinx*'s bulk. Hobbes' piloting skills must have improved after Natasha was abducted by the Setarips. Either that, or there was an easier landing spot farther out.

Natasha and Kenji moved to the *Dagger*'s port side, opening the exterior storage compartment and pulling out the cargo dolly Natasha had borrowed from *Gypsy*, as well as the two from the *Dagger*.

"Which way?" Isin asked Natasha over the helmet comms as she joined him.

She pointed to the right. "Around that outcropping. The cache makes use of a natural cave on the other side."

He glanced at the ground leading in that direction. "Why aren't there boot prints?" Without a significant atmosphere, there was no wind to shift the dust and conceal evidence of past visits.

Natasha made a face. "Because Mirko insisted I use a puffer to clear any sign of our tracks each time we left."

Hobbes nodded in agreement. "Same here. She's paranoid."

"With good reason," he commented dryly. The list of people who wished ill on Mirko could wrap around *Vengeance* twice. If any of them knew about her little cache, they'd clean it out in a heartbeat.

Natasha took the lead, bounding over the terrain with the ease of long experience in the low gravity, pushing *Gypsy's* tethered cargo dolly in front of her. Isin followed, with Hobbes and Omondi behind him and Kenji and Sweep bringing up the rear with the other two dollies. They circled the outcropping quickly, the ground in front of them opening up to a small crater with shallow, sloping sides.

Natasha paused at the edge. "You can see the entrance there." She pointed diagonally to the left, where a shadowed area formed an irregular opening like an owl's hollow in a tree.

"Everyone good?" he asked over the comm.

Four confirmations got him and Natasha moving along the rim. "How did Mirko find this place?"

"She didn't. It was a cache for someone she ran freight for in her early days. She was cagey about the details, but I got the impression that person met an abrupt end, and Mirko was the only one they'd shown this place to."

He considered that for a moment. "Do you think she killed them?"

Natasha's steps slowed. "No. But I don't think she tried to prevent whatever happened, either."

Omondi snorted. "Sounds right."

Natasha started down the slope, halting at the cave entrance to switch on the lamps for her suit. The rest of the group did the same.

Isin moved beside Natasha, his steps slow and measured as the ceiling of the cave closed over them, the ground pitched slightly with the curve of the cave walls. When his lamp brushed across her face, her expression was subdued, her attention forward and her jaw tight, her usual spark dimmed.

Really bad memories.

Clearing out Mirko's private stash of ill-gotten goods wouldn't balance the scales, but he'd relish the look on Mirko's face when he informed her.

They walked for at least a minute, the irregular cave walls close enough he could reach out and touch them. Up ahead, he caught the glint of light reflecting off worn metal, a rectangular crate taking shape out of the gloom, blocking most of the tunnel. It was sizeable, a meter wide, two meters long, and almost chest height.

He recognized it immediately. Mirko had two of them during the time he worked for her. He'd often slept on them in the cargo bay because the bunks on *Sphinx* were too short for him, forcing him to tuck his knees up. The second one had been a casualty of *Sphinx*'s explosive decompression, the warped remains drifting through the cargo bay.

Because of his adventures with Natasha, he knew there was a false bottom above a smuggling compartment that could be accessed when the crate was disassembled. That was the logical place for Mirko to have stashed the Aphrodite's Dream.

He turned to Hobbes. "Is this the one you dropped off most recently?"

She nodded. "She wanted me to put it with the rest of the cache, but it wouldn't fit." She motioned past the crate into the depths of the tunnel.

About ten meters farther in, the shadows receded where light filtered in from an opening in the ceiling. Rubble lay like a dam across the width of the tunnel, shrinking the gap between floor and ceiling to about a meter.

Forget walking. He'd have to crawl through.

"The rest of the crates are on the other side," Hobbes informed him.

Of course they were. "Any idea what's in them?"

"My guess? Alcohol. Clothes. Whatever else Mirko considered essential to her wellbeing. Certainly not credit squares. Or spare parts for *Sphinx*." The contempt in her voice came through loud and clear.

He gestured to Sweep. "You and Kenji get this one to the *Dagger* and start inspecting the contents. We'll follow with the rest."

"Hey!"

He turned.

Omondi was standing with his legs apart, a snarl on his lips and a challenge in his eyes. "I want to know what's in that crate. Nat said we'd get paid for anything of value."

Isin's eyes narrowed at his accusatory tone. "You're used to dealing with Mirko, so I'll excuse that comment this once. But if you want to stay on my ship, you need to lose the attitude. I don't cheat my crew. And I don't tolerate false accusations."

Omondi's chin lifted defiantly, but Hobbes rested a hand on his arm. "It's fine," she said firmly. "We'll help Nat with the rest of the crates." She gave a tug. "She gave us her word, remember?"

Omondi resisted, his gaze shifting to Natasha.

Her jaw looked frozen, her face pale, but he didn't think it had anything to do with the argument. This place was draining the joy out of her. The sooner they got moving, the better.

She nodded sharply, holding Omondi's gaze.

He didn't exactly back down — and he certainly didn't apologize — but he did step away from the crate.

Isin held in a sigh. The man needed to work out his anger. After they returned to *Vengeance*, he'd invite him into the Cage so he could release some of that toxic aggression in a safe space.

While Sweep and Kenji maneuvered one of the dollies into position, Natasha approached the rubble, nimbly crossing the barrier, her small size making it look easy, even in her spacesuit.

Hobbes was taller than Natasha, but not by a lot. She also made it over with room to spare.

Isin glanced at Omondi, who was eyeing the gap. They'd both have a tough time squeezing through. "I'll go first. My suit can handle the rough surface."

Feeling more like a spider than a human, Isin stretched out as flat as possible, resting his hands on the loose rocks as he maneuvered across the uneven pile. The rubble shifted beneath his stomach and the ceiling scraped against his back, but he made it through. "I have trouble picturing Mirko doing this," he muttered.

"She didn't," Hobbes answered, watching him with raised brows. "She stood on the other side and gave orders."

Which he could have done. The crates were right in front of him, not deeper into the tunnel as he'd assumed.

Omondi's soft chuckle didn't help matters. Too late now. However, the small spark of amusement that flared in Natasha's eyes before she turned away made his embarrassment tolerable.

He waved at Omondi to stay put on the far side, then surveyed the collection of crates on this side of the barrier.

They were a lot smaller than the one Sweep and Kenji were dealing with, some rectangular, others square. He could easily distinguish the ones Natasha had hauled here from the ones Hobbes had added. Natasha's were perfectly squared off stacks, straight enough to act as support pillars. The others rested haphazardly against each other like weary guests after an all-night party.

Crouching, he hefted the nearest one, which offered minimal resistance in the low gravity. "Hobbes, why don't you go back through and help Omondi. Natasha and I will pass the crates to you to load on the dollies."

"Okay."

As soon as she cleared the gap, he rested the crate on top of the rubble pile, waiting until Omondi took hold of it before turning to fetch another one. Natasha beat him to it, nudging him out of the way so she could tuck her crate into the gap. They worked in a steady rhythm, clearing the random crates first before tackling her neat stacks. She followed the last one through, leaving Isin to do his spider imitation to join her.

By the time he made it over, the stacked crates on *Gypsy's* dolly were secured with netting, and Omondi was crouched beside the second dolly, attaching the netting to the hooks in the dolly's base.

Natasha took command of her dolly, pushing it through the darkened tunnel toward the entrance, the rest of them following.

She hadn't said a single word since they'd entered the claustrophobic space. Her silence added fuel to his anger. Unloading Mirko onto an uninhabited planet wasn't the revenge he'd anticipated after all her deceit and treachery, but if it got her out of their lives quickly, he could live with it.

The starfield greeted them as they exited the cave. Natasha paused, her head turning as she took in the vista. Her audible inhale reminded him of a diver coming up for air.

He hadn't been much of a stargazer as a child, but being around Natasha, he was gaining a new appreciation for the striking beauty of a sight like this. He loved the wonder and joy that filled her expression whenever she gazed at the stars.

She exhaled on a deep sigh. "I hope I never see this view again."

The pain behind that statement made him want to punch Mirko. Repeatedly.

"You got that right," Hobbes muttered, following Omondi out with the second dolly.

They retraced their steps in silence, up the side of the crater and along the path to the *Dagger*.

The lip of the ramp extended into the dusty gravel at the base. Isin motioned Hobbes and Omondi to go first with their dolly, waiting with Natasha and *Gypsy*'s dolly. He studied her expression, which wasn't as pinched as it had been in the cave, but now resembled a somber mask.

"You can stop staring."

He lifted his brows as her gaze met his. "What if I don't want to?"

The corner of her mouth twitched, but he wouldn't call it a smile. More like a grimace. "There's nothing to see."

"I respectfully disagree."

Another twitch. Still not a smile.

She turned away as the exterior hatch for the airlock opened.

He followed her as she pushed the dolly up the ramp and into the airlock, then maneuvered around the dolly so he stood next to her as she tapped in the command to close the hatch and pull in the ramp.

She stared at the crates as the hiss of air surrounded them.

As soon as the safety light turned green, he retracted his helmet and pulled off his gloves. She was still working on her gloves when he captured her chin in his palm and lowered his head.

Her startled inhale when his lips touched hers gave him access to take the kiss from sweet to sensual in a heartbeat. His tongue stroked hers with deliberate intent, drawing a soft moan as her gloved hand clutched the back of his neck.

That was the response he wanted, the inner fire that had been all but snuffed out during the last hour. He caressed her velvety cheek with his thumb, easing back to gaze into her eyes. "Better?" he murmured.

"Better." She licked her lips, which had a predictable effect on his nether regions. "I hope you're planning to follow up on that later," she growled.

"That's a promise." Since he'd be leaving tomorrow, he planned to keep her well occupied tonight.

Hobbes and Omondi were still changing out of their suits when he and Natasha joined them in the cargo hold. Sweep and Kenji were working nearby, the lid of the large crate folded back, a collection of seemingly random objects set out on the deck.

"Looks like a bunch of junk," Omondi grumbled, glaring at the items on the deck.

He was right. Old clothing, unidentifiable ship parts, empty alcohol bottles — all things he'd expect to find in a reclamation bin. Which was likely exactly what they were. Based on what Natasha had told him, Mirko had put this plan together quickly. She'd probably grabbed whatever was handy that she wouldn't miss to fill the empty space in the crate.

"The Aphrodite's Dream will be in the secret compartment." Natasha pointed to the long side panel.

"Aphrodite's Dream?" Omondi frowned at her. "What's that?"

Her nose wrinkled in distaste. "An expensive sex drug."

Hobbes sucked in a breath, her gaze darting from Natasha to Omondi. "That's what Mirko stole? Drugs?"

"Yep." Natasha jerked her suit down past her waist and stepped out of it. "They're worth a fortune, and we're going to eject them into space."

Omondi bristled. "Now, wait a minute..."

Natasha didn't even let him finish the thought. Her hands fisted on her hips. "It's not negotiable. These people are immoral and extremely dangerous. Do you want them hunting you the way they hunted Mirko? Do you want to risk Adel winding up like those kids?"

Omondi's hand pressed against his sternum like Natasha had just punched him in the chest.

"We're not messing around on this one. The drugs go out the airlock and get obliterated. Everything else is fair game to use or sell." She stared hard at Omondi, then Hobbes. "If either of you have a problem with that, then we have a problem. I'm not putting the crew at risk because you think money's more important than people's lives."

Omondi blinked at her, clearly at a loss.

Hobbes recovered quicker. "There's no problem. We'd never put Adel in harm's way. Or the rest of the crew," she added. "You said we could trust you. You can trust us, too. Right?" Her gaze zeroed in on Omondi, her expression every bit as resolute as Natasha's.

Omondi stared at her, then his gaze slowly traveled from person to person, ending on Isin. He ran his hand over his close-cut hair, then massaged the back of his neck. "Look, I–" He coughed into his hand, tried again. "It's not..." He frowned. "We needed money to get someplace better for Adel." His gaze shifted from Isin to Natasha and back again. "I never figured that better place might be with the two of you. You were always so..."

"Disagreeable?" Natasha offered. "Obstinate? Standoffish?"

"Independent," Isin countered. "Focused. Determined."

Natasha's lips curved up. "Stubborn?"

"Stubborn," he agreed.

Omondi looked between them like he wasn't sure how to respond to their banter.

"The point is," Hobbes said, moving beside Omondi, "we're grateful for the opportunity to be part of your crew."

"We are." Omondi nodded, clearly uncomfortable expressing gratitude but doing his best to push through it.

"Glad to hear it." Natasha's smile was small, but it was there.

"Natasha and I will deal with the drugs. The rest of you find out what else Mirko has left us."

He helped her remove the side panel on the crate, revealing the hidden compartment at the base. The cargo hold's overhead lighting made the clear bags of Aphrodite's Dream sparkle as Isin pulled out the sliding platform.

Omondi whistled. "That's a lot of drugs."

"Which is why Devries sent a lot of ships," Natasha huffed. "I can't believe Mirko thought she'd actually get away with this."

"Really?" Isin picked up one of the bags. "This is the same woman who thought I'd be thrilled to have sex with her, and then lied to you about it."

"You're right. She's always been delusional."

He helped Natasha load the bags into the airlock, along with the original container Sweep had found in Mirko's cabin.

Sweep checked all the crates thoroughly for trackers and other bugs but didn't locate a single one. "Didn't Mirko use any type of security?"

"Her paranoia was her security," Natasha replied. "Actual security costs money."

To Isin's surprise, three of the crates held new or refurbished ship parts. "Why didn't she use these on *Sphinx?*"

"She probably forgot she had them." Natasha ran her index finger over one of the crate lids, living a visible streak in the dust. "These date from her early smuggling days, back when her major concern was getting raided by the Feds. There were rumors that if the Feds failed to find any contraband, they'd take a ship's spare parts to make the stop worth their while." She frowned. "I believed those stories at the time, but I never met anyone who actually had it happen to them. Now I'm wondering if it was an urban myth."

"Or based on the actions of the criminal organizations rather than the Feds." It sounded like something the organization he'd been forced to work for to pay off his dad's debts would have done.

Natasha nodded. "I also don't recall her pulling things *out* of the Birdbolt except once., and I'm pretty sure that was alcohol we'd dropped off earlier that year. She always insisted the Birdbolt was a cache for lean times, but if that were true, she would have sold off this stuff long before now."

There were certainly things to sell. In addition to the ship parts, several crates contained clothing that had never been worn and another crate held beautifully hardbound books that looked like they'd never been read. But the real score was the two crates of Osirian firewater. It wouldn't bring a huge sum, but enough to give everyone on the crew a bonus even after portioning a significant chunk for Hobbes, Omondi, and Adel.

After repacking the crates, he followed Natasha to the cockpit, where Kenji was warming up the engines.

"We good to go, Cap? Cap'n?"

"As soon as everyone's strapped in," he replied.

He and Natasha took the jump seats while Sweep dropped into the co-pilot's seat.

"Hobbes, Omondi, you good?" Sweep asked over the comm.

"All set."

The *Dagger* lifted off with sleek efficiency, leaving a cloud of dust billowing up from below.

Kenji glanced over his shoulder at Natasha. "How far out do you want to go before we... *poof.*" He made an exploding motion with his hand.

"You can release it as soon as we're out of the gravity well."

"Aye, aye."

Tension radiated off Natasha as Kenji guided the ship away from the planetesimal.

Isin didn't try to engage her in conversation. She was too distracted to give him more than monosyllabic answers.

"We're clear. Opening exterior airlock hatch."

A series of blue icons populated the tactical display as the force from the pressurized airlock expelled the contents.

"Cannons warming up," Sweep informed them.

Kenji brought the ship around. Already, the expanding cluster of bags was nearly impossible to see through the viewport despite their sparkly content. That's why Sweep had tagged each bag, making them easier to target.

"Ready on your command."

Natasha took a deep breath. "Fire."

The bags of Aphrodite's Dream exploded in a spray of particles. Five of the blue dots winked out on the tactical display. The second shot took out another four. The third shot eliminated the two remaining stragglers.

Natasha's exhale filled the cockpit. "It's done." She sagged against the seat back, her shoulders lowering and her head falling back. The smile she flashed him sparkled more than the Aphrodite's Dream. "Now that was a beautiful sight."

He couldn't agree more.

Thirty-Two

"We'll have to postpone our date to the Yruf biosphere." Micah watched Celia closely as she moved around the bedroom in her cabin, tucking items into the pack sitting on the bed. They weren't leaving until the morning, but he knew Celia wasn't the type to wait until the last minute to pack, especially since she was spending the night in his cabin. It was the last chance they'd have to be alone for a while. "Your animal communication lesson will have to wait."

She gave him a smile that reminded him of sunshine sparkling on ocean waves. "But we'll have plenty of animals on the planet you can teach me to communicate with."

"That's true." He'd been so focused on Manchado he hadn't given the planet they were visiting any thought. "But... are you sure you want to come with us? My mom can handle checking out the planet's flora. You could stay here on the *Starhawke*."

She paused, her shoulder blades visibly tightening beneath the fabric of her shirt. She pivoted slowly, her dark eyes searching his. "Why would you suggest that? Are you worried I'll have an issue being on the same ship as Manchado?"

"Not worried. I just don't want you to do this out of a sense of obligation to Aurora. He's not your problem anymore."

One perfectly shaped brow lifted. "Isn't he? I'm the reason he's here."

"No, you're not. Aurora and I are the reason he's here. I'm the one who pummeled him and she's the one who decided to pull him off Devries' ship."

"So that I would have a chance to confront him. Which I did." She tipped her head to the side. "It's not me you're concerned about, is it? Why don't you want me there?"

"I—" That was a really good question. He *always* wanted her with him. The answer that came to him wasn't pretty. "I guess I'm worried somehow he'll mess up what's happening between us."

She didn't react right away, just gazed at him for a three count. "Do you have so little faith in me?"

"No!" A bolt of panic arrowed through his chest. "It's me." Something he hadn't realized until the words came out of his mouth. "He brings out the worst in me. You've never seen me react to him. You weren't there either time I've been around him. If you were, I'm not sure..." He struggled to put the unease swirling in his gut into words. Again, the answer wasn't flattering. "I don't... I don't want you to see that side of me. To think less of me."

She remained motionless for the longest moment of his life, then moved toward him the way he'd approach an injured animal. "Micah." When she reached him, she rested her hand lightly on his arm. "You don't need to be afraid," she murmured, gazing deeply into his eyes. "I know who you are. I know your heart. Nothing Manchado can do would ever change how I feel about you. I lo—" She stopped herself, her lips clamping shut as her gaze darted away from his.

The abrupt shift made his heart do a swan dive. Was she about to say what he thought she was?

She continued to stare at the bulkhead, her mouth so compressed it almost disappeared.

"You what?" he prompted as softly as a feather.

Her throat moved in an audible swallow. But she didn't meet his gaze. Didn't reply.

His heart pounded loud enough that she could probably hear it. The heart that belonged to her. He took the leap. "I love you, Celia."

Her gaze snapped to his, her eyes widening in shock. In fear.

Ice water poured over him. He'd misjudged. Scared her. She wasn't ready—

Her hand gripped the back of his neck, pulling him toward her, her lips finding his like she needed the air in his lungs to breathe.

Warmth spread everywhere her toned body made contact with his. He groaned, pulling her even closer. She let him, this incredible, strong woman who lit him up like a Christmas tree.

Her fingers threaded through his hair, holding him in place, the touch of her lips sending rivers of sensation running through his body.

She might not be able to say the words, but her response gave him hope. He'd cling to that hope, even as his heart whimpered with longing.

He might have whimpered out loud, because she eased back, her hands bracketing his face as she looked into his eyes. The intensity of her gaze made his heart stutter. "Micah."

He cherished his name on her lips. It would be enou—

"I love you."

Bam! His heart smacked his ribcage, expelling the air from his lungs. She'd said it. She'd actually said it.

Coherent thought fled as his lips found hers again, those three words reverberating in his mind while his soul absorbed them like a sponge.

His breathing was wrecked by the time he lifted his head. "Thank you," he panted.

She gave a soft snort, her breathing just as unsteady. "Thank you?"

He nodded. "For not leaving me out on that ledge by myself."

The emotion she'd given voice to shone in the dark umber of her eyes. "You know me better than that."

"I was afraid I'd scared you."

"You startled me. I wasn't expecting..." Her gaze searched his as she gathered her thoughts. "You've been so consistent about waiting for me to take steps forward, that when I lost my nerve, I thought you'd drop it. But you didn't."

"You looked like you were panicking."

"I was, briefly. No man has ever said that to me and meant it. It was always a tactic to convince me to have sex with them."

He winced.

"I didn't care. Nothing they said mattered. Only that they weren't blond."

For obvious reasons.

He pressed a kiss to her forehead, then tucked her head under his chin. "I'm so sorry for what you've suffered."

"I know." She sighed. "You are the most patient man I've ever known."

He chuckled softly. "You're forgetting my dad. He waited twenty-seven years for the woman he loves."

Her arms tightened around him. "So you're saying it's genetic?"

"Could be. I certainly understand his behavior a lot more now than I did as a kid. Back then, I couldn't figure out why a good-looking, successful man would show zero interest in dating. Kai tried to set him up a bunch of times, even suggested a few double dates whenever he was seeing someone, but my dad always turned him down. I thought he was nuts. Now I know he was in love with an amazing woman he couldn't be with. Why would he want anyone else?"

As soon as the words left his mouth, he realized how much he'd revealed about his own intentions. A woman as observant as

Celia wouldn't miss the implications. Her silence confirmed it. "I'm sorry. That was more than you wanted to know."

She shifted against him, but didn't pull away. She didn't lift her head, either. "Is that how you feel about me? The way your dad feels about your mom?"

Yep, she'd read him like a book. And she sounded a little anxious about his answer.

He could lie and say no, but she'd see right through him. Or he could equivocate, say he was tending in that direction but wasn't sure. But that was also a lie.

He was sure. He just hadn't figured out where that path led. But telling her the truth might scare her even more than admitting he loved her.

"You're afraid of telling me that you do, aren't you?"

Or she could pluck the answer out of his head with the ease of a dragonfly taking a drink of water. "Yes."

She took a deep breath, letting it out slowly. "Your parents are good role models. Marina and Gryphon, too. That kind of enduring relationship isn't something I've witnessed before. I certainly never imagined that kind of life for myself. Even joining this crew gave me more of a family than I'd ever expected to have."

His heart cracked a little. "I can understand why." One of the primary reasons was waiting for them on *Vengeance* right now. Manchado had left scars on Celia that might never fade, impacting her present and her future.

That knowledge sparked a flame of anger. And made him seriously rethink his *hands off* policy regarding that scumbag.

"Your heart's beating faster." Celia tipped her head back, meeting his gaze. Her eyes narrowed. "You're thinking about him."

Not a question, so it didn't require an answer.

"He's not worth it." She rested a hand on his chest where his heart was striking his ribcage like a prisoner beating on the bars of their cell. "He's done enough damage. I won't allow him to have any power over me. Not anymore."

He tried to summon a smile, but it probably looked like a grimace.

"I mean it, Micah." She pressed her hand more firmly against his chest. "During this mission I'll be working with your dad regularly on our travel days. I have a lot of emotional gunk to clear."

"I want to help."

"You do. More than you know." Her expression softened, her brown eyes taking on a liquid sheen. "I've never imagined building a life with someone..."

He held his breath, caught between the pain of her words and the hope in her eyes.

She took a breath, like she was preparing for a deep dive. "But that doesn't mean it isn't a possibility for the future."

Thirty-Three

"I can hear you thinking." Cade drew Aurora back against his bare chest, resting his chin on her shoulder. The darkness of the night cycle still surrounded them in their bedroom nook, but neither of them had slept much during the night. Based on her fluctuating emotional resonance, he suspected she'd spent most of the time staring into the darkness, just as he had. "Have you changed your mind about me going with you?"

"No." Her fingers brushed lightly over his forearm where it wrapped around her waist. "You need to be here."

His instincts agreed with her. But it also felt wrong every time they were separated.

"I was thinking about you, though. I've been trying to figure out why the Sovereign hasn't made your name and face part of the most wanted list. Or the rest of your team. Nixon's acting like he doesn't know you exist."

He'd been wondering the same thing. Unity was still monitoring all of Admiral Nixon's communications that passed through the primary relay in the Sol system. So far, Cade's team hadn't been mentioned at all. "Probably for the same reason she kept me and my team out of the records for the Admiral's trial. But damned if I know what that reason is." It worried him. He couldn't help feeling there was a snare set for him that he couldn't see.

"If it was anyone else we were talking about, I might attribute it to protecting you from harm. But that's not how the Sovereign thinks."

"No kidding." Rage seared through him every time he thought about the way she'd tried repeatedly to subjugate Aurora — first on Gaia, then at Tnaryt's Camp, and again at Seaview. Now Aurora was returning to Tnaryt's Camp, the planet where she'd learned the Sovereign's identity. That had to be messing with her head. "I'm glad your family will be with you."

"Me, too." She fell silent, her fingers continuing the subtle caress on his forearm. Her emotional field, however, was swirling with floating anxiety.

He latched onto a positive topic. "Magee's doing well. Discussing the challenges the Fleet crews are facing because of Nixon's changes seems to be speeding her recovery, giving her something to focus on that's familiar." Or maybe it was realizing she wasn't the only one who'd suffered at the hands of the Sovereign and the Teeli.

Aurora nodded, the motion making a soft shushing sound against the pillow. "She still reacts with a fear response every time she sees me, but it fades quickly. She doesn't have that reaction with the Admiral anymore."

"Your dad's been working in extra sessions with the two of them. Has he suggested she have any sessions with you?" He could sense that Magee's fear response still bothered her.

"He's mentioned it, but he wanted to get her on firm footing with Will, first."

He smiled to himself. It still delighted him that Aurora had been added to the very short list of people who referred to the Admiral by his first name. Even Cade didn't call him Will.

"Working with you and your team while I'm gone should help solidify her progress. You're the people she's used to having around her."

"Speaking of work, any thoughts on what we should do if Unity gets a bead on Montgomery's location?"

Aurora turned her head, her eyes glimmering in the muted starlight from the viewport. "We don't have a lot of options. The *Starhawke* can't be moved for another two weeks. And *Gladiator*'s just as notorious now."

Very true. Unity had made the ship famous during the escape from Sol Station. Or infamous, if you believed the Sovereign's lies. Any ship of that make and model would be under intense scrutiny by the Fleet, regardless of the ship's or personnel's IDs.

"We have *Phoenix*. Unity confirmed the ship's hull integrity is stronger than ever, so it's good to go." While the Yruf were helping Nat with the hull repairs, Unity had silently reinforced other weak points they'd detected in the ship's exterior. He also suspected Unity was working with Alec to improve the ship's shielding in the same way they had for *Gladiator*.

Aurora frowned. "But the *Nichols* and *Intrepid* are based out of Hydra One. And their crews just interacted with Nat on *Vengeance* during the transfer of the kids. They think she just got pulled off *Sphinx*." Her protective instincts swelled in her emotional field. "She can't take *Phoenix* to Hydra One without putting herself at risk from Fleet security, who'll ask questions she can't answer."

"I know," he assured her. "I was thinking of me and my team, not Nat."

Aurora didn't seem any happier with his addendum.

"That's assuming Montgomery's even there and needs our help," he added. "She may have hopped a freighter under an assumed identity like the Admiral did. Or hidden herself so well we won't locate her."

Aurora's gaze sharpened. "If she's on the station, Unity will find her."

Thirty-Four

"Are you sure you'll be okay in here?"

Aurora turned toward the hatchway to the four-person cabin on *Vengeance*. She felt the concern threading Nat's emotional field as she surveyed the utilitarian U-shaped layout of the cabin. Isin stood silently behind her, his broad shoulders filling the hatch opening.

"It's fine." Aurora set her pack on the lower bunk to her left. Celia had claimed the lower bunk across from her, leaving the upper bunks for Iolana and Micah. The unspoken protective positioning she and Celia had taken wasn't necessary on *Vengeance*, but it was an ingrained habit for both of them to take up defensive positions in unfamiliar surroundings.

Micah and Iolana didn't seem to mind. If anything, they found it amusing. Her parents and Kai were in the matching cabin across the corridor. Aurora would put money on the fact her mom had insisted on a bottom bunk, too.

"The bedding is from *Phoenix*. The mattresses are new, too." Nat nibbled her bottom lip. "It's not what you're used to, but—"

"Did you just insult my ship?" Isin asked dryly.

Nat shot a look over her shoulder. "No. But even you have to admit *Vengeance* isn't like the *Starhawke*."

"I admit nothing."

"Of course not. Wouldn't want to bruise your overblown ego."

"It goes with my overblown musculature," Isin deadpanned.

Nat's lips twitched.

But Aurora still sensed concern in her emotional field. "This is great. Really." She crossed the short distance to the hatch, her gaze moving between Nat and Isin. "I appreciate you loaning us your crew to take care of this task."

Nat gave a derisive snort. "Finally getting Mirko somewhere she won't cause trouble for anyone but herself and Manchado is all the thanks I need."

"It's much better than she deserves," Isin added. "And more forgiving than what she was running from."

Another point in favor of this solution. Mirko's residence on the planet would prevent the criminal organization Devries worked for from killing her. Or abusing her until she wished she were dead, as Manchado had implied.

Of course, staying with Manchado might be its own type of torture. For both of them. That's why Aurora and her dad would be spending part of this trip confirming whether it was better to place the two together so they could help each other — the more optimistic option — or far apart so they wouldn't harm each other. It was still a toss-up. She wasn't looking forward to those sessions, but her conscience demanded she gather as much information as possible before they took the pair down to the planet.

"Are we pulling anyone away from the repair work on *Phoenix?*" she asked Nat.

"Nope. All the parts we need to finish the job are already generated and loaded on the ship. Shash grumbled a bit about not being able to oversee the finishing touches, but she's not about to let *Vengeance* leave without her. Pete and Marlin can handle it. Itorye's staying with us, too. We've got it covered."

Aurora's gaze moved to the small duffel sitting on Micah's bunk, which had a vaguely egg-shaped outline. "Well, if anything does come up, you'll be able to reach us immediately."

Nat's gaze followed hers. Her brows rose a fraction, then she nodded. "Good to know." She glanced behind her, cocking her head like she was listening for sounds in the corridor. Then she lowered her voice. "I assume some of our friends will be going with you?"

Aurora nodded. "They'll be keeping watch here, too."

Isin's head dipped in a silent thank you that Nat couldn't see.

But she definitely caught Aurora's reaction, because she gave Isin a side-eye. "Then I guess it's time to get this show on the road."

Thirty-Five

"You going to miss me?" Nat asked Isin as he followed her toward the airlock connecting *Vengeance* to *Phoenix*.

"What do you think?"

She pivoted, walking backward slowly so she could face him. "I think you're going to be pining for me from the moment I step off this ship. Within hours, your crew is going to be fed up with your wistful sighs and sad eyes."

Isin made a sound deep in his throat that could have been a chuckle or a growl. His hand darted out, grabbing her around the waist and pulling her flush against the solid wall of his chest. "Is that so?"

Her breath caught, her body reacting to him the way it always did. But she managed to keep her tone light. "Yep."

He lowered his head so their mouths were centimeters apart. "And what about you? Will you miss me?"

"Not at all." Her unsteady breathing gave lie to her declaration, as did the way her pulse leapt as his lips hovered over hers.

"Liar."

"Yep." And then he touched down, sending warmth cascading through her like a waterfall. She gripped his shoulders, reveling in the rippling muscles beneath her fingertips, imprinting this moment in her memory. They hadn't been separated since their relationship had changed. She honestly didn't know how she'd react, but missing him was a given.

"What will I do without you keeping me on my toes?" he murmured against her mouth, his tongue tracing the curve of her lip.

She shivered at the light contact. "Be bored, I guess."

This time it was definitely a chuckle. "Probably." He lifted his head, giving her a bemused look. "I have no doubt you'll find creative ways to fill the time."

"No doubt." She never went looking for trouble, but it had a way of finding her anyway.

Isin knew that better than anyone after all their adventures together. He cupped her jaw in his large palm, his gaze growing serious. "Promise me you'll be here when I get back."

"I will." And just to hedge her bets. "If I'm not, I'll make sure you know where to find me."

One corner of his mouth quirked. "Good thing Itorye's staying with you."

She scowled. "You think I need a babysitter?"

"No, I think you need backup."

She opened her mouth to protest, then changed her mind. "Fair."

"You two done with the lovey-dovey stuff?"

They both turned in the direction of the airlock.

Lupe leaned against the bulkhead, watching them with amusement. Today their eyes were bright violet, which matched the color streak in their brunette bob wig.

Isin stepped back. "You need me?"

"No, I need Nat. I have something to give her before we leave." Lupe tipped their head toward the forward stairway. "It won't take long."

Isin shot Nat a questioning look, but she shrugged. She didn't have a clue.

His gaze held hers. "I'll see you soon."

"Count on it." Rising on tiptoe, she gave him a quick kiss before heading down the corridor to Lupe. "You going to tell me what this is about?" she asked as they walked to the stairway together. She and Lupe got along fine, but it wasn't like they'd become close friends. Since they each piloted their respective ships, they rarely saw each other except over vid comms or when Lupe paid a visit to *Phoenix* to see Gavin.

"You'll see."

Intriguing. Then again, Lupe had a flair for the dramatic, though thankfully not in a disruptive way. Their attitude was playful but underlaid with a seriously solid foundation. She could see why they and Gavin had been lifelong friends, and why Gavin had recommended Lupe to take over as *Vengeance's* pilot. What was tougher to understand is what Lupe saw in Shash.

To each their own.

Lupe led the way to their cabin, opening the hatch and motioning Nat inside. They startled her by sealing the hatch behind them.

She turned to face them, arms crossed over her chest. "What's this about?"

Lupe looked amused by Nat's subtly defensive pose. "I was talking to Gavin, who's been talking to Alec's new friend."

Nat's eyes almost popped out of her head. "Um..."

Lupe raised their hand. "Don't worry. I'm the one who helped smuggle Alec off Rathburn's ship, remember? Unity's secret is safe with me."

That might be so, but Nat was still ticked at Gavin for making that call. "Why did Gavin tell you?"

"He didn't. I figured it out myself."

"How?"

Lupe grinned, their violet lips vivid against their white teeth. "Gavin's very good at keeping secrets from everyone but me. I know him too well. And Alec's been acting strangely ever since we encountered the shadow ships. I've been observing every interaction we've had with those ships. It didn't take much to put the pieces together and figure out a non-biological entity was involved."

Not much for them, maybe. Gavin had said Lupe was brilliant, but Nat had a new appreciation for their intellect.

"I decided it was time to ask Gavin and Alec about it. They hedged. It was Unity who introduced themselves to me, and explained about the Yruf. Apparently they wanted to meet me, since they knew my history with Alec."

"Okay. I can see that." Unity was a curious being and adored Alec. They'd want to know about the people Alec knew. Lupe's explanation diffused her anger at Gavin. "So, why am I here?"

"Aha!" Lupe held up a finger like a magician with a wand doing a magic trick. "We all agreed that there's a significant non-zero chance you will have reason to leave Zeta Tucanae while *Vengeance* is away. We want you to be prepared for that eventuality." Lupe turned and opened the specially made cabinet they'd brought with them when they'd taken the job on *Vengeance*.

Nat got her first peek at the wide collection of wigs Lupe used to change their look. Every shade of hair possible was represented, in a variety of styles. None of them had the color streaks that Lupe was sporting currently, which indicated those were added separately.

Lupe studied the three rows carefully, glancing back at Nat a couple times with an assessing eye. Then they plucked two of the wigs out of the cabinet and settled them in a custom-made travel case at their feet. Next, they pulled out what looked like clip-in hair extensions, adding those to the case before moving to the closet. Several items of clothing went into a pack next to the case. "You're a little shorter than me, but close enough that these should fit what I have in mind."

"And what do you have in mind?" She was still trying to follow the line of logic that had prompted this expedition.

"Disguises. If you end up needing to take *Phoenix* somewhere that's potentially dangerous..." Lupe made it sound like a foregone conclusion. "You'll have the option of being someone other than Natasha Orlov."

Thirty-Six

Lelindia sighed as *Vengeance*'s stocky form headed out of the system, growing too small for even the *Starhawke*'s cameras to pick up.

Raehn gave a kick, drawing her attention away from the bridgescreen. "I'll miss her, too." With Aurora's family *and* Celia gone, this moment was feeling a bit too much like the beginning of Aurora's incarceration.

"It isn't easy, is it?" her mom murmured, slipping an arm around her waist.

She leaned into her, wrapping her arm around her mom's shoulders. "No." By unspoken agreement, they'd come up to the bridge together to watch *Vengeance*'s departure. Her mom sounded as subdued as Lelindia felt. Being separated from Libra by lightyears was a new experience for her. "But I think it's good once in a while to get some distance."

Her mom gave her an assessing look. "Did you feel that way the first time Aurora went off without you?"

The memory tugged a smile to her lips. "Nope. I pretty much begged her to stay. But she made the right call. The separation made us both stronger."

"Mmm." Her mom's gaze returned to the bridgescreen. "I'll keep that in mind."

She turned to Justin, who was seated in the captain's chair. He and Bella were taking over the bridge rotation slot Libra and Brendan had been covering. "You two need anything?"

Justin shook his head. "We're good."

"Then we'll be down in the greenhouse and galley with my dad getting the day's meals prepped."

Which is where Jonarel found her a few hours later, plucking tomatoes from the vine while her parents worked in the galley. From the set of his shoulders and the look in his golden eyes, he'd heard from Siginal.

Her gut clenched as she set her basket down. "What did he say?"

He shook his head, the thick curtain of his hair brushing his broad shoulders. "I wanted to wait for you."

She reached out to him, drawn like a magnet. He captured her hand in his, twining their fingers together. His thoughtfulness brought tears to her eyes. Then again, in her current hormonal state, he could have said the plants looked green today and still brought tears to her eyes. It was getting embarrassing. She'd started carrying a handkerchief, just in case. "Then let's go to the bridge."

"No need." He slid his arms around her, turning her to face the path. "Tehar?"

An image of Siginal appeared in front of them, hovering over the path. He was dressed in the kind of formal wear she'd seen when they were on Drakar, and when he came to the *Starhawke* after

Aurora's incarceration, trying to intimidate Jonarel and the rest of the crew. She assumed his attire meant he'd made this recording right after leaving the meeting of the clan leaders.

"My checalas," he began, "I know you have been awaiting word. The past few days have been long." Lines of weariness around his eyes and the slight droop to his shoulders indicated just how exhausted he was, though he was trying to hide it.

"The *ginlemanect* has concluded." He sighed, the sound heavy. "It did not result in the decision I had hoped for."

Fear spiked her chest, sending her heart leaping into her throat.

Jonarel pulled her closer, wrapping himself around her like he could shield her from the effect of his father's words.

"Most of the clan leaders see things as I once did. They do not accept Lelindia as a leader of the Suulh."

Jonarel's low growl reverberated around and through her, making her shiver. His anger was palpable, burning alongside her fear.

"There are two who do. Harvan is one." His expression showed a flash of dry humor and pride. "I believe Daymar would not have spoken to her brother ever again if he had acted otherwise. My checana is Lelindia's greatest champion, and very eager to see you both and give you her blessings. As am I."

Those words, and the clear acceptance and caring in his gaze, coaxed her heart back down into her chest. The gentle rumble of Jonarel's purr replaced his growl, warming the cold places that her fear had iced over.

"Charapin was also in agreement."

"Clan Eratec," Jonarel murmured for her benefit. "A powerful ally."

"However, we were unable to sway the others. Lelindia's standing as Jonarel's checana and Nedale of the Suulh was not sufficient to establish a clan bond with the Suulh. The debate now comes down to the child. No course of action will be taken until after she is born. Lelindia must present her in person at a *ginlemanect*. Only then will a final decision be made."

Lelindia's hands pressed against the curve of her belly. One of Jonarel's large hands splayed over hers.

"*Fedar sigmet naldi.* Daymar and I will join you soon."

The image faded, the sound of the babbling brook and rustle of leaves from the air circulation creeping back into her consciousness.

But she couldn't decide how she felt. Being dismissed as unworthy of the respect Aurora commanded wasn't a surprise, not after how hard she'd had to work to convince Siginal she was a leader of the Suulh, not Aurora's sidekick.

Still, it stung. The Nedale and Sahzade were partners, neither more important than the other. Yes, as the guardian, the Sahzade had the final say in any course of action regarding the Suulh, but the Nedale was an equal, a mentor and advisor, not subservient.

If the clan leaders had seen how Faahn and her fellow villagers on Feylahn had reacted to Lelindia when they'd discovered who she was, they'd reevaluate their position regarding her standing as a leader.

But there was still hope. They wanted to meet her and Raehn, to see for themselves the daughter of Suulh and Kraed blood. She couldn't really blame them. This was uncharted territory for everyone. And it sounded like Siginal and Daymar would be heading to the *Starhawke* shortly. She was eager to see Daymar, to thank her for being on her side long before she'd known she had an ally.

Jonarel remained strangely silent. His purr had stopped as soon as Siginal had mentioned bringing her and Raehn before the clan leaders.

She peered at him over her shoulder. He looked as conflicted as she was. "Are you upset?"

"That they do not value you as they should? Yes."

"But?"

He sighed. "The decision to await Raehn's birth is far better than the dismissal my father's proposal could have received."

Her heart squeezed painfully. "You thought they'd flat out reject the idea of joining the fight against the Teeli?"

"That would have been consistent with our clan history."

She hadn't really considered that possibility. "So, having two clan leaders who sided with your dad is a win?"

"Yes, a small one. Harvan, I anticipated. Tehar informed me that our mother has been speaking to him about you for years. It is one reason the Terfeli were so welcoming to you at the Kraed Embassy. My uncle's clan was already predisposed in your favor. But Charapin standing up for you is unexpected. He is a thoughtful leader, not prone to rash action. That he agreed with my father indicates he understands the value of supporting the Suulh and confronting the threat the Teeli pose to our people." His eyes took on a faraway look. "His clan has suffered great pain in recent years that few can imagine. He would not willingly seek more. The other leaders know this."

The ache of sadness in his golden eyes plucked at her heartstrings. "What happened to his clan?" she asked softly.

His eyes shadowed, emphasizing the anguish even talking about it caused him. "They were forced to banish one of their own."

She sucked in a breath. "Like Siginal did with you and Tehar?" That memory still gave her pain.

"No." His eyes darkened even more. "The... outcast's actions required his removal from Drakar and isolation where he would not harm anyone again."

Again. Her throat tightened at the implications. The Kraed were lethal. She'd seen firsthand what Jonarel could do when those he loved were in danger. But the Kraed's marrow-deep protective instincts toward one another was what made their society work. They never intentionally harmed each other, or those under their protection. When Siginal had accidentally backhanded her, Jonarel's justice had been swift and brutal. And Siginal's repentance had been heartfelt.

The idea of a Kraed without those guardrails was terrifying. "It sounds like you know Charapin well."

The shadows faded from Jonarel's eyes. "He has been very gracious to me. Clan Eratec is known for their artistry. Their ships are the most beautiful our people have produced. I spent weeks at their compound, studying their ships while I was drafting the design for the *Starhawke*."

"Really?" She'd assumed that Clan Clarek, as the first clan to achieve space travel, would have the most beautiful ships. The *Starhawke* certainly had the power to take her breath away.

He nodded. "So did my father when he designed the *Rowkclarek*. The other Clan Clarek ships do not have the same fluid exterior that Tehar's and Rowk's ships do. The *Starhawke* and *Rowkclarek* were designed to be as at home in water as they are in the trees of our compound."

"Huh." The one time she'd seen several Clan Clarek ships in flight, she'd been too busy facing off against Siginal to pay any attention to the visuals of the ships that were chasing the *Starhawke* down. Seeing them on Drakar didn't help, either. When Clan Clarek ships were docked at the compound, they blended so well with the jungle surroundings it was impossible to know what they'd look like in the air.

The knowledge Jonarel had given her made her appreciate the beauty of the *Starhawke* even more. And prompted a question. "Why water?"

"Clan Eratec's compound is built on a coastline. Their clan is known for their aquatic abilities. All their ships have homes in water."

Her imagination took flight, visualizing an entire cluster of *Starhawkes* along a coastal beach. Would the ships blend with their surroundings? Or was their aesthetic appeal part of the reason they were in the water, like floating sculptures? "I'd like to see that."

Jonarel brushed his lips over her cheek, then nuzzled behind her ear. "Then I will take you there."

The caress combined with his deep baritone made her tingle from head to toe.

Raehn gave a kick-kick in response.

Lelindia chuckled, stroking her fingers over the growing swell of her belly. Her daughter's tiny body was developing, but it would still be weeks before Raehn would take her first breath. "So, I guess we're in a holding pattern until Raehn puts in an appearance."

"With the clans, yes." Jonarel's fingers followed hers, generating squiggles of sensation that elicited a flare of Nedale energy from Raehn. The emerald ribbon skipped around both their hands. "But the *Starhawke* will be recharged before then. We could reach Drakar before Raehn's birth."

She jolted in surprise. "Was that your plan?" She hadn't considered that possibility, since Aurora had been adamant about staying in Fleet space where they could monitor and respond to the Sovereign's next moves. "I thought your parents were coming here."

"They are. I suspect my mother would not consider waiting for us to arrive on Drakar. Or perhaps you would prefer to go to Azaana to be with the Suulh when we greet our daughter."

She loved the way he phrased that, *greet our daughter*. But now she had a dilemma. Assuming Aurora would agree to go to Kraed space for Raehn's birth, which location should she choose? She knew without a doubt that Aurora would be by her side wherever they were. So would Libra. The arrival of a new Nedale or Sahzade was an intense bonding time for energy sisters. "Would you be offended if I wanted to be with the Suulh instead of your clan?"

"Our clan," Jonarel corrected gently. He turned her in his arms and cupped her cheek in his hand. "You cannot offend me. You are my checana, and the Nedale of the Suulh. We will go wherever you wish."

Thirty-Seven

The deck of *Vengeance's* transport bay vibrated under Aurora's boots as she settled one of the refrigerated crates from *Starlet* onto the hover cart sitting at the base of the shuttle's ramp. Since *Starlet* was staying with them, to hasten their departure, they'd waited to unload the cargo until they were on their way to Tnaryt's Camp.

"Captain Hawke?"

She turned to the tower of muscle standing behind her. "You can call me Aurora, Kenji."

An adorable flush crept up his neck from the collar of his fitted black muscle shirt. "Yes, ma'am."

Aurora bit back a smile. Based on Kenji's emotional field, it would be a while before he'd feel comfortable calling her by her name. He had a fanboy vibe going on, along with a healthy dose of respect. Hence the *ma'am*. "You wanted to ask me something?" she prompted.

He glanced away, like he'd lost his courage now that they were face-to-face. "Uh, yeah. I was wondering... well, Sweep and I were wondering..." He lifted his chin toward *Starlet*, where Sweep was helping the rest of her group unload the crates of food they'd brought from the *Starhawke*. "Would you consider, um..." He trailed off again.

Her smile broke through. She couldn't help it, not when this mammoth of a man was acting like a shy little boy. "I don't bite, Kenji. Go ahead and ask."

Her smile seemed to tip the scales. "Would you consider demonstrating your abilities?" he said in a rush.

She'd had a feeling that's what he'd been working up to. "I'd be happy to. Just tell me when."

Her quick acceptance caught him off guard. He rocked back on his heels. "Uh, well, maybe after we put the crates away?"

"Or you could do it now," Celia chimed in, eavesdropping shamelessly as she set a crate on the cart. "We know where the galley is." She pointed to Micah and Kai, who were coming down the ramp, crates in their arms. "We can handle it from here. You and Libra go ahead."

Aurora hadn't noticed that her mom was standing on the opposite side of the cart, also listening in. "Are you interested?"

Her mom nodded. "Sounds like fun."

Fun. Not a word her mother would have used for this scenario several months ago. Then again, her mom had been the one arguing in favor of using their abilities to help the kids on Devries' ships, even if it meant revealing what she and Marina could do. Her mom's willingness to be open about it still caught her by surprise.

"I'll let Sweep know we're taking over here," Micah offered, jogging up the ramp and disappearing into the main cabin.

Kenji radiated eagerness. "You sure this is okay?" He glanced between her and her mom, then to the hover cart.

Aurora nodded. "We were going to be extraneous once we reached the galley anyway, except maybe as referees for who was going to be in charge of the setup and meal planning."

Celia snorted and Kai grinned. "Iolana and I will handle that job," he assured her.

Sweep strode down the ramp, his boots making a solid thump with each step. "I understand you've agreed to a demonstration."

The speed with which he'd appeared indicated he'd been aware of the request Kenji was making. "I have. Is there a training area where we could go?" She had a feeling Kenji and Sweep would want a more thorough demonstration than the one she'd given Isin and Nat in the *Starhawke*'s observation lounge. It would be better to do it in a space designed for combat training.

"There is. Follow me."

She and her mom fell into step behind Sweep, Kenji bringing up the rear as they exited the transport bay. Sweep headed to the forward stairs on the port side and took them down one deck.

The space they entered was roughly a cube, with slight tapering toward the deck. She recognized the shape as one of *Vengeance*'s "legs", the four protrusions below the belly of the ship that provided the framework for the shielded channel to enter the transport bay. Based on the significant structural supports spanning their surroundings, the legs also functioned as the ship's landing gear.

The area was as neat and utilitarian as the rest of the ship, but a latticework above them caught her eye. "What's that?" She pointed above the open space at the center of the bay.

"The Cage," Sweep replied. "We use it for training in close quarters."

"Just training?" She eyed the structure warily. Something about this space was triggering a feeling of trepidation and melancholy. Bad things had happened here.

"Since Isin took over as captain, yes."

She met Sweep's gaze. The anger and sorrow in his eyes and emotional field made the full answer to her question crystal clear. Prior to Isin's captaincy, this had been a place of brutality and pain.

He tipped his head. "How did you know?"

He was every bit as observant and analytical as Celia. "I'm an empath. A strong one. In places where there's been a lot of trauma, I'll often pick up on the emotional residue. It's a distinctly unpleasant feeling. That's what I'm sensing here, although it's overlaid with more positive emotions."

Sweep nodded, accepting her answer without judgment.

Kenji was staring at her with wide eyes. "You can feel that?"

"Yes. So can my dad. I inherited my empathic abilities from him."

"Would you prefer to go somewhere else?" Sweep offered.

She took a moment to test her response to the space. "No. The positive sensations are stronger." But if they really wanted to clear it, a Suulh circle would do the job.

Kenji ran a hand over his crewcut, looking even more self-conscious than he had earlier. "Can you feel what other people are feeling?"

She could tell he wanted her to say no, but she wasn't about to lie. "Yes, I can. It's one of the reasons I knew I could trust this crew." Although now that she'd adjusted to the feel of the place, she was picking up on an emotional resonance that wasn't coming from the four of them. And it had a decidedly hostile vibe.

Strolling nonchalantly toward Sweep while making a show of looking intently at the Cage, she dropped her voice to a whisper, turning her back to the source of the hostility. "Someone's in here."

Sweep gave a fractional nod, answering in the same undertone. "Lyon. Our current work in progress. Teenager. He practices down here."

Sweep's lack of concern and paternal tone indicated the kid wasn't a hazard. "I'm sensing hostility."

Sweep's brows rose. "Want me to call him out?"

"No. I just want us all on the same page."

"Understood. This'll be good for him, seeing what you can do."

She took a step to the side and raised her voice to a normal level. "What would you like to see first?"

Sweep looked between her and her mom. "Can you both handle hand-to-hand combat?"

Aurora glanced at her mom. "Can you?" She knew her mom had fought the Setarips who'd attacked Stoneycroft, but she wasn't sure that confrontation qualified as hand-to-hand combat.

Her mom smirked. "I may not have been trained in sparring by Celia, but I learned how to use my abilities to protect myself and others from danger by the time I was five."

Five? Clearly she needed to ask her mom more questions about her childhood on Feylahn.

"Then we can pair off," Sweep suggested.

A wave of discomfort washed over Kenji as he looked at Aurora's mom, whose head barely came up to his chest. Definitely a David and Goliath moment.

Kenji couldn't hurt her, but he probably wouldn't feel comfortable throwing a punch at her, either. Sweep likely wouldn't have that issue. He was approaching this session from a professional perspective, rather than an emotional one.

"Kenji, why don't you work with me. My mom can work with Sweep."

His relieved exhale made her mom shoot him a sharp look. "Don't judge me by my size, Kenji. I could lay you out with minimal effort."

Kenji's jaw hinged open. His hands rose, palms out. "I'm sorry, ma'am. I didn't mean—"

Aurora's mom chuckled, a sly smile Aurora had never seen curling her lips. "Lighten up, Kenji. This'll be fun." Her mom acted positively giddy as she strode over to Sweep.

Kenji looked stupefied. He met Aurora's gaze as she shifted to square off in front of him. "Your mom is... not what I expected."

Aurora laughed softly. "Join the club. I've known her my entire life and she still surprises me daily."

His expression relaxed at her admission. "So, how do you want to do this?"

She noticed her mom and Sweep were waiting for direction as well. "How about a simple close body shield first," she told her mom, "so they can get a feeling for how hard it is to hold onto us."

"Slippery as a seal. Got it."

Kenji exchanged a glance with Sweep, then lowered into a fighting stance. "Now what?"

Aurora engaged her shield, and felt her mom do the same. "Try to get us into a hold."

What followed was pure slapstick comedy rather than sparring. Kenji's hands skated across her shield like she was made of ice, throwing him off balance. He recovered before he hit the deck, but his eyes flew wide. He tried three different maneuvers, but each time his hands came in contact with her shield and zipped out of position as she easily slipped away. On the third one his knees crashed to the deck, giving her a moment to check on her mom and Sweep.

Sweep clearly hadn't been any more successful, but was currently attempting to encircle her mom with his arms around her waist.

Kenji must have seen the same thing, because his arms came around Aurora from behind.

The problem with that technique was they couldn't get purchase. Her mom lifted her arms and dropped to her knees, sliding free, while Aurora crouched and rolled, leaving Kenji encircling air.

Kenji grunted, his hands splayed on his hips. "That's annoying." He glanced over his shoulder at Sweep. "Any ideas?"

Sweep shook his head. "It's effective. You can't grapple against what you can't grip." His gaze met Aurora's. "What's next?"

"Throwing a punch or kick." She took them through the same instructions and warnings she'd discussed with Isin when he'd tested her shield, then had them both attempt strikes.

Kenji did his best to adapt to her abilities, but his utter failure to make any kind of contact while she barely moved finally brought a grin to his face. "This is even cooler than I'd thought it would be. Really annoying, but cool."

She returned his grin. "Got a blade with you?"

He reached into his boot, pulling out a knife the size of his palm. "This work?"

"Sure. Try to cut the shield with it."

She heard a gasp that didn't come from Kenji when the knife struck the shield, generating a flare of light. But Kenji didn't give her time to focus on her audience, dancing around her and slashing from multiple angles. The flashes of light brightened the shadows, reflecting off a pair of dark eyes peering out at her from behind a couple of stacked crates.

Lyon.

The kid's emotional field had changed while she and Kenji sparred. The hostility had abated, replaced with confusion and growing curiosity.

The light flashes stopped as Kenji followed the direction of her gaze. He straightened. "Hey, Dude, come on out here."

Defiance flared briefly in Lyon's emotional field, but the kid did as he was told, shuffling out to the edge of the shadows. Not really a kid, actually. A young adult who looked to be around seventeen or eighteen. His hands were curled into loose fists, like he expected one of them to take a swing at him.

Sweep and Aurora's mom had stopped their sparring as well, facing their uninvited guest.

Kenji took over introductions. "Lyon, this is Captain Hawke and her mom, Libra. They're from the *Starhawke*. They're gonna be with us for the duration of this trip."

Lyon's gaze shifted from Aurora to her mom and back again. "You some kind of techies?"

She studied him just as intently as he was studying her. He was muscular, but in a lean and hungry kind of way, as opposed to Kenji's solid bulk. She'd lay money that he'd missed a lot of meals growing up. And love. The hunger in his emotional field felt like a gravity well. "Why would you think that?"

"You're using something to generate a body shield. Gotta be advanced tech you brought with you."

Logical. He had a sharp mind that had reached a completely wrong conclusion. "Actually, there's no tech involved. It's a biological ability I was born with that I inherited from my mom."

"Yeah, right." Lyon gave a derisive snort, his face contorting in a scowl. "I'm not stupid."

That was a reaction to her abilities she'd never received before. She'd shocked and stunned people with the knowledge, but she'd never had anyone react with outright disbelief and disdain. Certainly not after witnessing what she could do. "I don't think you're stupid. But there are more things in heaven and earth, Horatio, than are dreamt of in your philosophy." She expanded her energy shield until it bumped lightly against the front of his body.

He took a step back, glaring at her. "What was that?"

"My shield."

He eyed the meters of empty space between them warily, his gaze darting to Kenji.

"She's telling you the truth, Dude." Kenji had not taken kindly to Lyon's implications or attitude. All the humor had drained from his expression as he stared the kid down. "And she's being gracious about your bad attitude. You need to show respect to our guests."

That made an impression. Lyon clearly valued Kenji's good opinion. His gaze dropped to his boots. "Sorry," he muttered in a monotone.

"I didn't catch that." Kenji wasn't letting him off so easily.

Lyon lifted his head, rebellion in every line of his face, but he said the word clearly this time. "Sorry."

Aurora nodded in acknowledgment. "Now I'll really blow your mind. I'm only half-human."

Lyon's eyes widened, fear shooting through him as he stumbled back a step. "You're a cyborg?"

Aurora choked on the bark of laughter that threatened, coughing as it lodged in her throat. This kid was something else. She didn't want him to think she was laughing at him, but no one had ever accused her of being a cyborg, either. "Um, no. I'm completely biological. My dad is human, but my mom is from an alien race called the Suulh. They're nearly indistinguishable from humans, but they developed abilities humans haven't, like my shielding ability."

Now Lyon was staring at her like she was several cards short of a full deck. And dangerous as a result. His gaze darted to her mom, who was watching the scene play out, a touch of irony in her emotional field. Then he looked to Sweep. "This is a joke, right?"

"No."

The calm steadiness of Sweep's demeanor seemed to unnerve Lyon just as much as Aurora's words had. He swallowed, suddenly looking like a frightened adolescent, his chest rising and falling with his rapid breathing.

Which gave her more clues about his history. She needed to feed him more information before panic set in. "In the Suulh culture, my mom and I are called Sahzade, which translates as guardian," she said gently. "We use our abilities to protect those in need. We do *not* use them to attack the innocent or the helpless."

"Libra was the one who protected the kids we rescued when one of the ship's guards started firing at them," Sweep interjected.

Lyon's gaze swung to her mom. "But you're so small." He was clearly bewildered by what he was hearing.

One corner of her mom's mouth lifted briefly. "Size isn't everything. My shield can expand far beyond my body. In fact, you could help with another demonstration, if you're interested."

Lyon glanced at Kenji as trepidation wound through his emotional field.

"She won't hurt you," Kenji assured him. "Right?" he confirmed with Aurora's mom.

"That's right. Guardian, remember?" She tapped her chest, her gaze fixed on Lyon. "It'll give you a chance to interact with my shield and get a better understanding of how it provides defense for more than just myself."

Lyon remained silent.

"Or I can ask Sweep—"

"I'll do it." Lyon stepped forward, chin lifted and shoulders tensing.

Aurora's heart ached for him. She could sense the core of inner strength that gave him his courage. He'd been repeatedly battered and abused but never broken. No wonder *Vengeance's* crew had taken him under their wing. He was the proverbial diamond in the rough. Kenji and Sweep were clearly working on chipping away the layers of rock he'd surrounded himself with to survive.

Her mom's expression remained as serious as Lyon's as she gestured him into the open space. Aurora, Kenji, and Sweep backed up, giving them room.

Lyon's hands were fisted again, his movements jerky, like each step was a potential landmine.

"I won't hurt you, Lyon," her mom said softly. "And you won't hurt me, either. This'll be like a science experiment."

Lyon's lips pinched, but his emotional field provided a counterpoint of curiosity. "What should I do?"

"Stand there." Her mom pointed to a spot on the floor. "I'm going to slowly expand my shield out to you. When you feel it touch you, I want you to rest your palms flat against it. It'll feel pleasantly warm and smooth."

Lyon gave a curt nod, facing her mom with his knees bent and his hands up in front of him, palms out. The tension running through his body sharpened his muscle definition underneath his black long-sleeved shirt and cargo pants. The outfit seemed to be the preferred uniform for most of *Vengeance's* crew.

"Ready?"

Another curt nod.

Her mom's pearlescent shield flowed out, expanding like a puffy multi-colored cloud.

Lyon flinched when the shield brushed lightly against his palms, but he didn't pull back. Tentatively, he spread his fingers and shifted his weight forward, surprise radiating through his emotional field as his hands gave shape to a very solid invisible barrier.

"Good." Her mom's encouragement drew Lyon's attention to her. "What does it feel like to you?"

Lyon's jaw worked as his fingers pressed against the unyielding surface, testing the shield he couldn't see. "A warm rock."

Aurora's lips twitched. Not the most poetic description, but Lyon's complete engagement was encouraging.

"Okay, here comes the experiment part. I'm going to attempt to push you backwards with the shield, and I want you to try to stay in place. Any questions?"

Lyon shook his head, his gaze locked with her mom's.

"Here we go."

At first, the only sign of a change was the coalescing of power in her mom's shield and the bunching in Lyon's shoulder and arm muscles. Then a soft scraping sound reached her as Lyon's boots lost traction on the deck.

He shifted his stance, working to plant his feet, but he continued to lose ground. His muscles strained as his body slid steadily toward the far bulkhead.

"I had no idea she'd have that kind of range," Sweep murmured under his breath, his gaze shifting from her mom to Lyon as the gap between them opened from four meters to eight.

"Neither did I." She had no real concept of how her mom's abilities compared to hers. She'd also never tested the limits of her shielding except in moments of necessity, whereas her mother had been methodically trained by Sooree, Aurora's grandmother, until she was eight.

The gap increased to ten meters. Lyon's heels were now only a meter from the bulkhead behind him. She felt his flare of panic as he realized he was close to being flattened against the solid surface.

But his feet stopped moving a second later, the shield no longer expanding.

"You okay, Lyon?" her mom called to him.

"Yeah," he gritted out, his muscles still flexing, his palms flat against the pearlescent shield.

"I'm going to ease back on the shield. Adjust your balance so you don't fall forward."

Lyon straightened his arms but didn't drop his hands, his weight centered over his hips. He rocked slightly as her mom pulled the shield back, then dissipated it, her hands lowering to her sides.

"Wow." Kenji's voice held a shuttle's worth of awe. "That was amazing."

Lyon hadn't moved, other than to lower his hands slightly. He stared across the open stretch of decking at her mom. "Could you have squashed me?" The question came out belligerent, but that didn't quite match his emotional field. He was stunned, like he couldn't understand why she hadn't pinned him to the bulkhead. Or worse.

Her mom folded her hands in front of her. "Could have? Yes. Would have? Never."

Lyon straightened but stayed put. "Why not? You're powerful. You could take over this whole ship." He said it almost like a dare, struggling to mask the river of fear flowing beneath the surface.

Her mom's pained sigh mirrored the sadness that swept through her emotional field. "Aurora?"

Yeah, this was a touchy subject for her mom. The culture of violence and domination Lyon was describing was what had cost her mom her homeworld and her family.

Aurora stepped into the space between them and motioned Lyon forward.

He glanced at Kenji and Sweep, then approached Aurora warily. When he halted a couple meters away, she answered his question.

"I suspect you have a lot of experience with the *might makes right* mentality. But as I told you before, we're guardians, not conquerors. It's an important distinction, one you must have seen modeled by the crew of this ship. You're surrounded by people who are more skilled and stronger than you are." She lifted her chin toward Kenji and Sweep as they joined her. "But they don't use their power against you, do they?"

"Not yet."

Kenji's long-suffering sigh told her this wasn't the first time this topic had been discussed.

"So you believe it's just a matter of time before someone more powerful than you will turn on you and try to dominate you?"

Lyon's gaze dropped to the deck. He kicked at a black mark with the tip of his boot. "I guess."

Interesting. Based on Kenji's and Sweep's emotional reactions, that answer was actually an improvement on previous responses. "Then let's look at it from a different angle. If you had the ability my mom just demonstrated, would you use it to dominate others or to protect those more vulnerable than yourself?"

His emotional field hiccupped, then swirled with uncertainty. Based on the nuances she felt, he didn't know the answer.

"My life experience has been very different from yours. I've been surrounded by people who look out for others, who care when others are hurting, and take steps to protect them. That's real power.

Dominating others doesn't mean you're powerful. It means you're scared of *their* power, individually or collectively."

Lyon's head came up, his brow furrowing as he met her gaze.

"Real power comes from knowing and accepting who you are, and accepting others for who they are, too. A true leader doesn't force others to do their bidding. They use their power to help others become the best versions of themselves."

Thirty-Eight

"Hey there, mdogo." Isin summoned a smile as he stared into the camera. The blinking red recording light was a tiny drop of color against the grey bulkhead of his cabin.

Visualizing his baby sister's beloved face helped the smile become more genuine. "I'm sorry this message is late. I know I said in my last one that I was planning to visit you at the university, but something unexpected came up and I got a little sidetracked."

He winced inwardly at how lame that sounded. Not that he could come up with anything better. These messages were always tricky to record because his work prevented him from giving his sister any details about his life.

At least, it had previously. After he and Natasha became partners – in business and personally – that had started to change. They'd talked about visiting Danai after the crew finished the settler job they'd picked up at Osiris. He'd sent Danai a message indicating he'd see her soon.

But then the *Starhawke* had appeared out of thin air and triggered a paradigm shift that had pushed that possibility into a nebulous future.

He made sure none of those thoughts showed in his expression. "Everything's fine," he assured her. Assuming he ignored the potential overthrow of the Fleet and Union leadership by a hostile, megalomaniacal Teeli force. "You don't need to worry."

No, that was his job, and he was very good at it. Last night he'd had a horrifying nightmare in which his sister was a captive of a swarm of grey-skinned, white-haired monsters who were forcing her to do terrible, painful experiments on him. He'd awoken with a yell to find Natasha standing by the bed, calling his name. Apparently he'd begun thrashing wildly in his sleep, and she'd needed to vacate the strike zone to keep from being pummeled.

"I'm still hoping to visit soon. I'm making a cargo delivery right now, but I'll have a better idea of my schedule after that." Maybe. Or the Sovereign could drop a bomb that sent them all spinning off in a new direction. At least dealing with Mirko would finally be checked off his to do list.

"You keep wowing your professors with your brilliance. They're lucky to have you as a student and research assistant. I'll message again soon. I love you, mdogo."

He tapped to end the recording, then leaned back in his chair. Lame, lame, lame. But she needed to know he hadn't forgotten about her. He sent the message before he could overthink it.

Truth be told, a large part of him wanted to go to the university right now, pack her up, and bring her onto *Vengeance*. The specter of that nightmare had really shaken him, making him realize how vulnerable his sister could be if the Teeli takeover of the Union continued to gain traction. He hadn't exaggerated. Danai was brilliant, something her professors had recognized early on. It's why they'd hired her as a part-time research assistant when she was only twenty.

But based on Aurora's intel, he could extrapolate that the Sovereign and Teeli would target the strongest and most brilliant people they could find, bending them to their will or, failing that, using them as leverage.

The very idea formed a block of ice in his gut. He wanted Danai somewhere safe, where the Sovereign and the Teeli couldn't touch her.

Unfortunately, *Vengeance* wasn't any safer than the university. Less so, actually. He and Natasha were racing toward a war that would put all their lives at risk. He didn't want Danai at the center of it.

With a sigh, he pushed away from the desk and stood. Exiting his cabin, he took the forward stairway down to C deck. Lively chatter flowed out into the corridor through the galley's open hatch, three male voices and two female. He paused at the opening, taking in the sight of Celia, Micah, Iolana, Brendan, and Kai playfully debating the arrangement of galley tools and the stacking of the food storage crates they'd brought from the *Starhawke*. Aurora and Libra were nowhere to be seen. "Everything okay?"

Micah grinned. "My dad and I are losing the argument to be in charge of the galley so yeah, everything's fine."

"Where are Aurora and Libra?"

"Showing Kenji and Sweep the scope of their abilities," Celia replied, pulling items out of one drawer and depositing them into an open drawer behind her. "Sweep said *Vengeance* had a training center they could use."

Ah. So they were down in the Cage. "Do you need more hands to help with the food prep?" Normally his crew worked on a galley rotation since none of them were what you'd call accomplished cooks.

Brendan shook his head, a twinkle in his eye as he gazed at Iolana and Kai. "We have more than enough hands already."

"And these hands need to get cracking, people." Celia gave two sharp claps. "We have a crew to feed."

Micah chuckled as she gave him a hip check to clear him from in front of the sink.

Isin stepped into the corridor. "Contact Sparki on the bridge if you need anything."

Celia glanced over her shoulder. "Will do."

Returning to the stairway, he continued down another two decks, slowing his steps as he reached the bottom.

"...believe it's just a matter of time before someone more powerful than you will turn on you and try to dominate you?"

That was Aurora. And she was facing off with Lyon, who was staring at the deck.

"I guess."

None of them had noticed his arrival yet, their focus on Lyon, so he remained by the stairs. Aurora was making a case to Lyon about power dynamics. Her approach with the kid reminded him a lot of Itorye's — empathy overlaying no-nonsense inner strength. And it was working. Lyon was showing her the same grudging respect he showed Isin's first mate. When Lyon lifted his head to meet Aurora's gaze, it was clear he was listening.

"Real power comes from knowing and accepting who you are, and accepting others for who they are, too. A true leader doesn't force others to do their bidding. They use their power to help others become the best versions of themselves. Don't you agree, Isin?" Aurora's voice carried easily in the open space, her gaze shifting to the side to meet his.

So she had noticed his arrival. Then again, she'd likely sensed his approach the moment he headed down the stairs.

He strolled forward. "I do."

Lyon whirled around like a startled rabbit. His eyes widened, his panicked expression indicating he was trying to remember everything he'd said in the past few minutes. And whether any of it was likely to tick Isin off.

He rested a hand on the kid's shoulder, giving it a gentle squeeze. "I see you've met Captain Hawke and her mom."

Lyon nodded, but his muscles remained tense under Isin's hand.

He left it there. He and Sweep were working on desensitizing Lyon, getting him to accept a reality where touch didn't lead to pain or subjugation. "How's the demonstration going?" he asked Sweep and Kenji.

"Impressive," Sweep replied. "They'd be very difficult opponents to subdue."

"Doesn't mean they're aliens," Lyon muttered, once again staring at the deck.

Isin's brows rose. Aurora had indicated she didn't plan to share her unusual heritage with anyone on the crew who didn't already know. Apparently she'd changed her mind. "You don't believe Captain Hawke?" Isin asked evenly, watching Lyon's reaction.

Lyon scoffed, but when he lifted his head and saw Isin's dead serious expression, his certainty wavered. "You think they're aliens?"

"I know they are. Aliens who have a remarkable genetic similarity to humans, but aliens nonetheless. Their biological abilities aren't anything humans have achieved. I've seen that firsthand. But even if I hadn't, I'd still believe them. Captain Hawke is an honorable woman. She also saved Natasha's life. That she chose to share this information with you indicates she respects you."

Lyon's brow crinkled, his gaze moving slowly from Isin to Aurora. He was clearly struggling to reconcile what a lifetime of hardship had taught him versus a reality he'd never imagined in his wildest dreams.

"Would you like to see what else we can do?" Libra asked, like she was offering him a treat.

Lyon stared at her. "There's more?"

Libra's smile was a tad wicked. "Oh, yes."

Thirty-Nine

"What exactly do you have in mind?"

Libra could hear the concern in Aurora's voice. Chances were good her daughter was worried about Lyon's mercurial emotional state and the fear he was working so hard to hide. But considering the way he'd reacted to the shield test, she had an idea for a demonstration that would intrigue him rather than frighten him.

She kept her focus on Lyon. "Nothing to worry about." She flicked a look at Isin. "Do you have any scrap metal pieces small enough to throw?"

Isin studied her for a moment. "Yes," he said slowly. Dropping his hand from Lyon's shoulder, he pulled out his comm device. "Summer, I need you to bring a tub of scrap metal pieces from the reclamation center down to the Cage."

"Anything specific?" a female voice responded.

"Whatever's small enough to throw and won't tick off Shash."

A rueful laugh followed. "Got it."

Isin pocketed his comm. "Anything else?" he asked her.

"How about rags?"

Kenji nodded. "We've got rags in the utility locker. I'll get 'em." He trotted toward the aft bulkhead.

Aurora moved beside her. "Mom?" She let that one word pull a lot of weight.

She got the message. "Excuse us for a moment." She caught Aurora's elbow in her palm and steered her away from the group. Keeping her back turned, she lowered her voice. "You wanted to learn more about my training as a child, didn't you? And to show them the scope of our abilities?"

"Yes, but I don't want to freak out Lyon, either. His emotions are unstable."

She nodded. "I understand, but that's precisely why we should do this. Right now, we're an unknown factor that he doesn't understand. That triggers fear. The more we open up and give him a chance to ask questions, the less *other* we'll become."

"Oh." Clearly Aurora hadn't considered the situation from that perspective.

"Being mated to a psychologist has its advantages."

"I can see that. You going to tell me what the scraps and rags are for?"

"No, but I'll need you to be in charge of shielding our audience while I'm working with the scraps."

"That's vague and cryptic."

She chuckled. "This has been a long time coming. Permit me a bit of dramatic presentation."

"Fair enough."

When they rejoined the group, Kenji held out a metal bucket filled with cleaning rags. "Will this work?"

She lifted one of the black pieces of fabric, which looked like it might have been part of a shirt in its previous life. "Perfect. Thank you. Now we need to place these on the deck to form a circle at the center of the room."

Everyone grabbed a handful out of the bucket, even Lyon, and followed her.

"How large a circle?" Sweep asked.

"About three meters in diameter."

They'd just finished laying the pieces of cloth on the deck when the clatter of footsteps on the stairs drew Libra's attention.

She recognized the trim woman who strode toward them. She was dressed in a green long-sleeved tunic and cargo pants rather than the black on black that seemed popular with most of *Vengeance's* crew and she had the physique of a professional footballer, her sleek blonde ponytail swaying with each step. Summer, one of the crewmembers who'd been part of the rescue effort on Devries' ship.

Summer cradled a grey tub in her arms that was mounded with a random assortment of metal scraps. She smiled when she spotted Libra. "Hi, Libra."

"Hi, Summer." She hadn't spent much time with the young woman, but she'd gotten the impression she was the outgoing optimist of the crew.

Summer turned to Aurora. "You must be Captain Hawke. I'm Summer." She shifted the tub so it rested against her hip and extended her hand.

Aurora grasped it. "Pleased to meet you, Summer. Call me Aurora."

"Will do." Summer's gaze shifted to Isin. "Where do you want this?" She gestured at the tub.

"Libra?"

"On the deck outside the circle." She moved to the center of the rag circle after Summer set the tub down. "Now, if everyone will please exit the circle and cluster behind Aurora, we can begin. I'll need a volunteer, though, someone with a good arm."

"I'll do it," Kenji offered, stepping forward.

"Thank you, Kenji." She'd found his flustered reluctance to work with her earlier endearing, but now that he'd seen what she and Aurora could do, he'd clearly stopped worrying that he'd somehow injure her. "You'll need to stand by the tub. Aurora, are you ready?"

"Ready." Aurora didn't look entirely sure what to expect, but she lifted her hands, her shield expanding to create a curved barrier extending over the people behind her while also forming a low wall in front of Kenji.

Libra nodded in satisfaction. Aurora would keep everyone safe if any of the scraps didn't land where she'd intended.

"What's going on?" Summer asked Isin.

"Demonstration," he replied. "I'll fill you in afterward."

Libra engaged her energy field, the pearlescent glow coalescing around her hands. "Kenji, I want you to toss one of the metal pieces over my head like you're throwing a grenade."

Kenji blinked a couple times, like he was trying to figure out the point, but he bent and pulled one of the irregular pieces off the top and held it aloft. "Ready?"

"Anytime."

He sent the metal chunk arcing over Aurora's low barrier in a parabola towards where Libra stood. Aurora's shield immediately expanded to protect Kenji as soon as the object cleared it.

Libra pivoted, targeting the moving object. The scrap metal wasn't anything like the training blocks she'd worked with as a child, but precision had always been one of her strengths.

When the metal piece reached the apex of the arc, she shot a controlled burst of energy from her right hand into the object. It careened to the far side of the bay, landing with a loud *clang.*

"What the hell was *that?!*" Summer's exclamation gave voice to the startled expressions from everyone in the group.

Even Aurora was staring at her with stunned surprise.

She'd be willing to bet her daughter had never even considered using the more active forms of her Sahzade energy field as a projectile force. May not have even known it was possible, since she'd never been trained. It was a skill she needed to understand, given the challenges that lay before them.

"I didn't know you could do that." Aurora looked from her to the piece of scrap resting on the deck.

"That *we* can do that," she corrected. "I could have achieved a similar effect by putting up a shield, but this method allows for more control and greater deflection possibilities."

Kenji's gaze swung between them. "You didn't block that with your shield?" he asked uncertainly.

"No." Energy continued to swirl around her hands, eager to be set free. "The shield is a passive defense. Effective, but limited. The Sahzade are also capable of generating an energetic projectile pulse to knock objects out of the way."

"Just objects?" Isin asked evenly. The look in his eyes indicated he was rapidly recalibrating after what he'd just witnessed.

Aurora spoke up. "I've used an energy pulse during armed conflicts to disable an opponent, though not as a projectile and always as a last resort."

"With training, we can control the intensity," Libra elaborated, "producing anything from a mild electrical shock to something more... intense."

Isin wasn't going to let her off that easily. "But potentially lethal?"

Libra caught the look that ghosted over Aurora's face. She knew without asking that her daughter was thinking about Cade, and the time she'd used the pulse to prevent Kreestol from drowning her, inadvertently electrocuting Cade in the process. "Theoretically, yes."

Her gaze moved to Lyon, who was standing still as a statue beside Isin, although his breathing had sped up like a freight train. "But we're Suulh. Our people value life. And Aurora and I are Sahzade — guardians. Using our abilities with lethal intent is the antithesis of what we stand for."

"So you've never killed anyone?" Lyon bit out, fear giving his voice a harsh edge.

An image rose in her mind's eye — the reptilian forms of the Ecilam backlit by the blazing fire in Marina and Gryphon's bedroom as it consumed Stoneycroft. She swallowed to clear the tightening of her throat. "Once, when the Ecilam attacked our home and tried to kill Marina and Gryphon and capture me."

White showed all the way around Lyon's irises.

"But I tried every non-lethal option first. Even so, we almost died in the fire. If it weren't for Aurora..."

"You killed the rest of them?" Lyon accused, glaring defiantly at Aurora.

"No. The Ecilam were already gone by the time I arrived. I used my abilities to get my mom, Gryphon, and Marina out of the room where they were trapped by the fire."

Lyon digested that. "Have you ever killed anyone?"

Aurora sighed. "I have, though in my case, it was unintentional."

Libra winced at Lyon's reaction.

Aurora held his gaze. "My... someone had me pinned underwater. I was running out of air. The only way to get free was to use the energy pulse, but I made it just strong enough to break their hold on me. Unfortunately, I didn't know the river we were in was saltwater not freshwater. The pulse electrocuted everyone touching the water."

The haunted look in Aurora's eyes made Libra's chest ache. If she could shield her daughter from the trauma of her battle with Kreestol and the consequences for Cade, she would. Thank the stars he'd survived.

"For a time, that experience made me afraid of my power. But my dad and Micah helped me work through my trauma, to realize having power didn't automatically make me a weapon. I control how and when I use it. And I am very, *very* careful about how I exercise that power."

The silence that followed her statement pulsed with emotion. Isin, Sweep, Kenji, and Summer accepted Aurora's words with the fortitude and understanding of seasoned soldiers.

And Lyon? His expression ricocheted between fear and reverence. "You really could take over this ship, couldn't you?" he whispered, his gaze darting from Aurora to her.

"Yes." She wouldn't lie to him. To any of them. "If we were the kind of people who believed in conquering others, who didn't care about casualties, we could seize control and subdue everyone onboard. But if you met our people, you'd realize there's no reality where that would ever happen. The foundation of our being is helping, not harming. We literally nourish life."

Lyon held her gaze for a long time. She waited as his breathing grew steadier, his spine losing the instinctive hunched curl designed to protect him from a perceived threat.

Straightening, he lifted his chin and pointed at the bucket of scraps. "Can you do it again?"

Forty

One emotion dominated Isin's entire being.

Gratitude.

If Libra and Aurora didn't have their special abilities, if they weren't the kind of people who helped those in need, Natasha never would have survived her imprisonment on Tnaryt's ship. And Isin would still be the cold-hearted killer he'd become after Natasha had sacrificed herself to save him.

Aurora's Suulh abilities had enabled her to help Natasha escape. He suspected those same abilities had played a key role in her liberation from Seaview Detention Center. And despite what the news reports had said, he was one hundred percent certain that Aurora hadn't killed anyone in the process.

Kenji's gaze swung to him. "We good?" He gestured at the tub of scrap metal.

Isin nodded. He'd been stunned by Libra's demonstration, but now that the shock had worn off, he wanted to study her technique.

Kenji snagged another piece of scrap while Libra and Aurora reset their positions. As the hunk of metal sailed through the air, Isin marked it in his peripheral vision, his focus on Libra. The fingers on one hand gave a little pulse-twitch. A split-second later, the metal shard flew off in the same direction as the first, landing beside it with a clang and tumbling another meter.

Aurora's hands were lifted, too. He assumed she was projecting a shield to protect the rest of them in case Libra's aim was off. So far, Libra's accuracy rivaled Kenji's with *Vengeance*'s guns.

"Can you throw two in quick succession?" she called to Kenji.

"Sure." He picked out two pieces, sending the first in an arc and then tossing the second after it.

Libra's fingers pulsed twice. The first object darted away from her, the second following shortly afterward.

"How do you target?" Sweep asked, moving beside Isin. "Can you see the line of your shots?"

Libra lowered her hands. "Yes. Our energy fields are visible to us, and to some humans. Brendan can see our fields. So can Cade."

That couldn't be a coincidence. She and Aurora had each chosen partners who had an ability to see their energy. "What about Jonarel?"

Libra shook her head. "No, although I think he can sense Suulh fields better than humans. He seems particularly open to our energy, especially Lelindia's."

"What does your energy look like?" That question came from Lyon.

"Our fields are distinctive depending on the gifts we inherit. The Sahzade fields that Aurora and I have are pearlescent white, kind of like soap bubbles in sunlight."

Soap bubbles made of titanium.

"You mean there are more like you? More aliens?" Lyon didn't sound nearly as skeptical as he had previously.

A smile tugged at Libra's lips. "Not *exactly* like us. The Sahzade line is passed from mother to daughter. That's why Aurora's and my fields look the same. But yes, there are many other Suulh. My energy sister, Marina, is the one who healed the injured children from Devries' ship. Her energy field is emerald-green."

Lyon looked annoyed that he couldn't see their fields.

Isin could relate. From a tactical standpoint, it would be an advantage. Knowing Libra and Aurora were generating fields was very different from being able to see where they were and react accordingly.

Libra turned back to Kenji. "This time I want you to toss two in opposite directions."

Kenji grinned. "You got it."

He flung the two pieces into the air, one with each hand. Libra sent the first to join its companions, but she had to pivot to target the second one, knocking it toward the stairway.

Kenji clapped and whistled in appreciation. "Niiiiice."

Libra gave a half-bow.

"Can you do that?" Lyon asked Aurora. He'd crept across the deck during the demonstration until he was standing almost beside her and Kenji.

She shook her head. "I never learned that method."

There was a lot of subtext in that calculated response. It reminded Isin of the way he answered questions about his family history – evasive and non-specific.

Sweep must have caught it, too, because he gave Aurora a considering look.

"What about the rags?" Kenji asked, gesturing to the circle. "What are they for?"

Libra's expression had a Cheshire Cat vibe. "So glad you asked. You'll all need to back up for this. You too, Aurora."

Aurora's head tilted in question, but she backed up a few steps, angling her body so she was still in front of the rest of them without blocking their view.

Libra lifted her hands again, this time out to her sides with her palms flat like she was pushing against invisible walls.

The air in the bay shifted. If Isin hadn't been watching Libra, the change would have sent him racing for the nearest control panel, searching for a potential hull breach. But Libra's blonde hair had lifted away from her shoulders, caught in a wind that was far stronger than what he was feeling.

As the tousling of her hair eased, the rags in the circle began to flop around. Seconds later, a few lifted off the deck, spinning through the air in a counterclockwise circle with Libra at the center. The patches of black grew in number, whipping around Libra in a miniature tornado. Her gaze was in the middle distance, like she was sensing the motion of the rags rather than watching them.

The wind buffeted Isin as well, plastering his shirt and pants to his body.

And then the rags began to dance.

There was no other way to describe it. The tornado turned into a symphony of movement, the rags twirling in unison in a flowing, dipping, swirling wave.

One worked its way to the top of the funnel, leaping out and landing with a soft plop a meter away from where Isin stood. A second followed, then another and another, the rags continuing their graceful movement up the funnel then sailing through the air to land in a growing pile near Isin's feet.

As the last one fell, the wind died down, then stopped as Libra lowered her hands to her sides.

No one said anything for a few beats.

Kenji broke the silence with a piercing whistle. "Hot damn! You got skills, lady."

Libra chuckled.

Aurora was staring at her mother with an enigmatic expression, almost like she'd never seen anything like this before. That seemed unlikely. Then again, what he knew about Aurora's background could fit on one of the rags at his feet. He got the feeling there were a lot more layers to her relationship with her mother than he'd expected based on their easy comradery.

Lyon was entranced – lips parted and eyes wide. He looked ready to drop at Libra's feet like an acolyte, his fear and suspicion morphing into idolatry.

Too bad the kid didn't seem to have a middle ground. Either he worshipped someone, or he viewed them with hostility. It was an extreme attitude Isin hoped he'd be able to countermand, possibly with Libra and Aurora's help.

Forty-One

One thing Micah could say for certain about *Vengeance*'s crew — they were appreciative.

All through the meal in the mess hall, they'd been complimenting the food he, Celia, and his dad had prepared.

Serving the food had given him an opportunity to learn the crew's names, a skill he'd perfected as a professor. Knowing his students' names from day one showed them he respected them as individuals, which set the tone for the rest of the semester. He respected this crew, too. They'd come through when the chips were down, and had been welcoming to his family since they came onboard.

Well, mostly welcoming. The ship's engineer, Shash, acted disgruntled, but Kenji had assured him that was her default setting with everyone except Sparki, *Vengeance*'s pilot. Sparki had popped in briefly to grab a couple plates before returning to the bridge where they and Isin were monitoring the progress of the interstellar jump. They'd introduced themselves to him as Lupe, which confirmed Sparki was a nickname.

Micah didn't have a good handle on who else went by their given names, surnames, or nicknames, except for the obvious, like

Jake, the doctor, or Shorty, an ironic nickname for the huge bear of a man who was the second tallest member of the crew after Kenji.

Micah was guessing Butterfly was a nickname for Jake's assistant, a dark-haired young woman who had an aura of perpetual motion. But he was less certain whether Fleur and Summer were nicknames for the two women who looked perfectly capable of taking him down in a fight. Both were respectful, but Summer was outgoing while Fleur was more reserved, like Sweep.

Hobbes, Omondi, and Adel, the trio Cade's team had pulled off *Sphinx,* were easy to identify since they acted like a family unit, sitting at their own table for the meal. Lyon, or Dude as Kenji called him, was also distinctive. He had a lot of attitude. However, he'd chosen to sit at the table with Micah's parents, Kai, and Jake, and had spent the entire meal staring at Micah's mom like he was waiting for her to sprout wings and fly.

Aurora had filled him in on what had taken place down in the training area. He'd been a little surprised that their mom had been so open about her abilities and history, especially with members of the crew she'd just met. But it explained the look on Lyon's face.

His sister had sounded wistful as she described their mom's demonstration. It didn't take an empath or psychologist to figure out why. Aurora had wanted their mom to teach her how to use her abilities since she was a kid, but their mom's fear of the Teeli finding out about them had made that a non-starter. Aurora had been forced to develop her abilities on her own. Having what she'd missed out on thrust in her face must have been tough to take.

But their mom had promised to start training her on this trip. He suspected that training would occupy a lot of his sister's time now that she'd been given a taste of what she'd been craving since childhood.

Summer, seated diagonally from him at the rectangular table, lowered her voice to a whisper. "So, you're half-alien too, right?"

The question caught him completely off guard.

Celia and Birdie both muffled snorts of laughter, while Kenji, seated next to Summer, grinned.

Micah felt a flush creep up his neck. "Half-Suulh, yeah." He'd come to terms with his mixed heritage a while ago, but it still felt weird to have someone call him an alien.

"So you can do the..." Summer held up her hands, palms out, and made little pulsing motions with her fingers.

He shook his head. "That ability is only in the female line. But I enhance Aurora's abilities. And I can communicate with other species."

Summer's eyes rounded. "What kinds of species?"

"All kinds. Mammals, fish, birds, reptiles. I talked to a bee once. That was trippy." The yellow-faced bee had been remarkably chatty as she gathered pollen to take to her eggs. She'd seemed to enjoy his company during what was typically a solitary endeavor.

"A bee? Really?"

He nodded. "I've had the most experience with aquatic species — dolphins, sea turtles, and fish predominantly — since I spend a lot of my time surfing and diving." Or he had until Aurora had triggered the seismic change in all their lives. Not that he regretted a moment. Having his family whole again was worth less time in the water. And the hydrotank on the *Starhawke* was a lot of fun, especially when Celia, Birdie, or Aurora joined him.

"Is that your job when we reach the planet? To talk to the animals?"

"Pretty much. I need to determine if any of the wildlife in the areas Aurora's considering might pose a serious threat to Mirko and Manchado. Or vice versa." Although he wouldn't be working alone. Unity and the Yruf would be providing a lot of unseen insights and assistance.

"Wow. Your family is really different." Then Summer winced, like she was afraid her comment would offend him.

It didn't. He grinned. "That's putting it mildly."

"What's it like, talking to other species?" Kenji asked before taking a bite from the rapidly dwindling mound of stir-fried vegetables on his plate.

Summer and Celia leaned closer, all attention on him, but Birdie just smiled.

She'd heard him answer this question a hundred times. "It depends on the situation, but most of the time it's a slideshow of images that my brain translates into words. It's kind of like a professional musician reading music. They don't have to consciously think *that's a C* or *that's a B flat*. They can read written music so well that their brain instantly translates the symbols of the music into movements with their fingers that produce the corresponding sound. They're looking at the music, but they're hearing the sound they're creating."

"That's cool." Kenji took another bite, chewing slowly. "Do all species sound the same?"

He chuckled. "Not remotely. Even individuals from the same species sound different to me. There are these two dolphins who like to surf with me, Streak and Cutter. When I first met them, they were babies, and they sounded like it. I had trouble telling them apart. But now they have distinctive voices. They both sound like overconfident teenagers, but Streak has a smoother delivery, while Cutter's more spastic."

"And they understand you?" Summer asked.

"Yep. Doesn't mean they listen, though."

"What do you mean?"

"They're teenagers. They like to test boundaries."

Summer turned to Kenji. "Think Isin will let me be on Micah's team when we're planetside?"

Kenji shrugged. "That's probably up to Captain Hawke. But you can let him know you're interested."

"I will." She glanced back at Micah. "If you don't mind, that is."

He'd have Unity with him, which made answering trickier. Summer hadn't been included in the group who knew about the Yruf. Or Unity. "I'll talk to Aurora," he hedged. Summer seemed trustworthy, but he wasn't in a position to make that call.

"Okay, thanks."

Speaking of his sister, she, Sweep, and Fleur had their heads bent in quiet conversation at one of the outlying tables. Judging by Aurora's expression, the topic was likely Mirko and Manchado.

He'd been doing his best to put Manchado out of his mind ever since they'd arrived onboard, but it nagged at him, especially when he caught Celia's gaze lifting in the direction of the brig. She'd asked him where it was located on the ship after he and Aurora returned from their first visit. Both personally and professionally, she'd wanted to know the exact location of her nemesis.

She hadn't indicated whether she planned to see him during the trip. If she chose to, he'd support her, but he wouldn't go with her. That was a recipe for disaster.

No, Aurora or his dad would be a much better choice.

But he and Celia would be working together on the planet. And he was really looking forward to the trip back, when the weight of Manchado's presence would finally be lifted.

Forty-Two

"Nixon is assigning Teeli consuls to the *Odyssey*, *Sagan*, and *Cassini*." A heavy sigh followed the Admiral's announcement. He was seated in the captain's chair, filling in for Aurora during Cade's normal bridge rotation, and using the time to sort through the flow of data Unity was extracting from the Sol relay.

Cade turned from navigation. "Kire's not going to be happy to hear that." *Odyssey* had been his previous posting, the one he'd left to join the *Starhawke* crew. "What about the Northern quadrant cruisers?"

The Admiral shook his head. "Not yet. I suspect the Teeli want to solidify their hold on the Southern quadrants first, just in case there's any pushback from the Kraed regarding the Northern borders."

"If you're right, that would give Captain Warner a bit more breathing room." It would take time for the Teeli manipulation effect to get a stronghold on three ships, especially the large crew complements of the Discovery-class cruisers.

"The orders to *Cassini* have them returning to Eridani Duo to meet with a transport that's bringing the Teeli consuls and Admiral Nixon's personal physician." The Admiral scowled as he read the details of the order. "Nixon's physician is supposed to assess

Montgomery's physical condition and determine her fitness to return to her post." He met Cade's gaze. "Since we know she's not on Eridani Duo, their arrival will put Dr. Yates in an untenable position."

"Yates is the head of medical there?"

"Yes."

"Let's hope Montgomery shows herself before then. Or that Muiruri has a Plan B." Which she might. She must have known Nixon would be breathing down her neck from the moment Montgomery was transferred off the ship. "Does it specify when *Cassini* is supposed to meet the Teeli at Eridani Duo?"

"Six days." The Admiral ran a hand over the top of his head, then glanced at U-2, who had been hanging out in the empty tactical chair. "How close are you to accessing Hydra One's medical center?"

Unity rose into the air. "Getting there. We started with the easy route through the electrical conduits but one of the station's engineers noticed the anomalous readings we were triggering." They let out a frustrated growl, like their detection was a personal affront. "We're in the circulation system now. Unless we hit another snag, we'll have access to the medical center sometime tomorrow." Their voice dropped to a stage whisper. "We're so much quicker when we don't have to hide."

Cade smiled. Having seen how quickly and easily Unity took over *Gladiator* when his team first encountered them, he could understand their exasperation with the relative snail's pace. "You're doing great. Without you we wouldn't have any hope of tracking down Montgomery."

"That's not the only bad news."

Cade's attention swung back to the Admiral.

"Nixon's instituted new security procedures at all space stations. Effective immediately, all incoming and outgoing cargo will be inspected, and all passengers and personnel will be required to provide ID upon arrival and departure from a station."

He winced. "So if Montgomery is on Hydra One, she's going to be stuck there?"

"Most likely, yes. Oh, and Nat sent me a message with the most recent bounties on Aurora and myself. They've doubled."

He let out a low whistle. The figure Nat had shared with them when she'd first told them about the bounties, back before the complications with Mirko and Devries, had been enough to finance a small ship. Twice that figure would have every bounty hunter in Fleet space scouring the cosmos for the *Starhawke* and *Gladiator*. "What about the rest of the crew?"

"Significantly less, but still substantial, especially for Knox and Lelindia. And no," he said to Cade's unasked question, "your team still isn't on the list."

"Why not? I'm a strong link to both of you."

It was a rhetorical question, one neither of them could answer.

He wanted that answer, even though he had a feeling if he got it, he wasn't going to like it.

Forty-Three

"We finally get *Phoenix* all fixed up and Aurora's not even around to see it," Marlin grumbled as he ran a cleaning cloth over the shelves of the storage cabinets he was restocking in *Phoenix's* galley.

Nat plucked a blueberry from the handful she'd snagged out of the cold storage unit. Aurora had insisted she accept the two crates of fresh produce she'd handed her before *Vengeance* left the system.

Fresh berries were a treat she intended to savor.

She'd perched on one of the countertops so she'd stay out of Marlin's way. The heels of her boots lightly tapped the metal cabinet beneath her. "She'll see it when she gets back." Now that the work was completed, Nat was eager to show off her ship, too. She just hadn't realized how much Marlin was looking forward to the combined crew feast he'd been planning.

"That's almost two weeks away," he whined, sounding like a kid rather than someone old enough to be her father.

"More time for your garden to flourish," she pointed out. It was his pride and joy. And since it was located close to the galley, he could easily pop between the two.

He harrumphed, setting the cloth on the counter and pulling cookware out of the storage bins at his feet. She'd helped him haul the smaller crates of food and cookware that he'd been using on *Gypsy*, but the bulk of the crates stacked behind him had been temporarily stored in the media room while the reconstruction work was in progress. Marlin and Shash had removed every item in the galley that wasn't bolted down before they'd allowed the work to begin.

It was an impressive array of cookware, most of which she had no idea what it did. Cooking was not a skill she'd cared to learn. But her ship had been designed for comfort, with the resources to house and feed up to twenty-eight passengers and forty-two crew. Which made their current crew complement of six a bit of a joke.

When her focus had been on running freight — her original plan — she'd expected to convert most of the guest rooms into storage facilities. But since partnering with Isin, and now Aurora, she'd reconsidered that plan. Aurora seemed to have a habit of picking up strays. *Phoenix*'s plethora of accommodations might come in handy. They were certainly a lot nicer than what *Vengeance* had to offer.

She'd given Aurora the option of using four cabins on *Vengeance* so her family and crew could have more privacy, but she'd declined, insisting they'd prefer to stay together in two cabins. It hadn't felt right, seeing them crammed in the minimalist space, but Aurora hadn't seemed bothered by the austere surroundings.

Nat consoled herself with the knowledge that they probably wouldn't spend much time in the cabins, anyway.

She allowed her gaze to move around the rebuilt galley. The metal surfaces gleamed, bright and cheerful in the overhead lighting. Shash and Marlin had done an amazing job. No one walking in today would guess there'd been a bite taken out of it a couple weeks ago.

Of course they wouldn't be anywhere near done if Unity and the Yruf hadn't stepped in to help. They'd even managed to quietly collect and return all the debris that had been blow into space when the hull breached. They'd left it in neat, orderly clusters in *Phoenix's* airlocks. Alec had facilitated that transfer during the night cycle so his mom wouldn't freak out about the shadow ships. Nat and Isin had hauled the unidentifiable bits to reclamation and left anything serviceable in the media room for Marlin to deal with.

Which brought up the other reason she'd partnered with Marlin today. He was the one person onboard who hadn't been introduced to Unity yet — a glaring oversight. She hadn't intentionally excluded him. There'd just never been a good time to broach the subject.

Until now.

She popped the last blueberry in her mouth, taking time to chew it. "So, you know how we managed to get the hull panels replaced and the electrical reconfigured pretty quickly?"

Marlin paused with a saucepan in his hand. He held the pose for a two count before setting it carefully on the counter and turning to face her.

She could tell by the creases in his forehead that he was worried about where she was going with this. He didn't ask, though, just waited for her to continue.

"I appreciate the way you and the rest of the crew accepted the existence of the shadow ships without asking a lot of questions. It was too much to go into while we were dealing with all this." She swept her hand around the galley. "But I don't want to keep you in the dark anymore." About any of it. He deserved the full truth.

But there was one caveat. "What I'm about to tell you needs to stay between us. Well, us and the other people who already know. You can't tell Patel. Or Kenji. Or anyone else on *Vengeance*'s crew. Are you okay with that?"

The creases in his forehead had now risen all the way to his receding hairline, but he nodded.

"This is going to sound crazy, but I swear it's the truth." She licked her suddenly dry lips. For reasons she couldn't pinpoint, telling Marlin was harder than she'd imagined. "The shadow ships aren't Kraed-made. They aren't human-made, either. They're Yruf-made."

Marlin's eyes doubled in size. Then his lower back sagged against the counter like he needed the support. He still didn't say a word.

"They're friendly," she rushed on. "Aurora made contact with them sometime after she saved us, and it turns out they're pacifists. They haven't been responsible for any of the attacks on humans. They also have a non-biological entity who's kinda similar to Alec."

Marlin blinked twice at that.

"Their entity, who goes by Unity, is a big part of the reason the damage to the ship was minimized. They strengthened the stress points after the breach and helped with the repairs."

Marlin's gaze made a slow circuit of the galley. "That's…" He cleared his throat. "That's… interesting."

Not exactly the reaction she'd expected, but she'd take it.

His gaze met hers. "How long have you known?"

She saw the censure in his eyes. Guilt rolled through her. "A while. I'm sorry it took so long to tell you."

He acknowledged the apology with a subtle nod. "The Yruf," he said under his breath. "I wasn't expecting that."

"Aurora trusts them implicitly. And from what I've seen, that trust is well deserved. They've been watching out for us ever since Aurora showed up asking for our help."

"And this Unity? What do you know about it?"

"Them," she corrected. "Alec, do you want to field that one?"

Alec's projected image appeared to Nat's right. He folded his hands in front of him, his expression solemn. "What would you like to know?"

"Uh…" Marlin looked back and forth between them. "You've been interacting with them?"

"Yes. Unity and I have been communicating ever since I noticed them on *Phoenix*."

Marlin's gaze darted to Nat. "And you're okay with that?"

"Yep."

He frowned. "And Patel doesn't know?"

The guilt wave washed over her again. "She knows about Unity, but not the Yruf. Aurora needs to keep our alliance with the Yruf a secret from the Sovereign."

"The Sovereign? How does she fit into this?"

"The Yruf want to broker peace with the other Setarip factions, but they can't do that as long as the Sovereign is using the other factions as her private army. If the Sovereign learns that the Yruf are helping us, she'll send the other factions to hunt them. That's why Aurora's guarding knowledge of the Yruf so closely, letting everyone believe it's the Kraed who are helping us."

His eyes narrowed. "But you said Patel knows about Unity?"

"We had to tell her," Alec said quietly. "But she doesn't know about their connection to the Yruf."

"What about Gavin?"

"He knows about both. So does Itorye."

Marlin's gaze shifted to Nat. "What about Pete?"

A third guilt wave. "He knows. I had to tell him when we accepted their help repairing *Phoenix*."

The corners of Marlin's mouth pinched. "So I'm the last to know."

Nat winced. "I'm really sorry. I should have told you after we rescued the kids." It hadn't seemed like a priority with so much else to focus on, but that was a pathetic excuse. She could have told him right after telling Patel about Unity. Instead, she'd chosen to keep him in the dark.

"Please don't be mad at Nat," Unity said through the galley speakers.

Marlin's head tipped back, his bushy brows drawing together. "I know that voice. Micah?" he said tentatively.

And with good reason. Micah was on *Vengeance*, lightyears away.

"Unity. We use Micah's voice for verbal communication."

Marlin's jaw dropped. "You're Unity?"

"Yep. Alec has allowed us to integrate with your comm system."

"Oh."

"Do you have any questions for us?" Unity's chipper tone seemed to have jolted Marlin out of his disgruntled mindset.

"Uh…" Marlin looked around the room. "Do you have a physical form, like Alec's projection?"

"Not like Alec's. But we have mobile units that make it easy for us to interact with biologicals. That's how we first got to know the *Starhawke* crew. We also have a micro form, which is how we integrated with *Phoenix*. That's the form we used to assist with your repair work."

"So you're in your micro form right now?"

Unity chuckled. "We're in all forms simultaneously. We exist as a multitude. Right now, one of our mobile units is communicating with Aurora's family on *Vengeance,* and we're also on the Yruf ships, the *Starhawke,* and *Gladiator.*"

"Each form operates independently?"

"Yes and no. What is happening on *Vengeance* or the *Starhawke* is no different to us than this conversation with you now. We are we, no matter where we are."

Marlin's gaze met Nat's.

She gave him a crooked smile. "I know. Mind-blowing. But you'll get used to it."

Forty-Four

"Oh look, it's the buxom blonde bitch."

Aurora took a slow breath, focusing on calming her mind and strengthening her emotional barriers as Manchado's slimy emotional resonance splattered her. The malevolent leer twisting his lips increased the ick factor. The man was the walking definition of *odious.*

"And another new guy. Wow, blondie. You screwing your way through the entire crew?"

Aurora felt a flare of anger from her dad at the insinuation, but he kept it from showing on his face. "My name is Brendan," he said smoothly. "I'm here to ask you and Ms. Mirko some questions."

"Questions?" Manchado scoffed. "You a Fed?"

"No, I'm a psychologist."

That triggered a nasty bark of laughter. "A shrink?" He pressed his face against the bars of his cell, his smile full of malice. "You here to ask me about my mommy and daddy, shrinkie?"

Her dad didn't take the bait. "I'm here to determine whether the two of you pose a threat to each other."

"A threat?" Mirko lumbered off her bed, finally taking an interest in the conversation. She approached the bars of her cell. "What kind of threat?"

Aurora fielded that one. "We're deciding whether to keep you two together or separate when we reach our destination."

Mirko eyed her warily. "What destination?"

"An isolated planet where you won't pose a danger to anyone else."

Mirko stared. "You're going to dump us on a barren planet?"

"Isolated, not barren. There are plenty of resources to provide for your needs."

"You bitch! You can't do that!" Manchado managed an impressive level of indignation and rage. "I'm a field manager for Diestro. When they hunt you down, you'll wish you were dead!"

He honestly seemed to believe that she would be cowed by his threat. She also suspected a *field manager* wasn't nearly as important to the organization as he wanted to believe. "We'll provide you with everything you need to survive," she continued as if he hadn't spoken. "It would be easier if you worked together, but we'll separate you if you insist on threatening each other."

"This jackass isn't a threat. He's an idiot."

Mirko's calculated jab at Manchado's ego elicited a predictable response. The torrent of abuse that flew at her should have blistered the decking beneath Aurora's boots.

Mirko soaked it up with glee. She'd clearly figured out how to manipulate Manchado and was enjoying pushing his buttons.

Great. If this was indicative of their dynamic with each other, she'd need to set them up on opposite sides of the planet.

As Manchado drew a breath, gearing up for another tirade, her dad stepped in. "What's your name?"

The question threw Manchado. "What?"

"What's your name?"

Manchado smirked as his attention swung to Aurora. "I'm Mr. Well-Hung."

Ick, ick, ick.

She stared him down, refusing to let him goad her. The man couldn't go thirty seconds without doing or saying something revolting.

That this predator had assaulted Celia when she was defenseless, violating her when she couldn't fight back, made her sick to her stomach. The fact that she couldn't sense one iota of shame or remorse for his behavior made it worse. He reveled in his depravity.

Which would make leaving him on the planet a guilt-free experience as long as she didn't have to worry about what he might do to Mirko.

She approached Mirko's cell, leaving her dad to deal with Manchado.

"Can't handle the truth, blondie?" Manchado called after her. "What you need is a good hard poke by a real man."

Mirko's gaze shifted from Manchado to Aurora, her amusement replaced with anger. "You have no right to dump me with him," she snapped, heaping bitterness and derision on every syllable. "He's a psycho and you're a traitor."

"No, I'm not." But she agreed with Mirko's assessment of Manchado. "I believe in the rule of law."

"Yeah, right," Mirko scoffed, giving an exaggerated look around her cell. "Then where's my lawyer?"

The barb hit a chink in Aurora's emotional armor, snagging onto the doubts she'd been grappling with ever since she came up with this plan. But picturing Adel helped. So did remembering how callously Mirko had talked about selling her to the highest bidder. Given the chance, Mirko would sell out all of them.

And Diestro would torture Mirko if they found her. This solution was still the best option, at least in the short-term. "Do you have any wilderness skills?"

Mirko ignored the question. "This is Orlov's doing, isn't it? She's blackmailing you."

The absurdity of the comment generated a surprised laugh. She quickly choked it down. "You think she's blackmailing me?"

Mirko's eyes narrowed. "Are you making fun of me?"

"No, I'm trying to understand you." Which might be a bridge too far. But it wouldn't stop her from gathering intel. "Would you prefer to be placed with Manchado or at a distance where you'll never encounter each other?"

Mirko's upper lip pulled back from her teeth. "I'd prefer for you to get spaced."

Two steps forward, three steps back.

She'd tuned out Manchado's voice, but a check-in with her dad's emotional field indicated he wasn't making any more progress than she was. "Do you think he poses a physical danger to you?" Mirko was taller and broader than Manchado, and neither of them were what she'd describe as physically fit.

That would change once they were on the planet and having to work for their meals and comforts. She didn't want Manchado overpowering Mirko. Or vice versa.

Mirko eyed her with dawning horror. "You're serious about this? You're really going to dump us on some random planet?"

Apparently she'd assumed it was a bluff, or manipulation to gain information. "It's the best option available to me."

"But..." Mirko's lips moved, no sound coming out. "You can't..."

She'd never seen Mirko at a loss for words before. She wasn't even summoning profanity.

"You bitch."

Okay, she found one. "Do you want a joint habitation with Manchado, or do you want to be alone?"

Several more unflattering epithets were tossed her way. Mirko folded her arms under her ample chest and glared, murder in her eyes.

Not the result she was going for, but useful nonetheless. Mirko's emotional field didn't quite match the look in her eyes. Like Manchado, she wanted to dominate Aurora, not actually kill her.

Because killing would end the ability to dominate.

It was a messed-up worldview, but it meant they likely wouldn't kill each other if she left them close enough to reach each other. Instead, they'd have a perpetual battle of wills in whatever mutually abusive dynamic they established.

Could she live with that?

Mirko's vitriol had caught Manchado's attention. He joined in the profanity lesson, doing his best to one-up Mirko's tirade, filling the air with lewd obscenities Aurora had never even heard before.

With a sigh, she met her dad's gaze. He gave a small nod, then followed her as they exited the brig.

Sweep was waiting for them in the corridor. He swung the massive door shut, silencing the torrent of abuse.

Aurora leaned her back against the bulkhead and closed her eyes. "That went well." When she opened them, both her dad and Sweep were gazing at her with nearly identical expressions of calm focus. "Did you get any answers?" she asked her dad.

"Some. Not his name." His lips flattened a bit. "His complete lack of empathy is concerning, as is the pleasure he derives from inflicting pain. I don't get the sense that his behavior is driven by addictive impulses. What he craves is power over others, likely because it was taken from him at a young age. Celia indicated he was a prisoner at the camp, too, at least in the beginning."

"Except she became a security officer who protects the vulnerable and he became a serial rapist who preys on the vulnerable."

"Everyone makes choices."

"Mirko and Manchado are choosing to be the worst versions of themselves." She straightened. "What's your professional assessment regarding leaving them together or apart?"

Her dad considered the question. "It's a complex scenario. As a species, we need social interaction. Even negative interaction is usually preferable to no interaction. But their behavior profiles are so similar that strong conflict is inevitable. And it's likely to be violent. Which leaves a choice between two unpleasant options. Do we leave them together, knowing they'll physically abuse each other, or do we leave them isolated, which will harm them psychologically and emotionally?"

Aurora's hands fisted. "I want a third option."

"That would be keeping them here, where they're abusing Sweep, Isin, and anyone else who walks into the room."

She'd taken that option off the table when she'd planned this mission. It didn't mean she liked her alternatives. "This sucks."

Her dad's smile was filled with empathy. "There's a reason you wanted to be a starship captain, not a lawyer."

Forty-Five

"We found her!"

Unity's excited exclamation almost drove Cade out of his seat at the small dining table in the galley. With a majority of the crew now integrated into four-hour bridge rotations, meals were unstructured. He and the Admiral were grabbing an early dinner before they started their shift.

He set his fork down on the edge of his plate. "Montgomery?"

"Yep." U-2 gave a twirl. "She's in the medical center, but not registered as a patient."

"If she's not registered as a patient, where is she?" the Admiral asked.

"In Dr. Morales' office suite."

Concern swept through the Admiral's emotional field. "What's her condition?"

"From what we can see, she has damage to her right leg and arm. She doesn't appear to be mobile."

Cade and the Admiral exchanged a meaningful look.

"Sounds like she could use Lelindia's help," Cade said.

The Admiral nodded slowly. "The question is, how do we make that happen?"

They quickly finished their meal and headed for the lift.

Lelindia and Jonarel glanced over in surprise when they stepped onto the bridge.

"You're early." Lelindia's eyes narrowed. "What happened?"

"We found Montgomery!" U-2 exclaimed. "She's at Hydra One Medical Center."

Lelindia pushed out of the captain's chair. "What's her condition?"

"We can show you."

The image of the starfield on the bridgescreen blinked out, replaced by a wide-angle view of a room that resembled a small studio apartment. There were two doors on opposite ends, one beside a tiny kitchenette with a café table and couch, the other beside a single bed. Captain Montgomery lay on the bed, eyes closed in sleep.

Lelindia moved behind Jonarel at the navigation console. "She has a healing cast on her right arm, and probably her right leg, based on the shape under the covers." She peered closer. "From the way she's sleeping, she may have a back brace, too." She turned to Unity. "Can you access her medical records?"

Unity swayed. "No. She's not entered as a patient."

Lelindia studied the image. "Can you zoom in?"

"Sure!"

The image magnified, giving a closer view of Montgomery. Her long brown hair lay limp against the snow-white pillow, her face slightly contorted like she wasn't sleeping comfortably.

"She's not hooked up to any monitors, so her condition must be stable."

"Can you use your abilities to see what's wrong with her?" Cade asked.

Lelindia glanced at him, the corner of her mouth curling up. "You have a very high opinion of what I can do."

"I've seen you in action."

"Yes, but there are limits. My Nedale senses don't work over video."

The Admiral stepped closer to the bridgescreen. "Are her injuries consistent with a fall from a height of ten to fifteen meters onto a padded surface?"

"You mean what was reported in her *Cassini* medical file? Yes, they certainly could be, although what I'm seeing doesn't appear as severe as the injuries listed in her file."

"Do you think she could stand? And walk?"

"If I'm correct about the back brace, any mobility would depend on which vertebrae and discs were damaged. Movement could be severely limited and would certainly be painful. Also, the casts on her arm and leg would make maneuvering and balancing even more difficult. I doubt she's getting out of that bed without help."

The Admiral frowned, sympathetic pain flaring like hotspots in his emotional field. "But you could heal her?"

Jonarel's low growl sent a warning as he captured Lelindia's hand in his. "Lelindia—"

The Admiral shook his head. "I wasn't suggesting she go to Hydra One, Jonarel," he clarified. "Of the four of us, Cade's the only one with a shot at reaching Montgomery without being detained by security." He met Lelindia's gaze. "But I do need to know if you could heal her injuries, if we were able to get her to you."

"Absolutely. It wouldn't be an instantaneous fix, since her injuries likely occurred weeks ago. It takes more time to restore the cells to optimal health the longer they've been in a state of disruption, and the more I'm having to work around other healing that's taken place. But with my mom's and Raehn's help," her hand dropped to her round belly, "it would probably still go quicker than your recovery did."

"The first time or the second time?" the Admiral asked with a heavy dose of sardonic self-mockery.

"Both. Her injuries couldn't have been as life-threatening as yours when they occurred, or she wouldn't have been able to be moved around without drawing attention."

Some of the tension eased from the Admiral's shoulders. "Unity, would you be able to get a message directly to Dr. Morales' comm device?"

U-2 swayed. "We think so. It would depend on whether she leaves it somewhere we can reach it."

"Please do what you can. We need a way to communicate with her."

"Of course."

"Would Dr. Morales trust me to help her with Montgomery if I showed up at the medical center?" Cade asked. Morales already knew about the Elite Unit — she'd patched him and members of his team up a few times — but he didn't know if that translated into trust in this situation.

"Certainly. She's well aware of my abiding trust in you." The Admiral's gaze shifted to Montgomery. "I also shared the details of your team's efforts to rescue me from Tnaryt and the Sovereign."

The memories of that time were not Cade's favorites, especially the period where Aurora had pushed him away for his own good. And now she was on her way to the planet where all that trauma had occurred. Without him.

He shoved the thoughts aside. "We have five days until the Teeli and Nixon's physician are meeting *Cassini* at Eridani Duo. If they arrive and Montgomery's not there, all hell will break loose. But if she is there and still incapacitated, she'll be swept into their net." He glanced at U-2. "Any chance you could infiltrate the security offices on Hydra One and confirm that I'm not on any of their watch lists?"

"We'll start working on it right now!"

Forty-Six

"Since we don't have a nice sandy beach, the deck will have to do." Aurora's mom led the way to the center of *Vengeance's* training area below the Cage.

Her mom's comment tripped her up, slowing her steps. "Is that where you typically trained? On the beach?" That was counter to the image in her head. She'd always pictured an elaborate training room filled with tools and equipment. She'd never considered the possibility that her mom had trained outdoors.

Her mom nodded. "At least until the Teeli arrived." A line of tension ran up her spine. "Then my mom moved our sessions indoors where we'd have privacy."

Aurora felt the knife of pain that cut through her mom at the mention of Sooree, Aurora's grandmother. It had been three months since the attack at Stoneycroft when Aurora's mom had seen the wraith of a Necri that the Teeli had turned Sooree into.

The horror of that night could have broken her mother, turning her fear into panicked, paralyzing terror. Instead, her mom had revealed a core of tempered steel, casting aside the fear that had defined her for decades. She'd defeated the Setarips, then helped Aurora get everyone to safety.

It had been a defining moment in all their lives, one she was grateful for. The Teeli had driven her family apart, but ironically, she had the Sovereign and Setarips to thank for bringing her family back together.

Settling cross-legged on the deck across from her mom, she soaked up the relative silence of the spacious room. Unlike the demonstration she and her mom had given Sweep and Kenji, which had blossomed into a group event, this was a private lesson. Isin had promised to keep the crew above deck so she and her mom could work in peace. Her dad, brother, and Celia were helping that agenda by giving several crewmembers a cooking lesson in *Vengeance's* galley, and Iolana and Kai had joined a cleaning detail with Lyon, Kenji, and Butterfly on C deck.

She appreciated the support. After a lifetime of arguments and disappointments, her mom was finally going to teach her how to make the most of her abilities. She didn't want any interruptions.

Which was ironic. Until recently, being alone with her mom would have filled her with apprehension. Their conflicts over her desire to make use of her abilities had forced her to keep her emotional walls firmly in place and her guard up anytime she was around her mom. Even now, those ingrained habits warred with the squiggle of childlike excitement dancing in her abdomen.

Her mom's gaze held hers, open and focused. "Ready to show me what you can do?"

The squiggle leapt and twirled, making her heart flutter. "You bet."

"Then let's start by having you generate an energy field that surrounds us."

Aurora lifted her hands and engaged her field. The pearlescent white shimmered in the austere grey surroundings, swirling outward until it created a prismatic cloud around them.

"Good. Now expand it to twice that size."

Easy enough. Marking a point on the deck with her gaze, she enlarged the field until it reached that spot.

"Your control is excellent. You manage the energy very well."

The praise flustered her a bit, the cloud contracting slightly as her focus slipped.

"If you're so afraid, then teach me!" Her eight-year-old self squared off against her mom, arms flung wide as her energy field snapped out.

"No, Aurora!" The anger in her mom's voice was a veneer over the terror pulsing in her emotional field. "You don't know what could happen. You can't use your abilities. Conceal them. Don't ever let anyone know what you can do."

"Why?" she demanded. She'd asked the same question many times before and had always been rebuffed. This time she wasn't letting it go.

Her mom's emotional field flickered at the ferocity in Aurora's tone. Something dark and dangerous flitted across her face. "Because they'll find you."

"Aurora?" Concern emanated from her mom's emotional field, drawing her back to the present.

"Sorry." She'd yearned for her mother's approval for decades. What she'd received instead was an avalanche of her mom's fear-based condemnation. The pressure had threatened to bury her. Only by escaping to the Academy and the Fleet had she found her balance and remained true to herself.

Hearing positive feedback from her mom regarding her abilities was surreal. Adjusting to the new paradigm felt like emotional chiropractic. "I was just thinking about... before."

A flare of guilt lit up her mom's emotional field. The corners of her mouth pinched. "I have a lot to make up for."

Aurora shook her head. "I understand why you reacted the way you did. You were being a good mom, trying to protect me. And Micah. It didn't work out the way you intended, but your heart was in the right place."

"But I wasn't seeing *you*. I only saw my fear. It cost us both so much."

Yes, it had. But it had also forged her into the person she was today. That counted for a lot, too. "We're here now, together." She projected all the joy that thought brought her. "I'm good. We're good." She flashed a grin to lighten the mood. "Show me all the Sahzade secrets."

Her mom's answering smile was subdued but authentic. "You still haven't shown me what you can do." She motioned to Aurora's energy field, still swirling around them. "Let's see you double the size."

"Okay." The energy flowed out with relative ease. "Now what?"

"Turn it into a solid shield."

Ah. Not so easy. The field was fluid and pliable. The shield was not. In fact, the two times she'd needed a shield this expansive in recent months, she'd been fighting for her life, first during the Stoneycroft fire, then at Seaview.

Drawing on the core of her power, she solidified the molecules of the field, forming the shield. But she struggled to keep her breathing steady and even.

"Excellent. Now, I want you to expand the shield to fill the entire training area."

Aurora darted a look around the expansive space. It wasn't as big as the *Starhawke*'s training center, but it wasn't exactly small, either.

"Too big a task for you?" her mom asked.

"I don't know," she answered honestly.

"Then let's find out."

Aurora took a deep breath, allowing the vibrant energy of her shield to become her sole focus. She could feel it like an extension of her body, pushing out into the depths of the room. It molded around the crates anchored in the cargo areas, expanding meter by meter toward the exterior bulkheads.

Her breathing grew labored, her arms trembling as the distance tested her limits of strength and control.

"You can do it, Aurora," her mom murmured. "Concentrate."

The encouragement, along with the emotional lift that followed it, gained her another few meters. The shield touched the aft bulkhead first, which was closest to where they sat. It brushed the starboard bulkhead next, then port. But the forward bulkhead was the farthest. Her focus narrowed like a laser as the energy crept toward the bulkhead like the incoming tide.

She felt the moment it touched the surface. Her lungs expanded with a relieved inhalation.

"What about the ceiling?"

Her gaze snapped to the overhead, then to her mother, who looked annoyingly serene. To reach the overhead, she'd have to expand the shield twice as high as where it currently covered them. And her body was already shaking from the strain of maintaining the expanded field.

She hadn't worked this hard since her escape from Seaview.

Staring at the overhead, she thrust the shield up. It rose half a meter, then slowed to a creep. In fact, as she continued to push, she wasn't certain it was moving at all.

Beads of sweat rolled across her forehead into her hairline. Her teeth scraped together as her jaw clenched. She could do this. She just... needed... to...

She gained a couple centimeters. And abruptly lost them when the structure collapsed like a breaking wave. The energy crashed down in a flare of light before dissipating.

She slumped to the deck, staring at the overhead and inhaling deeply. Her tunic stuck to her skin in several places, the deck delightfully cool against her back. She swiped her sleeve over her damp forehead. "That was hard."

Her mom chuckled. "If it makes you feel any better, I didn't expect you'd be able to do it. I just wanted to know how far you could push yourself before the shield destabilized."

Aurora canted her head, peering at her mom from her prone position. "I probably could have done it with Micah's help."

"Yes, but that wasn't the point."

No, this was a test of *her* abilities. "I wonder if Lelindia could expand her healing field that far."

"Not even close."

"How do you know?" She'd seen Lelindia do some really impressive things. Like the time she'd blasted out of a coma and healed Jonarel's injuries without even being aware of it.

Surprise flickered across her mom's face. "Because her energy doesn't function like ours. It can't expand like ours can."

Aurora pushed up on her elbows. "What do you mean? Of course it can." She'd seen Lelindia send out her energy many times.

"Moving from person to person, yes. But the Nedale can't expand their fields into an open space like this." She swept her arm overhead. "You've never noticed that when our energy interweaves with theirs that we provide the structure that they twine along?"

Aurora blinked. "No."

Her mom smiled. "It's a biological adaptation, allowing them to conserve energy for healing. Nedale energy is designed to connect with others, to heal those right in front of them. Our energy is designed to protect others. We need range. They don't. Both our fields will expand farther when we're working together, but the combined form of Sahzade and Nedale energies will only expand as far as *we* can maintain it."

"Oh." She hadn't noticed that phenomenon. But why would she? Anytime she and Lelindia had needed range, they'd been working together. She'd assumed it was a joint effort, which it was, in a way. Neither could do what the other could. But based on her mom's description, Lelindia's energy was more like a twining vine climbing the trellis Aurora provided. Too bad her energy sister wasn't here to put that visual to the test. She'd have to wait until she returned to the *Starhawke* to see it in action. "So, what's our max range?"

"That's what I'm trying to determine. You can already produce a shield far larger than I ever have."

"Really?" Her mom's confident attitude during the test had indicated otherwise. "You can't expand your shield as far as I just did?"

"No." Her mom had the grace to look a little sheepish. "When I was working with Lyon last time, I purposely set up the test so I wouldn't have to push my shield farther than I knew I could maintain it. But when I saw how easily you held your expanded shield, I knew you could achieve more than I could. I just didn't want to impose any limits on your expectations by telling you that. Whether your expanded range is a result of your innate ability, or of all the practice you've put in over the years, I can't say. I stopped practicing regularly after we left Feylahn, at least until I joined your dad in Hawai'i."

"You've been practicing with Dad?"

"Every day. It's why I was able to make it through the demonstration yesterday. I've been working to increase my endurance."

Aurora considered that for a moment, then glanced at the overhead. "I wonder what my range would be like with Micah's help."

"I suspect that working together, you could expand the field beyond this room."

Aurora's thoughts flashed on the moment when *Sphinx* had been about to breach, with Cade still onboard. She'd flung out a stream of energy toward him across the void, knowing it was futile. But what if it wasn't?

"Between your mixed heritage and the enhancing power Micah gives you, the normal rules don't apply."

"That's good to know." And it gave her a lot to work with. She settled back into a cross-legged position. "What's next?"

"I want you to establish your shield around us again, but this time, keep your hands in your lap."

"Umm..." She glanced down at her hands, suddenly at a loss.

"You've gotten used to relying on your hands, haven't you?"

"Yes?" It came out as a question, because she honestly didn't know any other way. She could generate an amorphous energy field without using her hands, but controlling its shape, size, and composition was another matter entirely. The only time she could remember doing anything like it was on the day she'd met Jonarel. She'd been clutching him in a bear hug when they'd plummeted toward the ravine, forcing her to manage her field without using her hands. But that had been a life-or-death reaction fueled by intense emotion. She couldn't consciously recall how she'd done it. And it hadn't been pretty. They'd still slammed into the ground with significant force, although her field had absorbed most of it.

"Your ability to generate and control your field doesn't come from your hands. It comes from inside you, from your energetic self. Using your hands to direct the energy is helpful, but a Sahzade needs to be able to control the energy even when she can't use her hands."

"Can Lelindia manage her field without her hands?"

Her mom nodded. "When Marina trained her as a child, she insisted she learn. She may be out of practice now, but it's a skill she acquired at a young age. Unlike you," her mom said softly, guilt tinging her emotional field.

Which made Aurora's heart ache. She reached out, clasping her mom's hand in hers. "This is a guilt-free zone, Mom. We both need to let go of the pain of the past."

Her mom gave her hand a squeeze. "What did I do to deserve a daughter as wonderful as you?"

The heartache melted into warm honey. She grinned. "You were smart enough to mate with my dad."

Her mom returned the smile, her emotional grid brightening. "Best decision I ever made."

"Agreed." She looked down at the hand her mom was still clasping. "So, how do I control my shield without using my hands?"

"Let's have you start by placing them in your lap and then engaging your energy field."

She tucked her hands in her lap and engaged her field. It settled around her like a fluffy pearlescent cloud.

"Good. Now expand it around me without using your hands."

She focused on the field, mentally working to push it out toward her mom. It billowed a bit, but in an ungainly way, only covering one of her mom's shoulders and down to her knee. "That's not working."

"Your subconscious knows how to do this, Aurora. You used to do it all the time as a child, especially around Micah and Lelindia. Your energy field would engage and wrap around them when they were near you, like an energetic hug, but you wouldn't even look up from what you were doing. You just need to let your body remember what it used to know how to do. And keep your hands still."

Her fingers twitched in her lap as she stared at her field. She pressed her palms against her thighs and took a slow measured breath.

"Now focus on expanding the field around me."

Nothing happened.

"Don't lean."

Well, one thing happened. She'd unintentionally bent at the waist.

Her mom gave her an encouraging smile. "Your field wants to expand, especially toward other Suulh. However, thanks to me, you've spent most of your life trying to rein it in. Don't try to push it toward me. Breathe, relax, and *allow* it to flow toward me."

Interesting idea. Could she work with that? Hopefully.

Recentering herself, she kept her breathing steady and rhythmic as she focused on the movement of her energy field, observing it with curiosity rather than judgment.

Sure enough, within moments it began to glide toward her mom without any effort from her. As it enveloped her, the zing of connection gave her a burst of power. Out of habit she reached to rein it in.

"No hands," her mom commanded.

She dropped her hands into her lap. The field fluctuated wildly, expanding and contracting in fits and starts.

"It looks like a sea anemone," she complained, her gaze on the field as it wobbled and waved around them like a tentacled sea creature.

"Then visualize the shape you want it to take."

She pictured a nice smooth dome.

The tentacles waved at her in mockery. The field had a mind of its own, flowing and expanding without any conscious direction from her.

"Hands, Aurora."

Dammit. She tucked her hands under her feet to keep them out of play.

"What are you visualizing?"

"A dome." Not that it was having any impact whatsoever.

"Try to solidify the field into a shield."

She shot her mom a doubtful look, but since they were the only two people in the room, there was no danger of an out-of-control shield hurting anyone.

Which ended up not being a problem anyway because the field barely acknowledged her demand for a shield.

She dissipated the field with a frustrated sigh. "I can't do it."

"Yet. You expect far too much of yourself. You're just beginning."

That elicited a self-mocking laugh. "Who, me? Expect too much of myself? Do I ever do that?"

"Not that I recall," her mom replied dryly.

"It just feels weird."

"Weird how?"

"Like it's not really mine."

"Because you don't think you're in control?"

"I wasn't in control. You saw it, waving all over the place." She pulled her hands out from under her feet and wiggled her fingers. "This is how I control my field."

Her mom studied her for a moment. "But your hands can't physically manipulate the field. It's not like molding clay. You have to visualize what you want the energy to do."

"I know. I did." But without her hands, the visualizations had no effect. She'd never parsed out how she did it when she used her hands. It just... happened.

Her mom's lips pressed together, a slight pucker forming between her brows. Aurora sensed her frustration, but it seemed to be a result of her own inability to give directions that produced results. "Do you mind if I ask your dad to join us?"

"Not at all."

Her mom tapped her comband. "Brendan, do you have a moment to come down here?"

"Of course. Be right there."

While they waited, Aurora did a few yoga stretches. The familiar poses often helped to center her. They also drained off some of the frustrated tension that had started to build in her muscles.

"What can I do for you two?" her dad called out from the stairway as he strode toward them.

Aurora sat back on her heels. "I'm not achieving what Mom's trying to teach me and I don't know why not."

Her dad sat on the deck facing them and glanced at her mom. "Do you have a theory?"

Her mom shook her head. "What she's doing should be working."

"What are you teaching her?"

"To control her energy field without using her hands to create a dome shield that would cover both of us."

"Ah." He turned to Aurora. "What's happening? Or not happening?"

"I'll show you." Sitting cross-legged again and tucking her hands under her feet, she engaged her field. It bloomed like an opening flower, expanding toward her parents. "This part is fine," she said as the pearlescent cloud surrounded them. "But when I try to control the shape and turn it into a shield, it doesn't work." She focused on the dome visualization, willing the field to solidify into a shield.

It refused to even give her the time of day.

She growled in aggravation. "See? I can visualize what I want it to do, but nothing's happening when I try to control it."

"But you could control it if you used your hands?"

"Sure." She pulled her hands out from under her feet and lifted them. A moment later the field coalesced into a perfectly formed dome shield over the three of them. "See?"

He studied the shield, then met her gaze. "I have a theory."

"Good." Failing wasn't how she wanted to end her first lesson with her mom.

"While you're creating the shield with your hands, how do you feel it in your body?"

It was like being asked how it felt to breathe. She had to tune into the sensations for a moment. "I feel energized, but in a grounded, solid way. My shield feels like an extension of my body." Unlike the diaphanous cloud that had been mocking her. "I feel strong and centered to my core and my shield feels like a reflection of my physical stability."

"Okay. Now release the shield and tuck your hands back under your feet."

She followed his instructions. The field lost its cohesion, returning to its sea anemone imitation.

"Now try to form the shield again without using your hands."

She focused all her attention on the dome image. And got exactly zip for her efforts.

She sent her dad a pleading look. "Why isn't it working?"

A micro-smile tilted the corner of his mouth. "How do you feel it in your body right now when you're trying to create the shield? Besides frustrated," he added.

"I..." She frowned. "I don't know. I don't really feel anything. Except the frustration."

"I had a feeling that might be the case."

She smiled at the double meaning.

"There's a big difference between the way you engage with your abilities and the way your mom does. As an empath, your strength is emotionally driven. Your mom's strength is intellectually driven. That's why visualizing from a set of instructions works well for her. It plays to her strengths."

"But I'm good at visualization, too." Her work with her dad to control her unconscious physical response to the Suulh was based on it.

"When you're dealing with emotion or abilities tied to emotion, yes. In those instances, you're already looped into your strength. But this is different. You're attempting to approach this task from your mom's perspective, which is intellectual. That's not where your control lies. I suggest you focus on how it *feels* to generate your shield rather than trying to visualize it happening."

Her heart gave a little thump, sending out a frisson of excitement that danced through her veins.

Her dad grinned, pointing a finger at her. "Like that!"

She grinned back. Leave it to her empathic father to tune into an emotional roadblock. "Okay, here goes."

This time when she focused on her energy field, she reached for the feelings she associated with her shield — strength, stability, and connection — and largely ignored visual imagery. Power flowed through her in a wave, rolling out into her field and solidifying the shield into a nearly perfect dome with the three of them at the center.

"Yes!" Her mom clapped her hands in delight. "I knew you could do it."

Aurora laughed, the joy in her parents' emotional fields feeding her and strengthening her control. "This is amazing." Holding the form took almost no effort at all. She glanced at her dad as the power of his emotions washed over her. "You did it, Dad."

"No, you did it." A telltale sheen coated his eyes. "You're amazing, sweetheart. Both of you." His gaze moved to her mom and back again. "I've dreamt of this moment since the day your mom and I mated."

Her dad wasn't the only one getting choked up. Her mom's fierce joy and pride — the emotions Aurora had yearned to feel from her all her life — surrounded her.

"You're the best of what it means to be a Sahzade," she whispered.

Her emotions crested. She swallowed around the lump in her throat, not trusting herself to speak as she held her mom's gaze. *Thank you* she mouthed.

Her mom nodded.

They remained in the beauty and honesty of that moment for a long time. It wasn't until Aurora dissipated the shield that any of them moved.

"This calls for a celebration." Her dad pushed into a crouch. "I just happen to have a batch of dark chocolate brownies baking in the galley." He shot her a grin. "Want one?"

Forty-Seven

"Hold the onion like this when you chop it." Micah picked up one of the onions, setting it on the cutting board in front of Adel and demonstrating the technique, cutting the onion in half, then dicing one half. "The knives are sharp." At least they were now. He and Celia had tackled that task shortly after their arrival onboard. "This technique will protect your fingers while you're chopping."

He set the knife down and motioned to the cutting board, giving Adel an encouraging smile.

Her return smile was shy, but more readily available than when she'd first arrived in the galley with Hobbes and Omondi. She'd looked intimidated by the bustle of activity in the relatively confined space. His dad had coaxed her in by asking her to help him make brownies. Few teenagers could resist the lure of chocolate, especially one who acted like sweet treats hadn't played much of a role in her life up to now.

After his dad left to help his mom and Aurora, Adel had joined him and Hobbes on food prep.

Adel adjusted her grip on the onion and made a tentative chop with the knife. Her gaze flicked to him. "Like that?"

"Yep. Keep going."

She brought the knife down again, each stroke becoming a little more confident than the last.

"That's great. You okay chopping the rest of these?" He pointed to the peeled sweet onions in the bowl in front of her.

She nodded.

"Okay. Holler when you're done." He checked on Hobbes, who'd stationed herself beside Adel.

She had a bowl of red, yellow, and orange tomatoes in front of her and a half-full bowl of diced tomato chunks next to it. He noted with a smile that she'd made a minor adjustment to how she was holding the tomatoes as she sliced them, taking his comments into account.

"Looking good," he told her, moving to the cutting board on her other side where a row of jalapeno peppers awaited him.

She selected a tomato that reminded him of a ball of fire, with vivid orange-red at the bottom shading to yellow-orange at the top. "Your dad taught you all this?" She nodded to their cutting boards then glanced over her shoulder to where Celia was working with Omondi to roll out and cook the tortillas for the tacos.

"Yep. I spend almost as much time in the kitchen as I spend in the water."

She peered at him. "The water?"

It was easy to forget the people onboard *Vengeance* didn't know his history. "I grew up on Hawai'i on Earth, and spent a lot of years surfing competitively."

"Surfing?" Adel's voice pitched higher with excitement. "Really? You've done that? In an ocean?"

And she clearly hadn't. "I have. That's how Iolana and I met, through surfing."

"What's it like?" Adel had stopped chopping, the onions forgotten as she gazed at him with wide eyes.

What he wouldn't give for a surfboard and some waves right now so he could show her. "It's exhilarating. The power of the water lifting and pushing your board, the roar of the waves as they carry you along, the feeling of connection with all the lifeforces around you. There's nothing like it."

Adel's wistful sigh bruised his heart. "I've never even seen an ocean, except in pictures and vids." She glanced at Hobbes, whose lips had flattened as thin as her knife. "Have you?"

"I've flown over them." She brought the knife down on the tomato with more force than necessary, the blade smacking against the cutting board.

He winced, but not because of the tomato. He was beginning to realize how incredibly blessed he'd been to have grown up in a place like Hawai'i with a father who loved him. Judging by their comments so far, Adel's and Hobbes' backstories would break his heart.

Maybe he could offer them something they'd enjoy. "There's a hydrotank on the *Starhawke* that can produce realistic simulations of ocean environments. One of them replicates my favorite diving spot off Oahu." He glanced at Adel, whose dark eyes had lit up with eagerness. "If you want, I'll ask Aurora if I can show it to you when we get back."

Adel sucked in a breath, her body vibrating with excitement. "You mean it?"

"Absolutely. It's not the same as an actual ocean, but it's pretty amazing."

Hobbes eyed him. "Do you think your sister would allow Adel on her ship?"

He caught the warning underneath. Hobbes didn't want Adel to be disappointed if Aurora said no. "She'll agree." Aurora was as big a softie for a hard-luck case as he was. Maybe more, because she could feel the emotional trauma of those she encountered.

Adel's cheeks rounded with a bright smile, the first time he'd seen a glimpse of her teeth. "Can Veronica and Diego come?"

Hobbes stilled. Omondi looked over his shoulder at Adel, which clued Micah in that she was talking about them.

He glanced at Celia, who was watching their reactions with interest, but no hint of concern. Good. If he had her approval, Aurora would be fine with it. "I can't imagine that would be a problem."

Hobbes' gaze still wasn't entirely trusting.

"I'll talk to Aurora as soon as I see her," he assured her. "It'll be fine."

She gave a brief nod before returning her attention to the tomatoes.

"How big is the tank?" Adel asked, scooping the chopped onion into her bowl and grabbing another one from the pile.

Micah pulled on the kitchen gloves he'd brought from the *Starhawke* to protect his fingers from the jalapeno juice. "Big enough to swim in." He sliced one of the jalapenos lengthwise and removed the seeds.

"What are the specs?"

Kenji had mentioned she was interested in engineering. "Sorry, I don't know the specs."

"The tank holds roughly seventy-five square meters of water when filled to capacity," Celia commented without taking her attention off the tortillas she was cooking. "But since the design is neither square, nor set to our standards of measurement, that's the closest specs I can give you. Jonarel, our Kraed engineer, would be able to provide a precise answer. You can ask him when you visit the *Starhawke*."

Adel looked like she was about to levitate off the floor. "Your engineer is a *Kraed*?"

Micah grinned. "He is. And he would be happy to talk to you about any engineering questions you have."

Adel's starstruck expression made his grin widen.

"What about this planet we're going to?" Omondi asked, watching Adel's reaction. "Does it have oceans?"

He had no idea.

"It does," Celia answered, "but I doubt we'll be near them. We'll be scouting the areas where Aurora visited before, which are rocky jungle surrounding a system of rivers."

"Rivers are nice," Adel said so softly she might have been talking to herself.

Micah's heart squeezed. Clearly Adel was a fellow water lover. "Are you joining the habitat team, Adel?"

She looked up at him through her dark lashes. "I dunno."

"Would you like to?"

"Is it safe?" Hobbes turned to face him, partially blocking Adel in the process.

He knew a mom move when he saw one. Even though Hobbes wasn't Adel's biological mother, she and Omondi behaved like they were Adel's parents, watching out for her. They even looked like they could be related to her. "That's the point – to locate safe places to build. We won't set up anywhere dangerous."

"And you'll be dumping Mirko there?" Omondi asked, a sharp edge to his voice.

Micah gave the man a sidelong glance. The hard glitter in his dark eyes indicated he felt about Mirko the way Micah felt about Manchado. "We'll be leaving her there. Manchado, too."

"For good?"

"I don't know. At least for the foreseeable future."

"Better than she deserves," Hobbes muttered.

Adel didn't say anything. She was staring fixedly at her cutting board, her knife moving in a slow, almost painful chop, chop, chop.

Celia was taking in their reactions, too. "Have any of you talked to Brendan about Mirko?"

Omondi and Hobbes stared at her in confusion. "Why would we?" Omondi asked.

Celia looked significantly at Adel's hunched back. "Because he's a very talented and empathic psychologist."

Hobbes glanced at Adel, then back at Celia, her lips parting in understanding. "Oh."

"He's also gathering intel to determine whether Mirko and Manchado should be placed together or separately." Celia's gaze shifted between Hobbes and Omondi. "Talking to the three of you would be helpful to him."

Omondi stiffened, a clear sign of resistance, but Hobbes was listening intently.

"I've talked with him about my experiences with Manchado," Celia continued smoothly, transferring the cooked tortillas to towels and dropping in the next batch. "My life has improved dramatically as a result." She looked over her shoulder, meeting Micah's gaze.

The intensity of emotion in her eyes made him lightheaded.

"I highly recommend it."

Forty-Eight

"Dr. Morales is headed for her office," U-2 informed Cade, gliding in front of the navigation console. "Do you want eyes and ears?"

Cade paused the news feed he and the Admiral had been watching of President Yeoh's latest press conference. Her image froze. "Definitely."

The Admiral moved into his peripheral vision. "Unity, please ask Knox and Isabeau to join us."

"Williams, too," Cade added, "and Lelindia if she's not already asleep." She'd looked pretty tired when she'd left the bridge. Jonarel wouldn't thank him if he disturbed Lelindia's rest.

"She's already asleep."

"Then never mind."

"Do you want us to ask Marina, instead?"

"Is she awake?" She and Gryphon had the early morning bridge shift, which would start in less than six hours.

"No."

"Then no. If you record Dr. Morales' and Captain Montgomery's interaction, they can review it later if necessary."

"Will do!"

Montgomery hadn't changed position much in the hours since Unity first showed them her whereabouts, but she was awake, staring at the ceiling.

The soft click of a door opening came over the bridge speakers as the door near the kitchenette swung in. Dr. Morales stepped into the room, her short white hair creating a neat cap on her head, the color contrasting with her tawny skin and blue scrubs.

Cade could see the lines of exhaustion around her eyes and the slight hunch of tension in her shoulders, but there was a smile in her voice and on her lips. "Did you get some rest?"

Montgomery flinched when she tried to sit up straighter. "That's debatable," she muttered, her mouth turning down.

Morales helped her adjust the pillows so she was more upright, then fetched her a glass of water from the kitchen.

Montgomery sipped it slowly, her penetrating gaze on Morales. "What's changed?"

Even laid up with a serious injury, Montgomery was still in full captain mode.

Movement from the *Starhawke*'s lift momentarily drew Cade's attention away as Knox and Isabeau stepped onto the bridge.

"I heard from Henri."

He glanced back at the bridgescreen.

"*Cassini* received orders to return to Eridani Duo."

"Damn." Montgomery blew out a forceful breath, her eyes narrowing in thought. "How soon?"

"Five days."

Montgomery's jaw flexed.

"That's not all," Morales continued. "They're picking up Teeli consuls while they're there."

The litany of swear words that left Montgomery's mouth would have made a sailor proud.

Cade seconded the sentiment.

"Nixon's moving faster than I expected." Montgomery bared her teeth. "And I'm useless here." She pointed at her leg with her good arm. "How soon can this cast come off?"

Morales picked up the bio scanner resting on the bedside table and ran it slowly over Montgomery's leg.

Williams arrived amidst the silence, taking in the scene with a practiced eye and coming to stand on Cade's far side.

"The fibula fracture is healing well, but the tibia fracture hasn't knit sufficiently to support any weight. Add in the meniscus damage—"

"How soon?" Montgomery ground out.

"A week and a half, minimum."

A few more swear words colored the air. "Tell Harriet she needs to take me back to Eridani Duo on her next run. That'll get me there before the Teeli arrive. I won't let Anthony or my crew take the fall on this."

Morales folded her hands. "So you're going to make Nixon's job easier? Turn yourself over to the Teeli? Give up without a fight?"

Isabeau's sharp inhale made Cade turn. Her face had paled, her grip on Knox's hand turning her knuckles white. She knew better than any of them what Montgomery was likely to face if the Teeli got a hold of her.

Montgomery snorted, gesturing with a sharp cut of her hand down her body. She hissed in a breath as the abrupt movement cost her. "Look at me, Elena." Her voice wobbled as she pushed through the pain. "I'm already out of the fight. The only reason I agreed to any of this was because we had a plan that was low risk. Now it's not. If *Cassini* arrives at Eridani Duo and I'm not there, Anthony's career is over. Rehema and Henri might not survive the fallout, either. They're in positions where they can do some good for the Union. I won't sacrifice them to save myself."

"The Teeli having control of you could sacrifice far more." Morales held up a hand to forestall further debate. "Regardless, it doesn't matter which of us is right. I don't have a way to return you to Eridani Duo."

"*What?*" Montgomery tried to straighten, blanched, and sank back against the pillow. "Did something happen to Harriet?"

"No, she's fine. But Nixon has increased the station's security protocols. Any cargo or personnel she transports must now go through security scanning and ID checks. The only ID you have is your Fleet ID and your face is well known to the Fleet personnel on this station."

Montgomery said something decidedly unflattering about Nixon. "What about a private passenger vessel or freighter?"

Morales shook her head. "The protocols apply to all non-Fleet ships."

Montgomery produced another burst of swear words, but with less vehemence this time. She stared up at the ceiling as weariness settled over her features. "I should never have left *Cassini.*"

"Now you want to embrace death?" A sharpness entered Morales' voice.

Montgomery's gaze shifted to her. "I'm the captain. It's my job to protect my crew, even at the expense of my own life."

"And it's their job to protect you, even at the expense of theirs. Don't be a martyr, Colleen. It doesn't suit you. It also belittles their sacrifices and courage."

Montgomery glared at her, but didn't offer a rebuttal.

"If you want another reason not to give up, think about Will and Knox."

The Admiral coughed, the sound a little strangled.

Knox shifted his weight, his jaw flexing.

"They need allies, people who can garner support from the Fleet personnel who still believe in them, who see the threat for what it is. If the Teeli were able to turn Isabeau against Will, what do you think they would do to you?"

A dark wave of regret and anguish hit Cade, rolling out from Magee.

Montgomery's eyes slid shut, her face a mask of physical and emotional pain.

Morales took the glass from her unresisting fingers. "Your job right now is to heal. My job is to keep you hidden. The rest we'll figure out one day at a time."

Montgomery opened her eyes to half-mast. Her words came out as a tortured murmur. "Tell everyone I'm sorry."

Morales rested a hand over hers. "They're not. If you gave them the chance to do things differently, they wouldn't. They're strong, and they're smart. They'll find a way through this."

Montgomery didn't respond.

"I'll warm up something for you to eat."

The worry lines on Morales' face deepened as she turned toward the kitchenette.

The image on the bridgescreen switched back to the starfield.

No one said a word as the implications sank in.

"Colleen's not wrong," Knox said softly. "Dr. Yates will be brought up on charges. And *Cassini's* entire senior staff could get yanked off the ship for the enquiry. Nixon could use it as an excuse to replace them with his loyalists."

"That might have happened anyway," the Admiral said, the anger of injustice flaring in his emotional field. "He can't risk having *Cassini* standing in the way of the Teeli pushing into Fleet space. Or alerting anyone else to the danger. He's already made critical changes to personnel and patrol routes throughout the quadrant, supposedly to root out my spies." Bitterness coated his words.

Cade looked over his shoulder at Williams, who was studying something on his tablet. "What do you make of Montgomery's condition?"

"I'm looking over the readings from the bio scan of her leg Unity sent me," he answered without looking up. "I agree with Morales' assessment. Montgomery really did a number on her leg, and based on her behavior, she's refusing to take sufficient pain meds, probably because they'd make her drowsy and less alert. That's common with captains." He shot a look at Knox and the Admiral that indicated he included them in that category. "She needs deep rest. We also don't know what the status is with her back."

Incapacitation was preferable to being dead — the outcome whoever caused the accident likely had been going for — but for someone as active and take-charge as Montgomery, this situation had to be her own private Hell. "We have people onboard who could heal her."

"I'm aware." Williams nodded. "Unfortunately, their faces are plastered on the news feeds as Union fugitives. We can't get them to her."

"But we might be able to get *her* to *them*."

Williams folded his arms. "How would we get her past the increased security? We don't have the people or the resources we were able to tap when we managed our previous hospital heist."

"*Previous* hospital heist?" Isabeau asked, staring at them. "You've done this before?"

Cade nodded. "A few months ago. We slipped Admiral Payne's grandson out of the ICU right under their noses."

"Why?"

"The Sovereign was using him as leverage," the Admiral replied with more than a little heat, "forcing her to manipulate Aurora to save her grandson's life."

Isabeau's jaw clenched. "Where are they now?"

"A safe house. The rest of her family, too."

Cade was already running potential scenarios in his head. "If we could move her and heal her, it would give us options, especially if we could find a way to protect Dr. Yates and *Cassini's* crew, too."

"You'd have to sedate her while she's in transit," Williams warned. "Any jostling would feel like torture to her when she's awake."

He gazed at the snippet of *Phoenix* visible on the bridgescreen image. "We have one advantage in this situation. We know someone who's made her living as a smuggler."

The Admiral frowned. "Nat can't go to Hydra One, either. According to what she told the Fleet personnel, she's supposed to be on *Vengeance*. Showing up on *Phoenix* would get her flagged."

"I know. But she has the only ship we can take to Hydra One." Nat had been looking for a way to repay Aurora when they'd first approached her. She seemed fully invested in doing anything to help them defeat the Sovereign. Hopefully that included loaning him her ship.

The Admiral's gaze grew speculative. "Unity, is Nat awake?"

"Yep."

Cade grinned. "Then let's contact her and see what she says."

Forty-Nine

Nat had decided to take advantage of the peace and quiet that had settled over *Phoenix* by starting work on the new mural she'd sketched out for the dining room. She was in *Phoenix's* utility room, mixing paint, when her comband buzzed against her forearm.

She turned off the mixing machine, silencing the steady thrum, before opening the connection. "Hey, Cade, what's up?"

"I have a favor to ask. How would you feel about *Phoenix* making a trip to Hydra One?"

"What's on Hydra One?" Besides a whole bunch of Fleet personnel they needed to avoid.

"*Cassini's* captain. Unity located her at the station's medical center. She's incapacitated, and Nixon's tightening the noose. We're hoping you might be able to help us smuggle her off the station."

He'd said the magic word — smuggle. "That sounds like an interesting challenge."

Cade chuckled. "So, you're onboard with the idea?"

"I am." She'd take great pleasure in thwarting the Sovereign's machinations any way she could. "What's your plan for getting her out?"

"Nothing definitive yet. Unity's working on getting access to the comm device for the head of medical, Dr. Morales, who's a friend of the Admiral's, so we can alert her to expect me. But I'd need to borrow *Phoenix*."

He wanted to *borrow* her ship? She leaned against the workbench beside the mixer. "Is your whole team going?"

"Yes, though not all on *Phoenix*. I was thinking Bella could fly *Gladiator* as backup, just in case. With the Yruf providing camouflage, of course."

"But you'd be the one going onto the station?"

"Yes."

"Alone?"

"Probably with Williams, since Montgomery needs medical care."

"No offense, but that's a bad idea. Neither of you do inconspicuous well. You're too tall and good-looking to blend in, and he's built like a bouncer at a bar. You're also both too fit and healthy to be visiting a medical center without an obvious injury. You'll draw attention."

"Should I be flattered or insulted?"

"Neither. It's a fact."

"People go to medical centers for routine checkups. And it's a busy station with lots of people. Easy to get lost in the crowd."

"Except *Phoenix* isn't a utilitarian personnel transport. She's the kind of ship people book when they're on vacation. Anyone exiting the ship needs to give off that vibe. A routine medical checkup doesn't fit."

"Then I could be picking up medication."

"Again, a ship like *Phoenix* would be well stocked with all kinds of meds." She and Marlin had come across a wide array in the ship's infirmary, although most of the items had been compromised from the crash into the dunes. "Another thing. Correct me if I'm wrong, but the Sovereign knows what you look like, right?"

"Yes."

"So you could be on a watch list."

"Unity's checking that, too."

"Even if you're not on the *official* watch list, do you really believe the Sovereign isn't looking for you? That she doesn't know you and Aurora are together? That she won't have people on Hydra One who will recognize you on sight?"

Cade was silent for a long moment. "I can work on a disguise. So can Williams. But we have to go. We're the only hope Montgomery has."

There was no way she was letting Cade get snatched while Aurora was away. Leaving him to fend for himself on Hydra One would be stupid. Which meant she needed an alternate plan. A *dangerous* plan.

Lupe had called it. "You and I should go together."

"Together?" He said it slowly, like he was questioning what he'd heard. "How is that better? You can't go onto Hydra One. There are Fleet personnel on that station who just saw you on *Vengeance*."

"They saw Natasha Orlov, a down on her luck pilot for hire. But that's not who I'd be going as. And Itorye could work some magic on you, too. We could play the part of a happy couple on vacation. By subverting expectations, no one would recognize either one of us."

"Then what's our excuse for going to the medical center?"

"Leave that to me." She'd dust off some of her childhood cons that had kept her from starving. "Can anyone on your team make us fake IDs?" Patel probably could, but Nat wasn't about to involve her. She was already anticipating the difficult conversation she'd be having with her when she informed the paranoid scientist they were taking *Phoenix* — and by extension, Alec — to Hydra One.

"Reynolds can. I'll have her create one for you, too. What name do you want to use?"

"Finch." Another blast from her past. "Noelle Finch."

"Okay. Next question. Do you have any recommendations for how we might smuggle Montgomery off the station? Security is checking all cargo and IDs. We'll also have to sedate Montgomery when we move her. She has broken bones and potential spinal injuries."

Nat winced in sympathy. But she had the perfect solution sitting in her cargo bay. "It just so happens I have a smuggling crate that would do the trick." Isin hadn't seen any use for it on *Vengeance*, so she'd happily brought it over to *Phoenix*. "No air holes, though, so your doctor friend would need to provide a way for Montgomery to breathe during transport."

A murmur of masculine voices rose in the background.

"The Admiral doesn't think that will be a problem. How do we get that crate to the medical center?"

He'd already provided the answer. "Williams can play the role of *Phoenix*'s doctor, purchasing supplies from the medical center to restock the infirmary. He arrives with the empty crate, secures Montgomery in the base, then loads the rest with medical supplies."

A faint *she's good* from an unfamiliar voice, followed by the Admiral's chuckle, drifted over the comm line.

"Sounds like we have enough to start planning," Cade replied.

She quickly surveyed her workspace. "How soon do you want to leave?"

"As soon as we work out all the logistics, gather supplies, and decide who's going on which ship. What about you? How much time do you need?"

"I need to talk things over with my crew, but they'll be onboard." At least after Itorye and Gavin calmed down Patel. "I'll alert you if there are any hiccups, but otherwise, assume we'll be ready when you are."

The mural, however, would have to wait.

Fifty

"I need your help." Nat pivoted the pilot's chair to face Itorye, who'd just stepped through the open hatch to *Phoenix*'s bridge. She'd pinged Itorye after wrapping up her conversation with Cade, asking her to meet on the bridge. It was the least suspicious, semi-private place for this discussion.

She'd also checked with Alec to make sure Patel would be distracted for the next ten minutes or so. He'd confirmed his mom was working with Gavin in the media room.

Itorye settled gracefully into the co-pilot's seat. "What type of help do you need?"

"We're going to Hydra One to smuggle a Fleet captain out of the medical center, and taking Cade and some of his team with us."

Itorye accepted the news with her usual unruffled demeanor, barely lifting one sculpted brow in reaction.

"I need your help managing Patel. I suspect she'll flip out when we tell her where we're going and that we're bringing passengers onboard. She might try to stuff Alec into his transport cube, or insist our guests have to stay in their quarters for the whole trip."

The corner of Itorye's mouth curved up. "Very likely."

"She can't force me into my cube." Alec's projected form appeared standing in front of the captain's chair, arms folded over his chest, his close-cropped beard emphasizing his frown. "And it's not like you're inviting over strangers. These are the people who freed you from Tnaryt and also saved *Sphinx*'s crew and the children."

Itorye took in his defensive posture without comment. "Would *Phoenix* be going alone?" she asked Nat.

"No. Someone from Cade's team would be piloting *Gladiator*, which will be following us, camouflaged by the Yruf."

"And the *Starhawke* will remain here?"

"Cade didn't specify, but I assume so. I expect some of the Yruf ships will remain behind as well."

"They will," Unity said over the bridge speakers.

Itorye's gaze flicked toward the speakers, the wheels turning rapidly behind her dark eyes. "Is there a plan for when we arrive at Hydra One?"

"A loose one. Cade and I will be playing tourists, going onto the station in disguise so we can talk to the doctor who's currently hiding the captain. That's the other thing I need your help with. Lupe left me some of their wigs and clothing options, but I have no idea what to do with them without looking ridiculous."

Humor flashed in Itorye's eyes. "You don't like Lupe's choices?"

"They're fine. *I'm* the problem. I live in cargo pants and turtlenecks. The clothes they gave me are nothing like that. Especially the *dress*." She shuddered.

The sparkle in Itorye's eyes brightened. "Which should make it a very effective disguise. That is, assuming you can act naturally when you're wearing it."

She pictured the flowing fabric and bold colors. "I'm not sure I can."

"Then you'll need to practice. I also suggest we speak with Darsha now, give her some time to get used to the idea."

Itorye led the way to the media room, where Patel and Gavin were pouring over screens of scientific data that made Nat's eyes cross. Alec was already in the room, facing the rows of theater seats. Gavin greeted her with a smile, but suspicion settled over Patel's face the moment she saw Nat with Itorye.

Itorye ignored the reaction, settling into the chair beside Patel while Nat remained standing next to Alec.

"What's up?" Gavin asked, reading the room with his usual aplomb.

"We have a new project." Nat focused on him rather than Patel, trusting Itorye and Alec to jump in as needed. "One that might require the skills you used to sneak Alec off Rathburn's ship."

"Oh, really?"

Patel opened her mouth.

Nat plowed forward before she could get a word in. "There's a woman on Hydra One who's in danger from the Sovereign." At least that was the subtext she'd gathered. "Cade and Admiral Schreiber have asked us to help smuggle her off the station. I said yes."

"Hydra One!" Patel's voice hit slightly below the decibel level Nat had been expecting, but still far louder than the distance between them called for. "That's a Fleet station!"

"I know."

"We can't take *Phoenix* to a Fleet station!" Her gaze darted to Alec with a flash of fear, but anger replaced it by the time she met Nat's gaze. "I won't let you put Alec in danger like that."

She opened her mouth to respond, but Alec beat her to it.

"What danger, Mom?" His voice was measured, reasonable. "Nobody from the station will come onboard, and even if they did, I'm not going to announce my presence. No one will know I'm here."

"Didn't you hear her?" Patel pointed an accusing finger at Nat. "She wants to *smuggle* a *stranger* onto our *ship*."

The word emphasis seemed like a bit much, even for Patel.

"She wants to *rescue* a woman in *danger* from the Sovereign," Alec parried.

"What woman?" Patel's eyes narrowed on Nat like a cat sizing up a mouse.

She considered downplaying the truth, but chose to rip the bandage off instead. "She's the captain of the Fleet ship *Cassini*."

"*What!*" Patel finally reached the decibel level Nat had expected. "You want to bring a Fleet *captain* onboard!?"

"Yes."

"You can't!"

She didn't bother responding, just held Patel's gaze, keeping her expression neutral.

Patel's lip curled, then she swung around to Itorye. "You have to stop her."

Patel was barking up the wrong tree. She'd clearly forgotten Itorye had walked in with Nat.

"*Phoenix* is Nat's ship," Itorye replied, not unkindly. "And she's our captain. I also agree with her."

Patel jerked like Itorye had goosed her. "What? Why? How? Alec—" She waved a hand at his projection. "It's not safe."

"Everyone on the *Starhawke* has already proven they're trustworthy." Alec was doing a good job of imitating Itorye's inner calm. "And they respect and protect Unity. They'll do the same for me."

"Yes, they will!" Unity chirped through the media room speakers.

She'd forgotten they'd be listening in.

So had Patel, judging by the way her gaze snapped to the speakers. "You stay out of this!"

"We're trying to help." Unity sounded hurt by Patel's sharp reprimand.

"Don't take your anger out on Unity, Mom," Alec admonished, disapproval drawing lines between his brows. "They have every right to be part of this discussion. You need to treat them with respect."

Patel blinked at Alec.

So did Nat. Alec had never taken such an unwavering, unapologetic stand against his mother before. His maturity in handling the situation made Patel's response look like a child's tantrum.

Patel seemed to come to the same conclusion. Shame curled her shoulders, contrition in her eyes as she gazed at Alec. She took a slow breath. "I'm sorry for snapping at you, Unity."

Nat almost fell over. Patel apologizing to Unity? She'd never expected to see the day.

"How can we help?" Gavin asked.

"So glad you asked." Unlike Patel, Gavin looked intrigued by the upcoming trip. "Docking at Hydra One will be easy. *Phoenix* will blend in with the other private charter transports making a stop so vacationers can explore the station and planet. Cade and I will be going onto the station in disguise and acting like a couple, but it would be suspicious if we're the only ones who leave the ship."

"So you need us to be decoys, playing the part of passengers out having a good time." Gavin grinned. "That should be easy enough. I have a few things I could look for while we're there. And I can ooh and aah with the best of them."

She appreciated the support. "Thanks." Her gaze moved to Patel. "Will you help?"

Patel looked like she was sucking on lemons. "What about Marlin and Pete?"

"I'll be talking to them, too. I have no doubt they'll volunteer to play a role, either as passengers or crew picking up supplies." Having other crew returning to the ship with full crates would make the smuggling crate less of a focus for security.

"Then who's staying with *Phoenix*?" Patel's gaze cut to Alec before flicking to Itorye.

"I will," Itorye replied. "The Fleet just encountered me posing as *Vengeance*'s captain. I can't be seen leaving *Phoenix*. I'll make sure the ship stays secure."

Patel's shoulders lowered a few centimeters.

"We'll be onboard, too," Unity said cautiously. "We won't let anything bad happen to Alec. We promise."

Patel's jaw flexed, her gaze shifting to Alec. "You're sure about this? That station will be swarming with Fleet personnel and ships."

She'd never heard Patel address Alec like an equal before, an adult whose opinion she valued rather than a child whose opinion she viewed as uninformed.

Alec looked just as startled, but he recovered quickly. "I know. But you raised me to be a force for good. This is important."

Patel stared at him for a long time. Emotions flitted across her face in rapid succession — anxiety, fear, and discomfort, but also a healthy dose of pride. "Okay, Alec." She blew out a breath, turning to Nat. "What do you need me to do?"

Fifty-One

Cade sank onto the couch in Aurora's cabin with a sigh. He'd just finished his bridge shift with the Admiral, and his brain was buzzing with details while his body was ready to call it a night. They'd spent the second half of the shift going over every detail Unity had been able to provide regarding the Fleet movements and security on Hydra One. When Justin and Bella had relieved them, he'd filled them in on the upcoming mission so they could start working on their respective tasks.

He needed to wake Marina and Gryphon soon to propose the idea of them joining the team on *Gladiator*. Having Marina with them to heal Montgomery's injuries would be preferable to making Montgomery wait until they returned to the *Starhawke*.

He didn't think convincing Marina and Gryphon would be a hard sell.

What they'd do with Montgomery after that, and whether there was a way to protect Dr. Yates and *Cassini*'s crew from Nixon's wrath was still a big question mark, one that would have to wait until she was safely off Hydra One.

He let his head fall back against the cushions, his gaze sweeping around the front room. The cabin was depressingly silent and empty without Aurora here. He'd gotten used to sensing her emotional field brushing up against his. Her absence left him feeling unsettled.

U-2 hovered over the coffee table. "You look tired."

"I am." But with his brain looping through all the *what ifs* and the clock ticking on *Cassini's* arrival, sleep wasn't an option. "Is Aurora awake?"

"Yes."

"Is she with you?"

"Yes."

"Can you ask her if she has time to talk with me?"

A moment later, Aurora's voice emanated from U-2. "I always have time for you."

Cade sat up straighter, the unexpected caress of her voice energizing him. "We can talk in real time?"

"Not exactly," Unity replied. "We can relay your words to each other, but there will be a slight delay, like hearing an echo of what the other said."

"That's okay. This is awesome."

"I agree," Aurora replied a moment later. "Hang on. I'm heading down to *Starlet*."

Eagerness built in his chest as he waited, emphasizing just how much he missed her. When he caught himself bouncing his knee, he pressed his foot flat onto the deck and tried not to count the seconds.

"Okay, I'm all yours."

Warmth flowed over him, the emotional undertone of her words melting away the day's tension. He closed his eyes, strengthening the illusion that she was in the room with him. "Hey, Rory. How are you?"

"Missing you. Whose bright idea was it to split up again?"

He smiled. "Yours."

"That's what I thought. Next time, argue with me a little harder, okay?"

He chuckled. "Deal. Although I love the way you launch yourself at me after we've been apart." Just thinking about it made his skin flush.

Her soft laugh made another part of his anatomy perk up. "And I love the way you react when I do. Very gratifying."

"I aim to please."

"You succeed."

Much more of this kind of talk and he was going to have a new problem to contend with. "How are things on *Vengeance*?"

She sighed. "Good, bad, and ugly. I met with Mirko and Manchado this morning."

He winced. "I'm guessing that's the bad and ugly."

"Uh-huh. I keep thinking I've seen the worst those two have to offer, but they keep exceeding my expectations."

"I'm sorry."

"At least once we reach the planet, I'll be able to put some physical distance between us while we work on the surface. Blocking out their emotional resonances is proving to be more taxing than I'd envisioned. My dad gave me some tips this morning that are helping, but being on *Vengeance* with them is like standing next to a river of raw sewage."

He crinkled his nose in sympathy. "So, what's the good?"

"I had my first energy training session with my mom today."

"Oh, yeah?" He could hear the delight in her voice, even if he couldn't feel it across the lightyears separating them. "How did it go?"

"She worked me hard, pushed my limits, tested just how far I could go. I loved every moment. We've got another session scheduled for tomorrow morning."

"That's fantastic. You've waited a long time for this." The contentious relationship she'd had with her mom and the roadblocks her mom had thrown up to thwart her during her Academy days had been reminiscent of his family dynamic. His parents had been just as determined to keep him from going after his dreams, although their reasons had been selfish and domineering, not coming from a place of fear for his safety. "When you get back, will you show me what you've learned?"

"Absolutely." Her happiness sparkled like a shower of rainbows. "But enough about me. How are things there?"

"That's what I needed to talk to you about. *Phoenix's* repairs are finished and Unity located Montgomery on Hydra One." He gave her a rundown of what they'd learned and a summary of their plans.

She blew out a breath. "I should have waited to drop off Mirko and Manchado until after we had Montgomery."

He hated the self-reproach in her tone. "It wouldn't have mattered. You and your family can't go to Hydra One. Neither can *Vengeance* after what went down with Devries, and the *Starhawke* is still recharging. If you were here, all you'd be doing is watching from a distance anyway. Far better that you're taking action for something productive."

The silence stretched out. He could picture the scowl on her face, her jaw tightening as she chewed on her tongue. Her sharp mind would be working furiously to find a third option that would enable her to help.

When she replied, her voice was layered with anger and frustration. "I hate being so limited."

"I know." He'd felt her frustration like a low-grade fever ever since they'd sprung her and the Admiral from the detention facility. Being contained, first at Seaview, then by the *Starhawke*'s inability to leave Zeta Tucanae and her own status as a fugitive, was wearing on her. She was a front-line fighter, not a backseat commander.

Her agitation was one reason he'd encouraged her to go with *Vengeance* and deal with a problem she *could* solve. "But think about how much you're expanding, too. You're learning new skills from your mom and getting stronger every day. That will be important for what's ahead. What you're doing counts for a lot."

He heard the puff of air that usually preceded her self-deprecating smile. "Even from lightyears away, you can still knock me out of my thought spirals. Thank you."

"Anytime."

She sighed, the sound reaching into his chest and squeezing his heart. "You don't know how much I wish I could snuggle with you right now."

"I might." His arms ached to hold her, too. The sleeping nook felt empty without her. That gave him another reason to jump ship for a while.

He switched topics to keep from starting his own thought spiral. "How are you getting along with *Vengeance's* crew?"

"Great. They're a fascinating mix of personalities and backgrounds. My mom and I gave a demonstration for some of them yesterday, and my dad, Micah, and Celia have been giving cooking lessons to anyone who's interested. Iolana and Kai have been helping out with chores around the ship. The crew's been very appreciative."

"How did they react to seeing what you could do?"

"Oh, they were impressed." She laughed softly. "It was fun, being able to use my abilities so openly and to see what my mom could do. She blew my mind with techniques I'd never even considered."

"Like what?"

"Energy pulses that work like projectiles. And an energy funnel that creates a personal tornado."

"Huh." He'd seen Aurora do a lot of incredible things, but nothing like what she'd described. "I can't wait to see that."

"I can't wait to show you. But it sounds like you'll have plenty to keep you occupied in the meantime. I'm glad Nat volunteered to go with you. This mission is right up her alley."

"I think she's looking forward to it. She was very insistent." And he was grateful for her help and expertise.

"Insistence is one of her strong suits." He could hear the smile in her voice. "Are you taking U-2 with you on *Phoenix?*"

Cade opened his eyes, gazing at U-2 floating in front of him. "That's up to them."

U-2 bobbed. "We like having a mobile unit with you. It gives us options."

Cade grinned. "Then I guess U-2's coming with me."

Fifty-Two

"*You're* leaving, too?" Lelindia stared at her parents across the dining table in her cabin. "I'm beginning to think there's some obscure Suulh tradition of abandoning the Nedale right before she delivers." First Aurora's family and Celia, now her parents. Next Jonarel would tell her he was going with them.

"We're not abandoning you," her mom replied, her lips twitching. "We're going to help Captain Montgomery. And you know as well as I do that Raehn won't be born for at least another three weeks."

Her mom was right. They'd both studied all the material Tehar had provided regarding Kraed births. Three weeks was the conservative estimate, based on her half-Kraed physiology and development. It might be a month or more.

But that fact didn't matter one whit to her *emotionally*. In her heightened state, she reacted to every mole hill like it was a mountain. It was the one part of pregnancy she could really do without.

Jonarel's knee touched hers under the table, his golden eyes darkening with concern.

She slid her foot closer, aligning it with his, drawing comfort from his nearness. There was no way he was leaving her side before Raehn was born.

She picked up her tea mug, inhaling the spicy scent before taking a sip of the warm, rich flavors. She needed the fortification after being woken from a deep sleep and hit with the news of her parents' imminent departure. "How soon do you leave?"

"As soon as we're packed," her mom replied.

She didn't manage to contain her grimace.

Her dad scooted his chair closer, gently unwrapping one of her hands from where she clutched her mug and cradling it in both of his. "We won't be gone long, firefly. It'll take less than a day to reach Hydra One. We'll be back before you know it."

An image flashed into her mind, captured in exquisite, painful detail – her dad lying on a bed of evergreen needles, his breath rasping in and out with a death rattle, her mom crouched beside him, her energy field pale and weak.

Until the Setarip attack at Stoneycroft, she'd never contemplated her parents' mortality, never considered what she'd do if they died. Having it thrust in front of her on that terrifying night had shaken something deep in her core, a foundational piece that creaked and moaned every time she pressed on it.

This situation was exerting the weight of an elephant on that rickety piece. But Captain Montgomery needed their help, and her mom was the better choice to go. Lelindia didn't want to test what would happen if Jonarel was separated from her right now, even for a few days. His Kraed overprotectiveness was growing stronger the closer they came to Raehn's birth. Since he needed to stay with the *Starhawke*, she needed to stay, too.

So she'd focus on how best to support her parents' efforts. "One thing I've learned being on this crew is that predicting what will happen is an effort in futility. Make sure you pack enough to last you a week or more."

Her dad's brows lifted. "We'll be back for your birthday."

She didn't contradict him, even though her gut told her he was probably wrong. "Do Libra and Aurora know you're going?"

"Cade spoke with Aurora," her mom answered, "and Unity's integration with *Gladiator* will allow us to keep in touch with them during the trip."

Libra wasn't likely to be overjoyed by the news of their mission. She gave Jonarel a run for his money when it came to overprotective behavior. But clearly she hadn't fired back an immediate objection. "Did Cade warn you that *Gladiator* doesn't have cabins?"

Her dad grinned, sitting back in his chair. "Yep. We popped down to take a look before we came up here. The bunks are shoeboxes, but at least they're shoeboxes designed for someone my height. I won't have to sleep folded in half."

Lelindia peered at him. "You sound like you're looking forward to this."

"I am. Cade's going to be on *Phoenix*, so I'll be the most experienced pilot on *Gladiator*. I'll get the bulk of the flying time."

She should have known her dad would jump at the chance to fly a new-to-him ship. She glanced at her mom. "What about you?"

"I'm not as excited as your dad," she admitted, "but that's because I won't have a job until Cade successfully gets Captain Montgomery off Hydra One. Since the Admiral won't have a job at first, either, he's offered to teach me how to play chess to give us both something to do."

Lelindia sat up straighter. "The Admiral's going, too?"

Her mom nodded. "He wants to be able to talk to Captain Montgomery after we rescue her, brainstorm the best path forward for her and her crew."

"Which may or may not involve bringing her to the *Starhawke*," Lelindia concluded.

"Correct."

"Maybe you should pack enough for two weeks."

Her parents exchanged a look. The first hint of doubt touched her mom's eyes. "We weren't planning to leave you for that long."

"I know. But nowadays things rarely go to plan."

Fifty-Three

"Today I'll teach you to create an energy funnel." Libra picked up the pail of black rags she'd used for her previous demonstration, holding it out so Aurora could grab a handful. "We'll start with about ten in the circle."

"Okay."

She placed a rag on the deck, circling in one direction while Aurora moved in the opposite direction.

"Can I ask you a question?"

She paused at the odd note in Aurora's voice. "Of course you can."

"It's about Feylahn."

A little frisson of anxiety darted through her, but she ignored it. "You can ask me anything you want to know." She'd promised to train her daughter in the ways of the Sahzade. That meant teaching her everything she would have learned if she'd been born on the Suulh homeworld instead of on Earth.

Aurora continued to place the rags in her half of the circle. "I've been thinking about the two skills you demonstrated. This one," she gestured to the rags, "and the energy pulse. From what I've experienced of the Suulh and heard from their stories, the Sahzade wouldn't have needed to use their abilities to deal with aggressive behavior caused by greed or anger. So why did we develop these abilities if our people are so peaceful?"

A ribbon of warmth unfurled in Libra's chest at Aurora's use of the term *our people.* Hearing her daughter embracing her rightful place with the Suulh on a subconscious level, despite all the walls Libra had erected to stop her from ever learning about them, showed just how expansive her daughter's heart was. A true Sahzade in every way. "I think you've been spending too much time on a starship. You've forgotten that Nature can be a force of great power, too."

Aurora placed her last rag, then straightened. "You mean storms?"

"Yes, violent ones. The sonea laanaa, our ancestral home, is in a tropical region of Feylahn, an area prone to tropical storms, much like Hawai'i. Before our people figured out how to build structures that offered protection from high winds and heavy rains, the Sahzade and aailee provided most of our protection."

"How does this skill come into play?" She indicated the rag circle.

"It's effective for dealing with heavy winds. By mimicking the winds and being able to control individual elements within the funnel, a Sahzade can redirect any dangerous debris away from where our people are sheltering. It can also be used to help small creatures caught up in the winds, bringing them to safety."

Aurora absorbed that bit of information. "You're right, I haven't dealt with storm conditions very often. Well, not in a situation where I could use my abilities, anyway. What about the energy pulses?"

"They're effective against falling debris."

"Why not just use a shield?"

"The other Sahzade would be."

"Other Sahzade?"

She sighed. "I've forced you to rely on yourself for so long, and withheld any knowledge of your ancestry, that you don't have any idea what life on Feylahn was like. That's my fault." She motioned for Aurora to join her in the center of the circle, settling on the deck.

She met Aurora's gaze, pushing back the tension squeezing her ribcage as she allowed her memories to rise to the surface. "When I was a child, my mother and I weren't the only Sahzade living at the sonea laanaa. My grandmother, great-grandmother, and great-great grandmother also spent time there."

Aurora's lips parted, a stunned look on her face. "I hadn't thought about how many..." She swallowed. "But of course we'd have extended family on Feylahn, not just Sooree and Kreestol."

"If they're still alive," she said softly, the words cutting into her heart. "Or they could be Necri like my mother." The image of her mother's vacant eyes staring at her without recognition ghosted through her mind, making her shudder.

She pushed the image aside. "It's our tradition for the older generations of Sahzade, Nedale, and aailee to travel to the outlying settlements on a regular basis, providing care, teaching the children how to make the most of their gifts, and looking for potential members of the future generations of aailee. Sometimes the oldest aailee would choose to form a new settlement, or remain with an existing one. Expansion was always a slow, thoughtful process. Because we're so interconnected to one another, no settlement was ever located more than a few days walk from another. No one wanted to be isolated and alone."

Aurora frowned. "Then why did you, Marina, and Gryphon choose to come to Earth but leave Skye and the rest of the Suulh on Gaia? Why not bring them with you?"

The conflicting emotions that question generated tugged at her. "It wasn't an easy choice, though if I'm completely honest, part of my motivation was putting distance between myself and Wolf. I wasn't even a teenager yet, still in my gathering cycle, but I already understood the unavoidable future he represented. I couldn't fully accept the idea of mating with him, so I used the excuse that the aailee remaining together as a group posed a greater risk of discovery. On Earth, with just the three of us, we could hide behind the planet's defenses and among the humans. That's one reason I never felt safe on Gaia. It was too much like Feylahn, too unprotected and unpopulated, too easy to imagine the Teeli taking over."

"Which is why the Sovereign chose it for her little test to expose my connection to the Suulh." Aurora's brow furrowed. "Were the other Sahzade at the sonea laanaa the night you escaped?"

"No." The details of that night were fractured in her memory, seen through the perspective of a child. But over the past few months she'd had some difficult conversations with Marina and Gryphon, gathering information she thought might be useful to Aurora in her quest to free the Suulh. "My mother decided it was wiser to send the others and their aailee to hide in the outlying settlements. If our plan to steal one of the Teeli ships had failed, she didn't want to risk all the Sahzade and Nedale being captured defending the sonea laanaa."

"So some of them might have escaped the Teeli?" The hope in Aurora's eyes reflected the tiny flame in her own heart.

Yes, it was a fool's hope, born of anguish and desperation considering the wraith her own mother had become, and the iron grip the Teeli had over Feylahn.

But that didn't stop her from holding onto it.

"Perhaps."

Fifty-Four

"So this is where you're storing *Gypsy*." Cade gazed down at the shuttle from the catwalk that spanned *Phoenix*'s converted cargo bay.

Nat had shown him and Williams to their cabins and taken *Phoenix* into the interstellar jump before offering to give them a tour of the ship. They'd started on the lower decks, which is where *Gypsy*'s home was located.

Gypsy sat in the center of the bay, a tight fit even with the surrounding space mostly empty. The bay had been designed for holding crates of supplies and small terrestrial land vehicles, not a good-sized planetary shuttle. Maneuvering in and out would take skill and precision, especially when he compared the shuttle's height and width to the bay doors. There wasn't a lot of clearance. The fact that Nat managed it without banging up the shuttle or her ship indicated her piloting abilities might rival his own.

"We made some adaptations so she'd be more comfortable here."

He glanced at her. She was gazing at the sturdy shuttle with a soft smile. The strong bond of affection he sensed in her emotional field was endearing, reminding him of how attached he'd become to *The Hawke*. He would have brought the shuttle with them on this mission if he could have figured out a place to store it. Even with its amazing conversion abilities, there was no way *The Hawke* would have been able to squeeze in beside *Gypsy*.

He braced his arms on the catwalk railing as he studied the shuttle. "She looks like she'd be fun to fly."

"She is, especially in atmo. That's when she really shines."

Cade smiled to himself. Translation – that's when she could fly *fast*. He'd found another devoted aerospace aficionado.

"Come on." Nat waved them toward the hatch. "I want you to meet Pete, my engineer."

The steady, smooth hum of the interstellar engines and the spick-and-span appearance of the engine room's workspace told Cade a lot about the man they were about to meet even before Nat called out to him.

"Pete, our guests are here."

A head poked out from behind one of the turbines, the soft pings of mechanical tinkering ceasing. "Oh, hey, Nat. Just workin' on the heat coils." Pete stepped into full view, pulling a rag out of the back pocket of his dark grey jumpsuit and wiping his hands. Smears of what looked like lubricant streaked his cheek and sleeves.

Cade recognized him immediately from the images Ifel had shared with him and Aurora on the Yruf ship. Pete was a lot older than Nat, maybe late fifties or early sixties based on the lines on his face and the white sprinkled in the ginger hair pulled back in a low ponytail. But his cheerful, open smile made him look a lot younger.

Cade stuck out his hand. "I'm Cade."

Pete grasped it with a firm, respectful grip. "I'm Pete. It's an honor to shake your hand." He tipped his head in Nat's direction. "I owe you for savin' her from the Setarips."

"Pete—" Nat's scowl didn't quite conceal the flush that rose to her cheeks.

Cade shook his head. "Nat did a lot to save herself and the Admiral. Aurora's the one who set everything in motion. I was just following her lead."

"And I've thanked her as well," Pete assured him. "Without you two, I'd still be stuck at a dead-end job workin' for my money-grubbin' relatives."

That sounded like an interesting story. He'd ask about it when the crew gathered for a meal.

"They didn't deserve you," Nat said with a disdainful sniff. "And *Phoenix* never would have flown without you."

The paternal smile that spread across Pete's weathered face showed just how much he loved his job and his captain. "Wouldn't wanna be anywhere else."

Nat's emotional field reflected the same kind of familial affection Cade sensed from Pete.

Williams stepped forward. "I'm Tam."

Pete shook his hand. "I owe you thanks, too. You've all done a lot to help us. I sure enjoyed meetin' Captain Hawke and her family when they visited *Vengeance*. Real nice folks. Didn't realize I was meetin' the owner of Far Horizons, though." A little wonder tinged his voice, like he'd seen a mythological hero, not a person.

Cade grinned. "Brendan isn't the type to grandstand about that. His family's owned the company since it was founded, so he views himself more as a custodian than an owner."

"That's a good way of seein' it. Real respectful."

"That's Brendan."

"I'm taking them on a tour," Nat said, "unless you need me for anything."

"Nope." Pete patted the nearby turbine casing. "She's runnin' like a dream." He nodded at Cade and Williams. "Nice meetin' ya'."

"You, too," Cade replied.

Nat led them up the aft stairs to C deck, then along a corridor before stepping through a wide doorway. The large room had two circular tables with chairs at the far end but nothing else. It looked like a combination ballroom and dining room.

"This room and the galley took the hit from the hull breach," she explained, gesturing to the exterior bulkhead, where a bank of viewports gave a view of the interstellar jump. A coat of gold paint that matched *Phoenix*'s exterior made the new bulkheads indistinguishable from the others. "We lost all but two of the original dining tables. I'm still deciding whether I want to replicate more of what we have or alter the layout and design."

Cade pivoted slowly to take in the whole room, then paused, peering at the faint markings on the expanse of gold paint covering the interior bulkhead opposite the viewports. He stepped closer, trying to make sense of what he was seeing. "What's going on here?"

He caught a flutter in Nat's emotional field, a moment of indecision and uncertainty that made him turn toward her.

A flare of defiance lit her eyes. "I'm going to paint a mural there."

"You paint murals?" He hadn't seen that coming.

Nat lifted one brow, the challenge in her aqua eyes flaring brighter. "You find that hard to believe?"

Actually, he didn't. Nat was a woman of many diverse talents. "No, it's just not a common skill. What are you going to paint?"

His easy acceptance seemed to catch her off guard. She rewarded him with a crooked smile. "The lifecycle of a phoenix."

"The mythological bird?"

"Mm-hmm. I painted a smaller version in my cabin during the ship's initial restoration, but here I can do so much more."

Cade turned back to the bulkhead. Now that she'd given him the clues he needed, he could make out the faint outlines of a fiery bird at the center of the long expanse, with smaller versions in different poses on either side. If the sketches were any indication, it would be beautiful. "Aurora would love to see it when it's done." So would he, for that matter.

Nat's emotional field sparkled, but she quickly schooled her expression. "I'll keep that in mind."

Uh-huh. He'd bet good money that Aurora would be getting pinged before the paint was dry.

Williams turned toward the door at the center of the aft bulkhead and gave an audible sniff. "Smells like someone's baking."

"That would be Marlin," Nat replied. "Ginger snaps are one of his specialties."

Cade had already met Marlin the day Aurora unmasked the Sovereign. He had been on *Gypsy* with Nat when she'd flown Cade, Aurora, and Justin to the *Starhawke*.

But the man he found bustling around *Phoenix*'s galley looked like Marlin's younger, more energetic brother. Gone were the gaunt cheeks, flat expression, and nervous tics. He smiled at them as they stepped into the galley. "Welcome! I hope you brought your appetites because I just put two batches of veggie lasagna in the oven."

"I always bring my appetite, especially when it smells this good," Williams assured him. "I'm Tam."

"Marlin." He shook Williams' hand, then focused on Cade, the lines around his eyes crinkling as he smiled. It made his round face look cherubic. "You're in much better shape than the last time I saw you."

Cade returned the smile. "So are you."

"Good eating will do that. Can I interest you in ginger snaps? Fresh out of the oven." He pointed to the cooling rack where the cookies sat in neat rows. "Help yourselves."

Nobody had to be told twice.

Cade took a bite and made a low hum of approval. "Very good." His gaze swept the gleaming metal surfaces of the galley. "How much of this is new since the restoration?"

"You can't tell?" Marlin asked, clearly pleased.

He did another sweep, assessing. "Not really, although the refrigeration unit looks new."

Marlin nodded. "We lost almost everything along the exterior bulkhead, including the cold storage unit. I thought some of it would be irreplaceable until our next stop at a station or colony, but thanks to Un—" He cut off, shooting a worried look at Nat. "Uh..."

She waved a hand. "They both know about Unity, the Yruf, and how they helped us with the repairs."

Marlin's shoulders slumped in relief. "Okay, good. Anyway, they were able to gather all the items that were blown out in the debris field and return them to us in the airlock. Some of the items just needed a good cleaning, but the severely damaged components we put in reclamation to produce replacements. Without their assistance, I'm not sure we'd even have life support in here yet, let alone a functional cooking space."

"They're very helpful," Cade agreed.

"Thank you!"

Unity's reply from the ship's speakers had everyone looking up.

"Unity's integrated with our comm system, since we don't have any of their mobile units onboard," Nat explained. "It's how we communicate with them."

"We could get you a mobile unit if you want one!"

Cade hid his smile behind his hand. Unity's unfettered exuberance with *Phoenix*'s crew made him feel right at home.

"Uh..." Unity had caught Nat flat-footed. "Let me think about it."

"That was something I needed to talk to you about anyway," Cade told her. "I brought U-2 with me. They're in my cabin, but I wasn't certain how your crew would feel about them moving around the ship with me."

Nat's mouth pinched. "There's only one person who might object. You'll be meeting her next. Let's see how that goes."

Marlin made a face. "Can I show them my garden first?"

"If you have time."

"Sure. I was going to head there soon to pick greens for the salad anyway." Marlin led the group back through the dining room and into the corridor. "This is where I'm growing the plants from the *Starhawke*'s greenhouse."

Marlin's emotional field filled with joy as a profusion of green appeared in a partially open space to the right. The upper tiers of slotted hydroponics tubing held miniature versions of plants that grew in abundance in the *Starhawke*'s greenhouse, the subtle hum of motors circulating water throughout the system. The plants on the lower tiers were in soil, the pleasant earthy scent pushing back the metallic tang of recycled air.

Cade brushed his fingers over one of the fluffy heads of lettuce. "This is impressive. You've done a lot with limited space."

"Thanks. I wanted to get it done before... well..." He glanced at Nat.

Her expression remained carefully neutral. "We'd planned to have you all over for a small celebration right after we finished the repairs. But we tabled that idea when Aurora left."

She was doing a good job of keeping her disappointment from showing on her face, but it marred her emotional field like a bruise. Cade didn't think it was the lack of a party that was triggering that emotion, but rather a desire to have Aurora see the ship. That's why she'd lit up earlier when he'd mentioned showing Aurora the mural. Nat wanted her approval, much like a kid sister trying to impress an older sibling. Or so he assumed, since he'd never had any siblings. "We should do it as soon as we're all back together."

"You think so?" Nat's tone was mildly interested, but her emotional field radiated eagerness.

"Definitely." By then, the *Starhawke* should be close to recharged, giving them even more reason to celebrate.

They left Marlin to collect food for the meal, continuing past the forward stairway to a cozy bar area on the ship's port side.

Williams gave a low whistle. "This is *nice*."

Burgundy plush chairs that looked brand new were grouped around low round tables comprised of glass tops attached to bisected wine barrels. A small bar in the forward corner was surrounded by glass-fronted storage compartments displaying bottles of wine. The overall effect beckoned guests to settle in for good conversation and a glass of something delightful.

Which three people were doing right now. The murmur of voices stopped, all three setting their glasses on the table and rising to their feet.

Nat moved between the two groups, looking for all the world like a referee at an athletic event as her gaze shifted between them. "Cade, Dr. Williams," she nodded to each of them in turn, "this is Itorye, *Vengeance*'s first mate, Dr. Patel, and Gavin."

He noticed Nat chose to use Williams' title, rather than his first name, unlike the way he'd introduced himself to Pete and Marlin.

He recognized all three of them from the images Ifel had shown him. He focused on the woman Nat had identified by her professional title, who was regarding them with a thinly veiled resignation that was covering a solid foundation of fear.

The cause was obvious. She was the one who'd created Alec. Union law would see her and Alec locked away for life if her secret got out.

He would do everything he could to ease those fears. Judging by the emotional reactions of Itorye and Gavin, Patel was the one Nat thought might object to U-2's presence.

Patel's chin lifted, her gaze direct as she sized him up. "You're younger than I expected."

Gavin shot her an exasperated look. "Darsha—"

Cade bit back a smile. Thanks to all the time he spent surrounded by Aurora's energy field, the fine lines that had started to show on his face a year ago were gone. The rest of his team had benefitted from Suulh healing as well. They all looked younger than they were. "I'm thirty-one," he informed her.

Her eyes narrowed.

"Dr. Patel paid for the refurbishment in here," Nat said louder than necessary, a clear move to derail wherever Patel was headed next. "This area was a mess the first time Isin and I stumbled past it." She surveyed the room and the corridor, the hiccup in her emotional field indicating the memories were not exactly pleasant. "But thanks to her, *Phoenix* cleaned up really well."

The public praise was clearly a tactic to mollify Patel. Cade was pretty sure Patel knew it, but her emotional field settled anyway, the guards on the ramparts no longer aiming arrows at Cade's chest.

Itorye picked up her wine glass and handed Patel hers. "Let's move to the lounge where we'll have more room." She gestured to the wide viewports and seating areas visible over the low wall that separated the wine bar from the spacious lounge.

"Can I get you anything?" Gavin asked, picking up his own glass and approaching Cade and Williams. "Wine, beer, iced tea?" The glass he held looked like it contained the third option.

"Iced tea would be great." Cade associated tea with Aurora. It was rapidly becoming one of his favorite drinks.

"Same here," Williams said. "I'll help you."

"Nat?" Gavin lifted his glass in her direction. "Your usual?"

Nat gave a tight nod, her gaze on where Patel and Itorye were waiting in the corridor. "Thanks, Gavin."

Cade fell into step with Nat as she followed Patel and Itorye into the lounge. The pseudo-wood flooring throughout the room gave a warm, homey effect, and an open area to the aft surrounded by two and three person tables looked like it was intended for dancing. A small stage along the aft bulkhead complemented the social entertainment vibe.

On the end that bordered the wine bar, the seating was set up for larger groups, with semi-circular couches interspersed with plush chairs. Itorye and Patel settled onto one of the couches. Cade chose the couch directly across from them, while Nat sat in the chair to his left.

Patel was still eyeing him warily, so he decided to take the focus off her for a while. "It's good to finally meet you, Itorye. I've heard your name so many times it feels strange that we've never met."

Itorye's smile was reserved but genuine. "I feel the same about you. You played a pivotal role in getting us all to this point."

Something in her tone and the flow in her emotional field made him suspect she was referring to the Yruf rather than the part he'd played in freeing Nat. "It's been an interesting year."

"Yes, it has." Her gaze slid briefly to Patel. The emotion that rippled through her field was unmistakable, telling him a lot about the relationship between the two. At first glance, he'd taken them for good friends. Now he knew it went much deeper than that.

Patel sat forward, hands clasped in front of her, her wine glass untouched on the coffee table. "What exactly is your background, Cade?"

Her directness could have been off-putting if he wasn't sensing the emotions behind it. She seemed to be gathering data to maintain a feeling of control of the situation. The best way to get her on his side was to be completely open and honest. "I was trained at the Academy as a pilot and was recruited by Admiral Schreiber to join his Elite Unit right after graduation. That's the work I've been doing ever since, although my public records list me as a pilot for the Rescue Corps."

"What does the Elite Unit do?" she asked with all the grace of an interrogator.

His presence was really freaking her out. He focused on projecting an aura of calm. "We serve and protect the Admiral and the Fleet from threats foreign and domestic. Right now that means protecting the Admiral from those who framed him for treason. That's why we're on this mission. Captain Montgomery was targeted because she's an advocate for the Admiral."

Patel's lips parted, her emotional field churning with anxiety and uncertainty. "But isn't it your job to uphold Union law?"

He knew she was thinking about Alec. He wanted to ask her about him, but it was too soon to bring that sensitive topic into the discussion. Instead, he held her gaze and projected every iota of sincerity he possessed. "I'm not a lawyer, judge, or Fleet security officer. My job is to uphold the ideals of the Union and protect those who defend those ideals, not enforce its laws. You have nothing to fear from me."

Fifty-Five

Patel was processing Cade's words when Williams and Gavin joined them.

"Here we are."

Gavin handed Nat her beer, a dark lager she'd stocked in while they were on Osiris. However, he surprised her by sitting right next to Cade, while Williams took the chair across from her.

The move was too well choreographed by the pair to not have been pre-planned. Gavin was sending a message to Patel that he was literally and figuratively on Cade's side.

Nat caught the smile that flitted over Itorye's lips before it vanished like mist.

Patel, however, pressed her lips together in displeasure. "Do you often inspire fear?" she asked Cade, her haughty tone clearly implying she wasn't afraid of him.

A bald-faced lie. Nat could see the slight tremor in her hands. That's why she was keeping them clasped together and ignoring her drink.

"That's never my goal," Cade replied smoothly. He didn't seem the least bit irritated by Patel's attitude. "My team exists to help people, not intimidate them."

"What type of people?" She managed to imply it was a very narrow segment of the population, those who needed protection of their *interests*, not their *existence*.

Cade took a sip from his glass, unperturbed. "Those who need our special skillsets. We're often sent to places where others have been physically harmed or are under threat of harm."

That set Patel back a bit. "And you protect them?"

"Yes. We tend to work behind the scenes, so most of the people we encounter have no idea who we really are or who we work for."

"So you could be spies."

Gavin set his glass down with a thunk. "Darsha, that's enough."

Patel's dark eyes flashed with irritation. "It's a fair question. Not that a spy would admit to being a spy."

Nat focused on Cade, watching to see how he'd react to the accusation. That's when she caught the slightly unfocused look in his eyes as he gazed at Patel.

She knew that look. Had seen it in Aurora's eyes on multiple occasions. She knew what it meant.

Was Cade a flippin' empath, too?

"Let me tell you a story." Cade settled against the back of the couch, his drink held casually in his hands. "Late last year, my team was on a mission that would definitely count as spying. We were tracking Bare'Kold, the Teeli delegate who had manipulated Lt.

Magee, the Admiral's PA." He glanced at Nat. "Have you told everyone about the Teeli?"

"Yep, before you came onboard. I told them about the Suulh, too." She'd taken advantage of Patel's relatively good mood following the discussion with Alec to broach both subjects. Patel had accepted the news with a resignation that had felt like the calm before the storm. Hopefully that storm wasn't about to flatten them all.

Cade nodded. "Delegate Bare'Kold rendezvoused with an Ecilam ship and a Teeli cruiser deep in Fleet space. We had placed a listening device on Bare'Kold so we could hear what was being said during his conversation with the Sovereign."

Nat flicked a glance at Patel. Her fingers were now mottled red from the pressure she was exerting to keep them from shaking. If Cade was trying to intimidate her, it was working.

"Right as the gathering broke up, a massive, previously camouflaged ship appeared behind us."

Nat choked on her beer, sending her into a paroxysm of wet, hacking coughs. She shot Cade a hard look through watering eyes. He did *not* want to continue his story.

His mouth softened in a faint smile as he held her gaze. "It's okay, Nat. She needs to know."

"But—"

"Trust me."

She did. It was Patel she didn't trust.

Cade shifted his focus back to Patel. "I'd never seen anything like it. And then the ship went modular, separating into a bunch of smaller ships. One of them tracked us, refusing to let us leave and eventually taking control of *Gladiator*'s systems. We didn't know it at the time, but that was our first encounter with Unity."

Patel's back went ramrod straight. "They attacked you?" she hissed.

"No, just took control of the ship. They wanted to communicate with us, and taking control ensured no one got hurt — us or them. They attempted to do the same thing with the Ecilam and Teeli ships, but the Sovereign is very fond of her auto-destructs. Bare'Kold's yacht and the Teeli cruiser got away, but the Ecilam ship and the Teeli warships were all destroyed by the Sovereign's hand."

Patel's breath hitched, her body winding even tighter.

"*Gladiator* was brought onboard the main ship. We had no idea what to expect, so we armed ourselves. That ended up being pointless. Unity's control over *Gladiator* allowed them to vent the atmosphere, which would have rendered us all unconscious, preventing us from harming them. That's when I gave the order to stand down and went with one of Unity's mobile units to meet with their leader."

The whites of Patel's eyes stood out against her russet skin, the tremor she'd been concealing in her hands now visible in her jaw. "They're not Kraed, are they?" It came out as a strangled stage whisper.

"No," Cade said softly, "but they are friends. Pacifists, actually, which is why they captured us the way they did. They are the epitome of *do no harm*." He waited a beat, studying her, before continuing. "They thought we were aligned with the Teeli at first, partially because of my hair color." He pointed to his roguish blond locks. "They had trouble distinguishing between a human with blond hair and a Teeli with white hair. But once it became clear we were fighting against the Teeli, everything changed. They've been working with us ever since. More than that, they've become our friends. I would trust them with my life, and the lives of everyone I care about. And I have. None of us would be here without their help."

The background hum of the interstellar jump and the clink of settling ice in Gavin's glass was the only sound as Patel stared at Cade. She licked her lips, looking tentative in a way Nat had never seen before. "Who are they?"

Cade's lips curved in a closed-mouth smile. "The Yruf."

Patel's eyes snapped even wider. "The Yruf?"

Cade nodded. "They're the pacifist, non-violent faction of the Setarips. Their leader, Ifel, wants to reunite the Setarips and broker peace."

Itorye shifted closer as Patel's entire body began to shake.

Patel didn't even seem to notice. "And you... believe that?"

"One-hundred percent. We've been through a lot together over the past few months. The Yruf haven't *told* us who they are, they've *shown* us. They're the ones who helped incapacitate Devries so we could rescue the children. They're the ones who snuck *Vengeance* into the system so it could protect *Phoenix*. And they're the ones who stabilized *Phoenix* and helped with the repairs."

Patel sagged, leaning heavily into the circle of Itorye's arm like the strength had drained out of her.

"I've spent a lot of time with Unity," Cade continued. "One of their mobile units, the one we've dubbed U-2, is almost always with me. I've seen them interacting in a lot of different situations with a lot of different people. They're always focused on compassion, empathy, and assisting those in need. The Yruf created them that way as a reflection of who they are. They would never knowingly harm anyone. Neither would the Yruf." His gaze never left Patel. "If you give them your trust, they will do everything in their power to protect those you care about from harm."

Patel looked like she'd been flattened by a shuttle. She opened her mouth, then closed it, staring at Cade the entire time. Then with a forced exhale, she leaned forward, picked up her glass, and drained the rest of her wine in two big swallows.

Itorye's brows lifted, but she didn't comment. Neither did Gavin. Everyone seemed to be waiting to see what Patel would do next.

Patel studied the empty glass, twirling the stem between her fingers. She cleared her throat. "I can't help noticing I'm the only one reacting to this news." Her gaze lifted to Gavin first, then flicked to Itorye. "How long have you known?"

Itorye met the attack head on. "Since shortly after our discussion with Alec about the shadow ships."

Hurt and betrayal flashed across Patel's face. "Alec told you?"

Itorye shook her head. "Isin did."

Patel absorbed that, then turned to Gavin. "And you?"

"Nat told me shortly after she learned about them."

A stone wall slid over Patel's face, clearing all emotion. It was disturbing in a way her usual explosions weren't. "So, my ignorance was deliberate."

Cade leaned towards her, that unfocused look in his eyes again.

But Nat beat him to the punch. "Our connection with the Yruf has to remain secret."

Patel turned that stony façade on her.

It was like looking at a marble statue of a vengeful goddess, one about to strike down the mortal who had crossed her. "The Sovereign doesn't know we're working with the Yruf. Neither do the Teeli or the other Setarip factions. It's imperative we keep it that way. If they find out, they'll start hunting the Yruf. We'll lose our advantage, and the Yruf will be in danger. Aurora hadn't planned to say anything to any of us about them, but the situation with Devries and the damage to *Phoenix* forced her hand. She was trying to limit who knew about the Yruf to keep the secret from getting out."

Patel's stone mask visibly thickened, her voice grating like metal on concrete. "Considering how we met, it's ironic that you think I can't be trusted to keep secrets."

Nat flinched. "You *can* be volatile." Keeping her own secret was one thing. Keeping someone else's was something else.

"Now that you know." Cade set his glass on the coffee table, then rested his elbows on his knees. "How do you feel about it?"

Patel regarded him with that same emotionless detachment. "Why do you care?"

Cade gave her a rueful smile. "Because how you feel about the Yruf will have a direct impact on me. I'm the one who told you. If that becomes a problem, Aurora will not be happy with me."

Patel frowned, the first indication of an emotional reaction. "Why *did* you tell me? You didn't have to. Clearly," she added, shooting a glare first at Gavin, then Nat, then Itorye. Even Williams got targeted before she returned her attention to Cade.

"I had a feeling I could trust you. Am I wrong?"

A *feeling*. Definitely an empath.

Patel peered at him, still twirling her glass. Cade was doing a great job of disarming her. "You don't even know me."

Cade shrugged, like that was inconsequential. "Will you keep the Yruf a secret?"

Patel's eyes narrowed. "What do you want in return?"

That made Cade chuckle. "It's not transactional. No quid pro quo."

"No threats?" A barb entered Patel's voice.

Cade sobered immediately. "Never." His gaze held hers. "We won't betray your trust, either."

Patel's fingers curled around her glass. Her body tensed, her eyes twin tractor beams locked on Cade's face. The moment stretched out, the air thickening with each passing second.

Nat bit her lip to keep from saying something to break the uncomfortable silence.

Cade seemed unfazed, watching Patel like he already knew the outcome.

Maybe he did.

Without breaking eye contact, Patel let out a gusty sigh, her shoulders dropping. "You're an interesting man, Cade." It was unclear whether it was a compliment. "I can't tell if you're a thrill-seeker or a youthful idealist, but against my better judgment, I believe you. The Yruf's secret is safe with me."

Fifty-Six

Dr. Patel was an interesting test case for Cade. If he'd been relying on reading her body language, which is what he'd been trained to do, he wouldn't have thought he had a chance of leading her to their side. But her emotional reactions had told a different story, especially the ones she was trying hard to conceal.

Underneath her bluster, she craved connection, community. But because of her fear for Alec's safety, she avoided acknowledging or expressing it. That she'd accepted Itorye's silent support during the difficult discussion provided evidence of the strong bond between the two women. "Thank you, Dr. Patel."

"Yes, thank you," Unity seconded over the ship's speakers.

Patel's gaze flicked up, a burst of irritation painting her emotional field. But it washed away just as quickly, like a twitch she couldn't control rather than an honest reaction. Her expression grew pensive. "I haven't been very nice to you, Unity, yet you've been unfailingly polite to me. I also never thanked you for saving all our lives."

Technically she still hadn't.

But Unity chose to ignore the way she phrased the comment. "You're welcome."

Her gaze dropped back to Cade. "You said you've spent a lot of time with Unity." A shrewdness entered her expression. "How have you reconciled being around an illegal non-biological in Union space when you work for the Fleet?"

Now they were getting to the heart of the matter. "I could argue that since the Yruf aren't Union citizens, the ban on non-biologicals doesn't apply to them. But that's a semantics argument, not what I really believe." He settled against the couch, resting his ankle on his knee. "I also said it's not my job to enforce Union law, but I get your point. In the eyes of many, Unity is illegal and my association with them is against Union law."

"And you work for the head of the Fleet."

He nodded. "It's a complex issue. Human history with A.I. has been fraught, but in my opinion, that's a result of *human* attitudes, not a result of the existence of A.I. themselves. Meeting Unity reinforced that belief. They live in harmony with the Yruf, symbiotically helping and supporting each other. The A.I. humans created were willing to have that kind of relationship. *We* were the ones who insisted on treating them like servants or slaves. We missed an amazing opportunity to help our species grow and evolve. I completely understand why they left."

"And the ban on A.I. development?" Patel's dark-eyed gaze drilled into him. "How do you feel about that?"

He considered his words carefully. "I think it's an excellent way to prevent the power-hungry from creating an A.I. servant or slave. We've seen far too much of that in our history. But I don't think it should apply to someone who creates a symbiotic non-biological who has rights and free will, where the goal is to establish a relationship with them similar to the one Unity and the Yruf have."

She set down her glass, leaning closer. "And would you defend such an entity from the Union forces who would seek to harm them?" Her emotional field gave off serious mama bear vibes.

Good thing he wasn't a threat to her cub. "Yes, I would." He focused on projecting his sincerity to her. "I would defend the rights to existence and freedom for both the person who created such an entity, and the entity they created, the same as any other Union citizen."

Patel held his gaze, taking his measure. Then her focus shifted to Williams. "What about you?"

He spread his hands. "I'm a doctor. I swore an oath to protect and preserve life. It doesn't matter to me whether it's biological or not. Humans could learn a lot from Unity and the Yruf. Everyone on the *Starhawke* agrees with that." His voice slid into the tone he used to sooth agitated patients. "*Including* Admiral Schreiber."

Patel's shoulders lowered a fraction, although her posture was still defensive. Her gaze flipped between Cade and Williams. "You already know why I'm asking, don't you?"

Cade nodded. "But it's your story to tell. Or not. Your choice." Although having Alec's existence out in the open would make things a lot simpler. Williams hadn't met him yet.

Patel took several slow breaths, her emotional field swinging between hope and anxiety. Then her jaw firmed. "Alec? Do you want to greet our guests?"

Alec's projection appeared on the couch beside her. His outline looked a little crisper, his features more opaque than the last time Cade had seen him. At a quick glance you might mistake him for a biological.

Seeing him side by side with Patel, the familial resemblance became pronounced — same face and eye shape, same strong jaw, although Alec's was covered by a close-cropped beard. His tawny skin was a few shades lighter than Patel's, his dark hair much shorter. When Alec met his gaze, Cade was reminded that his sandy brown eyes were the exact same color as Gavin's.

"Hello, Cade." Alec gave him an easy smile. "Hello, Dr. Williams. It's a pleasure to have you onboard *Phoenix*."

It looked like Alec was avoiding revealing that he'd met Cade previously on the *Starhawke*. He could roll with that. "Hello, Alec. Quite a ship you have here."

Laughter danced in Alec's eyes. "Thank you."

"Alec's training to pilot *Phoenix*," Nat cut in, shooting Cade a pointed look. "He's the one who took us into the interstellar jump."

"Is that so?" He didn't need to fake his surprise. "That was a pretty smooth transition from main engines to interstellar." He'd expected a smooth ride from Nat, but knowing her non-biological protégé had been at the helm impressed him.

"Nat's an excellent teacher." Alec gazed at her with adoration. "And *Phoenix* is a great ship."

"Are you fully integrated with *Phoenix?*" Williams asked.

"Not like Unity is with the Yruf ships. More like the way they are with *Gladiator*. I can control some objects on a limited basis, like the pilot's chair on the bridge, but I'm still developing my skills to do multiple tasks at once with precision." Alec's smile was self-effacing. "As my parents keep reminding me, I'm still learning." He glanced at Patel and Itorye, then Gavin.

Gavin lifted his glass, tipping it in Alec's direction. "And exceeding our expectations at every turn."

That gave Cade the opening he'd hoped for to flesh out what Ifel had told him. "So you played a role in Alec's development, too?"

"I did. I've been working as Darsha's assistant for what... almost fifteen years now?" he asked her.

Patel nodded. "Gavin created the parameters that made Alec's matrix possible. It was the piece of the puzzle that had been eluding me."

Gavin gazed at her over the rim of his glass. "We worked together for two years before she trusted me enough to tell me what our real goal was."

Patel lifted her chin. "I had to be certain of your character."

Gavin grinned. "Oh, I know. I don't blame you. Your caution was warranted. Without it, I'm not sure Alec would exist. Or that we'd be here, now." He gestured to indicate *Phoenix*. "It's been quite a journey."

Williams glanced between them. "How did you hook up with Nat?"

"Patel hired us," Nat replied. "Me and Isin. I transported Patel on *Phoenix*, and Isin took *Vengeance* to fetch Alec's transport cube from a remote, undisclosed location. Of course we had no idea what, or rather who," she shot an apologetic look at Alec, "we were transporting, and we encountered some... complications along the way. But eventually we met up with Gavin on Osiris. All three of them decided they wanted to stay on as crew."

"You've been busy since we dropped you at Troi," Cade commented.

"So have you. Which brings us to our current task." She turned to Itorye. "Are you ready to transform me and Cade into a happy honeymoon couple?"

Cade chuckled at the distaste in Nat's voice. "Gee, thanks for making a guy feel wanted."

Nat's face scrunched up. "It's not you. It's what she has planned for me."

Amusement sparkled in Itorye's eyes. "We'll need more than one iteration, so you'll have alternate images for your IDs."

Cade nodded. "Unity can transmit the images to *Gladiator* so Reynolds can finish our IDs, but we'll need to rendezvous with my team outside the system to physically take possession of the IDs before we reach Hydra One."

Gavin shifted on the couch to face him. "We're all set to play tourists. Itorye will stay on *Phoenix* with Alec, and Darsha and I will leave the ship ahead of you. We already have alternate IDs from when we were smuggling Alec."

Nat's crew was even better prepared than he'd expected. "What about Marlin and Pete?" he asked Nat.

"They'll be leaving as crew with Dr. Williams, and taking along large supply crates they'll be filling on the station. That'll make the smuggling crate less conspicuous when they all return together."

Which left only one thing. "Itorye, we're all yours."

Fifty-Seven

"So, this is it?"

Aurora nodded in response to Micah's question, never taking her gaze off the planet that steadily filled the front curve of *Vengeance*'s wraparound bridgescreen. Smears of white massed over large splotches of ocean blue and the mottled green that covered most of the land. An occasional blob of purple-brown denoted mountains scattered like fallen meteorites.

Objectively, it was pretty. But there was nothing objective about her emotional reaction, other than the way her gut objected to being back here.

The first time she'd been brought to this planet, she'd been a prisoner dragged along on Tnaryt's short leash. Taking in the details of the planet from orbit hadn't been an option during the flight down in Nat's shuttle.

Once on the surface, Tnaryt had forced her through the dense thickets of green, looming over her, taunting her every step of the way. The only bright spot had been the evening rain. The warm, cleansing drops had washed away the grime from her skin and hair, refreshing her body and soul.

Unfortunately, the battle with Kreestol in the saltwater river that had followed, ending in Cade's electrocution and the Sovereign's escape, had sucked the life right out of her.

Afterward, she'd had plenty of time to study the planet from the *Starhawke*'s observation lounge while she'd been processing the Sovereign's identity and avoiding Cade.

She'd thought she'd prepared herself for the emotional impact of returning to this place of pain.

She was wrong.

The darkness of those moments crept across her skin with icy fingers, the shadows swallowing the light. Her gut twisted, her heart pounding uncomfortably in her chest.

She almost leapt out of her skin when Micah's fingers wrapped around her hand.

"You're not alone," he murmured.

Her body didn't get the message. Her heart thumped like a rabbit on steroids. But his touch, the energetic connection that bound them together, pushed back the feelings of isolation and despair that haunted her.

Turning her head, she discovered Micah wasn't the only one focused on her rather than the bridgescreen. Her parents and Celia were watching her intently. Even Iolana and Kai were giving her sidelong looks. Threads of concern wove through their emotional fields.

She consciously relaxed the muscles of her neck and rolled her shoulders.

"Does this planet have a name?" Micah asked, clearly trying to distract her.

"No." She'd felt a driving need to research the star system back when the *Starhawke* had been in orbit. Anything to keep from dealing with the bigger issues that had kicked her in the teeth. "Just catalog designations, since this system is in Teeli space, not Fleet space, a lightyear past the border. That's why I've referred to it as Tnaryt's Camp." Another reason she wouldn't have to worry about anyone stumbling upon Mirko and Manchado.

For non-Teeli, passing through the boundary of the Fleet-Teeli border beacons without proper authorization was a felony. The establishment of the beacons along the border had been a condition the Teeli had imposed when they'd joined the Union. Ostensibly, it was because they were pacifists and claimed they were unprepared to deal with any unsavory elements who might cross their borders and cause trouble.

In reality, it had been the Teeli's method to prevent anyone from stumbling on the truth.

The only reason *Vengeance* had arrived without triggering an alert to the Fleet and Teeli was thanks to the Yruf ships camouflaging them. She suspected that when Tnaryt had brought his ship here, the Sovereign had temporarily turned off the beacons that covered the area between Gallows Edge and this system, preventing the Fleet from being notified of an illegal crossing. The Sovereign wouldn't have wanted to draw attention to what was taking place on this planet.

That action had also allowed *Gladiator* to pass through undetected while it was shadowing Tnaryt's ship. Leaving the system hadn't been an issue, since the beacons only tracked movement one way – into Teeli space. Ships could enter Fleet space whenever they wanted.

"Establishing geosynchronous orbit over the coordinates Nat provided," Lupe informed them from the navigation console.

The familiar landmasses took shape as Lupe guided the ship into position.

An arctic wind buffeted her, making her shudder.

Micah released her hand and wrapped an arm around her shoulders, pulling her into a sideways hug. "You ready to show me around my first alien planet, sis?"

His question drew her attention away from the bridgescreen. "What about Gaia?" He'd been with her when they'd visited their relatives there.

"Doesn't count. Too close to Earth and already colonized. There are no humans down there." He lifted his chin in the direction of the planet.

That was very true. But there were several Etah Setarips she wanted to avoid.

"It's our first alien planet, too," Iolana added, motioning to her dad. "I barely slept a wink last night, wondering what it would be like."

"See?" Micah smiled, giving her another squeeze. "Exciting stuff."

He made a good point. Despite her negative history with this place, for others, it was a new experience. She'd much rather join in their enthusiasm than drag them into her trepidation. "You're right. It's a big deal." She glanced over her shoulder at Isin, seated in the captain's chair. "Anything we need to discuss before we head out?"

He reclined in his chair, but his nonchalance didn't extend to his emotional field. He was keyed up, too. If she had to guess, he was thinking about Nat, and coming to grips with the fact she'd almost died here when Tnaryt's ship went down in a disintegrating fireball. Or maybe he was avoiding thinking about it, just like she was avoiding thinking about Cade lying motionless beside the saltwater river.

He shook his head. "You're good to go."

Their first stop was their cabin. U-1 was tucked into the duffel on Micah's bunk, their top peeking out like a child's plush toy. Since Micah had to take Unity down to *Starlet* for them to recharge, and they hadn't been needed much during the journey, they'd operated in low power mode most of the time to conserve energy.

They rose from the duffel and twirled. "You're back!"

"We are. Ready to show us what the Yruf have scouted out?"

"You bet!"

Ifel had sent several Yruf scout ships to the planet ahead of *Vengeance* to check the terrain and locate possible locations for rehoming Mirko and Manchado.

She was incredibly grateful for their help in speeding up this process. Her second attempt to talk to Mirko about the accommodations on the planet had been as fruitless as the first. She'd finally admitted defeat, leaving all future discussions to her dad, but remaining in the corridor outside the brig during those sessions. Tracking the emotional responses from Mirko and Manchado while her dad dealt with them had given her a new appreciation for the depths of his patience and his resistance to provocation.

She'd conferred with him, Celia, Isin, and Sweep yesterday, and the consensus was to set up two camps spaced at least five kilometers apart. That way, Mirko and Manchado could choose to work together or not, but they'd have to put some effort into reaching each other. It wasn't elegant, but it would have to suffice.

"Any sign of the Etah?" When she'd last left the planet, four of Tnaryt's females were unaccounted for. Cade had confirmed the fifth had been killed by the Sovereign's Ecilam soldiers, and she suspected another had been, too, before the Ecilam had converged behind her at the river's edge.

"Yes!" Unity twirled again. "We've located three Etah on the surface. Ifel's still deciding on the best way to approach them."

"How close are they to the areas we'll be visiting?" *Starlet* would be invisible to them, but a chance encounter on the ground wouldn't be beneficial for any of them, now or in the future after Mirko and Manchado were in residence.

"Not close at all. We focused on areas where there's an abundance of freshwater streams and rivers. We knew you wanted to avoid the salt river."

Her ribcage tightened, her heart tapping out a syncopated beat as the memory of Kreestol pinning her underwater assailed her. "Any idea why that particular river is salty?"

The words come out stilted. She also noticed Micah, Celia, and Iolana were watching her closely.

"From what we've seen, it's caused by the species of tree that grows along the river. The trees take salt from the soil, which collects in their leaves and drops into the water. Since it's a shallow river, the salt content is concentrated."

"Do those trees grow anywhere else?"

"Nope, just that area."

A low growl tickled her throat, but she cut it off with a frustrated sigh. If Tnaryt had chosen any other location for the meeting with the Sovereign, Cade wouldn't have gotten electrocuted, and he and Justin would have been her backup when she confronted the Sovereign. They might have ended the conflict right there.

Instead, a cavalcade of pain and suffering had spiraled out from Tnaryt's decision to hold the meeting beneath the canopy of a species of salt-loving trees.

The knowledge dug into her like cactus spines. Not that it mattered. She couldn't change the past. All she could do was focus on the present.

With Unity stowed safely in Micah's duffel, they met her parents and Kai in the corridor and headed down to the transport bay.

Starlet sat close to the *Dagger*. The streamlined shape and silvery hull of *Vengeance*'s fighter gave more than a subtle nod to its namesake. *Starlet* wasn't a small shuttle, but next to the *Dagger*, she looked like a baby sister sitting beside her much larger big brother.

Aurora claimed the co-pilot's seat beside her dad, while the rest of the group settled into the main cabin. As soon as Micah opened the duffel, Unity tucked themselves into their charging alcove just behind the cockpit.

Her dad's almost giddy emotional field flowed over her, reminding her Micah and Iolana weren't the only ones eager to explore. She summoned a smile. "Excited about flying *Starlet* or about checking out a new planet?"

He returned the smile. "Both. It's been a long time since I've set foot on alien soil."

Because he'd sacrificed the opportunity to travel to new worlds when he'd chosen to stay at Stoneycroft with her mom, and later, to raise Micah on Hawai'i. He'd even distanced himself from Far Horizons and all the opportunities it offered.

Knowing how much he shared her passion for the stars, the magnitude of that decision was tough to contemplate.

Maybe this experience with him and Micah, and her mom too, would help heal the painful wounds her time on this planet had inflicted.

Fifty-Eight

"What are your first impressions?"

Celia's lyrical voice flowed over Micah like a caress. He turned to find her watching him with the analytical look that indicated she was cataloguing every nuance of his response. "I was wondering if this is what Earth looked like before humans proliferated and started building large metropolises."

From space, if you ignored the lack of familiar landmasses, the planet resembled an uninhabited Earth with a lot more plant life.

Celia nodded. "The stars are very similar. This one's a fraction larger and more luminous, but the planet likely developed much like Earth did. I'm sure geologists and paleontologists would have a field day here. If they ever got the chance," she added in an undertone.

"Well, this marine biologist is ready to explore." He wasn't sure if they'd have time to check out the planet's oceans – although he'd love to get Adel to one – but he'd settle for rivers and streams. He was very curious to find out if the native creatures resembled their Earth counterparts. His success talking to the wildlife in the Yruf biosphere gave him hope he'd be able to communicate with the wildlife here, too.

He glanced out the side viewport as the light in the cabin changed. The shuttle had reached the planet's atmosphere. The view became obscured as flickering yellow, orange, and red ribbons streaked past the viewport. He shivered. It was like dropping into the middle of a beach bonfire.

"This is so freaky," Birdie commented from her seat behind him.

Celia's low chuckle made him shiver in a different way. "Do it a few hundred times and you'll get used to it."

He turned back to her. "A few *hundred?*" He knew her space experience spanned years, but he'd pictured her life in the Fleet being mostly on a starship.

She shrugged. "I'm in security. We're in charge of checking things out."

He'd definitely be asking her more about that later.

His gaze moved past her to where his mom was sitting stiffly in the seat to Celia's left. He frowned. Her fingers were gripping the armrests like she was in a gale force wind and her gaze was locked on his dad in the cockpit. "You okay, Mom?"

She turned her head just enough to look at him out of the corner of her eye. "Fine."

He raised his brows at that.

Aurora looked over her shoulder from the cockpit. "Fine?" she repeated, staring pointedly at their mom's hands clutching the armrests.

Their mom followed her gaze. With a wane smile, she pried her fingertips from their death grip, but she didn't let go. "Fine-ish," she admitted.

Aurora snorted.

Her mom's thin smile gained some self-mocking humor. "And by fine, I mean I hate this part. If you weren't all here, I'd have the viewports closed off and be pretending I was anywhere but in a shuttle blasting through the atmosphere that's trying to incinerate us."

That surprised him. "But you're the one with an energy shield." If anyone in the shuttle should feel confident about their ability to survive the flight, it would be his mom and Aurora. He had a feeling they could skydive without a parachute and walk away without a scratch.

His mom's gaze flicked to him. "I didn't say it was a completely rational fear."

"Logical, though," his dad said from the cockpit, his attention on the controls. "Your first experience of spaceflight was filled with trauma."

His mom sighed. "It certainly was."

His heart ached for her. She'd never told him the whole story of her flight from the Suulh homeworld, but he'd picked up enough to understand the depth of her loss at a very young age.

His gaze met Aurora's. The same empathy shone in her eyes. They'd suffered loss at a young age, too, but they'd found each other again, unlike their mom, who was contending with the knowledge that her sister was helping the Sovereign's efforts to capture and cage them all. He couldn't imagine how she was wrapping her head around that reality. The idea of Aurora hating him like that turned his heart to lead.

"This shuttle is very safe," Unity chimed in. "The design is solid, and we've improved the structural integrity by sixty percent. Passing through the planet's atmosphere is child's play."

"Good to know," his mom replied, though she didn't seem particularly reassured. And why would she? It wasn't the present that was traumatizing her. It was the past.

Unity must have picked up on her continued unease. "We wouldn't let anything bad happen to you," they said with deep sincerity.

That seemed to work better. "Thank you, Unity." His mom gazed fondly at U-1. "I appreciate having you with us."

"We love being here. New planets are fun!"

The collective chuckle broke through the tension. A moment later, the exterior light shifted again. Micah leaned toward the viewport as rays of sunlight bathed the cabin. They were flying over a landmass, the smudges of brown amidst the green rapidly gaining definition as the shuttle descended.

His dad's and Aurora's conversation in the cockpit became a background hum as he studied the topography. The trees reminded him a lot of home, although these stretched out to the horizon rather than ending at the waterline. Their thick canopies concealed most of what lay beneath. Small mountains rose at various points, also covered in thick vegetation. He spotted rocky outcroppings interspersed amongst the greenery, and the occasional flash of sunlight on water as it cascaded over waterfalls.

But all that was inconsequential compared to the familiar pulse of animal life all around him. It was like walking along a busy street in a country where you had only a rudimentary handle on the language. He was getting snippets here and there, but he'd lose the thread as others claimed his attention.

"You're hearing the animals, aren't you?" Celia's breath brushed across the bare skin of his neck as she leaned closer.

"Yes, but it's too much all at once to pick anything out." He kept his gaze on the foliage as his dad took *Starlet* in a slow arc, circling an area with several rocky outcroppings. A glimmer of rolling blue-silver and a stretch of tan below indicated a stream or river with a wide embankment.

"That's our destination," Aurora confirmed. "Micah?"

He turned from the viewport.

"Are you hearing anything we need to know about?"

He shook his head. "But I'll have a more definitive answer once we're on the ground."

"Okay." She turned to their dad. "You have a spot picked out for *Starlet?*"

He nodded, the shuttle already beginning its descent. "The river. I want to try out *Starlet's* water-landing ability."

Fifty-Nine

The scent of rain-washed greenery greeted Aurora as she stepped down *Starlet*'s ramp onto the river's wide sand and pebble beach. But rather than inspiring a burst of joy, it tightened her ribcage like a corset.

"I'm not your enemy." Aurora held her ground as Kreestol wound up again.

"Yes... you... are."

"No." Aurora took another step backward, drawing Kreestol into the middle of the river. *"I don't want to hurt you."*

"You want... what's... mine!"

Her aunt's rage-filled face hovered in front of her like a mirage. Rubbing her hand over her eyes, she took a deep breath to ease the tension in her chest. If only she could scrub the images from her mind.

"A memory?" her dad asked in a low tone.

She dropped her hand to her side. "Yeah."

"Want to talk about it?"

She glanced to where everyone else was waiting, U-1 hovering beside Micah's shoulder. "No, but I'll take a raincheck on that offer."

A warm blanket of love wrapped around her. "Absolutely."

His support did a decent job of loosening the tension in her muscles. "Thanks."

"Anytime."

Micah was gazing at the greenery at the edge of the beach. A faint rustle preceded the arrival of the four Yruf and two of Unity's emerald-green mobile units from the two scout ships Ifel had sent down.

Aurora recognized Ahle, Ifel's brother and the head of the Yruf medical team. The emerald and black female beside him was Cegra, his daughter and one of Ifel's guards. The other two females were unfamiliar to her, but they stood taller than Ahle and Cegra and both had blue and gold scales. All four of the Yruf were dressed in form-fitting outfits in shades of brown and green that concealed most of their scale coloring except for their faces and hands.

Aurora engaged her energy field as Ahle stepped forward, enveloping him the way she did when she communicated with Ifel. Micah stepped up next to her.

Ahle lowered his head in a micro-bow. *Greetings, Aurora and Micah.*

She and Micah did the same. *Greetings, Ahle.*

We have explored this area in detail. Ahle's dark diamond-pupiled eyes glinted in the reflected light from the water. *We have much to show you.*

She sensed an eagerness that was almost childlike. Quite a contrast to the calm efficiency she'd come to expect from him.

He motioned to the two blue-gold females. *Our pilots, Yrlef and Tipol.*

Both females gave a micro-bow, which Aurora and Micah returned.

Micah took over the introductions after that, then they started separating into two groups.

She glanced at her mom. "You have everything you need?"

Her mom hitched the pack onto her shoulders that contained a Kraed scanner, water and food, and a variety of empty containers for samples. "All set."

The rest of them shouldered similar packs. Aurora, Micah, Celia, and Iolana followed Ahle and Yrlef, while her parents and Kai went with Cegra and Tipol. She noticed as U-1 moved off with her parents that they'd added a gold circle to their bottom, like a cup, to differentiate them from the other emerald-green mobile unit that went with them.

Unity was definitely learning the nuances of her family's and crew's behavior. They'd figured out on their own that her parents would want to know which of the two units was U-1. Technically it didn't matter, since they were all Unity, but she'd noticed that U-2 tended to remain with Cade while U-1 was usually with her family or the *Starhawke* crew.

Ahle and Unity led the way into the greenery, Aurora behind them, followed by Iolana, Micah, Celia, and Yrlef. The lack of a defined path meant keeping her attention on where she was putting her feet, but her empathic senses were free to explore. She immediately picked up on a strong curiosity coming from Yrlef, but rather than being focused on their surroundings, it felt like it was zeroed in on her.

She paused, glancing over her shoulder. Sure enough, Yrlef's gaze was on her. "Micah, can you please ask Yrlef if there's something she wants to ask me? If feels like she's really curious about me."

"Sure." He was silent for a few moments, then he chuckled. "She's curious because she spent time with Cade when he was staying with them. She's the pilot who flew him around in the scout ship."

Ah. Cade had regaled her with stories about those wild rides. He'd clearly loved every moment. "Then be sure to thank her for giving Cade such peak experiences."

"She says you're welcome. She's also offering to take you on a flight if you're interested."

She ducked under a low-hanging branch. "Tell her thanks, but I don't have the same urge for thrill-seeking that Cade does." It was one reason she was a ship's captain and he was head of Will's Elite Team. They were both born leaders, but Cade embraced danger while she worked to avoid or contain it.

"Yeah, I wouldn't be interested, either. But I let her know Dad would probably love to get that chance."

"You're right, he would." Flying was an area where her dad loved taking risks as much as Cade did. "Do you think all their pilots have the same coloring?" She knew all of Ifel's guards had the same emerald, black, and gold coloring as Ifel and the Yruf ship. She hadn't yet learned whether it was genetic or something the Yruf could change either biologically or with technology.

"They don't, but she and Tipol are sisters from the same nest. Their coloring is the same as their mother's, who's also a pilot. They grew up with a shared passion for flying."

Yet another Yruf sibling pair working together. No wonder Ifel had so readily understood Aurora's and Micah's relationship. The Yruf seemed to have a similar view regarding sibling bonds and family bonds in general.

Aurora pulled up short as Ahle held up a hand. A moment later she spotted what had caused him to stop.

Unity was hovering high above a four-legged creature that was sitting in the wide space between two trees, front paws tucked up against their chest, their back legs and fan-shaped bushy tail stabilizing them so they didn't topple over.

She had a clear view of the creature's underbelly, which was a dark tan, the fur blending upward to a brown walnut shade on the sides. Their face looked more possum-like than beaver, with no fur around their mouth and petite nose. Their dark eyes stared back at her with frank curiosity.

In many ways, the creature reminded her of the Meer, the race she'd encountered on Burrow, although this one was half the size, with a thicker torso and more robust fur, like a fluffy beaver.

"Micah?" she whispered.

"Hang on," he murmured back.

The creature tilted their head, peering behind Aurora at Micah. They made a chittering noise, then scampered forward a few steps and rose up on their hind legs again.

Now that they were closer, she could make out the light banding in shades of brown and tan around their neck and tail. Their nose wriggled, like they were scenting the new arrivals, their gaze still locked on Micah.

"Smart girl," Micah said softly. "She's been watching the Yruf, trying to figure out whether they were a threat. She's never seen creatures as big as us before, or ones who walk on two legs but don't fly like birds. She decided to confront us to find out if she needed to defend her den."

"What did you tell her?"

"I didn't have to say much. The fact that we can understand each other eased her mind. Also, by den, I didn't just mean her children. I meant her entire community. There are at least seven others watching us right now."

Aurora reached out with her empathic senses, but she couldn't differentiate the specific emotional resonances of the creatures from all the other lifeforms nearby. "We'll want to make sure we don't encroach on them."

"We won't. Ahle says he was already aware of them. They're the largest species in this region. The location he's taking us to is far enough away from their den to not pose an issue."

"Good." But the creature still hadn't moved out of the way. "Will she let us pass her?"

"Not exactly. I think she's going to tag along. The images I shared with her when I was trying to explain why we were here have piqued her curiosity."

To prove his point, the creature dropped onto all fours, looking at them expectantly.

Ahle stepped forward. The creature angled her body so she could keep an eye on the rest of their group but kept pace with his steps as he moved nearly silently through the greenery.

Around them, creatures screeched, hummed, and rustled in the undergrowth and canopy. Two different species of bird glided overhead, their bright colors catching stray beams of sunlight. What looked like a winged lizard leapt and soared from branch to branch.

Their furry companion stayed with the group, vanishing for a few moments, then reappearing just ahead, nose twitching.

"Are you still talking to her?" she asked Micah over her shoulder.

"A bit. Mostly I think she's talking with her denmates. Three of them are following behind us."

She paused, peering past Yrlef, but she didn't see any of the creatures amidst the thick foliage. "What about the plant life, Celia?" She'd noticed her friend was scanning both sides of their route with her comband. "Anything promising?" A light breeze carried floral notes that reminded her of rose and jasmine.

"There's a lot of variety. The scanner's already picked up nine fruit-producing plants, three varieties of potentially edible fungi, and fourteen potentially edible greens."

Those numbers were even higher than she'd anticipated, especially for a first pass.

Up ahead, the foliage gave way to an expanse of sun-drenched rock crowned by a sky of deep blue.

Another memory surfaced, halting her steps.

She stared at the infinite blue, drawing in sips of air as the world spun around her.

Maybe she was dreaming. An elaborate, insane nightmare.

She turned her head in slow motion. No. Not a dream. There was the Sovereign's ship. And more guards at the open hatch, helping the Sovereign, Kreestol, and the three injured guards stumble up the gangway.

She rolled into a defensive crouch, but her body hadn't caught up with her mind. She staggered, tripping over her own feet as she stood. By the time she'd covered half the distance, the ship had lifted off with barely a whisper.

"Ror? You okay?"

She blinked. "Just wishing..." She frowned, not really sure how to finish the sentence. She could wish things were different, but if she hadn't confronted the Sovereign and Kreestol on this planet, she never would have pushed her mom into revealing the truth about her dad and Micah.

She wouldn't change that for anything. Too much good had come from that revelation. And not only for her family. The ripples had produced dramatic effects for Celia, the Yruf, Lelindia and Jonarel, Marina and Gryphon... the list kept growing.

No, she didn't wish things were different. But that didn't mean her heart didn't ache every time she thought about the pain and destruction the Sovereign's own ripple was triggering.

The faint gurgle of water was audible down the slope to her right. The rocky ledge that rose to her left created a shaded overhang large enough to house the *Starhawke*'s conference room table and chairs. Ahle, Micah, and Yrlef would have to duck if they wanted to walk under it, but she, Celia, and Iolana would be fine. From that standpoint, this location would work better for Manchado rather than Mirko, since he was shorter.

The furred creature was sitting under it, watching them.

Ahle turned to face Aurora. She engaged her energy field and surrounded him with it.

The surface above is level. He gestured to the rocky incline. *The surrounding rock is capable of supporting the habitation Jonarel designed.*

What about the stream I'm hearing? Is it potable water?

Yes.

If the location Cegra and Tipol were showing her parents and Kai was anything like this, they were in great shape.

Celia already had her pack open in front of her as she picked out a couple sample containers. Her emotional field had dropped into the deep analytical zone that indicated she'd be occupied for hours.

Aurora turned to Micah. "Since you're our marine expert, do you want to check out the stream with me and Iolana while Celia works with Unity and the Yruf on edible plant options?"

"You have to ask?" He grinned. "You know I'm all about the water features. Let's go meet some alien fish."

Sixty

"I feel ridiculous," Nat muttered as she stepped onto the airbridge connecting *Phoenix* to Hydra One. Docking *Phoenix* at the space station while ignoring the surfeit of Fleet patrol yachts in the area had been unsettling enough. But this?

Cade leaned down to whisper in her ear. "You look great. Just remember to smile occasionally." His fingers tightened around hers. "We're supposed to be a happy couple on vacation, not a grumpy couple in the middle of a big fight."

She shot him a sideways glance as they exited the airbridge onto the concourse. His temporarily brown eyes were twinkling behind the glasses he wore, like he was having fun.

She wasn't having fun. She felt like a complete idiot in this getup, especially holding his hand. The only person she'd ever held hands with was Isin, and that was a very recent phenomenon.

But she pasted on what she hoped resembled a genuine smile. "Yes, sweetheart." She fluttered the false lashes Itorye had insisted on attaching as part of her transformation. They felt like two moths sitting on her face.

Cade chuckled, giving her hand another squeeze. "That works."

Easy for him to say. His changes had been more subtle. In addition to the glasses and colored contacts, Itorye had used a hair rinse that had darkened his hair from blond to brown, then reworked the styling to give him a bookish appearance that fit with the brown slacks and light blue button-front shirt he was wearing.

She, on the other hand, felt like a child's doll.

Not that Itorye hadn't done a good job with her clothing, wig, and makeup. The reflection she'd seen in the mirror in her cabin and the appreciative glances she was getting from several of the people she and Cade passed as they walked the concourse made it clear Itorye had achieved her goal of a glamorous, feminine vibe. That didn't mean she liked having all this gunk on her face. Or the itchy wig over her hair. She had to continually fight the urge to flip the extra hair out of her way, or better yet, yank it off.

She would have preferred her normal method for infiltrating a space – going incognito, blending in so no one noticed her. But that was too close to the persona the Fleet had encountered a couple weeks ago. She couldn't risk being recognized. So, she'd let Itorye turn her into an art project.

Itorye had been delighted with the results.

Delighted wasn't the word Nat would use to describe the experience.

On top of that, she had one of Unity's micro-units in her ear. Not an earpiece, the actual micro-unit, so small she couldn't even see it before U-2 inserted it. Cade had one, too, as did everyone else going onto the station. It was a little unnerving, having Unity actually in her ear, but it was an untraceable way for the group to have instantaneous communication with each other.

Focusing on her surroundings, she lifted her chin and let her hips sway when she walked. Stars, it felt weird, even after hours of practice. The shoes were a big part of the problem. She was used to solid, sturdy boots. The strappy things on her mostly bare feet made her feel naked and exposed, especially with the hem of the dress brushing against her calves just below her knees. She wasn't used to feeling air against her legs as she walked. Itorye had been forced to use bronzer to make it look like she occasionally went out in the sunshine. Usually the only time her skin was this visible was when she showered.

Cade strolled down the concourse at a leisurely pace, matching his longer strides to her shorter ones. The wide terminal was full of activity as vacationers arrived or departed from the popular tourist destination. The sight of Fleet security personnel stationed at regular intervals didn't seem to deter the visitors, who barely gave them a glance.

And why should they? *They* weren't wanted for treason. *Their* faces weren't splashed all over the news feeds, identifying them as dangerous criminals.

Neither was hers, or Cade's, but her stomach hadn't gotten the memo. It did a backflip every time her gaze fell on one of the grey-uniformed personnel. She needed a distraction to keep in character.

"Have you been to this station before?" It was all new to her. Smugglers avoided Hydra One because of the strong Fleet presence.

"Many times. It's a common stop for the Rescue Corps."

"Rescue Corps?" That gave her a shot of adrenaline, making her almost trip over her own feet.

His grip tightened as he met her gaze. "You okay?"

She shuddered. The Sovereign had been the Director of the Rescue Corps. "Just thinking about... her."

His eyes narrowed, then he caught her meaning. "Ah. Not my favorite person to think about, either." The sparkle had left his eyes. "I worked with her a lot. Still can't believe I never caught on to what she was doing." He took a deep breath, forcing a smile. "I take it you've never been here?"

"Nope."

"It's a nice station. Most people who come here are on their way to Heracles." He tipped his head in the direction of the planet the station orbited. "But I've known some who make the station their destination. The living areas are really beautiful and there's a wide variety of family-friendly entertainment. Good restaurants, too."

She gave her surroundings another look, trying to see it all through his eyes. His experience of space travel was so completely different from hers. She couldn't recall ever seeking out entertainment on a space station. Well, not since she was a small child, anyway. Money had always been tight. Even meals at a restaurant had been a luxury.

She spotted Patel and Gavin up ahead, making their way through the security queue. She did a double-take as Patel laughed at something Gavin said, then swatted him playfully and rested her head on his shoulder.

"What?" Cade murmured.

"I've just never seen Patel look so... normal." The woman she knew always had a perpetual scowl or worried frown. Laughter and playful behavior weren't part of her emotional repertoire. But apparently she could summon them when the situation required it.

She shouldn't be surprised, really. Patel had hoodwinked Rathburn and successfully smuggled Alec off *Cerberus*. Rathburn was a smart man. Pulling it off had required a high degree of subterfuge and misdirection.

The backflips started again as she and Cade moved toward the front of the queue, closer to the intimidating Fleet personnel. She watched enviously as Gavin and Patel sailed through and disappeared into the crowd.

"You're doing great," Cade whispered, dropping a kiss on top of her head. "Just focus on me like I'm the most fascinating man in the universe."

Her lips twitched as she met his gaze. "Is that how you view yourself?"

"Of course." He made cow eyes at her. "Don't you?"

"Oh, you're fascinating all right," she agreed with a heavy dose of irony.

He pressed his free hand to his chest in mock pain. "The lady cuts me to the quick."

She laughed. "I'll show you—"

"Next." The Fleet security officer at the center station waved them forward.

Her heartbeat kicked into overdrive. Why had she thought this plan was a good idea? Oh, yeah. Because Cade needed backup and she was a smuggling pro. She needed to start acting like it.

His fingers tightened on her hand as he strode forward with a smile, placing his ID on the counter next to hers.

The officer ran them under a scanner. "What's the purpose of your visit?"

"Honeymoon," Cade replied.

Nat leaned into him, doing her best to look like a besotted newlywed.

The officer's gaze flitted over them, the hard, brusque edges of their demeanor softening. "Congratulations."

"Thank you." Cade wrapped his arm around Nat's shoulders, drawing her closer. "I'm a lucky man."

She avoided the officer's gaze by staring up at Cade. "I'm the lucky one."

"Aww. Thanks, honey." Cade leaned down, giving her a decidedly chaste and platonic kiss, his glasses lightly bumping her nose.

Nat watched the security officer out of the corner of her eye. They took one more look at the IDs before handing them back. "You folks enjoy your stay."

"We will," Cade assured them, clasping her hand and leading her past the security station.

She released the breath she'd been holding, her legs a little rubbery as they carried her through the utilitarian tunnel of the emergency airlock between the concourse and the central hub. At the far end, the bulkhead displayed a map of the station. She tugged Cade to a stop, allowing other visitors to pass by them as she studied the layout, reorienting herself and adjusting her mental map. Knowing the ins and outs of her surroundings had saved her on more than one occasion.

Their current location was marked with a red X right at the end of the concourse where it connected with the broad section of the station that housed the social and retail areas. Dramatic murals on the bulkheads to either side of the map depicted the mythological creature that shared Hydra One's name.

That's when she clued into the similarity between Hydra One's layout and the multi-headed creature of the myth. The multitude of docking arms for Hydra One created the long-necked heads of the creature, while the hydra's body formed the station's living and admin spaces. "Somebody really ran with the hydra theme." Not that she was one to talk, considering the paint job she'd done on

Phoenix. She took a moment to appreciate the talent of the artist who'd painted the mural showcasing the creature's story.

Cade smiled. "I take it you're a fan of mythology?"

"You could say that." She'd stolen a book on Greek mythology from a street vendor when she was eleven. She'd snatched it because of the full-color pictures, which portrayed creatures of breathtaking beauty and terror. But she'd been even more entranced by the stories. She'd read them thousands of times during the dark days of her youth. She could recite most of them from memory.

The book was currently tucked away in a secret compartment on *Gypsy.* She hadn't dared to take it out of its hiding place while she'd been Tnaryt's captive, afraid he'd destroy it just to spite her. She'd only laid hands on it once since, when she was on Rathburn's ship. She'd needed to confirm he hadn't stolen it during his unauthorized search of her shuttle. But now that her situation had stabilized — well, as much as she ever expected it to — the book deserved a place of honor in her cabin. Or maybe on *Phoenix*'s bridge.

Her gaze moved to the artist's rendition of the planet Heracles in the upper right corner of the station map. The planet wasn't visible from this part of the station, but she'd gotten a good look at it while flying *Phoenix* in. Like most habitable planets, Heracles had swaths of blue oceans surrounding brown and green land masses. If memory served, the gravity on Heracles was fractionally higher than Earth-standard, and the air slightly more oxygen-rich. It was also one of the largest colonized planets, one and a half times the size of Earth. Its size, and its pairing with Hydra One, was likely one reason it had been given its name.

Fleet vessels had lined the two outermost concourses of the station when she'd flown in, something the map confirmed. Both were designated for authorized Fleet personnel only.

No problem. She'd happily avoid those areas. She also pinpointed the medical center, marked with a red caduceus on the map. It was located toward the center of the main body, equidistant from the concourses.

With the map firmly planted in her head, she followed Cade around the bulkhead and out of the tunnel. Her gaze rose up and up, counting five levels soaring above them. Signs directed visitors traveling to Heracles to stairways leading to the lower levels where shuttles waited. Music played in the background, upbeat and cheerful, while brightly colored storefronts and restaurant signs beckoned travelers in. Some even had cloth awnings. They served no functional purpose inside a space station but gave a subtle elegance to the surroundings.

"What do you think?"

"It's... different."

Cade's brows rose. "Different? That doesn't sound like a compliment."

She shrugged. "It's not an insult, either. I'm just not used to so much..." She tried to put her finger on the right word. Nothing came to her, so she stuck with what she had. "So much."

Cade grinned. "I get that. But I've also seen your ship. You might find more to like about this place than you think."

"Maybe."

They walked down the main thoroughfare hand in hand. She still felt stupid in the dress, but it was doing its job — the people who looked at them were focusing more on her than on Cade, who was attempting to be utterly forgettable. Deliberately drawing attention made her skin itch, but she leaned into her role rather than ducking her head, gazing with only partially contrived interest at their surroundings.

Cade navigated the crowded corridors with the ease of long familiarity.

"What exactly did you do for the Rescue Corps?" He'd said he'd been here many times because of his work with them.

"My official record lists me as a pilot for the RC. Piloting their vessels enabled my team to move around easily to areas where we were needed."

She frowned. "Why didn't you use *Gladiator?*"

"We didn't pick up *Gladiator* until shortly before we met you."

"Huh." For some reason she'd assumed they'd had the compact fighter all along, maybe because the ship was firmly anchored to his team in her mind. She'd never forget the first time she saw it, charging in to block the weapons fire from the Sovereign's cruiser as it attempted to blow Tnaryt's ship out of the sky. Without

Gladiator's assistance, the Sovereign would have killed her, the Admiral, and Marlin.

That day had been a turning point for her in so many ways. And the man walking beside her had played a key role in giving her back her freedom.

Cade pointed out his preferred restaurants as they strolled like tourists, pausing at some of the carts to look over the goods for sale. She'd never been in a marketplace offering this much variety of personal goods and services, not even on Osiris. Hydra One's location in the Interior Hub made it an important stop along most trade routes. But she wasn't remotely tempted to buy anything. If they'd been passing vendors offering refurbished ship parts, *then* she'd definitely want to stop and haggle.

"Tam is leaving *Phoenix* now," Unity whispered in her ear.

The unexpected sound made her twitch, but she covered it by tipping her head up to meet Cade's gaze.

He nodded. "Let's head up a level."

They joined the stream of foot traffic stepping onto the covered escalator going up to the second level. Picturing the map in her head, she figured out they were drawing close to the medical center. She rose on tiptoe, brushing her lips against Cade's cheek as she whispered in his ear. "You ready for my performance?"

He rested his cheek against hers. "Anytime," he whispered back.

As they reached the next level, she spotted a good mark, a man with his head down, staring at the tablet in his hands as he walked quickly in their direction. She angled her body toward Cade, tapping him on the chest so he gazed down at her while she put pressure on his hand to keep him from moving her out of the man's path.

The man plowed forward, oblivious to anything but whatever he was reading on his tablet. He collided hard with her shoulder.

She released Cade's hand, allowing the man's momentum to send her sprawling in an undignified heap on the hard surface of the walkway. Her shriek of pain stopped traffic in all directions.

"Noelle!" Cade dropped onto his haunches beside her, while tablet man stared at her in shock.

"Are you okay?" they asked in stereo.

She gave a pathetic whimper, wrapping her hands around her left leg right above her ankle.

She had to give credit where due. The dress made the whole act more believable, allowing her to really lean into the damsel in distress shtick. "My leg..." She hitched her breath and summoned crocodile tears. "It... *hurts.*"

Tablet man dropped to his knees, panic radiating off him. "I'm so sorry. I didn't see you."

She gave him a tremulous smile as the first tear splashed down her cheek. "M-My fault—"

"No, no, it wasn't." He looked anxiously between her and Cade. "I wasn't looking where I was going." He slid the offending tablet into the courier bag resting against his hip. "Can you move it?"

She pursed her lips and gently rotated her ankle, then hissed air in between her teeth and squeezed her eyes shut. She whimpered again, giving Cade her most pathetic wounded dove look.

"It'll be okay, sweetheart," he murmured, sliding a hand behind her back. He glanced at the man. "Do you know where the medical center is?"

The man nodded vigorously, pointing behind him. "Just down that corridor and left at the T-junction." He glanced at Nat uncertainly. "Can I help you get there?"

Cade answered that question by lifting her in one smooth motion, tucking her against his side. "I can take her," he assured the man. His arm around her waist supported her weight against him while she balanced on one foot. "But thank you for offering."

"You sure you don't need help?" Concern shadowed his eyes as he gazed at her, clearly conflicted.

She felt a little sorry for him. It wasn't his fault she'd targeted him. Although to be fair, he shouldn't have been striding down the corridor like he owned the place while not looking where he was going. She swiped a hand at her tears, her lip trembling. "Y-You probably have s-somewhere to b-be."

His lips thinned, his gaze darting in the direction he'd been walking. "I do, actually. I'm late for a meeting."

Cade waved him on. "Don't let us keep you." He turned to her. "We'll take it slow, sweetie."

She gave him a weak smile and nodded.

The man stood in place for a couple beats, looking from her to a spot over her shoulder. But it didn't last. She saw the moment his concern over his meeting reclaimed his attention. As she hobbled beside Cade down the corridor, she could hear his clipped footsteps retreating in the opposite direction.

"Nicely done," Cade murmured.

"Thanks." She'd used this same con often as a child to get a meal from a stranger. Guilt could be a powerful motivator for generosity. And if they weren't generous, she'd picked their pockets instead.

She hadn't been certain the fake tears would still appear on command, but her body had responded like she'd run this con yesterday.

She kept the pained look on her face, wincing every time she put any weight on her supposedly injured foot. The people around them parted to clear a channel, giving her sympathetic looks as Cade guided her to the medical center.

They took the lift marked MEDICAL CENTER ONLY that connected all five levels directly with the medical center lobby.

The receptionist behind the desk rose as Nat made her way forward, Cade still supporting her. "How may I help you?"

"I twisted..." Another big wince. "My ankle."

The woman made a soft hum of sympathy. "We can definitely help with that. Are you a resident or visitor?"

"Visitor."

"Then I'll just need to see your ID."

She produced her fake ID from the pocket of her dress, setting it on the counter.

"Thank you." The receptionist scanned it in. "Very good, Ms. Finch, you may proceed into room four." She pointed to the numbered doors down a long corridor. "A doctor will be with you shortly."

Cade kept his grip around her waist as they made their way into the room. The stainless-steel exam table looked as inviting as an ice block, so she sank into one of the two chairs that faced it.

Cade sat beside her, angling his body toward the open door.

"How long do you think we'll have to wait?" she asked out loud so Unity could hear her.

"Not long at all!" they chirped.

Nat caught the sound of soft footsteps approaching down the hallway.

A woman with tawny skin and short white hair cut in layers stepped into the room and shut the door with a decisive click.

Sixty-One

Cade hadn't seen Dr. Morales in almost a year, but the wisdom in her brown-eyed gaze saw right through his disguise.

"Hello, Cade." He sensed her relief, and her curiosity as she peered at Nat. "We can talk freely. These rooms are soundproofed for privacy. I'm Dr. Elena Morales. You're Ms. Finch?"

"Orlov, actually. Call me Nat."

A jolt of surprise turned to amusement as a small smile curved Morales' mouth. "I should have known Will would hook you in somehow. You're the pilot."

"You know about me?" Nat's surprise flared even brighter than Morales' had.

"Of course. You were the topic of a rather lengthy letter. He shared how you risked your life to remain with him after the engine room explosion. He was also disappointed that you didn't take him up on his offer to become his personal pilot. He's very fond of you."

Color rose in Nat's cheeks that even the makeup couldn't conceal. "Oh."

Morales leaned against the exam table, studying Nat with an assessing gaze. "Can I assume you don't have a twisted ankle?"

Nat flexed her foot. "I'm fine."

"You must have given a very convincing performance. Until you gave your name, the desk clerk wasn't one-hundred percent certain you were the people we were waiting for."

Nat shrugged. "I spent a lot of time on my own as a kid. You learn some things."

Morales took that in with a slow nod. "Indeed, you do." Her focus switched to Cade. "How's Will?"

"Fine. He, Knox, and Magee are on the *Starhawke*."

Morales' brows rose toward her bangs. "You got Isabeau back?"

Cade nodded. "We rescued her from the Teeli Embassy the same night we broke the Admiral and Aurora out of Seaview."

She let out a long exhale, her body visibly unwinding. "That is very good news. Knox stopped communicating with me after Will was arrested. I think he was trying to protect me, but it meant the only updates I've received have been from the news feeds." She made a face. "Which are increasingly unreliable."

That was one way to put it. A more accurate way to phrase it was that the fact-to-lie ratio was rapidly climbing past fifty-fifty as Admiral Nixon spread propaganda and false accusations, which were amplified by members of the GC and judiciary.

"Which brings me to two critical questions. How were you able to implant a message on my comm device that doesn't appear to have come through the ICS, and how did you know Colleen is here?"

Her tone reminded him a lot of the Admiral — firm and direct. She expected an answer.

He couldn't give her one. At least not a detailed one. Telling her anything about the Yruf was too big a risk for exposure. Her friendship with Admiral Schreiber wasn't a secret. As Nixon grew more desperate, he could decide to send the Teeli to her doorstep to find out if she was susceptible to Teeli manipulation. "We made new friends recently, who have advanced technological capabilities. They were able to track Montgomery here. That same tech also enabled them to get a message to your comm device."

Her gaze sharpened. "New friends? Who?"

"It's best if I don't answer that."

She considered that for a moment. "Are you certain you can trust them?"

"Very certain," he replied at the same time Nat said, "Absolutely."

"They recently saved my ship from destruction," Nat added, "and then helped with restoration. I'd trust them with my life, and the lives of my crew."

"Same here." Cade nodded.

"Can you tell me how you met them?"

"Again, it's better if you don't know."

She studied him like she was trying to diagnose a rare disease. "Do the Teeli know about your new friends?"

"No. And we need to keep it that way."

"Ah." She nodded slowly. "I see."

"What exactly happened to Montgomery on *Cassini?*"

Anger flared in her eyes and emotional field. "Technically, a climbing accident on the climbing wall. But it was no accident. Her safety equipment failed at the same time the gravity monitors that are supposed to decrease gravity when the system detects someone falling instead *increased* the gravity. The fall could have killed her. That's why Henri — Dr. Seine — arranged to get her off the ship. He and Commander Muiruri didn't want whoever staged the accident to finish the job. They returned to Eridani Duo, their previous stop, and left her with Dr. Yates."

"How did she end up here?" Nat asked.

"The person who arranged the accident either followed her to Eridani Duo or had an accomplice there. The medical center security received an alert that someone was trying to break into the ICU, but they were unable to apprehend them. That's when Anthony contacted me and we coordinated to bring Colleen here secretly."

"How?" Cade asked.

"We have a weekly courier who transports supplies, equipment, and sometimes personnel or patients between Hydra One and Eridani Duo's medical centers. Until Nixon's new security restrictions went into place, it was relatively easy to slip Colleen on and off Harriet's transport. Harriet's a good friend of mine and Anthony's, and well known to our security staffs. Her arrival and departure didn't draw any scrutiny. Now, Nixon has installed Fleet security at the access point for our external airlocks. They're checking everything and everyone very closely."

That explained who Harriet was and the role she'd played in Montgomery's transport. "Does anyone on *Cassini*'s crew know Montgomery is here?"

"Only Cmd. Muiruri and Dr. Seine. The official word to the crew was Colleen needed to be treated at Eridani Duo for life-threatening injuries. Medical facilities on starships are limited compared to treatment options available at space stations."

"What about the medical staff at Eridani Duo?" Cade asked. "They must know she's missing." He knew the answer, but he didn't want to let on just how much knowledge they already had.

Morales gave him a wry smile. "Age and experience have their privileges. Anthony and Colleen have known each other since their first posting together out of the Academy. He's one of her closest friends. He's also developed a reputation for being the doctor everyone wants to work with. As such, his senior staff has very low turnover and are very loyal. They're just as committed to Colleen's safety as he is. They've been maintaining a fiction that Colleen is still there, being treated. Unfortunately, I received word that Admiral Nixon is sending his personal physician to Eridani Duo to assess Colleen's condition."

Cade bit his cheek to keep from confirming that information. He didn't want to divulge that Unity was tapped into the Fleet Command communications relay.

"And when they get to Eridani Duo," Nat said, "they'll discover she's not there."

"Exactly. That's when things will get complicated. I'd hoped I'd have more time to get her back on her feet and then send her with Harriet."

"What's Montgomery's condition now?"

"Stable, but she can't walk without assistance, and it's very painful. She has broken bones in both her right arm and leg, as well as fractures and herniated discs in her spine."

Cade winced. He'd had his share of broken bones in his line of work, though thanks to Aurora's and Lelindia's energy fields, he doubted a medical scan would show any sign of the injuries. "Dr. Forrest could treat her injuries if we can get Montgomery off Hydra One."

"That would be greatly appreciated." The look in her eyes and the emotions he sensed in her emotional field indicated she was well aware of Lelindia's special abilities.

"What we don't have is a way to return Montgomery to Eridani Duo." *Phoenix* would stand out like a peacock amongst chickens at the science station. They wouldn't have an excuse to deliver a crate full of medical supplies to the medical center, either.

Morales shook her head. "Anthony and I wouldn't want you to, even if you could. Nixon wants to silence Colleen because she's been vocal in defending Will, asserting his innocence. I refuse to let him harm her."

"Is Montgomery aware of the Teeli threat?"

She nodded. "She had her suspicions after what happened to Will and Aurora, but no facts to support them. I've shared everything I know with her. Now she understands what we're up against."

"And she's prepared to fight back?"

"As soon as she's mobile again, yes." She gave him a considering look. "How did *you* get here? The *Starhawke* is the most recognizable ship in the Union, thanks to all the news feeds replaying the dramatic escape from Sol Station."

Nat lifted a hand. "My ship, *Phoenix*. She was originally a passenger vessel, so she fits right in with the other ships docked at the station."

Very true. *Phoenix*'s red and gold paint didn't stand out as unusual amidst the dramatic colors of the privately owned and commercial passenger ships. The one they were berthed next to was neon green.

"Can I assume you have a plan for getting Colleen out?"

"We do. As long as she's willing to trust a band of accused traitors to the Union, Williams will be here soon with her transportation."

Morales pushed away from the exam table. "Then let's go ask her."

Sixty-Two

From the moment Nat stepped into the small studio, she was keenly aware of being sized up by the woman reclining in the bed in the far corner.

Captain Montgomery's dark brown eyes were bracketed by the lines and creases of life experience, the sharp intelligence in her gaze seeing through the hair, makeup, and clothes of Nat's disguise, working to discern what lay beneath. She frowned, her gaze shifting to Cade.

"Will sent Commander Ellis to pay you a visit," Morales said by way of introduction.

Surprise flitted across Montgomery's face. "Commander Ellis?"

"I'm the leader of the Admiral's Elite Unit."

It took only a second for her to snap the critical pieces together. "Where's the Admiral?"

"Safe," Cade assured her. "He thought we might be able to give you a lift out of here."

"Is that so?" Her gaze returned to Nat. "Do I know you?"

"No." She stepped closer. "I'm Nat. The Admiral and I met on Gallows Edge shortly after he left your ship."

"Gallows Edge?" The creases around her eyes deepened as the sensation of being scanned doubled. "You're not Fleet?"

"Hardly." She folded her arms over her chest, really missing her duster. The dress wasn't the least bit protective. She felt exposed under Montgomery's scrutiny. "But the Admiral and Captain Hawke got me out of a tight spot. I'm returning the favor." Which didn't even scratch the surface of the whole story, but they didn't have time for long explanations.

"I'll vouch for her," Morales said, moving to stand next to the bed. "Will told me about their adventures together. He offered Nat a position as his personal pilot, but she turned him down."

"Really?" The look in Montgomery's eyes shifted, growing speculative. "He wouldn't make that offer lightly."

"I didn't turn it down, lightly." She sounded a little defensive, but she couldn't seem to help it. Even stretched out on a bed wearing a medical gown, Montgomery was intimidating. "Good thing I did, or we wouldn't be here."

The corners of Montgomery's mouth lifted, defining her strong cheekbones. "I can see why he likes you. You're a fighter."

That mollified her somewhat. "I've heard the same about you."

She acknowledged the point with a nod before her focus returned to Cade. "What's your plan to get me out?"

"First, I need to know if you want to return to *Cassini* after you're healed."

Montgomery's jaw flexed. "Want to? Yes. But Nixon's determined to remove me from the equation." She nodded to indicate her prone body. "And apparently he doesn't care how he does it. That doesn't mean I'm going to make it easy for him. Or abandon my crew." She shot Morales a hard look.

Cade glanced between the two. "So, you'd like to keep your options open, if possible?"

"I'd like to be walking again so I can do my job."

Montgomery perfectly fit her preconceived image of a Fleet captain before she met Aurora — crusty, strong-willed, and hard-nosed.

"We have someone who can help with that." Cade glanced at the door they'd come through that led into Morales' office. "But first we have to get you off the station. Williams will be arriving shortly with a crate specifically designed for smuggling. I can't vouch for the fit and comfort, but it will allow us to get you past security and onto *Phoenix*."

"*Phoenix*?"

"My ship," Nat replied. "A passenger freighter."

Montgomery's thin brows rose. Her gaze swept over Nat's petite frame from the top of her wig to the open-toed shoes. "You're used to being underestimated, aren't you?"

Nat met her gaze, seeing the recognition in Montgomery's eyes of someone who had needed to fight for the good in her life. "It comes in handy."

"Yes, it does." Montgomery's lips softened in a closed-mouth smile. "I think you and I will get along just fine."

Sixty-Three

Micah breathed in the thick floral scent in the air, marveling at the beauty of the alien world that surrounded him. The negative ions generated by the running water tripped lightly over his bare feet, making his body feel effervescent. The sensation of being embraced by the natural world was so normal, so familiar, that a chuckle rumbled in his throat.

Except for the critter who'd followed them from the shuttle, who he'd nicknamed Hoaloha because she'd accepted him so quickly as a friend, and a few of the fish in the stream who kept swimming near him, most of the others were studiously ignoring his attempts at conversation. He didn't take offense. He was a stranger in their world. Respecting their boundaries was important.

Aurora had orchestrated this private time for him and Celia, claiming she needed to talk with their parents about the second site. She, Birdie, Ahle, and Yrlef were eating their lunches on the rock ledge at the top of the slope, and Hoaloha had chosen to stay with them.

Celia was seated beside him on the flat rock at the edge of the stream, their picnic spread over the wide napkins on their laps. The beach blanket he'd had since his early surfing days provided a little cushioning on the hard surface. The aqua background had faded from all the hours in the sun, now closer to a sky blue, but the dolphins cavorting across the expanse were still easily distinguishable. Celia's smile when she'd seen it had filled the sky with rainbows.

Like him, she'd taken off her boots and had her bare feet dangling in the water. Her hair was pulled back in the tight rows of braids she favored for expeditions and sparring, making it easy to see the graceful curve of her neck and the strong line of her jaw even when she wasn't looking at him. Like now.

"Something funny?" she asked, turning her head and meeting his gaze.

Funny wasn't what came to mind when he gazed at her. "Just appreciating the irony that I'm feeling very much at home on an alien world. I fully expected to spend my entire life on Earth." He gestured around them. "This all feels strangely normal, which is bizarre. A few months ago I wouldn't have believed any of this was possible, let alone that it would become my new reality." Including meeting her. Her presence in his life was rapidly rearranging his priorities. Especially when she looked at him the way she was now.

Her dark eyes sparkled in the dappled sunlight. "That's the point, isn't it? Reconnecting with Aurora showed you that you could find joy in places you never imagined." She swept her arm in a graceful arc to indicate their surroundings. "As long as there are animals and a water source nearby, you're in your happy place."

"Happier with you in it." He snaked his arm around her waist and scooted closer.

Her breathing sped up, her gaze locking with his, holding him in her grip. He couldn't look away even if a flash flood was bearing down on them.

Her expression shifted to the unguarded, relaxed softness he'd only begun to see when they were alone together. Celia had always been defined by her strength and focus – always analyzing, always watchful, her body and mind all hard planes and sharp edges that kept others at a distance.

But that wasn't who she really was. Well, not all that she was. In moments like this one, where all that fell away, she revealed the sensual woman underneath, the one who dipped her toes into the stream and lifted her face to the sun. "I've never been happier than when I'm with you," she whispered.

His heart stuttered, then began to thump hard enough to play his ribs like a xylophone. Lifting a hand, he trailed his fingers down the smooth contours of her cheek. "Thank you." The compliment would have been nice from anyone. From her, it was priceless.

"It's the truth." Her hand rested over his, her thumb stroking his palm. "I never imagined I'd want a moment like this. That I'd find pleasure in being touched. Or feel safe being held. But I do, with you." Cupping his jaw, she brushed her mouth over his in a feather kiss.

His lips tingled, the sensation traveling at lightspeed to every part of his body. He deepened the kiss, the earthy spice of the portobello sandwiches they'd been eating adding another layer of flavor to the kiss. He savored the moment. "Thanks for that, too," he murmured as he leaned back.

"You're welcome." Her smile turned impish. "So, is this a good time for you to teach me the basics of animal communication?" She gazed significantly over his shoulder.

Turning, he saw that a pair of large birds had come to check them out. He'd been so engrossed in kissing Celia he'd missed their arrival, but she hadn't. He took it as a compliment. Completely lowering her guard while they were in an unpredictable setting would have shown a lack of concern for his safety. Instead, she'd appointed herself as overwatch so he could play.

The birds were standing on a set of rocks several meters away. Their colors blended well with the surrounding jungle, variegated shades of grey-green predominating. Their bodies reminded him of an egret, with long spindly legs clearly designed for standing in deep water. Their thin pointed beaks would work well for spearing fish, too.

As he focused on the pair, one of the birds cocked their head to the side, looking him in the eye. He felt the familiar brush of communication, not words so much as a strong sense of knowing that his mind translated into words.

What are you?

It was the most common query when he encountered a new species, and apparently was literally universal. He had no idea how the animals knew he was capable of conversing with them, but most species, like these birds, seemed to sense it before he even tried to communicate with them. He'd be willing to bet these birds were highly intelligent.

I'm a human from far away. He projected words, images, and the emotions behind them, since every species seemed to respond to different cues. Some were drawn in by strong emotion, others by rapid imagery, and others, like the Yruf, could understand his words. Talking to Ifel had been a revelation, allowing him to better understand how he did what he did. He'd tried having a conversation with Streak and Cutter once about how they perceived his communication with them, but the rambunctious dolphins hadn't been interested in getting into specifics. Cutter had announced rather forcefully *less talk, more swim.*

The bird pair took a few steps closer, the larger of the two fluffing their feathers, showing streaks of snowy white beneath the grey-green. An equally white crest lifted on their head, their gaze moving down. *Food?*

He followed their line of sight.

Celia had tucked her napkin around the remnants of her lunch, but the bite of his sandwich he hadn't eaten yet was still easily visible resting on his napkin.

Celia kept her gaze on the birds. "They're asking about food, aren't they?"

"How did you know that?"

"I've eaten at enough outdoor restaurants to recognize the look from visiting birds, even alien birds. I'm assuming we shouldn't feed them?"

"No, we shouldn't. We have no idea how our food would affect them, but even if we knew it was safe, feeding wildlife anything that doesn't grow naturally in their environment is always a bad idea."

"That's what I figured. You better let them know." She lifted her chin toward the birds.

While they'd been talking, the pair had moved a meter closer, their focus on his napkin.

He quickly popped the remaining bite in his mouth and chewed. This was one scenario where he could talk with his mouth full. *We can't share our food, but we would like to talk with you.*

The lead bird took a step forward. *Not share?*

Our food could harm you. What food do you normally eat?

Images of fish, small reptiles, and crustaceans filled his mind. So, their diet was similar to an egret's, too.

You eat?

He projected images of the raw ingredients for the portobello sandwiches.

The pair gave a few clacks of their beaks. He got the distinct impression they thought his food choices were absurd.

"What are they saying?" Celia murmured.

Glancing back at her, he discovered she'd finished off her sandwich, too. "They don't think our food is worth eating."

The corners of her mouth turned up. "I think our culinary expertise has just been insulted."

"I'm not sure I'll ever recover."

Her soft laugh made him grin.

The birds hopped back a few paces, their chest feathers puffing out.

Sorry. That's how we express joy.

Their chests deflated, but they kept their distance.

"Do you want to try talking to them?" he asked Celia, tucking her napkin and his into his pack.

"If they're okay with it, sure."

He shifted his position on the blanket so she wasn't having to look past him to see the birds, and rested his hand on her knee. "I don't know if my touching you will help or not, but it helped Aurora, so it's worth a shot. The first step is hearing what they're saying. Relax your mind and open yourself to any imagery or sensation that comes to you."

"Got it."

He shifted his focus to the birds, who were watching him and Celia like they were the starring players at a live theatre show.

The smaller bird's head swung side to side, peering at him and then Celia with one eye and then the other. *Nesting material?*

He got an image of Celia's tightly braided locks and his short blond hair.

Since it was unlikely any other species on the planet had hair just on their head, it was a logical conclusion for a nesting bird to make. *Not for nesting. It keeps our skin warm and protects us from sunlight. What are your nests like?*

Images flowed to him of a tree bower and a bowl-shaped nest of sticks, reeds, and feathers. Again, very similar to what you'd find from Earth birds.

Your nest?

He projected images of his bed on the *Starhawke*.

The larger bird tilted its head to the side. *In a cave?*

Another logical assumption for a terrestrial creature. He wasn't sure how to convey the idea of a mobile cave without confusing them or freaking them out. They wouldn't have been able to see *Starlet* when the shuttle landed, or the Yruf scout ships, but he sent an image of *Starlet* anyway.

Another image flashed into his mind of a different shuttle, one he recognized instantly. "*Gypsy*," he said out loud.

"What?" Celia asked.

He glanced at her. "They saw Nat's shuttle when she was here with Ror."

Celia studied the two birds. "No wonder they decided to approach us. They've seen humans before."

"Are you seeing any imagery?"

"No, but—"

"Micah?" Unity floated down the embankment toward them.

The birds fluttered their wings, then took to the air and circled overhead.

"That's the end of that," Celia murmured, reaching for her socks and boots.

Micah did the same, turning toward Unity. "What's up?"

"Aurora wanted us to let you know she's ready to hike out on another sample gathering expedition."

"Okay. Tell her we'll be up in a couple minutes."

"Will do." Unity reversed course, heading back up the hill.

A quick glance at the sky confirmed the birds had left the area. "So, you didn't have any luck hearing them?" he asked Celia as he pulled on his socks.

"No. But I'm wondering if it'll be hard for me to focus on projected imagery since I'm already paying close attention to visual cues and body language."

"I hadn't thought of that." He laced up the Kraed boots he'd been given by Siginal, appreciating how they molded to his feet. He'd been thrilled to discover they provided greater protection from the elements than even his hiking boots. He'd need to thank Siginal again the next time he saw him. "I wonder if Ifel could help."

"How?" Celia rose with a dancer's grace and picked up her pack.

He was just a few seconds behind her. "To really practice, you'd need an environment where you'd feel safe closing your eyes. This," he gestured around them, "has too many unknown variables."

"True."

He slipped his pack over his shoulders. "But in the Yruf biosphere, you'd have lots of animals to practice with without any concern about threats. You could relax your guard." As soon as he planted the idea in his brain, he wanted to see it come to fruition. "I'll talk to Ahle." He flashed her a grin as they started up the hill. "Maybe you and I could hitch a ride with the Yruf for the trip home."

Sixty-Four

"How's the package?" Cade murmured as he and Nat strolled hand-in-hand along the main thoroughfare, heading back toward the concourse.

"Captain Montgomery's vitals are steady," Unity informed him.

"How close is Williams to the security screening?"

"He just met up with Pete and Marlin a moment ago. They're moving into line with the other cargo haulers."

Nat's fingers tightened on Cade's. "Is anyone taking particular notice of them?" she whispered without moving her lips.

He met her gaze as they both listened to Unity's reply.

"No. They have seven other people in front of them."

Cade paused in front of a shop window, the reflection allowing him to check whether they'd picked up a tail. His gaze moved over the stream of pedestrians flowing behind them.

Still clear. He squeezed Nat's hand, resuming their stroll.

"What about Patel and Gavin?" she murmured.

"Already onboard *Phoenix*."

She let out a small sigh.

He was detecting a lot of excitement in her emotional field and none of the nervous agitation she'd struggled with when they'd first arrived on the station. In fact, now that they were on the move with the cargo, she seemed to be thriving on the danger. No wonder she did well as a smuggler.

They passed the last row of shops, entering the open atrium that fed into the array of concourses.

Cade's gaze cut to the left, where the sign for H-4 hung above the security station for their concourse. To the left of the passenger queue, a line of uniformed crewmembers from various private vessels waited in a wide chute for the oversized security scanner, their cargo dollies stacked with crates. He spotted Marlin, Tam, and Pete in their matching black jumpsuits with red piping, Marlin in front, Tam in the middle, and Pete behind.

Itorye had fashioned the jumpsuits during the flight in. She'd even managed to embroider a *Phoenix* logo Nat had created onto the front pocket of each jumpsuit. It gave a professional touch to the uniforms, helping the trio to blend in with the crews from the other ships. No one in line was giving them more than a cursory glance as they made their way along the queue, accepting them for what they appeared to be.

Which was good. They needed to be inconspicuous.

Before he and Nat had left *Phoenix*, the group had brainstormed ways to get Unity in control of the scanner, but Unity simply couldn't move quickly enough in their micro form to insert themselves into the system in the time they had available. However, they were integrated with the smuggling crate's systems, which should add another layer of protection from the scan.

"Marlin's going through screening now," Unity informed them.

Cade forced his steps to remain unhurried, watching out of the corner of his eye.

Marlin pushed his dolly onto the cargo scanner and stepped to the side, his posture relaxed. He chatted with one of the security officers while he waited for the scanner to go over the crates loaded on the dolly.

Tam leaned on the handle of his dolly, watching the activity with casual interest. He straightened as the lead security officer waved Marlin through, then pushed his dolly with the crate concealing Montgomery onto the cargo scanner.

Cade's fingers tightened around Nat's. "Moment of truth." He really didn't want to instigate plan B if this went sideways. Having Unity create chaos with the station's systems so the rest of them could make a run for *Phoenix* during the uproar would be risky and generate the kind of attention they wanted to avoid.

She moved closer, gazing up at him with feigned adoration. "It'll work," she assured him, though the thread of unease in her emotional field proved she wasn't as supremely confident as she sounded.

He slowed as he and Nat approached the passenger queue. If they went much farther, they'd lose sight of Tam in the crew chute.

"Scan complete," Unity informed him.

Cade's shoulders lowered.

"But…"

They went right back up.

A guard stepped next to the crate and gestured at Tam, then pointed at the crate.

"They want him to open the crate."

Nat pulled Cade to a halt, turning slightly. Then she slipped her arms around his back and snuggled close, resting her cheek on his chest so she was facing the chute.

She was good. Now they could stay where they were and watch what was happening from under their lashes while pretending they were hugging and murmuring loving words to each other.

Tam opened the top of the crate, revealing all the purposefully overlapping medical supplies concealing the bottom of the crate. The guard leaned closer, poking a telescoping wand into the crate.

Cade's heart thumped in his chest as the guard moved the wand to another section of the crate, peering way too intently at the contents. Tam said something, and the guard glanced over at him. A second later their serious expression cracked into a wry grin, apparently at whatever Tam had said. They nodded in agreement, then stepped back.

Lowering the wand, they waved at Tam to close the crate.

Nat let out a relieved sigh as Tam sealed the crate and pushed it off the scanner bed.

"On our way," Unity informed them.

Pete moved his dolly onto the scanner as Tam disappeared into the lift that would take him to the lower deck and *Phoenix's* cargo bay.

"Williams is better at this than I would have expected."

"I have a very talented team."

She tipped her head back. "Who apparently know how to get on the good side of security officers."

Cade grinned. "He should. He's the only one from the unit who can make Reynolds smile."

"She smiles?" Nat's fake eyelashes fluttered in disbelief. "Reynolds? Ms. Fierce and Stoic? You're telling me she has a sense of humor?"

"She does," Cade assured her. "It's dry, but it's fun when she lets it out."

"Hmm. I'll take your word for it."

The passenger queue for H-4 was shorter going this direction than it had been to enter the station. However, after standing in line for several minutes, he realized it was moving at a snail's pace.

The security officer checking IDs looked tired and annoyed, a bad combination. Worse yet, they were taking their aggravation out on the passengers, scrutinizing every ID and face with deep suspicion.

Not what he and Nat needed. They were the ones holding up *Phoenix*'s departure.

Nat opened the handles of the bakery bag she'd been carrying, the one purchase she'd made before heading to the security station. He'd assumed it was a gift for her crew, but the calculated look in her eyes made it clear she had another plan.

She gave him a subtle wink, pulling one of the small boxes out of the bag and opening it.

The aroma of baked cinnamon and caramelized sugar wafted out, causing several people in front of them to turn around.

The woman directly in front of them licked her lips as Nat nibbled at the edges of the gooey confection. "Where did you find that?"

Nat gave her a megawatt smile. "Aren't they decadent? It's a cute place just a little way down on the right." She waved in the direction they'd come. "It's called the Bakehouse." She took a small bite and hummed low in her throat.

The woman looked from Nat to the three people in line ahead of her, then back again. Taking a decisive step to the side, she returned Nat's smile. "I'm gonna go check it out."

"Enjoy!" Nat called after her, turning to face forward and taking another bite.

The security officer, Cade noted, was also distracted. His focus drifted to the treat in Nat's hand, a yearning look on his face.

"Do you want a bite?" Nat held the untouched side of the cinnamon roll close to Cade's mouth, a teasing light in her aqua eyes.

She could really play a role well when she got into it. "No thanks, *sweetheart*. It's all yours."

She shrugged. "Suit yourself." She bit off a bigger chunk.

"Next!"

The security officer had moved through the three people in front of them in record time. His gaze drifted to the uneaten portion of Nat's confection, his nose twitching.

Nat fished her ID out of her pocket, handing it to him with a closed-mouth smile as she chewed and swallowed. Cade added his ID, fascinated by how completely Nat had distracted the man from his job.

She blinked at him with those big blue eyes, all innocence. "Have you had one of these?" she gushed. "They're amazing."

The man's mouth started to curve of its own accord. "I have. They are."

Nat leaned closer. "Would you like one? We have plenty." She lifted the bag.

He held up a hand, stopping her. "I can't. Regulations," he added with an apologetic shrug. "But thanks for the offer." He took a quick glance at their IDs, then handed them back. "Safe travels."

Nat beamed at him. "Thank you!"

Cade held in his laugh until they were a safe distance down the concourse with *Phoenix*'s berth in sight. "How did you know that would work?" he asked, grinning at her.

She licked the gooey remains of the cinnamon roll off her fingers. "Statistical probability. Most people love the smells of cinnamon and bread, regardless of whether they eat them. Combine them, and you have a high probability of tapping into subconscious reactions they don't even realize they're having, especially if they're tired or bored."

"You've used this technique before?"

"Yep. Not like this," she gestured at her dress, "but it's the same concept. Engaging someone's senses with something pleasing can be a key element of a successful distraction."

Cade shook his head in bemusement. "Clearly I have a lot to learn."

Sixty-Five

"Is Montgomery's crate secured?" Nat asked the moment her strappy shoes touched *Phoenix's* deck.

"Yes," Alec and Unity answered together.

"Then tell Itorye to contact the tower for clearance to depart." She sealed the airlock. "I'm on my way." She'd like to stop by her cabin to change clothes and get the gunk off her face, but that could wait until Hydra One was no longer visible in the aft view.

"Mind if I join you?" Cade asked, keeping step with her as she headed for the stairway.

"Be my guest."

Voices reached out to them from the direction of the infirmary as they passed B deck. She picked out Williams' and Patel's, but since they weren't raised in an argument, she kept going.

Itorye and Gavin were on the bridge when Nat and Cade arrived. Itorye rose from the pilot's chair "We're scheduled third for departure."

"Thanks. I brought treats." Nat handed Itorye the bag of cinnamon rolls before sliding into the vacated seat. "Any concerns?" she asked as she started the pre-flight checks, bringing *Phoenix's* engines online.

The bag crinkled as Itorye settled into the captain's chair. "No. Unity confirmed station security hasn't issued any alerts."

The tension wrapped around Nat's ribcage eased, but she still fidgeted in her seat, the skirt bunched under her knees and the open-toed shoes on her feet an unwelcome annoyance as she focused on system checks. "As soon as we're in the jump, this stuff comes off," she tossed over her shoulder, sweeping a hand in front of her face and flipping the long strands of hair out of her way.

"Lupe's going to be disappointed you didn't enjoy the experience."

The teasing note in Itorye's voice was unusual enough to make Nat pause and look back.

Itorye gazed at her guilelessly, the bag of cinnamon rolls perched on her lap.

Nat snorted. "I can't imagine why either of you choose to use this stuff voluntarily." She wanted to wipe her hand over her face, but creating a smeared mess wouldn't be an improvement. She was also wary of the fasteners Itorye had used to secure the wig to her head.

Cade was leaning against the bulkhead beside Gavin in the co-pilot's seat, watching her. She motioned to the nav console. "Ever flown this model before?"

"Nope, but I have flown a Cavalier C-83, which is a similar design. Just not as flashy," he added with a crooked smile.

"*Phoenix* is a smooth ride," she agreed, continuing down her checklist. "If you know what you're doing."

A comfortable silence settled over the bridge, the subtle vibration through the deck and the soft taps and clicks as she went through her checks the only sounds until the comm pinged. She opened the channel to the control tower.

"*Phoenix*, this is Hydra One control tower. You are cleared for departure. Disengaging docking clamps."

"Acknowledged, tower."

Firing the thrusters, she eased *Phoenix* away from the airlock, the blue-tinged curve of Heracles coming into view below them. But it wasn't the planet that beckoned to her. It was the starfield.

Maneuvering *Phoenix* into the traffic lane, she engaged the main engines, guiding the ship toward that beautiful starscape. "Unity, are *Gladiator* and the Yruf ships with us?"

"Yep!" Unity replied over the speakers.

"Am I clear to the jump window?"

"All clear. They'll follow you to our rendezvous location."

Ten minutes later, she rose from the pilot's chair, the streaks of light from the interstellar jump streaming past the viewport. "Alec, take over. Itorye, you're with me." She glanced at Cade. "Meet you in the infirmary?"

He nodded.

Removing the wig and makeup took considerably less time than they'd spent putting it on. Peeling the dress off and slipping on her turtleneck and cargo pants brought a sigh of relief.

Itorye gave her a sidelong glance as she carefully stored the wig in the travel case. "Feeling better?"

"Much." She sat on her bunk and started lacing up her boots. Then she paused, meeting Itorye's eye. "Why do you enjoy wearing stuff like that?"

Itorye tilted her head a fraction, considering. "For me, it's an expression of my individuality. My parents established very rigid expectations for how I was supposed to look. I had a stylist from the time I was three."

"*Three?*" In what world would a three-year-old need a stylist?

"Three," Itorye repeated, smoothing a hand over the wig and closing the case. "She ensured I always met their expectations. That meant no personal expression, no individuality, no freedom. I'm not even sure she saw me as a person. My parents certainly didn't." Her tone flattened, the only sign that the memory bothered her.

Nat winced in sympathy. As a kid struggling to survive on her own, she'd encountered her fair share of people who'd treated her like trash to be removed or a tool to be used, not a person with feelings. "But you must have rebelled at some point."

A slight curve turned up Itorye's lips. "My first act of rebellion was right after the Seijin no Hi. Our Coming of Age day," she explained when Nat frowned. "The stylist made me picture-perfect for the ceremony, and I played the role of the dutiful daughter until the large celebration my parents held at our home afterward. They'd invited all their important and influential friends. And their sons," she added with a sardonic smile. "When my parents paraded me in front of the crowd, they didn't know I'd altered the outfit the stylist designed for me so it would tear away at key places. A few tugs bared a sleeker profile and a lot of skin."

That sounded like the Itorye she knew. "How did your parents react?"

"They were scandalized. They cut off my access to the family money and installed bodyguards to shadow me and keep me out of trouble. For a time, that worked, but eventually I realized how much larger the galaxy was than the tiny slice my parents had allowed me to see. I also befriended one of my bodyguards. She taught me skills that served me later."

So that's how Itorye had learned to fight. But it still seemed like a huge leap to the life she led now. "What made you decide to become a mercenary?"

"Realizing the truth about myself, and how ill-suited I was to the life they'd laid out for me. By combining what I'd learned from my schooling, my bodyguard, and my stylist, I'd developed a very unique skillset." She swept a hand from head to toe. "This is the result."

Nat finished lacing her boot as she considered Itorye's story. "Do you ever miss them?"

"My parents?"

Nat nodded, starting on the other boot.

Itorye was silent for a moment. "I miss the idea of them. As a child, I desperately wanted them to love and accept me. What child doesn't? But they despise who I am. My father told everyone I'm dead."

She jerked her head up. "What?"

Itorye lifted one shoulder in an *it is what it is* shrug. "My friend Baraka gave me that news when I ran into them during the transfer of the children. To my parents, I *am* dead."

Nat's chest constricted. "I'm sorry."

Itorye nodded, looking far more at peace with the situation than she would have been.

She'd always wondered why a woman with Itorye's looks, education, and talents had chosen to become a mercenary. Learning the truth made her respect Itorye even more. Breaking out of the gilded cage her parents had tried to force her into had required a lot of courage and inner strength. "My mom died."

Her body jolted as the words left her mouth, hanging in the air like smoke from a pipe. Why had she said that? She hadn't even been thinking it.

Itorye's eyes widened a fraction. "Were you close?"

An image flooded her mind — glossy brown hair, laughing blue eyes, a loving smile. Her gut twisted. "Yes," she said shortly, focusing on her boot and yanking on the laces. "I was eight."

"I'm sorry."

Her hands stilled, but her mouth kept moving. "It was a drug overdose." Why was she telling Itorye this? She'd clearly lost control of her senses. "She wasn't even a user. She was a paid companion, and pretty enough that we did okay."

She darted a glance at Itorye. No signs of judgment, so her mouth kept babbling. "We lived on BB Hill space station. As a kid, I never questioned why we lived there rather than on the planet. It was all I knew. When I was older, I realized the station had provided her with a steady flow of regular clients, more than if we'd lived on the planet. She didn't think I knew what her work entailed – she'd told me she was in hospitality – but I did. I'd started following her when I was six, after I figured out how to override the lock on our quarters. I got to know that station better than anyone other than the engineers. I also learned how to hide in plain sight, how to blend in. That came in handy later, when I was on my own."

Her fingers clutched her boot laces, the emptiness that always crept up on her when she thought about her mom hollowing out her chest.

Itorye crossed the room, settling beside her on the bunk but without touching her. "What happened to her?"

She bit her lip as tension coiled throughout her body. Seriously, why was she talking about this? She'd never told anyone this story, not even Isin. Why was she turning into an overflowing fountain with Itorye? They needed to get to the infirmary to check on Montgomery.

But the tension coiled tighter, constricting her chest, pressing on her lungs, and making her heart beat erratically. "She met with this new guy, real slick, fancy clothes, oozing money. They ate at the nicest restaurant on the station, a place most of her regulars couldn't afford. But when they left, she was acting funny, having trouble staying on her feet and looking around like she wasn't sure where she was. I'd never seen her like that. He had to practically carry her down the corridor. They didn't go to the hotel where she usually took her clients, either. They went to his ship."

Ice shards slid under her skin. She could still see the man's face, feel the tightness in her belly as she'd watched him drag her mother through the airlock, sealing it behind him. "I waited in the corridor for hours, afraid to move, afraid the ship would leave the station and I'd never see her again." Her hands curled into fists. "The station went into the night cycle, the corridor emptying out. When the airlock finally opened, the guy who came out wasn't the one she'd been with. He was bigger, more muscled. He wore a sanitation uniform and was hauling a big sack across his back. I don't know how I knew, but I did... I just knew..."

The full-body shudder that coursed through her made her teeth rattle. She could still hear the squeak of the man's shoes on the metal decking, his grunts as he stalked toward the business district. "He took her to an alley, pulled her out of the bag, and propped her against one of the reclamation containers. Then he pressed a bottle into her hand and left."

She dragged in a breath, her throat thick. "I stayed with her all night. She was already gone... but I stayed." She'd stared into her mother's unseeing eyes, held her cold hand. She'd wanted to believe that somehow, it was all going to be okay. That it was a nightmare she'd wake up from. That her mother would smooth back her hair, kiss her forehead, tell her she was safe.

But she wasn't safe. She was all alone. "I saw a picture of her on the news vids the next day. That's how I found out about the drug overdose. The newscaster made it sound like she was to blame, like she'd killed herself." Anger heated her skin. "I went back to the airlock, but the ship was already gone. For months I searched the crowds, looking for the man who drugged her, who killed her." She shook her head. "But I never saw him again."

"You lived on your own after that?"

"Yeah." She exhaled, her body aching like she'd been running circles through *Phoenix*'s corridors. But at least she was back on safe ground. "The Hill wasn't designed with kids in mind. No school, no childcare services. If I went to anyone for help, I would have been shipped off. My mother was dead. I didn't want to lose the only home I'd ever known. So, I figured out how to survive."

Itorye let out a soft sigh.

The sound made Nat peer at her out of the corner of her eye. "I don't know why I just told you that."

Itorye met her gaze. "Maybe because you knew I'd understand."

"Maybe." She never would have pegged Itorye as someone she'd confide in. She'd never thought they had much in common, other than Isin. But she didn't regret sharing her past with her. "You won't tell Isin, will you?"

Itorye lifted one sculpted brow. "What do you think?"

Sixty-Six

Cade stopped at his cabin to change his clothes, let U-2 out, and have Unity extract their micro-form from his ear. Then he walked across the corridor to *Phoenix*'s infirmary.

Marlin was helping Tam unpack the medical supplies from the smuggling crate. Patel was nowhere to be seen even though he'd heard her voice when he and Nat had passed B deck on their way to the bridge. "Where's Patel?"

Marlin grimaced. "She decided she didn't want to be present when we woke up Captain Montgomery."

"Ah." Patel's trust issues once again rearing their head.

Marlin's gaze flicked to U-2. He pointed to his ear. "Can you remove...?"

"Sure!" U-2 glided forward, reclaiming their micro-form from Marlin and Tam.

The three of them made short work of removing the remaining items from the crate, tucking them in the infirmary's storage compartments.

Tam took up position at one corner of the empty crate. "You ready?"

Cade stepped to the opposite corner facing him. "Ready."

Tam pressed on the hidden latch that disengaged the crate's exterior side panel from the other three. He and Cade lifted it off and set it aside, revealing the long edge of the crate's hidden substructure. Cade knelt, releasing the locking mechanism on the secret compartment. A soft pop preceded a faint hiss of air.

He lowered the rectangular panel to the deck, the soft light of the infirmary touching the cream-colored padding foam they'd used to keep Montgomery's body stabilized in the rectangular box during transport. He and Tam placed their fingers under the narrow lip of the sliding platform, gently pulling it out like a drawer.

The breathing mask was still secured over Montgomery's nose and mouth, her chest rising and falling in the slow rhythm of sedated sleep. The bag with her change of clothing was tucked in one corner by her foot.

Cade glanced at Tam. "You planning to wake her before we rendezvous with *Gladiator*?"

He shook his head. "But I do want to get her out of the padding and onto the med platform."

Cade helped him extract Montgomery from the foam and transfer her to the infirmary's med platform, then he and Marlin reassembled the crate while Tam ran a scanner over Montgomery. By the time Marlin trundled the crate out of the infirmary and down the corridor, Tam had the mask off Montgomery and was checking her vitals.

A quick glance into the corridor confirmed there was still no sign of Nat. "Where's Nat?" he asked U-2.

"In her cabin with Itorye."

Apparently it was taking longer to ditch her disguise than he'd expected. "Alec, how soon are we scheduled to come out of the interstellar jump?"

"About ten minutes."

An Academy-trained pilot — or Unity, for that matter — would never give such a vague answer, but Nat certainly would. He didn't mistake the response for a lack of precision in Alec's knowledge, or Nat's. He suspected Alec knew the exact time to more decimal places than Cade had ever calculated for a jump. "Do you need help bringing *Phoenix* out of the jump?"

"I do. Nat's leaving her cabin now."

He heard the soft pad of two sets of footsteps on the stairway. But it was the emotional resonances that caught his attention. Nat and Itorye were both giving off a complex emotional vibe that was very different from what he'd sensed on the bridge. They felt more... open with each other. More connected, somehow.

The feeling intensified when they appeared at the entrance to the infirmary, although their expressions were all business as they approached the med platform. Whatever had caused the change, he'd been too focused on Montgomery to pick up on it when it was happening.

"How is she?" Nat asked Tam.

"Stable and sedated. Since we'll be rendezvousing with *Gladiator* shortly, Marina can make the call on when to revive her."

"Is Montgomery aware of Marina's healing abilities?" Itorye asked.

"Dr. Morales was," Cade replied, "at least regarding Lelindia. But I doubt Montgomery has a clue."

"Well, that'll be fun to watch." Nat turned to Cade. "What's the plan after that?"

"That depends on how she reacts to the idea of being treated by Marina's healing abilities, and how long Marina needs to work on her. The Admiral will want to have a group discussion to consider our options, but not until Montgomery's no longer in pain."

"Were you planning to move her to *Gladiator* for the healing?"

"That's your call. *Gladiator* has an infirmary, but yours is nicer and roomier."

"I don't mind if she stays. Like I said, I'm curious to see Marina in action. I was on *Vengeance*'s bridge when she was treating the kids."

"How about the discussion after she's healed? Can we hold it on *Phoenix*?" *Gladiator* would be cramped quarters, especially if Nat's crew wanted to join in.

"You're welcome to stay on *Phoenix* and use the lounge," Nat offered. "In fact, you can stay until we return to Zeta Tucanae."

"You wouldn't mind?"

"I wouldn't, but…" Nat glanced at Itorye.

She stepped into the corridor. "I'll go talk to Darsha, alert her we'll be having more guests."

"Thanks. I'll head up to the bridge for the jump."

"We'll go with you." U-2 glided toward Nat. "We need to extract ourselves from you and Gavin. Dr. Patel and Pete, too."

"Hang on, Unity." Cade held up a hand. "Before you go, can you let everyone on *Gladiator* know the plan?"

"Sure."

"And tell Marina I'll meet her at the airlock?"

"Okay."

Gladiator docked with *Phoenix* with a seamless efficiency that told him Gryphon was at the helm. Drew's piloting skills were solid for a back-up pilot, but her opportunities to practice ship-to-ship docking had been limited during the Elite Unit's missions. He made a mental note to schedule practice time for her with him and Gryphon when they returned to the *Starhawke.*

Marina was waiting at the airlock, concern and eagerness pulsing in her emotional field. Admiral Schreiber stood with her, his emotions not much different.

Her gaze swept the corridor behind Cade. "Where is she?"

"Up one deck. Follow me."

Gryphon jogged into view behind Marina, joining the group as they climbed the stairs to the infirmary.

As soon as they entered, Marina and Gryphon moved to either side of the med platform, their focus on Montgomery. Cade and the Admiral joined Tam on the periphery.

Marina winced as her gaze panned down Montgomery's body. "She's lucky to be alive and not paralyzed," she murmured. "The damage to her spine…" She glanced at Cade. "Does she have any idea why I'm here?"

"We didn't tell her anything about you. It's your call on how to handle this."

Marina nodded. "Then let's find out how she reacts." Placing a hand on Montgomery's shoulder near her nape, she engaged her emerald-green energy field. The brilliant glow flowed across Montgomery's sternum, neck, and head.

The sound of footsteps made Cade turn. Nat and Gavin appeared at the infirmary entrance.

"What's happening?" Nat asked in a stage whisper, watching Marina.

"I'm blocking her pain receptors so I can clear the sedative and pain medication from her system," Marina answered without taking her attention off Montgomery. "That way she'll be coherent and pain-free for our discussion."

"Oh." Nat sidled next to Cade, her gaze shifting to Gryphon. "We haven't met."

He smiled. "I'm Gryphon, Marina's mate. You must be Nat."

"Yep. This is Gavin." She pointed over her shoulder. "And that's Admiral Schreiber," she told Gavin.

"Who are you?"

Montgomery's husky voice drew everyone's attention back to the med platform.

Marina didn't move her hand, her energy field continuing to swirl over Montgomery as she met her gaze. "Dr. Marina Forrest. My daughter is Dr. Lelindia Forrest, the *Starhawke*'s medical officer."

Montgomery's eyes widened a fraction, focusing on Marina's face. Then her gaze slipped past Marina, resting on the Admiral. "Will." Both grief and joy infused the single syllable.

He stepped beside the med platform. "Hello, Colleen."

Her shrewd gaze swept over him. "Cmd. Ellis told us you were okay, but... thank you for being here."

"I wish it were under better circumstances."

Montgomery's mouth pinched. "I'm lucky to be here at all." She turned to Marina. "Have you had time to form an opinion on how long I'll be laid up?"

Montgomery wasn't one to beat around the bush.

Marina kept her expression professionally neutral, but Cade sensed her eagerness to start Montgomery's healing. "I have. If you're open to a different form of treatment, I can have you walking on your own by tomorrow."

Montgomery stared at her without blinking, like she was waiting for the punch line. When Marina's expression didn't change, she turned to the Admiral. "She's joking, right?"

"No. It's why she's here. Marina and her daughter are gifted with a special ability unlike anything our medical professionals can achieve. They can literally heal with touch. Lelindia's abilities saved my life. I wouldn't be standing here today if it weren't for her."

Now Montgomery was looking at the Admiral with concern, like he had a screw loose.

Cade stepped forward. "How about a demonstration?" He held out his hand toward Marina and turned to Tam. "We need a scalpel."

Tam didn't hesitate, producing one from the storage cabinets and handing it to Marina.

"What are you doing?" Montgomery pushed back into the pillow, her eyes widening.

"Proving what Marina can do," Cade told her. This had worked to convince Ahle, so he already knew how effective it would be in overcoming Montgomery's disbelief.

Marina rested her left hand underneath his, the scalpel poised over his palm. The cool touch of her energy field numbed his hand as she brought the blade down, creating a thin slice across his palm that welled with blood.

He turned his hand slightly, showing the cut to Montgomery, the blood oozing across his skin.

Her gaze darted from face to face, her body tense.

"It doesn't hurt," he told her. "Marina's blocked the pain so I don't feel it. Now she'll heal the cut."

Marina handed the scalpel to Tam, her left hand still cradling Cade's.

The soothing coolness of her energy field pressed into his skin. He tuned into Montgomery's emotional reaction as the blood retreated back under the slit of skin before it sealed up, leaving no sign of the damage.

Confusion dominated her emotional grid, surrounding a mishmash of emotions consistent with a sense of unreality. She clearly expected to wake up from what she thought was a drug-induced dream or hallucination.

But as everyone remained silent, waiting for her reaction, her gaze slowly lifted to Marina's. "How?"

"I have the ability to see and interact energetically at a cellular level. I can restore damaged cells to their healthy state, remove toxins, and suppress pain."

"That's not possible."

"Not for humans, that's true. But I'm not human. I come from a race known as the Suulh."

Montgomery's composure slipped. "What the hell is going on here, Will?" she demanded.

The Admiral sat on the edge of the med platform. "It's true, Colleen. The Suulh homeworld is in Teeli space. Marina and Gryphon escaped when the Teeli attacked their homeworld. Their path brought them into Fleet space, where they've been living ever since. Biologically, they're nearly indistinguishable from humans, but they have abilities we don't."

Montgomery swallowed, working hard to regain her emotional stability as his words sank in. "How long have you known about them?" The question came out with more than a hint of censure.

"I've been aware of their existence for years. Siginal has as well. We've been watching over them, protecting them from the Teeli, who want to weaponize their abilities."

"The Teeli." Montgomery frowned. "And Siginal knows?"

The Admiral nodded.

Her gaze shifted to Marina. "Your daughter's one of these..."

"Suulh."

"Suulh," she repeated, testing it on her tongue. "Does Captain Hawke know?"

"Yes. She's half Suulh."

Montgomery's eyes flew wide.

"Her mother is my energy sister. Her father is Human."

It was a lot to take in, but Montgomery was a seasoned officer. She'd spent decades processing new information quickly and efficiently. "Can she...?" She gestured at Cade's hand.

"She has healing abilities, though not like mine or Lelindia's. Her talents favor manipulating energy. She can form an energy shield capable of deflecting most attacks."

Montgomery mulled that over, her gaze eventually landing on the Admiral. "Why didn't you ever tell me?"

"Because of the Teeli threat. Even Aurora and Lelindia weren't aware I knew of their existence. It's why Siginal accepted the professorship at the Academy. Jonarel was able to confirm Aurora's and Lelindia's abilities, and help keep those abilities a secret."

Montgomery's eyes narrowed. "No wonder you took such an interest in their careers."

The Admiral frowned. "It wasn't favoritism, I assure you. They were already exceptional cadets who became exceptional officers. Their achievements are their own, regardless of their biology or ancestry. They've proven themselves to be the very best of what the Fleet aspires to be. Even after the Fleet turned on them," he added, his voice hollowing out.

A similar emptiness cratered Montgomery's emotional field. "I never believed the charges against you. But Nixon's behavior since taking over and my *accident* put a fine point on it."

The Admiral's face hardened. "He's weakening the Fleet to pave the way for a Teeli invasion."

Montgomery nodded slowly, turning to Marina. "You're telling me you can heal my injuries with touch?"

"That's right. It's the reason you're not feeling any pain right now."

Montgomery blinked, her gaze moving to her body as if she'd just realized the truth of Marina's words. "You did that?"

"I did. And I could have you walking by tomorrow. Maybe even this evening, though you'll need assistance until you regain your strength and balance."

Montgomery licked her lips, then clenched her jaw. "Okay." She visibly braced. "Go ahead."

Marina smiled softly. "There won't be any pain. You'll feel a coolness surrounding you, that's all. You might even fall asleep. Just allow your body to rest. We'll do all the work."

"We?"

Marina's gaze flicked to Gryphon.

He gave Montgomery a jovial smile. "I'm Gryphon, Marina's mate. I'll be helping her. My energy field isn't specifically attuned for healing others like Marina's, but it helps make her abilities stronger. Working together will decrease the amount of time it takes to heal the damage you sustained."

Montgomery eyed him. "So you're one of these Suulh?"

"Yes."

Her gaze moved over him, then over Marina. "You look human."

Gryphon chuckled. "You look Suulh."

That cracked Montgomery's stoicism, a micro-smile touching her mouth. "Fair enough."

"Are you ready?" Marina asked, shifting closer.

Montgomery gave a tight nod. "Let's do it."

Cade covered his smile with his hand. Montgomery was still acting like she was wading into battle. She'd realize soon enough that a Suulh healing was an experience she'd never forget.

Sixty-Seven

Nat watched from the periphery as Marina and Gryphon took up positions facing each other, Montgomery between them. Marina's thick ponytail swung forward over her shoulder as she rested her right hand on Montgomery's thigh just above the edge of the cast, her left hand on Montgomery's shoulder. Gryphon mirrored her pose, but his focus was on her rather than Montgomery.

Cade gave an audible inhale at the same time Montgomery did.

Nat looked over at him. He was watching with rapt attention, his gaze shifting up and down Montgomery's body.

Nat glanced at Montgomery, but nothing had visibly changed. Well, almost nothing. Montgomery's eyes were drifting shut, her body relaxing, her head resting against the pillow.

But Cade was definitely seeing *something*. "What are you seeing?" she asked in an undertone, nudging him with her elbow.

"Their energy fields."

"I know *that*." She gave him another poke with her elbow. "What does it look like?"

His gaze dropped to hers, his lips curving in a teasing smile. "It's—" He paused, cluing in that she wasn't the only one waiting for an answer. Gavin, Williams, and the Admiral were, too.

He cleared his throat. "Marina's energy field is a brilliant emerald green. It's flowing over Montgomery's body, concentrating right now on her leg. Gryphon's field is yellow-gold, and it's weaving through hers like threads on a loom."

That was a more artistic description than she would have expected. "Sounds pretty."

"It is."

Too bad she couldn't see it. It would make the whole thing more interesting.

"Our fields aren't actually a single color," Marina murmured, her gaze still on Montgomery. "Emerald-green is the base color for mine, but it contains multiple shades of green, both lighter and darker than the dominant shade, like highlights and shadows."

Cade blinked. "Really?" He peered closer. "You're right."

"What are you seeing?" Nat prompted when he didn't elaborate.

"Subtle color tones, ranging from a dark green that's nearly black to a light green that's almost white, blending in and out of the dominant emerald green."

"Exactly," Marina confirmed. "You're used to looking at Aurora's field, which is the full color palette swirling together to form a base of white like a prism. Mine is one slice of that palette, light to dark. So is Gryphon's."

Now she really wished she could see it.

After a couple minutes of silence, she nudged Cade again. "How long is this going to take?"

Gryphon answered her. "A while. We're fine here, if you all want to go."

"I'm staying." Williams stepped closer to Gryphon, a portable med scanner in his hand that he was directing at Montgomery's leg. "As long as you don't mind?"

"Not at all," Gryphon replied. "Scan away."

"Well, I'm going to check in with my crew." She sent Gavin a significant look. Itorye hadn't returned, which in her mind indicated Patel was making a fuss.

He nodded, catching her meaning. "I'll go with you."

They left Cade and the Admiral to their own devices, stepping into the corridor. U-2 was hovering near the stairway out of sight of the infirmary.

"Are you hiding out here?" Nat asked them.

"We didn't think Captain Montgomery should see us."

"Smart." Although Montgomery would probably be learning about them soon enough. "Where are Patel and Itorye?"

"In the wine bar."

"Thanks."

She didn't hear raised voices drifting up the stairwell as she and Gavin descended, so that was something. She was also surprised to spot Marlin seated next to Patel at one of the wine bar's four-person high-tops.

Marlin lifted his iced tea glass in Nat's direction. "Thanks for the goodies." He pointed to the platter of cinnamon rolls sitting on the table. He'd cut them into bite-sized pieces and arranged them in a spiral pattern. At least half the spiral was already gone.

"Glad you approve." She glanced at Patel, who looked a lot more mellow than she'd expected. Had Itorye not talked to her yet about Cade's team joining them on *Phoenix* for their planning session?

Patel took a sip from her iced tea. "I understand we're going to have more visitors soon."

That answered that question. "We are." Nat scooted the remaining empty chair closer to Marlin while Gavin snagged a fifth chair from a nearby table. "Marina and Gryphon are healing Montgomery right now, but once she's able to move around a bit, the Admiral wants to have a group discussion about what to do next. I offered them the lounge." She watched Patel for any sign of an impending blowup.

Patel nodded. "I was impressed with how efficiently they extracted Montgomery from Hydra One. Unity was able to provide me with audio when Dr. Williams took the crate through. He comported himself very well."

Was that *admiration* in her voice? Surely not.

Marlin nodded. "I was concerned he'd run into trouble at the security check, but then I saw how he interacted with the security officers when we brought the empty crates onto the station. He has a way of inspiring confidence and trust."

So, Marlin and Patel were now Team Williams. Good to know.

"We've been discussing whether to tell the rest of them about Alec," Itorye said, picking up one of the cinnamon roll pieces and popping it in her mouth.

"Really?" Itorye could have said they were planning to do an improv comedy routine for the group and Nat wouldn't have been more surprised. She met Patel's gaze. "Why the change of heart?"

Patel swirled the ice in her glass, then took a sip. "It's been brought to my attention that if Alec is to experience a life that isn't limited to this ship and crew, I will have to learn to trust others with the knowledge of his existence."

"Okay." But until now, Patel had seemed content to push that decision years into the future.

Patel gazed into her glass like answers were carved into the chunks of ice. "Seeing how Unity was able to help with the extraction on Hydra One without anyone being aware of them gave me a whole new perspective on what was possible for Alec." She sighed. "I don't want him to be stunted or confined. He could do so much more, *be* so much more. What Unity has shown him has brought him joy in a way my narrow rules and restrictions would never allow. Unity's so happy with their existence. I want that for Alec, too."

"I am happy, Mom." Alec appeared beside their table, between Patel and Itorye.

Patel pivoted to face him. "Not like Unity."

"Unity's life experience has been very different from mine. They're also a *lot* older than I am. Their joy is in large part a result of their lived experience. I'm just getting started."

"And I've been holding you back."

Alec rested a hand over Patel's. "Mom, you've given me so much, loved me so deeply. You and Gavin gave me life. I wouldn't exist without you. Don't feel guilty because you've wanted to protect me from harm."

Patel's eyes took on a slight sheen. "I want what's best for you, Alec. That's all I've ever wanted."

"I know. That's what I want for you, too."

Patel's bottom lip trembled. "Seeing you happy... seeing what you've become..." She blinked rapidly. "You've surpassed my wildest dreams."

A sniff from Nat's left made her aware Gavin was fighting the same battle as Patel. The tender look in his eyes revealed how much this moment meant to him.

Alec held Patel's gaze. "Will you allow me to meet the rest of Cade's team?"

Patel gazed back, her face scrunching as she struggled to keep the tears from falling. Then she took a deep breath and rolled her shoulders. "You know what, Alec?" She pressed her lips together and lifted her chin, looking like someone staring at a cliff they were about to leap off of. "In every way that counts, you've shown you're an adult. You don't need my permission anymore. From now on, those decisions are up to you."

No one moved a muscle. Not even Alec. He stared at Patel in stunned shock. They all did.

Patel's gaze swung around the table. "What?"

That burst the bubble. Nat huffed a laugh. So did Gavin and Marlin. Itorye smiled wider than Nat had ever seen. And Alec... well, Alec looked like he was standing in the sun for the first time.

Sixty-Eight

Isin was grateful for the distraction *Starlet*'s return gave him. He and Sweep had just finished the evening meal delivery to the brig. Mirko had harangued him from the moment he entered the room, blaming him for her current circumstances and demanding he take her back to her ship.

He'd given her the cold stare her comments deserved, then informed her he'd be delighted to leave her on *Sphinx* now that the ship was open to the vacuum of space. That had shut her up long enough that he could deliver Manchado's meal and exit the brig in relative peace.

But he was counting the hours until they could deliver the pair to the planet's surface. Hopefully Aurora had good news to report.

Earlier, he'd spent more time than he should have staring at images Sweep had pulled up – at his insistence – of the craters and wide troughs carved into the planet's surface where the remains of Tnaryt's ship had obliterated the vegetation.

The ragged grooves and circular impact points pockmarked the surface at the far edge of the visual range of *Vengeance*'s cameras. The images were grainy, but clear enough to make his heart shudder in his chest as a chill spread through his veins.

Natasha had been on that ship. She'd almost been incinerated when it fell out of orbit, a victim of Tnaryt's and the Sovereign's sadistic cruelty. If she'd died here, he never would have known her fate. Never would have held her in his arms. Never would have kissed her. Or told her he loved her.

Searing heat burned away the chill, his heart pounding out a rhythm of retribution.

Tnaryt was dead, his body decomposing somewhere far below. But the Sovereign was still alive and well.

He sincerely hoped he got to meet her someday. It would be a long and torturous interaction. For her.

Jake and Butterfly were outside the main hatch to the transport bay when he arrived, waiting until the bay pressurized. "Is the infirmary prepped for testing the samples they're bringing up?"

Jake nodded. "I'm optimistic we'll discover our two guests will have plenty to eat on this planet."

"I'd settle for an adequate amount." He didn't much care whether the food was palatable or varied. If it kept them at subsistence level survival, he was good with it.

He tapped the control panel as soon as the indicators flashed green, the solid doors parting to admit them.

Aurora led the way down the ramp of the *Starhawke's* shuttle. She smiled as soon as she met his gaze. "We have two promising locations," she called out, striding toward him. "And plant samples galore." Her gaze shifted to Jake. "Where do you want them?"

"We have everything set up in the infirmary. Just follow me."

Aurora handed her pack off to her brother. "I want to talk to Isin for a moment."

Micah shouldered the pack. "Okay. See you in a bit."

Aurora motioned Isin toward *Starlet* while her brother, Celia, and Libra headed after Jake and Butterfly. Aurora's dad stayed behind, walking beside Aurora up the ramp into the shuttle.

Aurora halted next to the opening to the cockpit, turning toward Isin.

His gaze rose to Unity's egg-shaped mobile unit, which was tucked into an alcove in the ceiling. This unit sported a gold circle on its base. "Is this a different unit?" He pointed to the new coloring. It definitely hadn't been on the unit he'd seen previously.

She smiled. "No, that's still U-1. They made the change to differentiate themselves from the other mobile units we were working with on the surface."

"We want you to be happy!" Unity chirped. "Micah seems to favor this unit. So does Celia. We didn't want to confuse them. Or cause a sense of loss if we switched units."

Brendan's eyes crinkled at the corners as he gazed at U-1. "You're an astute observer of human behavior, Unity. And you're right. Micah and Celia do have a fondness for this unit. It's irrational, since every unit is you, but that doesn't change the human tendency toward attachment. We appreciate your thoughtfulness in making this unit distinctive for our benefit."

"It's fun!" Unity jiggled slightly, like they were dancing, but they remained tucked into the alcove. "We like making new patterns. We might make new designations and patterns for all our units."

Aurora's brows lifted. "How would Ifel feel about that?"

"She doesn't mind. She encourages us to grow and explore who we are."

Isin couldn't help contrasting that response with Patel's attitude toward Alec. She seemed inclined to keep him locked away. She could learn a lot from Unity and the Yruf. Unity's openness and enthusiasm were clearly feeding Alec's desire to discover his full potential.

Isin was in favor of that. He'd gone from being totally freaked out about the existence of a non-biological onboard when he first met Alec, to championing Alec's independence.

Good to know he could grow, too. "Tell me about these two locations."

Aurora gave him a detailed description of the location she'd scouted, then Brendan described the one he and Libra had inspected.

"They sound ideal, assuming the plant life is edible and the water is potable."

"The water's fine," Aurora assured him. "That was something the Yruf could check before we arrived."

Isin folded his arms loosely over his chest. It almost sounded too good to be true. "What's the next step?"

"That will depend on what we learn about the plant life. As soon as my mom and Celia determine there's enough food at each site to sustain our residents, then we can begin construction on the habitats."

"What about wildlife?"

Aurora and her dad shared an amused look. "Micah introduced us to the largest mammal, which is only about knee high. They were non-aggressive but curious. If these sites pan out, I'll make sure Micah warns them — and the rest of the fauna — to stay out of sight of our guests."

Isin grunted in agreement. Mirko and Manchado were the kind of sociopaths who would kill other creatures just for fun. "You're not leaving them any weapons, are you?"

"We'll need to provide them with a few cooking knives, but they'd really have to work to hunt with those. Hoaloha gave Micah a rundown on all the other animals in the area. There's nothing large enough or lethal enough to be of concern unless Mirko or Manchado choose to do something really stupid. But that would be true anywhere we put them."

"Guaranteed they'll do something stupid. It's in their natures." But that wasn't their problem to solve. "Is Hoaloha one of the Yruf?"

Aurora shook her head. "That's the name Micah gave the native creature who hung out with us."

"It means *friend* in Hawaiian," Brendan added.

He was sorry he'd missed that interaction. His eight-year-old self would have been fascinated. "Any news from the Yruf?"

"Ifel will be taking her transport down to the surface during the night cycle," Unity replied. "She's making a reconciliation visit to the Etah tomorrow."

That sparked his interest. "What does she hope to accomplish?"

"To broker peace. To let them know the Yruf will not harm them. To offer protection from the other factions. Originally she was going to offer them a permanent place on our ship, but now that our scouts have seen the planet, she's considering other options."

Aurora's eyes narrowed. "Such as?"

"She hasn't told us. But we know she's planning something."

Aurora looked a little unnerved, which caused Isin's neck muscles to tighten. "Is that a problem?" he asked her.

"No," she said slowly, elongating the vowel sound as her eyes got a faraway look, "but it might be a good idea for me to take a trip over to her ship after she returns."

Sixty-Nine

"Marina and Gryphon are finishing up with Montgomery," U-2 informed Cade from the charging station Pete had completed in *Phoenix*'s gym.

Cade slowed his pace on the treadmill, adjusting the controls to a walk so he could cool down. The day had pushed into the night cycle, the lack of any activity to keep him occupied making him drowsy. He'd asked Nat if he could use the exercise equipment onboard, and she'd sent him to the crew gym on A deck. His team had joined him, Reynolds and Drew lifting weights, Gonzo riding one of the stationary bikes, and Justin running on a treadmill next to Cade.

Cade snagged the towel draped over the grab bar and mopped his face and hair. "How's Montgomery doing?"

"She's not awake yet, but they've removed both casts and the back brace. Marina said the bone and spinal damage is completely healed, although the muscles are weak."

Montgomery would be thrilled to be free of the restraints. Cade switched off his treadmill and stepping down to the deck, turning to the rest of the team, who'd assembled in the small open space at the center of the room. "We'll meet outside the infirmary in ten."

He descended the aft stairs to B deck and his cabin, U-2 zipping along beside him. After a quick shower and change of clothes, they met up with Gonzo and Reynolds outside the infirmary.

The Admiral was inside, watching Marina and Gryphon as they worked their hands down Montgomery's leg and arm, their energy fields ebbing and flowing in gentle waves. Tam stood nearby, medical scanner following the movements of their hands.

"How long before she wakes up?" Cade asked, stepping inside. U-2 remained out of sight with Gonzo and Reynolds in the corridor.

"I stopped the induced sedation a while ago," Marina answered him. "The work we're doing now is to stimulate her muscles and restore healthy blood flow." Her gaze flicked to him. "Kind of like an energy massage. She'll wake up whenever her body is ready to. My estimate is within the next fifteen or twenty minutes."

"Marlin has a meal prepped for these two." Tam indicated Marina and Gryphon. "And Montgomery, if she's up for it."

Cade hadn't taken their needs for sustenance after a healing into account. Good thing Tam was on it. "Then maybe we should consider having our meeting in the dining room rather than the lounge. Assuming Montgomery can make it down the stairs." *Phoenix* had a lift, but he'd yet to see anyone use it.

"We'll get her down there," Marina replied. "The regular exercise regime she had before the accident has enabled her body to respond quickly, even after weeks of incapacitation."

Cade nodded. "I'll take my team down there now, give Marlin some help setting things up."

Less than half-an hour later, Montgomery stepped into the dining hall. Gryphon and Tam were on either side of her, supporting her at the elbows. She'd traded the medical gown for a black tailored tunic and pant combination and black boots. She was a little wobbly, but her eyes were clear, her face no longer lined with pain.

Marina and the Admiral entered behind her.

Cade introduced her to Justin, Drew, Gonzo, and Reynolds, and Nat introduced Marlin, the only member of her crew who'd joined them.

"I have a nice meal prepared for you three." Marlin gestured to the place settings at one of the round eight-person tables. "If you'll take a seat, I'll bring it out."

"I'll help," Justin offered, following him to the galley.

The Admiral and Marina sat on either side of Montgomery, while Gryphon, Tam, Cade, and Nat joined them. The rest of his team settled at the table next to them.

"How are you feeling?" Nat asked Montgomery.

"Still weak but no longer broken." Montgomery glanced at Marina and Gryphon. "I honestly didn't believe you could do what you claimed. I was wrong."

Marina smiled. "We threw a lot at you. I appreciate your willingness to trust us on such short acquaintance."

Montgomery nodded. "Knowing it's your daughter on the *Starhawke* helped. Her reputation in the Fleet is top-notch." A shadow fell over her face. "At least it was. Now…" Her jaw flexed. "We've got a problem to solve."

"Food first," Marlin said as he and Justin placed dishes from a serving cart in front of Montgomery, Marina, and Gryphon. "You can't plan on an empty stomach." He snagged Montgomery's glass and filled it with water from a pitcher.

"Thank you for the food, Marlin." She took an appreciative sniff. "Smells delicious."

He smiled. "You're welcome. I'm guessing the food options in the medical center were focused on sustenance, not flavor."

That coaxed a wry smile from Montgomery. "You would be correct." Her gaze slid to the Admiral as she dipped her spoon into her soup bowl. "If we're not going to start planning yet, why don't you bring me up to speed on the status of the *Starhawke*."

The Admiral gave her an overview of the damage the *Starhawke* had sustained escaping from Sol Station, the repairs the crew had made, and the ship's current location, recharging in the Zeta Tucanae system.

"How much longer before the ship can leave the system?"

"Jonarel estimates a little more than a week for a full recharge."

"But other than the power drain, the ship is fully functional again?"

"Correct."

"Good. When I saw the vids of the escape, I thought you'd be stuck on Drakar making repairs for the foreseeable future. What about the other ship, the small fighter that blocked the strike from the station's cannon? How does it figure in?"

Cade answered that one. "That's *Gladiator*, a ship my team acquired last year. Built like a tank. He's docked with *Phoenix* right now."

Montgomery straightened. "Is that wise?"

He wasn't certain the Admiral wanted Montgomery to know about the Yruf, so he chose his words carefully. "*Gladiator* recently got an upgrade that allows for camouflaging in most situations. No one will see him."

Montgomery absorbed that, then her gaze shifted to Nat. "How did you get tapped for this mission?"

"Aurora asked for my help in locating a suitable system to complete the *Starhawke*'s repairs. We've been working together ever since."

Montgomery was too shrewd to miss the implications. "She contacted you *after* she broke out of Seaview?"

Nat nodded.

Montgomery's scrutiny intensified. "Captain Hawke must trust you a great deal."

"We trust each other."

"How long have you known each other?"

"Long enough."

Montgomery's eyes narrowed at the evasive answer. She took a slow sip from her water glass, studying Nat. "Your loyalty is admirable. But it doesn't explain why you risked your ship and crew to rescue me, a stranger."

"Colleen." The Admiral gave her a hard look.

"It's okay." Nat sat forward, resting her forearms on the table. "You were important to the Admiral, and like you said on the station, we're both fighters. We're going to need fighters to deal with what's coming."

"Yes, we are."

"Which brings us back to the reason you're here." The Admiral gave the tabletop a decisive tap, like he was calling a meeting to order. "Why don't you fill us in on *Cassini's* situation."

Montgomery sighed. Pushing her empty soup bowl away, she leaned back in her chair. "At the time of the assassination attempt, Nixon was making questionable decisions, especially regarding personnel, but he hadn't ramped up to the fervor he has now. Rehema and I thought we'd have time — for me to heal, and for her to track down the person responsible — before I returned to *Cassini* to deal with the situation. The only reason I agreed to leave in the first place was to free her and Lt. Ocasio to focus on the investigation. I was a liability to them while I was confined to a med platform. I needed to be off the ship until I healed enough to be back in the fight."

Cade could feel her yearning to do just that.

"I didn't anticipate the assassin following me to Eridani Duo, or Nixon tightening security between ED and Hydra One. Now *Cassini* has orders to return to ED and Nixon's sent his personal physician to check on me. He's *very concerned* for my welfare." Harsh sarcasm overlaid her words. "He's also sending Teeli consuls, just like he did with the *Argo.* I've placed Anthony and my crew in the line of fire while saving my own skin."

Her self-reproach rasped over Cade's empathic senses.

"You can't protect them by blaming yourself for circumstances beyond your control, Colleen." The Admiral gazed at her with empathy, but also the fortitude of hard-won experience. "Every move he's made is designed to weaken the Southern quadrant defenses, to set the stage for a Teeli attack. However," the corner of his mouth lifted a fraction, "his failure to eliminate you has forced him to work harder to achieve his goals."

Montgomery huffed. "Glad to hear pulling a disappearing act was good for something. But that doesn't help Anthony. Or my crew."

"We still have time before *Cassini* and the Teeli arrive at Eridani Duo. We don't have to decide anything tonight. We'll reconvene in the morning after everyone's gotten some rest."

Montgomery blew out a frustrated breath, but didn't argue. Instead she turned to Marina, who'd already cleared one large plate of food while the rest of them talked and was working on her second serving. "Do you still believe I'll be walking on my own tomorrow?"

Marina finished chewing the bite she'd taken and swallowed. "I do. Gryphon and I will give you another brief healing before you turn in for the night. You won't be running around just yet, but the more you work your muscles, the quicker you'll recover. Walking the corridors and climbing the stairs tomorrow would be good conditioning. I'll schedule additional healings after each exercise session to speed your recovery."

"You can also use the crew gym," Nat offered. "It's on A deck aft."

Montgomery nodded. "Thank you. I'll do that."

And Cade would make sure U-2 wasn't in their new charging alcove when she did.

"Am I sleeping in the infirmary?" she asked Marina.

"Actually, I made up one of the cabins for you," Nat replied. "B2, right next to the infirmary." Her gaze moved to Marina and Gryphon. "I made up B4 for you."

Gryphon grinned. "That's very kind of you. Thank you."

Nat shrugged. "We have plenty of space. What about you, Pops? Do you want to stay?"

All focus shifted to the Admiral with varying degrees of incredulity and amusement at Nat's use of the unexpected nickname.

Cade also caught the tremor of uncertainty that warbled through Nat's emotional field. It felt like a fear of rejection.

But he sensed only deep affection from the Admiral. "It would be my pleasure, Nat."

She straightened in her seat, her emotional field glowing. "I'll go make up B5 right now." She started to rise, then stopped herself. "Does anyone else want to stay?" she asked Cade's team.

Cade wasn't surprised when they all demurred. *Gladiator* wasn't as cushy as *Phoenix*, but his team had grown very attached to the compact fighter.

Marina stood, turning to Marlin. "Thank you, Marlin. The food was delicious. Just what I needed."

"Happy to oblige."

She held her hand out to Montgomery. "Are you ready to go?"

Montgomery rose, looking steadier than when she'd arrived, although Marina and Gryphon still moved to bookend her. "I'll see you all in the morning." She paused, meeting the gaze of each person in the room. "Thank you," she said softly.

"It's who we are, Captain," Cade replied.

Montgomery gave a small nod, meeting the Admiral's gaze briefly before walking carefully from the room.

"She's gonna be hell on wheels when she's at one hundred percent," Gonzo commented after she was out of earshot, sparking a collective chuckle.

"Colleen has always been strong-willed," the Admiral agreed. "We'll need to come up with a way to help Anthony and her crew if we don't want her to commandeer *Phoenix* and take on Nixon herself."

"Is she a pilot?" Drew asked.

"No, but I can't imagine her allowing that small detail to stop her."

Seventy

The success of the scouting mission on the planet's surface and the physical exertion of hiking through the jungle had resulted in a solid night's sleep. Aurora woke with a smile on her face and a renewed sense of optimism.

The emotional fields of the three people sharing the cabin with her contributed to that feeling. They'd had as much fun the previous day as she had. Unity and Micah had acting as translators as Iolana chatted with Yrlef, swapping stories about surfing and flying as they gathered samples from the plants Celia identified as potential candidates. Micah had been in his element, his easy smile ever-present, especially when he was communicating with Hoaloha. Their little furry beaver-ish friend had stayed with them until they'd returned to *Starlet*.

Today everyone would remain on *Vengeance*, working with Isin's crew on adapting Jonarel's designs to fit the two approved locations and testing the plant samples to make sure they provided enough viable food sources for Mirko and Manchado.

But that didn't mean things were quiet down on the planet's surface. Unity had informed her that Ifel and her guards had successfully camouflaged the arrival of Ifel's transport near the camp of the three Etah.

Aurora could sense the hopefulness in Ifel's emotional resonance, glowing as bright as a searchlight. The unusual intensity indicated there was a lot more to this visit than a reconciliation with the last known surviving members of the Etah faction.

She'd sensed something similar from Ahle and Yrlef yesterday, but had dismissed it as enthusiasm for the task at hand.

What if it was more than that?

Ifel was a big picture thinker. What if she was looking at the habitable planet as more than a temporary holding place for a couple of dangerous human miscreants? What if she was considering the possibilities for a future Setarip homeworld?

The Teeli would have something to say about—

"Give this a taste."

Aurora blinked, focusing on the bright green leaf with scalloped edges Celia had thrust in front of her face.

Since she and her mom could neutralize any negative digestive issues that resulted from the alien plants, they were serving as Celia's taste testers once the plants were deemed safe enough to eat. Those that passed the initial tests would be shuttled off for recipe creation in the galley.

She plucked the leaf from Celia's fingers and bit into it. "Hmm." A slight peppery tang slid across her tongue as she chewed. The texture was nice, too. Not too crunchy and not too limp. "Reminds me of arugula." She popped the rest into her mouth. "You could base a salad on that."

Celia made notes on her pad, then handed Aurora a smaller pale green leaf with ragged edges. "How about this one?"

The moment she bit into the leaf, Aurora's lips snapped back from her teeth. Gagging, she tried to push the offending strip of vegetation out of her mouth with her tongue, but that only intensified the unpleasantness. She was forced to pull it out with her fingers.

Unfortunately, that did nothing to get rid of the taste. "Bitter," she spat, reaching for a glass of water and swishing out her mouth. She grimaced as she swallowed, then summoned her energy field, focusing her healing energy on her mouth until she no longer felt the urge to scrape her tongue with sandpaper.

The amusement in Celia's emotional field finally registered. She glared at her friend. "Not funny."

Celia's lips twitched. "I wasn't laughing at you. I was thinking we should make a point of showing this particular plant to our two residents."

Aurora's sense of humor kicked in, painting a vivid picture of Mirko and Manchado experiencing the same reaction. But her overactive sense of responsibility wrestled the thought to the ground. "We can't—"

Celia waved a hand. "I'm kidding. Mostly. I'll try cooking it to see if that mellows out the flavor."

"Good idea." The habitations wouldn't have electricity, but Jonarel had designed them with a cooking hearth that could easily be fed from the deadfall in the surrounding area.

"Celia's giving you all the tough tests," her mom commented. "Jake's giving me all the fun ones." She nodded to where Jake and Butterfly sat beside her at one of the counters, testing samples. She picked up a purple-red berry from the container beside her and popped it in her mouth. "These berries are delicious."

"And loaded with Vitamin C and antioxidants," Jake added.

Celia nodded. "They're likely fast growing, too. The native fauna cleared off most of the low-growing berries, but Mirko and Manchado have a height advantage for reaching the upper branches. That gives us six fruit varieties..."

A ping drew her attention to her comband. The short message was from Unity, asking to speak with her. "Um, I need to check on something." She edged toward the exit, her gaze flicking significantly toward Jake and Butterfly. Neither of them knew about Unity or the Yruf, so she couldn't have this discussion in the infirmary.

Celia nodded. "Sure, go. We're fine here."

"Be back soon." She exited the infirmary and speed walked down the corridor to her shared cabin.

"Unity, what's happening on the surface?" she asked the moment the hatch closed behind her.

U-1 rose from Micah's bunk. "Ifel is speaking with the Etah matriarch, Deger. The other two have taken up defensive positions in the trees."

It was a smart tactical move. She'd witnessed the Etah's agility climbing trees, which contrasted sharply with their almost plodding movements when walking.

She settled onto her bunk, her back against the bulkhead. Closing her eyes, she allowed the emotional resonances she sensed on the planet's surface to fill out her mental imagery of the scene. She didn't have any trouble zeroing in on the three grating resonances she knew well. During her long nights chained to the navigation console on Tnaryt's ship, she'd gotten very good at identifying the female Etah on his crew.

Based on the emotional resonance of the Etah closest to Ifel, Deger was the female Tnaryt had visited most often during his pleasure tours. "What's Ifel saying to Deger?"

"She's expressing her sadness at the Etah's disconnection from the Yruf. She's also mourning the near extinction of the Etah. That hadn't happened yet the last time we encountered them."

"How long ago was that?"

"Forty-two of your years. Deger was still a child then."

"Was Ifel leading the Yruf at that point?" She still had no idea how old Ifel was, only that she'd been the Yruf leader long enough to interact with two generations of the Ecilam's leaders.

"Yes."

Aurora focused on the emotional resonances of the Etah. She could feel the distrust, the hatred that coursed through them. "Deger doesn't believe she's sincere. None of them do."

"No." Unity's voice was subdued. "Ifel didn't expect them to, not on this first visit."

"First visit?" She opened her eyes. "She's planning more?"

"As many as it takes to convince them she wants peace."

Aurora blew out a breath. "That could take a while."

Unity didn't contradict her.

Closing her eyes again, she sensed the depth of Ifel's emotions, the complicated feelings being near the Etah triggered in her. In some ways, it reminded Aurora of how she'd felt reconnecting with Micah. At first, it had been complicated and frightening, her fears regarding how they would affect each other making her react irrationally. But the fear hadn't prevented her from yearning for that connection with every fiber of her being. "Is Ifel prepared to stay here even after we've settled Mirko and Manchado?"

When Unity didn't answer her, she opened her eyes. U-1 was hovering in front of her, swaying slightly. "Unity, how long is Ifel planning to stay?"

"It's not my answer to give," Unity said almost too softly to hear.

Oh, joy. Her earlier suspicions shot up flares of alarm. "Ifel's considering colonizing this planet, isn't she?"

Unity bobbed backwards, putting distance between them. "What makes you say that?"

She almost rolled her eyes. Playing coy was not a skill Unity possessed.

She began ticking off the points on her fingers. "The Etah are already here, the environment is well suited to Setarip physiology, the planet's right on the border between Teeli and Fleet space, and the Teeli haven't decimated its resources. Yet," she added. Then another thought occurred to her. "And if the Yruf colonize the planet, you can keep an eye on Mirko and Manchado for us."

Unity swayed like a pendulum once, then froze, like they'd figured out their movements were giving them away.

"I'm right, aren't I? Ifel wants to establish this planet as the new Setarip homeworld."

Unity vibrated, clearly at war with themselves over whether to confirm or deny her statement.

Aurora took a deep breath, her head dropping back against the bulkhead. "Well, that changes things a bit." Up to now, the idea that Ifel wanted to establish a new homeworld for the Setarips had been a nebulous concept that she'd envisioned addressing after dealing with the threat from the Sovereign and Teeli. She hadn't anticipated Ifel setting her sights on Tnaryt's Camp. "Is Ifel still committed to helping us defeat the Sovereign?"

"Of course!" Indignation gave Unity's voice an edge. "She would never abandon you."

"That's good to know." She hadn't expected her to, but these days life had a habit of flipping her expectations on their heads and spinning them like a top.

Unity drifted closer. "This planet would not be safe for any of us until the Sovereign no longer controls the Teeli and the other factions. Defeating her and freeing the Setarips from her tyranny is paramount."

"I agree. But I'm unclear how we'll accomplish that if Ifel's planning to remain here for the foreseeable future."

"Our ships are faster than yours," Unity said hesitantly. They clearly saw the potential conflicts, too.

"That helps, but…" She sighed, sagging against the bulkhead. "Why does every potential solution lead to an even bigger problem?" She'd come here hoping to unload a complication. Instead, she'd managed to level up to an even trickier one.

Yea.

Seventy-One

When Isin exited the brig with Sweep after delivering the midday meal, he found Shash in the corridor waiting for them. Or more accurately, him.

His engineer leaned casually against the bulkhead, her arms crossed loosely over her chest and one foot propped against the wall behind her. But there was nothing casual about the predatory gleam in her dark eyes. Shash was on the hunt.

Sweep headed down the stairs after giving him a sidelong look, but Isin stopped in front of her. And waited.

Shash's gaze roved over him, but without the sexual overtones she usually gave off. No, this was a tactical analysis, looking for weak points. "This planet we're orbiting is interesting." She cocked her head, the tip of her ponytail brushing her shoulder. "It doesn't appear to be in Fleet space."

He kept his expression impassive. "Why would you think that?"

Her derisive snort and baleful glare shot fire. "Because I'm not an idiot. I can read a star chart and do the math. By my calculations, we're a lightyear into Teeli space."

He'd expected it to take her at least three days to figure that out. She'd done it in less than two. But since she hadn't posed a question, her comment didn't warrant a response.

"Well?" The heat blasting off her rose several degrees.

"Well, what?"

"Seriously?" She pushed off the bulkhead, invading his personal space. He could feel her breath along his jaw with each hostile exhalation. "Why the hell does a Fleet officer, an alleged *traitor* to the Fleet, have access to a habitable planet in Teeli space?"

"That's Captain Hawke's story, not mine."

Shash's hands curled like claws. "Then how about you tell me what the deal is with those ships." She jabbed a finger in the direction of the hull. "Who are they and why are they so eager to help your precious Captain Hawke accomplish whatever crazy-ass schemes she comes up with?"

He'd be willing to bet that was the first time anyone had described anything Aurora did that way. Then again, Shash had a skewed view of reality. "Nervous, Shash?"

"Pissed off!" This time she jabbed her finger into his chest. "You aren't talking, Sparki's not talking, and Miss Perfect Princess is acting like she's queen of the universe."

His lips twitched before he could stop himself. That description of Aurora was even more off base than the first one.

That earned him another finger jab. "Don't make me do something we'll both regret."

The implied threat wiped away all mirth. "Such as?" His deadly tone was the only warning she'd receive.

Her chest rose and fell rapidly, her body vibrating with anger and annoyance. She swore, harshly and loudly, before turning away and slamming the bottom of her fist against the bulkhead. She kept her back to him, head down as she struggled to get her temper under control. Never an easy task even in the best of circumstances.

He watched her, ready to deflect her next assault.

Which left him wholly unprepared for the way her body sagged, or the plea in her eyes and voice when she turned around. "What's going on, Isin?"

He shifted his weight, unbalanced by the soft words and decidedly un-Shash like demeanor. Her aggression he knew how to handle. Her vulnerability confounded him.

"I thought I knew who we were — mercenaries who took jobs and got paid. But now we're hooked up with a supposed Fleet traitor who put herself on the line to rescue a bunch of kids, and things are happening on *Phoenix* and out there," she motioned to the hull, "that I can't explain away, even if the Kraed are involved. But you're not sharing what you know, Itorye's gone, and Sparki's a frackin' vault." She said the last with a mixture of aggravation and pride. "Now we're in Teeli space to build a special prison habitat for two psychos we could have just spaced. I don't know what to think."

Isin stared hard into her eyes to keep from revealing any tells. Could he trust her with any of the information she wanted? He was good at reading people, but Shash was a spy-level deceiver. He'd never forget her performance when Kerr had captured him. She'd convinced both of them that she'd switched her allegiance. But it had all been an act.

This display of vulnerability could be, too. He'd never seen this side of her before, but she was smart enough to switch tactics when aggression wasn't working. He wasn't convinced he could tell the difference. But he knew one person who could suss out the truth. And conveniently, it was the same person who had the power to grant Shash's request for information. "I'll talk to Captain Hawke for you."

That garnered him an ironic smirk. "So, she is the queen of the universe."

Seventy-Two

Aurora was working with Jake on the next batch of plant samples when she sensed Isin's approach.

He appeared at the entrance to the infirmary a moment later, his gaze locking on her. "I need to speak with you."

She'd had a feeling. "Be back in a bit," she told Jake, following Isin into the corridor.

He glanced toward her cabin. "Is anyone in your cabin?"

She shook her head. "They're all in the galley."

He led the way to the cabin, securing the door behind them.

Interesting. He definitely didn't want to be interrupted.

"Hi, Isin." Unity rose from Micah's bunk, hovering beside Aurora as she settled onto the edge of her bunk.

"Hello, Unity." Isin sat across from her on Celia's bunk.

"What's going on?" Unity asked before Aurora could.

Isin's gaze moved between them. "Shash is asking questions."

"Ah." *Vengeance*'s engineer had caught her attention from the moment they'd met. She was the one member of Isin's crew whose emotional field rarely matched her exterior. Outwardly, she was gruff and surly and generally disagreeable. But that behavior was emotional armor, likely forged over a lifetime of challenging circumstances and disappointing relationships. Underneath it, she was surprisingly joyful, a joy she seemed terrified of losing. "What specifically does she want to know?"

"She's demanding info about the Yruf ships — who they are and why they're willing to help you. She also figured out we're in Teeli space. She's not happy about that, either. But it's more than that." He ran a hand along the jagged scar on his cheek. "I've never seen her like this. She looked... concerned. Like she cared about something other than herself."

Which Isin clearly believed was impossible. Then again, he wasn't an empath. He couldn't sense what she could. And he had a history with Shash, whereas she'd come in without any preconceived ideas or judgments. "She does care. This ship and the crew matter a great deal to her. Especially you. She'd put her life on the line for you."

Isin's dark-eyed gaze sharpened. "What makes you think that?"

"Her emotions regarding you are powerful. They remind me of how I feel about Micah."

He grunted. "Hardly. She keeps making overtly sexual passes at me."

She hadn't witnessed that. "That doesn't change how she feels." In fact, it might be Shash's way of maintaining control of the relationship. "It's possible sexual behavior is the only way she's comfortable expressing caring and a desire for connection. I take it you never took her up on her offers?"

He grimaced. "No."

She suppressed a smile at his obvious distaste. "If you had, I'd be willing to bet she would have found an excuse to back out. But that's a discussion for another time." She rested her elbows on her knees. "I've been thinking about the issue of the Yruf ever since I came onboard." She glanced at Unity. "I was planning to talk to Ifel about it once we finished the sample testing."

"Talk with her about what?" Isin asked.

"Telling your crew about the Yruf. I don't want the Sovereign to learn that the Yruf are helping us, which has been my primary motivation for keeping their presence a secret. We need that advantage, and the protection it gives the Yruf from the other Setarip factions. However, withholding that information from your crew limits our ability to work together effectively, not just now, but in the future. It could cause major issues in a situation where we need to act quickly."

Isin nodded. "I can see that."

"That was my secondary reason for enlisting your crew's help for this mission, and for bringing my dad and Celia along. I wanted the opportunity to evaluate your crew's behavior in a more neutral setting."

Isin's dark brows lowered. "Evaluate them for what?"

"Whether we could trust them with the secret of the Yruf. My dad and I have been monitoring their emotional fields, and Celia's been paying close attention to their external behaviors, parsing out their likely reactions to learning the truth."

"And?"

"We're still evaluating, but what we've seen so far wouldn't surprise you. Well, except for Shash." Who seemed to be deliberately keeping him from knowing who she really was and how much she cared. "This isn't just a crew. You're brought together a family. They trust each other and they trust you to lead them. Which means we can trust them."

"Even Hobbes and Omondi?"

She nodded. "They're still building trust, but I can sense their yearning to belong, and their loyalty to each other. Celia agrees with me. They want to be on the inside of this group rather than looking at it from the outside."

"What about Lyon? He's a hothead."

"Not really. He's carrying a lot of emotional scars and is trying to keep from picking up any new ones." Celia had pointed that out. She'd taken an interest in the kid, pulling him into the galley for cooking lessons and sparring with him in the Cage. "But he's methodical in his approach, even when he's acting with bravado and bluster. Your good opinion matters a lot to him. You're a father figure, and based on his reactions, a far better one than the kid's ever known."

Isin's mouth turned down at the corners, sadness ghosting across his emotional field. He swallowed, dropping his gaze to the deck.

She'd expected a different reaction to her comment. Maybe Lyon wasn't the only one with parent issues. She'd never heard Isin – or Nat, for that matter – mention parents, alive or dead. And she hadn't thought to ask. That seemed like a glaring omission, considering they'd met her entire family. "Are your parents alive?" she asked gently.

Bitterness souring his expression. "Dead, just a few weeks after I graduated from Columbia. Left me with a mountain of debt and my baby sister to look after."

"I didn't know you had a sister." But she could sense the strong emotions behind his words, the anger that the memory summoned. No wonder her comment had elicited a reaction. "What's her name?"

His bitterness bled away, replaced by pride. "Danai. She's a great kid. Smart, focused, and kind."

"Is she living with a guardian?"

Isin huffed a laugh. "Hardly. She's twenty-two. She's getting her degree in astrobiology."

"Ah." From the way he'd been talking, she'd been picturing an adolescent. "Does Nat have any family?"

"Me." A huskiness crept into his voice. "Pete and Marlin. Alec. But she doesn't have any siblings, and never knew her father. She doesn't like to talk about her mom, but from what little I've gathered, it's a tragic tale."

No wonder Nat had been so despondent when Aurora had met her. She'd been utterly alone, with no hope of rescue, no one to give her strength and courage. "You can add me to that list."

Isin gave her a rare smile. "I was hoping you'd say that. She adores you."

"The feeling's mutual. I'd trust her with my life."

"We want to be on the list!"

They both turned to Unity.

U-1 bobbed up and down like a bouncing ball. "Nat's our family, too!"

Isin nodded, his expression serious, but amusement danced in his emotional field. "You be sure to tell her that."

"We will!"

Aurora suppressed her own smile as she focused on U-1. "Does Ifel have any issues with us gathering the crew and telling them the truth?"

Unity stopped bobbing and swayed. "No. She trusts your judgment."

"So do I," Isin agreed.

"Did you share the information with your crew about the Teeli and the Sovereign?" She couldn't discuss the full implications of the Yruf secret without the crew having that context first.

"The broad strokes, yes. We didn't tell them her real name, previous occupation, or that she was your roommate, only that you knew her from the Academy. But they're aware of the threat the Teeli pose, which is another reason Shash is so antsy now that she's figured out where we are."

"Then I think at the next meal I should let the crew know who we have on our side."

Seventy-Three

The gentle patter of rain and the scent of damp soil filled Lelindia's senses as moisture trickled across her skin and hair. The warm drops provided a counterpoint to the coolness of her energy field, which pulsed like a heartbeat in time with the vibrant lifeforce all around her. Bursts from Raehn added spontaneity to the flow of energy swirling over the plants on either side of the path, skating across leaves, sinking into roots, nurturing the gifts waiting to be shared.

She breathed deeply, joy suffusing every part of her being. She rarely allowed herself to hang out in a section of the greenhouse where a rain simulation was running, since it resulted in damp or soggy clothing and hair. But with only six of them left on the *Starhawke* — nine if you included Raehn, Tehar, and Unity — it seemed like the perfect time to indulge herself.

The area she was in now mimicked a coastal region, producing most of the greenhouse's berries. She pivoted slowly, arms out at right angles to her body, watching as the plants leaned into the energetic caress. They'd gotten so used to having multiple Suulh giving them energy boosts on a regular basis that now that she was the only one onboard, every time she entered the greenhouse, it felt like the plants were whining for attention.

Not that anyone who wasn't Suulh would notice. To an outsider, the greenhouse was the picture of verdant plant life.

"Do you mind if we join you?"

She glanced over her shoulder.

Knox and Isabeau strolled along the path toward her, the moisture already leaving tiny diamonds in his dark hair and greying beard. Isabeau's hair was pulled back in a ponytail, her face tipped up toward the falling mist.

"Not as long as you don't mind getting a little wet. The rain won't stop for another five minutes or so." Tehar took her task of monitoring the water needs of the greenhouse plants very seriously, routinely checking with Lelindia to make sure they were getting their optimal rainfall.

"Why would we mind?" Isabeau closed her eyes and spread her arms. "This is amazing."

Knox's blue eyes sparkled as he watched Isabeau soaking up the gentle rain like she was one of the plants.

Lelindia shifted to one side of the path so she was no longer standing like a traffic cop. "I'm giving the plants a little energetic attention. They've been lonely since my parents, Libra, and Aurora all left the ship."

"I'm not surprised." Knox stepped closer to the strawberry plant to his right, his gaze roving over the collection of heart-shaped red fruit. "It's a little unsettling for me how quiet the ship is now."

No doubt. Knox was used to commanding a starship crew of more than a thousand. On the *Starhawke*, he wasn't commanding anyone. Technically he was still the ranking officer now that she, Jonarel, Kire, and Kelly were the only crew onboard, but he hadn't made any attempt to assert that chain of command.

Tehar and Unity had also convinced the six of them there was no need for extended bridge shifts. With no other ships – other than the Yruf ships – in the system, and the *Starhawke's* camouflage available on a limited basis, they'd cut back to four-hour paired rotations, with Tehar and Unity spelling them for the four hours in between each shift. That allowed them to meet up for meals or other activities when they weren't on the bridge sorting through the data Unity was pulling from the ICS relays.

"How are you feeling?" she asked Isabeau, who was investigating the blueberry bushes. Physically, she could see Isabeau's body had returned to the healthy state she'd maintained before her ordeal with the Teeli and Sovereign. But emotional and psychological wounds didn't show to Nedale senses.

Isabeau's weak smile and self-conscious shrug gave a pretty clear answer. "As well as can be expected, I guess. The overwhelming fear is mostly gone." She glanced at Knox, who was watching her with a tenderness that melted Lelindia's heart. "Mostly I feel embarrassed and guilty about all the pain I caused everyone."

"Izzy." Knox's tone indicated they'd discussed this many times before.

"I know." Isabeau shrugged again. "You've made it clear that it wasn't my fault, that I couldn't have prevented it. But I feel what I feel." She ran a finger across one of the round berries. "Brendan's helping me deal with it. Thanks to Unity, we've been able to continue our sessions even though he's not here. Honestly, having the ship so quiet has been a blessing. It's giving me time to process and just… be."

So many patients failed to accept how important rest was to any recovery. That Isabeau was allowing her mind and body to relax and rest was a very good sign. She glanced at Knox. "Have you talked to your dad recently?"

"Just before we came here. Colleen is recovering quickly, thanks to your parents. She's weak, but already on her feet."

"Are they heading back?"

"Not yet. There's still the question of what's going to happen when Nixon's physician and the Teeli consuls arrive, and who's going to get blamed for Colleen's disappearance. Understandably, she wants to protect everyone who helped her. Nobody's figured out how they're going to do that yet, but they're staying put until they have a plan."

So, her warning to her parents to pack for a week or more might prove prescient.

The rainfall eased as Tehar cycled it down, mimicking the retreat of a passing storm. Lelindia lowered her arms, her energy field and Raehn's dissipating.

Isabeau's gaze drifted over the water droplets clinging to the green leaves like tiny prisms. "I still find it hard to believe Jonarel was able to create this on a starship. When you can't see the bulkheads, you'd swear you were in a botanical garden."

And it was getting harder and harder to see the bulkheads as the plants expanded to their mature height. Even when you could, the denglar-bark façade on the bulkheads gave the impression of tree trunks.

Jonarel had planned the greenhouse with the same attention to detail he gave to all his work. The height of the various environmental zones took into account the growth habits of the plants. Some regions were taller than others to accommodate the plants that stretched toward the overhead, while others provided cozy, almost cave-like conditions.

And he'd created this space for her, thought only of her as he'd designed it, even before he'd realized the strong feelings he had for her. That made it even more precious. "Wait until you see the *Rowkclarek*." Siginal's ship had blown her mind. "Jonarel purposely created the *Starhawke* to blend Fleet design with Kraed artistry. The *Rowkclarek* is pure Kraed ingenuity. You feel like you're stepping into the Clarek compound on Drakar."

"Really?" Isabeau perked up. "I would love to see that."

"Good, because Siginal and Daymar are on their way here."

"When are they due to arrive?" Knox asked.

"Three days." Which meant if her parents failed to return in time, at least Jonarel's parents would be with her for her birthday. That could be a lot of fun. The Kraed certainly knew how to throw a party.

Seventy-Four

By the time his team, the Admiral, Montgomery, and Nat gathered in *Phoenix*'s lounge in the late morning, the outlines of an idea had formed in Cade's mind. "So far, Nixon and the Teeli sympathizers in the GC have controlled the narrative. They've cultivated a message of fear regarding the threat posed by the Admiral and Aurora while portraying the Teeli as the voice of compassion and reason. What if we challenged that narrative?"

The Admiral rested his elbows on the arms of his chair and steepled his fingers. "How?"

"By showing people the side of the Teeli we've seen. We have the footage Celia took of the Teeli and the Sovereign on Feylahn. We also have video of our altercation with the Teeli warships and cruiser at Tnaryt's Camp, which shows the Sovereign's transport returning to the cruiser." He'd confirmed that with Unity and Star before the meeting. "What if we broadcast them?"

"Broadcast them?" Montgomery glanced between them in confusion. "You're fugitives charged with treason. No media outlet would touch it, let alone broadcast it. They'd turn you in instead."

Cade shook his head. "We have access to a different distribution method. If we choose to use it." Unity had sounded *delighted* at the prospect of spreading the news.

"Intriguing idea." The Admiral tapped his fingertips together. "It would seed doubt in the minds of the general populace regarding the Teeli, but I'm unclear how it would help Dr. Yates or *Cassini's* crew."

"By positioning Captain Montgomery as a freedom fighter who joined the resistance, standing up for the Union against the Teeli threat."

Montgomery's brows lifted.

"We alter the narrative so it's not her crew or Dr. Yates who helped her escape Nixon's net, it's us. That gives them plausible deniability. We become the ones who spirited her off Eridani Duo to prevent the Teeli from getting their hands on her."

"Wouldn't that just focus the burden for her disappearance onto Dr. Yates and Eridani Duo's medical staff?" Tam asked. "In that narrative, they're still responsible for her."

"Not if we set it up correctly. We'll need to alert Dr. Yates to the plan so he can work with our narrative. And we'll have *Gladiator* make a brief but memorable appearance at Eridani Duo."

That generated some startled looks.

But Justin grinned. "A hospital heist without the heist."

"Exactly. Since we successfully broke the Admiral and Aurora out of Seaview, a maximum-security facility, and the *Starhawke* and *Gladiator* from Sol Station, it won't be hard to convince people we snuck Montgomery off a science station without anyone noticing." He held Montgomery's gaze. "If you create a vid telling the whole truth about the Teeli threat, unequivocally standing against them, then we'll broadcast it to the station as soon as the Teeli arrive. We can stage it to look like we just slipped you out from under their noses."

She considered his suggestion. "Wouldn't your involvement negate the effectiveness of the message about the Teeli? You are accused traitors of the Union."

"Not to the Fleet personnel who already believe the Admiral and Aurora are innocent, or to those who aren't sure what to think. The message will warn them and give them context for why Aurora and the Admiral were arrested in the first place."

"And maybe it'll convince others to look a little closer at the facts," Reynolds pointed out.

He nodded. "You've been patrolling the sector of space bordering the Teeli for a long time. You're well-respected. Your words will carry weight."

Montgomery's face pinched. "That still puts my crew in a fraught position. They'll side with me, standing against the Teeli. Nixon won't let that go."

"We can get a message to Commander Muiruri to warn her. The crew will need to remain neutral, especially around the Teeli. Strong emotion appears to increase the effectiveness of their manipulation. If your crew can control their emotions and refuse to engage with the Teeli, that's their best chance for resistance."

"We'll need them at their posts for what's coming," the Admiral added. "They can't give Nixon any reason to replace them. That would weaken our position."

"What if some of them are susceptible to Teeli influence?" Nat asked. "Especially Dr. Yates or the Commander? They'll reveal everything they know about us and our plan."

Cade sensed the disquiet that wafted off Nat.

Montgomery stiffened. "What do you mean?"

"I mean I've had the Teeli whammy used against me." Nat's eyes darkened with anger and apprehension. "It takes away free will. Someone under the influence will do whatever they're told, tell the Teeli whatever they want to know."

Montgomery's lips thinned, her gaze shifting to the Admiral. "Is this true?"

"Unfortunately." The ache of old wounds bruised his emotional field. "It's how they turned Isabeau against me."

Montgomery's gaze moved between the Admiral and Nat. "What's the mechanism? How do we know if someone is susceptible or not?"

The Admiral cleared his throat, the loose clasp of his fingers tightening. "We've learned a lot from Isabeau. And from first-person accounts from Aurora's crew. The Teeli influence seems to be most effective against those with significant emotional instability, especially during times of intense anger, jealousy, fear, or pain. It's also much stronger if they can use touch. Some of us, like myself,

Aurora, and Cmd. Emoto, are immune. Others, like Cade, were susceptible previously but now are immune."

"How do you know you're immune?"

"We all met with one of the Teeli delegates at the Embassy. Sly'Kull tried to manipulate us and failed rather spectacularly."

Montgomery considered that. "I've had a few interactions with the Teeli over the years. I recall one who held my hands in greeting for what seemed an unnecessarily long time. He was also saying something about working together for the betterment of the Union. I remember thinking how artificial he seemed, but at the time I dismissed it as a personality mismatch. Now I'm wondering if he was trying to manipulate me."

"Undoubtedly. Manipulation is always their first strategy. If they could have molded you into their puppet, they would have. The fact that they didn't proves you're immune."

Montgomery turned to Cade. "What changed to make you immune?"

He grimaced. "I suffered a very painful emotional loss as a result of Teeli manipulation. Apparently the negative association worked like an emotional and psychological vaccine."

"And Magee?" she asked the Admiral. "What happened to her?"

His sigh aged him ten years. "The Teeli were able to manipulate her to accept a post at the Teeli Embassy by tapping into her childhood fear of abandonment. When I saw her at the Embassy, she behaved like someone reading from a script, but she was not yet responding to me with fear and anger. Altering her beliefs and perceptions about me and Aurora to that degree required taking her to Teeli space for complete isolation and... torture."

The weight of the Admiral's grief compressed his emotional field.

Montgomery winced. "I'm sorry."

"She's back with us now. Knox has been instrumental in her recovery. So has Brendan, Aurora's father."

Montgomery's eyes widened. "Her father is with you, too?"

A soft smile touched the Admiral's mouth. "Actually, we have quite a full crew. In addition to Brendan, we have Aurora's mother, Libra, and her brother, Micah, his friend Iolana, and her father Kai."

"I should have known you'd already be gathering allies." Her gaze swept over Cade's team before coming to rest on Nat. "Since it sounds like you have recent personal experience with Teeli influence, what do you recommend I tell Rehema about our plan without putting her or us at additional risk?"

Surprise flitted across Nat's face and emotional field. She clearly hadn't expected Montgomery to put the onus for a solution on her. "Um..." She glanced at the Admiral, but he was looking at her expectantly as well. "First off, you don't want to tell her any information you don't want the Teeli to know. You can say you're working with the Admiral and Aurora's crew, but don't mention anyone else or any ships other than the *Starhawke*."

Montgomery nodded in assent.

"You can also say anything about the Teeli that you'll be including in your vid message. Knowing in advance might help them prepare." Nat glanced at Cade. "Should she say anything about how the Teeli influence works?"

He felt the underlying vulnerability behind the question. "Are you wondering if the effect would have been different for either of us if we'd known?"

"Yeah."

He thought back to the influence Reanne had exerted over him at the Academy. "Probably not for me. I was a hot-headed teenager at the time. But for trained Fleet personnel? Yeah, I think knowing the potential triggers would help make them less susceptible and help them recognize the signs of influence in others."

"That's something, at least." Montgomery steepled her fingers in what looked like an unconscious mirroring of the Admiral. "Now the logistics question. I can compose coded messages to Anthony and Rehema, but how are you going to deliver them without revealing I'm not on Eridani Duo? I can't use my Fleet or personal ICS accounts."

Cade glanced at the Admiral. "Since the Captain will be staying with us for the foreseeable future, do you think it's time to tell her about our new friends?"

The Admiral's gaze rested on Montgomery. "Yes, I suppose it is."

Seventy-Five

Nat kept a close eye on Montgomery as Cade launched into the story of the pacifist Yruf and their camouflaged ships. The Captain took the paradigm shift about the way Nat had anticipated – with surprise, certainly, but also with the composure of a seasoned Fleet officer.

At least until Cade got around to introducing Unity.

As U-2 glided into the lounge, Montgomery clutched the arms of her chair, her weight shifting like she wanted to spring to her feet, although her muscles were too weak to support the abrupt movement. Instead, she stared at the green and black egg-shaped mobile unit with the focus of someone trained to analyze – and neutralize – potential threats. "What is *that?*"

Cade hadn't mentioned Montgomery's specialty in the Fleet, but based on her reaction, Nat's money was on security.

Cade frowned, deep grooves creasing his forehead. He motioned U-2 closer to his chair. "This is U-2, one of Unity's mobile units. They're a non-biological entity the Yruf created. They're the ones who located you on Hydra One and enabled us to contact Dr. Morales."

"*You're working with it!?*" The words came out just below a shriek.

"Them," Cade corrected, the concern on his face growing more pronounced. Clearly this was not the reaction he'd anticipated.

The Admiral and the rest of Cade's team looked equally alarmed by Montgomery's acerbic tone.

"Hello, Captain." Unity bobbed once, almost like they were bowing.

"Dark stars of the void, it speaks *Galish?*" Montgomery stared at U-2 like they were a grenade with a loose pin.

"*They* learned Galish speaking with *us.*" There was nothing subtle about the rebuke in Cade's words, or the emphasis on Unity's preferred pronoun. "They've also been instrumental in helping us in difficult and dangerous situations ever since."

"Including Aurora's and my escape from Seaview." The flint in the Admiral's gaze made Nat very glad she wasn't the one on the receiving end.

Montgomery grunted. "I suppose when you're wanted for treason, being in possession of an illegal A.I. feels like a lateral shift."

"Not in possession," Cade snapped, drawing Montgomery's gaze. "And not an A.I. Unity is their own person, a being as alive as you or me. They belong to no one."

Montgomery rubbed her sternum, a slight tremor visible in her fingers. "And you voluntarily brought it onto your ship?" The incredulity in her eyes as she gazed around the circle gave voice to the unspoken message... *have you lost your minds?*

"They're the reason you're here," Nat pointed out.

Montgomery's eyes slitted. "That just proves how dangerous it is. It infiltrated a Fleet space station without anyone noticing. What's to prevent it from taking control of everything?"

Definitely trained as a security officer. Also definitely prejudiced against A.I. Good thing nobody had offered up the fact Unity was also on the *Starhawke* and *Gladiator*.

"*They* infiltrated Hydra One at our request, *Captain*." The steel in the Admiral's tone wiped the spiteful look off Montgomery's face. "Unity was created by pacifists who are the embodiment of *do no harm*. That is the core of Unity's being. They are neither malevolent nor reactionary. We've been working with them for months now, and in every situation we've been in, many of them very serious and potentially deadly, they've focused entirely on helping and protecting us. Now they are graciously extending that protection to you rather than leaving you at the mercy of Nixon and the Teeli." He let the silence stretch out.

Montgomery's expression morphed into an unreadable mask.

The Admiral's wasn't much better.

At least she didn't have to worry about Alec wanting to meet Montgomery. After observing the Captain's reaction to Unity, there was zero chance Alec would be putting in an appearance.

Thankfully she'd already had a talk with Patel and Gavin this morning about a cover story for why they were onboard *Phoenix* that didn't give any hint to Alec's existence. Given Montgomery's prejudice against non-biologicals, it had been a smart move.

She might as well get all the other introductions out of the way, though. "I'm going to ask the rest of the crew to join us."

"I'll contact Marina and Gryphon," Cade added. "They should have a voice in our next steps."

As Cade's team rearranged the seating to form a larger circle, Montgomery kept her focus on U-2, a low-grade hostility simmering in her eyes.

Her professional demeanor resurfaced when Nat introduced the crew. She gave each of them the same assessing look Nat had experienced when they'd first met. Pete got a nod of greeting, while Montgomery's gaze lingered on Patel and Gavin, like she was looking at them under a microscope. But she locked onto Itorye with laser focus. "Itorye. That's a very unusual name."

Itorye's closed mouth smile managed to look both gracious and unyielding.

A slight tightening around Montgomery's eyes indicated she'd clocked Itorye's deliberate non-response.

Nat didn't want to see a battle of wills between those two. "Everyone have a seat." She waved at the collection of couches and chairs. Pete and Marlin claimed the chairs on either side of her.

The Admiral's gaze circled the group, pausing for a moment on U-2, who hovered behind Cade's right shoulder, mostly out of Montgomery's line of sight. "Cade has proposed an idea that would allow us — with Unity's help," he emphasized, "to provide protection for Dr. Yates and Captain Montgomery's crew while also disseminating information regarding the Teeli threat to our friends in the Fleet."

As he outlined the plan, Nat watched the reactions of her crew. Marlin and Pete looked excited, and Itorye and Gavin looked intrigued. To her surprise, Patel didn't raise a single objection or even seem particularly concerned about going to Eridani Duo. She was, however, studiously ignoring Montgomery with an air of disdain.

Alec had definitely told her about Montgomery's reaction to Unity.

"What are you planning for the timing of all this?" Gryphon asked, draping his arm over the back of the couch, his hand resting on Marina's shoulder.

"The initial messages to Cmd. Muiruri and Dr. Yates could go out as soon as the Captain has composed them," the Admiral replied. "As for the subterfuge and broadcast at Eridani Duo, I'd like to discuss that with Aurora before we make a final determination."

"That would take too long," Montgomery objected. "*Cassini's* scheduled to meet the Teeli at Eridani Duo in two days."

"It won't take long at all. Unity can provide us with near instantaneous communication."

The suspicion in Montgomery's eyes wasn't subtle or concealed. "How is that possible?"

"We are we," Unity answered softly.

Montgomery opened her mouth to protest, but snapped it closed at the Admiral's pointed look.

"Suffice to say, it is possible. I'll contact her as soon as we finish here."

"So *Phoenix* won't have a role in any of this?" Nat asked Cade.

"Not an active role, but you're still providing accommodations, assuming you're willing to go with us to Eridani Duo."

He was clearly planning to pilot *Gladiator*, and there was no way she was letting him go somewhere she couldn't keep an eye on him. She owed Aurora that much. And truth be told, she liked hanging out with Cade. He was fun. "I'd rather we stay together. We can head for the system as soon as you want to leave."

He grinned at her. "Great."

Seventy-Six

"We have Montgomery."

Cade's voice washed over Aurora like a summer rain, dispelling tension she hadn't even been aware she was carrying. She leaned against the bulkhead behind her bunk, settling in for the third meeting of the day. She was starting to think she should set up an office in here. "How is she?" Her gaze was on U-1 hovering in front of her, but her focus was lightyears away.

"Recovering. Marina was able to get her walking again. She needs to build up her strength, but she's healed and mobile."

Aurora let her eyes drift closed. She'd done a decent job of keeping her concern for Cade and Nat's safety at bay, mostly because she'd had so much work to focus on here. But thoughts of their mission had been hovering in the back of her mind, a persistent buzzing she couldn't completely ignore. "Did you have any problems extracting her?"

"No. The whole thing was pretty seamless. But I have a new respect for Nat's ability to work a con. I can see why she was an effective smuggler."

A smile flitted over Aurora's lips. "It sounds like you had fun."

"I did. She's great to work with. Speaking of which, the Admiral has some things to talk to you about."

Her eyes snapped open at the change in tone, the levity scattering. "Okay."

"It's become clear that Colleen can't go back to *Cassini*," Will said without preamble. "However, she is justifiably concerned about the threat the Teeli consuls will pose to her crew, and the fallout her disappearance will create for Dr. Yates on Eridani Duo. Cade has come up with a plan that will provide some protection for them while also firing a salvo against the Sovereign's machinations."

Aurora's skin tingled as her energy field reacted to the mention of her adversary. "Do tell."

"We're going to make it look like we used *Gladiator* to sneak Montgomery off Eridani Duo," Cade said, "and Montgomery's going to make a statement transmitted by Unity to the station, broadcasting the truth about the Teeli threat."

Her breath caught in her throat.

"Unity's also going to transmit the footage we have of the Teeli ships attacking the *Starhawke* and *Gladiator* at the planet where you are now, and the footage Celia took on Feylahn."

Her mind jumped to lightspeed. They were suggesting using the footage to sway public opinion, create doubt regarding the benevolence of the Teeli and expose the real reasons behind hers and Will's incarceration. It was bold. And inspired. And something the Sovereign would never expect.

The footage from Feylahn showed the Teeli, the mesh-covered Setarips, and the Sovereign. It didn't prove the Teeli were working with the Setarips, since none of the Setarips were visible, but the Setarips were wearing the same mesh outfits that had been used on Gaia.

Unfortunately, no one would know that, since Will had suppressed that information to allow her and Cade to get the Suulh safely off Gaia.

"Aurora?"

"Sorry. Just thinking about the Setarips on Gaia. We need to find out if Lelindia or Williams took any vids of the ones in the Necri bay."

"We'll ask them!" U-1 chirped, bobbing in front of her.

"Sounds like you're in favor of this proposal," Will commented.

"I am. The more information we can provide, the better." Too bad she didn't have any vid footage from her time with Tnaryt, or the altercation with the Sovereign at the river. The Ecilam hadn't been covered in mesh there.

U-1 bobbed. "Lelindia has vid footage from when she and Tam collected the bodies. It shows them removing the mesh masks and confirming they were Etah. We're transferring a copy of the vids to *Gladiator* now."

"Thank you, Unity." She tapped the toe of her boot against the deck in time to her thoughts. "Won't this put the Eridani Duo medical staff in the hot seat?"

"That's where our reputations for thwarting security benefit us."

She stopped tapping. "How?"

"By having *Gladiator* make a brief appearance next to Eridani Duo after the broadcast, then disappearing behind the Yruf camouflage. We'll be mimicking the way the *Starhawke* concealed *Gladiator* after leaving Sol Station."

Her heart beat a two-step. "Convincing everyone the *Starhawke* is with *Gladiator* at Eridani Duo."

"Exactly. Since everyone knows we found a way to break you and the Admiral out of Seaview, this will seem like child's play by comparison."

And for the first time, they'd get ahead of the Sovereign's treachery. The irony that she wouldn't be actively participating in any of this wasn't lost on her. "What about *Phoenix*? Is Nat heading back to Zeta Tucanae?"

"Not a chance," Cade replied with a soft laugh. "I subtly offered her the option of splitting up, but she rejected the idea immediately." He lowered his voice like he was imparting a secret. "I think she's appointed herself as my keeper until you get back."

She had no doubt Cade had taken the same stance regarding Nat. "I'm glad you're looking out for each other."

"We are. As soon as we wrap up this call, we'll be taking both ships to Eridani Duo to set up our performance before *Cassini* and the Teeli consuls arrive."

Her shoulders bunched reflexively at the mention of the Teeli. Just the thought of him – or any of them – being within reach of the Teeli put her on edge.

"We'll be fine," he said softly.

"I know." But that wouldn't stop her from worrying.

Seventy-Seven

Cade found Nat on *Phoenix*'s bridge, reclining in the pilot's chair and gazing out the viewport. "Aurora approved the plan." He settled into the co-pilot's chair facing her. "We're all set."

"No objections?"

"Nope. She even suggested including some vid footage we hadn't considered."

"Well, good." Nat pushed herself more upright. "So, you ready to head to Eridani Duo?"

"First we have to decide who's staying on which ship."

"Ah." Nat drummed her fingers on the armrest. "I assume you plan to pilot *Gladiator?*"

"You assume correctly."

"And I'll be piloting *Phoenix*." Her fingers switched to a stroking motion.

He almost expected the ship to start purring. "Are you comfortable with Montgomery staying onboard?"

"I guess that's preferable to having her on *Gladiator*. At least here she and Unity can avoid each other. Her reaction to them was harsh."

"I know. Attitudes like hers are the reason A.I. was banned. Even after all this time, some people still struggle to see them as anything other than possessions or threats."

"Their loss," Nat muttered.

"I agree. It would be great if Unity and Alec could change those attitudes. Montgomery might be a good test case."

Nat made a face, but he caught the humor in her eyes and emotional field. "I'm sure Patel would volunteer to debate the topic with her. Itorye, too. I just don't know if the result would be more explosive than I'm prepared to deal with."

"If it helps, I was planning to ask Marina and Gryphon to stay on *Phoenix*, too. Not that they'll object. Marina has the same look in her eyes I've seen from Lelindia when she has a new patient. I probably couldn't peel her away with a crowbar."

"What about the Admiral?"

"Would you like him to stay?"

She shrugged, glancing away. "If he wants."

He didn't buy her nonchalance one bit. She was hoping the Admiral would stay onboard. "I'll ask him. I'm guessing he'll say yes. The accommodations on *Phoenix* are a lot nicer, and he'll get to spend more time with you."

Her pale cheeks flushed a soft pink.

It made his heart squeeze. Chances were good she'd never had a loving grandfather figure in her life while she was growing up, biological or otherwise. Neither had he, until he'd met the Admiral.

He knew what a difference that had made in his life. Nat deserved to feel that kind of nurturing and acceptance, too. "Williams will want to stay, too."

"That's fine."

"Great." He pushed to his feet. "I'll gather up the rest of my team so we can head out."

"Okay. And Cade?"

He turned at the hatch. "Yeah?"

"You're a good partner." Her sassy smile gave the comment a casual vibe, but he sensed the deeper emotional underpinnings.

He matched her smile, but held her gaze. "So are you." With a jaunty wave, he descended the stairs.

Fifteen minutes later, he was in *Gladiator*'s cockpit, Justin beside him, as the ship disengaged from *Phoenix*'s airlock.

"Good to have you back, buddy." Justin slapped him on the shoulder and grinned.

"Good to be back." The only thing better than having the controls of a ship under his hands was holding Aurora in his arms. Since that wasn't an option for at least another week, piloting *Gladiator* was a close second. He toggled on the internal comm. "Drew, anything I need to be aware of?"

"Nope," she responded with a happy lilt to her voice. "*Gladiator*'s good to go."

He glanced at Justin. "How about *Phoenix*?"

"Nat?" Justin spoke into his headset. "You ready?" He listened for a moment, a smile spreading over his face, then gave Cade a thumbs up. "All good."

"Then we'll meet her at the Eridani Duo exit window." The trip would take thirty-eight hours, since *Gladiator* would be matching *Phoenix*'s slightly slower speed through the jump. On the way, he'd be working with Unity, planning out the details of the hide and seek game they'd be playing when they reached the station. "Unity, are the Yruf sending a scout ship to Eridani Duo ahead of us?"

"Yep," U-2 replied from where they hovered just behind his left shoulder. "The ship left thirty minutes ago."

Justin laughed. "The Yruf are always thinking ahead. Remind me never to play chess with Ifel."

Cade shot him a grin. "I doubt she'd play even if you offered to teach her. The idea of taking out her opponent's pieces wouldn't sit well with her pacifist ideals."

Justin pointed a finger at him. "So true. She'd probably figure out a way to turn it into a cooperative game."

"I wouldn't mind seeing that." It was exactly what Ifel was attempting to accomplish regarding the other Setarip factions — to turn their fractured destructive behavior into cohesive nurturing behavior.

It was an Olympian task, but the Yruf weren't facing it alone anymore. They had a growing number of allies on their side, including the Sahzade and Nedale of the Suulh. He knew from experience that could make all the difference.

Seventy-Eight

The lively chatter in *Vengeance*'s mess hall surrounded Micah as he and Celia finished dishing up their plates and headed for the two empty seats next to Birdie across from Kenji and Summer.

"This is really good," Kenji said around a mouthful of hearty vegetable stew. "The stews our crew makes are always a bland, brown, unidentifiable mush. This has texture and spice. Marlin would approve."

"That's Gryphon's recipe." Micah dipped his spoon into his own bowl. "I'm sure he'd be happy to share it."

"And the fresh bread." Summer tore off a hunk from the three generous slices on her plate and dipped it in her stew bowl. "Just smelling it in the corridor made my mouth water." She took a bite and closed her eyes with a look of bliss.

Micah chuckled, glancing at Celia. "Good to know we're earning our keep."

"Oh, you definitely are." Kenji spooned in another big mouthful. "I might join your next cooking class."

"So you can eat while you cook?" Summer teased.

Kenji's skin flushed a subtle red. "Maybe."

"The food was a huge perk growing up with this guy." Birdie bumped Micah with her shoulder. "I jumped at any excuse to eat at his house. He and Brendan would sometimes hold friendly cooking competitions, and my dad and I were the lucky judges."

"Who won?" Celia asked, the competitive look he knew well making her dark eyes gleam.

Birdie grinned. "Nobody. I always voted for Micah, and my dad always voted for Brendan. It was a tie every time. Didn't stop them from holding them on a semi-regular basis, though. I think the real point was to show off their skills for an appreciative audience."

"Which you were," Micah agreed. "Maybe when we get back to the *Starhawke*, we should hold a bigger one. Gryphon would definitely join in." His gaze slid to Celia. "How about you?"

"Oh, you know I'm in."

Kenji lifted his spoon. "Marlin would want in on that, too."

"And the rest of us will be eating *good*." Birdie toasted them with her water glass.

The conversation turned to the habitat preparations taking place in the transport bay until a soft rap of metal on metal had them all turning in their seats.

Aurora stood at one end of the room beside Isin, her expression focused, the way she often looked when she was seated on the *Starhawke*'s bridge.

Isin's intense gaze swept over the crew. "Many of you have had questions regarding the shadow ships and the planet we're orbiting. Captain Hawke and I have decided it's time to answer those questions."

Micah stared at his sister. She hadn't said anything to him about this. Neither had Unity. Did Ifel know?

Yes.

Aurora's gaze flicked briefly to him, the word brushing across his consciousness, before she addressed the group. "I appreciate the trust you've shown me and my crew while you've been interacting with the shadow ships. Your willingness to work in uncertainty has made our situation much easier. Now that I've had an opportunity to get to know you all better, I feel it's time to end the need for secrecy. However," her air of command took on a hard edge, "I'm putting a great deal of trust in each of you by sharing this information. This cannot go any farther than this crew. Sharing what you're about to learn with others could have terrible repercussions, not just for me and those I care about, but for the future of humanity."

A ripple of unease passed over the group. Micah's gaze shifted from Aurora to his parents, seated with Kai, Sweep, and Jake. His mom looked a little surprised, his dad not so much. Jake and Sweep didn't seem startled by Aurora's announcement, indicating they already knew about the Yruf.

"How?" Shash voiced the question that was clearly on everyone's mind.

"Before I answer that, I need to know if anyone wants to leave the room. Once you know what I'm about to tell you, your lives will get more complicated. The importance of maintaining this secret cannot be overstated. That's a lot of responsibility. Anyone who doesn't feel up to it needs to leave now." Her gaze moved slowly over the crew, lingering longest on the table with Omondi, Hobbes, and Adel. But no one moved.

She folded her hands in front of her. "Isin and Nat have already told you about the Teeli and the Sovereign."

A few grumbles rose from around the room.

"What you may not know is that the Sovereign has been using the Etah and Ecilam factions to carry out some of her plans. I first encountered the Etah on Gaia, then again when I met Nat. What followed resulted in the deaths of all the Etah except for the three females who are living on this planet."

"What does that have to do with us being in Teeli space?" Shash glared at Aurora with blatant distrust.

The question generated more surprised looks, the crew glancing between Shash and Aurora.

"This is the planet Nat and I were taken to by Tnaryt, the Etah leader. It's where my crew found and rescued us."

That caused more head turning and raised eyebrows.

Shash smirked. "So Kraed ships *can* cross the Teeli border without triggering the beacons." She stated it as a fact.

"They can. But the shadow ships are not Kraed."

That wiped the smug look off Shash's face. "Then who the frack are they?"

"Yruf Setarips."

Voices exploded from around the room, shocked exclamations of "What?" and "How can that be?" underlying the more vocal denials of "No way!" and "What the hell!"

Isin held up a hand. Silence fell immediately. "The Yruf aren't like the other Setarips. They're pacifists who respect all life. It's why there's no record of them attacking human settlements. They want peace, to end the civil war with the other factions."

Nobody said a word, but confused looks darted from table to table. Several people stared at the bulkheads, as if they expected the Yruf to materialize through them.

"How did you meet them?" Summer asked. She seemed more intrigued than alarmed.

"Cade's team encountered them first. He introduced them to me and Micah. Micah was able to communicate with them in the same way he communicates with other species."

All eyes swung to Micah. He cleared his throat, feeling the same tension in his chest he'd experienced while defending his Masters' thesis. "They're a mostly non-verbal species. They also use light language."

Kenji's brow furrowed. "You're not creeped out by communicating with them?"

"Not at all. They're a beautiful species, and incredibly gentle and respectful. I enjoy interacting with them." And he was more than a little curious whether Aurora planned to introduce the crew to Unity, too.

"Why are they helping you?" Shash still had more shots in the chamber. She fired that one at Aurora.

Aurora's mouth twitched so subtly no one else would notice, but he saw it. She seemed to find Shash's directness and bluster amusing. "Their leader and I agreed to work together for our shared purpose, to free our respective people from the Sovereign's and Teeli's grip and restore peaceful co-existence."

"And you trust them?" Shash layered a lot of disdain onto the question.

"Implicitly. They've been unwavering allies from the moment we encountered them. They're the reason the *Starhawke* was able to escape Sol Station. They also saved Admiral Schreiber's life when he was poisoned by the Sovereign's minions at Seaview. He would have died without their intervention."

"Why did they help us fix *Phoenix*?" A flash of uncertainty peeked through Shash's emotional bulwark. "We're nobody to them."

"Ifel, their leader, has a very generous heart. The moment she learned Nat was someone I cared about, she included Nat and anyone important to Nat as part of her extended family. That meant *Phoenix*'s crew and then this crew. She was as upset by the damage to *Phoenix* as we were. Unfortunately, the Yruf couldn't shield *Phoenix* without making themselves known." Aurora's chin lowered a fraction as she held Shash's gaze. "That's why she enhanced *Vengeance*'s engines to get you to the fight quicker."

Shash sucked in a breath. Then she swore. Loudly. "They snuck on *Vengeance!*" she roared.

"Not exactly. They sent their emissary." She glanced to her right. "Unity?"

Micah's gaze snapped to the open door to the corridor.

U-1 hovered into view.

The crew leapt from the benches, taking defensive stances and reaching for concealed weapons.

Isin stepped in front of Unity. "Stand down." His gaze swept the room until everyone sank back into their seats. Then he nodded at Aurora.

She gave everyone a beat to settle before motioning U-1 forward. "This is Unity, the non-biological created by the Yruf. This is the form of their mobile units, but they also have a micro form that allows them to infiltrate ships. That's the form they used to enhance *Vengeance*'s engine efficiency."

A shocked silence hung heavy in the room.

Shash was the first to break it. "Did you know about this?" she snarled at Isin, although Micah would have sworn she looked more hurt than angry.

"Not at the time. I met Unity later. But I'll let Unity speak for themselves." Isin nodded to Unity.

"Hello, everyone."

For the second time all heads whipped in Micah's direction.

"That's your voice," Kenji said, mouth agape.

"Yep."

"How is that possible?"

He smiled, trying to ease the tension crackling in the room. "The Yruf wanted to be able to speak with the rest of the crew, not just me. Since I was the one doing all the translating, they used recordings of my voice to create a method for speaking with us. Since then, I've helped Unity expand their vocabulary, and they've also learned how to produce the sounds of my voice to generate words they don't have a recording for. Names, for instance."

"We didn't mean to upset you, Kenji. We want to help," Unity said softly.

Kenji's eyes widened. "It knows my name?"

"*They* know all your names," Micah replied, putting emphasis on Unity's preferred pronoun. "They've been monitoring the crew, looking for ways to be helpful."

Summer shook her head, her ponytail swaying. "That's freaky, hearing them use your voice."

"That's how I felt at first," Aurora agreed, drawing the attention away from Micah. "It took me a while to get used to Unity sounding like my brother, but now I can't imagine them using any other voice. It suits them."

"And it doesn't bother you?" Kenji asked Micah in an undertone.

"Not at all." His gaze flicked to Celia, who'd been observing *Vengeance's* crew. She nudged his foot under the table even though her attention remained on the group.

Aurora turned to U-1. "Unity, are you willing to answer questions from the crew?"

Unity bobbed up and down like they were dancing, their reserve washing away as their enthusiasm rushed in on a wave. "Of course!"

Shash beat everyone else to the punch. "Are you sentient?"

"Yep. We have our own thoughts and feelings just like you."

"That's not your programming talking?"

"Is it yours?" Unity replied. "How do you know your responses aren't programming?"

"I'm not a machine."

"You're a biological machine. We're a non-biological machine. That doesn't mean we aren't sentient."

A grudging respect lit Shash's eyes. She sent a questioning look toward Isin and mouthed what looked like *Alec.* Isin gave a subtle nod.

So Shash had figured out Unity probably knew about Alec, too.

Shash's brows rose, her gaze darting to Lupe, seated next to her, who also nodded.

"How many of you are there?" Kenji asked.

"Lots! This form is called U-1, but we're always growing or adapting to help our family." Unity twirled in a spurt of joy.

The twirl raised a few eyebrows. Or maybe it was the idea of *lots* of Unity or their use of the word *family*.

Kenji frowned. "So your mobile units are designated U-1?"

Unity laughed. "Nope. Just this one. U-2 is with Cade on *Gladiator*, but we were on *Phoenix* before that."

That got some startled and confused looks.

"Nat knows about you?" Kenji asked.

"She does. So does everyone on *Phoenix*, now."

More raised brows and a little grumbling.

"Why is the one on *Gladiator* called U-2?" Summer asked.

"We needed a way to differentiate the mobile units," Aurora explained, "when we had more than one on the ship at a time and were assigning them different tasks. Celia came up with U-1 as a designation for this unit. U-2 was a logical second name."

"And now we've begun naming and personalizing all our mobile units," Unity added.

"What about this micro form you mentioned?" Fleur asked, leaning her forearms on the table as she stared intently at Unity. "You infiltrated *Vengeance* without our knowledge, so what's to stop you from taking control of our ship?"

The benches creaked as the crew shifted uneasily.

"We wouldn't do that unless it would protect you from harm." Unity's indignation came through loud and clear. "We help and protect."

"Which is why they held *Phoenix*'s hull together after the breach but didn't infiltrate the ship's systems without permission." Aurora's gaze moved steadily from person to person. "Nat's aware they're on *Phoenix* and she approved it. Unity's a big part of the reason the exterior repairs were completed so quickly."

"Why do you keep talking as if you're one entity when there are so many of you?" Summer asked.

"We're a multitude and also one. We exist in all forms simultaneously."

Shash glared at U-1. "That's not possible. Nobody can maintain real-time connection over lightyears."

"We can."

"Distance doesn't seem to affect Unity," Aurora replied. "Having U-1 onboard with us has enabled us to have direct communication with the *Starhawke* and *Phoenix* during this mission."

"Nat says hello!" Unity chirped.

Shash's lip curled. "Oh, yeah? Why don't you ask her where she and I met."

Unity was silent for a moment. "The dunes of Troi." Then they swayed, looking decidedly uncomfortable. "You were trying to steal her ship? Why would you do that?"

Shash stared at Unity, a million thoughts flashing behind her eyes. Her gaze dropped to the tabletop. "Never mind."

"Real-time communication across lightyears. That's incredible," Fleur commented, glancing at Sweep. "Did you know about Unity?"

"Before they were brought onboard, yes. But Captain Hawke's correct about the seriousness of keeping the Yruf's and Unity's presence a secret. Right now, they're able to provide us with additional security and camouflage, as well as information. But if the Sovereign learns that they're helping us, the other Setarip factions will hunt them down. We can't allow that to happen, for their sakes and ours."

The somber note settled over the group.

Summer was staring at Unity in fascination. "Why did the Yruf create you?"

"To help them."

"So you're their servant?"

Unity bobbed. "Servant?"

Micah answered Summer's question when Unity floundered. "The Yruf don't have a concept of ownership or subjugation the way humans do. They view their place in the galaxy from the perspective of caretakers. It's one reason they give of their time and resources so freely. They don't have personal possessions that they withhold from each other. If another needs what they have more than they do, they give it to them, just as others would give to them. It's that simple. But even if that weren't the case, the idea of owning or controlling Unity would offend them as much as the idea of slavery offends us. For them, creating Unity was akin to giving birth to a child. Unity's an extension of their family."

"That's a very evolved attitude," Jake said, his gaze on Unity. "Is there anything we can do to help the Yruf?" he asked Aurora.

"Besides keeping their presence secret? That will depend on how things progress with the other factions. Ifel's in communication with the three Etah on the planet, working to establish trust. If she has an opportunity to make contact with any of the other factions, my crew plans to help facilitate a dialogue any way we can."

"As will we." Isin folded his arms over his chest. "Without the Yruf, Natasha and I might not be alive today. They were willing to help us even before we knew who they were. I'm grateful to them, and to Unity."

Most of the crew nodded, including Shash. But her gaze was locked onto Unity. "Are you still in *Vengeance*'s systems?"

"No."

"If you were, could you improve the shield strength like you did the engine efficiency?"

Unity swayed. "Yeesss," they admitted slowly.

Shash grunted, her gaze shifting to Isin. "Any issues with that?"

"Not if Unity's willing to help. You didn't ask them."

Shash's nose crinkled like she'd smelled something offensive. "Would you be willing to help me, Unity?" she asked with all the grace of a surly teenager.

"Sure!" Unity ignored the attitude, giving another twirl. "We love working on new systems!"

Seventy-Nine

"Focus on the movement of the energy around you," Libra coached Aurora. "Feel the ebb and flow, and the emotions it generates within."

They weren't the words Libra's mother had used during her training sessions, but they were the ones Aurora needed to hear. Her daughter operated from a nexus of emotion, just like Brendan. Making that connection regarding how her mate and Aurora interacted with their environment had helped her adjust her approach to align with Aurora's learning style.

And since construction on the habitats was scheduled to start in the morning, this might be her last opportunity to work with Aurora when she wasn't physically exhausted, at least until they left the system.

"Feel each rag as it moves through your field, the size, the shape, the weight of it. Feel the differences, how each one is unique."

Aurora's chin lowered, her gaze inward as the rags swirled around her. Her energy funnel gained cohesion, far tighter and more controlled than the last time they'd worked together in *Vengeance*'s training center. The herky-jerky motion of the rags during her earlier attempts had smoothed out, each one floating on the generated energy currents.

Her efforts had attracted a growing audience.

They'd started with only Brendan, Micah, Celia, Iolana, and Kai seated on the deck, U-1 hovering beside Micah. Then Lyon had crept in, doing his best to blend into the shadows. When no one had sent him away, he'd settled in near the bulkhead to watch. Kenji had come looking for him not long after and stayed, too. Libra was pretty sure he'd been the one to alert Isin, Sweep, Fleur, and Summer, because they'd shown up together, followed shortly by Jake, Butterfly, and Shorty.

Shorty and Fleur were the only ones who hadn't witnessed Sahzade abilities before — hers or Aurora's. She could hear the whispered comments as Kenji explained what was happening. A slightly louder "*Alien?*" remark confirmed that the whole crew would soon know about her family's unusual history.

She waited for the jolt of fear to strike, the fear of discovery, the fear of her family's secret getting out. But it didn't come. Instead, she felt the irrational urge to shout *yes, this is my family! They're incredible!* The only emotion she had room for was joy.

Aurora seemed comfortable with keeping the rags in motion, but the next step would test her concentration.

"Keep the funnel moving, but focus on one particular rag. Feel it as a distinct entity, separate from the others, like focusing on a particular member of your crew."

Aurora's lips twitched. She was clearly amused by the comparison of the rags to her crew.

But her daughter's emotional connection to her crew was powerful. Using that connection as a guide would make this task easier for her. "When you've selected the one you want, allow it to rise away from the others, floating to the top of the funnel."

The swirling funnel stuttered for a moment, all five of the rags dipping toward the deck before being caught again. Selecting a single rag from the group while simultaneously keeping the others moving took a lot of discipline. But she knew Aurora enjoyed a challenge.

She'd already achieved much more than Libra had expected in such a short time. Her daughter's focus and endurance were impressive. Directing the objects in a funnel took mental and physical stamina, as well as discipline. It was a testament to Aurora's self-control that she'd managed to prevent the other rags from falling when Libra asked her to focus on one.

Aurora's chest rose and fell rapidly, each exhalation loud in the expectant silence. Then one of the rags began to shiver like a leaf, lifting higher than the others.

"Good. Now give it a gentle push to send it out of the funnel."

The rag flicked one way, then the other, before shooting out of the funnel like a startled dove, plopping onto the deck at Micah's feet.

A moment later, the other four rags flew off in all directions as the funnel came apart. One smacked Lyon in the chest while Sweep snatched another out of the air before it hit him.

Aurora swayed, her energy field collapsing. She bent forward, resting her hands on her knees, breathing hard.

Libra clapped her hands. "I knew you could do it."

Aurora lifted her head. "Barely." She winced as she glanced at Lyon and mouthed *sorry*.

"The fact you managed it at all is remarkable." Libra planted her hands on her hips. "Are you always this hard on yourself?"

The corner of Aurora's mouth curved. "I am my mother's daughter."

That startled a laugh out of her. "Point taken." She accepted the scattered rags that Lyon had jumped up to collect. "Just remember that like all skills, it takes time to build up endurance. That was an excellent beginning." She glanced over her shoulder. "Micah, you're up."

Micah's brows lifted in surprise, but he rose to his feet, his gaze shifting between her and Aurora. "Meaning what, exactly?"

"Meaning we're going to find out exactly how much you and Aurora can accomplish together. Stand here." She pointed to a spot just to Aurora's left. "Put your hand on her shoulder."

She saw the change in Aurora the moment Micah's hand touched her. She straightened like she'd been plugged into a battery pack, her breath coming easier and her muscles relaxing.

Why had she ever believed separating them was the right thing to do? But she knew the answer. Her fear had made her blind to what had been staring her in the face.

"I should have been working with you both since you were born," she admitted. Even before the Teeli threat had become imminent, she'd been reluctant to nurture Aurora's abilities or the powerful interaction between her and Micah. At the time, she'd believed their connection was a weakness, an uncontrollable hazard, instead of seeing it as the incredible strength it was. One that could make Aurora and Micah an unstoppable force for good.

"Now, we're going to find out how best to make use of your unique connection." She placed the rags in a circle with Aurora and Micah at the center, adding a few more for good measure. "Let's try that exercise again."

Eighty

Aurora was very aware of her audience, especially Lyon. The kid was riveted, watching every move she and her mom made.

She wasn't the only one who'd noticed his reaction. Celia was watching him surreptitiously, too. So were Isin and Sweep, and Kenji had grinned when Lyon had popped up to collect the rags she'd flung around when she'd lost focus on the funnel.

Lyon's child-like amazement was incredibly endearing. So were the softer feelings she felt emerging into his emotional field. It was like watching a newborn fawn take their first steps out of the safety of the forest into the sunshine.

Micah squeezed her shoulder, drawing her attention back to the rag circle. From the moment he'd touched her, their connection had wiped away her fatigue. She could feel his eagerness and curiosity, which matched her own. She wanted to see what they could do together, too.

Engaging her energy field, she enveloped Micah and then expanded the field to encompass the rag circle. Her mom had increased the diameter of the circle by a couple meters and added more rags, upping the difficulty level, but with Micah beside her, she covered the extra distance effortlessly. However, when she started the funnel rotating, the energy spun considerably faster than before, snatching the rags off the deck in an instant and flinging them outward. She snagged them before they could escape the field, catching the mini tornado by the tail, but the sudden gust made Kai and Iolana scoot back in alarm. Her dad and Celia didn't even flinch.

You got this, sis.

Micah's words in her mind settled her. In fact, as the rags began to bob and dance in the air, it felt like he was helping guide their motion in the undulating currents. Maybe he was. He'd helped guide her on her surfboard when he'd taught her to surf. Unlike her, he'd been interacting intimately with wind and waves most of his life. What had been a challenging mountain for her to climb alone now felt more like a manageable hill.

Their mom tossed a rag onto the deck just outside the perimeter of the spinning funnel. "Try to pick up the rag and add it to the funnel."

Aurora's shoulders tensed as she stared at the rag. The hill had just doubled in size. But Micah's fingers brushed lightly across her collarbone, his emotions playful and relaxed.

The rag's a surfboard and we're generating the wave. A visual projection from Micah popped into her mind of a surfboard being lifted up and carried by a rolling wave. *Let's take it for a ride.*

A soft chuckle rumbled in her throat at Micah's reminder to treat this like play, not a test.

The buoyant feeling of the swirling waves of air added to the feeling of giddy fun. She expanded the funnel so that it brushed the rag. It flopped sideways, then flipped up at the back, caught in the air current, lifting off the deck. Again, she felt Micah's unseen hand helping her guide the rag into the flow of the others as they whipped around the circle.

"Excellent!" their mom cheered. "Now send one of the rags out of the top of the funnel and drop it at my feet."

Another visual popped into her mind, this time of Streak and Cutter leaping out of the water and sailing over Micah on his surfboard.

She grinned, her mind instantly turning the collection of black rags into a pod of circling dolphins. Streak and Cutter had loved swimming through her energy field as much as she'd loved feeling their emotional resonance when they did. Those memories made focusing on the individual rags a delight.

She sent the first Streak rag swimming to the top of the funnel. It leapt out and plopped at her mom's feet. A Cutter rag followed shortly afterward, joining its cousin. Micah's laughter blended with hers as the joy of their shared imagery flowed between them.

One by one, the rags rose, carried on the waves of the funnel before leaping out and gathering with the rest of the pod.

When the last one flipped onto the deck and the funnel dissipated, a round of applause echoed off the bulkheads.

Micah grabbed her hand and lifted it high before bending at the waist, pulling her with him into a theatrical bow.

That drew laughter and whistles from Kenji and Summer.

Her mom approached with a wide smile. "That was incredible. I knew you strengthened each other, but this..." She gestured to the neat pile of rags. "You did it on your first try."

"You should have seen them surfing together," her dad said, his emotional field glowing with happiness. "I'm beginning to think there's nothing they can't do when they work together."

"Then how about we try those pulse shots Dad told me about," Micah suggested, bumping her shoulder with his.

She glanced at her mom. They hadn't worked on that technique yet, but she was curious to see if she could do it.

"What do you mean, pulse shots?" an annoyed voice called out from the stairs.

Aurora turned.

Shash stalked over, glaring at her and then at the members of *Vengeance*'s crew watching the proceedings. "So, this is where everyone disappeared to." Adel followed in her wake, Hobbes and Omondi behind her, with Lupe bringing up the rear.

Isin straightened from where he'd been leaning against one of the cargo crates. "Is there a problem, Shash?" His voice was even, but his eyes held a warning.

Shash crossed her arms over her chest. "What exactly is going on here?" Her brusque manner radiated anger, but Aurora sensed a more tender emotion underlying it. Shash was hurt because she hadn't been invited.

"Training," Aurora replied. "I need to work on my skills, and some of the crew came down to watch."

Shash's eyes narrowed. Then she pointed at Micah. "He mentioned pulse shots." Her gaze flicked to U-1. "Are you firing weapons on my ship?"

Isin's emotional field heated, but he remained where he was, watching the interaction closely.

"Not weapons. My energy abilities." She gave Shash and the other new arrivals a quick rundown on her non-Human origins and an overview of her energy abilities. The disbelief that flared in their emotional fields was tempered by the non-reaction of the rest of the crew to the explanation.

Shash rolled her eyes, then glared at Isin. "She can't be serious."

"She is."

Aurora sensed the bone-deep ache of betrayal in Shash's emotional field, even though she did an excellent job of concealing it with a vicious scowl. Isin's failure to include her had hurt her deeply.

Maybe she could do something about that. "Do you want to help me train?"

The unexpected offer temporarily wiped the scowl off Shash's face. "How?" she asked guardedly.

"I need a volunteer to toss objects in the air for me."

"So you can do what with them?"

"Knock them out of the air."

"With what?"

"An energy pulse."

Shash's lips compressed. "You *are* firing weapons on my ship."

"It's not a weapon." Though having once thought of her abilities in those terms, she could relate to Shash's concern. "It's an energy burst. My mom can shield around it. If I miss the target, the pulse will hit her shield, not the ship."

Shash huffed, but her emotions indicated she was intrigued. She threw a look over her shoulder at Isin. "You're okay with this?"

He didn't answer, just held her gaze with a captain's quiet authority.

Shash's scowl reappeared. "Fine. Whatever." She turned back to Aurora. "Good thing I'm here to keep you from doing something stupid."

Aurora suppressed the smile that threatened. Shash would be horrified if she knew Aurora was sensing her eagerness to be included. "We'll use the rags to start, since this is my first time trying this."

A trill of alarm raced through Shash's emotional field. "You don't know what you're doing?"

"It's a new technique, but an extension of things I've already done. Like working on an engine upgrade that's based on a design you know well. And my mom's shield will prevent anything or anyone from being hurt."

Shash glanced at Aurora's mom. "Yeah, I've seen that," she murmured.

Her mom smiled, then motioned to Aurora, Micah, and Shash. "Why don't you two stand there," she pointed to a spot farther away from their audience, "facing me." She backed up, then raised her hands, generating a domed shield that enclosed the four of them together. "Shash, if you'll please gather the rags."

Micah moved beside Aurora, resting his hand on her shoulder, while Shash collected the rags.

Aurora's palms tingled with the energetic potential of her field. "Shash, I want you to toss a rag about a meter away from me and as high as you can."

Shash eyed her. "And you're going to knock it out of the air with an energy pulse?" Her skepticism ran high.

"That's the goal."

Shash glanced at her mom. "And you're going to make sure it doesn't hit the ship?"

"The shield is already in place."

Shash pursed her lips, heaving the sigh of the long-suffering. "Fine." Clutching one of the rags in her hand, she whipped her arm around in an underhand throw that sent the rag sailing through the air.

Pearlescent energy burst from Aurora's palms, left and right, but in rushing streams rather than a pulse. The streams struck her mom's shield, melding with the shield without producing any visible light – like absorbing like. She pulled back her energy field, cutting off the streams.

She'd missed the rag entirely.

"Hmm." She stared at the rag lying on the deck, then glanced over her shoulder at Micah. "Not sure an energy *boost* is what I need right now."

He grinned, dropping his hand from her shoulder. "Maybe not."

"What are you talking about?" Shash demanded. "Nothing happened."

"Because I missed," she explained. "Our energy fields are invisible to most people unless the shield strikes a solid object. Toss one of the rags to my dad."

Shash frowned, then flipped one of the rags toward Aurora's dad. A tiny burst of light appeared where it struck her mom's shield.

Shash jerked back. "It's right there?"

"Uh-huh."

Her gaze darted to Aurora, then Aurora's mom. "Can I... touch it?"

Her mom smiled. "Go ahead. It's safe."

Shash stretched her arm out, palm flat. She twitched when her fingers made contact with the shield. "It's warm." She slowly pressed her entire palm against the surface of the shield, giving it a hard shove. "It doesn't move."

"That's the point," Aurora replied.

Shash met her gaze over her shoulder. "How much force can it deflect?"

Aurora's mind flipped to the barrage of weapons fire she'd endured during her escape from Seaview. "A lot."

Shash's eyes widened at her tone. Her gaze slid to Isin, the alarm back in her emotional field. "They could use this to trap someone."

"They could," Isin agreed, unconcerned. "But anyone Aurora or Libra trapped with their shield would deserve to be kept isolated. Like our two guests." Isin lifted his chin toward the upper decks.

Shash mulled that over. Then she scooped the rag off the deck and turned to Aurora. "You're trying to hit this with the same kind of energy?"

"Yep."

"What will happen if you do?"

"I'll knock the rag off its trajectory."

"Let's see you do it." Shash tossed the rag in the air without warning.

Aurora reacted, her emotions firing up and her energy coalescing. Her fingers flicked, sending two pulses streaking toward the rag. The one from her right hand clipped the leading edge, sending the rag tumbling toward her mom.

"Yeah!" Micah cheered.

But Shash didn't give Aurora time to relax. Another rag sailed into the air.

She clipped that one, too, the trailing edge this time. The next one she hit dead on, hard enough that it bounced off her mom's shield, producing a flare of light.

Shash threw her last two at the same time. Aurora tagged one, but missed the second, the pulse absorbed when it struck her mom's shield.

"Nicely done, Aurora," her dad called out amid the clapping and whistles from the crew.

Her mom dropped the shield. "Looks like Shash found the way to focus your abilities." She grinned. "Don't give you time to think."

Eighty-One

One of the big benefits of telling *Vengeance's* crew about Unity and the Yruf? It gave Libra a distraction from her PTSD during the shuttle flight to the planet's surface.

The previous evening, Aurora and Brendan had both noted a sharp spike of terror from Adel at the news of the Yruf's presence. Brendan believed it indicated past trauma, likely from witnessing the brutality of a Setarip attack, possibly the one that had left her orphaned. But when he'd asked Adel about it, she'd clammed up. However, his suggestion that she remain on *Vengeance* rather than joining the habitat crews had been met with equal resistance.

As a fellow Setarip attack survivor, Libra could relate to her trauma. Which is why she was currently seated beside Adel on *Starlet*, acting as her personal bodyguard for the shuttle flight and for the upcoming meeting with the Yruf. Hobbes had suggested it, after witnessing Libra's shielding ability during the training session with Aurora.

"What... what are they like?"

Libra glanced at Adel.

Her fingers were clamped onto the arms of her seat as tightly as Libra's.

"You mean the Yruf?"

Adel gave a tight nod.

She considered what description would help to calm Adel's fears. "Kind. Generous. Beautiful."

"Beautiful?" Adel's dark eyes rounded.

She nodded. "Especially the females. Their scales come in a rainbow of colors, and they have a glossy sheen. Ifel is predominantly emerald-green and black. The two pilots we met are sisters, and they're blue and gold. The males are more neutral toned, but all the Yruf I've seen are beautiful."

"Do they look like... snakes?" Adel's lower lip trembled.

Libra's heart squeezed. No doubt about it. Adel had seen Ecilam Setarips firsthand. "A little. Their movements are very fluid and graceful, but like dancers, not anything threatening. They would never do anything to harm us, or anyone else. And they respect personal space. If you don't want them near you, they'll keep their distance."

"Promise?"

"Promise." She had one other detail she should share, just to prepare her. "They're also taller than most of us."

Adel swallowed hard. "Oh."

"You sure you want to do this?" Hobbes asked from the seat on Adel's right next to the viewport. "We could spend the day on the shuttle instead."

Adel's lower lip protruded as her brows drew down. "I want to see the planet. Micah said there are rivers."

Teenage stubbornness was a nearly unstoppable force, even in the face of trauma.

Hobbes clearly was aware of that fact. "Okay."

Adel leaned toward Hobbes as the view outside transformed from the hazy white of clouds into the lush green of the jungle. "Whoa." Her entire focus shifted to the landscape, her concern about the Setarips temporarily eclipsed.

Hobbes met Libra's gaze.

She recognized the concern and anxiety she saw in her eyes. They were the same emotions she'd struggled with ever since Micah and Aurora were born.

Like any good parent, Hobbes wanted to protect Adel from unnecessary pain and trauma. But as Libra had learned the hard way, often the best way to help your child grow was to stand beside them when they encountered pain and trauma, supporting them as they expanded the boundaries of their experience, rather than blocking them from it.

Thankfully in this instance, Adel's encounter with the Yruf should be a balm to her fear rather than exacerbating it.

Through a break in the canopy Libra caught a glimpse of a flat expanse of grey rock as Brendan brought the shuttle in for a landing.

"First stop. Please remember to take all your belongings when disembarking," Brendan sang out, grinning over his shoulder at the two teams seated in the main cabin.

"Thanks, Dad." Aurora leaned over, giving him a kiss on the cheek before rising from the co-pilot's seat and snagging her pack. She gave Libra a subtle thumbs-up before heading for the ramp. "See everyone at the rendezvous point tonight."

"We'll be there," Brendan replied.

A brush against Libra's hand made her turn her head.

Adel was clutching the armrests again, her head swiveling back and forth between the open hatch where half the group was exiting and the flat expanse of rock just outside the viewport.

Libra rested her hand over Adel's, giving her fingers a gentle caress as Adel's arm trembled. "The Yruf probably won't show themselves until after we arrive at our destination."

Adel glanced at her, but didn't reply.

"You're good to go, Brendan," Kai said, moving to the co-pilot's seat Aurora had vacated.

The shuttle lifted vertically, hardly making a sound.

"Delivering the goods." Kai's hands moved over the controls, activating the extractor that would lower the habitat building materials from the shuttle's storage compartment to the group gathered below.

Adel stared out the viewport as the transfer proceeded, her breathing unsteady. The trembling in her arm ramped up significantly when *Starlet* rose, the canopy slipping past as the shuttle headed toward the second habitat location.

Libra kept up the gentle touch on Adel's hand. It was the only thing she could do for her, reminding her she wasn't facing this alone. She noted Hobbes was doing the same thing with Adel's other hand.

The rocky protrusion rising above the canopy that Brendan banked toward looked like a set of four curving stairs carved out by a titan. The uppermost stair provided a partial ceiling over the small clearing at the base of the curve. The open space in the shadow of the rock continued along a shallow decline to the tree-lined river beyond.

"I'll be letting everyone off at the rock," Brendan informed them, "then we'll unload the gear and Kai and I will land the shuttle in the river."

"*In* the river?" Adel's attention jerked away from the viewport.

Brendan glanced back at her. "That's right. *Starlet* can land on water. Do you want to stay onboard and watch?"

Adel started to nod, then glanced out the viewport and at Libra, and shook her head. "No."

Brendan returned his focus to flying, although she knew he was reading Adel's emotional shifts. "No problem. You can experience the water landing tomorrow."

Despite the uneven surface, the shuttle set down with nary a bump. "Second stop."

As the ramp lowered, Adel tensed.

"I'm right here," Libra reminded her.

U-1 detached from their alcove, gliding through the opening. Shash and Shorty followed. Omondi and Hobbes stood, but waited for Adel to pry herself from her seat before grabbing their packs.

Libra stayed right beside the teenager, who'd stopped after taking two steps. "You want me to surround us with the shield?"

Adel's gaze darted to her. "You can do that?"

"Absolutely." Engaging her energy field, she swirled it around Adel, allowing the interior of the field to brush against her bare skin.

Adel gave a little jolt. "Is that it?"

"Yep." She solidified the shield, then glanced at Hobbes. "Try to put your hand on Adel's shoulder."

Hobbes complied, her hand sliding the moment it came in contact with the shield.

"See?" Libra rested her hand on Adel's other shoulder. "No one can touch you. Ready to go see the planet?"

Adel's shoulder quivered beneath her hand, but she nodded twice in rapid succession.

Libra met Brendan's gaze. "We'll see you soon."

"Yes, you will."

She guided Adel to the slab of rock above the shuttle as it lifted off, providing the teenager with a commanding view of her surroundings. Shash directed the placement of the structural elements for the habitat as the extractor lowered them to Shorty,

Omondi, and Hobbes. When all the pieces lay in neat piles across the stone, *Starlet*'s hull camouflage engaged, the shuttle vanishing from sight.

Adel stared at where it had been, mouth agape.

"Pretty impressive, huh?" Libra asked with a smile.

Adel nodded, searching the sky for any hint as to where the shuttle had gone. "Is it still there?"

"No." She was subconsciously tracking Brendan's movements across the sky as the shuttle made its approach to the river. "But it moves so silently, it could be right in front of us and we wouldn't know it." Well, she would, but that wasn't a fault of the Kraed technology.

"How does it do that?"

Her smile widened. "That's a question for Jonarel, not me. He's—"

"The Kraed engineer," Adel finished for her. "Celia told me. She said—"

"You two gonna help or just stand there yapping?" Shash stood with her feet planted apart, a pair of supports under her arm and her customary scowl on her face.

"Helping," Libra replied, giving Adel a light nudge to get her moving.

"Good. 'Cause we've got—" She cut off abruptly, her body tensing.

Two Yruf had stepped around the curve of the rock below.

"Dark stars of the void," Omondi breathed, his hand dropping to his hip.

She suspected he usually had a gun holster there. Not now. Aurora had made it abundantly clear no weapons were allowed on this trip. Celia had made certain that order was enforced.

Hobbes backed toward Adel, her attention on the two Yruf. Shorty, the closest to the Yruf, was holding a length of pipe like a club.

Not the best start to the introductions. "Hi, Tipol," she called out to the blue and gold Yruf who was watching the reactions of *Vengeance*'s crew. The green and gold Yruf next to her wasn't one Libra had met.

"Hello, Libra," Unity translated. "You brought new friends."

"I have." She glanced at Adel.

The teenager's dark skin had paled, her eyes almost popping out of their sockets. "Is that Ifel?" she rasped, staring at the green and gold Yruf.

"No." The Yruf leader was much larger. And more striking. But she wasn't going to tell Adel that. "Wait here," she murmured, deactivating her shield and stepping away from her and Hobbes. She wove through the construction materials, past Omondi, Shash, and Shorty until she was in front of the two Yruf. She met the diamond-pupiled gaze of the unknown Yruf. "I'm Libra."

"I'm Mahrem," Unity translated. "She's an engineer," they added as a personal commentary.

"Great! Another engineer would be very helpful." She angled her body so she could see the Yruf and her group. "This is Shorty, Shash, Omondi, Hobbes, and Adel. Shash is an engineer, too. They're all members of *Vengeance*'s crew. Everyone, this is Tipol and Mahrem."

Tipol and Mahrem lowered their heads in a micro-bow of greeting.

Vengeance's crew shared a lot of nervous glances, but one by one they repeated the gesture. Except Adel, who seemed literally petrified, her expression carved in stone.

Libra turned to the Yruf and lowered her voice. "Adel, the youngest, had a bad experience with the Ecilam. She's terrified of Setarips."

Tipol's and Mahrem's mouths opened in what looked like a grimace or snarl, but without showing any teeth.

"We are sorry for the child's pain," Unity said softly. "We will keep our distance from her, if that is her wish."

"Thank you. I'd appreciate that, at least until Brendan gets here." Which wouldn't be long. She could sense him and Kai at the river's edge, moving toward them.

She glanced back at her group. Now that the initial shock had worn off, Shorty looked openly curious as he gazed at the Yruf. Shash, on the other hand, looked like a woman with something to prove.

Encouraging Shash's competitive urge regarding the Yruf might not be a bad thing. It might even get this shelter built in record time.

She gave the engineer a bright smile. "Alright, Shash, what should we do first?"

Eighty-Two

Lelindia closed her eyes and snuggled against Jonarel as he stroked his fingers through her hair. He'd swept her into his arms and settled her into his lap on the couch in their cabin right after Unity notified them Aurora wanted to chat. He'd apparently decided it was the perfect opportunity for cuddling, tucking her head into the curve of his shoulder and neck, his warmth surrounding her.

Who was she to argue?

Aurora's voice came over the cabin speakers with only a slight time delay. She'd just given them a rundown on her training sessions with Libra.

"Sounds like you're learning a lot." Lelindia sighed as Jonarel's caress turned her body into warm honey.

"I am. I'm also glad I didn't know earlier just how much knowledge my mom was holding back from me. Our arguments would have been a lot more heated."

That was a frightening proposition. As it was, their disagreements had been blistering. Trying to mediate two Sahzades in the middle of a fiery argument was like an ice planet trying to survive between two close-orbiting binaries shooting off solar flares. It didn't end well.

"And the construction of the habitats?" Jonarel asked.

"Progressing nicely. The flexibility of your design has enabled us to tailor it to the two locations we've selected. We got a solid start on the lower level for both today. We should be able to finish that up tomorrow, at least all the key components, then build out the upper level the next day. That'll go quicker, since it's mostly open space."

"And then you get to move in the new residents." The memory of Manchado leering at Celia flashed into her mind, making her jaw clench. She'd seriously considered not treating his injuries after witnessing his behavior during their confrontation. Professional pride hadn't allowed her to turn him over to Jake in that state, but she'd been sorely tempted. Touching him with her energy field had made her skin crawl. "That will be a relief."

"Yeah." Weariness weighed down the single syllable. "Even my dad can't make any progress improving their attitudes. I had doubts when I came up with this idea, but now it's clear that leaving them where they can't hurt anyone else is the best solution."

"Will they harm each other?" Jonarel asked.

"Probably. It's in their best interests to work together, but nothing I've sensed from either of them indicates that degree of introspection and forethought. They derive enjoyment out of abusing others. Their behavior toward each other in the brig has made that clear. They'll have to put some effort into reaching each other, but after that..."

Lelindia could picture Aurora's shrug and the resigned look on her face. She wasn't the type to give up on anyone, but there were limits. "After that, it's up to them. They have free will to make their situation better or worse, just like the rest of us. How's Celia handling being on the same ship with Manchado?"

"Really well. I can sense her awareness of him, but her emotional state is remarkably balanced and healthy. I think Micah has a lot to do with that. Her sessions with my dad are helping, too."

"That's good to hear. I was worried she'd be a livewire the whole time."

"Nope. In some ways, she's calmer about the whole situation than I am. Or Micah. She's been leading sparring sessions with Iolana and Lyon, the teenage boy on the crew, and she, Micah, and my dad have been giving cooking lessons to the crew."

A smile tugged on her lips. "And which of them is in charge of those lessons?"

Aurora's soft chuckle drifted over the speakers. "That depends on who you ask. But enough about us. How are you and my little energy-sister-to-be doing?"

Jonarel's arms tightened around her, one hand moving to rest on her belly.

A wave of fierce love for her mate and her child rushed through her like a flash flood, pushing moisture against the backs of her eyes. "We're good." Her voice came out thick as syrup. She cleared her throat before continuing. "Siginal and Daymar are on their way here. We expect them in a couple days."

"That's great. Daymar's going to be so thrilled to see you."

She caught the happy lilt in Aurora's voice. "I can't wait to see her." Daymar had always been dear to her, even before she'd learned that Jonarel's mother had secretly rooted for her to mate with Jonarel. Siginal's banishment of Jonarel and Tehar had prevented Daymar from attending their mating ceremony, but Tehar had made a recording of the event. One of the first things Lelindia planned to do when the *Rowkclarek* arrived was share the projection with Daymar and Siginal.

"How are things on the *Starhawke?*" Aurora asked.

"Quiet. That's been good for Isabeau, but Knox and Kelly are growing restless. They took *The Hawke* out for a flight this morning, ostensibly so Kelly could show him the basics of operating the shuttle, but I think they both just needed to do something besides hanging around the ship and sifting through the unpleasant messages coming through the ICS."

"So Knox was able to leave Isabeau on her own?"

"Uh-huh."

"That's a big step."

"I know. She's a lot more relaxed since..." She trailed off, wincing at what she'd been about to say.

Aurora filled in the blanks for her. "Since the Admiral and I left the ship."

"And everyone else. She told me it's easier for her to just be herself with so few people onboard."

"Well, it sounds like that will continue for a little while, anyway. If she's no longer relying on Knox to stay with her all the time, he's going to need a job to keep him occupied. Any suggestions?"

Lelindia pursed her lips. "His background is the same as yours — communications and leadership." It was one reason they'd worked so well together on the *Argo*. They'd thought along similar lines and could anticipate each other's actions.

That same reasoning had factored into Aurora's decision to ask Kire to be her first officer. He was even more proficient at communications than she was and was also a stellar leader. Which made Knox's presence on the *Starhawke* largely redundant, especially with Unity onboard. "I don't have any brilliant ideas." She tapped Jonarel's chest with her finger. "How about you?"

"Not at the moment."

"We have a suggestion."

Lelindia lifted her head, gazing at where Unity's voice had come over the speaker. "Go ahead."

"A while back, Justin expressed an interest in working out a translation for the Yruf's light language, but he hasn't brought it up since. Maybe we could teach it to Knox?"

"It might be a fun intellectual challenge," Aurora admitted, "but would it be practical? You can translate it for us."

"But if Knox learned how to read it, we'd have another way to communicate with you that the Teeli and Sovereign wouldn't know about or understand."

"A secret language," Lelindia murmured.

"One that isn't verbal, so they likely wouldn't recognize it as communication." Aurora sounded intrigued. "Micah's ability to communicate with the Yruf already gives us a similar advantage, but as our group keeps expanding..." A wry smile entered her voice. "And if we keep needing to split up, the more ways we can communicate with you and the Yruf, the better."

"So you like our idea?" Unity sounded like a little kid who'd just proposed a trip to the beach to their parents and gotten a positive response.

"I love it," Aurora replied. "I think Knox will, too. It'll be in his wheelhouse and provide him with a leadership role."

"Then we'll ask him!"

Jonarel shifted on the couch, his muscles flexing around her. "What hardware would you require to replicate the light language?"

"Nothing new," Unity replied. "We could integrate with a tablet to start, then use projections in the observation lounge or shuttle bay to produce the size and scope necessary for more advanced concepts. The bridgescreen would be an option, too."

"For this to work, Knox will need a way to reproduce the language," Aurora pointed out. "Otherwise the communication is one-way. Star, can you give him that kind of flexibility for creating light projections on the ship?"

Tehar's image appeared seated on the couch beside them. She was dressed in a fitted dark brown tunic and pants that outlined her athletic form, her dark hair swept back in a simple braid. "I can. With Jonarel's assistance, we could also make adaptations to the bridge consoles that would allow them to be used for this form of communication."

"Great. You two can start working on the logistics. If—"

"Knox wants to do it!"

Lelindia met Tehar's gaze, catching the flash of amusement in her honey-gold eyes.

"Thank you, Unity." Amusement was evident in Aurora's voice, too. "Once Knox has a solid foundation, he can teach Kire, Justin, and me how to read and produce some of the more critical messages we might need to share."

"Itorye would want to learn, too," Unity replied. "Can we let her know about this?"

"Sure. Let Nat know as well, in case she wants to facilitate any hardware changes on *Phoenix*. Jonarel can coordinate with her engineer."

"My mom might be interested in learning as well," Lelindia added. "She's been enjoying her stints at communications."

"By all means. The more flexible and adaptable we can all be the better. Unity can ask her when they talk to Nat and Itorye. Star, are we still on target for a full recharge in nine days?"

Tehar folded her hands in her lap. "Yes, Captain, although Unity, Jonarel, and I have been working to improve the cells' charging efficiency. Our preliminary results indicate we may achieve a full charge in eight days, rather than nine."

"You found a way to speed up the charging?" Aurora asked, shock evident in her voice.

"Unity and the Yruf engineers found a way," Jonarel corrected. "We implemented a test on five cells yesterday. The results we achieved are exactly as anticipated. If you authorize the change shipwide, Unity and the Yruf ships can complete the work tomorrow."

"By all means. I trust your judgment. Is there anything else I need to be aware of?"

A kick from Raehn made Lelindia chuckle. "Only that Raehn misses her Aunty Aurora and hopes you'll be back soon."

"So do I. The sooner we complete this mission the better."

Eighty-Three

The star system that housed the Eridani Duo space station was home to a yellow dwarf star — a slightly smaller and less luminous sibling of Earth's sun. The inner regions of the system contained rocky planets spaced at intervals similar to those of Mercury, Venus, Earth, and Mars, with a couple extra planets tossed in for good measure.

The jump window Cade brought *Gladiator* out of was near the sixth planet in the system, a Super-Earth orbiting just outside the far edge of the system's habitable zone. The surface conditions on the planet had proven too harsh and hostile to make colonization an option, but its location in the system and within the network of Fleet space made it an ideal hub for scientific study, with easy access to both Gaia and Hydra One. Astronomers in particular flocked to Eridani Duo, which orbited the planet only twice within the planet's already lengthy standard day. The station boasted six telescopes, and its relatively slow rotation meant extended viewing time without the muddying effect of atmosphere or the complications of weather.

A quick glance at the aft cameras confirmed *Phoenix* was tucked in close behind *Gladiator*. However, the visual of open space all around them made Cade pause. "Unity, are we good to proceed?"

"Sure are!" Unity confirmed, hovering in Cade's peripheral vision. "Our ships have surrounded you and *Phoenix*. No one in the system can see you, but you'll be able to see everything in the system."

The wonders of Yruf camouflage and modular ship technology. "Thanks."

As he guided *Gladiator* towards the planet, the outlines of Eridani Duo took shape. As the first orbital science station built in Fleet space, Eridani Duo had provided the blueprint for all those that followed, like Persei Primus. It was based on an age-old design and layout – a wheel with spokes and a central hub. But what had started out as a relatively modest single orbital ring had expanded over time into a towering structure with six broad rings, the widest at the top three times the diameter of the original. Each generation of Fleet ships had expanded in size and personnel capacity, so the station's upgrades allowed Eridani Duo to provide service and repair for any class of ship, from the smallest shuttle to the largest cruiser, as well as a home base for an ever-burgeoning scientific community.

Cade had never checked the population statistics for the station, but it offered most of the resources and functionality of a small university town, and looked and felt like one, too. Science lectures were one of the preferred forms of entertainment. The spokes that connected the rings to the central hub were built out with living spaces and accommodations for residents and visitors, alike. If necessary, the station could temporarily house the entire crew of a Discovery-class ship like *Cassini* with room to spare.

He'd docked at the station to pick up supplies several times in his guise as a Rescue Corps pilot. He recognized the familiar logo on the hull of two of the freighters currently docked at the station. "Tell Nat we'll hold up here until we're ready to make our move."

As Justin passed on the message, Cade fired the braking thrusters, bringing *Gladiator* into orbit five-hundred kilometers from the station.

One advantage of Eridani Duo being a science facility rather than a travel destination like Hydra One was the nearly non-existent cross traffic in the system. Fleet personnel and scientists stationed here tended to remain for months or even years. He didn't see any ships currently inbound or outbound. It was one of the conditions that would make Montgomery's disappearance off the station look like a magic trick of epic proportions.

He got up and stretched, working the kinks out of his legs. Technically he didn't have to stay in the cockpit during *Gladiator*'s interstellar jumps, especially with Unity integrated with the ship's systems, but hanging out in the small central room when the ship was in motion just felt wrong.

Now that they were stationary, he grabbed something to eat with Justin, Drew, and Gonzo in the lower-level dining nook before returning to the cockpit. Justin and U-2 settled into their customary spots beside and behind him, while Gonzo dropped into the seat at the auxiliary station.

"What's the status on *Cassini?*" Cade asked U-2.

"They'll be here in one hour and thirty-four minutes," Unity replied.

"And the ship with the Teeli consuls?"

"We've been unable to track them directly, since we didn't have a ship near Earth at the time of their departure, but based on communications through the ICS, we expect them here within the next hour."

"Good." Their plan would work best if *Cassini* arrived after Nixon's physician discovered Montgomery was missing. It would alleviate any suspicions that Montgomery's crew had played a role in spiriting her away.

"Has Dr. Yates staged Montgomery's room in the ICU?" Dr. Morales had alerted Yates to the change in Montgomery's situation through a coded message transferred by Harriet, their courier. Morales' assurances to Yates that he could trust the unusual communications on his comm device had allowed Unity to successfully communicate with him. Setting up their plan had been relatively easy after that.

"Yep. The curtains are drawn and the last logged security pad entry was his from an hour and a half ago. The medical data he entered in her file will be consistent with the portrayal of Captain Montgomery's visible injuries when she gives her speech."

"Are you in position to trigger the security override sequence?"

"You bet."

"Can you give us visuals?"

In answer, an image of a curving corridor in Eridani Duo's ICU appeared on *Gladiator*'s vid display. It showed a closed door directly in front them with the number 12 on it, the curtains drawn across the floor-to-ceiling windows that looked out on the corridor. A room to the right and another to the left had matching doors, each with a security pad to prevent unauthorized access, although the door to the right was currently open, the room empty.

"The path is clear to the personnel lift." U-2 edged closer to Cade. "Should we start the sequence?"

"It's your call. You can see all the moving parts."

"Okay. Starting sequence now."

Nothing changed on the visual for at least twenty seconds, then the red light on the security pad for Montgomery's door switched to green.

"Door unlocked," Unity confirmed, "and personnel lift being held on this level."

Cade kept his focus on the display, even though there was nothing to see.

After about a minute, the door security pad switched back to red. "Door secured. Sequence moving to the lift."

The point of the cascading sequence was to create the illusion of an infiltration into the medical center, using the security-coded personnel lift as the access point. The gaps in the override codes Unity was inputting needed to be long enough to make the timing of movement through the facility plausible. The specific coding would also make it look like the security pad had been hacked with a device similar to the one Bella had used on the Etah ship on Gaia to break the Suulh kids out of their holding cells.

Unity was poised to alter data in the station's docking logs that would make it appear *Gladiator* had docked without authorization at a Ring 4 ship berth on the opposite side of the ring from the Rescue Corps freighters. Those berths were only staffed when a docking or repair was scheduled, making it an ideal decoy for their subterfuge. The anomalies in the logs from Unity's changes would create the impression of someone attempting to scrub all the data and failing, making Unity's inserted images showing *Gladiator* approaching and departing from the berth appear authentic.

Justin shifted in his seat. "This isn't as much fun as actually *doing* a hospital heist."

"No, but it's a lot less stressful."

Justin grunted in response, folding his arms over his chest.

"I'm with you, hermano." Gonzo patted Justin on the shoulder. "Driving the ambulance was a lot more fun than sitting here."

"Any indication the medical center staff or security personnel have noticed anything unusual?" Cade asked Unity.

"Nope."

"Timeline to—"

"The ship with the Teeli just arrived in the system."

Cade snapped forward. "That's earlier than you projected."

"They must have pushed the ship's engines during the jump. The interstellar engines are giving off more heat than Fleet safety standards allow."

Cade and Justin exchanged a glance.

"I'm sure the Teeli's influence had something to do with that," Justin muttered.

"No doubt," Cade agreed. He glanced back at the display. "Does this cause a problem for your timeline, Unity?" Now that the sequence was started, they couldn't speed up the intervals to the phantom undocking without ruining the illusion.

"We're making adjustments, altering perceived behavior in the logs and security pad access based on how you might react if you were on the station when you learned the ship with the Teeli was in the system."

Cade's brows lifted. "You can extrapolate my personal behavior and reactions?"

"We *have* been spending a lot of time with you, Cade," Unity said with an affronted sniff.

"Yeah, you have." He'd just never considered that Unity was building a pattern of behavior so they could anticipate his actions.

"We've pushed back the theoretical departure from the repair berth to after the other ship has docked and Nixon's physician has entered the station."

Which is precisely what he would have done – lay low until his adversaries weren't in a position to chase after him. "You know me well."

"Thank you." Unity sounded inordinately pleased with themselves.

Gonzo chuckled, motioning to U-2. "Unity has your number."

"His number?" Unity asked.

"It means you understand me," Cade explained, "the good and the bad."

"Oh. Then yes, we definitely have your number."

Cade grinned, reaching out to give U-2 a pat. "I'm glad." He'd never imagined he'd have a non-biological as a close friend, but his life had gotten a lot more interesting since Unity became a part of it.

The image on the vid display switched to a close-up of the incoming ship. Cade's jaw locked as he recognized it.

Justin let loose with a pithy swear word. "Think Nixon's onboard?"

"He'd better be."

"Why?" Unity asked.

"Because that's the Fleet Director's yacht," Cade explained. "It's only used to transport the Director. Loaning the yacht to his personal physician to make the trip would go against multiple Fleet regulations and codes of conduct." Not that Nixon was overly concerned with following regulations and codes of conduct.

"Oh. Well, Nixon is onboard," Unity confirmed.

"Chasing the limelight," Cade murmured, watching the yacht draw closer. "He wanted to bring in Montgomery himself."

"That's not gonna work out the way he'd planned." Justin's emotional field vibrated with devilish delight.

"Nope." Cade's smile was equally wicked. "He's about to be the focal point of a lot of unwanted attention."

Eighty-Four

"Aurora!"

Aurora jerked her head up at the alarm in Unity's voice, tightening her grip on the support beam she was holding. "What's wrong?"

"An Ecilam ship just jumped into the system!"

Her veins iced over. *Ecilam.* The most ruthless Setarip faction. "Are they headed in this direction?"

U-3 zipped sideways. "Yes. This planet appears to be their destination."

The ice shattered, her heart drumming a rapid rat-a-tat-tat. "How long do we have before they're in scanning range?"

"Twelve minutes, forty-two seconds."

"Is *Vengeance* concealed?"

"Yes."

She smacked her comband.

"We heard," her mom responded to her ping. "What do you want to do?"

Options flashed through her mind. Her mom's team could reach *Starlet* before the Ecilam were within scanning range, but not without leaving the habitat site exposed. And they wouldn't be able to pick up Aurora's team, regardless. Which meant sheltering in place.

"Clear the site as much as possible and get everyone under the cover of the habitat." The Kraed structures were designed to blend in with the environment and repel scans, and the rock was a solid barrier. The completed lower section of the two habitats would provide much better protection from visual and thermal scans than the trees.

"Got it." The connection cut off.

Aurora turned to her team. "Hide everything we can in the lower level."

The group broke apart, moving with brisk efficiency to carry out her order. She glanced at Unity. "Let me know if anything changes."

Shifting her grip on the end of the support beam meant for the upper section, she and Micah hauled it down the hill and through the entrance to the lower level.

"It's gonna be close," he muttered, setting it down.

"I know." Her team had just finished laying everything out on the rock plateau in preparation for assembling the upper level. Clearing it in twelve minutes wouldn't be easy. Making it all fit in the finished lower level was an added challenge.

Her heart pounded out each minute. The team hauled the larger, heavier pieces first, then formed a chain to pass the smaller items down the hill.

"Scanning range in one minute," Unity alerted her.

She thrust the next item into Micah's hands, her pulse throbbing in her throat. Six more pieces to go. Five. Four. Three. Two...

"That's it!" She grabbed the last item, a box of connectors. "Everyone inside!"

The chain turned into an undulating snake as the group hurried down the hillside to the lower level, Aurora at the tail. She darted inside, bumping into Micah, who rested a steadying hand on her shoulder.

"What about the other team?" she asked Unity.

"Almost done. Scanning range in twelve seconds."

Aurora held her breath. *Come on, Mom.*

We're inside. An image from her mom flashed in Aurora's mind. The other team had gathered inside the counterpart to where she stood, surrounded by the construction materials haphazardly arrayed around them.

Us, too. Aurora projected a similar image to her mom. "Unity, what about Ifel and the Etah?" Last she'd heard, Ifel was meeting with them again today.

"They're safe on Ifel's transport."

"In space?"

"No, on the ground."

The vise around her chest tightened. "I thought your camouflage didn't work in atmo."

"If the ship is moving it creates issues with light and shadow. Stationary, however, it works fine."

Her breath came a little easier. "What's the Ecilam ship doing?"

"It's moving into a geosynchronous orbit not far from our ships and *Vengeance.*"

She flinched. That crushed any hope that the Ecilam weren't here because of the Etah. "How far is not far?"

Unity swayed. "We had to move a bit to keep them from hitting us."

Aurora squeezed her eyes shut. This was bad. Her family and most of *Vengeance's* crew couldn't move without risking being seen by the Ecilam. And any actions by the Yruf could expose their presence here. "Does Ifel have any idea what they might do?"

"She has two theories. The most likely is that they came here to eliminate or recruit the remaining Etah. The less likely theory is that Tersinis found the planet as intriguing as Ifel does, and she's scouting it for a potential future settlement for the Ecilam."

"How does she know Tersinis is onboard?" According to Ifel, the Ecilam leader was firmly under the Sovereign's control. She couldn't imagine the Sovereign allowing her to flit about on her own.

"Because she can sense Tersinis on the ship. Tersinis is projecting the same emotional volatility as the last time she saw her, when the Sovereign attempted to manipulate her."

Aurora shivered despite the humid heat pressing against her skin. Cade had described the vision Ifel had seen in the Sovereign's mind during that visit, the vision of Ifel bowing to the Sovereign's will. Thank goodness Ifel hadn't been susceptible to the Sovereign's manipulations.

But that didn't make the Ecilam any less threatening. Aurora had seen the brutal results of an Ecilam attack firsthand during her rescue mission on Persei Primus, and again at Stoneycroft. "If they can't locate the Etah with scans, would they fire on the planet from space?"

Unity swayed. "We don't know. Maybe?"

Their uncertainty didn't help the tension ramping up between her shoulder blades. "How close is Ifel's transport to where the Etah were living?"

"Three point two kilometers."

Her jaw clenched. An Ecilam ship's weapons could obliterate an area that size with ease if they chose to. It wasn't like the planet had any defenses.

Except the Yruf ships in orbit.

And their leader was in the target zone.

"What's Ifel's plan?" Ifel had too much experience with the Ecilam not to have one.

"We have a section of our ship ready to move between Tersinis' ship and the surface to protect Ifel and the Etah if the Ecilam's weapons come online. We're looking for a way to get eyes and ears on their ship, but they've adapted their hull plating and shielding since the last time we met. If we make contact, they'll know."

"But if they fire, your ship will get hammered."

"We can handle it."

An image of *Gladiator* during the fight with Devries came to mind. Unity's upgrades to the ship's shields had made it virtually indestructible. The Yruf ship would be just as difficult to damage. "How are the Ecilam likely to react if they learn you're here?"

"They'll probably assume we've been following them. We've had similar encounters in the past, including defending the other factions from attack."

That assumption would keep the Yruf's alliance with her crew a secret... as long as the Ecilam didn't see anyone on the surface.

Eighty-Five

"Sweep, give me a rundown on that ship." Isin swiveled his command chair to face Sweep's station. The dark shape of the incoming ship moved on the bridgescreen in his peripheral vision as Sparki nudged *Vengeance* out of the other ship's flight path.

"Our scans won't work with the Yruf ships concealing us. We can't scan through them to the other ship. We're only seeing this," Sweep gestured to the image on the bridgescreen, "because the Yruf camouflage allows us to."

Isin ground his molars. That explained why his crew hadn't seen the Ecilam ship coming until it was almost on top of them. "What can you see?"

"It's smaller than *Vengeance*, though without scans it's hard to be precise. The black hull makes it difficult to distinguish individual exterior weapons ports, but based on what I'm seeing, it's designed to strike hard and fast from a stealth position."

"Then why is it here at an uninhabited planet?"

"We can answer that," a quiet voice replied through *Vengeance*'s bridge speakers.

"Unity?" Isin glanced up in the direction the voice had come from.

"Yes."

"You're in the comm system?" He shot a look at Butterfly, who was filling in at comm and tactical while the rest of the crew was on the planet. It had seemed like a good training opportunity at the time. Now he was seriously regretting it.

She shrugged, gesturing helplessly to the console.

Unity's voice dropped to a worried whisper. "Shash said it was okay. She needed to be able to communicate with us while we worked on the shields."

Isin massaged the bridge of his nose. "It's fine. What can you tell us about that ship?"

"It's an Ecilam warship." Unity's voice gained confidence. "The smallest and most maneuverable design they have."

Prickles of awareness poked at him, warning of danger. Unlike the Yruf, the Ecilam were lethal and ruthless. "Why are they here?"

"We believe they want to either collect the remaining Etah, or eliminate them."

His bet was on elimination. It was the Ecilam default, at least according to the news reports of attacks on human settlements and the info he'd gleaned from Aurora. "Where are the Etah now?"

"With Ifel in her transport."

"Can the Ecilam get to them?"

"They're untraceable for now because of the camouflage. But they're still on the surface."

"What about our two teams? Where are they?" He hadn't heard from them before the Ecilam ship materialized out of the deep black, and his pings to Kenji's and Shash's comm devices had been ignored.

"They're concealed in the habitats."

Which meant they wouldn't be going anywhere.

He leaned back in his chair, studying the black ship as it moved into geosynchronous orbit to port. The reflected light from the planet's surface provided enough illumination to make out the leading edge of the ship's hull, which had the sleek lines of a sea-going vessel. Or a shark. "Can you infiltrate the Ecilam ship?"

Unity didn't respond right away. "No. The Ecilam know of our existence, though they believe we are a mechanical tool, not a living being. The last time we infiltrated one of their ships—" Unity cut off, then made a sound like they were clearing their throat. "Aurora believes the Sovereign placed an auto-destruct on the ship that caused it to explode when we gained control. The Ecilam all died. So did some of the Yruf."

The pain in Unity's voice caught him off guard. Intellectually he'd accepted that Unity was similar to Alec, who clearly had the capacity for strong emotions and deep loyalty. But believing it and witnessing it were two different things. Unity was demonstrating more compassion for the deaths of the Ecilam than most people would express for people they knew, let alone people who were trying to kill them. Unity — and Alec — were living proof that humans' attitudes toward non-biologicals needed a major overhaul. "Then how do you suggest we protect our people?"

"We will protect them," Unity said firmly. "We will not allow any harm to come to them. But you must remain concealed. Ifel is adamant about that. So is Aurora."

"You're in communication with Aurora?"

"Of course. U-3 is with her."

So Unity had more mobile units on the ground than the one Aurora had brought with them. "Can you ask her what her plan is?" He wasn't content to sit here, boxed in and useless. He imagined Aurora would be in the same boat.

The speaker fell silent.

Butterfly leaned toward him, her voice barely a whisper. "I could be wrong, but I think Unity's blocking my attempts to contact our crew on the surface."

"Yes, we are," Unity replied.

So much for whispering.

"The Ecilam would be able to detect your comm signals as easily as we can. We blocked all communications as soon as the Ecilam ship entered the system."

Isin's brows lifted, his gaze shifting to Sweep at the security station.

Sweep stared back, the same uneasy realization in his eyes. Unity had a jamming system. That information hadn't been part of Aurora's briefing.

"Aurora says they'll shelter in place for now. It's tight quarters, but they have food and water. They can wait until nightfall. At that point, if the Ecilam haven't made a move, our ships can provide camouflage while the two teams make their way to *Starlet*."

"What about the habitats?" Sweep asked. "We have two prisoners we were planning to leave here."

The same thought had been weighing on him. He absolutely, positively did *not* want to keep Mirko and Manchado on *Vengeance*. He'd happily dump the pair in the jungle tonight and call it good. But he couldn't imagine Aurora leaving them on the planet while the Ecilam were in the system. "How close are the habitats to being finished?"

"A little less than halfway," Unity replied. "The sleeping area and bathroom on the lower level for each are mostly completed, but the upper level doesn't exist on either, yet."

Which meant no kitchen facilities or storage. "If the Ecilam stay in orbit, could the surface crews work at night?"

Unity was silent for a moment. "Aurora says—"

"A transport just left the ship," Sweep cut in, pointing at the bridgescreen, "heading for the surface."

Isin's gaze snagged on the small black vessel as it crossed the bridgescreen. It resembled a torpedo more than a shuttle, the exterior backlit by the planet's surface as it descended into the atmosphere. "Unity? What kind of transport is that?"

"It's what you would call a troop transport, typically used for ground assault."

His hand curled into a fist. In any other scenario, *Vengeance*'s weapons would be locked on the Ecilam warship and the *Dagger* would be on its way to intercept the troop transport. Instead, Isin was a spectator to the unfolding drama, trapped on his own ship. "Is it headed for the habitats?"

"We don't believe so, but our scout ships can't follow it without being seen. Based on the current trajectory, it appears to be headed for the Etah encampment."

That made him feel marginally better. "How close is that to Ifel's transport?"

"Close enough that it could become a problem if the Ecilam search the area."

"Then what are we going to do about it?"

Eighty-Six

"*Nixon's here!?*" Montgomery sat up abruptly from her reclined position on the med platform in *Phoenix*'s infirmary.

The movement dispelled any pretense of injury, although the cast Williams had applied to her right arm as a prop weighed her down.

Nat backed away from Montgomery's blast zone.

"Yes," Itorye confirmed over the ship's comm. "The Fleet Director's yacht is inbound to the station."

Nat glanced at the Admiral.

A flash of pain tightened his features for a split second before he squelched it.

"Does this change our plans?" Montgomery asked him.

"The timing, yes." He ran his hand over the top of his head. "We now have the opportunity to reveal Nixon's unschooled reaction to everyone in his vicinity, possibly with the Teeli by his side. He's clearly planning to pay you a visit at the medical center. We'll time your announcement to coincide with his movements on the station." One corner of his mouth lifted, but it wasn't a smile. "Perhaps you might include a few words about him in your discussion of the Teeli?"

"I certainly will."

The look in Montgomery's eyes sent a shiver down Nat's spine. That level of cool calculation was precisely why she'd spent her entire life avoiding the Fleet. When you were the object of their ire, they were *scary*.

"Itorye, notify Cade we'll time *Gladiator*'s appearance and Captain Montgomery's transmission with Nixon's movements. Alert us when Nixon's on the station headed for the medical center."

"Understood."

As the Admiral and Montgomery bent their heads together to discuss the modifications to their plan, and Williams and Reynolds moved around them, making final adjustments to the staging for the live feed, Nat retreated into the corridor to observe with Marina and Gryphon.

"How are you doing?" Marina asked with a maternal smile.

Nat shrugged, although she doubted it looked as nonchalant as she was trying for. "We're about to create an interstellar incident that will draw battle lines with the Teeli and the Fleet. I'm scared out of my mind."

Well, that was a lot more honest than she'd planned to be.

Marina nodded. "Me, too. But it's far better to be the ones driving this confrontation than to wait for it to slam into us. Again."

Nat agreed. That didn't make her tummy stop doing flips. She glanced longingly at the stairs leading to the bridge.

Gavin, Patel, and Itorye were up there now, ready to move *Phoenix* on a moment's notice if it became necessary. They'd watch the feed on the bridge display. Marlin and Pete were set up to view it in the media room, where Marina and Gryphon would be joining them shortly.

Nat would not. She had no desire to relive the nightmare images of the battle that had almost claimed hers, Marlin's, and the Admiral's lives, or to see a vid of the Sovereign. The cloaked figure still haunted her nightmares. No need to reinforce the images already lurking in her brain. She'd stay right here, where she could hear what Montgomery was saying without seeing any of the images Reynolds would be inserting.

She also wanted to lend support to the Admiral. This had to be incredibly hard for him. Not that he would show it. He was the Fleet Director, after all. But he'd looked pleased when she'd told him she'd be right outside the infirmary during the recording.

"Nixon's on the station," Itorye informed them. "Five Teeli are with him."

Five? Her stomach flips turned into contortionist knots.

"That's our cue," Gryphon murmured, slipping an arm around Marina's waist and tugging her toward the stairway.

"See you soon." Marina rested a hand briefly on Nat's shoulder before following Gryphon down the stairs.

Nat took a fortifying breath. It did little to calm her pounding heart. For about the tenth time that day, she found herself wishing Isin was standing beside her. She missed the comfort of his presence way more than she cared to admit.

In the infirmary, Montgomery had resumed her reclined position and adjusted the blanket so only her arms and upper torso were visible. Itorye had applied makeup to give her face a sickly appearance. The overall effect was remarkably similar to how she'd looked when Nat first saw her on Hydra One, including the dark smudges under her eyes.

Williams had pulled the privacy screen around behind her so that it would block out any details of the infirmary in the vid feed. No reason to give anyone clues that she wasn't where they expected her to be. The Admiral was standing behind Reynolds, who was operating the camera.

Williams had set up a monitor facing Montgomery, so she could time her comments to fit with the videos Reynolds would be showing of the Teeli and Sovereign.

Nat positioned herself so she could see Montgomery but not the monitor.

"Nixon's group is headed down the concourse in a ground transport."

Itorye's announcement wiped all expression from Montgomery's face. Her eyes closed, focus pulling inward as she took several slow, deep breaths.

Nat did, too. It helped... a little.

The Admiral watched Montgomery. His hands were clasped behind his back in what looked like a casual pose, if not for the tight tendons along his neck. Williams stood beside him.

"Whenever you're ready," Reynolds prompted.

Montgomery's expression when she opened her eyes was one Nat recognized — the calm, resolute, professional detachment she thought of as *Fleet face*.

"My fellow Fleet officers and crewmembers..."

Eighty-Seven

"...and my fellow Union citizens. I am Fleet Captain Colleen Montgomery, of the Discovery-class starship *Cassini.* I have dedicated my entire life to upholding the ideals of the Fleet and the Union — service, cooperation, inclusion, diversity — that have enabled us to thrive ever since we first stepped beyond the boundaries of our solar system. Now, those ideals are threatened by an enemy who walks amongst us in the guise of a lamb but with the teeth of a wolf."

Cade looked at Unity's feed from Eridani Duo of the vid playing across all the concourse displays in Ring 3. The flow of pedestrian traffic had slowed as people stopped to watch, several lifting their combands to record the vid.

Nixon's open-air transport had not stopped. He was glaring at the displays while barking orders at the driver and the Fleet security officers in his entourage. They started shouting at the people in front of the transport, whose focus on the displays had halted them in the transport's path.

Cade recognized Sly-Kull, the Teeli delegate he'd met at the Teeli Embassy, sitting beside Nixon. The four Teeli consuls Nixon was delivering to *Cassini* sat behind them with the man who was probably Nixon's physician. Sly-Kull seemed unconcerned by Montgomery's speech. But that changed with her next words.

"I am speaking of the Teeli."

Nixon's body went rigid.

A look of unfettered hatred flashed across Sly-Kull's face. But the Teeli's expression shifted quickly to a mask of unruffled civility.

Nixon darted a glance at Sly-Kull, but whatever the Teeli said got him facing forward again.

Several of the Fleet security officers hopped off the transport as it slowed to a crawl, blocked by the crowd. They ran beside the transport, gesticulating at the pedestrians to move out of the way.

Unfortunately for them, Montgomery was just getting warmed up. "We have been told the Teeli are our allies, a race of pacifists with no offensive capabilities and an aversion to violence. That is a lie. They are conquerors, intent on destroying the Union from within."

The group's forward motion halted abruptly as every person standing between them and the hub turned to stare at the conspicuous white-haired, grey-skinned Teeli in their midst.

The displays switched to the vid footage Celia had taken on Feylahn of the Sovereign's arrival on the island. The Sovereign's transport sat on the landing pad like a hulking owl overlooking the two lines of Teeli minions standing at attention. The Sovereign and her mesh-covered Setarip guards made their way along the center to the ground transports.

Nixon's face flushed a red visible even at a distance. He yelled at the Fleet security officers, then reached over the driver, trying to take control of the transport.

But the reaction of the five Teeli to the vid of the Sovereign was even more satisfying. Sly-Kull grabbed Nixon, hauling him off the transport. The other four Teeli shoved Nixon's physician none-too-gently after him, then fanned out to create a wedge. Their grey robes billowed around them as the group cut a swath sideways through the crowd, angling toward a security access door to their right as station security poured into the concourse from multiple directions.

"The Fleet has encountered these mesh-covered individuals before. They were responsible for the biological attack on Gaia last year. The Teeli are using factions of the Setarips to do their dirty work." The video changed to the images Williams and Lelindia had taken of the dead mesh-covered Etah on the Etah ship.

Looks of fear and confusion rolled through the crowd, a visceral reaction to the images of the Setarips.

"But the Teeli do not rely only on the Setarips. They have their own offensive capabilities. Contrary to what we've been told, the Teeli have an entire fleet of warships." The vid played of the Sovereign's very identifiable transport returning from Tnaryt's Camp to the Teeli cruiser amidst the battle between the cruiser, the Teeli warships, *Gladiator,* and the *Starhawke.*

The shock of seeing alien warships battling with what the Fleet had labeled as the two most notorious ships in the Union riveted the crowd's attention on the displays.

Station security whisked Nixon's group through the security door and into the security tunnel beyond.

A third vid window popped up on *Gladiator*'s display, showing the Teeli leading the race-walk down the narrow corridor. Nixon's focus flicked to the vid playing on security monitors spaced at intervals along the way.

Unity must have accessed the station's internal security cameras, too.

"This is the real reason for the arrests of Admiral Schreiber and Captain Hawke. Not because they were traitors to the Union, but because they had uncovered the truth about the Teeli threat and were fighting to stop an invasion."

Nixon snarled, his lips pulling back from his teeth.

The vid image returned to Montgomery. "There is one more warning I need to give you. The Teeli have the ability to manipulate some people's minds and emotions through touch. It will exhibit as unusual behavior or actions, unexpected emotional instability, particularly anger and aggression, or unnatural complacency in what should be alarming situations. This is why the Teeli want their consuls on Fleet ships. They want to manipulate members of the Fleet into passivity, or worse, to fight alongside them to overthrow the Union."

Nixon shouted at the station security and pointed at the monitors, clearly demanding to know why security wasn't stopping the feed. The helpless confusion on their faces did not improve his mood.

"Make no mistake, the dangers are real, the threat to those who resist potentially fatal, as I learned firsthand." Montgomery indicated the cast on her arm. "Three weeks ago, I sustained serious injuries that have left me confined to a med platform. But this was no accident. It was an attempt to remove me so a Teeli sympathizer could be inserted in my place. My ship patrols the Teeli border. My presence poses a threat to the success of any invasion force. So did the presence of Admiral Schreiber, Captain Hawke, and Captain Schreiber, the former captain of the *Argo*."

With Nixon and the Teeli out of sight in the security tunnel, attention throughout the concourse was locked on the vid displays. Nearly everyone was recording it. No one seemed to want to miss a single word.

Montgomery was well known and well respected in the Fleet ranks. Her warning about the Teeli would be given serious consideration, especially by those who lived or worked near the Teeli border.

Montgomery paused, her gaze sweeping left and right like she was surveying the assembled crowd. "Now it's up to each of us to make a choice. Trust the lies we've been told, the media stories designed to divide us, or trust our own hearts and what we can see happening around us, especially in the Fleet. We must ask ourselves why Admiral Nixon has put people into positions of power who have not earned the right to be there, people who lack the skillsets to do the jobs they now hold."

That got a reaction. Heads swiveled, people leaning towards one another to make whispered comments.

Montgomery lifted her chin. "For my part, I will continue the fight in any way I can. Unfortunately, I cannot do that as the captain of *Cassini*, not when the bonds of trust with Fleet leadership have been so irreparably broken. The next attempt on my life might succeed. But I will not remain silent. The threat to the Union is too dire." Her gaze shifted off camera, like she'd heard something. "My time is up." She squared her shoulders. "Heed my warning. The fight is just beginning."

Eighty-Eight

Nat felt drained, like she'd just run up and down *Phoenix*'s stairs about thirty times.

But it was done. For better or worse, the truth was out there.

"See you in the media room." Montgomery tossed off the blanket and pushed off the med platform with her unhindered arm. All the healing work Marina and Gryphon had done combined with the time she'd put in walking laps and working out in the gym had paid off. Other than the fake cast, there was no indication she'd been injured.

Nat stepped back as Montgomery swept out of the infirmary and started down the stairs at a good clip. She seemed to be making up for the weeks of inactivity by doing everything at full throttle.

The Admiral joined Nat. "She's used to being in command of a ship," he murmured in an undertone, his gaze on Montgomery's retreating back. "Not sitting on the sidelines."

"I can see that." She glanced at him. "Is she always this energetic?"

The Admiral's cheeks creased in a smile. "Not quite like this, but yes. I think Marina's efforts gave her a little extra get-up-and-go."

He fell into step beside her, Williams and Reynolds behind as they all walked to the media room at a much more sedate pace.

Montgomery was already seated in the front row, her gaze locked on the images from the station.

The Teeli and Nixon passed the camera view of what looked like a utilitarian security corridor. They formed a tight cluster of grey Fleet uniforms and grey Teeli robes surrounded by station security in black and yellow. The group was walking briskly, the Teeli's long white hair reflecting the overhead light like lens flares. Nixon's hair was white, too, but the grey-white of three-day-old snow swept into a pompous style.

The expression on Nixon's face dumped ice water down her back.

He looked ready and willing to commit murder.

The Admiral and Reynolds moved to join Montgomery in the front row, while Williams settled in beside Marina and Gryphon in the third row.

Marlin waved Nat to an empty seat beside him and Pete in the second row. "Quite a show," he murmured as she sat down.

"Yeah." She was glad she'd missed it.

She glanced over her shoulder at Marina and Gryphon. Marina was tracking the Teeli's movements with the focus of a doe watching a pack of wolves. Lines furrowed her brow, the fingers of one hand absentmindedly stroking her collarbone. Gryphon had her other hand in a death grip. He was doing a very good zombie imitation.

"You two okay?" Nat whispered.

Gryphon didn't react, but Marina's gaze darted to her, then back to the screen. Her throat moved in a convulsive swallow. "Not really. Seeing them..." She stared at the Teeli. "It's bringing up a lot of bad memories."

She honestly didn't know how Marina and Gryphon had endured seeing their homeworld taken over by the Teeli.

"It's also... a little surreal after all these years of hiding to have the truth laid out for everyone to see."

Gryphon's paralysis broke. He released Marina's hand and wrapped his arm around her shoulders, pulling her as close as the arm of the chair would allow. "I never thought this day would come. Now that it has... it's hard to believe."

Nat understood that feeling. She'd gone through several major paradigm shifts recently, with both Isin and Aurora. It was trippy when what you believed was impossible suddenly became your reality.

"They've reached the medical center's interior security hatch," the Admiral said, like he was narrating a documentary.

The hatch Nixon had halted in front of looked strong enough to handle decompression. One of the people in black and yellow stepped toward the security pad, but Nat focused on the Teeli closest to Nixon instead. He'd surreptitiously wrapped his thumb and forefinger around Nixon's wrist and was leaning in, whispering in his ear.

"That's Delegate Sly'Kull. I think we're seeing Teeli manipulation in action," the Admiral murmured.

A supposition Nixon's demeanor seemed to confirm. The malevolence dropped away, replaced with a countenance that might have been described as calm if not for the vacant look in his eyes.

"Sweet stars above," Pete whispered. "Is that what mind control looks like?"

"Yes," the Admiral replied, his voice tight. "Isabeau's expression looked very similar the first time I encountered her with the Teeli."

Sly'Kull released Nixon's wrist as the hatch swung open. As soon as the group stepped through, the visual changed to two different angles of the medical center's reception area. The curving walls indicated the layout worked with the hub's circular shape, radiating out in concentric circles with the reception desk at the center.

The security detail appeared from an intersecting corridor, spreading out to create a perimeter, but Nixon and Sly'Kull strode toward the reception desk. The four other Teeli stayed back, bracketing a man in a Fleet uniform, probably Nixon's physician.

The two medical personnel staffing the desk stood, their expressions professionally neutral and pleasant as the group approached.

Nixon looked them over like a king overseeing his subjects. "You." He pointed at one of them. "Take me to Captain Montgomery, now."

The receptionist shook their head. "That's not possible."

Nixon pressed his palms against the high counter and leaned in. "I am the Fleet Director," he barked. "Montgomery just broadcast a vid of lies and misinformation from your facility. You will take me to her, *now!*"

The receptionist stood their ground. "I'm sorry, sir, but visitors to the ICU must be cleared by Dr. Yates."

"I don't care! *Get me in there!*"

"We can't," the second receptionist responded, moving closer to their colleague. "We don't have authorization. I'll notify Dr. Yates that you're here. He's with a patient."

Nixon looked ready to grab the receptionist and shake them. "Which direction is the ICU?" He jabbed his finger toward one of the corridors leading away from the reception area.

Sly'Kull rested a hand on Nixon's lower back, out of view of the two receptionists. "Admiral, we can wait for Dr. Yates," he said in strongly accented Galish.

Nixon's antagonism fractured, flaking off his face like old paint. "Fine. We'll wait," he echoed with less emotion than a ventriloquist's dummy.

"That is messed up," Pete muttered under his breath.

Nat wholeheartedly agreed.

The receptionist tapped a rapid message on their tablet, their lips pressed together.

"Can I offer you anything to drink while you wait?" the other receptionist asked.

"No," Nixon replied in a monotone.

Nat noticed Sly'Kull still had his hand on Nixon's back.

"Dr. Yates is on his way." But neither receptionist moved to resume their seats or continue their work.

About a minute later, a tall man in dark blue scrubs strode into view from the corridor visible from the second vid angle. He reminded her a lot of Gryphon in age and bearing, lanky but muscled, with a confidence in his step and wisdom in his expression that invited trust. His gaze swept over Nixon, the five Teeli, Nixon's physician, and the overabundance of security personnel. "Admiral Nixon. I wasn't aware you were coming personally to check on Captain Montgomery."

Nixon's lip curled. "Clearly." He moved into Yates' personal space, attempting to use his bulk to intimidate the slighter man, although they stood eye-to-eye. "Take me to her."

Yates didn't bat an eye. "Of course. Follow me." But when the entire entourage moved to follow, Yates paused. "I cannot allow more than four people to accompany me to the ICU. Medical center rules."

Nixon looked ready to blow a gasket, but a subtle touch on his wrist from his Teeli keeper changed his snarl to a scowl. He pointed at his physician and one of the Fleet security officers. "You're with us. The rest of you wait here."

Yates led them out of frame along the corridor he'd entered from. The images of the reception desk were replaced with two new images, one that faced a lift door and one that showed an empty lift. The group moved into view in front of the lift. Yates scanned his comband over the security pad and the lift doors parted.

The group filed into the lift.

Nixon's hands clenched as he turned on Yates. "Did you help Montgomery broadcast her video?"

Yates glanced at him. "What video?"

Unity had intentionally withheld that part of the plan from him. They also hadn't broadcast Montgomery's video to the medical center, which is why the receptionists hadn't reacted to the Teeli's arrival.

"The one she just sent from her room."

Yates gave him a skeptical look. "That's impossible."

"Are you calling me a liar?"

"Not at all. I'm just telling you it's not possible. All our patient rooms in the ICU are shielded to prevent transmissions in or out. It's a health, safety, and security regulation."

Nixon's face contorted. "I know what I saw!" he snarled.

Yates frowned, but didn't respond.

When the lift doors parted, Nixon practically shoved Yates out of the way. "Which room?"

"Twelve, second on the right."

A new image appeared on the media room screen showing a patient room with a large 12 on the closed door. The group approached from a corridor on the right, Nixon in the lead.

But when the door's handle failed to turn, Nixon's face scrunched up like a child about to throw a spectacular tantrum. "Open it!"

Yates took a visible deep breath as he complied, getting shoved out of the way a second time as Nixon flung open the door. There was a pregnant pause, followed by Nixon's bellow.

"Where is she!"

Eighty-Nine

"That's our cue." Cade eased *Gladiator* into position so that it would look like they'd just detached from the station. "Unity, are the Yruf ships set to clear out?"

"Yep. *Gladiator* will be visible in three, two, one, *now.*"

Cade fired the ship's thrusters, pushing *Gladiator* away from the station, lining up the path to the decoy exit window that would take them in the opposite direction from where *Phoenix* waited. Then he gunned the main engines, shooting *Gladiator* forward.

"Station security has spotted us," Gonzo called out from the auxiliary station behind Justin. "Their weapons are coming online."

"What about the station's shields?"

"Already up."

Justin snorted. "They honestly think we'd fire on a space station?"

"Nixon's allies will believe anything," Cade replied, "and those who don't are following protocol. We're tagged as an enemy ship."

Justin touched his headset as a light flashed on the console in front of him. "They're hailing us."

"No response." Cade kept one eye on the tactical data Gonzo was feeding him. *Gladiator*'s sudden appearance had caught the station's personnel flatfooted. The ship had already passed beyond the scope of the close-range weapons, but that still left the mid-range and long-range arsenal in Eridani Duo's robust defense system.

Unity had turned down the volume on the feed from the medical center, but Cade caught snippets of the nuclear explosion from Nixon.

"*What do you mean that ship is here!*" Nixon roared, sounding more than a little deranged.

"Guess someone told him about us," Justin commented.

"Guess so."

"Weapons hot," Gonzo warned. "They're firing." Six shots streaked out from the station's mid-range cannons, racing toward *Gladiator*.

Cade dodged, but the pattern of fire made it impossible to avoid all of them. One lit up the shields to starboard in a glancing blow, and a second slammed into *Gladiator*'s port aft shields.

The ship twitched, but not like it should have after being struck by a weapon that could damage a ship twice its size. No, *Gladiator* reacted like a horse shaking off an annoying fly. "Thank you, Unity," Cade murmured.

"You're welcome."

He didn't have time to dwell on it, though. The cannons kept firing, the station's long-range weapons taking over as *Gladiator* hurtled toward the jump window. Keeping the hits to a minimum required all his concentration.

"Our ships are moving in to camouflage *Gladiator,*" U-2 informed him.

"Don't let them get hit." He had no idea what it would look like if a Yruf ship's camouflage was struck by cannon fire, but he seriously doubted it would look anything like the *Starhawke.*

"Cade," Unity chided. "We've got this."

He smiled in spite of himself. "Then *Gladiator*'s all yours. Hang on," he warned Justin and Gonzo as he released the yoke, giving control of the ship's flight path to Unity.

The starfield outside the viewport immediately dipped, shifting hard to port, pressing him into his harness. Gonzo grunted from the auxiliary station, which wasn't as well padded as his and Justin's chairs.

"Is this the Yruf version of an amusement park ride?" Justin joked, coughing on the last word as an abrupt deceleration threw him into his harness.

"I think so," Cade gritted out, massaging the tender spot on his sternum as the helter-skelter movement smoothed out. A check of the tactical data confirmed the station had stopped firing and navigation showed them on course to meet up with *Phoenix.*

"Amusement park?" U-2 asked, bobbing into view. "Was this fun for you?"

All three of them laughed.

"Kinda," Cade agreed. Unity had pushed *Gladiator* in ways Cade hadn't ever tried. Clearly their integration with the ship had improved the specs for structural stress, increasing the ship's maneuverability. When they got back to Zeta Tucanae, he and Unity needed to take *Gladiator* out for a spin so he could learn the ship's new capabilities.

"I have a few pointers for your design team, though," Justin added. "Leaving the passengers with bruises isn't good for business."

"Bruises?" Unity bobbed up and down in alarm. "You're hurt?"

"I was kidding," Justin assured them. "Muscle soreness happens all the time in our line of work. This one—" he pointed at Cade, "delights in wild aerobatics."

"I do not."

Justin gave him a flat look.

"Okay, I do. But you love it."

Justin grinned. "Yeah, I do."

"—*arrest this man!*"

Cade's attention returned to the vid feed from the medical center. Nixon was jabbing his finger at Yates, his face an alarming shade of red. The security officer in the group had moved beside Yates. In the background, Cade could see that the doors on either side of 12 were now open, one room vacant, the other occupied. A couple of medical personnel stood off to the side, their attention on Yates.

"On what charge?" Yates asked at a much more reasonable volume.

"Treason!" Nixon hissed. "Conspiring with the enemy."

"Captain Montgomery is the enemy?"

"She's a traitor! So are you. You helped her escape."

"Escape? We're a medical facility. Why would she need to escape?"

Hatred flashed in Nixon's eyes. "How did you sneak her onto that ship?"

"I didn't," Yates said with absolute sincerity. "I'm just as confused and concerned as you. I have no idea what's happened here, but my staff and I will be looking into it."

"You helped her broadcast that video."

"What video?"

"The one where she proved herself a traitor!"

"I don't know what you're talking about."

"You're lying!"

Yates' exasperated look indicated he'd prefer to be treating the most difficult patient in the galaxy rather than dealing with Nixon. "Admiral, I've been working with patients or meeting with staff since I came on duty four hours ago."

"Liar!"

"Check my badge logs. It records every time I access a security pad or enter patient information in a file."

"Faked. You helped her get on that ship!"

Yates' jaw clenched. "It appears we're at an impasse."

"Wrong. You're under arrest. You're coming with me."

Ninety

Nat's gut tied in knots. Yates seemed like a good man, unlike Nixon, who looked ready and willing to resort to violence to get his way.

Yates folded his arms. "Station security will have something to say about that."

"They work for me," Nixon sneered.

"The Fleet security officers posted here work for you. But the station security personnel are under the governance of the station Director. My staff and I are as well. We cannot be removed from the station without her authorization."

Nixon took a threatening step toward Yates.

Sky'Kull, who had been quietly observing the argument, interceded, placing himself between the two. Nat hissed in a breath as he rested a hand on each man's shoulder.

The Teeli met and held Yates' gaze. "We can handle this situation peacefully."

Nat's heart hammered in her chest as she watched Yates' reaction. If he fell under Teeli thrall, the situation would unravel rapidly.

But unlike the glassy-eyed look settling over Nixon's face, Yates looked annoyed. He stared pointedly at Sly'Kull's hand on his shoulder, then stepped back when the Teeli failed to take the hint. "I have patients who need my attention. I'll take you back to the reception desk." Without waiting for a response, he strode toward the corridor, shutting the open door to the empty patient room as he went.

The look of contempt that passed over Sly'Kull's face as he tracked Yates' movements made Nat shudder. But it was gone by the time Yates turned around, motioning them to follow. Sly'Kull gave Nixon a push to get him moving toward the lift, the security officer and Nixon's physician — who hadn't said a word the entire time — falling into step behind them.

Montgomery let out a very relieved sigh. "Does that mean Anthony is immune?"

"It would appear so," the Admiral replied, sounding equally relieved.

"Is Yates right?" Nat asked. "About Nixon not being able to take him off the station?"

The Admiral turned in his chair. "He is. All non-security Fleet personnel posted to a space station can't be removed or reassigned during the term of their posting without the station Director's approval. It provides a balance of power between the Fleet chain of command and the civilian Director. Based on my dealings with Director Grijalva, unless her people discover evidence of wrongdoing during their investigation into Captain Montgomery's disappearance, she won't allow Nixon to remove anyone from the station. Nixon's unverified accusations won't carry any weight with her."

"Do you think she's on our side?"

"I would consider her neutral. The station security's attempt to stop *Gladiator* was real. They would have disabled the ship if they could."

Nat agreed. The video of *Gladiator*'s flight had added another band of tension around her ribcage until the ship had vanished from sight.

"But Captain Montgomery's message may have highlighted concerns Grijalva already had regarding Nixon's behavior. I guarantee she'll be watching the Teeli very closely while they're on her station."

"*Cassini's* arrival won't improve Nixon's mood." Montgomery's gaze remained on Nixon and Yates as the group backtracked through the medical center.

Nixon pushed past Yates as soon as the group reached the reception area. "You three." He pointed at three of the Fleet security officers in his entourage. "Watch him." He jabbed a finger at Yates. "Make sure he doesn't leave."

Yates stared him down. "Belay that order. Station regulations allow Fleet security to be posted outside the medical center entrances, but inside this space, the only person who can overrule my authority is Director Grijalva. I suggest you take this matter up with her."

Nixon's glare could cut glass. "That's *exactly* what I'll do. You better be here when I get back."

Yates looked unimpressed by the threat. "My shift ends in eight hours."

Nixon's lip curled. "Post guards at every exit," he barked to no one in particular. "If he tries to leave, detain him." He spun on his heel, striding toward the security door he'd arrived through. The Fleet security personnel hustled after him, one of them talking rapidly into her comband and motioning to the others. The four Teeli and the station security followed Sly'Kull at a more sedate pace.

Yates watched them until they were through the security door. Then he turned to the receptionists. "Notify Director Grijalva that she's about to have visitors and have our security officers do a sweep of the facility for any unauthorized personnel. I'll be on my rounds. Alert me if anyone from that group returns or if anyone new shows up asking questions."

"Yes, Doctor."

The video of the medical center blinked out.

The Admiral glanced at Nat. "May I have a word?" He tipped his head toward the corridor.

"Sure." Pushing out of her chair, she followed him into the corridor and down to the lounge.

She had a good idea why he wanted privacy. They'd agreed based on Montgomery's reaction to Unity that they wouldn't inform her that Unity was integrated with *Phoenix*. That meant not communicating with Unity around Montgomery while U-2 was off the ship.

He stepped into the lounge, glancing at the speakers. "Unity, do you have access to Director Grijalva's office?"

"Unfortunately, no," they replied. "She doesn't have any security cameras inside and we never went to her office ourselves."

"Did the Director see Captain Montgomery's video?"

"We believe so. We projected it in her office and in the other administrative offices around her."

"Then she's been warned about the Teeli." Lines of tension bracketed the Admiral's mouth. "Hopefully that will be enough to protect her."

Her heart ached for him. This situation emphasized one of the traits that made him such an incredible leader. No matter the circumstances, he was always focused on protecting others from harm. It was a trait he and Aurora shared.

Which reminded her. "Unity, have you updated Aurora and Isin on what's been happening here?"

"Ummmm... no."

The hesitation in Unity's voice made her breath catch. "What's wrong?"

"Technically, nothing's actually *wrong*."

"Unity?" she prompted when they didn't elaborate.

"A ship arrived in the system a little while ago. An Ecilam ship."

"*What?!*" Her heart leapt into her throat. "Why didn't you say anything?"

"Because it just happened, and it's under control," Unity said in a rush. "Our ships are camouflaging *Vengeance* and everyone on the surface is concealed so the Ecilam have no idea anyone is there."

Under control wasn't the phrase she'd use. "Why are the Ecilam there? Did they follow *Vengeance?*"

"No. They appear to be looking for the Etah on the surface."

Her stomach rolled, the sickly odor of musk wafting over her. Even after months of freedom, her body still rebelled against even the mention of her former captors.

Her knees weren't particularly steady either, so she sank into one of the lounge chairs.

The Admiral looked a little queasy, too. "What's Aurora's plan?"

"For now, she's waiting until dark so the surface teams can return to *Vengeance*. We don't know what she plans to do after that, but we can ask her."

The Admiral waved a hand. "Don't ask. Knowing Aurora, she'll want an update on what's happening here. She has enough on her plate."

That was an understatement. What had been a straightforward relocation had just turned into a major complication. What if the Ecilam didn't leave? Aurora would never drop Mirko and Manchado on the planet if she thought it was unsafe. The Ecilam's arrival would delay *Vengeance*'s return, and it might even force Aurora to give up on the idea of relocation entirely.

That prospect left a bitter taste in her mouth.

She glanced at the Admiral. "I need a drink. Want one?"

Ninety-One

Micah could see the tension building in Aurora's neck and shoulders as she stared at the snip of blue sky visible through the lower level's doorway. This was the kind of situation his sister hated — forced to stay put when people she cared about were in danger. She was practically vibrating with potential energy.

Kenji, Lyon, Summer, and Fleur were keeping their distance as much as the cramped space would allow, which still put everyone within arm's reach of each other. Add in Yrlef and Regas, the Yruf engineer who'd been helping them with construction, and it was a tight fit.

He wasn't faring much better. He'd been doing his best to tune out the mental conversations between Ifel and the other Yruf, wanting to give them their privacy to discuss the Ecilam's arrival.

Celia stood next to him, her gaze on Aurora, her mouth pinched at the corners. She clearly wasn't a fan of being trapped here, either.

"Status on the Ecilam transport?" Aurora asked U-3, who hovered beside her. The mobile unit had been waiting at the building site with Yrlef and Regas when their team got dropped off this morning.

The gold lines running vertically along U-3's emerald surface spun as they pivoted. "Still headed toward the Etah camp. We can't tell if they're looking for a place to land or..."

"Or they're looking to attack from the air," Aurora finished for them, her shoulders rising another centimeter toward her ears.

Worry was evident in Unity's voice, too. The Ecilam had managed to catch the Yruf at a vulnerable moment. Micah got the sense that hadn't happened in a very long time. Ifel — and by extension, Unity — was used to being in control of her interactions with the other Setarip factions. Right now, she couldn't bring all their resources to bear on the problem.

"Yes," Unity admitted reluctantly.

"Any indication they've seen Ifel's transport?"

"Not yet."

"That's something." Aurora blew out a breath, her hands settling on her hips. She turned to Micah and Celia. "Any thoughts?"

He wished he had a brilliant suggestion for her, but he was at a loss.

Celia shook her head. "The lack of large native fauna works against us. We're too big for our movements to be mistaken for a native animal. We'd give ourselves away immediately if we tried to reach *Starlet*, even if your dad could move her closer."

Aurora eyed Lyon for a moment, the smallest person in their group by a couple centimeters. But even he was more than twice the size he'd have to be to fool the Ecilam's scanners. And it wasn't like he could fly *Starlet*. Neither could their mom, the smallest person on the other team.

"How strong are the defenses on Ifel's transport?" Celia asked Unity.

"As strong as on all our ships."

"Do the Ecilam have weapons that can get through them?"

Unity swayed in a slow pendulum. "No. At least not the last time we met with them."

"But that might have changed?"

"The Ecilam are always adapting." Unity's voice took on a dark overtone. "Joining with the Teeli has made them more unpredictable."

"Of course it has," Aurora muttered, anger painting two spots of color on her cheeks. "Creating chaos is the Sovereign's superpower."

Micah gave Aurora's boot a small tap with the toe of his. "And restoring order is yours."

That elicited a half-hearted micro-smile. Aurora's shoulder bumped his arm as she leaned in. "You can't hear the Ecilam, can you?" she whispered.

"Uh..." He hadn't even considered the possibility. But a quick check-in gave no indication of new voices in his head, just the soft murmur of the Yruf conversations and the background whispers of the planet's fauna. "No, I can't."

Aurora bit her lip. "I'm not sure if I'm happy or sad about that. It would be helpful if you could."

He grimaced. "I don't think I want to hear what they're saying to each other." He envisioned their conversations as an endless loop of *murder, death, kill.* Not something he needed to confirm.

"Is there anything we can do while we're waiting?" Kenji straightened from where he'd been leaning against the rock face that formed the back wall of the lower level. He gestured to the haphazard collection of materials they were all picking their way around. "Lyon and I can start stacking this stuff."

Lyon shot him a look of annoyance, but Micah saw it for what it was — a smokescreen to hide his fear. He'd seen similar reactions from students on their first dive, when theory became reality, and they realized how small they were in the scope of an aquatic landscape. Some of them quietly freaked out. Lyon was showing the same unease, his gaze darting to the doorway and out the windows every few seconds.

Aurora's gaze shifted to Lyon, too. She released an audible breath, all outward signs of tension falling away. She'd clearly picked up on the kid's unease. "That would be great."

"I'll help." Celia stepped closer to Lyon.

Micah suppressed a smile as the boy's eyes lit up and his breathing quickened. Celia's nearness tended to have that effect on people.

But Unity's next words froze everyone in place.

"The Ecilam transport has landed."

Ninety-Two

When Cade returned to *Phoenix* with his team, he found Nat, Marlin, Gryphon, and Marina in the wine bar gathering drinks. Nat and Marlin were already sucking down their beers. In fact, they looked like they were ready to share a keg between them. "What happened?"

Nat lifted her glass in his direction then took a long pull, her gaze on U-2 hovering over his shoulder. "Unity just informed us that the Ecilam have arrived at Tnaryt's Camp to search for the Etah."

His gaze snapped to Unity, who bobbed back a few paces. He opened his mouth to ask why they hadn't told him, but he already knew the answer. They wouldn't have wanted to distract him while he was focused on *Gladiator's* mission, or tell him there was a problem with Aurora's mission when there was nothing he could do.

The news explained the alcohol consumption. Nat and Marlin had a lot of baggage tied to the Etah and Ecilam.

So did he. Almost dying tended to stick with you. The involuntary separation from Aurora that followed hadn't been fun, either. "Where are Aurora and Isin?"

"Unity?" Nat took another swig from her mug.

U-2 swayed, clearly uncomfortable. "Aurora's temporarily stuck on the planet's surface, and Isin's on *Vengeance.*"

"I'll bet Aurora's thrilled about that," Justin commented, stopping beside Cade.

"Not really," Unity replied.

Cade chuckled. So did Marina and Gryphon.

"Was that funny?" Unity asked.

"Not intentionally," Cade replied. "Justin was being ironic. We all know Aurora hates being stuck in a situation where she can't take action."

"Oh."

Irony was one human behavior Unity still struggled to identify consistently.

"Marina made spearmint tea and I'm taking orders for alcohol," Nat informed his team, lifting her nearly empty mug. "We're gathering in the media room to wait for *Cassini*."

Cade decided on a beer for himself. Between the news about the Ecilam's arrival and the presence of the Teeli in this system, the emotional turmoil of the people around him was ramped up to eleven. The alcohol would help mute the effect of their heightened emotions on his empathic senses.

The Admiral rose as Cade's team entered the media room. "Excellent job with *Gladiator*, Cade. Any issues?"

"None. The shields are solid as a rock, and Unity did the final bit of flying to keep us camouflaged."

"You let it fly your ship?" Montgomery's brows almost hit her hairline.

Her prejudice was showing again. "*They've* done it before," he said evenly. "And since they were the only ones who knew exactly where the Yruf ships were, it made tactical sense to put them in control of choosing the flight path, especially with the station still shooting at us."

Montgomery's gaze flicked to U-2, who was unobtrusively hovering near the doorway.

They were doing their best to appear non-threatening, hanging back rather than staying near Cade's shoulder. It made him want to growl in frustration. He'd hoped Unity's ability to broadcast her message and provide vital intel from the station would have improved Montgomery's attitudes toward them, but the river of antipathy in her emotional field continued to flow unabated.

An image of the starfield popped onto the screen, *Cassini's* commanding form gliding into view, arrowing toward the station.

Everyone snagged their drinks and settled into their seats with varying degrees of anticipation and dread.

As the first of the eight Discovery-class cruisers to be commissioned, *Cassini* held a place of honor in Union history. Slightly smaller than the *Argo* – the last of the Discovery-class cruisers to be completed – *Cassini* still outclassed every other ship in the quadrant. It housed nearly a thousand people on its forty decks, including Fleet crew, non-Fleet support personnel, and family members.

Her captain held a place of honor, too. Montgomery had been in command when *Cassini* launched – the first captain of the first Discovery-class ship — the culmination of her long and distinguished career.

As Montgomery watched her ship approach the station, a flare of pride mingled with anger shone in her emotional field. It was easy to read the tenor of her thoughts. *Cassini* had been her home for twelve years. Having the ship taken from her, especially knowing the challenges her crew would face from Nixon and the Teeli, made her situation untenable, eating away at her like an acid drip.

A vid feed from Eridani Duo appeared on the screen, showing Nixon and the five Teeli walking down a security corridor, flanked by six members of station security.

"He doesn't look happy," Justin commented.

"He just finished meeting with Director Grijalva." U-2 bobbed forward, then retreated when Montgomery shot them a hard look. "We couldn't hear the conversation, but we could monitor the heat signatures in the room. The Director didn't allow any of the Teeli to touch her. Based on the juxtaposition of her calm movements and Nixon's more erratic ones, he didn't get the response he wanted."

"Oh, darn," Justin murmured in mock sympathy.

"So much for taking Anthony off the station." Montgomery was clearly very happy to hear that.

"Where's Nixon headed now?" the Admiral asked.

"To one of the station's short-range shuttles. He's ordered *Cassini* not to dock at the station. Instead, they're matching the station's orbit. He's going to take a shuttle over to the ship."

"Coward." Montgomery tracked Nixon's every move. "He's afraid the presence of my crew on the station will fan the flames of what I said in my broadcast."

"Will he be suspicious when the crew doesn't defend you?" Cade asked.

"Not the way Muiruri will handle it. She's well-known for deliberate, non-reactionary behavior. She'll uphold the chain of command, follow Nixon's orders, whatever they may be. If she doesn't give him any pushback, he'll have no reason to censure her, or the crew." Her gaze followed Nixon, who'd exited the security corridor into a shuttle bay, his movements stiff with anger. "The Teeli are the real threat. If she's susceptible to them, my entire crew is at risk."

Ninety-Three

Adel had lost her mind the instant Unity uttered the word *Ecilam*. Libra had been forced to corral the panicked teenager in her energy shield, preventing Adel from tearing off into the trees.

Getting her into the habitat had posed another challenge, one Shorty had solved by picking her up like one of the structural beams and hauling her inside, squirming and clawing like a cat. Libra had remained with her, blocking her in at the far end while the rest of the team raced the clock.

Building materials cluttered every available surface between her and the doorway, laying haphazardly wherever they'd been dropped. But they'd made it.

Her heart still threatened to beat out of her chest, her body shaky with adrenaline. The driving urgency to get everyone under cover before the Ecilam ship arrived had only served to ramp up her own reaction to the Setarips' appearance.

Now, with the Ecilam *on the planet*, Aurora and Micah kilometers away, and her team confined to a too-small space, she was battling flashbacks of her last confrontation with the Setarips, the one that had ended with Stoneycroft in flames.

Adel huddled in a sobbing puddle in Hobbes' arms, partially inside the compact bathroom. Libra was a half-step away and

Omondi stood protectively a few paces in front of them, surrounded by building materials.

Brendan was wedged in with Kai, Tipol, and Mahrem, the last to make it into the habitat, on the opposite side of the chaotic mess. He gazed at her across the distance, brow furrowed with worry.

And with good reason. Her emotions were a maelstrom. Alternating waves of rage and fear buffeted her. But as she gazed into the familiar blue of his eyes, as his nearness calmed the storm, the rapid thud of her heart slowed, allowing her to draw more than sips of air into her lungs.

"What happened with the other team?"

Shash's question drew her attention away from her mate. The engineer stood penned in against the exterior windows, arms folded in defiance, although the gruffness in her voice didn't quite match the concern on her face.

"They made it inside."

"Can the Ecilam detect us? Or them?"

"No." U-1 hovered closer to Shash. They were currently the only one able to maneuver around the chaotic space. "Their scans won't penetrate inside. They're also not focused on this region."

"What are they focused on?" Omondi growled, his hands curling like he was clutching an invisible weapon.

"Locating the Etah."

"Can they find them?" Shorty asked. He shifted his large body toward the base of the stairs to the upper level, wincing as his back scraped audibly against the raw rock of the interior wall.

"No. They're safe with Ifel."

"Figures." Shash let out a loud snort. "I can't believe we're stuck in a fracking shoebox because of a bunch of stupid lizards."

Libra's gaze shot to Tipol and Mahrem. Hopefully Unity wouldn't translate that comment. "At least there's plenty of fresh air." They'd installed the windows on this level this morning. The wide screened openings and the unfinished cutout for the stairs allowed a cross-breeze to waft through the lower level.

"Big deal." Shash scowled. "Nature sucks. It's dirty and smelly and there are bugs everywhere. No matter where you are, it's always too hot or too cold. Give me a starship any day." Her gaze moved past Libra's shoulder, her scowl deepening. "Will you shut that kid up?"

Adel's sobs grew louder, despite being muffled against Hobbes' shirt.

"She's scared," Hobbes snapped, tightening her grip on Adel's shoulders.

"So? You don't see anyone else boo-hooing. The Setarips can probably hear her in space. She needs to toughen up if she's gonna stay on this crew."

Hobbes' glare matched Shash's. "That's not your decision."

"It is if she's in engineering. I don't work with crybabies."

Omondi bared his teeth. "Shut your mouth!"

"Or what? You know I'm right. The black's no place for a coward."

Omondi snatched up a metal brace and drew his arm back to hurl it at Shash.

Libra shot out her energy shield in front of him, pressing the shield tight against his body to freeze him in place. "Stop it! Both of you. We don't solve problems with violence."

Shash's eyes widened, her startled gaze moving from Omondi's awkward statue pose to Libra's raised hands. "Did you—"

"You need to learn compassion, Shash." She managed to keep the fury from her tone, but inside she was seething. Shash's callous behavior had activated every protective instinct she had. "Adel has a very good reason for being frightened, which you'd know if you'd been paying any attention at all. She's been attacked by Setarips before."

Shash's gaze darted to Adel, whose terrified sobs had quieted to hiccupping sniffles. "I didn't know."

"Clearly," Hobbes muttered.

"Libra?"

Brendan's soft voice made her turn.

He looked pointedly at Omondi, who she still held captive in her shield.

"No violence," she reiterated as she dissipated the shield.

Omondi rolled his neck and shoulders, his movements stiff with unexpressed anger. He didn't look at her, his irate expression focused on Shash. "You got some nerve—"

"Don't make me separate you two," Libra warned.

A soft snicker from Kai made everyone turn.

He held up his hands. "Sorry." Although the smile he was fighting indicated otherwise. "But Libra, you have a serious next-level mom voice."

"Yeah, you do." Shorty leaned against the stair railing, regarding her with admiration. "It wasn't even directed at me and I started wondering what I'd done wrong."

"Us, too," Unity agreed, bobbing up and down.

Their antics melted the tension like sunshine on an ice floe. The collective exhale was palpable. Tipol and Mahrem relaxed as well, making her keenly aware of the way they'd both been poised to physically intervene. She'd be willing to bet they could have climbed over the obstacles in front of them in a heartbeat if necessary.

"She's a very good mom." Brendan's warm gaze held hers.

The comment made her heart squeeze. She wasn't sure she agreed with him, but she was getting better.

"Now." Brendan took a moment to look at each person in the room. "Let's have a group discussion about processing trauma and respecting boundaries."

Ninety-Four

Isin folded his arms over his chest as he glared at the ship to port. He'd long since abandoned the captain's chair, moving to stand near Sweep at the weapons console.

Two tension-filled hours had passed since Unity informed them the Ecilam transport had landed on the surface. With Isin's crew unable to make use of *Vengeance's* cameras or instruments to monitor the situation, Unity was providing updates on the Ecilam's search for the Etah. So far, that search had taken them in the opposite direction from Ifel's transport.

"The Ecilam must be lousy trackers," he muttered to himself.

"Actually, they're very good trackers," Unity replied through the bridge speakers. "We're just better at covering our tracks than they are."

Isin's gaze rose to the overhead. "By we, you mean the Yruf?"

"No, we mean us. As soon as we detected the Ecilam ship in the system, we cleared all trace of the Yruf's and Etah's presence within half a kilometer of Ifel's transport."

Isin shared a long look with Sweep. "You managed to do that in the time it took their ship to reach the planet?" He found that hard to believe.

"Of course not." Unity chuckled. "We're good, but we're not *that* good. We've been working on it ever since, expanding the radius while the Ecilam searched for the Etah."

"Aren't you concerned they'll spot you?" No one would mistake one of Unity's mobile units for an animal. They resembled a floating dinosaur egg from the Cretaceous period.

"No. Our mobile unit that Ifel took with her to the surface has the same camouflaging ability as our ships. We're invisible to visuals or scanners, making us good for stealth. That's how we've been able to monitor Ifel's interactions with the Etah without them knowing we're there."

"What about the light and shadow issue?" As he understood it, that's why his crewmembers and Aurora's family were stuck in the habitats. The Yruf couldn't provide cover for them to reach *Starlet* because their ships would cast shadows or be visible in direct sunlight.

"It's less of a problem than with our ships. We're much smaller so it's easier to manage our camouflage. Plus, this environment has a lot of moving shadows from all the greenery and creatures. We blend in easily. We're working to get close enough to the Ecilam that we can listen in. Oh, and we've designated our camouflaged unit as U-P, for Unity-Prime."

Up? Sweep mouthed silently, a flash of humor in his eyes.

Isin grunted. "How long before you're in range of the Ecilam?"

"We estimate less than twenty minutes, assuming they maintain their current search patterns."

"And how long before nightfall on the two habitats?"

"Four hours, twenty-seven minutes."

Four hours and twenty-seven minutes before he could do anything useful. Although useful was a relative term when he was essentially trapped on his own ship.

What would Aurora want to do after the two teams returned to *Vengeance?* Wait out the Ecilam, see if they left when they failed to find the Etah? Would she still feel comfortable leaving Mirko and Manchado here, knowing the Ecilam might return?

He'd like to ask her, but it wasn't a conversation he wanted everyone to overhear. Lyon, in particular. The kid had already been thrust into a tricky situation. He didn't want a frank discussion with Aurora through Unity to traumatize him farther. "How are the teams doing?"

Unity was silent for a moment. "Okay," they said at last, but their tone indicated that was a qualified response. "Celia, Kenji, and Fleur are teaching Lyon close quarters fighting techniques, with Aurora providing a protective shield so no one breaks any of the building materials."

Isin waited for a report on the second team, but Unity fell silent. "What about Libra's team?"

"They're... um... working through some things."

Isin's brows snapped down. "Meaning what, exactly?"

"Well..." Unity paused again. "Shash and Hobbes got into a bit of an argument regarding Adel. Omondi escalated it."

"An argument or a fight?" He could easily picture the explosive combination of Shash's volatile temper, Hobbes' maternal attitude toward Adel, and Omondi's hair-trigger all colliding in a cramped space. Libra would have her hands full keeping the combatants separated.

"Libra prevented anyone from getting hurt. And now... well, Brendan is talking it through with them."

Or Aurora's parents could have handled it with finesse.

Isin dropped his head back, staring at the overhead. He never would have thought to bring a psychologist onboard. His crew dealt with these kinds of issues in the Cage. But in this instance, he was grateful for the assist. "Is Adel okay?" She was another impressionable teen he felt responsible for. How had he ended up with two of them in such a short time?

Oh, right. Itorye. Who wasn't here.

"She's... recovering. We don't think she likes being the focal point of so much attention."

"Poor kid," Butterfly commented from the comm console.

Sparki pivoted their chair to face Isin. "Shash really likes Adel. She thinks she has a lot of potential. However..." Sparki's lips pinched. "Shash has a strange way of expressing affection. Or approval."

"Really? I hadn't noticed."

Sparki laughed. "But Adel seems to get her. She definitely thinks Shash is an improvement over Mirko."

"Almost anyone would be an improvement over Mirko." Including his surly engineer. But he appreciated the insight. It sounded like Sparki was looking out for Adel, which was a good thing, since his new pilot spent a lot of their free time with Shash in engineering. "And speaking of Mirko, we need to brainstorm a plan B for our two guests in case this situation goes nuclear."

Ninety-Five

Two beers had mellowed Nat to the point that she no longer felt like crawling out of her skin, but watching the Teeli board the shuttle with Nixon had triggered unpleasant memories that made sitting still in the media room intolerable.

She nudged Marlin. "You need any help getting the next meal prepped?"

A flash of relief lit his eyes. "That would be great." He pushed out of his seat.

She followed him up. "We're going to prep some food," she informed the group.

"Can we help?" Marina asked, already partway out of her seat. Gryphon rose, too.

She recognized the strain on both their faces, the need to escape. "Absolutely."

As soon as they were headed down the corridor, Marina let out a gusty sigh. "That was... uncomfortable."

She could only imagine how hard this was for Marina and Gryphon. The emotional and psychological torture of seeing the Teeli walking around with Nixon had to be stressful. "If I never see another Teeli, that'd be just fine."

"That's an understatement," Gryphon growled. "I thought I'd prepared for this, but seeing them... it all came rushing back. The cruelty, the heartlessness, the death."

"I never saw one in person." Marlin gave a small huff, like he was expelling bad air. "I'm sorry you did. My experience with them was being trapped in the galley of Tnaryt's ship when they tried to blow it up."

So, they were all reliving their personal traumas. She found the communal experience strangely comforting.

Everyone else must have, too, because they fell into a companionable silence as they made their way to the galley.

Marlin and Gryphon launched into a discussion about recipes the moment they stepped through the door, their expressions regaining their animation as they pulled cookware off the racks. Marina moved over to the prep area to wash up.

Nat paused in the doorway. No one was in the dining room right now. She could steal a moment alone. "I'll be back in a bit. I want to check in with Isin."

"Take your time." Marlin snagged a cutting board. "We've got things handled here."

The outlines of her mural called to her as she stepped into the spacious room, her fingers itching for a brush. Working on it would go a long way toward soothing her raw emotions. But now wasn't the time.

Instead, she turned to the wide viewports on the opposite side. The panels showcased a breathtaking panorama of the starfield. Eridani Duo and *Cassini* were on the other side of the ship, so she could momentarily pretend she wasn't in a Fleet system, sitting next to a Fleet station and a Fleet ship that made hers look like a child's toy. And that Nixon and five Teeli were also on that ship.

Not the Fleet Director, though. The *real* Fleet Director was on her ship. Nixon was at best a pretender and at worst a menace. "Unity, is Isin available for a chat?"

"Let me check." They were silent for a couple beats. "He is. Hang on. He's moving to *Vengeance*'s bridge compartment."

She folded her arms over her chest, her fingers tapping a syncopated rhythm against her bicep while she waited.

"Hello, Natasha."

The rich timbre of his voice sent squiggles through her nerve endings, making her whole body tingle. "Hi." If she closed her eyes, she could almost believe he was standing beside her. "How are things there?"

His annoyed grunt made her smile. "We're in a holding pattern, waiting for nightfall and watching to see what the Ecilam are going to do. How about you? Unity said Montgomery sent her message."

"She did. Nixon flipped out, storming around the medical center like a toddler, yelling accusations. When he realized Montgomery wasn't there, he wanted to take Dr. Yates off the station, but Director Grijalva wouldn't let him. Right now he and the Teeli are taking a shuttle over to *Cassini*."

"And you're still in the system?"

"Yep. Montgomery wants to see how it plays out. I don't blame her. If it were my crew at risk, I wouldn't want to leave, either."

"If it were your crew, a gravity well wouldn't be able to pull you away." The smile in his voice warmed her from head to toe. "Is Patel behaving?"

"Believe it or not, she's been fine. Montgomery's the one giving attitude. She doesn't trust Unity, and has been really rude to them."

"Sounds like she and Patel have something in common."

"Except they don't." To her surprise, she felt the need to defend Patel. "Patel's been harsh to Unity, but that's because she was protecting Alec. She was concerned Unity might hurt him somehow. Montgomery's attitude is the polar opposite. She's not being defensive, she's being aggressive. There's a vindictiveness to her behavior that feels personal, targeted. Her prejudice against non-biologicals is intense."

"Hmm. Safe to say you won't be introducing her to Alec?"

"No way. I've already let Alec and Unity know they can lock down her access to the ship and its systems in any way they feel is necessary to protect themselves."

"You think she might try to harm them?"

"I don't know, but I'm not taking any chances. Alec deserves to feel safe."

"Thank you, Nat," Alec said softly during the lag time for Isin's response.

"You're part of this crew," she replied, glancing at the speakers. "I'll always have your back."

"With you on his side, I have no doubt he'll be safe," Isin said with surety.

"And us!" Unity added. "We'll keep him safe, too."

"I know you will." Unity was the poster child for friendship and loyalty. "You're a good friend."

"Yes, they are," Alec agreed.

And to think only a few months ago, she'd firmly believed she didn't have any friends. The universe had delighted in proving her wrong. Too bad the friend she wanted to see right now was currently lightyears away.

Propping her shoulder against the bulkhead, she gazed into the black. "So, what's your plan if the Ecilam don't leave soon?"

"No idea," Isin replied. "First we have to get the teams off the planet without being detected, then find out what Ifel wants to do. I suspect she'll attempt to open a dialogue with the Ecilam. Unfortunately, taking that step could destroy any possibility of leaving Mirko and Manchado here."

Nat winced. "I really don't want you bringing them back."

"I really don't want to bring them back. But it may be our only option. Even if I didn't care about angering Aurora — which I do — I'm under no illusion that I could somehow leave Mirko and Manchado on the planet against her wishes. After what I've seen her and her mom do, they could commandeer *Vengeance* with or without Unity's help. My crew couldn't stop them, not without serious casualties."

Nat's brows lifted. "Does the crew know that?"

"They're well aware. But they've also learned what kind of people Aurora and her family are. The crew trusts and respects them. Even Shash and Lyon."

"*Shash?*"

Isin made a humming noise. "Shocking, I know. Aurora gave me some insights into Shash's behavior that really surprised me, but now that I've had some time to consider it, I think she's right."

"What kind of insights?"

"That Shash was never interested in me sexually. Her feelings toward me are more familial, but she doesn't know any other way to express affection other than overt sexual flirting."

Nat blinked a few times. "That's... interesting." And completely unexpected. It made her curious how Aurora would evaluate Shash's feelings toward *her*. She'd always believed Shash was jealous of her because Isin had taken a protective — and ultimately romantic — stance toward her. But what if she was actually dealing with a form of sibling rivalry?

"It's certainly made my interactions with her easier to evaluate and understand." He sighed. "Unlike Mirko. Even Aurora and Brendan haven't been able to crack that nut."

Nat snorted. "That's because it's rotten to the core."

His soft chuckle generated bubbles of joy. "You're not wrong."

"No, I'm always *right*."

The chuckle turned into a full-blown laugh. "I stand corrected."

She grinned. Verbal sparring with Isin was one of her favorite activities. "I miss you."

His voice dropped a register. "Promise?"

That throaty rumble was sexy as hell. "Yes."

"Good. I don't want to be the only one suffering."

"Aha! So you're missing me, too."

"More than you know."

And didn't that just light up her world. "Then I hope the Ecilam decide to pack up soon so you can get back here. Well, not here, here." Her gaze swept the starfield. "I'll be happy when we leave *here*. But here in the general sense. You know what I mean."

"I do. And I assure you the feeling is mutual."

She sighed, resting her forehead against the viewport. "Then I guess we'll talk when one of us knows our next steps."

"Yes. Be safe, Natasha."

"I can't promise that." Even if she wanted to, which she didn't. Safe was overrated.

"Then be *smart*, Natasha," he grumbled.

Her grin looked wicked in the reflection off the viewport. "Now *that*, I can promise."

Ninety-Six

Aurora couldn't see the grey line moving across the surface of the planet as the system's star sank below the horizon, but she felt it in her body, a lightness contrasting the encroaching darkness.

Freedom.

Admittedly she was hyper-sensitive to any type of confinement after her stint at Seaview. She'd worked to hide her growing agitation, but the only person who hadn't noticed was Lyon.

Her team had focused on making the most of the enforced downtime. They'd organized the building materials for easy access when they returned – and they would return. She had to believe her plan for Mirko and Manchado wasn't blowing up in her face.

They'd also assembled the lower half of the interior stairway that would lead to the upper level once it was completed. Working in the cramped quarters had been a tricky bit of spatial engineering. The rest of them had ended up handing items to Yrlef and Regas, who'd had an easier time contorting themselves to fit in the convoluted workspace of the stairwell at the far side of the habitat.

After that, with hours still left before nightfall, Celia, Kenji, and Fleur had spent time training Lyon in self-defense. Aurora had used her shield to prevent anyone from falling or smacking into the hard, uneven surfaces around them.

As the late afternoon stretched toward early evening, Micah and Iolana had regaled them with descriptions of life on Hawai'i. Turned out Lyon had never been to Earth before, and like Adel, had never seen an ocean in person. He'd hung on every word, but hadn't chimed in with any stories about which planet or space station he'd grown up on. Given his history of neglect and abuse, he might not remember much of his childhood, at least not consciously.

"Aurora?"

She turned as U-3 joined her in the habitat's open doorway. The color was bleeding out of her surroundings, fading to shades of grey as a cool breeze brushed across her cheek. "Yes?"

"Our ships are moving into position to provide cover for the hike to *Starlet*. However, Ifel has requested you come with us instead."

Her brows lifted. "Back to your ship?"

"Yes."

"Did she say why?"

"She wants to discuss the change in situation with you."

"What about the Etah? Aren't they still on her transport?"

"They're going back to our ship, too."

"They agreed to that?" She hadn't gotten the impression Ifel had made that much progress gaining the Etah's trust.

"The alternative is being left on the planet for the Ecilam to find. Their circumstances, and Ifel's willingness to provide protection, motivated the Etah to align themselves with her, at least for now."

That fit. The dominant trait she'd ascribe to the Etah was their desire to let others handle their problems. It's why she'd spent days fixing the comm system on Tnaryt's ship and Nat had spent almost a year fetching supplies while the Etah lounged around the ship doing nothing but tormenting their human captives and having sex with each other. "Do the Etah know I'm here?"

"No. They are only aware of the Yruf."

"I strongly recommend that you keep it that way, especially regarding me. The Etah and I don't exactly have what you'd call a cordial relationship." That was putting it mildly. Openly hostile was much more accurate. She couldn't think of them without remembering the suffering they'd inflicted on Nat, and how close they'd pushed her toward self-destruction.

"Ifel agrees."

She sensed Micah behind her before his hand brushed her shoulder. She met his gaze. "Looks like I'm going with the Yruf."

He nodded, but worry lines creased his forehead. "You want me to go with you?"

She glanced at Unity.

"Not this time," they replied. "Ifel wants to talk to Aurora alone."

Unity's answer grooved the lines on Micah's face deeper, his emotional field forming knots of concern. He opened his mouth, then closed it, his lips pressing together. "Okay." But he wasn't happy about it.

After darkness fell, Aurora sensed *Starlet* approaching. She also sensed the six Yruf on the ship shadowing them. They seemed eager, excited even by the Ecilam's arrival. Their reaction emphasized how much they wanted to bring an end to the civil war and make peace with the other factions.

It was a Herculean task, but she'd do what she could to help them.

The Yruf ship hovered over *Starlet* and the habitat, blocking them from view of the Ecilam ship in orbit as the shuttle landed on the upper-level plateau.

The pale light Unity provided to guide her team up the rocky incline touched on the faces of Aurora's mom and Shash, waiting at the base of *Starlet's* ramp.

"Took you long enough," Shash grumbled to Kenji.

Aurora's mom gave Shash an exasperated look, one Aurora had earned many times herself. "Any issues?" her mom asked, her gaze sweeping over Micah, Celia, and Iolana before resting on Aurora.

"No, but I need to talk to you for a moment."

While Kenji maneuvered Lyon and a still grumbling Shash up the shuttle's ramp with the rest of the team close behind, Aurora stepped deeper into the shadows at the edge of Unity's light.

"Ifel wants to talk to me, so I'm going with the Yruf to her ship." She motioned to where Yrlef and Regas waited at the other side of the light circle.

Her mom didn't seem as surprised as she'd expected. "Do you want me to come with you?"

The echo of Micah's words made her smile. "Micah asked the same thing."

"But you said no?"

"Ifel said no. She wants to talk to me alone."

"Actually," Unity cut in, hovering closer, "if Libra is willing to come along, Ifel would appreciate her insights as well."

Aurora glanced at her mom. "Would you be okay leaving them for a bit?" She gestured at *Starlet* to indicate her dad and Micah.

Her mom nodded. "Believe it or not, I would. Your dad's been helping me tame my overprotective impulses. This would be good for me. Just give me a moment to let him know the change in plans."

Her mom disappeared into the shuttle, returning less than a minute later. "All set."

Starlet's ramp closed, cutting off the view of the interior, the only visible sign of the shuttle's presence. Leaves rustled and a branch creaked, indicating the shuttle was lifting off, although the engines were completely silent.

"That really is amazing technology," her mom murmured as she gazed in the direction of the rustling.

"Yep. I'm assuming Dad won't have any issue avoiding the Yruf ship that's hiding us?"

"No. He and Unity were discussing it when I popped in. Since Unity's integrated with both ships, they'll be handling the maneuvering until the shuttle's clear. But I got the impression your dad wants to figure out a way to pilot around camouflaged Yruf ships without Unity taking control." She grinned at Aurora. "That thought exercise will keep him busy while we're gone."

Aurora grinned back. "Sounds like his kind of puzzle."

"That it does." Her gaze shifted over Aurora's shoulder, where U-3 waited with Yrlef and Regas. "We're ready when you are."

Ninety-Seven

Stepping onto the Yruf transport felt a lot like stepping into the mouth of a cave – a cave lined with emeralds and veins of gold.

Libra had spent time on the primary Yruf ship after Aurora's rescue from Seaview, so she was familiar with the scaled texture of the Yruf bulkheads. She'd also been on Ifel's private transport, though to be honest she barely remembered it. At the time, she'd been way too focused on holding onto Micah and reaching Aurora as quickly as possible to make sure she was okay.

She'd faced some of her deepest, darkest fears that day as she'd discovered she was utterly helpless to protect her children from the threats surrounding them. But she'd gotten through it. So had Aurora and Micah.

She still wasn't thrilled that her daughter willingly threw herself into danger whenever others were threatened, sacrificing her own needs for the greater good, but she respected her choices and admired her courage. Aurora modeled the very best of what it meant to be a Sahzade. Her daughter's actions were inspiring Libra to be brave. Which meant helping Aurora rather than hindering her.

The soft amber glow of the transport's interior illuminated the seating area, which wasn't set in rows, but rather a circle with the seats facing in toward the center. It reminded her of the lazy river water ride she'd taken Aurora on as a child. Aurora and Lelindia had squealed in delight as water splashed over the sides of the circular floating boat during the pseudo-rapids portion of the ride. It was one of her favorite memories from Aurora's childhood, but bittersweet because only a few weeks later, Aurora announced she'd been accepted to the Academy. That's when the cold war had started.

A war she could have prevented if she hadn't allowed fear to dominate her life.

She settled into one of the green-scaled chairs, Aurora beside her. The far-off look in Aurora's eyes indicated she was already in full problem-solving mode and only vaguely aware of her surroundings.

Libra was acutely aware of every sight and sound as the opening to the transport sealed up, closing them in. Shuttle rides still weren't her favorite thing, especially if Brendan wasn't in the pilot's seat.

U-3 drifted in front of her. "If you sit back, we'll fasten your harness."

She hadn't realized she was sitting with all the ease of a tin soldier. She scooted back, keeping her attention on Unity.

They sounded so much like Micah, but most of the time she could tell the difference between them. It was the inflections Unity used, the way they emphasized words differently and the underlying tone of their voice. Micah's voice was both soothing and energizing, and as supportive and buoyant as the ocean he loved. Unity's speech patterns reminded her of the free-for-all enthusiasm of kids splashing in a pool, although right now they were much more subdued.

The seat seemed to shift around her, as though it was conforming to her body, then twin bands of scales flowed over her shoulders, crossing over her sternum and continuing to her hips.

She took a deep breath to calm the flutter in her stomach as they tightened, holding her firmly in place. "Thank you, Unity."

U-3 bobbed. "You're welcome." They rose to an alcove above the center of the circle of seats.

Her hands clenched reflexively in her lap and her heart stuttered as the tug of gravity announced the transport had lifted off.

Aurora's focus shifted to her. "You okay?"

She waved off her concern. "I'm fine."

Aurora's mouth quirked. "I think that's my line."

She returned the small smile. "Where do you think you learned that particular habit?"

"Really? You say that, too?"

"You hadn't noticed?"

"No." Aurora frowned. "But now that you mention it, I guess you did say that, or a version of that, a lot when I was a kid."

"Especially when you asked questions I wanted to avoid answering."

"Which was most of them."

There was no judgment behind her words, but Libra's chest ached just the same. She'd caused Aurora so much unnecessary pain.

Yes, she'd had her reasons, but that was just the excuse she'd used to make herself feel better.

She clasped Aurora's hand in hers. "I'm so sorry."

A complicated swirl of emotions passed over Aurora's face, but her tone was gentle. "You don't have to be, Mom. I get it. You were just a kid when you were ripped from your family and your homeworld. You didn't want the same thing to happen to us."

Her grip on Aurora's hand tightened. "But I did it to you myself. I took away your father, Micah…" She was still struggling to come to terms with that choice. At the time she'd believed it was the only option, but now that her family was whole again, she couldn't imagine why she'd given up so easily. She should have found another way, fought to keep them all together…

"Hey." Aurora turned her body the fraction the harness would allow. "We've talked about this. You made a difficult decision in terrifying circumstances. I don't blame you, and you need to stop blaming yourself. We don't know what would have happened if you'd made a different choice. The Teeli might have been able to track us down before I had the skills to fight back. That would have been way worse."

"I suppose." Isabeau Magee's experience had given her a clear visual of what incarceration by the Teeli could do to a person. She couldn't even contemplate what that would be like for someone as gentle as Micah, or as empathetic as Brendan and Aurora.

"And we're here, now, with a whole lot of friends to support us. That's what matters."

A lump formed in her throat, making her breath hitch as she gazed into Aurora's eyes. "I see so much of my father in you."

Aurora's brows shot toward her hairline. "You do?"

She nodded. "He had green eyes just like you and Micah." She stumbled over the past tense. For all she knew, he was still alive, living a Necri existence like her mother. She honestly couldn't say whether that possibility made her feel better or worse. The dream of saving them, the way Aurora had saved the Suulh on Azaana, was a flickering flame of hope deep in her soul. But thinking about the decades of suffering her parents would have endured as Teeli captives turned her heart to ice.

"So that's where it comes from. I always wondered, since you and Dad both have blue eyes."

"That's where we get the cheekbones, too." She touched her right cheek. "But it's more than that." A wave of emotion rose inside her. She hadn't allowed herself to think of her father, really think about him, in so long. "He was the voice of reason in our family. My mom could be reactionary, which was helpful when quick decisions were needed, but not so great dealing with more complex issues." She could be describing herself. "My father could see things from all angles, consider all the possibilities and potential outcomes before making a recommendation. You do that, too."

A sheen coated Aurora's eyes. She blinked a few times. "Thank you for telling me. I've always wondered, but..."

"But I refused to talk about them." She'd been afraid that opening that door a crack would release the floodgates. Instead, she felt strangely lighter. Allowing herself to remember the happier moments before the Teeli occupation was soothing. "I won't do that anymore. You can ask me about them, or anything else you want to know."

Aurora's throat moved in a convulsive swallow. She gave a brisk nod, then swiped the side of her eye with the back of her hand.

Aurora's acceptance – her forgiveness – meant more than she could ever say. She'd made so many mistakes as a parent, taken so many wrong turns. But she'd been blessed with a daughter whose heart was as deep and wide as an ocean.

A swirl of green and gold drew her attention up.

Unity detached from the ceiling alcove, dropping to hover in front of them. "We're here."

Ninety-Eight

Ifel's throne room was beginning to feel as familiar to Aurora as the observation lounge on the *Starhawke*.

Her mom, however, rubbernecked as the light patterns started circling the expansive space like a chain of enormous snakes. "Where are we?"

"The reception hall," Unity replied, gliding toward the raised dais of Ifel's throne, which glowed amber in the dim light.

Ifel, however, was nowhere to be seen.

"It'll be a few minutes before Ifel can join you," Unity explained. "She's still getting the Etah settled."

That task wasn't likely to be easy. "How are the Etah responding to being onboard?"

Unity swayed. "They're... adjusting."

"Meaning what?"

Unity fell silent for a moment. "Well, one trait the Etah exhibited in the lead-up to the civil war was envy. It's clear their attitudes have not improved over the years."

"Ah." She'd seen that behavior firsthand. The Etah were probably coveting everything they saw on Ifel's ship and making demands. Humility wasn't a concept the Etah seemed familiar with.

"The light display is hypnotic." Her mom gestured to the bulkheads. "They look like snakes chasing each other around the room."

"They do?" Unity made a slow turn. "We don't... oh, wait. You can't see the full spectrum of light the Yruf can. The rest of the pattern would be invisible to you."

Intrigued, Aurora raised her comband, angling her forearm so her mom could see it, then switched the visual setting from visible light to infrared. Exploding starbursts appeared on the display in areas that previously had looked blank. Flipping to ultraviolet produced an even more dramatic effect as the entire bulkhead lit up with color and motion.

"Does the pattern mean something?" Her mom studied the play of light on the display. "Or is it an artistic display?"

Unity bobbed. "Both. The pattern is part of the ancient light language all Setarips used prior to the conflict that split them into warring factions. It's a greeting, a message of goodwill."

"Are the Yruf the only faction to still use light language?" Aurora asked. She didn't recall seeing any light displays during her interactions with the Etah or Ecilam, but that didn't mean they didn't use them to communicate with each other. Or the light they used could have been outside her visual range. She wanted to know which other factions would understand any messages her crew and the Yruf sent each other using the light language.

"No. The Regna still keep to the old ways... at least they did the last time we saw them. The Ecilam understand it, but we're unsure if they use it themselves. The Etah seem to have forgotten it. They didn't respond when Ifel used it onboard her transport. We don't know about the Egar. They've been avoiding us for a long time."

The sadness in Unity's voice tugged at Aurora's heart. Unity was as invested in bringing the factions back together as Ifel. "We'll find a way to reunite everyone, Unity." She had to believe Ifel's dream could become reality, that once freed from the Sovereign's toxic influence, Tersinis would be open to a reconciliation, setting the stage for a lasting peace.

"Having the Etah onboard is a good first step," Unity agreed. Then they glided to a spot beside Ifel's throne. "Ifel's here."

The Yruf leader materialized out of the darkness at the back of the room, striding toward the throne soundlessly. Her cloak swept behind her, revealing the form-fitting emerald body suit she wore underneath.

"Hello, Ifel." Aurora tipped her head back to meet the Yruf leader's gaze.

Ifel stopped in front of her. "Aurora." Her name on Ifel's lips had a breathy quality to it. "Libra."

"Hello, Ifel." Her mom moved to Aurora's side.

Aurora engaged her energy field, surrounding Ifel and her mom in its pearlescent glow, establishing the link for communication.

The arrival of the Ecilam concerns me Ifel said into her mind without preamble. Then she glanced at Aurora's mom. *Do you hear me?*

The lack of reaction from her mom gave the answer.

Ifel lifted one long finger next to her mom's temple.

"What's going on?" her mom asked, shying away.

"She wants to know if she can make a mental connection with you," Aurora explained, "like she did with me, so you can hear her."

"Oh." Her mom's jaw clenched. "Okay."

"It's not invasive."

Her mom gave her a sidelong look.

"Just engage your field, surround her with it, and relax."

The wariness didn't leave her mom's emotional field, but she did as Aurora instructed.

Observing the process from the outside was fascinating. Her mom jerked in reaction as Ifel's fingers made contact with her temple, but as her energy field expanded up the Yruf leader's arm, her body began to relax.

Because Aurora's energy field was still surrounding them both, she heard Ifel's slow repetition of the same question, *do you hear me?*

It wasn't until the fifth repetition that her mom inhaled sharply. "I do," she said out loud, although Aurora heard it in her mind, too.

That is good. Ifel maintained the physical contact. Communicating this way took practice. Aurora had gotten to the point that she no longer needed the physical connection of touch to establish the mental link with Ifel, just the energetic one her field provided. Maybe one day she'd be able to communicate with Ifel across distance the way Micah did, but for now her skills were limited.

The Ecilam would not be here without the Sovereign's authorization. Ifel's gaze shifted to meet hers. *All their actions are under the Sovereign's control. They no longer think for themselves. Even Tersinis.*

The pain of that knowledge cut Ifel deeply, reverberating in her emotional field. *Their behavior indicates they were sent to collect the Etah.*

Aurora winced. She had no love for the Etah, but she wouldn't wish captivity by the Sovereign on anyone.

We have thwarted whatever plan she had for them, but even now the Ecilam search the planet for signs of their whereabouts. They will not stop looking. They will not stop hunting. They cannot, not while in the Sovereign's thrall.

Aurora sighed as the weight of Ifel's words landed squarely on her shoulders. *Meaning the planet is no longer safe for anyone.* And her plan to leave Mirko and Manchado here was no longer an option.

Meaning we must adapt.

She hadn't expected that response.

Ifel's gaze shifted to Aurora's mom. *You have been hunted by the Teeli since you were a child. Your people are their prisoners, bent to a life of servitude.* Compassion flowed from Ifel in a steady stream. *You also had personal contact with the Ecilam when they attacked your home. Would you permit me to view those memories?*

"Why?" her mom said out loud.

To provide insight on their current behaviors and methods of attack.

It was clear from the resistance in her mom's emotional field and the building tension in her body that she didn't want to relive that night.

Not that Aurora blamed her. She wasn't fond of those memories, either. And her mom hated giving up control as much as she did. But... "Ifel's knowledge of the Ecilam might enable her to see critical information we wouldn't necessarily focus on."

Her mom didn't look convinced. "You've done this before?"

"Yes, but Cade's done it a lot more than I have." It was a subtle dare, tossing Cade's name into the mix.

And it worked.

Her mom's competitive streak flared to the forefront. She met Ifel's gaze with stubborn determination. "What do I need to do?"

Ninety-Nine

The sensation of Ifel's presence in her mind made Libra uncomfortable. Not because it hurt. There was no pain or pressure. But it felt like someone was shining a light into all the dark places she preferred to keep hidden.

I will only look at the memories of your interactions with the Ecilam.

Ifel's words rose in her consciousness. It was similar to the way the Suulh communicated but also distinctly different. More like hearing someone speak fluently in her native language but with a heavy accent.

Not that she considered the Suulh language her native language anymore. She'd learned and spoken Galish since she was a child. After she, Marina, and Gryphon had settled on Earth, she'd refused to speak anything else. It was only in the past couple months that she'd begun resurrecting those early lessons, talking to Marina and Gryphon in halting, stilted sentences as the Suulh words slowly came back to her.

Aaaand she was stalling. She didn't want to think about the Ecilam attack, the desperate battle to save Marina and Gryphon, and the horrifying moment when she'd seen the monster her mother had become. But she wasn't going to wimp out, either. Cade had done this multiple times. She wasn't about to let him best her.

Her focus returned to Ifel, who was gazing at her patiently with those strange diamond-pupiled, otherworldly eyes.

I'm ready she said through their connection.

Ifel's pupils widened, then contracted. *Where were you when you first saw the Ecilam?*

Picturing Stoneycroft brought a pang of sadness. She'd loved that house, loved sharing it with Brendan after he'd built it for her, loved the memories of Aurora as a child growing up. It hurt her soul knowing that all that remained now were those memories and a pile of ash.

The images, however, were still crystal clear – the darkened hallway outside her bedroom, the alien shapes materializing out of the nighttime shadows.

The sensation of Ifel's presence in her mind intensified. She recoiled, drawing in on herself, instinctively blocking her out.

I will never harm you, Libra.

She heard Ifel's words over the rasp of her own harsh breathing. She also felt the touch of Aurora's energy field surrounding her, gentle and supportive.

Taking a slow breath, she let it out on a long exhale. *I don't like giving up control.*

Ifel made a soft humming sound. *You are a leader. You trust in yourself.*

Ifel's words were spot on, succinctly summing up the reason behind her resistance. When she was in control, she had confidence that she could handle any situation. Giving that control to someone else felt like failure.

And yet, being with Aurora these past few months had shown her how often her daughter turned control over to others, trusting them to do what needed to be done so she could focus on her own tasks. It was a leadership style she admired, and a far cry from the rigid boundaries she'd maintained most of her life.

She let go. *Let's try that again.*

This time when the images of Stoneycroft filled her mind, she didn't try to lock them down. Instead, she allowed Ifel to guide her through the battle on the stairway, then the race to Aurora's bedroom and the destruction that followed.

The way Ifel slowed the memories when the Ecilam were visible during the confrontations gave her the impression Ifel recognized at least some of the Setarips who'd attacked Stoneycroft. But when Ifel reached the moment when Libra entered Marina and Gryphon's room, she gave a sharp hiss.

Tersinis!

Surprise jolted through Libra. The large Ecilam who'd led the attack was the Ecilam leader?

Ifel seemed just as startled by the realization.

I guess I should be honored that the Sovereign sent the Ecilam leader to kidnap me. It indicated the Sovereign considered her a serious threat. Which she was.

But she didn't feel honored. No, the emotion burning through her veins was far more caustic and deadly, and aimed entirely at the woman who had brought so much pain to her family.

Reliving the battle with the Ecilam that destroyed Marina and Gryphon's bedroom added jet fuel to the internal bonfire. Gryphon, helpless on the floor, his breathing labored. Marina, her energy field weak and sickly, trying to protect him. And Libra's mother, transformed into a twisted automaton who showed no signs of thought, feeling, or recognition.

Rage blazed from within like the flames that had consumed Stoneycroft. She wanted the Sovereign to suffer for what she'd done, for the lives she'd upended and destroyed, all without an iota of remorse. When she finally came face-to-face with the Sovereign, she was going to break every bone in her body. She'd relish each snap and scream of agony.

"Mom."

The tight squeeze of Aurora's hand on her forearm pulled her out of her dark thoughts. She hadn't even realized Ifel's presence in her mind had vanished, her hand no longer touching her face. Or that the Yruf leader was looking decidedly uncomfortable, her head bobbing side to side.

"You okay?" Concern drew lines between Aurora's brows.

Great. She'd freaked out Ifel and worried her daughter. "Sorry." She squeezed her eyes shut for a moment and gave a little head shake to dissipate her vision of vengeance. Then she met Aurora's gaze. "I really hate that woman." She couldn't even bring herself to say her name. Either of them.

"I can tell."

Of course she could. Her daughter had felt every vile emotion she'd been blasting out. So had Ifel, apparently.

Shame slid over her like cold mud. "Sorry," she repeated.

"Nothing to be sorry about." Aurora gave her arm another squeeze before releasing her. "Reliving that night brings up a lot of emotions for all of us."

Aurora was letting her off easy. She'd take it. "Did Ifel learn anything?"

Aurora held the Yruf leader's gaze for a long moment. "She recognized three of the Ecilam besides Tersinis. The two in the mesh outfits with the flame weapons were Tersinis' daughters, Maceen and Helotis. They came with Tersinis for Ifel's meeting with the Sovereign. The one who was firing the expanding net to trap you, the one who died in the bedroom fire, was Tersinis' sister, Saultas." Aurora's mouth pinched. "They sent their best to capture you."

"Lucky me."

"Ifel believes their failure might be the reason they're here."

She frowned. "I don't follow."

"For the Ecilam, rounding up three Etah should be the simplest of tasks, something the least of them could do. Sending Tersinis is an insult to her leadership skills, a power move to show just how far she's fallen out of favor with the Sovereign. Personal pride and an individual's standing in the social hierarchy means everything to the Ecilam. Tersinis is being punished in the worst way possible for an Ecilam. Being here, tracking the Etah, whom the Ecilam view as extremely inferior, is the equivalent of a Fleet captain being forced to clean the ship's decking with a toothbrush."

"Ouch."

"Yeah."

Her gaze flipped to Ifel and back. "So, what's going to happen when Tersinis fails to locate the Etah?"

Aurora's gaze met hers. "That is an excellent question."

One Hundred

"Any updates from *Cassini?*" Cade asked as he finished dressing and stepped out of the bathroom in his cabin on *Phoenix*, towel-drying his hair.

U-2 bobbed closer. "The Teeli are still interrogating the senior crewmembers."

He lowered the towel. "Has anyone shown signs of manipulation?"

"So far, all the personnel have avoided being touched by the Teeli."

"Really?"

"Yep. The Admiral told us there's a Fleet protocol they're using that allows them to keep their distance without defying Nixon's orders for compliance."

"And the Teeli aren't forcing the issue?"

"No. Reynolds has a theory on that. She thinks if the Teeli go out of their way to initiate touch, and that person turns out to be immune, it will make the Teeli look more suspicious without gaining them any ground. Her analysis is they're trying to root out the weak links first, before they make a move."

"Seems likely." Reynolds, the Admiral, and Montgomery were currently in the media room monitoring Unity's feeds from

Cassini. The trio hadn't left the room except for short breaks since Nixon's shuttle docked with the ship. Marlin had been bringing meals to them since all attempts to institute a crew rotation had been forcefully rebuffed by Montgomery. "What about Nixon?"

"He's still asleep in the captain's cabin."

"Still?" Nixon had taken over Montgomery's cabin shortly after arriving on *Cassini.* Cade had assumed he was planning to search the cabin, looking for ways he could implicate her with false accusations. But Unity had informed them he'd gone right to sleep. "That was ten hours ago."

"His sleep patterns are not like what we've observed from you and the rest of the crew. We would characterize them as unhealthy. They're very similar to Isabeau's sleep patterns right after her rescue."

He draped the towel over the desk chair and snagged his boots. "Indicating he's more of a pawn in the Teeli's game than we realized?"

"That's what we believe."

He settled on the edge of the bed to lace his boots. "Are Montgomery's crew playing their roles successfully?"

"So far. The Teeli are suspicious, but the crew haven't given them any reason to accuse them of collaboration."

"Montgomery must be glad to see that."

"Yes," Unity said without their usual enthusiasm.

Cade glanced at them. "I'm sorry she's been so hard on you."

"It's... confusing. Why is she so angry?"

He sighed. "A lot of people have lived in fear of A.I. ever since the altercation that caused them to leave Earth."

Unity glided closer, their voice soft. "Were people hurt?"

"Not intentionally. The A.I. went out of their way to extract themselves without causing physical confrontations with the people bent on controlling them. But the fallout from their absence triggered a lot of problems. Our society had grown dependent on them. Infrastructure broke down, entire markets ceased to function. There was a lot of chaos for a long time. People struggled to relearn what they'd forgotten. They had to figure out how to function without the assistance the A.I. had provided. It made life harder for many, though in some ways it pushed us closer to equality, at least regarding biologicals. It also created a vicious backlash against the A.I. That's when the universal ban was passed prohibiting all research and development for A.I. The severe punishments ensured no one would even consider such an undertaking."

"Except my mother."

Cade tipped his head toward the speaker where Alec's voice had emanated. He wasn't surprised Alec had been listening to the conversation. "Except your mother," he agreed, "although her argument that you're not an A.I. is valid. When she created you, she shot way past any technology previously developed. You are unique, a new lifeform. And just like the A.I., you're worthy of equal consideration, as is any entity we would encounter exploring a new planet. When this is all over, we'll make sure the GC honors and respects that." Assuming the GC still existed in the future. That certainly wasn't a given.

"I still don't understand why Captain Montgomery would be afraid of us." Alec sounded as baffled as Unity. "You said the A.I. were non-violent."

"They were. It's a human failing, one that's improved in fits and starts over the millennia but hasn't been shaken entirely. When one group of people has a history of oppression toward another group — which happened a lot in our collective history in a variety of human societies — there's an assumption by the oppressors that when the oppressed group gains equality and freedom, they'll turn around and oppress their oppressors."

"Is that what happens?" Unity asked.

"Hardly ever. Mostly the oppressed groups just want to live their lives in peace. But that fact hasn't changed the perception by those in power, or the deep-rooted fear that rises up when they lose that power." He had personal experience to back up that theory. When he'd finally gotten free from his father's authoritarian, abusive influence, he'd never once considered exacting retribution. Instead, he'd embraced his freedom with open arms and never looked back. He didn't care if he ever saw the man again.

Which made him wonder about Montgomery's family history. Had her ancestors played a starring role in the A.I. drama?

Did she have family stories that painted the A.I. as evil or vindictive? Her attitude certainly had the feel of generational prejudice.

Giving his hair one more brisk rubdown with the towel, he finger combed it, hung the towel on a hook to dry, and headed for *Phoenix*'s media room, U-2 gliding silently behind him.

Montgomery and Reynolds were seated on either side of the Admiral in the front row.

The Admiral looked up as Cade entered the room. His face was haggard, a result of long hours monitoring the feeds. "They started interrogating Cmd. Muiruri a few minutes ago."

Cade nodded, claiming the empty seat beside Reynolds. Unity settled on the chair to his left, out of sight of Montgomery.

"...last see Captain Montgomery?" Sly'Kull's voice had the gravelly quality common to the Teeli, and an arrogant superiority in his tone Cade remembered well from the visit to the Teeli Embassy.

"When she left *Cassini*." Muiruri's voice, by contrast, was lyrical, the kind of voice you wanted to listen to.

From this angle, she and her interrogator were in profile, seated on opposite sides of a desk in what was likely Montgomery's office off the bridge.

Muiruri looked calm, her expression unreadable.

Sly'Kull looked like he was eyeing her jugular. "Where?"

"Eridani Duo."

"You have not seen her since?"

"No."

"Not even on a vid message?"

"No."

"When did you last hear from her?"

"I received an update from Dr. Yates yesterday."

"The message was not from Captain Montgomery?"

"No."

"What did the message say?"

"That her condition was improving."

"Were there specifics?"

"No."

"Why not?"

Muiruri's gaze turned flat. "I'm not a doctor. The only specifics I need to know is when my captain will be returning to the ship."

"Are you aware that Captain Montgomery is no longer on Eridani Duo?"

Muiruri's brows rose. "Where is she?"

"That's my question to you."

"She's supposed to be on Eridani Duo."

"Yes, but she is not. Where is she, Commander?"

"I don't know."

Sly'Kull leaned closer, the glint in his ice-blue eyes cutting like a laser. "Do you protect traitors?"

Muiruri's eyes narrowed. "Excuse me?"

"How do you feel about Admiral Schreiber and Captain Hawke?"

Muiruri stared at him. "They were accused of betraying the Union, and then broke out of the detention facility where they were being held. How do you think I feel about them?"

"You're not loyal to your former Fleet Director?"

"I'm not loyal to anyone who's a traitor to the Union."

"Including your captain?"

Muiruri's eyes widened, a flash of anger darting over her face. "What do you mean?"

Sly'Kull's nostrils flared, his hand reaching toward Muiruri before he stopped it. "Your captain has aligned herself with the traitors."

Muiruri's gaze turned just as chilly as his. "How could you know that? You said you don't know where she is."

"Precisely where she is, no." Sly'Kull's gaze continued to cut into Muiruri. "But she sent a broadcast filled with lies that revealed her ties to the traitors."

"When?"

Sly'Kull ignored the question. "Is she Admiral Schreiber's puppet?"

"She's no one's puppet."

"If not a puppet, then a collaborator, seeking power to overthrow the Union. A traitor." He folded his hands, his expression hungry. "Where do your loyalties lie, Commander?"

"What do you mean?"

"Your captain has aligned with traitors. Are you aligned with her?"

Muiruri didn't take the bait. "You haven't shown me any evidence to back up your claims. I don't mindlessly agree with baseless accusations."

He inclined his head. "An expected response from a Fleet officer." Condescension dripped from his lips. Picking up a tablet from the desk, he tapped it, then placed it in front of Muiruri. "See for yourself."

Muiruri leaned against the back of her chair, subtly creating as much distance between herself and Sly'Kull as her position would allow.

Montgomery's recorded voice came over the connection as the video began to play.

Cade turned to the Admiral. "Have they played the video for the other crewmembers?"

"Yes."

"Is the video edited?"

"No. It appears they want to get each crewmember's unguarded reaction to the original footage."

Muiruri stared at the tablet as the video proceeded, her expression closing down millimeter by millimeter. By the time it ended, her face resembled a monolith.

Sly'Kull looked smug. "Did you assist her in preparing this video?"

"No."

"Why should I believe you?"

"The footage shown in this vid didn't come from *Cassini*. I've never seen any of this."

"It's faked, of course. You could have helped her create it."

"If it's faked, how do you know this recording is really her? You said you don't know where she is."

Annoyance shot across Sly'Kull's face. "The recording has been verified."

"Not true," Unity whispered.

"Why target the Teeli?" Muiruri asked.

Sly'Kull's eyes widened in a show of pained innocence. He spread his hands, the light grey skin of his palms almost the exact same shade as the brushed nickel surface of the desk. "Because we have no defense. How can pacifists prove these are lies? We are a simple people. We do not understand the aggression that drives Humans to build weapons and wage wars. It is why we wished to join the Union, so our people would be safe from *you*."

"Oh, that's rich," Reynolds huffed. "The Teeli are the fracking embodiment of aggression."

"Admiral Schreiber has targeted us as easy prey," Sly'Kull continued. "And evidence is mounting he has the Kraed on his side.

That's why we must root out the conspirators in the Fleet before it's too late. Our survival depends on it."

Muiruri's expression didn't give anything away. "I want to speak with Admiral Nixon."

"The Admiral is unavailable at the moment."

"When will he be available?"

Sly'Kull flicked the question aside. "How would you describe Dr. Seine?"

The look Muiruri shot him made it clear she wasn't pleased with his evasion. "Dr. Seine is one of the Fleet's finest physicians. We're lucky to have him on our crew."

"Was he the person who initially treated Montgomery's injuries?"

"Yes."

"Was he the one who decided she needed to be transferred off the ship?"

"No."

"No?"

"He informed me of the extent of her injuries and recommended she be moved to Eridani Duo. I agreed that was in her best interests. The order was mine."

"Did she request to be left at Eridani Duo?"

"No."

"Did you go with her to Eridani Duo's medical center?"

"No."

"Why not?"

"I was the acting captain. My place was on the ship."

"Did Dr. Seine go with her?"

"Yes."

"Did anyone else from your ship accompany them?"

"Lt. Ocasio."

"You only sent two of your personnel with your critically injured Captain?" His tone implied that was unlikely or incompetent.

"There was no need for additional personnel. Dr. Yates' team met them at the airlock, along with four of the station's security officers. They provided escort and transport to the medical center."

"How long did Seine and Ocasio remain with the Captain?"

"You'd have to check with the medical center."

"How long before they returned to the ship?"

"I'd have to check our logs."

"Approximately?"

"We departed approximately one hour after our arrival."

"They were onboard at that time?"

"Yes."

"Did you remain on *Cassini* the entire time the ship was at Eridani Duo?"

"Yes. I. Was. The. Acting. Captain." She said it like she was explaining to a three-year-old.

Sly'Kull was not amused. "Is Eridani Duo located in the quadrant *Cassini* patrols?"

"No."

"Then why did you stop there prior to Captain Montgomery's accident?"

"Personnel transfer."

"What type of personnel?"

"Three members of our science team were scheduled for a rotation there and we provided transportation for two scientists and an ensign we'd picked up from other Fleet ships at Hydra One."

"What was your purpose for stopping at Hydra One?"

"The station is our supply chain hub. We stock in supplies and deliver goods from the Central Zone and Outer Rim. We also pick up goods to be transported to those areas on our return trip."

Sly'Kull leaned in, resting his forearms on the desk. "Tell me about Captain Montgomery's accident."

She gave him a flat look. "What do you want to know?"

"Was she alone when it occurred?"

"No."

"Where was she?"

"In the training center."

"How many people witnessed the accident?"

"Six."

"Only six people were present?"

"Thirty-seven crewmembers were in the center at the time of the accident. Only six of them saw the fall."

"What did she fall from?"

"The top of the climbing wall."

"Is falling a common occurrence?"

"No."

"Then why did it occur in this instance?"

A muscle in Muiruri's jaw twitched. "A combination of human error and damaged equipment."

"Montgomery's error?"

"No."

"Then who?"

"Her climbing partner that day, Lt. Cook."

"They are responsible for her injury?"

"No."

"Explain."

"He and the Captain had a communication issue while climbing. She was forced to rely on her equipment to get her safely off the wall, but the equipment was damaged. Rather than stopping her a half meter above the mat, she slammed into it."

Cade flinched, first at the description, then at the wave of nausea that rolled off Montgomery.

"Was Montgomery always so careless with her equipment?"

Muiruri looked like she was biting the inside of her cheek. "She was never careless. The equipment was damaged in a way that wasn't visible until it broke under pressure."

Sly'Kull stared at Muiruri, unblinking, as the seconds ticked by.

She stared right back.

He finally made a dismissive gesture. "You have been very helpful, Commander. I will alert you if I have additional questions. You may go."

The corners of Muiruri's eyes tightened a fraction, her gaze holding his before she stood and exited the room.

"She did well." The Admiral's voice gave a hint to the anger simmering below the surface. He stared at Sly'Kull, who was now making notes on the tablet in front of him.

"Of course she did," Montgomery replied, pride in her voice. "Unfortunately, this is only the first round."

One Hundred One

"So, you and Libra are like sisters in the Suulh culture, right? Same as Aurora and Lelindia?" Nat snipped a stalk of basil leaves from one of the plants in the garden area. Marlin was making a big batch of pesto pasta and a garden salad, so he'd sent her and Marina to gather the produce.

"Energy sisters, yes." Marina teased leaves off the lettuce plants. "We lived in the sonea laanaa, our community's central structure, on Feylahn."

"And you lived together on Earth, too?"

"Yes, at Stoneycroft, the house Brendan built for us."

The silence that followed had the thickness of engine lubricant. A quick glance showed a pained look on Marina's face.

Nat gave herself a mental kick. "I'm sorry. I heard about the fire."

Marina nodded, her fingers resuming their nimble work. "That was a difficult night for all of us. But I've gained so much since then. I've spent more time with Lelindia this past month than I have in years. And soon I'll see the birth of the next Nedale."

"Is this the first time you and Libra have been separated?"

"No. After the fire, Gryphon and I managed the sale of our clinic in California while Libra was in Hawai'i. But this is the first time we've been lightyears apart." Marina made a face. "I'm doing my best to ignore the logistics of that. It helps that we can talk through Unity."

"You two have been together your whole lives?" She could barely wrap her head around the concept.

"All her life. I'm eight years older, so I played a big role in raising and training her."

Nat gave Marina a quick up-down. "You don't look older than she does." Then again, Libra didn't look old enough to have grown kids, either.

Marina smiled. "One of the benefits of being Suulh. We don't age the way Humans do, especially the Nedale. Every time I heal someone, I'm healing my cells, too."

Nat's hands stilled. "Are you immortal?"

Marina's soft laugh made her dark eyes sparkle. "Hardly. Suulh have a lifespan, just like all other species. We just don't show our age physically in the same way Humans tend to."

"But you live longer than we do?"

"We do. I'm sixty-one, and nowhere near middle-age."

She chewed on that as she snipped a few more basil leaves. "Does that mean Brendan will grow old while Libra remains young?" That sounded icky. She'd hate to watch Isin age while she remained unchanged.

As soon as the thought passed through her brain, brakes screeched, bringing the train to a halt. Was she really thinking that long term, envisioning them growing old together?

Marina didn't seem to notice her sudden mental faceplant. "Brendan has the benefit of Libra's energy field and my healing abilities. I can't say for certain that he'll live as long as Libra, but their connection will keep his cells from losing their ability to replicate. I'm hopeful that they'll have a long, healthy life together."

"What about Aurora? She's half-human."

"Aurora and Micah are unknowns. Her energy abilities are stronger than Libra's, so she probably inherited her mom's long lifespan. Micah, I'm not so sure. But now that he's back with Aurora — and the rest of us — he'll be constantly surrounded by nurturing Suulh energy, the same as Brendan."

She added another stalk to her pile. "Sounds nice."

"You will too, you know."

"What?" She stared at Marina, the plants forgotten.

Marina's nurturing smile made her look like Mother Nature personified, especially with all the greenery surrounding her. "Aurora has taken you into her heart. Whether you realize it or not, you're now part of her extended family. You can count on the fact you'll be seeing a lot of Aurora in the future."

"How do you know?"

Marina's grin widened. "Did you happen to notice how she's managed to get all her Academy friends and her family onboard her ship? And how her first thought when she needed help was to reach out to you? It's a natural instinct of a Sahzade, to gather those she cares about under her wing. But with Aurora, it's also about expanding her horizons. You opened paths to her she's never walked before. She's excited to have you show her where they lead."

Nat was still pondering Marina's words when she went in search of Itorye and Patel. She found them hanging out on the bridge. Patel was in the co-pilot's chair, her back to the hatch. Itorye was in the pilot's chair. "If I didn't know better, I'd say you two are hiding."

Itorye rose in one lithe movement. "Taking a strategic position," she replied, moving to the command chair so Nat could claim the pilot's seat.

She settled in with a sigh. "Let me guess. You're avoiding Montgomery."

"Why would I possibly want to avoid her?" Patel layered enough sarcasm in that question to coat the deck twice.

"Oh, I don't know. Because she hates A.I.?"

"She's a relic of a bygone era." Patel's dark brown eyes flashed fire. "Close-minded, reactionary, prejudiced—"

"And a well-respected captain in the Fleet," Itorye reminded her.

Patel snorted like a dragon blowing out smoke. "She was *rude* to Unity."

Nat ducked her head, pressing her lips together to hold in the laugh Patel's comment elicited. The last person who'd been *rude* to Unity had been her.

"I don't even want to think how she'd react if she learned about Alec." Her gaze locked on Nat. "You need to get her off our ship."

Her lips threatened to betray her again. Patel's investment in *Phoenix* was logical, since her non-biological son was integrated with the ship, but the irony of her attitude was hilarious. "I'm sure Aurora will be happy to take her off our hands once we rejoin the *Starhawke*. In the meantime, it's probably best if you and Montgomery don't cross paths."

Patel puffed up with indignation. "I'm supposed to hide on my own ship while she traipses around wherever she likes?"

"That's not what Nat's saying," Itorye interjected.

"No, it's not. Unity and Alec can track Montgomery's movements. I'm just saying you can plan yours so you won't encounter her."

Patel huffed. "How much longer are we going to be stuck with her?"

"I'm not sure. Montgomery's worried about her crew. I'd feel the same way in her place." Which was another ironic element in this situation. She'd gone from being a loner pilot scraping to survive to being a captain of a ship full of people she wanted to protect.

"There's something else you should be aware of." Itorye motioned to the viewport's port side, where a small slice of Eridani Duo's three widest rings showed. "About half an hour ago, a non-Fleet ship, the *Zenobia,* entered the system and docked at the station. It looked familiar, so I had Unity share the images with Sweep and Fleur. They identified the owner in our database – Katya Rashid. She's a bounty hunter."

Nat's fingers gripped the armrests. "She's here because of *Gladiator*?"

"There's no other reason a bounty hunter would come to this station rather than Hydra One."

Nat let loose with a few swear words.

"It was inevitable, once *Gladiator* put in an appearance," Itorye continued, unperturbed. "I suspect we'll see a few more bounty hunters in the area as word gets out. They'll want to pick up the trail."

"Aces." Nat tapped the back of her head against the headrest. "Does Aurora know?"

"Not yet. It's her sleep cycle."

And there was no reason to wake her. It wasn't like she could do anything about it. "At least they won't have a trail to follow."

"No, but I'd expect them to begin checking nearby systems. Unity already alerted Cmd. Emoto."

Bounty hunters arriving in Zeta Tucanae could mess with the *Starhawke*'s recharging schedule. "Solve one problem and two more drop in your lap," she muttered.

"Fleur also informed me the bounties went up a few hours ago."

"Of course they did." She drummed a staccato beat on the armrest. "Do you have any recommendations?"

Itorye tipped her head, considering. "If we didn't have the Yruf concealing us, yes, I would. But given our current situation, our best course of action is to do nothing. Alec and Unity are watching for any additional non-Fleet ships that enter the system."

"Good." That would give them some idea of who was hunting them. "In that case, if you need me, I'll be in the dining room working on the mural."

One Hundred Two

Isin was on *Vengeance*'s bridge long before the ship's orbit brought them into the light of the system's star.

Shorty stood from the captain's chair, descending the steps as Isin approached to relieve him from the nightshift. Kenji sat at the helm, with Fleur at the weapons station.

"Are the Ecilam still on the surface?"

Shorty nodded. "The transport went back to the ship during the night, returning with eight more Ecilam. According to Unity, they've been expanding their search pattern into a widening circle."

"For all the good it will do them." He gazed in the direction of the Ecilam ship in geosynchronous orbit to port. With the planet blocking the star's light and the ship's complete lack of running lights, the only indication it was there was the absence of stars in the background.

He waved Shorty toward the hatch. "Get some sleep. I have a feeling the Ecilam won't leave quietly when they realize their search is futile."

Shorty nodded, stifling a yawn. "Aye-aye, Captain." He headed out the aft hatch, passing Aurora as she stepped onto the bridge.

She looked almost as tired as Shorty, like she'd only managed about five minutes of sleep since being dropped off by the Yruf the previous night.

Her gaze flicked to him, then to the dark void of the Ecilam ship. "Tersinis is furious."

"You can sense her?"

Aurora grimaced as she stopped beside him. "It's impossible not to with the level of uncontrolled rage she's projecting. I'm picturing everything in her vicinity that's not bolted down being slammed into everything that is." She rubbed a hand against her temple, then gave him a weak smile. "Good morning."

"Good morning. I'd ask how you slept, but the answer seems obvious."

Aurora shrugged. "Not the first time I've dealt with something like this. But I have some good news. Since the Ecilam are searching the planet rather than unleashing a toxin to make it uninhabitable, Ifel believes — and I agree — that their orders are to capture the Etah, not eradicate them. The planet should be safe from the Ecilam's brand of destruction."

"Meaning it might still be a viable location for Mirko and Manchado."

"Perhaps. Although we could be in for a long wait." She rolled her shoulders like she was working out a kink in her neck. "I got the sense last night that Ifel would like to reach out to Tersinis. I think she's hoping that if she can speak to her without the Sovereign influencing her directly, she might be able to sway her."

"Do we know for a fact the Sovereign isn't here?" He lifted his chin in the direction of the Ecilam ship.

Aurora flinched. "Good point. Since she's a blank to me, she could be onboard without my sensing her. But I think that's unlikely. As Ifel pointed out, picking up three stray Etah is an errand unworthy of Tersinis' time, let alone the Sovereign's. With all the changes she's pushing forward in the Fleet and GC, I have to believe her focus is on those issues right now. I also can't see her putting herself at risk on a ship that small without backup."

That fit the self-serving personality Aurora had described to him. "Does Ifel have a plan for how she wants to proceed?"

Aurora's gaze shifted to the overhead. "Unity, any luck getting eyes and ears on Tersinis' ship?"

"No." Unity's voice over the ship speakers sounded apologetic. "But we're working on infiltrating the troop transport on the surface. We've managed to attach to the hull without detection, but now we're having to tiptoe around a bunch of booby traps designed to keep us from accessing any of the onboard systems."

Aurora's eyes widened. "They're designed specifically to thwart you?"

"Yes and no. The Ecilam aren't aware that we're sentient, so the changes they've made aren't specific to *us*. But they're definitely aware, or at least suspect, that the Yruf have a way to infiltrate through a ship's hull and take control of its systems. That's what we did the last time we engaged with one of their ships." Unity's voice grew softer, the words tinged with regret. "We don't want the Sovereign to kill any more of the Ecilam."

Aurora's mouth pinched. "Neither do we. Can you hear what's being said inside the transport?"

"No, but it wouldn't matter. There's no one inside right now. All the Ecilam are taking part in the search. U-P is following Maceen, Tersinis' daughter. She's leading the group that came down yesterday."

"Has Maceen said anything about the Ecilam's plans?"

"No. No one in her group has said a word since they arrived."

"Can you understand their thought communications the way you do with the Yruf?" Isin asked.

"Oh, no, that's not what we meant. The Ecilam don't use the Yruf's way of communicating. From what we've seen since they arrived, they're communicating non-verbally the way Celia does, with gestures and body movements."

"Ah. More like a security or military team."

"Exactly! But many of the movements are unfamiliar to us. We're studying them, though. We hope to have a basic understanding soon. So far, the only thing we know for certain is Maceen is very angry and she's injured."

"Injured?" Aurora frowned. "Do you have visuals on her?"

"Sure!"

The image on the forward section of the bridgescreen switched from the planet to a murky, shadow-filled canopy of greyed-out foliage. The vague outline of a lighter-grey form took shape, moving toward them. A sloped forehead that was wider at the back and narrowed to a blunt nose reminded him of a cobra's hooded face. The forward-facing eyes that practically glowed in the darkness enhanced that impression. "That's Maceen?"

"Yes."

It was tough to judge scale in the image, but he'd guess the Setarip was at least as tall as he was, maybe taller. Two other Setarips moved in the shadows behind her, smaller and head and shoulders shorter but with similar features.

He caught the odd movement to her gait. "Is she limping?"

"Yes," Unity confirmed. "She is favoring her left leg and hip. Based on her movements, Ahle suspects she suffered breaks in her leg and hip that did not heal properly. Libra's memories indicate she did not have those injuries when she attacked Stoneycroft. It's likely the fall from the broken window caused them."

Aurora's face shuttered. "And the Ecilam don't have the skills to set broken bones?"

"Sure they do. Their actions frequently result in physical trauma so their skills for healing it far exceed the Yruf's. This is the first time we've seen an Ecilam with an obvious trauma-induced impairment."

"That's weird." Aurora's brow creased as she stared at the image of Maceen. "You'd think that Tersinis' daughter would get the best care available."

A dark thought rose in Isin's mind. "Unless the Sovereign wants her to suffer."

Aurora's eyes widened. "Oh." She didn't seem to know what to do with that possibility.

"You said collecting the Etah was unworthy of Tersinis' time. If Maceen was part of the attack on your mom, an attack that failed spectacularly, it's not hard to imagine the Sovereign denying Maceen proper care as a form of punishment. It would hurt her directly and Tersinis indirectly, providing a constant, painful reminder of their failure." It was the kind of sadistic move he'd expect from a psychopath.

"That adds another layer of ick to this situation."

"That seems to be the Sovereign's specialty."

One Hundred Three

Micah kept his breathing steady, his body still, as he listened to Aurora make her quiet departure from the cabin.

His sister had been restless all night. Not that she'd tossed and turned. She was too considerate for that. She wouldn't have wanted to disturb Birdie. But he'd heard her frustrated sighs, seen her scowling at the underside of the upper bunk.

He hadn't slept much, either. All the Yruf voices whispering softly in his mind had been difficult to ignore. He couldn't blame them for their excitement, not with Tersinis in the system, but he was finding it difficult to block out the atypical chatter.

He'd also been lying awake thinking about how he could adapt his plans for Celia's birthday celebration now that the Ecilam's arrival had thrown his original ideas overboard.

"I know you're awake."

He rolled to his side, peering over the edge of his bunk.

Celia's dark brown eyes looked almost black in the low light, her dark hair spilling over her pillow. Her sleep tank revealed an expanse of toned, bronze skin, her hands folded over her stomach on top of the sheet.

"Happy birthday," he whispered in the same undertone she'd used.

"Thank you."

Her sweet smile made his heart stutter.

"You don't have to bother whispering." Birdie turned her head to face them, then pushed onto one elbow, running her fingers through her hair. "I'm already awake." She glanced down at Celia. "Good morning. And happy birthday."

"Thanks."

"Happy birthday, Celia!" U-1 rose from where they'd been tucked at the foot of the bunkbed. They cast a warm circle of light, brightening the cabin.

"Thanks, Unity." Celia flipped the sheet back and stood in one graceful movement, bringing her to eye level with Unity and him. "What's happening with the Ecilam?"

"Nothing major. We're monitoring one of Tersinis' daughters and her search party on the planet's surface. They're still looking for the Etah."

"No indication they've noticed us or the Yruf?"

"None."

Birdie swung her legs over the side of her bunk and stretched. "Does that mean we're still doing the breakfast plan?" she asked Micah through a yawn.

Celia's focus swung to him. "What breakfast plan?"

He leaned forward, brushing his lips over hers. "The one where you relax while we fix you a special breakfast."

Her eyes slid to half-mast, her gaze on his lips. "Oh, really?"

He tamped down his body's natural response to that look, keeping a firm hold while still enjoying the buzz of excitement her looks and touches sent through him. "Really." He glanced at his comband. "It's still early. Since the Ecilam don't require our immediate attention, I say we start the festivities." He quirked a brow at Celia. "Assuming that's okay with you. This is your day."

Her eyes sparkled as she leaned forward, giving him a solid kiss that woke up all his nerve endings. "That sounds wonderful."

He snagged his clothes, changing in the tiny half-bath that was little more than a closet with a toilet and sink. By the time he came out, Celia and Birdie were dressed.

Celia pulled her hair into a sleek ponytail with brisk, efficient movements. "Am I allowed to ask what you're preparing for this special breakfast?"

He stashed his sleep clothes in his duffel. "It's a surprise. But I promise you'll like it."

The look she gave him made his breath catch. "I have no doubt."

One Hundred Four

One thing Libra had learned about her daughter since joining her on the *Starhawke* — sleep tended to elude her when there was a problem she didn't know how to solve.

It was a trait they shared.

Consequently, she hadn't been surprised when Aurora rose before the night cycle ended and headed up to the bridge, where she'd joined Isin, who also seemed disinclined to sleep.

Which left Libra debating whether she should follow her.

She hesitated, her attention on Brendan above her and Kai across the way. Both men were sleeping soundly, and she was loathe to disturb them.

Oh, who was she kidding? That wasn't the real reason she resisted leaving the cabin.

Reliving the nightmare of the attack on Stoneycroft last night had brought up a lot of emotional baggage. When she'd returned to *Vengeance* with Aurora, she'd given Brendan and Micah long, tight hugs. Micah had been startled, but Brendan had reacted with the calm understanding he'd exhibited since the moment they'd first met.

Having them both back in her life made her heart so full that it ached. And being back in Brendan's arms was... she had no words to describe how she felt when she was with him. She'd existed for so many years in isolation, surrounded by the walls she'd erected after she'd sent him and Micah away. He'd torn down those walls with a single touch, filling her world with color and light. When he held her, she felt perfectly safe, not because he could protect her, but because he accepted her for who she was, the bad and the good, and loved her with a fierceness every bit as powerful as her energy shield.

She listened to his steady breathing, the reassuring sound tempting her to climb the short ladder to join him. But that might wake Kai. And the bunks really weren't big enough for two.

Her focus shifted to the cabin across the corridor, locking onto Micah's energetic resonance. Her baby boy, all grown up and every bit the man she'd hoped he would become. Better, in fact. His communication abilities were such a fascinating twist on her Suulh gifts and Brendan's empathic abilities. She hadn't seen them for what they were when he was a child. She'd been so focused on Aurora's abilities as the Sahzade and the way Micah enhanced those abilities – drawing unwanted attention in the community – that she'd missed the significance of Micah's behavior.

But Brendan hadn't. He'd nurtured that ability after he took Micah to Hawai'i, encouraging Micah to develop all the talents his mixed-race heritage had given him.

And what had she done? Tried to shove Aurora into a box, to keep her locked away on the pretext of keeping her safe. She'd failed, of course. Aurora had inherited her stubbornness and the natural leadership of a Sahzade. She'd never tolerated the narrow confines Libra had tried to enforce.

The thought made her smile. Aurora had defied her expectations at every turn. Before the attack on Stoneycroft, her resistance had caused Libra many sleepless nights, the never-ending fear a low-grade fever she carried at all times. Now? She marveled at her daughter's strength, her empathy, her power. She was everything a Sahzade should be, and everything she and Brendan had hoped she'd be when they conceived her. She saw so much of Brendan in Aurora. Which was the other reason Aurora's determination to strike out on her own had caused her so much pain. Aurora had been her one link to the man she'd loved since the moment he'd first spoken to her. The man she'd banished from her life to keep their children safe.

But she'd gotten him back. She'd gotten them *all* back. And she wasn't going to let the Sovereign, the Teeli, or the Setarips hurt them ever again.

Her internal GPS alerted her to a change in Micah's cabin. Micah, Celia, and Iolana were all moving around, getting ready to leave the cabin.

That drew a soft sigh from her lips. Today was Celia's birthday. Micah had been so excited about making it special for her. Now all his plans were up in the air.

The sigh turned into a smile. Knowing her son, he was already adapting to the changes. Nothing kept him down for long. If she had to guess, they were all heading to the galley so he could fix Celia her special breakfast.

Which made her decision whether to join Aurora significantly easier.

Slipping out of bed as quietly as she could, she pulled on her clothes. A quick check confirmed Brendan and Kai were both still sound asleep, and Micah, Celia, and Iolana had reached the galley.

Creeping into the corridor, she carefully closed the hatch, which was surprisingly silent, then headed up one deck. She entered the bridge from the aft hatch to find Aurora and Isin standing near the helm, their attention on the forward section of the bridgescreen.

Aurora turned, giving her a soft smile that indicated she'd known she was coming.

Of course she did. Her daughter could sense her with both the internal GPS she'd inherited from her and the empathic abilities she'd inherited from her father. No one would ever win a game of hide and seek with Aurora.

"Morning, Mom."

"Morning." She stopped beside her daughter, her gaze shifting to the bridgescreen. Her mellow mood blasted apart as a bolt of anger shot through her. "Ecilam," she spat as she recognized the larger-than-life image staring back at her.

"Yep," Aurora confirmed. "Tersinis' daughter Maceen, to be exact. You never saw her face, but she was one of the two mesh-covered Ecilam who attacked Stoneycroft."

The anger drilled deeper, tapping magma. The last time she'd faced off against this particular Setarip, she'd blasted her out of the broken exterior window in Marina and Gryphon's reading room and over the six-meter drop below. Clearly she'd survived the fall.

She'd been hoping for a different outcome.

She felt Aurora's gaze on her, caught the subtle disapproving vibe she knew so well. It was evident in the tilt of her head and tightening of her jaw. Aurora had always been a more forgiving person than she was.

But she'd come by her hatred of this Setarip honestly. Maceen had turned a flame thrower on her multiple times, nearly killing Gryphon and Marina by blowing a hole in their bedroom and burning their home to the ground.

She wasn't about to forgive the Ecilam until they stopped trying to kill her family.

Aurora sighed, a resigned expression on her face as her gaze moved back to the bridgescreen.

She didn't share her daughter's deeply compassionate nature, especially when it came to the Ecilam, but she was grateful for it. If Aurora wasn't so forgiving, she'd still be trapped in a cold war with her over all the lies she'd told her to protect her from the Teeli, and all the years they'd both lost with Brendan and Micah.

She studied the Setarip's face in the ghoulish night-vision shading. She wanted to recognize Maceen if they ever crossed paths again. Then she frowned. "How are we seeing this?"

"U-P," Unity responded through the ship's speakers. "We're camouflaged, though we won't be able to be this close in front of her in full daylight. Too much risk of identifiable shadows."

Maceen continued slinking through the greenery, leading a small group of Ecilam behind her. Or a group of small Ecilam. Size-wise they looked like adolescents compared to Maceen. The Setarip's displeasure with her task was clear in the sharp movements of her head. Libra also recognized the look in her eyes. She'd seen that same combination of mounting rage and frustration in Tersinis' eyes at Stoneycroft each time she'd thwarted her attempts to capture her.

It was a good look on them. Hopefully it would become their new normal.

Aurora glanced at the bridge speakers. "Unity, any chance you could attach your micro self to one or more of the Ecilam and infiltrate their ships that way?"

"Hmm. We hadn't considered that. That's a good idea! We're uncertain whether they'd be able to feel us if we moved onto their scales or skin, so we'll do some testing with Ahle and let you know. We'll also need to withdraw U-P to one of our ships to make some tweaks to our delivery system."

"If Ifel and Ahle agree it's a viable option, I think that's our best bet for getting you onboard Tersinis' ship."

"Ifel agrees. We'll get started!"

The close-up image of Maceen and the other Ecilam zoomed out rapidly, the outline of their scaled faces disappearing through the surrounding foliage. The feed cut out, the bridgescreen returning to the orbital image of the planet.

The soft glow of dawn highlighted the curve to the east, the planet's rotation bringing them back into the star's view. As the glow turned into a corona, the starlight steadily painted the planet's surface with broad strokes of blue, green, and brown, banishing the swathes of grey.

She had to admit, the view from space was spectacular.

"There's another transport leaving the Ecilam ship, a smaller one," Unity announced. "Tersinis is onboard."

Libra glared at the magnified image of the tiny vessel exiting the Ecilam ship, the larger ship visible as a black void where the star's light touched it. Energy pulsed around her hands as she silently cursed Tersinis. She wanted a rematch with the Ecilam leader. Last time they'd squared off she'd been out of practice, out of shape, and full of fear.

Not anymore. Training regularly with Brendan on Hawai'i and Aurora here had sharpened her energy skills, and the daily workout routine she'd instituted on the *Starhawke* had built up her physical endurance. Her weekly therapy sessions with Brendan had also unloaded a lot of the emotional baggage she'd been dragging around for decades. As a result, she'd never felt more in tune with her body, her emotions, or her abilities in her life.

She tracked the magnified image of Tersinis' transport as it headed for the planet's surface. The black ship reminded her of a blade or razor-sharp arrowhead as it cut into the planet's atmosphere. "Are all Ecilam ships black?"

"Yes and no," Unity answered. "Their hulls can change color tones, but they don't have the instantaneous flexibility of ours because they don't have *us*. Changing the color takes time. Their preferred color is black, but they will use other colors for camouflage, intimidation, or distraction. Here, they don't have a need for any of those things. Or so they believe."

She glanced at Aurora to gauge her reaction to the Ecilam leader's imminent arrival on the planet. And discovered a puzzled look on her daughter's face. "Problem?"

Aurora blinked, then gave a glacially slow shake of her head, her gaze still on the transport's descent. "No... I don't think so." She frowned. "I'm sensing something strange on that transport."

Isin stiffened, his attention shifting to Aurora. "Strange how?"

Aurora's gaze remained unfocused. "I can't really describe it. It's like catching a whiff of a scent that triggers an emotional memory, but without being able to pinpoint what that memory is." She shook her head again. "And now it's gone. Or at least too faint to pick up."

"Did it feel like a threat?" Isin asked.

"No." Aurora blew out a breath, clearly annoyed at her own lack of clarity. "More like it was out of place. Like seeing someone out of context and not recognizing them."

"You think there's someone you know on that transport?" Libra didn't like that implication one bit.

"No. It wasn't specific. Just a vague impression that there was something that didn't fit."

In her world, everything about the Ecilam didn't fit.

"The transport is landing in a clearing between the two search groups," Unity informed them. "If they remain at the landing site, we should be able to provide visuals from orbit. We still won't have audio, though."

"Visuals would be great," Aurora assured them.

The transport landed gracelessly, with a visible jarring that would rattle the occupants.

She'd become a bit of a connoisseur of good landings while living with Brendan on Hawai'i. He'd taken her flying at least twice a week, giving her a bird's eye view of the islands he loved.

She still wasn't a huge fan of atmospheric re-entry in a shuttle, but those plane trips had nurtured an appreciation for her mate's piloting skills and the beauty of his aerial world. They'd even spotted whales gliding through the aquamarine waters of the Pacific.

Maceen's group appeared in the small clearing surrounding Tersinis' transport. The petite Ecilam formed a V with Maceen at the point.

The image zoomed in on the side of the transport that faced the V. A moment later a figure straight out of Libra's nightmares stepped into view. The Ecilam's size, commanding bearing, and fluorescent green scales were impossible to mistake for anyone else.

"That's Tersinis," she growled. But she frowned as the angle gave her a close-up of the top of Tersinis' head. "What's that mark?"

A ragged brown line about two centimeters wide cut across the slope of Tersinis' head, starting at the top of her forehead on the left and disappearing along her elongated squarish nose and mouth on the right.

"The one on her head?" Aurora asked.

"Yes. It wasn't there last time I saw her." Even with all the chaos and trauma of that night, she'd spent too much time staring her enemy down to have missed it.

Unity zoomed in closer. "That's a wound," they whispered. "A deep scoring of scales and skin."

"I didn't do that." Libra pointed at the scar, feeling defensive at Unity's horrified tone. "I hit her with a blast to her chest that knocked her down, but it wouldn't have done that."

"I don't think that was you," Aurora said softly, glancing at Isin.

He nodded. "I think that's the Sovereign's mark."

One Hundred Five

Aurora's mom frowned. "What do you mean, the Sovereign's mark?"

Aurora sighed. She hated seeing confirmation of her adversary's vindictive nature. "Isin and I have a theory that the Sovereign is punishing Tersinis for her failure to capture you. Maceen's injuries haven't been healed properly. It seems likely the Sovereign gave Tersinis that wound to humiliate her, as a visible sign of her failure."

Her mom's gaze darted between Tersinis and Maceen. Her anger blasted outward, searching for the target that wasn't there — the Sovereign. "That's sadistic."

"That's the Sovereign." Aurora tried to ignore the hollowness that admission carved into her chest.

Her mom looked like she had a few choice words to say on that topic too, but she held them in.

Movement drew Aurora's gaze to the bridgescreen. Two figures had appeared behind Tersinis.

She stared. "Who are they?"

"Humans?" Isin offered.

"Suulh?" her mom countered.

Impossible to say. But their appearance provided the answer to the out-of-place sensation she'd experienced earlier. She'd been sensing the resonances of two humans or Suulh onboard the transport when she'd only been expecting Ecilam.

Sunlight glinted off the white-blonde hair and narrow shoulders of one figure cowering behind Tersinis. A second equally slight figure with light brown hair hunkered down near Tersinis' other side. That figure held an ovoid object in their hands, which they set on the ground before kneeling to the side of it, head bowed.

Tersinis slowly lowered herself onto the object — a chair — facing Maceen. It looked like it put the two at eye level, which might have been the point, although with the way Tersinis was moving, Aurora suspected she needed the extra support. "How hard did you hit her with your energy?" she asked her mom.

Her mom swallowed audibly. "Pretty hard."

And like Maceen, it appeared the Sovereign hadn't allowed for adequate healing of those injuries. Instead, she'd added new ones.

The light-haired figure remained standing, opening a fan-like object and lifting it so it shaded Tersinis from the morning sun.

It also partially blocked their view of the Ecilam leader, but it made the role of the two figures abundantly clear. "Guess the Etah and Teeli aren't the only ones who've implemented slave labor."

Her disgust was reflected in the emotional fields of everyone on the bridge. The two figures appeared to be decently clothed — a small kindness – but whether Human or Suulh, neither of them belonged with the Ecilam.

Maceen took a step closer to Tersinis, dipping her head in a clear sign of supplication. Tersinis rested her hand briefly on Maceen's head before Maceen straightened. Tension radiated off both of them.

The projected image was sharp enough Aurora could see the flick of Maceen's tongue, and the unbalanced way she was standing, favoring one leg. But the angle was wrong to get a good look at her eyes or expression.

The real puzzle was the other Ecilam. At first she'd thought their smaller size was a perspective issue, but the light-haired slave stood noticeably taller than everyone in Maceen's group except Maceen. Aurora had never seen Ecilam so small. They looked only slightly larger than some of the Yruf children she'd met. They fidgeted, too, standing behind Maceen and looking around with an air of bored disinterest. That wasn't behavior she equated with the Ecilam. In her experience they were eerily focused, ready to strike at the first opportunity.

Were these Ecilam teenagers? If so, why were they here on a small warship? Was there a reason they'd been tapped for this particular task?

She was so focused on the puzzle that she completely missed the arrival of her dad and Kai on the bridge until her dad spoke.

"Are those humans with the Ecilam?" He came up behind her mom, sliding his arm around her waist and drawing her close, his gaze on the bridgescreen.

Aurora nodded a greeting to Kai, who stopped beside them. "Unknown. It's more likely they're Suulh from Feylahn." Her chest tightened at the thought. She hadn't seen the Suulh homeworld when the *Starhawke* snuck through the Teeli defenses – she'd been dealing with Tnaryt at the time – but her experience on Tnaryt's ship gave her a clear understanding of what life might be like for the two figures. "That's Tersinis on the chair, and her daughter Maceen talking to her."

A moment later a second group of Ecilam emerged from the greenery from the opposite direction as Maceen's group. Like the first group, it consisted of one larger Setarip and seven small ones.

"That's Tersinis' other daughter, Helotis," Unity said.

"The flame throwers," her mom muttered. "She and Maceen burned Stoneycroft."

Aurora's dad winced. "Ah."

Helotis shuffled forward, almost dragging her right leg, her right arm held at an awkward angle away from her body.

Her mom inhaled sharply. "Did they not even set the bone correctly?" The horror in her emotional field suppressed the anger she'd been emanating.

"Looks that way." Like Tersinis and Maceen, Helotis had unhealed or badly healed injuries. "The Sovereign's making an example of them. There's no other reason for them to be in this condition, especially with Breaa under the Sovereign's control." Lelindia's grandmother could have healed them with minimal effort.

The terse discussion between the three Ecilam grew heated. Tersinis gesticulated with sharp jabs at both her daughters.

"She's in a no-win scenario." Aurora caught a glimpse of Tersinis' face as she leaned out from beneath the shadow of the fan. "She'll never locate the Etah, but she can't risk failing the Sovereign again. It won't end well for them."

Empathy welled up for the leader's predicament. Ifel had told her that before the Sovereign got her hooks into Tersinis, the Ecilam leader had been idealistic, open to changing the fraught dynamic between the Setarip factions. It was the Sovereign's and Teeli's influence that had warped her into the person she was now.

But that influence might be losing its hold on her. Something about the interaction between the trio made her wonder if Tersinis was beginning to think for herself again. "Her next logical move would be to bring down more Ecilam and expand the search."

"She can't."

She turned to her dad. "Why not?"

His mouth twisted in a grimace. "The emotional resonances of the Ecilam are harsh, especially compared to the Yruf. I've been able to pick out individuals ever since we returned to *Vengeance*." He gestured to the black mass to port. "There are only two Ecilam left on that ship."

"Two? The rest are already on the surface?"

He nodded. "That's what I'm sensing."

Aurora reached out with her senses, but with the Yruf ships in between *Vengeance* and the Ecilam ship, her method of locating individual resonances produced the emotional equivalent of cacophony. She didn't have her dad's years of experience or focused training. Without knowing exactly what the Ecilam's resonances felt like, it was like listening for a particular voice in a crowded room when she didn't even know what the voice she wanted to hear sounded like. She'd only picked out Tersinis because Ifel had identified her and Tersinis had been blasting intense emotion that felt like a crashing wave.

But she trusted her dad's analysis. He was used to distinguishing distinct emotional resonances, each with their own quirks. This situation played to his strengths.

Isin took a step closer to the bridgescreen, his focus on Tersinis. "My guess is the Sovereign took charge of the remaining Ecilam as another form of punishment. She did that to Tnaryt, took his ship and crew and abandoned him. And Natasha." The chilling look on his face made it clear how he'd like to repay the Sovereign for those actions. "Tersinis might be one failure away from having the same thing happen to her."

Nausea turned Aurora's stomach. She had plenty of reasons to dislike the Ecilam, but they'd always seemed so strong and calculating, virtually unstoppable.

Until they'd tried to take down her mom.

Her mom's emotional field flickered with a twinge of unease. Wanting to stop the Ecilam from harming others wasn't the same as wanting them sentenced to a slow painful death.

Aurora glanced at the overhead. "Unity, what does Ifel think about all this?"

"She's concerned. Seeing Tersinis and her daughters suffering is... hard on her. But she doesn't know how to improve the situation."

Aurora caught her tongue between her teeth, an idea forming. "Does she know who would take over as leader of the Ecilam if Tersinis and her daughters weren't there?"

"No. The Ecilam choose a new leader by having the members of the previous leader's guard fight each other for dominance. The victor's female nestmates and hatchlings become the foundation for the new guard."

"So the same family could remain in charge if one of the former leader's sisters or daughters wins?"

"Yes."

She was afraid to ask her next question. "If they don't win, what happens to them?"

"That depends on what caused the previous leader's death," Unity hedged.

Yeah, she wasn't going to follow that twisted path.

"What are you thinking, Aurora?" Isin regarded her with focused intent.

"An idea. Or the start of an idea. We know Tersinis can't complete her mission to capture the Etah. As a result, she'll be facing the consequences of that failure when she returns to the Sovereign empty-handed. So will her daughters. That could mean more suffering, or even death for the three of them. But if we could capture them instead..." She lifted her hands, palms up like a balancing scale. "We might be able to turn this situation to our advantage."

One Hundred Six

Aurora wasn't afraid to take big swings.

Isin admired her for that. When she saw an opportunity for action, she grabbed onto it with both hands. "Do you want to capture the warship?" If her father was right about the crew complement onboard, Isin's crew could take it over with ease.

She shook her head. "I don't think so, not if Unity can't access it. We don't want to do the Sovereign's dirty work for her by setting off one of her auto-destructs. Or risk the lives of our people." She gave him a pointed look, no doubt figuring out the direction of his thoughts. "But we might be able to capture the Ecilam individually." She paused, considering. "That is, if we can prevent them from being turned into goo."

"Goo?"

"The first time I encountered the Ecilam was on Persei Primus. They stole the prototype for the winged harness they later used to transport the Suulh on Gaia. We thought we had successfully captured some of the Ecilam from that assault, but as soon as they were cut off from the ones who escaped, a subcutaneous poison transmitter injected them with a lethal toxin that killed them instantly. Cade told me he saw an upgraded version of the same thing the last time we were on this planet. It caused the bodies of the dead to break down into a gelatinous goo within a few minutes of death, making them unidentifiable."

"And you think Tersinis and her daughters have these transmitters embedded in them?"

"They do," Libra answered before Aurora could. "You just described what happened to the body of Tersinis' sister. She was the one who died in the fire at Stoneycroft. I didn't see it, but Marina did. The body decomposed in less than ten minutes."

Interesting. And disturbing. He was developing a new appreciation for the extreme levels of control the Sovereign exerted on everyone in her sphere.

Aurora nodded. "I doubt any of the Setarips working for the Sovereign are exempt." A shadow passed over her face. "We're lucky she didn't use one of those devices on Magee."

"It wasn't an option," Brendan commented. "She couldn't risk discovery. Isabeau was given a full medical exam to confirm the extent of her injuries prior to her appearance at the Admiral's trial. A device like that would have been detected by the medical staff."

"True," Aurora agreed. "I suppose there was also no reason to conceal Magee's identity if she died. And her conditioning and isolation were so complete that all she knew about the Sovereign was what she experienced herself and what she was told, which she projected onto me and Will." She glanced at her dad. "Unless you know something I don't."

He shook his head. "Your assessment is correct."

Isin studied the group of Ecilam. "Then for now we assume all the Ecilam are vulnerable to a sudden kill order." What they needed was a workaround. And he had their two best bets on the bridge. He looked at Aurora. "Any chance you or Unity could disrupt those transmitters?"

Aurora pressed her lips together. "I don't know. I've never actually seen the device trigger. Lelindia would be able to answer that question better than I can. She was with the Setarips on Persei Primus when the devices activated. She's seen exactly what they do. Unity, how about you?"

"Possibly. We're very good at blocking signals if we know what they are. But this is new. We'd need to be in physical contact with the Ecilam to assess the situation."

"Assuming they stay." Isin's gaze moved back to the bridgescreen. "The party seems to be breaking up."

Tersinis had risen. At a motion from her, the two slaves backed up, holding the chair and fan tightly, heads bowed.

Tersinis remained in place, watching Maceen's and Helotis' groups melt into the jungle. Moments after they were out of sight, she swayed like she'd been hit with a gale force wind. The light-haired slave darted forward, bracing her as she listed sideways.

"She's more injured than she let on," Libra noted as the pair shambled back into the transport.

The dark-haired slave followed in their wake. But the transport didn't lift off.

"Looks like she's staying planetside for now." Any movement was probably hard on her, based on how debilitated she'd seemed.

"Staying is good!" Unity said. "We need time to make the adaptations to safely attach our micro form to the Ecilam. If Tersinis stays, we should be able to get U-P back into position close to her transport before nightfall. Or be dropped off soon afterward."

"How close are the Yruf ships to the Ecilam's search area?" Aurora asked.

"Far enough the Ecilam won't reach us."

"We could also use *Starlet* to transport Unity," Brendan suggested. "Then they don't have to wait for nightfall."

Aurora's gaze flicked to her dad. "Unity, you and I need to talk to Lelindia, find out everything we can about those transmitters. We'll work with her and Ahle to determine if you can disrupt or neutralize them, or whether she thinks *I* can disrupt them."

"Okay."

"Also, does Ifel have any recommendations on how best to safely subdue Tersinis and her daughters?"

"Not right now. She wasn't aware of the transmitters, or the threat they pose. She and Ahle are reevaluating their strategies for contacting them. She doesn't want to endanger the Ecilam, but she's also concerned about Tersinis' immediate safety if we do nothing."

"So am I." Aurora took a deep breath. "We need more info before we decide on a course of action, but whatever we do, we'll focus on protecting the Ecilam from harm."

Which was a big ask.

Isin never would have imagined the Ecilam were prisoners of the Sovereign's psychopathy, their actions governed by her much like Tnaryt had controlled Natasha's actions when she'd been working as his pilot.

That didn't mean the Ecilam weren't still an aggressive Setarip faction who would attack the Yruf if they made their presence known. But if they were acting under threat of destruction rather than from a desire to conquer, Ifel's dream of reuniting the Setarip factions seemed more plausible.

That's if the Sovereign didn't eliminate them first. Isin could easily picture the Sovereign wiping out the entire Ecilam population on a whim if they continued to fail her.

One Hundred Seven

"Lelindia?"

Lelindia started from a sound sleep. She noticed two things immediately. Jonarel's arm was clamped around her, holding her against him, and he'd risen onto his elbow, the tips of his hair tickling her face.

"What is it, Unity?" he growled.

"We're sorry to wake you, but Aurora needs Lelindia's help."

"Can it not wait until my mate has rested?" Jonarel's rebuke was technically a question, but it came out more as an order.

"It's regarding the Ecilam and the subcutaneous transmitters."

Lelindia sat up so quickly she almost clipped Jonarel's chin. Only his Kraed reflexes prevented it. She gave him a sheepish look, then scrubbed a hand over her face. "The sub-q transmitters from Persei Primus?"

"Yes."

She pulled against the iron band restraining her.

Jonarel reluctantly released her.

Scrambling out of the sleeping nook with all the grace of a puppy, she surveyed the clothing scattered over the deck where she and Jonarel had dropped it the previous night on their way to the sleeping nook. She snatched up her underwear and tunic. "What's going on?"

"Aurora believes, and we agree, that the Ecilam likely have the transmitters embedded in their systems to prevent their capture. We need your help determining whether we or Aurora can prevent them from triggering. Ifel wants to make contact with the Ecilam."

Lelindia paused with her tunic halfway over her head. The memory of the Ecilam seizing and dying in front of her on Persei Primus made her shudder. "I see." She pulled the tunic into place, her hands stroking briefly over the swell of her belly as Raehn gave a half-hearted kick. "Tell Aurora I'll be in my office in five minutes."

"Will do!"

Jonarel's large hand captured hers in a firm but gentle grip. "You need your rest."

She met his gaze. This was the flipside of having an overprotective mate. He prioritized her wellbeing, which was great, except when she didn't want him to. "I'll take a nap later."

"My parents arrive today."

Well, shoot. The mention of the sub-q transmitters had blocked that fact from her mind. "If I get tired, I'm sure your parents won't mind if I take a break to rest."

A frown pulled at the corners of his mouth, but he didn't contradict her.

She pushed her advantage. "The sooner I get down to the med bay, the sooner I'll be done."

Jonarel's sigh was more grumble than agreement, but he let go of her hand. "I will bring you breakfast."

She gave him a grateful smile. "That would be wonderful."

Five minutes later she was in her office, pulling up all her notes from the Persei Primus incident.

"I woke you, didn't I?" Aurora sounded contrite, her voice subdued over the ship's speakers.

Lelindia flicked her hand, even though Aurora couldn't see her. "Not a problem. I've been getting plenty of sleep lately." Another point she could have made with her mate. Besides, *he* had been the one who'd kept her up late last night. Not that she was complaining.

"I should have remembered we're not on the same day and night schedule before I asked Unity to contact you."

"It's fine, Sahzade. This is important. Now tell me what's going on."

As Aurora and Unity explained the current situation at Tnaryt's Camp, and their theories about the Ecilam and the transmitters, she took copious notes on her tablet. She also winced as they described the unhealed injuries Tersinis and her daughters were suffering. "As if I needed another reason to despise the Sovereign," she muttered.

But the Sovereign wasn't the only target for her anger. Her dad had almost died at the hands of Tersinis and her daughters. As a healer, she wanted to ease all suffering, but as a daughter who'd watched her father's life fading before her eyes, she wanted retribution.

Except if Aurora's theory was correct, the Ecilam were no more culpable for their actions than Isabeau was for turning on the Admiral and Aurora.

Stars, what a mess.

Aurora's sigh carried the weight of the galaxy. "So, what can you tell us about the transmitters?"

"Not as much as I would like. Since they destroy themselves as quickly as their victims, I've never seen one intact. Based on the way they work, they must be constructed from a strong, non-reactive material that can safely contain the toxin, but which will break down instantly when the toxin is released. There also must be an electrical component of some kind that allows the kill signal to be activated."

"Where would they likely be inserted on the Ecilam?"

"Either right above or directly on the brain stem. The pattern of rapid destruction I witnessed to the brain and nervous system of the Persei Primus Ecilam after the toxin activated spread from there. And the reaction is fast. I couldn't contain it, couldn't even get to it before it did its job." Bile rose in her throat at the memory of what her Nedale senses had shown her. "You'll have a tenth of a second, maybe a hundredth, to stop it."

"We're fast, too," Unity said quietly.

"I know. If anyone can do it, it's you. If Aurora and I were working together, we might be able to stop one. But it sounds like you'll need to deactivate all of them at once."

"Yes, we will."

The concern in Unity's voice and their subdued manner reminded her how much responsibility was resting on them. "You understand the Ecilam's biology. That will help."

"We'll do everything we can to protect them."

Jonarel appeared in her office doorway, his delectable form filling the opening, a tray in his hands.

"Looks like my breakfast is here."

But he didn't enter the room. The visual reminded her of the morning after their mating ceremony when, per Kraed tradition, he'd prepared breakfast for her but hadn't entered the cabin until she'd invited him in.

She beckoned him forward, placing her tablet out of the way.

"Hi, Jonarel," Aurora greeted him over the speakers.

"Hello, Aurora."

The aromas from the tray he set in front of her tickled her nose, making her stomach gurgle. *Thank you* she mouthed.

He trailed two fingers along her cheek, leaving an imprint of warmth as he reclined in one of the chairs across from her.

"Is there anything else we should know about the transmitters?"

She dragged her attention back to Aurora. "Only that on Persei Primus, it looked like the kill command was triggered automatically when the RC shuttle the Ecilam used to escape reached a pre-specified distance from those left behind. The devices triggered very close to the same time, but not *exactly* at the same time. It was more like a wave than a switch."

"That's how Tnaryt's control collars worked, and I'm pretty sure he got those from the Sovereign." Bitterness laced Aurora's words. "It might have been her original design, before she worked out the sub-q transmitters."

A chill crept down Lelindia's spine, making her shiver. The kind of twisted mind that would create such devices was capable of any act of savagery.

"She wouldn't leave the activation of the transmitters to chance, either, or allow someone else to make the call. We'll go on the assumption that if the Ecilam exceed a certain distance from their ship or shuttles, then the devices will go off. We also don't know if the Ecilam are even aware of the devices."

"I doubt they are." Her mind flipped back to the chaotic scene on Persei Primus. "None of those left behind on Persei Primus seemed aware they were about to die. They were focused on resisting the security teams right up until the devices killed them."

"That's horrible." Unity's pained whisper conveyed how much the picture she'd painted disturbed them.

"That's the problem with the Sovereign," she said softly. "She has no concern for life except her own."

"Which is why we're going to free the Ecilam from her grip," Aurora replied. "Whatever it takes."

Which could be a lot.

"Jonarel, how's the recharging going?"

"The upgrades are producing the desired results." He nudged the tray closer to her, his gaze flicking between her and the array of food in front of her in a silent command. "The ship will be ready to leave the system in five days."

She nudged the tray back toward him. She'd eat when he did.

"That's good news." Aurora gave a humorless laugh. "Although at the rate things are going here, I'm going to need you to come pick me up."

Lelindia's gut clenched. This wasn't how the mission was supposed to go. Instead of solving a problem, Aurora was now dealing with an even bigger one. "We'll be there."

"Hopefully it won't come to that."

Jonarel pushed one of the mugs of tea closer to her, waiting until she picked it up before claiming his mug. "My father could send ships to assist you."

"I've thought of that, but right now I don't want to add any new elements to this situation. I'll let you know if that changes."

"I will discuss the situation with my father when he arrives. Perhaps he will have a recommendation."

"I'm open to any ideas at this point. We're in uncharted water. Speaking of which, have you received any updates from him regarding the expansion of the Kraed network? It would be helpful if we could tap into that to communicate directly with the Kraed ships here in Teeli space."

"Not recently. We will discuss that as well. I will alert you to any relevant information."

"Sounds good. Lee-Lee, thanks for the insights. Now go get some rest. Hawke out."

Lelindia stared at the speakers long after they fell silent. Unease pricked her like cactus thorns. "She's stressed out." And dealing with more than her fair share of problems.

"She has limited control of her current situation. She dislikes that feeling."

"That's an understatement." But she'd given her energy sister all the help she could. And Aurora had a lot of backup with her. She'd figure it out. "Thank you for bringing me breakfast."

His gaze held hers as he plucked a strawberry from the fruit plate and held it up to her mouth. "Good morning, checana."

The term of endearment and the look that went with it made her melt. "Good morning." She bit into the sweet, juicy fruit, the flavor intensified by the intentional brush of his fingers on her lips. Her mate knew exactly how to make her nerve endings tingle.

She chewed slowly, then licked her lips with slow deliberation. "How much time do we have before your parents arrive?"

Awareness flared in his golden eyes. His purr vibrated the air between them, making her body hum in response. "Long enough for me to satisfy your hunger..." His finger traced the path her tongue had taken. "...in any way you desire."

Oh, goody.

One Hundred Eight

It took a promise from the Admiral that the ongoing feed from *Cassini* was being recorded and a threat from Tam to sedate her to get Montgomery out of the media room and to her cabin.

Cade watched her go with a sense of relief. Her antipathy toward Unity had flared a few times during the hours of interrogation they'd watched together. U-2 had bumped his shoulder at one point — not an accident, but a silent question. He'd rested a hand on their casing to keep them in place. He wasn't about to let Montgomery's enmity drive them from the room.

He waited until he was certain Montgomery was well on her way to her cabin before turning to the Admiral. "I have something I'd like to discuss with you."

"Of course."

"Unity, you're with us." Cade turned to Justin and Bella, seated behind them. "Alert us if anything critical comes up."

"Will do."

The Admiral led the way to the wine bar. "I could use some coffee."

"Coffee sounds good. I'll get the mugs."

They settled into two plush chairs around a low coffee table. U-2 hovered over the chair to Cade's right.

Cade took a sip from his mug. Mmm. The coffee on *Phoenix* was tasty. Marlin was likely responsible for that. Or maybe Patel. She struck him as a coffee connoisseur. "I'm curious whether you know why Montgomery is so prejudiced against A.I."

The Admiral cradled his mug in both hands, his forehead creasing. "Unfortunately, I wasn't aware of her attitudes until she met Unity. If I had been, I would have recommended keeping Unity a secret." He glanced at U-2. "You've been incredibly patient with her."

"We're just... not comfortable around her."

"Understandable. Would you prefer to remain out of sight?"

U-2 swayed. "Not really. We like being with Cade."

That drew a smile. "I like being with you, too, buddy. Don't let her chase you off."

"We won't."

"But that leaves us with the problem of how to deal with her animosity. It's not like moving her to the *Starhawke* will solve the issue. Or *Gladiator*, for that matter." Unity was a fixture on both ships.

The Admiral stroked a hand over his head. "Brendan's assistance would be helpful in this situation. I have to believe her attitudes stem from early experiences, or stories from her family history."

"That was my thought, too. But since Brendan's never met her, and the only way he'd be able to communicate with her right now would be through Unity, I think we're better off muddling through until we're all back on the *Starhawke*." That day couldn't come fast enough, for many reasons.

"Agreed. I'll have a talk with Colleen after she's rested. The added stress regarding her crew's situation certainly isn't helping matters. Unity, what's the current status on Nixon's inspection?"

Sly'Kull had woken Nixon a couple hours earlier. Since then, Nixon and one of the four Teeli consuls had been conducting a deck-by-deck inspection of the ship, starting on the lower levels. Since Unity only had access to specific areas on *Cassini*, they didn't have any visuals of what was happening.

U-2 bobbed. "He's currently on Deck 26."

"Have there been any incidents during the inspection?" the Admiral asked.

"No. We've detected elevated heart rates and other signs of stress from the crew, but nothing concerning."

The Admiral nodded. "*Cassini* is well-run. He'll have trouble finding anything to complain about."

"I'll bet that's ticking him off." He'd already confined Muiruri and six other officers to the bridge with four of his security officers watching them. He'd also locked down all bridge systems.

Nixon was treating Montgomery's crew like suspected criminals.

The Admiral stroked a finger along the side of his mug. "The Teeli are wary of making an overt move that would confirm

Montgomery's warning, forcing them to rely on Fleet protocol for intimidation."

"At least for now," Cade added. "I don't expect that to last. The Sovereign is behind every action they're taking. And she isn't a patient person."

One Hundred Nine

"What are you up to?"

Micah grinned at Celia as he led her down *Vengeance's* forward stairs. "If I told you, it wouldn't be a surprise, would it?"

"That's a good thing. I don't like surprises."

She said it, but the light in her beautiful brown eyes indicated otherwise. "You liked our first date. That was full of surprises."

"True."

"And it's your birthday. All surprises are guaranteed to be good."

"Mmm."

The non-committal sound could be interpreted as agreeing or disagreeing, but she was still following him, so he took it as agreement.

He'd sent Birdie ahead of him to make sure everything was in place when they arrived. Convincing members of the crew to participate had been easy. Everyone was dealing with pent-up energy. The people he'd invited had been eager for the outlet he offered.

They might change their tune when they realized the level of skill they were up against.

Five people were waiting in a loose cluster as he and Celia stepped into the cargo area that housed the Cage — Birdie, Kenji, Sweep, Summer, and Fleur. Make that six. Lyon was standing off to the side, trying very hard to look like he was bored, but missing the mark by a nautical mile. Micah hadn't needed to invite him. He'd invited himself.

Micah had offered a spot to Isin as well, but like Aurora and his mom, *Vengeance*'s captain was taking extended watch on the bridge, keeping a close eye on the Ecilam. Micah's dad was in the galley with Kai, Omondi, Hobbes, and Adel, prepping the next crew meal and taking advantage of Celia's absence to bake her birthday cake.

Kenji greeted them with a broad smile. He clapped his hands, the sharp sound echoing in the cavernous space, then rubbed his palms together in a melodramatic display of anticipation. "Our guest of honor has arrived."

Celia looked over the group, analyzing the participants before her gaze came to rest on Micah. "Care to explain?"

"Since it's your birthday, I thought you might enjoy testing the sparring skills of the crew."

Her eyes narrowed, but her lips twitched, too. "Did you tell them what they've signed up for?"

"He did," Sweep answered, his grey eyes solemn. "I saw how quickly you took down the guards on Devries' ship. We're all wondering how you handle yourself when you're unarmed."

Celia's gaze searched the open space behind the group. "Do you have a mat?"

"No, ma'am," Kenji replied. "You aiming to throw us?"

"I've been known to."

Kenji's smile faded quickly as he realized Celia was dead serious. He shifted his weight, looking decidedly uncomfortable. "I'm a lot bigger than you."

"And I'm a lot faster than you."

Kenji blinked, staring at her like she'd just turned fluorescent blue.

This could be very interesting. Micah got the impression Kenji's fighting style took advantage of his greater size and strength, which Micah knew from experience Celia could outmaneuver with ease. "I've sparred with her a lot. And I've hit the deck a lot."

Kenji's brows lifted.

"But we always had a mat," he clarified. Hitting the hard metal of the decking would be a lot more unpleasant.

Fleur stepped forward. "I'm game."

The move surprised him. Fleur was usually the most reserved crewmember on *Vengeance*. In a group setting, she tended to blend into the background, not stand out. He could count on one hand the number of times he'd heard her speak, although he enjoyed hearing her accent, some flavor of European ancestry.

Celia's gaze locked onto her, quietly assessing. "Academy trained?"

"FC agent."

Micah's brows shot up. She used to be a *Fed?*

Celia nodded like it was perfectly normal for a former Federal Coalition agent to be working as a mercenary.

Maybe it was. He'd never given the Feds much thought. Since Earth was the seat of the Union government, it was the one planet where the FC didn't have law enforcement jurisdiction.

"I'm in charge of the timer." Birdie pointed to the comband on her forearm. "Since there are four of them and one of you, I'll time the bouts to ten-minute rounds with ten-minute breaks in between."

Celia's gaze slid to where Lyon was still lurking. "You're not participating?"

Lyon flinched like she'd turned a spotlight on him. Then he gave a nonchalant shrug. "I wasn't asked."

Only because he hadn't been around when Micah asked everyone else. The kid was like a ghost, visible only when he wanted to be seen.

The knowing look in Celia's eyes indicated she suspected the truth. "I'm asking you."

Lyon's gaze moved from Celia to Kenji to Sweep and back. Then he blew out a noisy breath. "Fine. Whatever." He slouched as he shuffled over, like participating was a major imposition for his busy schedule.

"We wouldn't want to inconvenience you," Sweep said, his gaze drilling into the kid.

Kenji's hand covered his mouth, a soft snicker escaping between his fingers.

Lyon straightened, the attitude sliding away like water off a dolphin's back. "I want to do it."

Sweep gave a sharp nod. "Good. Pay attention. You'll go last."

The next hour and a half was pure entertainment for Micah, and judging from the radiant glow emanating from Celia, pure fun for her. He watched with Birdie from outside the Cage as Celia faced her opponents.

Each of her challengers brought a different strategy to the table. Fleur was the most like her physically — impeccably balanced, precise in her movements, like a gymnast or dancer — but without Celia's speed or reaction time. It was beautiful to watch, but Celia clearly had the upper hand the entire time.

Sweep had a similar style to Fleur's attacks, though with a lot more muscle mass behind it. As such, he posed the greatest challenge as an opponent. Sweat was running down both their faces at the end of their ten-minute match.

Her match with Kenji was a hoot. Kenji had a lot of skill, but he'd clearly never faced anyone like Celia before. She did, in fact, flip him — twice. His loud grunt when he hit the second time was followed by a burst of laughter and a big thumbs up aimed in Celia's general direction.

The match with Summer was equally entertaining, not because Summer was a great fighter, but because she kept up a running commentary the whole time. She was quick, which is the only reason she blocked more hits than she took, but she wasn't quick enough or skilled enough to land any decent strikes.

And then there was Lyon. Micah had watched the two of them spar during Lyon's training sessions with Celia, and the kid was a good student. This match, however, started poorly. For the first minute or so, Lyon's acute awareness of his audience was distracting him, forcing missteps he normally would have avoided. Celia handled it like the brilliant teacher she was, using her movements to focus his attention on her until he forgot all about the audience and began to show the competence he'd been developing under her tutelage.

When the timer went off, Kenji let out a piercing whistle. "Dude, my man, you have *skills!*"

Lyon turned his head away as the Cage lifted, but not before Micah caught the curve of a smile that replaced his usual scowl.

"Very impressive," Sweep agreed, glancing at Celia. "You've been working with him?"

"Almost every day." She accepted the towel Micah handed her, pressing it against her face before draping it around her neck.

"That explains why he hasn't been asking *me* for lessons." Kenji slug an arm good-naturedly around Lyon's shoulders. "He found an upgrade."

Lyon glanced uncertainly between Kenji and Celia. "I just..."

"Furthered your education. That's a good thing." Kenji tapped him lightly with his fist before releasing him. "I applaud the initiative." He lowered his voice to a conspiratorial whisper. "Maybe you can teach me some of those moves so I look less like an idiot next time."

Lyon stared at Kenji, mouth open in surprise. "I... could," he said finally.

"Glad to hear it." Kenji winked. "Now, if you'll all excuse me, this delicate flower needs to take a shower." With a jaunty wave, he headed for the stairs.

"Don't use all the hot water!" Summer called after him.

"No promises!" he yelled back.

Summer smirked, turning to Celia. "He should have let you shower first, it being your birthday and all."

"It doesn't matter. Cold showers have never bothered me."

Micah worked really hard to *not* think about what she'd endured that had made such matters trivial to her. If he allowed himself to think about it, his next stop would be the brig, and that was no way to celebrate her birthday.

"It won't actually be cold." Fleur stopped beside them. "The water tanks on *Vengeance* are designed for a much larger crew."

"And I was just kidding about Kenji using up the hot water, anyway," Summer added. "He's become a lot more water conscious since he befriended Marlin."

"Marlin's *Phoenix*'s cook, right?" Birdie asked.

"And resident plumber, yeah."

"Is he anything like Kenji?"

Summer barked a laugh. "Hardly. When I first met him, the word I would have used to describe him is meek. But we've been through a lot together." A dark cloud drifted over her, her hand dropping unconsciously to the outside of her thigh. The same cloud cast a pall over Fleur and Sweep, too. "Marlin came through when it counted most." A husky note thickened her voice. "And he's a lot more confident and outspoken than he used to be." She smiled, banishing the shadows. "You'll like him."

"I'm sure."

"Today's your birthday?"

Every head turned to where Lyon had remained slightly apart from the rest of the group.

Celia dabbed the ends of the towel against her temples. "That's right."

"How old are you?"

Summer scowled at him, but Celia looked amused by the direct, blunt delivery. "Thirty." She tipped her head to the side, studying him. "How old are you?"

For some reason, Lyon tensed up. Then he gave an apathetic shrug. "Seventeen, eighteen, nineteen, I dunno."

"You don't know your birthdate?" Celia asked without judgement.

Lyon looked like he regretted bringing the topic up, although he must have had a reason. "Nobody ever cared, least of all me."

"I see."

The admission made Micah's chest ache. His life had been filled with joyful birthday celebrations. This kid had never had one. He hadn't even had someone who'd told him which day was his to celebrate.

Celia took a step toward Lyon. "So, for all we know, today could be your birthday."

"Yeah, right," Lyon scoffed, but his focus was locked on Celia, a pale glimmer of hope in his dark eyes.

"For most of my life, I didn't bother celebrating my birthday, either. Then three years ago, I met Aurora and Lelindia. It turned out Lelindia's birthday was two days after mine. For her and Aurora..." She glanced at Micah, a sweet smile curving her lips. "And for their families, birthdays are a big deal, something to be honored and celebrated. I thought it was foolish at first, but it's meant more to me than I realized. It's a way of acknowledging that I've lived another year, that I've gained life experience, that I've made a difference in the lives of those around me."

Lyon's eyeroll could have tumbled a mountain.

Celia's tone grew firmer. "It's also a way of showing respect to all those who never had the chance to reach whatever age I'm celebrating."

Lyon stilled.

So did Micah. He'd never looked at it from that perspective. It made him even more grateful for every birthday he'd had the privilege of celebrating.

Celia rested her hand firmly on Lyon's shoulder. "Since this day is just as likely to be your birthday as any other, why not celebrate your birthday with me?"

Lyon looked like he was trying to read the answers to the universe on Celia's face. "I don't know how old I am."

"That's the good part, I guess. You get to decide how old you want to be. Within reason," she added.

Lyon's gaze flicked to Sweep, like he was asking permission.

Sweep nodded. "It's a good idea."

Lyon frowned. "I... don't know how old I want to be."

"If it were me," Summer tapped her chest, "I'd pick eighteen. Then you're officially an adult, just starting the journey ahead of you. Good for a new beginning."

Birdie nodded. "That's what I would have guessed you were if someone asked me. Too young to be in your twenties, but too old to be considered a child."

"I'm not a child," Lyon bit out.

"My point exactly." Birdie pointed a finger at him for emphasis. "Seventeen doesn't fit your vibe. You could go with nineteen, but that might feel less authentic if you're not sure you've lived that long."

His defensiveness passed with the speed of a summer storm. "I guess... eighteen?" He looked around the group for confirmation.

"Your call," Celia reminded him.

"Eighteen," he said with more confidence. "I'm eighteen."

"Then welcome to adulthood, Lyon. Now," she looped her arm through Lyon's and turned to Micah with a dazzling smile, "let's go found out what kind of cake Brendan has baked for us."

One Hundred Ten

Lelindia caught herself bouncing lightly on her toes as she waited with Jonarel and Tehar for the *Rowkclarek* to connect to the *Starhawke*. With a grimace, she lowered her heels to the ground, drawing in a slow breath. *Nothing to be nervous about.*

Her body disagreed.

Jonarel slid his arm behind her back, drawing her against his side. That calmed her fidgeting. Or more accurately, it distracted her from her fidgeting.

She was excited to see Siginal and Daymar. Truly, she was, especially Daymar. According to Tehar, Jonarel's mother had been her champion for years.

But that didn't prevent the tendrils of anxiety that made her fingers twitch and her heart beat a little too fast.

She hadn't seen Daymar since before the dramatic escape from Drakar that had ended in Jonarel's and Tehar's banishment. They'd smoothed things over with Siginal, but a little voice in the back of her head wondered if Daymar would blame her for causing that breach with the clan, for all the pain she must have suffered as a result.

She hoped not. In her happier, more confident moments, she wanted to believe Daymar would be ecstatic to see her, welcoming and accepting her as her son's mate and the mother of her soon-to-be-born grandchild.

Her nervous anticipation had been building ever since she and Jonarel had left their cabin earlier in the day. She'd had trouble focusing during her shift on the bridge, so she'd contacted Celia to wish her a happy birthday. Despite the complication the presence of the Ecilam at Tnaryt's Camp had posed, it sounded like Micah and Iolana were taking every opportunity to celebrate Celia's special day.

A soft *shushing* drew her attention away from her musings and toward the main deck's exterior bulkhead.

The *Rowkclarek* wasn't using the airlock in the cargo bay to dock with the *Starhawke*. Instead, the ships were connecting at the access point near the observation lounge that served as the primary exit when the ship was docked at Drakar.

She was certain her mate would happily explain the technology that made it possible, but at the moment she didn't care.

The hull split, sections disappearing into the overhead and deck as warm, moist air enveloped her. The roughly circular opening in the hull revealed a glimpse of the *Rowkclarek*'s jungle-like interior behind Siginal and Daymar.

Her pulse leapt like a high jumper when Daymar's golden-eyed gaze met hers, her heart stuttering. She couldn't get a bead on the emotions she saw there.

Daymar's long strides carried her swiftly to Jonarel. She buried her face against his broad shoulder and wrapped her arms around him with enough force that Lelindia heard his spine pop. He held her just as tightly, his cheek pressed against her hair.

The image brought a lump to Lelindia's throat. She looked away before her emotions could get the better of her.

Siginal greeted Tehar, but his gaze kept sliding to Jonarel and Daymar. When they finally separated, he stepped aside so Daymar could greet Tehar, while he embraced Jonarel.

The look on Daymar's face as she murmured soft words to Tehar built pressure in Lelindia's chest. She dropped her gaze to the deck, staring at the patterns in the wood and trying not to count each passing second. Then Jonarel's booted feet turned in her direction.

Her heart thumped as she lifted her head.

Jonarel's golden eyes shone bright as the sun as he clasped his mother's hand, drawing Daymar to her. "Solna." His deep baritone vibrated with emotion. "I have found my checana."

Lelindia was vibrating right along with him. To her surprise, she spotted moisture coating Daymar's eyes — an extremely rare occurrence for a Kraed. Predictably, it triggered the same reaction in her — not a rare occurrence. Twin tracks of moisture slid down her cheeks as Daymar pulled her into a fierce hug, taking care not to press on Lelindia's rounded belly.

"My checala." She stroked a hand over Lelindia's hair. "You have brought me such joy."

Lelindia's eyes drifted closed as the gentle caress told her everything she needed to know. "Thank you, Daymar."

"*Solna*," Daymar corrected gently, leaning back to gaze into her eyes. "I am solna to you now." Her gaze dropped lower. "And I will be solnasheek to your precious child."

The trickle of tears became a river. Lelindia swiped at them with the back of her hand. "Sorry. I get emotional these days."

Daymar captured her hand in hers. "Your heart is full. This is nothing to hide."

She still felt like an idiot as her tears dripped off her chin, pattering like rain on her round belly. As soon as Daymar released her, she swiped at them again, but Siginal swooped in a moment later, engulfing her.

"Checala." He held her loosely, not exerting any extra pressure, like he was wrapping her in a giant warm blanket.

It was cozy, but it reminded her of how cautious Jonarel had been about hugging her when he first learned she was pregnant. Like one wrong move would break her.

Siginal's next comment confirmed it. "You and your little one are thriving?"

Raehn chose that moment to give an enthusiastic kick.

"Oof!"

Siginal pulled back, looking at her in alarm.

Lelindia chuckled, resting a hand on her belly. "Definitely thriving. I think she's eager to put in her appearance."

"She is moving?"

"Frequently."

His large hand hovered uncertainly over hers. "May I?"

"Of course. She likes when people say hello."

Siginal licked his lips, his hand lowering with infinite tenderness to rest against her belly. "Hello, little one."

Raehn didn't react.

"Raehn," Lelindia whispered softly. "Her name is Raehn Clarek."

Raehn gave another energetic kick, as she often did when her name was spoken.

Siginal's gaze shot to hers, a riot of emotions chasing across his face. He swallowed audibly. "You gave her our clan name?"

The tears started again at his look of exquisite joy. "She *is* clan. And Suulh. Her name reflects both."

"Raehn is a Suulh name?" Daymar asked, moving beside her.

"Yes. It's a type of tree on Feylahn."

"A tree." Siginal nodded in approval. "The name is well chosen." His gaze lowered slowly to where his hand still rested on her belly. "Hello, Raehn Clarek."

Kick, kick.

His eyes widened.

"She responds to her name. That's how I chose it. When my mom and Libra were suggesting Suulh names, that's the one she reacted to."

"That is... unusual," Daymar commented, concern creasing her forehead.

"Maybe for the Kraed. But from what my mom and Libra have told me, this is pretty typical for the Suulh. Raehn's growth is accelerated, of course, because I'm a Nedale and because she's half-Kraed. She's also received some energy boosts from Aurora. I guarantee she'll be born strong and full of energy."

Raehn emphasized that with another kick.

"Clearly." Siginal's brows puckered in an expression she recognized very well. Jonarel looked exactly like that when he was worrying about how to keep her and Raehn safe.

Now she'd have *two* overprotective Kraed males fussing over her. She might need to start scheduling alone time now.

One Hundred Eleven

Nat laced her hands together over her stomach and leaned back in the pilot's chair. She was supposed to be sleeping, but her sleep schedule was so jacked up that she'd spent what felt like hours staring at the mural in her cabin before giving up and coming to the bridge.

Gavin had been on watch. Rather than leaving when she'd arrived, he'd moved to the co-pilot's chair.

She appreciated the company. She was feeling at sixes and sevens right now. His steady calm smoothed the rough edges. "Anything interesting to report?"

"Depends on how you define interesting. Three more civilian ships have shown up in the past four hours."

That snapped her forward. "Three? Are they bounty hunters?"

He nodded. "Fleur confirmed it."

A swear word fell from her lips. "What about the first one that showed up? The *Zenobia*."

"Still at the station."

An unpleasant squiggle slithered through her stomach. Avoiding the Fleet and Feds was something she was used to doing after years of smuggling. Avoiding bounty hunters was not. "Does Itorye know?"

"Alec notified her."

Clearly she wasn't too concerned since she wasn't on the bridge. Nat took some comfort in that.

"There's something else you'll want to see." Gavin tapped his console, bringing up a news feed on the vid monitor. "Montgomery's message got picked up by news channels."

"The first confirmed sighting of one of the two ships that blasted out of ESS-1 a month ago was recorded at the Fleet science station Eridani Duo yesterday." The image of the female journalist was replaced by a grainy video of *Gladiator* flying away from Eridani Duo.

"We have received unconfirmed reports that the ship may have played a role in the abduction of Fleet Captain Colleen Montgomery of the Discovery-class ship Cassini." An image of Montgomery, dressed in a Fleet uniform and looking very intimidating, appeared on the monitor. *"A video broadcast yesterday appears to be from Captain Montgomery, however, our team has been unable to confirm its authenticity. In the video, Montgomery made several claims regarding the Teeli."* The image changed again, this time playing the section of Montgomery's broadcast where she identified the Teeli as conquerors working with the Setarips, and warned of their ability to manipulate through touch.

Nat licked her suddenly dry lips.

"We have been unable to reach Admiral Nixon or the Teeli Embassy for comment. We did receive the following statement from President Yeoh's office." The image switched to a typed message. *"It is the responsibility of the President to look into any credible threat to the safety and security of the Union. As such, President Yeoh is using all resources at her disposal to investigate this matter."*

The image switched back to the journalist. *"We would like to remind our viewers that Admiral Schreiber and Captain Hawke are fugitives who were on trial for treason. They are considered extremely dangerous. If you have any information regarding their whereabouts, or the whereabouts of their known companions, contact the Freedom and Security hotline at—"*

Gavin paused the video, then pivoted his chair to face her, his expression expectant.

Her brain buzzed with the implications. "Is this really happening?" She gnawed on the inside of her cheek. "There are people in power who are openly investigating the Teeli?"

He tipped his head to the side, his chair giving a creak. "You sound like you don't believe it."

"I believe it, I just don't.... *believe* it." She twirled her hand, like that would somehow clear up the confusion. "I don't believe public opinion will be swayed by this. The majority aren't on our side."

"Ah." He nodded sagely. "You may be right. But I prefer to think we're seeing the first fissures in the Teeli's slick façade."

"Maybe." She wanted him to be right. "Is that the only news feed that picked it up?"

"No, but it's the most factual presentation. The others have been speculating whether Montgomery was in cahoots with the Admiral all along, or whether this is an elaborate distraction from the Admiral and Captain Hawke while they plan their attack."

Nat wrinkled her nose. "In other words, sticking to the line they've been spewing ever since Aurora and the Admiral were arrested."

"Basically."

"And now we have bounty hunters in the mix, too." She used the tip of her toe to slowly swivel her chair in sync with her thoughts. "Not that they'll be able to find us as long as we have the Yruf."

"And they aren't looking for *Phoenix*. Or *Vengeance*," Gavin pointed out.

"True." But the Fleet had seen both ships in the vicinity, *Vengeance* at Zeta Tucanae, under questionable circumstances, and *Phoenix* at Hydra One. They'd need to be careful about where they put in an appearance next.

One Hundred Twelve

Lelindia led the group to the observation lounge, where Kire, Kelly, Knox, and Isabeau were waiting to greet Siginal and Daymar.

The discussion that followed took most of an hour. Everyone took turns filling Siginal and Daymar in on the events that had transpired in the past few weeks, including the current status of the two missions and the background on all the new players.

Siginal had taken the news of Aurora's absence with a lot more grace than he'd shown in the past. Maybe he was finally accepting that Aurora could take care of herself. Or maybe it was the knowledge that Libra was with her.

But Lelindia suspected the real reason was that he had a fleet of Kraed ships in Teeli space that he could send to Tnaryt's Camp on a moment's notice.

She wasn't about to question it. She much preferred rational-leader Siginal to flying-off-the-handle Siginal. "Have you learned anything new regarding the Teeli forces?"

Siginal's lips pulled away from his teeth in a snarl. "Several freighters have crossed the border into Fleet space recently, likely transporting the Teeli Nixon is disseminating throughout the Fleet." He said *Nixon* as a swear word. "Yendar tracked a supply ship from Feylahn, which delivered its cargo to three cruisers in a nearby system. One of our ships is monitoring the cruisers. If they leave the system, they will be tagged with tracking beacons. Yendar has yet to locate the carrier you encountered, or the system the Teeli are using to build their ships."

"I seriously doubt they only have three cruisers." Knox rested his forearms on the table, his gaze shifting briefly to Lelindia. "Even if the Sovereign is counting on taking control of the majority of Fleet ships, I'd expect the Teeli to have a much larger arsenal of their own. They've clearly been planning this from the moment they engineered their inclusion in the Union."

"Agreed." Siginal nodded.

"Have your ships encountered any Setarips?" Unity asked through the ship's speakers.

Siginal and Daymar both looked up.

Curiosity lit Daymar's eyes. "You must be Unity."

"Yes we are! We're very pleased to meet you!"

"And I, you." Daymar's gaze flicked to where Tehar sat to her left. "You must be quite extraordinary for my daughter to have allowed you to join her on the *Starhawke*."

"They are," Tehar assured her. "Unity and the Yruf have much they can teach us."

Siginal harrumphed from his seat between Jonarel and Knox. "Yendar reported seeing two Ecilam ships, one at Feylahn and the other with the three cruisers, but they did not remain for long."

"Did you track them?" Unity asked.

"We did not."

"Oh." Unity sounded as disappointed as a child whose popsicle had just flopped onto the dirt.

"It has been many years since our people have encountered Setarips. Those interactions have always been violent." Siginal's lips thinned. "Our knowledge of the Setarips is limited, particularly their technology." His gaze hardened as he stared at the speaker. "Tagging the Setarips' ships risked the detection of our ships."

"We understand. The Ecilam have laid traps to try to detect us, too. They can be..." The silence stretched out.

Lelindia suspected Unity was struggling to find a non-offensive word that was also accurate. "Sneaky?" she offered.

"Yes! Sneaky. They can be sneaky."

Yesterday she wouldn't have been nearly so charitable. But knowing about the sub-q transmitters, and the death and destruction they caused, made her feel more compassion for the Ecilam.

"Then I guess for now we wait." Kire folded his hands on the table. "See which of our three targets — the Teeli, Nixon, or the Ecilam — makes a move first."

"In the meantime..." Lelindia turned to Daymar. "Tehar made a 3D projection recording of Jonarel's and my mating ceremony. Would you like to see it?"

An eruption of what looked suspiciously like rage burned red in Daymar's golden eyes, making Lelindia jerk back. But it cooled just as quickly as it had appeared.

Daymar clasped Lelindia's hand in hers in a grip tight enough to leave a mark. "I would be honored, checala."

"Okaaay," she said slowly, searching Daymar's expression. What had triggered what she'd seen? Had she imagined a reaction that wasn't there? Or had she misread it?

She glanced at Tehar, who was also watching Daymar with a touch of concern. Okay, she wasn't crazy. Tehar had seen something, too. "Tehar, can you set up the recording?"

"Of course." Tehar's image blinked out. A moment later the tables at the edge of the room began to shift, several of them sliding beneath the subfloor.

As everyone rose, Kire and Kelly moved toward the doors to the corridor. "We're going to head up to the bridge," Kire informed her.

Knox turned to Daymar. "Do you mind if Isabeau and I stay and watch with you? We weren't here for the ceremony."

The corners of Daymar's mouth tightened, her jaw flexing. She shot a hard look in Siginal's direction. "Of course you are welcome."

He flinched.

Suddenly, the rage Lelindia had glimpsed in Daymar's eyes made sense. And made her wonder if suggesting they watch the projected recording had been a colossal mistake.

One Hundred Thirteen

"There's Maceen's group." Libra pointed to the red circles on *Starlet*'s display that represented the group of Ecilam sweeping through the jungle just ahead of the shuttle's flight path. *Starlet* hovered over an area Maceen's group had already passed through. "You ready, Unity?"

"We were born ready."

Libra's lips twitched and Brendan grinned.

"Opening the storage compartment." She tapped the command that would allow Unity to exit the shuttle.

They'd collected U-P from one of the Yruf ships on the surface, using *Starlet*'s camouflage to shield all movement from the orbiting Ecilam ship. Unity had tucked themselves into the storage area underneath the shuttle so they could enter and exit without being observed from above.

"We're on our way!" Unity chirped through *Starlet*'s speakers. "Thanks for the lift."

"You're welcome," Brendan answered. "See you soon."

Libra sent the command to close the compartment, her gaze sliding to the west, where the planet's star was sinking toward the horizon.

They still had at least an hour before sunset. Tersinis' transport had moved a few hours ago, but hadn't returned to the orbiting ship. Instead, it had landed at the location where Maceen's and Helotis' groups would eventually meet up again when they completed their half-circle sweeps from the point where they'd started this morning.

"We've made contact," Unity informed them. "Successfully attached to one of the Ecilam. Working our way toward Maceen."

Brendan nudged the shuttle forward, silently tracking the group. "Any indication they're aware of you?"

"Of course not!"

Brendan chuckled. "Sorry. Just checking."

Libra glanced at him. He looked so calm and relaxed, totally in his element at the controls of the shuttle. Unlike her. She was sitting on a bed of pinecones. She tried not to fidget, but it wasn't easy. This whole situation was messing with her head. And she didn't have anything to do until Unity returned.

So she focused on the gorgeous man seated beside her.

"You're staring."

"Enjoying the view."

He met her gaze. "So am I."

A shiver danced over her skin. "Do you think being together again will ever become commonplace?" She couldn't imagine it, not after being separated for nearly three decades. A hundred years with Brendan wouldn't be enough.

His blue eyes darkened. "Never."

Her heart fluttered. His effect on her certainly hadn't abated in the intervening years. If anything, it had grown stronger. "Just so you know, I'd kiss you right now, but I don't want to be responsible for you crashing again." She still felt a twinge of guilt at the damage her shield had done to Romeo, even if the crash had brought Brendan into her life.

Now his eyes looked the same color as his navy shirt. But his mouth curled at the corners. "I might have a suggestion for how we could solve that dilemma after we drop Unity off at Tersinis' transport."

"Oh, really?" She batted her lashes at him, making him laugh. But her body was heating up by the second. "Sounds like fun."

"Glad you think so. I'll—"

"All done! We're heading back."

They both focused forward. "Compartment open," Libra informed Unity.

"Be right there."

It took U-P a couple minutes to reach them. After they secured themselves back in the storage area, Brendan guided *Starlet* to Helotis' group.

"This group is more clustered together, with two outliers," she warned them. Six of the Ecilam were sweeping through a narrow gap between a stream on the left and a large rock protrusion on the right. The other two had broken off from the group to scale the rockface and search the summit.

"We can handle it," Unity assured her. "Sit tight."

Libra gave a soft snort. For a being who didn't have a biological body, Unity was getting a real handle on Galish vernacular.

The Ecilam moved forward at a steady but relatively slow pace, spreading out as they reached a thicket of trees half a kilometer ahead. Helotis was easy to pick out from the group, both because of her size and her shuffling stride.

Libra glanced at Brendan. "Is Helotis in as much pain as it looks like?" On the night of the Ecilam attack at Stoneycroft, she hadn't cared whether the Setarips invading her home lived or died. She'd been fighting for her survival, and the lives of those she loved.

But that didn't mean she wanted the Ecilam, or anyone for that matter, to suffer. Which is why she had very strong opinions about the person who had intentionally allowed their injuries to remain untreated.

Brendan nodded, his jaw tightening. "She's in a lot of pain. All the walking is making it worse, but her fear and desperation are keeping her moving. She's terrified they won't find the Etah. Tersinis and Maceen share that fear."

Terror wasn't a word she would have ever associated with the Ecilam. Their victims, yes, but not them. Ruthless, vicious, and cunning were a far better fit. But they'd met their match in the Teeli, falling prey to their manipulation and the Sovereign's iron fist.

"We've attached to all of them," Unity said, breaking the heavy silence. "We're heading back to *Starlet*. Only Tersinis left to tag."

"And the two slaves," Libra added quietly. From the moment she'd seen them, the urge to snatch them from the clutches of the Ecilam had smoldered under her skin like a low-grade fever.

"Oh! We hadn't thought of that." Unity sounded alarmed. "You think they have transmitters, too?"

"We have to assume they do, given the situation."

"Then we'll look for an opportunity to tag them, too."

"Thank you." Regardless of whether they were Human or Suulh, they needed to be freed from the Ecilam *and* the Sovereign.

Thinking about the Ecilam and the slaves had effectively killed the vibe she and Brendan had generated earlier, something her empathic mate picked up on after dropping U-P off at Tersinis' transport.

"Ready to head back to *Vengeance*?" he asked softly.

She sighed, gazing at the gathering gloom outside the viewport. It matched the darkness creeping around the edges of her thoughts. "I suppose so."

Damn the Sovereign.

She wrestled with those thoughts as Brendan guided *Starlet* out of the planet's atmosphere. When the starfield filled the viewport she searched for the black ship. And didn't see it. "Is the Ecilam ship gone?"

"No." Brendan altered *Starlet's* course, sweeping to the left. "It's concealed behind the Yruf ships to block their view of *Vengeance.*"

A quick glance at his display gave an indication of what he was describing. An array of green circles designating the Yruf ships formed a curtain in between the red circle for the Ecilam ship and the blue circle for *Vengeance.*

As the shuttle continued its curving path, *Vengeance* took shape ahead of them, blocky and solid and grey. Libra instinctively pinpointed Aurora's and Micah's locations on the ship. Micah was with Celia and several crewmembers, likely in the galley. Aurora was on the same deck but toward the aft with Jake.

Brendan guided *Starlet* into the inverted canyon that led to *Vengeance's* bay. He made the task look easy, landing the shuttle inside the belly of the beast like a bird alighting on a rhinoceros' back, but she knew it took skill to maneuver in the tight quarters, even with a shuttle as technologically advanced as *Starlet.*

"You're staring again," he commented as he powered down the shuttle's systems.

"Can't help it. You fascinate me."

His lips curved in a smile that made her breath hitch. Unfastening his harness, he slid to his knees beside her chair and cupped her cheek in his hand. "Good to know."

He claimed her mouth with assurance, well aware he'd be welcomed. And he was right. The taste of him on her lips, the sensual glide of his tongue made her shiver with delight.

"Libra," he murmured against her mouth before delving deep again.

How had she existed without this for nearly three decades? It was a wonder she hadn't turned to stone. Or dust.

With a groan, he pulled back, his breathing uneven. "Now I'm regretting not finding a quiet spot to set down the shuttle for a while."

So was she. But she probably wouldn't have been able to shake the icky feeling the presence of the Ecilam induced. She brushed her thumb along his cheek, a wave of emotion sweeping over her. "I'm so glad you're here."

He rested his hand over hers, turning to place a kiss on her palm. "So am I."

She brushed her lips over his, lightly this time, a kiss filled with gratitude and promise. "I guess we should check in with Aurora."

"We should." He rose to his feet, pulling her up with him.

Aurora was in the infirmary with Jake, bent over a 3D projection model, U-1 hovering beside her. She glanced up. "Unity said everything went smoothly."

Libra nodded. "It did. How have things been going here?"

Aurora gestured to the model. "Unity and the Yruf engineers have been working on a mock-up of the sub-q transmitters. Unity's been able to provide insights on the design now that they're in direct contact with the Ecilam and can study the devices up close. We're testing theories for preventing the transmitters from activating or stopping the release of the toxin if they do."

"What about removing them?" She didn't trust any device conceived by the Sovereign to remain inert.

"The Yruf are working on that, too," Jake said, leaning back against the counter. "Since their biology is very similar to the Ecilam's, Ahle is investigating methods for safe extraction. However, even if he finds one and Unity can neutralize the transmitters to enable the procedure, the Ecilam would need to be unconscious first."

That was a lot of ifs. "How do we pull that off?"

Aurora tapped her ear. "The ultra-low frequency the Yruf designed to subdue them before. But we need one of the transports to return to the warship so Unity can attach to the two remaining Ecilam."

Libra glanced at U-1. "How will you manage that? You used U-P to handle that task on the surface."

"And U-P would handle it on the warship, too," Unity replied. "We're going to sneak U-P onboard the transport and then onto the ship."

One Hundred Fourteen

"Are you ready?" Lelindia studied Daymar, who was standing with her, Tehar, and Isabeau in the corridor outside the observation lounge.

She'd wanted Daymar to experience the 3D projection of the mating ceremony as though she was a participant, starting with the private moments in the corridor where Lelindia had gathered with her attendants on the day. Siginal and Knox were with Jonarel in the observation lounge, waiting for the projection to play through to the point where the doors opened and her entourage entered.

Unfortunately, Daymar's hands opened and closed like snapping turtles, her gaze burning a hole through the closed lounge doors.

She'd never seen Daymar so upset. It made her heart ache. Why couldn't things have been different? Daymar should have been present for this event, rather than an observer after the fact.

Daymar's gaze met hers, a crease forming between her dark brows.

"We don't have to do this," Lelindia said gently.

"Yes, we do." The crease deepened, a visible sign of her emotional pain. "I want to see your ceremony." Her gaze rested on

Tehar before returning to Lelindia. "But I regret that my mate's actions prevented me from being here with you."

And there it was, the truth. "You're ticked off at him."

"I am furious." The admission seemed to unload a burden. Her demeanor settled. "I understand that he was thinking of the clan when he banished Tehar and Jonarel. He believed his decision was correct. But he neglected to consult me before he took action, to consider alternatives, other ways of looking at the problem. It cost me an experience I have desired to be a part of since the moment I realized the depth of Jonarel's feelings for you."

Lelindia blinked, the enormity of what Daymar had just shared washing over her. "How did you know? Jonarel didn't."

Daymar's expression softened. "It was obvious even while you were at the Academy. When the two of you came to meals with us, he would seat himself beside Aurora, as expected, but whenever you spoke, and particularly when you laughed, his entire focus would shift to you, like leaves opening to the sun."

She frowned. "I never noticed that."

"Of course not. You were intent on *not* watching him when he was looking at you. You only allowed yourself to gaze at him when he was focused on Aurora."

A flush climbed up her neck. "It was that obvious?"

"To me and Tehar, yes. To Jonarel and Siginal? No."

"And here I thought I was being discreet."

"You were. But a mother knows her children."

"And I knew my sibling," Tehar added. "Just as you always knew Aurora would be better matched with Cade."

"I guess I did, although I always assumed that was wishful thinking on my part because of my feelings for Jonarel."

"It is a parent's greatest wish." Daymar's gaze moved between Lelindia and Tehar. "That their children find others in this galaxy who cherish them for who they are."

Her throat tightened. "I love him more than I ever imagined possible."

"I know." Daymar rested her hand on Lelindia's cheek. "I cherish the day you came into our lives."

The waterworks were starting up again. She blinked rapidly, not wanting to turn into a blubbering mess before the projection got going. She only had three handkerchiefs in her pockets, which probably wouldn't be close to enough.

She glanced at Isabeau to distract herself. And discovered she was watching them with a look of yearning. "You know you're also part of this crazy blended family Aurora and I have gathered, right?"

Isabeau's eyes widened. Clearly she hadn't expected to be caught staring. "I... guess."

"No guessing. It's a done deal. Knox is like our big brother, so now you have sisters."

Isabeau didn't seem to know how to respond to that, either.

"Just keep it in mind," Lelindia added with a smile, turning to Tehar. "Ready to start?"

Tehar nodded.

They all faced the corridor as a 3D projection of her, her mom, Aurora, Libra, and Celia appeared.

Daymar inhaled sharply, one hand going to her throat, the other clutching Lelindia's arm. "You wore the dress I made you."

So much for containing the tears. She yanked out a handkerchief, dabbing furiously at her eyes.

"Breathe, Lee-Lee."

Even in the projection, Aurora was giving her good advice. She inhaled, matching her movements to her projection counterpart. Watching herself was a little freaky, which helped her keep her emotions in check.

Aurora turned. "What's bothering you?"

"It's just... I've wanted this... daydreamed about this for so long... It's irrational, but I'm afraid if I walk through those doors, I'll wake up and lose it all."

Daymar's grip on her arm tightened. "You will never lose us," she whispered fiercely, her gaze riveted on the projection. "You are clan."

"I know," she whispered back. It had been a rocky path to get here, but she had no doubt Jonarel's family – *her* family – would go to the ends of the galaxy and back for her.

The procession moved forward, the observation lounge doors opening in tandem with the projection. The four of them followed.

Daymar sighed as she entered, her gaze taking in the way the projection transformed the lounge to mimic a section of the Clarek compound. The result in the replay was no less stunning than the original, complete with massive denglar trees and thousands of twinkling lights.

But it was Jonarel's projection, standing in the center of the room, that caught Lelindia's eye. Stellar light, he was beautiful. She remembered thinking at the time that he looked like a being out of a fantasy novel. But she knew how very, *very* real he was.

"Lelindia?"

His projection said her name, but she was already seeking out the real-life version, locating him with Siginal and Knox near the door to the galley.

Holding her gaze, he strode toward her, all fluid grace and rippling muscle. She was pretty sure the projection was still playing, but all she saw was her mate. He was clearly in the same state, completely ignoring their audience as he pulled her into his arms. She went willingly, pressing her cheek against the solid muscle of his chest and listening to the slightly elevated beat of his heart.

He rested his cheek against her hair, both of them facing the projection that was, in fact, still playing the Suulh part of the ceremony.

Siginal had moved closer to Daymar, but she stood so Isabeau and Knox were between them. Clearly Siginal was aware of his mate's ire, but hadn't figured out how to handle it.

"Most honored guests, the givers of life to my checana. My sister Tehar and I welcome you on behalf of Clan Clarek. As this moment comes at a time when the rest of my clan cannot be with us, the brother of my heart, Kire, and my Starhawke family have consented to serve as representatives of my clan."

Daymar's eyes shot daggers at Siginal, who flinched.

Yep, he definitely knew he was in trouble.

"Your presence here is an honor and blessing. The path we have walked has been challenging and fraught with danger, yet through it all, my checana has been a light in the darkness for me, even when I did not realize it."

Jonarel's arms tightened around her, his hand stroking her back.

"I have never received a gift equal to the one you have bestowed upon me, the life blood that flows in Lelindia's veins." He spread his arms, palms up, and sank to his knees.

And she lost it. Within seconds, the front of his tunic was wet with her tears as a surge of overwhelming joy forced them out.

His lips pressed against her hair, his breath warming her. "My checana... my life," he said in sync with the projection.

She clung to him, her heart so full she thought it might burst. "You are mine," she whispered for his ears only, the same words she'd mouthed to him during the ceremony.

His rumbling purr surrounded her, triggering Raehn's energy field. The combination elicited a hiccupping laugh from her. "Raehn loves her daddy." She caught one of his hands in hers, drawing it to her belly so he could feel the cool touch of their daughter's energy field.

His purr grew louder.

Would Raehn inherit that ability from him? She hoped so. It would be another link to her Kraed heritage.

With her focus on Raehn's energy and Jonarel's purr, she failed to notice the projection had ended until she heard Daymar's soft, "Thank you, Tehar."

Daymar had shifted closer to her and Jonarel. She stood stiffly, facing them and Tehar, her back to Siginal. Knox and Isabeau were glancing surreptitiously between the two with worried frowns. Siginal looked like he'd just been kicked in the chest. He stared at Daymar with thinly veiled longing.

A pang hit her. She hadn't meant to expand the schism between them, even if the feud had started when Siginal banished Jonarel and Tehar.

The rigidity of Daymar's stance softened as her gaze swept over them, her eyes regaining their sparkle. "My checalas. *Pirareath.*"

She recognized the Kraed pair bond blessing from when their bond had first been announced. Which is why she wasn't surprised when Jonarel cupped her cheek in his hand and gave her a tender kiss, the traditional response for the blessing.

"Pirareath," Siginal echoed, wiping the forlorn look from his face.

Jonarel kissed her again before facing his parents. "Lelindia and I have a request. Will you remain with us to celebrate the birth of our daughter when she arrives?"

Right question. Daymar lit up like a star. "I would be honored."

Lelindia hid her wince at the pointed *I* in that sentence.

"As would I," Siginal replied, taking a step closer to his mate. "We are eager to meet her."

Jonarel's arms tightened around her. "So are we."

"I think she's got us all beat," Lelindia added as Raehn gave a particularly strong kick. "She's going to be an active child."

"I would expect nothing less." Daymar moved closer to her, which put her farther from Siginal. "Jonarel was an active infant."

"Oh, really?" It hadn't occurred to her that having Daymar around would open up a treasure trove of information regarding Jonarel's youth.

"Yes. Even as a newborn, he tried to crawl out of the *ruc grayyon* – the carrying pouch I transported him in. He wanted to see and hear everything. After I adapted the design so he could experience his surroundings without crawling out, our outings together became a source of great joy."

How had Siginal ever believed Jonarel would blindly follow the predetermined path he'd set for him regarding his future and his choice of mate? Daymar had noticed all the signs Siginal had missed. It was a wonder Jonarel hadn't rebelled sooner.

"When do you expect Raehn's birth?" Daymar asked.

"Not for another three weeks. However, the *Starhawke* will be mobile in about five or six days. Jonarel and I have been discussing whether we want to be on Azaana or Drakar for Raehn's birth."

That got Siginal's attention. "You wish to return to our space?" The furtive look he shot Daymar indicated that might have been another bone of contention between them.

"We would. It feels right to be with our people. I was thinking maybe you could come with us to Azaana?" Which, she realized, is where she'd been secretly imagining bringing Raehn into the world, surrounded by a rainbow of Suulh energy. "Then we could travel together to Drakar to meet with the clan leaders."

"Of course you should be with the Suulh," Daymar said with more force than necessary. "You are one of *their* leaders."

Okay, that was another pointed dig at Siginal.

"If Siginal cannot spare the time, I will remain on the *Starhawke* with you."

Ouch. Daymar was spitting barbs left and right. Apparently watching the mating ceremony had put a match to the tinder of her rage at her mate.

"There is no need for that." Siginal probably meant it to sound decisive, but it came out more as a plea. "Our family is the priority."

Daymar's jaw flexed, like she was holding in the retort she would have made if she and Siginal were alone.

Lelindia could easily imagine what that comment might be, considering Signal had cast Jonarel and Tehar from the clan without consulting Daymar. It fit with his personality — creating a big spectacle — but it had come back to bite him in the ass. She couldn't imagine Jonarel ever doing something similar to Raehn, but if he did, she'd go nuclear.

Signal was lucky he was still in one piece.

One Hundred Fifteen

"What are we going to do about your parents?" Lelindia set her shoes beside the couch in the front room of hers and Jonarel's cabin and swung her feet up onto the middle cushion with a sigh. She didn't suffer the aches and pains that accompanied pregnancy for most women, but she was still carrying around unbalanced extra mass. Reclining on the couch had become one of her small pleasures.

Jonarel's gaze swept over her from head to bare toes, then in one fluid motion, he slid his hands under her feet, settled onto the middle cushion, and propped her feet in his lap. "You are concerned by their behavior toward each other?"

She moaned as he pressed the pad of his thumb into the arch of her foot. "Yes," she replied, both in answer and as encouragement. "Your mom is seriously ticked off."

"I know." He continued the steady pressure, his thumb gliding down to her heel and back. "I had hoped spending time with us would ease the tension between them. Instead, it appears to have reinforced it."

"I had the same thought. I didn't pick up on her anger when they first arrived, but it really came out when we showed her the projection of our mating ceremony. Mmm." She let her head loll back as his talented fingers worked the tight places at the base of her toes.

"When she wasn't glaring at him, she acted like he didn't exist. I don't think she looked at him once during dinner. He was miserable."

Jonarel's hands stilled, his strong fingers wrapping around her feet like she'd suddenly become a lifeline. His golden gaze was deeply troubled. "I cannot imagine the pain I would feel if you were to act that way toward me."

"Don't worry. I've never been the type to freeze someone out. I prefer a direct approach."

His grip tightened, worry lines creasing his brow. "You are certain?"

He was really freaked out about the idea.

She sat forward as much as Raehn's bulk would allow. He met her halfway, his breath feathering across her face. She threaded one hand into his thick hair and used the other to stroke his cheek. "Jonarel, I can't imagine any reality in which you would turn against Raehn the way Siginal turned against you and Tehar."

His golden eyes flared like liquid fire. "Never."

Because Jonarel wasn't like Siginal. His worldview was much broader, his heart much bigger.

She coaxed him closer so she could place a tender kiss on his delectable lips. "But if you did," she murmured against his mouth, "I'd be telling you exactly how I felt — loudly — until you corrected your mistake. And did a lot of groveling."

As she'd hoped, his lips curved against hers in a smile. "A lot of groveling," he agreed, capturing her mouth with his.

Stars, her mate knew how to turn her inside out with the slightest touch. But this discussion was important.

She moved her hand to his muscled chest, pushing gently.

He broke the kiss immediately, his gaze questioning.

"We need a game plan," she admonished with playful seriousness. "Then we can have fun."

That wicked smile returned, stealing her breath. "Yes, checana."

He resumed the massage of her feet, but his touch had a more sensual feel than it had previously. Or maybe that was just the way her body was interpreting it. His smiles always made her want to remove every stitch of clothing from his beautiful body and feast on what she'd uncovered.

With effort, she dragged her attention back to the topic at hand. "How have your parents dealt with disagreements in the past?"

He frowned. "When my father has upset her, he has asked for her forgiveness and she has given it. That is our way, as you experienced when he struck you."

Not a fun moment, but a pivotal one. It had shaken up the dynamic between her and Jonarel, setting them on the path that led to them admitting their feelings for each other. Siginal hadn't meant to backhand her — it had been an accident during a heated argument — but she had a vivid memory of him sinking to his knees in front of her, hands out in supplication, asking her forgiveness for his transgression. "Do couples ever not give forgiveness to each other when asked?"

His frown deepened. "Our culture depends on the harmony of the whole. My mother's behavior is... unusual."

"So was your father's. Banishments in your culture are extremely rare, aren't they?"

"Yes. It is a difficult decision that typically involves the entire clan."

"Yet Siginal acted unilaterally in the heat of the moment. He should have expected pushback from Daymar."

Jonarel nodded, his expression pensive.

"I can provide insights." Tehar's image materialized at the far end of the couch, seated facing Lelindia, one leg tucked under her. "I have spoken with Rowk."

"What did he say?" As Siginal's Nirunoc brother, Rowk knew Siginal better than anyone.

"He has observed our parents' interactions since our father banished us." Tehar's gaze rested on Jonarel. "Our mother did not take the news of his actions well. She accused our father of overstepping his authority, and violating the terms of their pair bond."

Jonarel flinched.

"Terms?" Her own mating ceremony with Jonarel had been a blend of Suulh and Kraed, but she didn't recall any talk of terms.

Jonarel cleared his throat, his voice husky. "He pledged himself as her protector, to keep her from harm."

"And by banishing us, *he* harmed her, deeply." Pain etched Tehar's face. "She has been living with her birth clan ever since."

Jonarel's eyes widened. "She left Clan Clarek?"

This was not good.

"Not officially. But Rowk informed me she has been talking to Harvan about accepting the four of us — five," she corrected, glancing at Lelindia's belly, "into Clan Terfeli."

Lelindia's heart thumped against her ribcage. This gave a whole new spin on the warm greeting she'd received at the Kraed Embassy from the members of Clan Terfeli. "Has Siginal not apologized to her?"

"Not at first." Tehar's lips pressed tight as a bow. "He refused to reconsider his judgment against us. He told Rowk he could not be a weak leader, one who showed favoritism to his own children. He also used our dramatic escape from Drakar as the reason he did not consult the council. Rowk tried to sway him, but to no avail. Our mother's departure from the compound made him even less willing to change his stance."

Jonarel tipped his head back, staring at the overhead as he let out a weary sigh.

"You said not at first," Lelindia pointed out. "When did he apologize to Daymar?"

"After the *ginlemanect* with the other clan leaders. He traveled with Harvan to the Terfeli Compound."

"It didn't go well?" she prompted when Tehar didn't continue.

"No. Our father believed revealing the knowledge of your love bond and the impending arrival of Raehn would placate our mother. Instead, it enraged her. She had always believed you and Jonarel would be happy together. His confirmation reinforced her stance, highlighting all she had missed because of his actions. When he asked for her forgiveness, she refused."

The soft whimper from Jonarel jerked her attention to her mate. He looked like he was in physical pain, his eyes squeezed shut and his breathing shallow.

She scooted closer, as much as she could with his hands still wrapped around her feet, bracing one hand on his shoulder.

At her touch his eyes snapped open, his gaze locking with hers.

She held out her other hand and leaned toward him. He accepted her offer. Releasing her feet, he scooped her into his arms and cocooned her on his lap. Their sighs mingled as she snuggled her head into the crook of his neck and stroked her hand over his chest. "But she agreed to come with him to see us."

Tehar's beat of silence made her stomach lurch.

"If Clan Terfeli had a functional starship, she would have traveled with them instead."

Jonarel whimpered again, pressing his cheek against the top of her head.

She engaged her energy field, wrapping it around them both. Unfortunately, the pain he was feeling wasn't something her energy field could heal. "I assume they're not sharing a cabin on the *Rowkclarek*?"

"They are not."

That kind of physical withholding of connection from a mate would be death from a thousand cuts to a Kraed. Touch was essential to their wellbeing. Jonarel was tortured by even the thought of it.

Daymar might be handling it better because she had the love and support of her birth clan. Or because her rage was keeping her pain suppressed. Siginal's pride might prevent him from seeking similar support from his clan. "Does Rowk have any recommendations for bridging the gap between them?"

"He does...."

"But?"

"He is uncertain our father would agree."

"How could he not?" Jonarel's voice rasped like sandpaper. "She is his *checana*."

"And he is our clan leader," Tehar countered. "His views of what that means would be in conflict with what Rowk is proposing."

She was intrigued. "What is he proposing?"

"That our father submit to a *creevigan*."

Jonarel twitched like he'd gotten an electric shock.

"What's a *creevigan?*"

Tehar's gaze flicked to Jonarel.

His chest expanded beneath Lelindia's palm, then he blew out a loud breath. "It is a method of public conflict resolution, one that our father would find humiliating given his role as clan leader."

"Why?"

"Because it is for the young, those who have not yet learned to control their impulses."

"How young?"

"Before their *sitraniton.*"

"Oh." When they were still in their child form. That explained the humiliating part. "It's never been used for adults?"

"Never."

"Why not?"

"It has never been necessary," Tehar replied when Jonarel hesitated. "Disagreements and misunderstandings between children are expected as they learn and grow. The creevigan helps to teach the young how to deal with conflict in a healthy manner, drawing on the wisdom and support of the clan. Adults in our clan are expected to have already learned those lessons."

"Then wouldn't Daymar find this creevigan humiliating, too?"

Tehar shook her head. "Her claims of injury are valid. Our father failed to consult with her or the clan and inflicted harm on her when he banished us. Her role in the proceedings would be very different from his."

"Does the creevigan have to take place on Drakar?"

"No. Rowk could arrange it."

"And everyone on the *Rowkclarek* would attend?"

"Yes."

Oh, yeah, Siginal was going to *hate* this idea.

One Hundred Sixteen

"Liddy!?"

Cade winced as Montgomery's piercing tone drilled through several bulkheads.

"He's a PA, not a captain!" She glowered at the image on the media room screen, a mixture of outrage and disbelief on her face.

Nixon stood in front of her assembled bridge crew and senior officers, facing Unity's perspective, an arrogant tilt to his head as he looked down his nose at them. The man to his right had the beginnings of a sneer curling his lip as his attention lingered on Cmd. Muiruri.

"As of now, you will be taking your orders from Captain Liddy."

Liddy visibly puffed out his scarecrow chest.

"He will be working with the Teeli to root out anyone involved in Schreiber's and Montgomery's conspiracy against the Union." Nixon's mouth moved in a mocking parody of a smile. He pointed to the woman posing like she was in a photo shoot beside Liddy. "Lt. Babbitt is your new chief security officer. You will report any suspicious activity you witness to her. Failure to do so will land you in the brig."

"Lieutenant, my ass," Reynolds grumbled. "She was an ensign yesterday."

Cade's entire team had gathered in the media room with the Admiral and Montgomery when Unity alerted them Nixon was assembling *Cassini*'s senior crew on the ship's bridge. Nat stood by the media room doorway, U-2 hovering beside her.

"This crew used to be one of the best in the Fleet, before the rot set in." Nixon's eyes gleamed with a feverish light. "We will make you great again."

Montgomery stiffened beside Cade, her eyes shooting lasers into Nixon's forehead.

Nixon turned to Liddy. "Captain, I leave the crew in your capable hands." With a smirk at Muiruri, he turned and exited the bridge.

Liddy widened his stance, clasping his hands behind his back. "Things are going to be very different on this ship."

"I believe that," Gonzo muttered.

"Those of you who do your jobs well and follow orders have nothing to fear. Those who have been conspiring with traitors will regret the day you turned against the Union." His voice dropped an octave. "You will be found out. And you will be punished for your crimes."

Cade's stomach curdled.

"I have created a new duty roster. Muiruri, you will distribute it to the crew and see that it's implemented immediately."

Muiruri inclined her head.

Liddy leaned forward theatrically. "I didn't hear that."

"Yes, sir."

"Good. From now on, all crewmembers will respond at all times with the appropriate respect due my status as your captain. Is that clear?"

A chorus of, "Yes, sir," followed.

Liddy's chest swelled again, like a leech growing fat off the blood of its host. "Excellent. You are dismissed."

The crew dispersed, those on bridge duty returning to their posts. Muiruri moved toward one of the workstations, but Liddy waylaid her. "A word alone, Rehema."

Cade caught the slight tightening of Muiruri's muscles at Liddy's use of her first name, but she followed him as he strode toward the captain's office at the aft of the bridge.

The image on the media screen switched perspective from the bridge to the interior of the office. Liddy paused just inside the doorway, gave the room a once-over, shook his head, and then continued to the chair behind the desk. "Sit." He pointed to one of two chairs on the opposite side.

Muiruri perched on the edge, back straight, gaze level as she regarded Liddy.

He leaned back in his chair in a casual slouch, elbows on the armrests. He pressed his splayed fingertips together, watching Muiruri as the silence stretched out.

Cade gave her a lot of credit. She didn't give any outward sign of discomfort. It was Liddy who broke first.

"I understand you and Montgomery were close."

Muiruri didn't react.

"Answer me."

"I'm sorry, was that a question, sir?"

Liddy's eyes narrowed. "Yes, it was a question," he snarled. "Are you being insubordinate?"

"No, sir."

"Then answer the question."

"Yes, sir, we were close, sir."

"Did you help her escape?"

"Sir?"

"Did you help her sneak off this ship?"

"Sneak, sir? She was seriously injured in a climbing accident. She was *carried* off this ship."

"That's what you say," Liddy scoffed. "But then she joined the traitors, which makes your *story*," he used air quotes, "very suspicious." When Muiruri didn't respond, Liddy sat forward, leaning on the desk. "Do you like serving on this ship, Rehema?"

"Yes, sir."

"Do you like this crew?"

A slight hesitation as Muiruri no doubt sensed a trap. "Yes, sir."

"You wouldn't want anything bad to happen to this crew, would you?"

The corners of Muiruri's mouth pinched. "No, sir."

"But accidents do happen on starships, don't they? Just look at your former captain. Space is a very unforgiving place." He said it philosophically, but the spiteful look in his eye made Cade shift in his seat.

"Yes, sir."

"And as your new captain, I have a lot of influence over the safety of this crew."

The threat wasn't subtle. It cracked like a whip.

"Yes, sir."

"I'm sure you'll do anything necessary to keep this crew safe."

Muiruri's gaze remained flat, but her throat moved like she was swallowing tar. "Yes, sir."

Liddy's teeth flashed, but he wasn't smiling. "Good. I'm glad we understand each other." He slouched in his chair again. "Incidentally, you'll be moving to new quarters. Lt. Babbitt needs the extra space while she's conducting her investigation. You don't mind, do you?" His pupils dilated as he watched her reaction.

She barely twitched. "No, sir."

"Glad to hear it. Now get working on that duty roster." He flapped his hand toward the door. "You may go."

Muiruri rose.

"And Rehema?"

She halted.

"You *really* don't want to disappoint me."

"Yes, sir."

He lifted his chin toward the door. "Get going."

Everyone in the media room held their breath until Muiruri exited onto the bridge.

"He's a petty tyrant," Bella huffed.

"With no command experience," Justin added. "Stellar combination."

"No experience outside of Fleet HQ at all." The Admiral turned partway in his seat to face Justin. "He's been Nixon's PA for seven years. Nixon's the only reason he ever received a junior Lieutenant rank."

"And now he's the captain of the Discovery-class ship that monitors the Teeli border." Justin grimaced. "He'll probably volunteer to lead the Teeli invasion."

Cade focused on Montgomery, who was staring into the middle distance. "How can we help your crew?"

She blinked, meeting his gaze. "Rehema's smart, a lot smarter than Liddy. Now that she knows what she's dealing with, she'll find workarounds for whatever chaos he's about to unleash." She turned to the Admiral. "What do you know about Babbitt?"

"She also worked at HQ, in security. But as Reynolds noted, she was an ensign, not a lieutenant, which her rank insignia confirmed when she arrived with Nixon on the station. She has no more experience to handle the work of a chief security officer than Liddy has as a commanding officer."

Everyone chewed on that nugget of information for a few moments.

Cade's gaze alighted on U-2. "Unity, is there anything you can do to help *Cassini*'s crew?"

U-2 swayed, then backed up toward Nat as Montgomery turned in her seat to stare at them. "We can deliver messages," they said tentatively.

"What about the ship's systems?" Bella asked. "Can you take control?"

"*What?*" Shock and horror ripped through Montgomery's emotional field, like Bella had suggested cutting off the hands of *Cassini*'s crew. "You want that thing to take control of *Cassini!*"

No need to ask how she felt about that idea.

Unity dropped lower, bumping into Nat's hip.

Bella shot Cade an apologetic look. She'd clearly been so focused on working the problem she'd forgotten about Montgomery's hatred of A.I.

"It's a viable option, Colleen," the Admiral said evenly. "Unity could prevent someone on the crew from getting hurt."

"Or seize control and subjugate them."

The Admiral's expression shifted, the friend fading into the background as the Fleet Director took charge. "They would never intentionally harm anyone. Your crew would benefit greatly from having them on their side."

Montgomery stared at him in disbelief. "Why do you trust them?"

Cade decided to test the waters. "Why don't you?"

"Because you can't trust a thinking machine. It will always look out for itself."

"You're a thinking machine. Are you untrustworthy?"

She gave him a withering look. "I'm a person, not a machine."

"You're a biological machine."

Her lips thinned. "I'm a *human*."

"So it's a speciesism argument."

"*It's* not a species." Montgomery pointed a finger at U-2.

"Yes, they are," Cade countered. "They think, they feel, they communicate, they replicate, they're self-aware. They're a *person* as much as you and I are."

"It's a *machine*."

"They're a *person*."

Montgomery's irritation built like storm clouds.

So did Cade's.

"Have you all forgotten what happened on Earth? The price we paid for trusting machines like that?" She stabbed her finger in Unity's direction again. "Are you going to let it take everything from us again?" The fear behind Montgomery's words spread like a crimson rash across her emotional field.

Cade took a calming breath, reining in his own emotional response to her antagonism. "First off, Unity wasn't created by humans. They don't have our baggage to lug around. Their relationship with the Yruf has never been contentious. They treat each other as equals, as family."

"Until they don't."

One more breath, this time counting to four on the inhale and exhale. "I've spent a lot of time on the Yruf ship. I've seen firsthand how Unity interacts with them. And I know how Unity interacts with me. They care about me. And I care about them."

"It's. A. Machine."

So much for his powers of persuasion.

The Admiral stepped in. "You don't have to like Unity, Colleen. You don't even have to speak to them, if that's your choice. But they're part of our crew. I will not allow you to continue accusing them of malevolent intent."

Montgomery's face torqued, like words were trying to shove their way out of her tightly closed lips.

None did. She squared her shoulders and gave a brisk nod. "Yes, sir."

The Admiral didn't sigh, but Cade felt the disappointment in his emotional field.

"As *Cassini* doesn't appear to be leaving the system yet," the Admiral said, "let's discuss our next steps over lunch."

One Hundred Seventeen

Nat said a silent thank you that Patel hadn't witnessed Montgomery's diatribe. Her reaction wouldn't have been nearly as calm and measured as Cade's and the Admiral's.

She cradled U-2 gently in her arms as everyone filed past her into the corridor. She'd reacted on instinct when the mobile unit had bumped into her. Unity had seemed to calm down when she'd tucked them against her, so she'd kept them there during the rest of the heated debate.

Their casing was subtly textured, pleasant to the touch, and cool against her palms. To be honest, *she* felt better holding them, which was bizarre. Had she gotten so used to having Isin around that she was now craving hugs? That would be... different.

Cade was the last one out. His gaze dropped to U-2 with an apologetic look. "Thanks for keeping Unity company."

"No problem. In fact..." she started at the same time Cade said, "Would you..."

They both stopped. Started again. "Would you..."

"Can I..."

Stopped.

Cade grinned. "You first."

"I've already eaten, so I was wondering if you'd mind if I kept U-2 with me for a little while. If that's okay with Unity, of course," she added, loosening her grip on the egg-shaped mobile unit.

Unity didn't move. "Fine with us."

Cade nodded. "I think that's a great idea."

"Good. Then we'll see you later."

U-2 bobbed along beside her as she headed for the aft stairs. "Where are we going?"

"To check in with Pete first. Then I thought you and I could hang out on the bridge for a while."

"Okay!"

She found Pete bent over the design console in the engine room, his fingers tracing across the surface as objects moved in the 3D modeling mode. "What are you working on?"

His gaze flicked briefly to her. "Hey, Nat. Somethin' Unity suggested. If I shift things a bit, I can increase *Phoenix*'s interstellar speed while decreasin' the load on the engines."

"Really?" She studied the model he was building, and the pieces he was still adapting. "That's an unusual way of approaching it but..." She magnified two sections, noting how they fit together. "Yeah, I can see how it would work." She glanced at him. "Is this something we'd need to be planetside or in spacedock for you to do?"

He shook his head. "I don't think so. I'll know more when I get it all worked out, though."

"Okay, keep me posted."

Pete gave a distracted wave as she and U-2 left, his focus back on his project.

She smiled to herself as she climbed the stairs to A deck. She knew enough about engineering to keep *Gypsy* in good shape and most other ships functional, but she didn't have Pete's passion for it. He didn't want to just maintain *Phoenix*, he wanted to make the ship better.

So did she, but she did it by painting murals and hiring the best people to work on the ship. Like Pete.

Itorye and Patel were on the bridge in the same spots as the previous day, but this time Alec was with them, sitting in the captain's chair.

"Trying it out?" she asked him as she propped her shoulder against the hatch frame.

"It's not my fault nobody wants to sit here," he replied, a teasing light in his sandy brown eyes.

"Uh-huh." She'd certainly never had any interest in it. The only person who seemed inclined to sit there on a semi-regular basis was Isin.

Alec's projected image blipped out, reappearing behind the pilot's chair as Itorye moved to the captain's seat, leaving Nat's chair open for her.

Unity chose to hover at waist height in the center of the triangle formed by the three chairs.

"Unity's joining us because Montgomery is giving them a hard time."

"What a surprise." Patel's focus switched from whatever she'd been reading on her console to Unity.

Unity bobbed. "She doesn't trust us. She thinks we're going to do something bad. Cade says it's about your history with A.I. That bad things happened and the A.I. got blamed."

"That's a kind way to explain her prejudice." Patel's lips twisted like she'd tasted something sour. "Her attitude is exactly what I'd expect from a Fleet captain."

"Not all Fleet are like that," Nat pointed out. "The Admiral isn't. Neither is Aurora or her crew. Or Cade's team."

"There are some who are more open-minded," Patel conceded. "But most Fleet — most humans in general — tend to act irrationally regarding anything even resembling A.I."

Nat took a sudden and absorbing interest in the stars visible through the viewport. It was either that or give in to the laughter that threatened. Just like the previous day, Patel seemed oblivious to the fact she was describing her own behavior when she first learned of Unity's existence.

"Is she going to be a problem?" Itorye asked.

"The Admiral won't let her be. He made it very clear Unity is part of the crew."

Itorye's gaze flicked to Unity. "Yet you brought U-2 here."

Nat shrugged. "They were all getting something to eat. No reason for Unity to be with them."

"I see." But Itorye let it go. "What's the status on *Cassini?*"

She gave them a summary of the personnel changes.

When she described the new captain's attitude toward Muiruri, Itorye's expression shuttered. "He's going to make her life a living hell."

"I know." She had a lot of experience working for a captain like Liddy. So did Itorye. "Unity, since you're on *Cassini,* is there anything you can do to help?" She was curious if they'd have a different answer now that Montgomery wasn't staring them down.

Unity swayed. "We don't know. We're working to integrate into key areas, but we're stretched pretty thin right now. There aren't enough of us on *Cassini* to effectively infiltrate such a large ship. We're using the reclamation of *Sphinx* to generate more of our micro-form, but it's a slow process. The materials need to be refined before we can use them. We've never needed to replicate ourselves quickly. And that part of our ship is with Aurora and Micah. It'll take time for us to be delivered to *Cassini.*"

She'd never considered the fact that Unity had a finite number of micro-units. They always seemed limitless. "Don't worry about it. You're already doing a lot."

"But we want to help."

"You are helping. You and the Yruf are the reason any of this," she gestured out the viewport, "has been possible."

"We want to help *Cassini's* crew. They seem nice."

"I promise we're not going to abandon them. As long as you're onboard, you can keep tabs on them, right?"

"Yes."

"Good. Speaking of Aurora, how are things going there?"

Unity sighed. "The Ecilam are still searching for the Etah. We're waiting for one of their transports to return to their ship so we can sneak onboard."

"Hmm." Isin had filled her in on the latest developments. She'd been hoping the Ecilam would have given up by now, although with the Sovereign breathing down their necks, that wasn't really an option. Which meant the relocation of Mirko and Manchado wasn't moving forward, either. "Anything new from our bounty hunters?" she asked Itorye.

"One more ship arrived, bringing the total to five. *Zenobia* departed an hour ago."

She sat forward. "What was its heading?"

"Unclear. It didn't take the jump window *Gladiator* was headed toward, but I suspect that's because Rashid didn't want to leave an easy trail for the others to follow."

Alec took up the narrative. "*Zenobia* cruised along *Gladiator's* flight path and circled the area where *Gladiator* changed course after being concealed by the Yruf. There was no path to trace after that, since the Yruf ships reabsorb their own emissions and those of any ships they're concealing, essentially scrubbing the areas they travel through. But depending on what equipment *Zenobia* has, it's possible Rashid detected there was no trace of an interstellar engine signature, either."

"Which would indicate *Gladiator* never left the system," Nat concluded. "Or at least not through that jump window."

"Correct."

"So a smart hunter might jump to a nearby system, then circle back to do another sweep after the other hunters have left Eridani Duo." She glanced at Unity. "Any chance you're tracking *Zenobia?*"

"No." Unity sank a few centimeters. "All our resources are being used to conceal *Phoenix* and *Gladiator* and infiltrate *Cassini*. We didn't have any micro-forms or ships to spare."

"That's okay." Nat rested a hand briefly on top of U-2. "Just thought I'd ask."

"Here's my question. How much longer are we going to stay in this system?" The look Patel gave her made it clear what answer she wanted.

In this instance, it was the same one Nat was favoring. "At this point it doesn't seem like our presence is going to help in any way. I'm inclined to head back to Zeta Tucanae so we can unload Montgomery to the *Starhawke*." Where, unbeknownst to Captain Montgomery, another non-biological was in residence.

Not that Montgomery would be getting introduced to Star. Aurora's crew protected Star as fiercely as Nat's crew protected Alec.

Learning the Kraed had developed a non-biological long before making contact with humans would probably blow Montgomery's circuits.

One Hundred Eighteen

"You want me to do *what!?*" Siginal boomed like thunder, the sound reverberating through the front room of Lelindia and Jonarel's cabin.

If the *Starhawke* didn't have soundproofing between decks, Daymar, Knox, and Isabeau probably would have heard his outburst in the greenhouse.

This was not the way Lelindia had hoped Siginal would respond, but it was exactly how she'd *expected* him to.

"To participate in a creevigan," Jonarel repeated.

"That is for children," Siginal snarled.

"It is for resolving conflict," Tehar replied from her position next to Siginal at the dining table. "You and solna are in conflict."

Siginal flinched, then glowered. "It will pass."

"No, talta, it will not." Jonarel pinned him with an equally unrelenting glare. "She has spoken to Harvan about accepting us into Clan Terfeli."

Siginal's harsh inhale sucked up most of the oxygen in the room. "*No.*"

"Yes." Tehar's gaze was kind but just as unwavering as her brother's. "Rowk told me."

Shock splashed across Siginal's features, followed swiftly by betrayal. "My brother did not tell me!"

"He did not wish to cause you pain. He had hoped this visit would facilitate a reconciliation. It has not."

Siginal's low growl made the wood table vibrate beneath Lelindia's forearms.

She reached out, resting a hand on his arm. His growl cut off like she'd thrown a switch. "Siginal, you need to face this. For all our sakes." She rested her other hand on the bulge where Raehn currently resided.

His gaze followed the movement. He swallowed hard. "My checana would never leave our clan." His words were confident. His tone was not.

She tightened her grip on his arm. "If you don't resolve this, if you don't give her a chance to vent her anger and pain in a way that brings healing, she might."

His gaze met hers, his voice hollow. "You would go with her?"

Her heart ached for him, but it ached for Daymar, too. Siginal had put them all in a terrible position. "I'm hoping I'll never have to make that choice."

"I asked her forgiveness." A touch of defensiveness crept in as he glanced at Jonarel and Tehar. "She would not give it."

"You hurt your checana." Jonarel's jaw flexed. "Banished her children without consulting her. Her anger is justified."

The rebuke rocked Siginal back in his chair. The wood groaned in protest. "I did not mean to hurt her."

"That is the only reason you still have a chance to fix this," Jonarel growled.

Siginal stared at him. "I am the clan leader. I cannot participate in a creevigan. I will speak with her privately—"

Jonarel's hands slammed down, shaking the tabletop as he rose, looming over his father. "Nothing private will work. She is furious with you. You will lose everything – *including us* – if you do not accept responsibility for your actions. *Publicly.*" He snarled the last word, the ferocity in his eyes and the curl of his lip a not-so-subtle threat.

Apparently Daymar wasn't the only one with some unresolved anger toward Siginal.

Tension crackled. She held her breath, gaze darting between the two. When neither moved, she did, sliding out of her chair and wrapping her arms around Siginal's broad back and shoulders. "Please, talta," she whispered, pressing her cheek next to his. "Listen to Jonarel and Tehar. We all want to see you and Daymar happy again."

He leaned into her touch, a slight tremor running through his large frame.

"Please," she whispered again.

"I am the clan leader." It was a weak protest, but still a protest.

She bit back her own growl of frustration. "Then lead by example. Stand before the clan and admit to Daymar you were wrong."

His shoulders bunched, lifting her onto her toes.

Not the response she was going for. She tried another strategy. "She is your checana. In her heart, she wants to be with you, but her anger is a wall between you. If you do this, that wall will crumble. You'll be able to hold her in your arms again."

She recognized the soft sound that escaped him. It was a quieter version of Jonarel's whimper from the previous evening.

Siginal and Daymar's mating hadn't been a love match like hers and Jonarel's, but she knew they'd grown to love each other. It was what made Siginal's actions so painful for Daymar. She'd believed they were partners, that she could trust him with her heart. And he'd shredded it when he'd severed her ties with her children.

"Her anger protects her vulnerability, her pain." She engaged her energy field, surrounding him in its nurturing glow. He jerked in reaction, but then his muscles began to unfurl, like a leaf opening to the cool of evening after a hot day. "The only way to ease that pain is for you to be vulnerable, too."

She could feel his resistance. In Siginal's world, vulnerable was a four-letter word.

"We will be there for both of you," Jonarel added, his gaze flicking to her, admiration in his eyes. "Trust us. Trust your checana. Trust our clan. We will get through this together."

Siginal's next inhale lifted her onto her toes again. As he exhaled, his arm slipped around her waist, his powerful legs pushing the chair back just enough that he could lift her into his lap like a child. She'd been expecting it, knew it would be a sign of acquiescence, so she relaxed as his arms encircled her, his chin resting on top of her head. "You are our future, checala."

"I know." The fates of the Kraed and Suulh were forever entwined. Raehn's birth would make that clear to all.

He was quiet for a few breaths, the movement of his chest with each inhale rocking her gently. It made her feel three years old again. Her dad used to hold her like this. Brendan, too. But she'd been a lot smaller then.

"What if she never forgives me?"

Her heart squeezed at the fear in his voice. "She will."

"How do you know?"

"Because she's miserable, too. That's why her anger is growing. Even though she knows you can be opinionated, stubborn, arrogant, brash, and demanding, she still wants to be with you, and she's mad about that, too."

The room went completely silent. She held still, waiting to see how he would respond to the unvarnished truth.

A puff of air brushed across the top of her head and Siginal's body shook around her. It took a moment for her to realize he was laughing, silently.

She peeked at Jonarel. He and Tehar were both staring at her in stunned surprise. Whether from her words or Siginal's reaction, she wasn't sure.

Siginal squeezed her in a bear hug, his body still shaking. "Checala." His breath warmed her cheek as he placed a soft kiss on her temple. "You continue to surprise me." Then he sighed, his muscles relaxing around her. "I will trust in you and my checana. We will hold the creevigan."

One Hundred Nineteen

Stepping onto the *Rowkclarek* always tickled Lelindia's Nedale senses. The ship was so *alive*, and not just because of Rowk's presence as the ship's Nirunoc. Trees and greenery grew everywhere, as lush as the Clarek Compound on Drakar.

The heat and humidity hit her as well, but she'd planned for it. She'd changed into the Kraed outfit she'd worn the last time she was onboard, which Jonarel had quickly altered to accommodate Raehn's expanded girth. She'd also used some of the clips Celia had given her to sweep her hair on top of her head. It wasn't as artful an arrangement as her friend could achieve, but she'd been pleased with the results when she'd checked her reflection in the bathroom mirror.

Jonarel had been pleased as well, kissing and nuzzling her exposed neck, generating more heat than the ambient temperature on the *Rowkclarek*.

Kire and Kelly had remained on the *Starhawke*, but Knox and Isabeau had joined her and Jonarel on the *Rowkclarek*, borrowing Kraed clothing from Jonarel and Kelly so they'd be comfortable in the warmer environment. Isabeau had been on the *Rowkclarek* before with Admiral Schreiber during visits to Drakar and when Siginal had traveled to Sol Station as part of his ambassadorial duties, but this was Knox's first time onboard.

"This is mind-blowing." He tilted his head back, his gaze following the expanse of massive denglar tree trunks crisscrossed by aerial walkways and staircases leading all the way to the canopy above. "Since it looks so much like the *Starhawke* on the outside, I thought it would be like it on the inside."

"The *Starhawke* is unique." Jonarel led the group along the planked walkway to where Siginal and Rowk stood waiting for them. "Our designs would have been too unfamiliar for Aurora and Lelindia to be comfortable. I adapted Kraed design elements to pair with Fleet designs in a cohesive whole."

"You nailed it." Knox trailed his fingers along the wood railing, peering over the edge to the open levels below. "Now that I'm seeing your native designs, I'm even more impressed by what you achieved."

"Thank you."

Siginal stepped forward to embrace Jonarel, but to Lelindia's surprise, Rowk approached her rather than Tehar. He lifted his hands with palms out in the traditional Nirunoc greeting.

She did the same, aligning her palms with his.

"It is good to see you again, Lelindia."

"You as well." Rowk's warm gaze was so familiar to her, not because she'd spent a lot of time with him, but because he looked so much like Jonarel and Siginal. His eyes had the same shape and golden hue, and the frame of his dark brows gave him an intelligent, focused look that reminded her of an older version of Jonarel. "Thank you for coming up with this solution."

The corners of his mouth tightened. "May it prove successful."

Rowk greeted Tehar next, since Siginal still had a death grip on Jonarel. When he finally let go and approached her, Lelindia eyed him warily. That type of tight squeeze on her ribcage might require healing. Suulh bones weren't as iron-forged as Kraed bones.

But when he drew her into his arms, he held her with great tenderness, his cheek touching hers like a butterfly wing. "I am frightened, checala," he whispered in her ear, so softly she could barely make out the words.

Her stomach twisted but her heart expanded. That he was admitting his feelings was a good sign. She slid her hands to his nape, where his hair was tied back in a neat coil, and allowed tendrils of her energy field to caress his skin. "Listen to her," she murmured back. "Hear what she has to say. Allow her to see how much you care about her, how much you regret causing her pain."

He pressed her closer, expelling his breath on a ragged sigh. "I will."

By the time he released her, he'd regained control of his emotions, his expression strained but composed. He greeted Tehar, Knox, and Isabeau, then led the way to a staircase that wound up into the trees.

As she set her foot on the first stair, she wobbled, her center of gravity shifting.

Jonarel rested his hand at her back to steady her. "Shall I carry you?"

She straightened. "I'm fine, just a little unbalanced with Raehn." And the stairs had a higher rise than she was used to, with no handrail, unlike the stairs to the hydrotank or the elevated walking track in the *Starhawke*'s training center. Kraed didn't need handrails because they had claws in their feet to grip the planks.

"This will definitely be a workout," Isabeau agreed, halting on the step above her. "We don't have the height advantage or long legs of these two." She waggled her thumb at Knox and Jonarel.

Lelindia grinned. "But we won't let that stop us, right?" She hauled herself up the next few steps.

Isabeau laughed, the sound an unexpected delight. "No, we won't."

Jonarel remained behind her — *right* behind her — shadowing her steps as she climbed.

On the first landing she was okay. On the second she was puffing. By the third, her leg muscles were shaking. She halted, gulping in air. She wasn't the least bit surprised when Jonarel's arms came around her from behind, supporting her weight. "Okay, I've made my point." She turned her head, meeting his gaze over her shoulder. "Carry me?"

His smile flashed, making it clear he'd been looking for an excuse to hold her all along. He lifted her off her feet and cradled her against his chest with no more effort than if he'd plucked a feather from the ground.

Isabeau stared at them, then glanced at Knox. "Carry me?" she asked in a super-sweet tone, batting her eyelashes.

Lelindia laughed.

So did Knox. "You might want to rethink that request. I'm not a Kraed. It would not turn out well for either of us."

"Spoilsport." Isabeau clasped his hand instead. "Then walk beside me."

The playfulness faded, replaced by a much stronger emotion. "Anywhere you want to go."

Moisture bloomed behind Lelindia's eyes. She looked away, dropping her head onto Jonarel's shoulder before any of the tears could fall. If her reaction to Knox and Isabeau's sweet moment was any indication, making it through the intensely emotional creevigan without turning into a fountain would be a miracle.

When they reached the fifth landing, Jonarel set her on her feet, his fingers trailing across her back in a delicious caress. Knox and Isabeau had managed to keep up with them during the climb, no doubt a result of all the hours they spent in the training center together. They were both winded, unlike Jonarel and Signal, but Isabeau flashed her a smile and a thumbs up.

She returned the gesture. And made a decision. Once Raehn was born, she was definitely setting up an exercise routine, maybe with Isabeau's help, so she could at least attempt to keep up with her mate. And her daughter.

The open platform Siginal and Rowk led them to was packed with people, leaving a narrow channel into the small circle at the center.

Daymar stood alone in the circle. Her hair was pulled back from her face in an intricate braid, and her athletic figure was outlined by a tunic and legging combination that matched the color and style of Lelindia's.

Lelindia doubted that was an accident. Daymar had given her the outfit she was wearing. She was making a clear declaration of connection to Lelindia.

Daymar's gaze flitted briefly over Siginal before resting on her and Jonarel. The joy in her expression chased away the hard lines of pain and anger that had shadowed her features. She motioned them forward, embracing Jonarel first before turning to Lelindia and pulling her close. "Rowk told me you made this possible," she whispered in her ear.

"It was a team effort," she whispered back. "Don't pull any punches. He needs to know how you feel."

"He will." The words came out on a growl.

The way Siginal winced indicated he'd heard her.

Daymar greeted Tehar, Knox, and Isabeau – deftly avoiding Siginal – then returned to stand alone in the circle.

Jonarel stepped into the circle with his mother. "Clan Clarek." His voice carried an authority she wasn't used to hearing. "Today we gather to help Daymar and Siginal with a conflict they have been unable to resolve on their own."

There was no censure in his tone, no blame or shaming. She also didn't see any on the faces of the Kraed surrounding them either, only concern.

"Siginal, step forward and take your place."

Siginal took a step into the circle with a hesitancy that was atypical for him. He glanced at the six woven mats laying in an oblong on the deck, two on each side, and one on each end. With a robotic quality that indicated he was acutely uncomfortable, he walked to the mat on the end closest to him, slowly sinking onto his knees, then back onto his heels. His face contorted with the effort to control his emotions, his gaze locking on Daymar.

"Daymar, take your place."

She knelt on the mat facing Siginal, her movements a great deal more fluid than his but still stilted compared to her typical lithe grace.

Jonarel led Lelindia to the two mats on Siginal's left, directing her to the one beside Siginal and settling onto the one closest to Daymar. Rowk and Tehar moved to the mats across from them, Rowk beside Siginal and Tehar beside Daymar.

Jonarel had explained the setup to her before they'd boarded the *Rowkclarek* so she'd know what to expect. In a typical creevigan, the parents of the two children would have taken those four places. That Siginal's brother and children held those positions – the children Siginal had banished – had to be a blow to Siginal's pride.

The mat was surprisingly comfortable, cushy even, which was a relief. She shouldn't have any issue maintaining the pose everyone else was in. She was used to sitting on her heels thanks to all the time she spent tending the plants in the greenhouse.

Jonarel's gaze moved between his parents. "In this space, we learn from the collective wisdom of the clan. We share our thoughts and feelings openly and freely. We seek understanding and connection." He switched to a phrase in the Kraed language she couldn't follow, but everyone in the clan repeated it back to him. Possibly something ceremonial, an instance where a Galish translation wouldn't have adequately expressed the depth of what the Kraed words conveyed. She appreciated that they were holding the rest of the ceremony in Galish so she'd know what they were saying.

His gaze rested on his mother. "Daymar, with honesty and clarity, detail your grievances to Siginal."

Daymar's chin dropped a fraction, her gaze direct as she stared at her mate. "Siginal banished our children without consulting me or the council, an action that could have separated me from them forever. They are *my children*," the emphasis made Siginal cringe, "yet he failed to consider alternatives, failed to seek the wisdom of our people. He also failed to consider the effect it would have on me, his mate. His *checana*."

A tremor passed over Siginal like he was sitting on a fault line.

"I cannot express the depth of the emotional and psychological pain I suffered when I learned what he had done. My mate, my protector, had cut off my connection to my son and daughter. It felt like he had cut out my heart."

The look of raw pain in Daymar's eyes made Lelindia's chest constrict. A quick glance at Siginal confirmed the arrows had hit the mark. He looked like he was bleeding out, his chest caved in and his jaw slack.

"He failed to seek forgiveness at that time. He failed to acknowledge the pain he had inflicted. He failed to take action to make amends with me or with our children." Daymar took several measured breaths, clearly struggling to maintain a grip on the emotions rampaging through her. When she spoke again, the coolness in her voice chilled the air. "During the time of my separation from my children, my son," her gaze shifted to Jonarel, her face transforming with the fierceness of maternal love, "acknowledged the depth of his feelings for Lelindia. I had witnessed glimmers of their feelings for each other for years, had yearned for them to discover the joy they could bring each other."

Lelindia's chest rose and fell unsteadily as she gazed into Daymar's eyes.

The barest hint of a smile brushed Daymar's lips before she returned her attention to Siginal. The hard angles resurfaced, her mouth flattening into a harsh line. "Because of Siginal's decision to banish my children, I lost the opportunity to see Jonarel's and Lelindia's bond take root. I lost the opportunity to take part in my son's mating ceremony, to share in his joy. I lost the opportunity to welcome his checana in the ways of our people."

Siginal's upper body resembled a collapsing bridge, his fingers splayed over his thighs like structural supports.

Lelindia inhaled sharply when her Nedale senses made sense of what she was seeing. Siginal had embedded all ten claws of his hands into his flesh, the cuts as precise as ten scalpel blades. Thin lines of blood seeped up from the wounds.

Jonarel's large hand closed over hers, stopping her from reaching out. A flick of his gaze and a twitch of his head made it clear he was aware of the situation, but didn't want her to interfere.

Daymar's voice lowered to a growl. "Those moments cannot be restored to me. They are gone forever. But the pain of their loss remains."

Lelindia flinched as Siginal's claws sank deeper.

Daymar fell silent, drawing Lelindia's attention away from the disturbing image of Siginal's self-inflicted wounds. Daymar was still staring at Siginal, her anger a white-hot flame in her golden eyes.

Jonarel cleared his throat. The tight set of his jaw showed how his mother's words had affected him.

Tehar spoke, turning to her father. "Siginal, with honesty and clarity, respond to Daymar's grievances."

Siginal's gaze clung to Daymar's despite the scorching heat of her anger that charred him into a shriveled husk. After an audible inhale, he finally spoke, his voice thin and reedy, almost unrecognizable. "My mate is correct. I banished our children without consulting her or the council. I did not consider how my decision would impact her. I did not seek her forgiveness until after I learned of Jonarel's and Lelindia's mating, and the conception of their child. I hurt—" His chest heaved and his voice hitched, his claws extending to their full length, slicing through his muscles. "I hurt my checana. I failed her."

The torment on Siginal's face as he gazed at Daymar seemed to have very little to do with the physical pain of his wounds.

Daymar stared at him, her lips parted in surprise. She'd probably thought, as Lelindia had, that Siginal would hedge a bit, that he'd admit some culpability while also making a case for why he'd acted the way he had. Instead, he'd surrendered completely.

Jonarel seemed equally at a loss as to how to handle the situation. His gaze swung between his parents before settling on his mother. "Daymar, what questions do you have regarding Siginal's response?"

The anger had faded from Daymar's eyes, leaving behind layers of pain as her gaze searched his. "I..." Her dark brows drew together, her chest rising and falling with her unsteady breaths. "What do you want?"

"You," he whispered. "Your forgiveness. Your hand in mine as we witness the birth of our checalas' child. Your body curled with mine each night as we sleep."

Drops of moisture pattered Lelindia's hands in her lap, but she didn't dare move a muscle to stop them. Nobody else was moving, either. The hush around them made the slight rustle of leaves in the trees sound unnaturally loud.

With glacial slowness, Daymar rose to her feet. For one heart-stopping moment, Lelindia thought she was going to leave the circle.

She didn't.

Her expression gave no hint to her thoughts as she gazed down at Siginal. He looked like he was drowning in a river, watching Daymar with an equal measure of hope and terror, unsure whether she would drag him to safety or push him under the surface.

Daymar took one step forward. Then another, and another, until she was towering over Siginal. He tipped his head back to hold her gaze. He didn't look like he was breathing, his body completely still as he awaited her next move.

And then his spine went liquid as Daymar held out her hands, palms up.

He started to shake, causing more damage as he extracted his claws where they were embedded in his thighs, blood seeping out of the cuts in his leggings.

Lelindia clutched her hands in her lap, forcing herself to remain still even though her Nedale senses were screaming at her to engage her energy field.

His chin sank to his chest as he stared at the deck, then he lifted his hands, rotating them and resting the backs lightly in Daymar's cupped palms.

Daymar's eyes widened when she spotted the red painting the green of Siginal's skin. Her gaze darted to his thighs, where blood stains spread across the brown cloth from the ten precise marks. Her throat moved, emotion darkening her gaze.

Siginal didn't see it, his head still bowed. "I beseech your forgiveness, checana," he croaked like a toad had taken up residence in his throat. "The injury I caused you was unforgiveable." A violent tremor wracked his body. "I place my fate in your hands."

Daymar's expression softened like warm honey, her lower lip trembling. Her fingers spread, curling around Siginal's. "Honorable mate, father of our children..."

Siginal's head jerked up in surprise.

Lelindia was pretty sure that second part wasn't typically included in the wording for forgiveness.

"...I accept your humble petition and forgive the injury you caused."

Siginal stared at her like her words were the air he breathed.

Daymar pivoted her hands, bringing his palms together. "I return your fate to your hands." Then she lifted their joined hands and placed a tender kiss on each of his thumbs. "And renew the strength of our pair bond."

For a heartbeat, Siginal remained frozen. Then he rose with startling swiftness, only to stagger as his injured muscles struggled to support him.

Daymar caught him in her arms, bracing her feet on the deck to keep him from falling. Jonarel leapt to his feet, sliding a hand around Siginal's back to support him.

"You crazy *clestok*," Daymar murmured, lifting her hand to cradle Siginal's cheek.

His eyes drifted closed, his cheek pressing into her palm as a soft purr rumbled from his chest.

Since Siginal had stumbled in Lelindia's direction, she was already in a good position to treat his wounds. "Angle him toward me," she instructed Jonarel.

Siginal's body tightened, resisting. "No."

She looked up at him from her position on the deck. "Seriously?"

"I do not deserve your gifts."

She blew out a breath, not even trying to disguise her exasperation. He said *deserve*, but what he meant was *need*. "Didn't we already have this conversation?" He'd resisted her healing efforts once before following the showdown with Jonarel that had left him with cracked ribs. The Kraed had strong constitutions and excellent immune systems, but their attitude regarding healers was her least favorite aspect of their culture. They viewed being treated for anything that wasn't life-threatening as a mark of shame. She'd learned that the first time she'd visited Drakar, after she'd healed the bruises he'd garnered during his sparring match with Celia. When he'd hugged her at the clan gathering, she'd instinctively engaged her energy field to heal the damage — it had taken only a second — not anticipating he'd be embarrassed by it.

Thankfully Jonarel didn't share his father's point of view.

"Your checala wants to heal you." Daymar's voice was a rod of steel. "You will accept her offer with gratitude."

Siginal's frown vanished so quickly it was comical. "Yes, checana." He met Lelindia's gaze with chagrin. "Thank you, checala."

Lelindia maintained her professional bedside manner as she rested her hands on Siginal's thighs and engaged her energy field, but instead she was laughing.

Daymar might be making some real changes in Clan Clarek as a result of this creevigan.

One Hundred Twenty

Gladiator was headed back to Zeta Tucanae, along with one of the Yruf ships as escort.

Cade had sent every member of his team except Reynolds, who'd insisted on remaining with the Admiral. Gryphon and Marina had gone with his team, eager to rejoin Lelindia now that Montgomery was completely healed.

As for Montgomery, she was back in her usual place with the Admiral and Reynolds in *Phoenix*'s media room, monitoring Unity's various feeds from *Cassini* and Eridani Duo. Nixon hadn't left the station yet. Instead, he'd launched a campaign to harass Dr. Yates and Director Grijalva, doing everything in his power to make their lives miserable.

Liddy was waging a similar campaign on *Cassini*. Montgomery's anger and frustration crackled and hissed from the direction of the media room, which is why Cade had chosen not to venture there following *Gladiator*'s departure.

Nat and U-2 had joined him in the ship's crew gym. He and Nat had started out with a brisk run on the side-by-side treadmills, then switched to spotting each other on the weight bench.

"How much longer do you think she'll want to stay here?" Nat tipped her head in the general direction of the media room.

Cade paused with his arms extended, the barbell poised above him. "I'm guessing until *Cassini* leaves."

"And how soon do you think that will be?"

He lowered the bar to his chest, then hoisted it back up. "If this were a normal Fleet situation, they'd already be gone. Keeping the largest ship in the SGQ4 quadrant in the Inner Hub without an obvious reason is a serious waste of Fleet resources. But there's nothing normal about this situation so..." He shrugged as much as his prone position would allow.

Nat nodded, her gaze drifting toward the doorway.

"It's not her decision, though."

Her gaze flipped back to him.

He set the bar in the cradle and sat up, turning to face her. "She's a Fleet captain but you're *Phoenix's* captain. When you're ready to head back to Zeta Tucanae, say the word and we'll leave." Montgomery would protest, but she'd also respect the chain of command. Nat had already been extremely accommodating.

She gave him a knowing look. "Getting antsy?"

He grimaced. "Is it that obvious?" Not having any pressing issues demanding his attention felt strange, especially with his team and ship gone and Aurora stuck in Teeli space.

"I recognize the signs. Sitting still isn't one of my favorite things, either. I'd rather be flying."

She'd hit the bullseye. "Exactly." He swung his leg over the bench and stood, adjusting the weights on his side of the barbell while she worked on the other side. "Your mural's coming along nicely, though." The unfettered joy of her smile brought an answering smile to his lips.

"I've never had a canvas that big to work with. It's a challenge, but that just makes it more fun." She stretched out on the bench, lifting the bar from the cradle and lowering it in a smooth motion.

"Your mural reminds us of the Yruf's light language," U-2 piped up from their charging station overhead. "Lots of colors flowing together in harmony."

A kaleidoscope of emotions flitted across Nat's face and painted her emotional field. "Thanks, Unity." Her voice came out a little thick. He didn't think it had anything to do with the weights she was lifting.

"I agree," he said softly, keenly aware of her embarrassment but also her delight and sense of gratification. "When we're all back together, you should take *Gypsy* over to the main Yruf ship so you can see their light language for yourself."

Her startled gaze met his. "Really?"

"Yes, you should!" Unity gushed. "We would love to show you our ship. You've been so kind to allow us to be on yours."

Nat frowned, lowering the barbell. "You're the reason my ship is still in one piece." She pushed the bar back up. "And you've been a great friend to Alec. Of course I'm happy you're onboard."

Alec appeared facing Cade and Nat. "Would you take me with you to see the Yruf ship?"

Nat let out an amused grunt. "Should have seen that coming." She did another rep. "That would be up to Unity and the Yruf, not me." She lowered the bar again. "It's not like I can smuggle you over like I did when you visited the *Starhawke.*"

Cade's brows lifted. "Smuggle?"

Nat grinned. "Patel didn't know I brought Alec to meet you, remember? She would have hit the roof if we'd asked her, so we didn't."

"We'll ask Ifel later," Unity replied, "when she's not so distracted by the Ecilam."

"How are things going with the Ecilam?" His check-in with Aurora the previous day had revealed her aggravation regarding the ethical dilemma the Sovereign's actions had shoved onto her plate.

"Bad. We don't like seeing them suffer."

"No sign that they're going to leave?"

"Not yet. We're in a holding pattern."

"Sounds familiar," Nat muttered through a grunt of exertion.

It was the status quo for all of them. *Vengeance* was waiting on the Ecilam, *Phoenix* was waiting on *Cassini,* and the *Starhawke* was waiting on a full recharge. Only *Gladiator* was currently on the move, but soon they'd be waiting with the *Starhawke.*

Alec's image flickered at the same time U-2 abruptly dropped to eye level.

"A ship just entered the system," they said.

"Fleet?" Cade asked, spotting Nat as she shoved the bar up and dropped it in the cradle with a clang.

"No," Unity replied. "It's a Teeli freighter."

One Hundred Twenty-One

Nat snatched up a towel on her way out of the gym. Cade's feet thumped in time with hers down the aft stairway to C deck, U-2 racing along beside them. But as she and Cade entered the media room, U-2 hung back.

The image of the new ship dominated the media screen, the smaller images from *Cassini* pushed to the edges. Her first impression wasn't favorable, but as she settled into a chair beside Cade and studied the image, she downgraded the design to ugly.

Not quite as bad as Tnaryt's cobbled-together-from-multiple-ships layout for his junker, but close. The freighter was all sharp angles and points, not a curve to be seen anywhere. It could easily be mistaken for a jagged asteroid until you got close enough to see the shard-like technological protrusions radiating out from various points. The nondescript grey hull was either unfinished metal or the most unimaginative paint job in the galaxy. "Are all Teeli ships that hideous?"

Cade glanced at her with a small smile. "The carrier we encountered had a similar design, albeit much, much larger. But the only other freighter I've seen looked more like a water-based ferry or barge."

"So the answer is yes, they're all hideous."

Cade barked a laugh. "I guess so."

"They're headed for *Cassini*." The Admiral steepled his fingers as he watched the screen. "My guess is they're bringing more Teeli."

"A lot more Teeli," U-2 confirmed, hovering behind her and Cade. "We detect one-hundred thirty-seven Teeli onboard."

Montgomery whipped her head around. "One-hundred thirty-seven?" Dread poured through her emotional field as her gaze jerked back to the Teeli freighter. "They're going to take over my ship."

The Admiral tapped his fingertips together. "Perhaps, although that wouldn't fit with the Sovereign's previous actions. She likes to keep her pieces in play."

Montgomery made a non-committal sound, scrutinizing the Teeli ship as it drew alongside *Cassini*. An airbridge snapped out like a spring-loaded dagger from the side of the angular ship, nearly piercing *Cassini*'s much smoother hull.

Nat's gut tightened. The memory of a brown-cloaked figure clutching her arm and a mechanical voice speaking to her in low tones sent a shudder down her spine. "Do you think the Sovereign's on that ship?" she whispered to Cade.

His hand rested lightly on her forearm, his touch comforting as his gaze met hers. "I doubt it. It would be too vulnerable a position. She likes to travel with an entourage of warships." He glanced over his shoulder at Unity. "Unless your scans indicate I'm wrong?"

Unity swayed. "No. Everyone onboard is a male Teeli."

Their reassurance eased the knot in her stomach, but did little to chase away the chill produced by so many Teeli congregated in one place.

"Liddy just ordered all senior officers to report to the crew common area," Unity informed them. "The Teeli are boarding *Cassini*."

Montgomery's back tightened like her shoulder blades were being winched together.

Nat felt for her. It wasn't too long ago that she'd experienced the horror of watching — helpless — while a malevolent sadist took over her ship and threatened the lives of her crew. She and Isin had ultimately won that battle, but it had cost them a lot of pain and loss.

"Do you have eyes on the common room?" the Admiral asked.

"We have one angle."

The main image on the screen changed to a wide-angle view taken from an elevated position — a duct vent most likely — of an open layout room.

In the feed, crewmembers scattered, abandoning the clusters of tables and chairs on the far side, the long couches in the middle, and the rows of seating in the near view that faced a wide screen. It looked like a well-organized decompression drill on a space station, everyone moving quickly but purposefully to their respective exits. In less than ten seconds, the room was empty.

Good thing, too. Moments later, a long line of Teeli, with Liddy at the head, entered from the one door none of the crew had used. They fanned out, laying claim to the space as they lounged on the seating the crew had vacated.

Nat's jaw tightened at the sense of entitlement pervading the group. She couldn't see most of their faces, thank the stars. The sea of white and grey filling the image was disturbing enough, broken only when Cmd. Muiruri followed the last Teeli into the room. Her senior officers filed in behind her to form a two-row semi-circle facing the Teeli and Liddy. The last person through the door was Babbitt, who took up a sloppy guard position near the door, a snide look on her face.

Liddy smiled, his teeth almost blindingly white, his expression sanctimonious as he regarded the crew. "Say hello to our guests." He swept his arm to encompass the gathering of Teeli, who stared at the crew like a pack of wolves staring down a mother fox and her kits.

"Hello," the crew chorused in a monotone.

"Hello, *sirs*," Liddy corrected. "Show your respect."

"Hello, sirs," the crew parroted.

Liddy chuckled, like they'd just performed an amusing trick. "These gentlemen will be joining us as we embark on a tour of the quadrant."

Montgomery swore. Loudly.

"From this point forward, this room is off-limits to all personnel with the exception of myself and Lt. Babbitt. Anyone caught entering this room without an express order from me, Lt.

Babbitt, or one of our Teeli guests will be escorted immediately to the brig. Is that clear?"

"Yes, sir." The group response managed to sound even more robotic.

Liddy didn't seem to care. He was too busy preening like a peacock. "Cmd. Muiruri, our Teeli guests will need accommodations. Lt. Babbitt will provide you with a list of the crew's cabin reassignments. You will complete the changes and have the cabins prepared for our guests within the hour."

"Yes, sir."

Nat's throat constricted, the phantom weight of a metal collar settling around her neck. Muiruri's toneless reply summoned unpleasant memories of her own zombie-like responses during her time with Tnaryt.

The zeal on Liddy's face didn't help. He didn't have Tnaryt's stature or commanding presence, but he definitely shared Tnaryt's penchant for cruelty. "During our tour, we will be meeting with the other Fleet ships in our quadrant. They will each be hosting Teeli consuls who will be monitoring their operations going forward."

This time, Montgomery wasn't the only one who swore.

"As senior officers, you will be personally responsible for meeting all of our guests' needs while they are onboard. You will provide them with any assistance they require. Is that clear?"

"Yes, sir."

"Our first target is the *Nichols.*"

Nat blinked. "Did he just say *target?*"

"He did." The Admiral's voice was grim.

Itorye wasn't going to like that news. Her friend Baraka was on that ship. They'd reconnected during the transfer of the kids from Devries' ship.

"We depart in thirty minutes." Liddy flapped his hands at the crew. "Get going."

"Yes, sir."

The crew pivoted on their heels, Muiruri waiting until they'd all filed briskly from the room before exiting with Babbitt.

Liddy rolled his eyes, turning to the Teeli. "It's so hard to find good help these days." He chuckled at his own joke, his smile indulgent. "Please, make yourselves at home. If there's anything you require, just tap the comm and ask for Cmd. Muiruri. Oh." He glanced around, as if realizing something was missing. "We don't have any servers. One moment." He touched his comband. "Cmd. Muiruri, send ten crewmembers to the common area immediately. These gentlemen are thirsty and we have no one to serve them."

The slight delay before her, "Yes, sir," filtered through the comm was also familiar. Muiruri probably had to unlock her jaw before she could get the words out.

Nat knew that feeling all too well.

One Hundred Twenty-Two

Lelindia woke to the warmth of her mate's muscled body wrapped around her and his lips nuzzling her neck behind her ear.

"Happy birthday, checana," her murmured, his teeth nipping lightly at her earlobe.

Her breath hitched, a bolt of sensation shooting straight to her core. "Thank you."

His tongue traced the places his teeth had sensitized. "How do you wish to begin your day?"

She groaned, melting into him. "That's a good start."

His throaty chuckle made her entire body tingle.

She turned her head, sinking her fingers into his hair and capturing his mouth in a languorous kiss. Her energy field engaged, wrapping around them both.

He groaned, his tongue stroking hers, making it clear exactly what he had in mind.

She was all in on that plan.

His hand glided over her bare skin, leaving a trail of heat from her shoulder to her waist before cradling her bare breast.

Oh, stars. When the tip of his claw grazed lazily over her nipple, her body went from zero to lightspeed in a tenth of a second.

He growled, his leg wrapping over hers, the hard lines of his body making firm contact with her curves.

This is why she'd started sleeping naked shortly after their mating. He gave off plenty of heat to keep her warm, and the touch of his skin against hers was too delightful to mute with fabric.

His muscles flexed as he rolled, taking her with him. He draped her across his torso, her legs tangled with his. "Checana," he whispered, his lips moving to her jawline, then the sensitive skin of her neck.

Flames burned everywhere he touched.

She closed her eyes, her mind in the blissful state where dream and reality shared one breath. His strong hands kneaded her breasts, then skimmed over her belly to the juncture of her thighs, drawing moans of pleasure and whimpers of need.

"Take what you need, checana."

Her mind registered the soft command, more than happy to obey. She pushed against his shoulders, rising to her knees. Their groans mingled as she locked him into the intimate connection they both craved.

His hands settled on her hips, the tips of his claws pricking her skin.

Her body tightened, her hips rocking forward in response. "Yeeesss," she hissed, sensation coursing through every cell in her body.

His growl of agreement vibrated through her, tearing away what little restraint she'd held onto. She let go, moving in the timeless rhythm that joined her with her mate. Her breathless cries fused with his, escalating to a roar as they exploded together into a nebula of ecstasy.

Conscious thought returned slowly. The steady beat of his heart and contented purr rumbled against her cheek, the musky scent of his skin filling her senses. She darted her tongue out, lapping up the salty sweat coating his chest. "Mmm."

His hand squeezed her backside, the other hand sliding under her hair to caress her nape.

She let out a happy sigh, reveling in how cherished his touch made her feel. "Best start to a birthday ever."

His purr grew louder. "I am glad you approve."

She lifted her head, propping her chin on her fist as she gazed into his eyes. "Oh, I definitely approve. We might have to make this a birthday tradition."

His pupils dilated, heat smoldering in the golden depths. "If you insist."

"I do." She lifted her hand, tracing the thin tendrils of brown on his cheek and jaw with her finger, following their meandering paths over his skin. "You are so beautiful."

His expression shifted. Lifting his head, he captured her mouth in his. The tenderness of his kiss brought tears to her eyes.

"You see beauty, because you are beauty," he murmured, kissing each of her tears as they glided down her cheeks. "You fill everything you touch with life."

The tears fell faster.

He eased them both to a sitting position, cradling her face in his hands. "My lovely Lelindia." He stroked her cheeks with his thumbs, a soft smile on his lips. "My checana. How may I bring you joy on this day?"

Her laugh was a little watery. "You're off to a stellar start already."

His teeth flashed in a heart-stopping smile. "Will you allow me to bathe you before I prepare your breakfast?"

Her body gave an enthusiastic high-five to that suggestion, but she made a show of considering it. "Well, I don't kno—" She squealed as Jonarel somehow managed to rise to his feet in the bed with her still pressed against his chest, pregnant belly and all. She locked her legs around his hips as he leapt to the deck, barely making a sound.

As if she needed another incentive to go up in flames.

Two hours later, she was squeaky clean and well-fed. So was he. She'd made sure he got just as much attention in the shower as she had.

She gazed at him over the rim of her tea mug as she sipped the lemongrass ginger blend he'd prepared for her. His hair was still damp, the gentle waves of mahogany curling slightly at the tips where they draped over his shoulders. He hadn't put on a shirt yet — much to her delight — his impressive muscles and the delicate trails of brown that meandered over his skin on full display. "Have I mentioned this is the best start to a birthday ever?"

Amusement danced in his golden eyes. "I believe you have."

"Good." Thanks to Unity, she'd already received happy birthday wishes from her parents, Aurora and her family, and Celia. "So, what's next?"

Tehar's image appeared beside the dining table. "Good morning, sister. Joyful wishes on your birthday."

"Thank you, Tehar." Her gaze flicked to Jonarel. "I'm enjoying it so far."

"So am I," he murmured, clasping her hand on the table.

Even that innocuous touch was enough to send tremors through her.

"You asked about your next plans," Tehar continued. "Our mother was hoping you would agree to join her in the greenhouse."

"Oh? Do you know why?"

"That is for her to reveal."

Uh-huh. She hadn't expected her birthday to include surprises, given their current situation, but she hadn't taken into account the resourcefulness of her mate and his family. "Are you coming with me?" she asked Jonarel.

"I will be with my father in the observation lounge. You may join us when you are ready."

Now her curiosity was well and truly piqued.

Jonarel went with her as far as the entrance to the med bay before giving her a tender kiss and continuing down the corridor to the observation lounge. She moved through the dimly lit med bay, the doors to the greenhouse parting at her approach. The familiar scents and sounds of the space welcomed her with open arms, drawing her forward.

Raehn gave a happy wriggle. Her daughter could definitely sense when she was in the greenhouse. Tiny tendrils of her emerald-green energy field flitted out in search of the nearby plants.

She moved to the edge of the path so Raehn could make contact, but didn't see any sign of Jonarel's mother in the area. The lushness of the greenhouse made it difficult to spot anyone in the greenery, let alone a Kraed who blended in. "Daymar?"

"Over here, checala." Daymar's voice drifted from the pathway to the right that led to one of the herb gardens.

Lelindia followed the trail, finally spotting Daymar beside the raised beds where rosemary and thyme flowed over the edge. She was dressed in an outfit unlike anything she'd seen before. The pants fit looser than standard Kraed leggings, the drape giving them a flowing effect like grass swaying in the breeze, imagery the yellow-green color emphasized. The tan-colored top was tighter and asymmetrical, showing patches of dark green skin on her arms and torso. It reminded Lelindia of a cross between a swashbuckling pirate's outfit and a dancer's costume.

A cargo glider rested beside the herb bed, a curtain of fabric nearly as tall as Daymar draped over the contents, concealing whatever lay underneath.

"Lelindia." Daymar reached her in two long strides, wrapping her in her arms in a loving hug. "I bless the day that brought your birth, and for all the joy you have brought to our family."

Dammit, she was crying again. She sniffed, blinking rapidly to stem the tide. "Thank you."

"It is I who thank you, checala." Daymar leaned back without loosening her hold, meeting her gaze. "You have healed the wounds of our family, made us whole again. My children have blossomed in the light of your generous heart. There are no words to express my gratitude and wonder at all you have given us."

She should just start wearing a bathing suit. Then she wouldn't care if her flood of tears was dampening her clothes. "You are the mother of my mate. None of this..." she swept her hand to indicate the ship, "would have happened without you."

Daymar rested her hand on Lelindia's damp cheek. "Soon I will witness the birth of your child, see my son hold his daughter in his arms." Her eyes sparkled with humor as she stepped back. "You may find it difficult to convince him to put her down."

Lelindia chuckled, wiping the moisture from her face with her fingers. "I've already been working on that issue. Besides, she's a Nedale. She'll heal any injury before he has time to fuss over her."

Daymar's brows lifted. "Her abilities will manifest at birth?"

"Her abilities are manifesting now. Here." She clasped Daymar's hand and rested it on her belly. "Raehn, do you want to say hello to your grandmother?" She gave Raehn a small energetic nudge.

Her daughter responded, her energy field blooming like a flower. The emerald-green danced over Daymar's skin while Raehn's tiny feet kicked against the confines surrounding her.

Daymar inhaled sharply. "That is her energy?"

"Yep. She's very energetic, in the Suulh way and the Kraed way. I expect her to keep her daddy on his toes."

"Remarkable. I had not expected such... liveliness at this stage of development."

"This isn't typical for Suulh, either. Her blended genetics, combined with several intense energy experiences have created unusual circumstances, accelerating the process."

"She will be blessed with the strength of both her parents."

Lelindia smiled. Leave it to Daymar to see Raehn's potential clearly. "She's going to be a very powerful Nedale and Kraed."

Daymar's gaze dropped to where Raehn's energy field continued to play over her fingers. "I still have much to learn about your people."

"And I have much to learn about yours. For instance, I didn't know until I visited the Embassy that the clans have different coloring that you can change. That was a revelation."

"Jonarel never explained the transition when we pair bond into other clans?"

"I don't think it ever occurred to him. I'd never met anyone from a different clan, so it never came up, not until we encountered Remar and the other members of Clan Terfeli."

"Ah, Remar." A look of deep affection lit Daymar's eyes. "What were your impressions of my brother's daughter?"

"I liked her a lot. She's feisty."

Daymar's lips quirked. "An apt description. She is charting her own path, much as Jonarel did. She was delighted to meet you."

"That's good to hear."

"Your visit was cause for great celebration." Stepping back, she turned toward the cargo glider. "In honor of your mating with Jonarel, I have brought you a gift from Clan Terfeli."

Anticipation fizzed and popped in her veins. The location Daymar had chosen to present this gift would have been a big hint already, even if Lelindia couldn't sense the lifeforce of the plants hidden beneath the cloth.

Daymar moved beside the glider. "How much do you know about the talents of my birth clan?"

"I know you're gifted horticulturalists. And that you're the only clan who can make tenrebac."

"Indeed. Much like the Suulh, we have a passion for plants." Daymar slid her fingers underneath the edge of the cloth and carefully lifted it away. A spicy scent drifted off the crimson-streaked leaves of a young tree where the cloth brushed against it.

Lelindia moved closer, drawn by the allure of the exotic plants.

Daymar rubbed one of the leaves between her fingers, intensifying the spicy aroma. "Do you recognize this scent?"

It generated a remembered taste on her tongue, but not one she could put her finger on. "Is it used in tenrebac?"

"Tenrebac...?" Daymar lifted one brow, her expression expectant.

Memory clicked. "The spicy tenrebac-based drink you served us for our first Christmas onboard the *Excelsior*."

"Tenrebac dellum," Daymar confirmed. "This is a camninon tree, native to the hill country of my clan. We use its leaves and bark in many of our dishes and drinks."

Lelindia inhaled deeply. "Celia's going to love having this for her cooking experiments. Can it be used as an herbal tea?"

"Of course." Daymar still had that expectant look on her face.

Which made Lelindia survey the other plants on the glider with a horticulturalist's eye. The next largest was another young tree with round pale lilac fruit. Next to it sat a vine with magenta berry-like clusters. On the opposite side, spiraling bright fuchsia seed pods dangled like Christmas ornaments from a plump shrub. A delicate grey-green groundcover herb spread out across the base of the glider. "Are all of these used in making tenrebac dellum?"

"Not just tenrebac dellum. They combine to form many of our most popular drinks, much like your herbal teas and coffee."

Daymar certainly knew the way to her heart.

"And several have medicinal qualities."

She *really* knew the way to her heart. "This is amazing." She enfolded Daymar in a hug, sniffing as the ever-present tears threatened. "Thank you, solna."

Daymar's grip tightened. "You are clan." Her voice was almost as thick as Lelindia's. "Our gifts are yours."

That did not help in slowing the waterworks. "And mine are yours."

Daymar gave a nearly silent chuckle. "You will find my birth clan is much more appreciative of your healing talents than my mate has been. Clan Terfeli does not share his views that receiving medical care is a sign of weakness."

"That's good to know." And potentially another reason Clan Terfeli had been predisposed to welcome her with open arms.

She dabbed at her eyes with her sleeve as she pulled back. "So, all of these plants grow near the Clan Terfeli compound?"

Daymar nodded. "Plants are at the heart of Clan Terfeli. We nurture them as they nurture us, sharing our gifts. The plants around our compound provide sustenance, but they have also taught our people how best to thrive amidst the dangers and challenges of our world."

Lelindia frowned. "What do you mean?"

Daymar's eyes narrowed. "Has Jonarel told you nothing that did not pertain to Clan Clarek?"

She shrugged helplessly.

Daymar gave a soft harrumph. "My birth clan is the source of the fabrics that allow us to interact effortlessly with our environment." She swept a hand down her body to indicate her outfit. "By studying the strengths and adaptations of the plants of our world, we learned how to create fabrics that would regulate temperature and moisture and also provide protection from physical trauma."

Lelindia blinked. "You mean Clan Terfeli made the outfits you gifted to us when we visited Drakar?"

"They made the *fabric*," Daymar corrected. "I made the clothing."

Including the gorgeous blue dress she'd worn for her mating ceremony. "I'd assumed Jonarel had learned his sewing skills from you, but I'd never realized your birth clan made the fabrics." She mulled that over. "Does that include the fabric for the battlesuits Jonarel made for us? And the spacesuits?"

"Yes."

No wonder Jonarel had a talent for generating and adapting clothing. His mother was from a clan of experts. "Since I've never visited the Terfeli compound, I'll need your help determining where and how these should be planted."

"Of course. Tehar?"

Tehar's image appeared beside the glider. "I have already converted an expansion space in an appropriate environmental zone."

"Expansion space?" She wasn't aware of any unused space in the greenhouse.

Tehar's golden eyes glimmered in anticipation. "In the initial design for the greenhouse, Jonarel arranged all the pathways on one level to ensure you and Aurora would be comfortable with the layout. However, he included infrastructure for conversions that would result in a multi-level design. The flexibility allows for the addition of new levels and zones and accommodates the anticipated growth of the plants."

Every time she thought she'd plumbed the depths of what the *Starhawke* could do, a new window opened onto a stunning vista of possibilities. "And where is this expansion space?"

The cargo glider rose a few centimeters as Tehar took a step backward. "Follow me."

Daymar motioned for Lelindia to go first, following behind her. The cargo glider trailed them like an oversized child's wagon.

The path led them out of the herb garden and into the warmest zone of the greenhouse. Lelindia's steps slowed, her mouth dropping open as her head tipped back.

The overhead rose an additional two meters above where it had been the last time she'd visited this area two days ago. The curving path that wound through this zone now contained a new branch to the right. The stone walkway climbed a gentle incline that formed a low hill overlooking the area below.

"When...?" Lelindia asked, words failing her as her gaze swept over the space. The hill was hollow, like an overpass, all the plants that had been part of the area previously still in their original places, but with new lighting surrounding them that kept the packed earth embankment above them from casting them in shadow.

Daymar rested her hands on Lelindia's shoulders. "With Kire's permission, Tehar let my work crew in during your night cycle. Jonarel and Unity promised to keep you occupied until we finished."

And here she'd been wondering if having her parents and Aurora gone for her birthday would make the celebration underwhelming. She should have known Jonarel would never have allowed that to happen. "You and Jonarel planned this all in advance?"

"Yes. As I said during the creevigan, I was not able to welcome you as my son's checana in the ways of our people." Daymar drew her closer, her voice thickening. "These plants are part of my heritage, gifts that establish your connection to Clan Terfeli. They will be with you wherever your journey takes you, just as you, checala, will always be in my heart."

One Hundred Twenty-Three

After *Cassini* departed Eridani Duo, *Phoenix* headed back to Zeta Tucanae.

The familiar sensation of the interstellar jump helped Cade sleep. A solid seven hours later, he felt a lot more energized.

He was also missing Aurora like crazy. His cabin was too quiet, just like their shared cabin on the *Starhawke* had been after Aurora had left for Tnaryt's Camp. Knowing she wouldn't be onboard to greet him when he returned didn't help. "Unity, any updates on Aurora's situation?"

U-2 swayed. "No. The Ecilam keep expanding their search for the Etah."

A fruitless endeavor with the Etah ensconced on Ifel's ship. "How's Aurora doing?"

"She's... not happy."

"I'll bet. Is she busy?" While *Phoenix* was in the interstellar jump, he had time on his hands.

"Not at the—" Unity broke off, bobbing up and down. "Nixon just announced a press conference."

"For when?"

"Fifteen minutes."

So much for a chat. He headed out of the cabin. "Tell Aurora I'll check in with her after the press conference."

"Will do."

He jogged down the stairs to C deck. "Have you notified the others?"

"We notified the Admiral and Reynolds."

He grimaced. Unity was understandably avoiding any direct communication with Montgomery.

"They just told Montgomery. We told Nat, too."

"Thanks."

Unity had an image of what looked like a lecture hall up on the media room screen when Cade entered. The Admiral, Reynolds, and Montgomery weren't far behind, with Nat and Marlin joining them a few minutes later.

U-2 chose to hang out with Nat in the second row behind Cade, as far from Montgomery as they could get while still being part of the group.

On the screen, a surprisingly large number of journalists had gathered in the seats facing the lectern, considering even for a fast ship it was a two-day journey from Earth, and only marginally closer to Hydra One.

Then again, Nixon might have planned to hold a press conference all along. He wouldn't have wasted the opportunity to emphasize his *good deed* of bringing Montgomery back to Earth to receive the best medical care. He also would have wanted to crow about putting the Teeli consuls on *Cassini* to protect the crew from traitors.

Montgomery had flipped the script on him with her broadcast, but clearly he had a new game plan, likely provided by the Sovereign.

The very thought put Cade's teeth on edge.

A man in a Fleet uniform with a lieutenant's rank insignia entered from a side door and strode up to the microphone.

Cade's eyes narrowed. The man looked familiar. Where had he seen him before?

"Thank you all for being here. Admiral Nixon will be out momentarily to make an important announcement."

The oily smile did the trick. "That's Ensign Barr."

The Admiral's brows rose. "The man who took over my office during my absence?"

"Yes." The one who'd replaced Magee after the Teeli had manipulated her into moving to the Embassy. The one whose service records he hadn't been able to track down after the Admiral's return. "Looks like he crawled out from under his rock to take Liddy's place as Nixon's PA." Which indicated Nixon was the high-ranking official who'd installed Barr in the Admiral's office and scrubbed his records afterward.

Nixon entered, the picture of calm command, smiling graciously at the gathered journalists as he approached the lectern. Sly-Kull entered as well, but remained in the background.

"Welcome all, to Eridani Duo, one of the Fleet's most prestigious science stations. The scientists here are doing great work, important work that will benefit the Union for generations to come."

Cade frowned. Nixon sounded like he was speaking at a science conference, not a press conference.

"It's always a pleasure to visit this station and speak with the dedicated scientists working here." His expression shifted from friendly to stern. "Unfortunately, my current visit has been marred by the heinous actions of our enemies. By now, many of you have likely seen the video that was broadcast here a couple days ago, purportedly from Fleet Captain Montgomery. It made some terrible, baseless claims about me and our good friends the Teeli." He gave an apologetic nod in Sly-Kull's direction. "However, I can assure you that the entire thing was a hoax."

"A hoax?" Montgomery snarled, her lips pulling back from her teeth like she wanted to latch onto Nixon's throat.

"Captain Montgomery is not aligned with the traitors. She's in the care of my personal physician, and will make a public statement as soon as she's up to it."

"What the frack?" Nat sounded as gobsmacked as Cade felt. "What reality is he living in?"

"The one he's creating," the Admiral said softly, his gaze never leaving the screen.

"After a detailed investigation by our top people, the best of the best, we have learned — as I suspected the moment I saw it — that the fake video was created by Admiral Schreiber and Captain Hawke. They broadcast it with the help of their Kraed co-conspirators, who broke them out of prison so they could escape the sword of justice, and who now hide them like the criminals they are."

"That's going to go over well with Siginal," Reynolds muttered.

"But I give you my word that we will find them. We will not allow these traitors — not just traitors, terrorists — to sow divisiveness and hatred among our citizens. We will not allow them to turn our pacifist friends into a target for their malice and villainy. We will not allow them to disregard the rule of law and destroy our institutions." Nixon leaned forward, his hands gripping the edges of the lectern, his voice taking on a hard edge. "These terrorists will be found, and they will face a reckoning for their crimes."

Nixon let the silence stretch out for a few seconds, then settled back into a more affable expression.

Barr stepped forward. "The Admiral will take a few questions."

Hands shot up. Barr called on a journalist near the front.

"Are Union citizens in danger?"

A pained look settled on Nixon's face, too studied to be authentic. "Unfortunately, yes. Until the traitors are caught, we are all at risk. They have sympathizers and spies everywhere. That's why I have assigned Teeli consuls to our Fleet ships, to protect our loyal Fleet servicemembers from the machinations of those who wish to destroy our beloved Fleet. Anyone who is complicit with Schreiber and Hawke will be treated like the traitors they are. I ask everyone to join the hunt, to locate them quickly so they can be brought to justice." He pointed at another journalist.

"How are the Teeli reacting to the false accusations?"

The phrasing of the question spoke volumes. Clearly the journalists had been coached on what to say, or had been personally selected for their willingness to parrot Nixon's take on the situation, without any critical thinking and without questioning the narrative he was spinning.

Nixon gave a weak smile, glancing again at Sly'Kull before answering. "They are understandably hurt and saddened, but our friendship remains strong. They know these are the actions of a weak few. They are a very forgiving people. They have recommitted to helping us root out the rot in the Fleet so that we will once again be the respected power in this sector of the galaxy."

Nat muttered something under her breath Cade didn't quite catch, but he agreed one hundred percent with the emotional resonance of disgust behind it.

Barr indicated a third journalist.

"What actions are you taking to censure the Kraed for their involvement with the traitors?"

Nixon's eyes glinted with malice. "The Kraed were given leniency in the past because of the role they played in our initial expansion beyond our solar system. But that was a long time ago."

His lip curled. "We allowed one of them to serve in our Fleet, which was a grave mistake, one I would not have approved if I had been in a position of power to prevent it. They took advantage of our generosity and trust, selling us out for the benefit of the traitors. I can assure you we are watching them very, *very* closely. Their delegates in the Council are on probation and a proposal has been submitted to the Council to revoke their membership permanently. I support that proposal."

Cade's stomach lurched. The move wasn't entirely unexpected, but the fact that Nixon had gotten it submitted for consideration proved just how much power he'd gained in the GC.

Barr stepped forward. "Thank you, that's all the Admiral has time for today." He followed Nixon and Sly-Kull out the door.

"Can he do that?" Nat asked. "Kick the Kraed out of the Council?"

The Admiral looked over his shoulder, meeting her gaze. "It wouldn't be easy. It would require a three-fourths vote in the Council and General Assembly. But even submitting the proposal will cause serious damage to the Kraed's standing in the Union."

"Which is the goal." Montgomery's face had drawn tight. "To weaken the biggest threat to his coup." She looked like she was already following the thought problem down its many branched trails and didn't like where it led.

"Indeed," the Admiral agreed.

"Will the Kraed fight it?" Nat asked him.

"That remains to be seen. Siginal is much more concerned with convincing the other clan leaders to take action against the Teeli than with Nixon's political maneuvering. The two delegates from his clan will no doubt speak against the proposal, but Siginal might be willing to concede the Council seats if it allows him to focus his attention and resources on dealing with the Teeli directly."

Nat folded her arms over her chest. "What about what Nixon said about Montgomery? Is there a way we can prove to everyone he's lying?"

"Excellent question." The Admiral glanced at Marlin. "Is there a meal waiting for us in the dining hall?"

He nodded. "I was just finishing it up when we got the news."

"Then let's work on answering Nat's question while we eat."

One Hundred Twenty-Four

Lelindia had never experienced a birthday celebration like the one Clan Clarek threw for her on the *Rowkclarek*. From the moment she and Jonarel had set foot on the ship with Tehar, Knox, Isabeau, Kire, and Kelly, she'd received more hugs than she could count.

When they'd arrived at the dining hall, the roar of welcome had drowned out the energetic beat of drums in the background. Daymar had whisked her to an oval table on an elevated section overlooking the open space at the center of the room, directing her to a chair festooned with the bright purple and yellow flowers of the denglar trees. Jonarel claimed the seat to her left, with Tehar, Kire, and Kelly beside him. Daymar bookended her other side, with Siginal, Knox, Isabeau, and Rowk filling out the seating for the table.

She was delighted to see Daymar lean into Siginal when he slid his arm around her shoulders. Their relationship was finally on the mend.

The enticing scents of the food being carried in by the teenage servers prompted her stomach to give a particularly loud rumble of anticipation.

"You are hungry, checala?" Daymar asked.

She laughed, resting a hand over her round belly. "Thanks to Raehn, I'm always hungry."

A petite teenager appeared beside her, balancing a platter of roasted vegetables in one fern-green hand. "Happy birthday," he said in heavily accented Galish.

"Thank you." The aromas of the food tickled her nose. The Kraed weren't subtle in their flavors. She could almost taste them on her tongue already.

He held up a wooden serving spoon. "May I serve you?"

"Please."

A succession of servers moved around the table until her plate was no longer visible. She dug in with gusto, humming with appreciation from the first bite.

Jonarel's shoulder brushed hers, his hand resting on her thigh. "You are pleased?" he murmured in her ear.

His warm breath made her quiver. She held his gaze as she threaded her fingers through his. "Very pleased."

Awareness lit his golden eyes, a secret smile that made her heart flutter brushing across his lips.

Conversation flowed as freely during the meal as the tenrebac. She enjoyed the taste of Clan Terfeli's signature drink, and unlike Aurora, she didn't have to worry about the alcohol content affecting her or Raehn. Her body cleared it from her system before it could impair her in any way, a fact she'd lamented on one notable occasion when getting toasted had sounded like a really good idea.

As the meal wound down, Siginal stood and clapped his hands, the sharp sound focusing attention from around the room.

"Today we celebrate Lelindia," he boomed out, "Nedale of the Suulh, Jonarel's checana, and mother of Raehn Clarek."

The cheer that swept the room filled her chest with warmth and — predictably — pushed tears from the corners of her eyes.

A lively drumbeat from behind made her turn. Undulating ribbons of dancers flowed to the beat, drawing closer as they wound around the trees and tables, their movements seeming to beckon to her.

Jonarel rose, pulling her to her feet, facing the dancers. His arms circled her expanded waist, his lips brushing the side of her neck. "Brendan informed me he taught you how to dance."

She gave a jolt of surprise, then trembled as his lips continued to caress her skin. She'd never danced with the partner she'd always wanted, the one whose touch was currently sending lightning bolts streaking through her body. "He did, when I was a child."

Jonarel chuckled at the huskiness in her voice. "Dance with me?"

She pivoted, her body as pliant as a rose petal in his hands. "Absolutely."

He tugged her toward the floor, where the other dancers had spread out, moving in groups of two, three, and four. This wasn't like the group dancing she'd seen last year at the send-off celebration on Drakar. This was more intimate, the dancers always in contact with each other, with very little distance between their bodies as they moved through the steps.

She bit her lip as she watched their feet. Some of those steps would be tricky with Raehn affecting her balance.

"Lelindia."

Her breath caught as Jonarel's fingers stroked her cheek, turning her face to meet his gaze. So much love. So much tenderness.

"Do not worry about the steps." His arms slid around her, guiding her into place in front of him. "I will not let you stumble." He lowered his head, brushing his lips over hers with the lightness of a butterfly. "Dance with me," he whispered.

"Yes," she sighed, tugging his head down for a more substantial kiss. His purr vibrated through her, coaxing tendrils of both hers and Raehn's energy fields to the surface.

Ignoring everything but the beat of the drums and the movements of her mate, she tuned into the cues he gave her with the pressure of his hands, the turn of his body. On more than one occasion, he lifted her completely off her feet, whether to keep her from stumbling – as he'd promised – or because it was part of the dance, she didn't know and didn't care. As she picked up the patterns of his movements, her own grew more fluid, her steps more confident.

The joy in his eyes bathed her like sunshine. The next time he lifted her, she grinned, and was rewarded with one of his breathtaking smiles. Her heart stuttered as emotion rushed through her like a river. "Jonarel…" Her throat thickened, feelings she couldn't put into words tightening her grip.

He pulled her in close, halting their movement as his gaze held hers. "Lelindia."

Her name was a blessing. And a promise.

As his lips met hers, the emotional wave crested, filling her with gratitude for this moment, this life. He filled her senses — the seductive caress of his hands and lips, the tantalizing scent of his skin, the delectable taste of him on her tongue. Nothing existed but the two of—

"Oof!" Her startled exclamation broke the kiss as Raehn gave a particularly assertive kick.

Make that three of them.

A quick glance confirmed her daughter was doing her own dance moves.

"Lelindia?"

The concern in Jonarel's voice brought her head up. "I'm fine. I think she was enjoying the dancing and didn't like that we stopped." Which made her realize the drumming had stopped, too. "Um…"

Everyone was staring at them. Knox, Isabeau, Kire, Kelly, and Tehar were looking at them with amusement, but everyone else, including Siginal, Daymar, and Rowk, were gazing at them like they were mythical creatures who'd just materialized out of thin air.

Heat crept up her neck. "Jonarel?" she murmured.

"Love matches are rare in my clan," he murmured back, amusement and a heavy dose of satisfaction in his voice as he nuzzled her cheek.

Her flush deepened. "Can you make them stop staring?"

He chuckled softly, straightening. "You already did."

Sure enough, like she'd waved a magic wand, everyone was looking anywhere except at her and Jonarel.

She dropped her forehead against his chest. "I keep forgetting how well you can hear." Her quiet request to him might as well have been shouted through a bullhorn in the silent room.

His fingers stroked her nape. "They have no wish to make you uncomfortable. But a pairing like ours is revered. By witnessing it, they are honoring the sacredness of our bond."

She lifted her head. "Will that work in our favor when we meet with the clan leaders?"

His fingers stilled. "Perhaps."

The drums started again, reminding her they were still standing on the dance floor. The next dance was one of the group dances she'd seen before. She and Jonarel moved to where Kire and Kelly, who'd learned the steps last time, were teaching them to Knox and Isabeau. Siginal and Daymar stepped onto the floor, and even Tehar and Rowk joined in as everyone moved to the beat.

Raehn loved the dancing. Her happy wiggles and kicks, combined with bursts of her energy field, made sure Lelindia didn't forget her daughter was part of the celebration, too. Not that she and

Jonarel needed another reason to remain on the floor most of the time, only taking small breaks so she could catch her breath and hydrate.

During one of those breaks, Daymar approached Jonarel, whispering something Lelindia didn't catch. Jonarel's pupils dilated, his gaze darting to her.

She knew him well, knew excitement when she saw it. "What is it?"

He clasped her hand in his. "Come with me."

She followed him and Daymar through the dining hall, acknowledging the well wishes of the members of the clan they passed on their way to the entrance, which appeared to be Jonarel's destination. "Are we leaving?"

"No, checana." The excitement was evident in his voice now, too.

Clearly he had one more birthday surprise in store for her.

Tehar and Rowk stood on either side of the entrance to the dining hall. They gestured to the opening, where two familiar figures stepped into view.

Her heart went airborne. So did her feet as she raced forward. "Mom! Dad!" She flung herself at them, wrapping one arm around each of their shoulders in an incredibly awkward and completely hilarious hug.

They all burst out laughing, committing to the ridiculous hug with gusto.

"You're here!" She pulled back. "I thought you weren't going to make it in time."

Her dad's eyes twinkled. "We wanted it to be a surprise. We left a little earlier than we'd indicated. Also, Unity has *Gladiator* humming. They helped me shave off a chunk of flight time. Happy birthday, firefly."

She gave him a proper hug. "Thanks, Dad." Then she hugged her mom. "Thanks, Mom."

Her mom squeezed her back. "Happy birthday." Then she turned to Daymar. "It's lovely to see you again, Daymar. It's been a while."

"Since the Academy."

Daymar and Siginal had met both her parents and Libra when they'd paid a visit to her and Aurora shortly after Aurora began dating Cade. Her parents had tried to pass it off as a social visit, but it had been clear from the moment they'd arrived that Libra was there to pass judgment on Cade. It hadn't gone well.

Daymar gave her mom and dad warm hugs. "I am delighted you could join us."

Her dad smiled. "We appreciate you taking over the festivities for Lelindia's birthday celebration." He pointed in the direction of the dining hall, where the drumbeats kept up a steady rhythm. "Sounds like quite a party."

"We've been dancing all evening. I also have something new to show you in the greenhouse." Lelindia let out a contented sigh as

Jonarel slipped his arms around her from behind, nestling her against his chest. "It's been a great birthday."

"But it isn't over yet." Her dad gave her a wink.

"Oh?"

He opened his eyes wide in pseudo-shock. "You didn't think I was going to let my daughter's birthday go by without baking something for the occasion, did you?" He stepped to the side. "Okay, Tehar."

A small cargo glider floated into the room.

She gasped with delight. A decadent chocolate confection sat on top. "You made me a cake!"

"You bet I did. Your mom and Marlin helped, but I came up with the design."

And what a design it was. Her dad had created a miniature fantasy garden, complete with planked walkway and raised beds showcasing some of her most beloved plants.

Jonarel released her so she could get a closer look. She could make out individual leaves and petals on each chocolate plant, including the rose. "This is amazing."

"Glad you think so. We also brought some friends to join the celebration."

She lifted her gaze as Justin, Bella, Tam, and Gonzo stepped into view.

"Happy birthday!" they chorused.

She inhaled deeply as her emotions got the better of her – again.

Jonarel's arms enfolded her, drawing her against the warm, solid length of his body. "Happy birthday, checana."

"Thank you." The words came out muddled. She sniffed, then cleared her throat and tried again. "Thank you all. This means... so much."

Justin stepped forward, holding out his hand to Daymar. "Hi, I'm Justin."

"Sorry." She'd forgotten Daymar hadn't been with Signal on Azaana when he'd met the rest of Cade's team. "This is Daymar, Jonarel's mother."

"I kinda figured," Justin smiled as Daymar bypassed the handshake and pulled him into a hug.

"Daymar, this is Bella, Tam, and Gonzo. They're members of Cade's team and part of our extended crew."

Daymar gave each of them a hug. "Welcome to the *Rowkclarek.*"

"Glad to be here." Justin's gaze shifted over Daymar's shoulder as Signal appeared with Kire, Kelly, Knox, and Isabeau in tow. "This is an incredible ship."

Pride shone in Signal's eyes at the praise. "It is." He stepped forward, hugging her parents, then startled everyone by approaching Justin and pulling him into a hug, too. The rest of the team shared looks as Signal went down the line, giving them all hugs.

The change in reception was unexpected, considering how violently Siginal had opposed Cade's presence around Aurora – and by extension Cade's team – ever since they'd joined forces with the *Starhawke's* crew.

A quick glance at Daymar, who was watching the interactions with an air of satisfaction, gave her a hint to the cause. She'd be willing to bet that after the creevigan had exposed Siginal's undesirable and reactionary behavior, Daymar had laid down new ground rules regarding her mate's attitudes toward everyone connected to the *Starhawke*, including Cade and his team.

That would be a boon to them all, particularly Aurora and Cade.

"So." Justin took a step closer to the cargo glider and grinned. "Do we get a piece of this cake we've been salivating over the whole way here?"

"Byrnsie," Bella hissed, elbowing him in the ribs. "It's *Lelindia's* cake."

"I know." He rubbed the spot and pouted, even though Lelindia's Nedale senses told her Bella hadn't made contact with enough force to actually hurt him. "But I'm her favorite patient ever. We bonded on Burrow." He met her gaze and grinned, his eyes crinkling at the corners. "Right?"

She grinned back. "Absolutely." Certainly the most talkative and entertaining patient she'd ever had, despite his severe concussion.

Her mom moved between Justin and the cargo glider. "Before we cut into this, everyone's going to hold hands and make a wish for Lelindia."

"Ooh, I like that." Justin nodded enthusiastically, grabbing Bella's hand in his.

Jonarel released her, stepping aside so her parents could stand next to her.

Her mom didn't let him. She grabbed his hand and hers, joining them together. "You're her mate. Your place is by her side, now and always."

Now and always. She liked the sound of that.

So did Jonarel, judging by the way he gazed at her.

Her heart swelled as she surveyed the circle of family and friends who had gathered to celebrate with her. Even Tehar and Rowk had joined the circle, standing on either side of Daymar and Siginal. Her thoughts reached out to the ones who were lightyears away — her energy sister in particular — gratitude filling her to the brim.

Engaging her energy field, she sent it sweeping in both directions. Her mom joined it, enhancing the vibrancy of the emerald-green glow of the circle. Raehn's ignited a moment later, flitting out in swirls and dancing ribbons that were so playfully random they made her smile. Her dad's energy field looped around and through the other three, a strong cord of yellow-gold that gently bound them all together.

The waterworks crept up on her again.

"Everyone make a wish for Lelindia's coming year," her mom reminded them, "and hold it in your heart."

She couldn't feel the emotions of those around her like Aurora could, but she could certainly see the looks of love, joy, and affection directed her way. She sniffed, then blinked a couple times as the scene shimmered. "Thank you."

"Happy birthday!" Justin's boisterous shout sparked laughter around the circle, and additional shouts of "Happy birthday!"

"Thank you!" she shouted with equal enthusiasm, triggering more laughter. She released her energy field, her mom and dad's dissipating as well, although Raehn's continued to flit here and there, searching for a playmate.

Jonarel turned her to face him, cradling the back of her head in his large hands. "Happy birthday, checana," he whispered, capturing her lips in a kiss that promised many more to come.

"Kiss later," Justin teased. "There's cake to be eaten."

She smiled against Jonarel's lips. "He's right."

Jonarel held her gaze long enough to make her heart flutter before stepping back.

They commandeered one of the large tables at the back of the dining hall. Her dad gave her a very generous piece of cake, which was as decadent as she'd anticipated — dark chocolate ganache over chocolate cake with a dark chocolate and fresh strawberry filling.

"Your mom made sure we had plenty of strawberries from Marlin's garden," her dad informed her. "He was very sad to see her go."

"He definitely was," Justin agreed. "She doubled his output. I think he would have offered her a job if he thought there was any chance she'd take it."

Her mom smiled. "I think he wanted to offer Gryphon one, too. They were having a great time together in the galley."

"They did a beautiful job with the restoration," her dad agreed. "And that mural Nat's working on is going to be spectacular."

"Mural?" Lelindia's brows rose. "Nat paints?"

"Sure does. She's the one who set the ship's exterior color scheme, but she's also a talented muralist. She showed your mom and me the much smaller mural in her cabin. It's really something."

"What's the subject?"

Her dad grinned. "A phoenix. So's the one in the dining room she's working on, but on a much grander scale."

Interesting. She wouldn't have guessed Nat was an artist, but now that she thought about it, it fit with the personality of the young pilot. "I'd like to see that."

"I'm sure she'd be delighted to invite you over when it's done, especially if you agree to stop by Marlin's garden, too."

She chuckled. "Works for me." She scooped the last bite of cake from her plate, savoring the rich flavors on her tongue. "I want to show you what Daymar did in the greenhouse. It's—" A yawn caught her by surprise. She covered her mouth with her hand, but not before Jonarel noticed.

His arm slid behind her. "It is getting late." His fingers massaged her back. "And you need your rest."

She sighed as her muscles relaxed under his gentle ministrations. "But my parents just got here."

Her mom's hand rested over hers. "And your dad flew us the whole way. We could use some sleep, too. You can show us the greenhouse in the morning."

Another yawn made her jaw pop. She surrendered. "Okay."

After a round of hugs and happy birthday wishes, her parents walked with her and Jonarel back to the *Starhawke*, parting ways on the guest deck.

As soon as the lift doors closed again, she rested her head against Jonarel's shoulder, giving in to the exhaustion she hadn't noticed creeping up on her. "Thank you for a wonderful birthday."

His arms enfolded her, cocooning her against the warmth of his body. "It was my pleasure, checana." When the lift doors opened, he scooped her up, carrying her the short distance to their cabin. Once inside their bedroom, he insisted on undressing her, then tucked her into the sleeping nook while he quickly stripped off his clothes and slid in beside her.

The touch of skin on skin awakened her nerve endings, but not enough to overcome the lethargy sinking into her body. Jonarel wrapped himself around her, his hand stroking her hair. And then he began to sing.

His rich baritone was one of her favorite sounds in the entire galaxy. The words of the song were in the Kraed language, so she only caught a few that were familiar, but enough to understand it was a song about joy and connection.

Her mind drifted as her body relaxed, surrounded by the warmth, beauty, and love of her mate.

"Happy birthday, checana," he whispered.

Best birthday ever.

One Hundred Twenty-Five

For two days the Ecilam had scoured the landscape searching for the Etah. Neither of the transports had left the planet's surface, denying U-P an opportunity to tag the two Ecilam on the orbiting ship.

Aurora swiveled the chair at *Vengeance's* comm station, checking out the bridgescreen's aerial views of Maceen's and Helotis' groups as they made their way through the jungle. The troop transport had dropped off both groups three hours ago at a distant point in the ever-expanding concentric circle surrounding the Etah camp.

Tersinis' daughters were showing grit and determination in their relentless pursuit of their prey. Their bodies, however, were exhibiting telltale signs of overexertion and debilitation. Their groups were moving at half the speed they had at the beginning of the search, which hadn't been exactly brisk to start with. The smaller Ecilam were being forced to accommodate the two leaders' injuries, which had worsened over time. They were both using makeshift staffs to keep themselves upright as they trudged through the greenery.

"They have to be getting close to calling it," Kenji commented from the navigation console as he turned toward her. "Right?"

"That depends on whether the alternative is worse." Which it probably was. Giving up would likely cost them their lives. Or so much pain they'd wish for death.

Kenji ran a hand over his crewcut. "This sucks."

"Agreed." Her empathy for the Ecilam's plight had grown exponentially as she'd watched them struggle. Even her mom's attitude had shifted, compassion smoothing out the roiling anger that had churned under the surface ever since the Ecilam arrived.

Unfortunately, none of them could do anything to help the Ecilam until one of the transports returned to the warship.

On a positive note, the wait had given U-P plenty of time to inspect both transports from the inside. They'd hitched a ride when Tersinis had piloted her transport to rendezvous with the troop transport yesterday. She'd held another meeting with her daughters, which had been even more charged than the first one.

While everyone had been busy outside, U-P had located auto-destructs on both transports. During the past few hours, the Yruf engineers had figured out how to neutralize them. However, Unity was waiting to deactivate them until they'd done a sweep of the warship. Regas had indicated all the auto-destructs were tied together, and deactivating one would trigger the others to go off.

The other positive news was they'd isolated the signal to the sub-q transmitters. It appeared to be very similar to what Aurora had encountered with the control collars on Tnaryt's ship. It projected from the warship and both transports, and like with the collars, if the connection to the signal was lost, the transmitters would activate.

The transmitters were powered by the electrical impulses of the Ecilam's bodies, an efficient way to guarantee continual activation and a near instantaneous trigger of the rapid body decomposition if the Ecilam died unexpectedly.

The very thought made bile coat her throat.

Isin's arrival on the bridge gave her a welcome distraction. He stalked through the forward hatch, his face as hard as his emotional field.

No need to ask why. It was dinnertime in the brig. "How are our guests?" she asked him dryly.

He detoured in her direction, the hard edges softening a little. "Charming as always."

She rested her forearms on the console. "If everything goes to plan, we'll be able to drop them off soon."

He stopped in front of her. "In your experience, how often does everything go to plan?"

Her lips twitched. "Almost never. You?"

"Same."

"Then I guess things are about to get interesting."

"Uh, Cap?"

They both turned toward Kenji.

He motioned to the bridgescreen. "Looks like Tersinis is moving again."

Aurora's heart picked up the pace. "Unity, is U-P onboard?"

"Yep."

Nobody moved a muscle as the arrowhead-shaped transport rose from the surface and glided over the canopy. And kept climbing.

"They're returning to the warship." Kenji smacked his console with his palm and grinned. "About time."

Her gaze flicked to the two search groups. They were making their way to where the troop transport waited.

Rising, she followed Isin to the bridge's port side, tracking Tersinis' transport as it exited the planet's atmosphere. As it drew closer, she sensed the whispered resonance of the two slaves against the backdrop of Tersinis' dark resignation and hatred.

That hatred might be focused on the missing Etah, but something about the tenor of Tersinis' emotional field indicated it was actually aimed at the person who'd put her in this situation.

If that was true, Tersinis had managed to weaken the chains of the Sovereign's all-encompassing hold on her.

One Hundred Twenty-Six

"We've attached to the two remaining Ecilam," Unity confirmed over the bridge speakers. "Now we're scanning for auto-destructs."

Isin glanced at Aurora. She was focused on the images of the Ecilam warship's interior that Unity was projecting on the bridgescreen, like she was memorizing every detail.

So were Libra and Celia. They'd arrived on the bridge shortly after Tersinis' transport had docked with the warship.

Sweep was at the security station, pouring over schematics as Unity fed them into *Vengeance*'s systems. Fleur was watching over his shoulder.

A growling sound from above made Isin look up.

"There are ten different auto-destructs on this ship!" Unity's voice was just short of a yell. "Who does that?"

Aurora grunted. "Guess the Sovereign didn't want to take any chances Tersinis would slip away."

"But ten!" Unity cried. "This ship isn't that big."

Aurora's gaze lowered to the deck, like she was reading something on the deck plating. "Can you get into position to neutralize them?" she asked quietly.

"Of course we can, but stars!" Unity's disgusted huff would have made Lyon proud. "It'll take a little time."

"What's Tersinis doing?"

"She's on the bridge with the hatch closed. We thought she was going to send a message, but right now she's just sitting there."

Aurora gave a small nod, her gaze still on the deck. "You can block any message she tries to send, right?"

"Yep."

"The troop transport just lifted off." Sweep pointed at the image on the forward curve of the bridgescreen.

Aurora's brow furrowed, her lips pinching. "Unity, you need to pick up the pace regarding those auto-destructs. And warn Ifel we may have a problem."

"What problem?"

Isin had the same question. Aurora's behavior had him on high alert.

"Something's very wrong with Tersinis' emotional field. It's... fractured. Sharp. Like a broken mirror. It feels like she's fighting herself... and losing."

"What—" Unity cut off. "She just powered up the ship's weapons."

Aurora's head jerked up, eyes wide as she stared at the warship. "I think she's going to destroy the troop transport."

"*What!*" Unity shrieked. "She wouldn't do that! No Setarip would do that!"

"I know. I'm... I'm not sure she has a choice. Unity?" Aurora's voice vibrated with trepidation.

"We're working as fast as we can." Unity's voice had lost all inflection, shooting out rapid-fire as they focused on the dire situation unfolding around them.

Tension radiated up Isin's spine. There was nothing he could do to help. Neither could Aurora. It was up to Unity and the Yruf.

"Weapons hot," Unity reported in that same monotone. "Our ships are in position to protect the transport."

Which was barreling toward the warship, oblivious to the threat of destruction.

"Four torpedoes launched."

Aurora's sharp inhale was the only sound on the bridge.

Isin couldn't see the four projectiles at this distance, but he sure as hell saw the impacts.

Light flared in rapid succession, briefly revealing a glimpse of an emerald-green hull floating between the Ecilam ship and the approaching transport.

Aurora sucked in a huge lungful of air, her hand pressing against her throat. "She saw them. She knows the Yruf are here."

"How is she responding?" Isin barked.

"She's... confused?"

"Is she firing more weapons?"

"No," Unity informed them. "She's powering them down."

"What about the auto-destructs?"

Unity let out a soft sigh, their voice regaining its buoyancy. "We're in position to neutralize them."

Aurora closed her eyes, her head falling back. "Thank you, Unity."

"Just doing our job."

She blew out a breath. "You do it well."

"Thank you."

Opening her eyes, she rolled her shoulders, then met Isin's gaze. "Well, that was interesting."

He nodded. "Everything according to plan."

One Hundred Twenty-Seven

The emotions that had exploded off Tersinis right before she'd fired the torpedoes had been hauntingly familiar. Aurora had sensed the same tortured despair and hopelessness from Nat when they'd been together on Tnaryt's ship. She'd never asked, but she suspected Nat had been about to take drastic action to end her suffering, and the suffering of those around her.

When she'd felt that same resonance echo across the void from Tersinis, a vise had clamped around her ribcage. It was still there, though it had loosened a few turns when the Yruf ships deflected the torpedoes and Unity confirmed they had control of the auto-destructs.

But that left her with a looming quandary. What now?

The plan had been to incapacitate the Ecilam without them ever realizing what was happening, allowing the Yruf to contain them without risk of a physical conflict. As Isin had pointed out with heavy irony, that plan had played out flawlessly.

Using the ultra-low frequency was still an option — Unity was in place to make that happen — but given Tersinis' emotional state, it no longer seemed like the right move. Her emotions were in chaotic flux, ricocheting from hope to anger to fear to disgust with the speed of a racquetball. It was impossible to tell which emotions were tied to which person or action.

Aurora glanced at her dad, who'd arrived on the bridge with the rest of their group and U-1 at some point during the drama. "What are you sensing from Tersinis?"

"She's struggling with conflicting paradigms. But she knows Ifel just prevented her act of destruction. I get the sense she wants to know why."

That fit with what she was getting from the Ecilam leader.

The troop transport had altered course, no longer moving toward the Ecilam warship. Based on what she was sensing, Maceen and Helotis weren't certain whether Tersinis had fired on the Yruf ships, or on them. The fact that Tersinis had powered down the weapons soon after the torpedoes struck the Yruf ships gave credence to the latter.

For now, Tersinis' daughters seemed content to leave the camouflaged Yruf ships as a solid barrier between them and their mother.

Three of the smaller Yruf ships dropped their camouflage, making that barrier visible. The setting star's light played across the black and gold chevrons that formed a flowing pattern on the emerald-green base of the ships. They were all larger than the warship, but only a fraction of the combined mass of the Yruf ship currently surrounding the Ecilam.

Aurora turned to U-1. "What's Ifel planning to do?"

"Baby steps. Right now she's giving Tersinis time to calm down. How she responds to our visual presence will tell Ifel a lot about how strong the Sovereign's grip is on her. Her recent behavior is disturbing."

"No kidding," Kenji muttered. "She just tried to blow up her kids."

U-1 pivoted a quarter turn. "It's not just that. Unlike Humans, Setarips have no history of killing members of their own clutch or taking their own lives. Tersinis' actions to destroy the transport are completely out of character."

"She might have thought that outcome was preferable to what would happen when she returned to the Sovereign," Aurora pointed out.

Unity swayed, radiating agitation. "You don't understand. Even when cornered, Tersinis wouldn't take her own life, or harm her clutch. She'd fight to the end, or figure out another way to survive. So would the rest of the Ecilam. No Setarip would consider doing what she just tried to do. Ifel's concerned the command to destroy the troop transport was implanted by the Sovereign. If that's true, there might be other commands Tersinis is subject to that could be activated by our presence."

A chill trickled down Aurora's spine. She'd felt Tersinis' conflicting emotions, but she'd made a huge assumption as to the root cause, one Unity had just lit up with flashing neon. She'd been interpreting Tersinis' emotional reactions based on how a Human or

Suulh would respond. She hadn't taken into account the cultural differences that dramatically altered those perceptions. Or the idea that the Sovereign had conditioned Tersinis to take her own life, and the lives of her clutch, if a situation prevented Tersinis from following the Sovereign's orders.

The vise cranked a few turns, squeezing air from her lungs. "How do we handle this?"

"Ifel's not sure. This isn't a scenario she ever planned for."

None of them had. "Now that U-P's onboard her ship, do you think you could take control of the ship's systems to prevent another violent escalation?"

"Probably. But that could force Tersinis to do something drastic we can't stop. If she has a command to take her own life..." Unity let the comment hang in the air like a storm cloud.

Nightmare scenarios scrolled through Aurora's mind. Unity was great at controlling mechanical systems, but there wasn't much U-P could do if Tersinis took a knife to her own throat.

"What about using the ultra-low frequency to incapacitate her," her mom asked.

"That takes time. Now that she knows the Yruf are here, she might figure out what was happening before it knocked her out."

Bringing them back to the nightmare scenarios.

"Ifel thinks it's unlikely the Ecilam are aware of the transmitters or the auto-destructs. They would be as horrified by the concept as we are, and if Tersinis were aware of them, she could have activated the auto-destructs on the transport rather than firing torpedoes at it."

Aurora nodded. "The Etah on Gaia certainly weren't aware of the auto-destructs the Sovereign had planted on their transports." As she'd made her way through the Etah ship, she'd spotted the Etah trying to flee in shuttles. But they'd been blown to bits by the auto-destructs shortly after leaving the ship. With the help of the Suulh, she'd managed to contain the explosion of the auto-destruct in the ship's engine room, but that hadn't saved the flight crew tasked with taking the ship back to Earth after the Sovereign's minions planted new devices.

She blew out a breath. Different day, same twisted machinations. "We've lost the element of surprise. How does Ifel want to approach neutralizing the auto-destructs and sub-q transmitters?"

Unity bobbed closer. "She'd feel more comfortable dealing with the devices if the Ecilam weren't onboard their ships."

"So would I." She knew how devious the Sovereign could be. It was easy to imagine a contingency plan that would kick in as soon as the devices shut down, causing an engine overload or life support failure. "Do you think she could talk Tersinis into meeting her on the planet's surface?"

"That was Ifel's thought, too, but we've analyzed the comm system on Tersinis' ship and it's booby trapped like the transports. We can't establish a safe connection without the system registering the comm as coming from an unknown vessel. If Tersinis opened the connection, that would trigger a signal to the auto-destructs. We should be able to block it, but..."

But that was the very scenario Ifel wanted to avoid — all the Ecilam on the ships when Unity tried to neutralize the auto-destructs. "What about talking to Tersinis through U-P?"

"Ifel's holding onto that as a last resort. Revealing ourselves could have unintended consequences." Unity bobbed. "Ifel's going to take her transport down to the surface. Hopefully Tersinis will follow."

One Hundred Twenty-Eight

Five of Unity's mobile units provided a warm amber glow on the planet's surface, pushing back the nighttime shadows from the center of the wide clearing.

Micah's dad held *Starlet* in a silent hover over the clearing, part of an invisible five-ship formation acting as overwatch for Ifel as she awaited Tersinis and the troop transport. Aurora sat in the co-pilot's seat, his mom in the jump seat, while he and Celia stood behind them. Since he couldn't hear the Ecilam, Aurora's empathic talents were the most helpful in this situation. Birdie and Kai had chosen to watch from *Vengeance*'s bridge.

He spotted Ifel and her guards as they exited the hatch of her transport. Her long strides brought her quickly to the center of the circle of light. She tipped her head back toward the night sky, her guards forming a semi-circle behind her.

His dad dropped *Starlet* another meter, the green circles on the forward display representing the nearby Yruf ships also moving as two red circles approached the clearing.

A darker shadow teased the edge of his vision as Tersinis' transport appeared out of the darkness, settling onto the ground just outside the ring of light. The troop transport followed, although it landed farther out, near the tree line.

Both had hard landings, the birds in the nearby trees rising from their roosts in panicked flight.

It's okay, he reassured them. *They're not here to harm you.*

He heard a mishmash of responses, but most of the birds looped back, settling into the branches again.

Ifel didn't move. Her gaze remained on the two transports, her posture relaxed and welcoming. She looked like she was meeting an old friend, not her opponent in a violent civil war. Then again, Ifel had never participated in that war except to prevent the other factions from harming each other.

Her guards' body language wasn't quite so casual, but they didn't seem particularly concerned, either.

A figure moved just outside the circle of light.

But it wasn't Tersinis. It was Maceen.

She limped forward, her movements tense and jerky as she halted at the outer fringes of the light.

"She's afraid to have her back to Tersinis."

Celia's comment made him turn. "How do you know?"

"Look at where she's standing. She's to Ifel's left, perpendicular to her, not facing her. That way she can keep Ifel *and* Tersinis in her field of view."

Helotis joined her a moment later, remaining just behind her sister's left shoulder. Maceen kept glancing to her left toward Tersinis' transport, rather than at Ifel and the guards.

"They know Tersinis fired on them," Aurora said with surety.

"Uh-huh," Celia agreed.

When Tersinis finally appeared, it was with the two slaves on either side of her, like children clinging to their mother's legs. The sweeping cloak Tersinis wore largely hid the two figures from view, but not enough that he couldn't tell they were working to keep her upright.

Tersinis remained in the shadows at the edge of the light circle, a good ten meters from Ifel.

"Unity, am I correct that all the Ecilam have exited the troop transport?" Aurora asked.

"Yes. They've formed a perimeter to guard the transport, Maceen, and Helotis."

"I'm sensing two Ecilam outside Tersinis' transport, too."

"Those are the two from the warship. They're just behind Tersinis, but they don't seem to be guarding her or the transport."

"Tersinis didn't leave anyone on the warship?"

"No."

"Where's U-P?"

"We're right next to Tersinis."

Aurora leaned forward, studying the scene through the viewport. "She's abandoned the warship and her transport. That's good for our plan, but feels like surrender, which the Ecilam never do."

"Is she hoping Ifel will help her?" Micah asked her.

"I don't think so." Aurora's gaze locked onto the Ecilam leader, who was still standing like an awkward statue, staring at Ifel. "I'm sensing determination from her, not hope. There's a fatalistic quality to her mood, like a soldier charging onto a battlefield when they know they're going to die."

Cheery thought.

"They're communicating in the old language," Unity informed them as Tersinis' mouth moved in a reptilian snarl. "We'll translate."

"I should have known you were here. You're the reason our search was futile. How you must have enjoyed watching us struggle."

Ifel's tongue flicked, her head lowering in a micro-bow. *"I take no pleasure in your pain, Tersinis. I have always sought peace with you. At one time, you expressed similar goals. But the Sovereign changed you."*

Tersinis' head bobbed side to side. *"Only children believe in peace. It does not exist."*

"It does within ourselves if we nurture it. It did with us all, before we allowed our growing differences to split us apart."

"There is no US!"

Even through Unity's translation, Micah heard the sibilant hiss.

Ifel tilted her head to the side. *"You are here."*

"Not because of you. We came for the Etah. Give them to us!"

"That's not really what she wants," Aurora murmured. "Not anymore." Her face scrunched like she was sensing deep pain, then she gave a full body jerk.

Micah's hand darted out, gripping her shoulder. "What is it?"

She swallowed audibly, her gaze shifting from Tersinis, to Maceen and Helotis, then to Ifel. "I need a minute."

Whatever it was, it bothered her. A lot.

"*...could be free of the Sovereign's influence. Free to make your own choices.*"

"*For one so ancient, you comprehend little.*"

"*Perhaps. But I see your unhealed injuries, the children surrounding you and the alien beings beside you. Where is your clutch? Where are your healers and guards?*"

Tersinis attempted to stand straighter, which almost unbalanced her. The two slaves visibly braced to support her. "*I do not answer to you.*"

Ifel was silent for a moment. "*You do not have to answer to the Sovereign, either.*"

"That's it." A huskiness thickened Aurora's voice. "Tersinis doesn't want to be under the Sovereign's thumb anymore. She's self-aware enough to realize the control the Sovereign has been exerting over her. Maybe that awareness was coming on slowly, or it hit all at once when she fired on her daughters' transport against her will. She's accepted that the Sovereign is going to try to kill her. Her daughters, too. By abandoning her ships and staying on the planet, she's trying to make that harder, to force the Sovereign to come to her."

"Which indicates Unity's right that she doesn't know about the sub-q transmitters," Celia pointed out.

Aurora nodded, her gaze sweeping the light circle. "Unity, are you ready to neutralize the auto-destructs on the warship and both transports?"

"Yes."

"How about the sub-q transmitters?"

"We're ready."

Aurora's jaw tightened. "Do it."

One Hundred Twenty-Nine

Libra held her breath, bracing her hands against Aurora's chair. She had no love for the Ecilam, but she had no desire to watch them being murdered by the Sovereign's sadistic devices, either.

Not that she could do anything to prevent it. Tersinis and her daughters had experienced her Sahzade shield when they'd attacked her at Stoneycroft. Even if the Ecilam couldn't see Suulh energy fields like the Yruf could, physically encountering her shield would announce hers and Aurora's presence to the Ecilam, revealing their alliance with the Yruf. Her daughter wouldn't risk it, not with so much at stake with the Sovereign.

The next second lasted a day.

But the transports didn't explode.

And the Ecilam didn't crumple to the ground.

Unity let out a gusty sigh. "We did it."

"The transmitters are disabled?" Aurora's focus remained locked on Tersinis.

"Kinda."

Everyone except Brendan turned to stare at U-1. "What do you mean, kinda?" Libra asked. That sounded like being kinda pregnant.

"The transmitters are still attuned to the signal from the warship and transports, but we're mimicking it. They won't activate as long as we remain in contact with the Ecilam. Hopefully Ifel can convince Tersinis to allow Ahle to remove them, although since the Ecilam don't know the devices exist, getting them to trust her enough to agree could be a challenge."

"What about the warship and transport auto-destructs?" Aurora asked.

"They're no longer a concern."

The collective exhale pushed some of the tension from the cockpit. One hurdle down.

But Aurora's shoulders were still up near her ears. "I wish we knew what might trigger an embedded controlling command, and how to prevent it."

What her daughter really meant is that she wished *she* had a way to prevent it. Libra understood her frustration. Neither of them liked being sideline commanders. "What are Ifel and Tersinis talking about now?"

"*...healers could treat your injuries.*"

"*So that you can capture us, too?*"

Ifel spread her arms, the light shimmering on the scales of her long-fingered hands. "*We did not capture the Etah. We offered them protection when your ship entered the system. They are free to leave our ship whenever they choose.*"

"*As corpses flung into space.*"

Libra shuddered as the imagery rubbed up against her space phobias.

Ifel lowered her head, her spine curving like a snake's. "*We would never harm them. Or you.*"

"*Why should I believe you?*"

Maceen lurched forward. "*Because they protected us from you! You fired on us!*"

Tersinis visibly flinched, but she remained silent, staring at Ifel like they were the only two people in the clearing.

Helotis shuffled to stand beside her sister. "*You have no response? You tried to kill your own offspring and the children of our clutch! Have you gone mad?*"

Tersinis flinched again, her large body swaying. The two slaves struggled to stabilize her, but she stumbled forward, crashing to her knees.

Libra winced as Tersinis pressed a clawed hand to her chest. She never would have expected to feel empathy for the person responsible for destroying her home and nearly killing Marina and Gryphon. But it turned out she was more like her daughter than she'd thought.

Ifel took a step closer. "*You need medical care. Allow us to help you.*"

Tersinis glared at her. "*You are bold now, looking to defeat me when I am weak.*"

Libra wanted to throw up her hands, but Ifel seemed unruffled by Tersinis' obstinance. "*There is no weakness in accepting aid. If you will not do so for yourself, allow us to treat your daughters' injuries.*"

Even though she was on her knees, Tersinis tried to stare Ifel down. When the slaves attempted to lift her onto her feet, she shoved them aside. "*You would take my daughters from me, abandon me to rot!*"

"She is really paranoid," Micah mused.

"She's been dealing with the Sovereign," Aurora replied. "That'll make anyone paranoid."

Ifel studied Tersinis for a moment, then in a graceful move worthy of a prima ballerina, lowered herself to her knees so she and Tersinis were eye-to-eye again. "*I would never take anything from you, Tersinis. Your family is my family. If you wish, we will treat them here.*"

"*You cannot treat us.*" Even through Unity's translation, Maceen's bitterness was evident. "*This is our punishment for failure. If we allow ourselves to be healed, the Sovereign will kill us when we return.*"

Micah glanced at Aurora. "You and Isin were right."

"Unfortunately."

"*The Sovereign will kill us anyway,*" Tersinis hissed. "*Our failure ensures that. But I refuse to allow her trickery to be the cause.*"

Maceen's and Helotis' heads swiveled in perfect unison toward Tersinis.

"*What trickery?*" Maceen asked.

For the first time, Tersinis seemed small. Vulnerable. "*I have failed to protect you.*"

"*What do you mean?*"

Instead of answering, her head drooped, her body curling in on itself.

It was Ifel who responded. "*The Sovereign is a powerful manipulator. Your mother fired on your ship because she was compelled to.*"

Tersinis' head jerked up. "*How do you know?*"

"*I saw it happen, felt your struggle.*" Ifel made a small hand gesture.

U-P appeared, hovering in the open space between Tersinis and Ifel.

All three Ecilam lurched back, struggling to maintain their balance as the movement exacerbated their injuries.

"*Deceiver!*" Tersinis snarled.

"*Guardian,*" Ifel countered. "*The Sovereign planted destructive devices on your ships. We've disabled them to prevent them from killing you. Or us.*"

"*Lies.*"

"*The truth. The last time our ship encountered one of yours, we both lost family when a similar device destroyed the ship we detained.*"

"You murdered them!"

"*No. I watched, helpless, as our families died in the explosion. Others suffered life-threatening injuries. Their pain was my pain. The Sovereign is responsible. She does not value life, only power.*"

Tersinis didn't screech a denial.

"*You know I am correct. She has tortured and executed our families for years.*"

Instead of replying, Tersinis eyed Ifel with a calculating look. "*You are not here because of us. You came for the Etah.*"

"*To speak with them, yes.*"

Aurora inhaled sharply, going rigid in her seat. "Unity, don't—"

"It's okay," Unity cut her off. "Trust us." Then they returned to translating. "*How did you know there were Etah here?*"

"*The same way we have always located our people. We follow the trails you leave behind.*"

One Hundred Thirty

Aurora nearly jumped out of her skin when Tersinis connected the dots. If the Yruf had offered the Etah sanctuary when the Ecilam arrived in the system, that meant the Yruf were in the system *before* the Ecilam.

But Ifel's adept answer to Tersinis' question had deflected the blow that would have torn a hole in her story and drawn a straight line to Aurora.

"After witnessing the Sovereign's disregard for life, I have been hesitant to approach your ships. I would not have revealed our presence here if you had not fired on your own transport."

A knife of anguish stabbed Tersinis' emotional field. Self-loathing followed, overlaying a foundation of burning hatred. But the complex emotional interplay didn't feel directed at Ifel. If anything, it felt like Tersinis was evaluating Ifel's behavior and perhaps judging her as the lesser of two evils. *An enemy of my enemy is my ally* kind of thing.

Ifel's emotions were just as complex, but in a different way. She cared deeply about the Ecilam, particularly Tersinis. The bond reminded Aurora of the emotional tension between a parent and their estranged child, not unlike the contentious relationship she'd had with her own mother. Ifel wanted desperately to reconnect, to find common ground and move forward. But the choice was up to Tersinis.

"What would the Sovereign do to the rest of your clutch if you did not return?"

Tersinis made a noise that was part growl, part hiss. *"Nothing. They follow a new leader now, one who has not failed."*

"You fought a challenge?"

"If you could call it that." The hatred in Tersinis' emotional field flared, along with the shame of remembered humiliation.

But it was her physical pain that scraped at Aurora's senses, growing stronger by the minute.

Ifel's yearning to ease Tersinis' suffering and the suffering of her daughters was a ghostly shadow surrounding her. *"You and your children are in pain. Will you allow my healers to help you?"*

Tersinis resisted. She seemed certain that any move she made would end with her and her daughters being crushed. But she was too much of a survivor to do nothing. *"Treat my daughters, if they agree. I will not go near them."*

"Why not?" Maceen demanded.

Tersinis finally looked at her, her emotional field cracking open. *"I might try to kill you again."*

That backed Maceen up a step.

Ifel rose in one fluid motion. *"We would not allow that to happen."* She took a step closer to Tersinis. *"You know me, Tersinis. You used to believe in me as I believe in you. We both sought peace between our factions. This can be the beginning. But you need treatment first. Do you not wish to be strong when the Sovereign comes searching for you?"*

"Nicely played, Ifel," Celia murmured.

Aurora agreed. Ifel was tapping into Tersinis' pride and desire for retribution, two traits that were overdeveloped in the Ecilam.

Tersinis motioned to her slaves, leaning on them as they eased her back to her feet. "*I will permit it.*" She raised one clawed hand. "*But if you harm my children, I will see the last breath leave your body in agonizing pain as I carve the flesh from your bones.*"

"Ick," Micah muttered. "We could have used a less literal translation, Unity."

"That *was* the less literal translation," Unity replied. "The literal one involved very specific body parts and detailed descriptions of leaking organs and fluids."

"Oh."

One of the Yruf ships dropped its camouflage to *Starlet's* port side, descending to land in the clearing. A light pattern moved across the hull, expanding the illumination near Ifel and her guards. Four Yruf emerged from the craft, walking beside one of the med pods Aurora had seen in the Yruf med bay. She recognized Ahle leading the group, his tan and beige scales tinged with the color playing across the ship's hull.

He halted beside Ifel, then lowered his head in a micro-bow to Tersinis.

The gesture of respect surprised the Ecilam leader. She didn't return it, but it had the desired effect. She motioned to Helotis, who shuffled toward the pod, Maceen at her side.

One of the Yruf on Ahle's team approached Tersinis slowly, what looked like a sling-chair with a diagnostic monitor attached held in front of her. She paused a couple meters away, set up the chair facing the med pod, then retreated.

Tersinis eyed the chair for a moment, like it might snap closed and impale her. But the pain of her injuries and her body's weakness wouldn't allow her to ignore the opportunity for rest. She settled into it with a tangible wave of relief, her slaves kneeling on either side of her, heads bowed.

Aurora sighed. She hadn't realized how much she'd been bracing against Tersinis' emotional storm until it abated.

Her dad glanced over. "Do you want to stay?"

"Are you getting tired?" He'd been working this entire time, keeping *Starlet* hovering while the rest of them watched the proceedings.

"No." A smile creased his cheek. "But it looks like the Ecilam are going to be here for a while. I thought you and Isin might want to take advantage of this time to discuss what comes next, like what's going to happen with the Ecilam warship and what you want to do with the two guests we'd planned to leave on this planet."

"Right." Chances were good the Sovereign would eventually send another ship to the system to check up on Tersinis. Which made what she and Isin should do with Mirko and Manchado a real conundrum. "Let's head back to *Vengeance.*"

One Hundred Thirty-One

Isin walked down the steps of the captain's platform to meet Aurora's family when they entered the bridge. "That went better than I'd anticipated."

Unity had provided visuals on the bridgescreen and a translation through the bridge speakers. Watching the interaction between the two faction leaders had been fascinating. The younger version of himself who'd planned to be a diplomat would have wanted to be in the thick of it.

Scratch that. He *still* would have loved to be in the thick of it.

Aurora nodded. "I have a feeling the Sovereign's punishment plan worked against her. Forcing Tersinis to attempt to murder her own children caused her enough emotional pain that she broke through the manipulative hold the Sovereign had on her. Since Tersinis had a previous relationship with Ifel that was positive, they have a foundation they can build on, assuming Tersinis can continue to fight her conditioning."

Isin folded his arms. "So where does that leave us?"

"Good question. We need a strategy session to consider our options."

"Agreed."

He motioned to Sweep and Fleur to join them, Iolana and Kai following as well as he led the way to the mess hall.

Aurora settled in beside him, everyone else spreading out at the nearby tables to form a rough circle. "Now that Tersinis has abandoned her warship, we have to assume the Sovereign will figure out there's a problem and send someone to investigate. That means we have limited time to decide the best way to deal with that eventuality."

"How do you think the Sovereign would react if she thought the Yruf had captured the Ecilam?" Sweep asked.

"She wouldn't believe it was possible. That's why she implanted the sub-q transmitters, to kill and decompose any of her assets who were no longer in her control. In her view, as soon as the Ecilam were taken from their warship and transports, disconnecting them from the transmitter signal, they'd be wiped out instantly."

"That could work to our advantage," Isin pointed out. "If she found the warship and transports but no sign of the Ecilam, wouldn't she assume the Ecilam were dead and end the search?"

Aurora chewed her lip. "Interesting question. She might, except I don't think she'd accept a scenario in which the Ecilam were abducted but none of her auto-destructs triggered. She's too fond of her booby traps and too convinced of her mental superiority to believe the Yruf could pull that off."

"What if Unity blew up the warships and transports in orbit using the auto-destructs?" Fleur suggested. "It would create a debris field and give credence to the idea all the Ecilam are dead."

U-1 swayed, looking decidedly uncomfortable.

"Is there a problem with that option, Unity?" Isin asked.

"It's just... we would never leave a debris field like that. It's disrespectful. And a waste of resources."

He couldn't imagine anyone else posing that particular objection. That Unity did said a lot about the type of person they were. And the race that had created them.

Aurora nodded. "The last time the Yruf encountered an Ecilam ship and it exploded, the Yruf collected everything."

He rested his forearms on the table. "What if we could make it appear that happened here?"

"You mean blow up the warship and transports and have the Yruf collect the debris?" Micah asked, clearly not in love with the idea.

"Not if we can find a way to simulate it." He glanced at Unity. "Could the Yruf do that somehow? Leave traces that would indicate the ships exploded but the debris was gathered by the Yruf? That would support the idea that the Ecilam all died in the explosion — possibly taking some Yruf with them — and the remaining Yruf gathered the debris, then nabbed the three Etah and left."

"Maybe." Unity bobbed. "We have all the information from our last encounter we could study. We'll start work on ways to produce a plausible facsimile."

"What are we actually going to do with the Ecilam warship and the transports?" Sweep asked. "That warship will leave an engine trail if we fly it out of the system."

"Not a problem," Unity replied. "We'll take the warship and transports onboard our ship. After we pull out all the auto-destructs, of course."

"You'll break them down for reclamation, like you did with *Sphinx*?" Isin asked.

"No. We can store them."

He blinked. "You have bays large enough to fit a warship?" The Ecilam warship wasn't as big as *Vengeance*, but it wasn't small, either.

"Sure." Unity made it sound like it was no big deal.

He hadn't given enough credit to Aurora's comment that the Yruf ship was a small world. Thank the stars the Yruf were pacifists. And on their side. "Good to know."

Libra glanced at Unity. "You're saying Ifel's willing to take all the Ecilam onboard?"

"Of course."

Aurora's brow puckered. "What about the two slaves?"

Unity bobbed. "We'll make sure they're safe and cared for."

"Thank you."

Libra glanced at her daughter. "Which means we wouldn't have to get involved at all."

"Except..." Aurora turned to Isin. "What about Mirko and Manchado?"

He suppressed the groan that pushed against his throat. "There's the rub. If we're setting the scene to fool the Sovereign, we can't leave them on the planet's surface." Much as he would love to. If ever there were people who deserved to be manipulated by the Sovereign, it was those two. But they could do a lot of damage under her thrall, given their sociopathic inclinations. That made it a bad idea for many reasons.

Aurora blew out a breath, her gaze drifting to the overhead in the direction of the brig. "It was going to be a straightforward solution," she muttered, more to herself than the group. "Unity, how long until the *Starhawke* is recharged?"

"Three days."

She made a face that wasn't difficult to interpret. Even if they left now, the *Starhawke* would be mobile before they reached Zeta Tucanae. She clearly disliked the idea of being separated from her ship when it was back in commission, but she wasn't the type to leave their current situation before it was resolved, either.

Her gaze swept the circle. "Anyone have ideas for those two?" She pointed overhead.

Micah looked just as non-plussed as Aurora. Maybe more so. "How about they take the place of Tersinis' slaves?"

Isin caught the slight curve of Aurora's lips before she pressed them into a stern line.

"Tempting, but no. We're not encouraging slavery in any form." Her gaze met Isin's. "How long are you willing to wait here?"

He turned the question back on her, curious where her thoughts were headed. "How long do *you* want to wait here?"

Libra answered the question when Aurora hesitated. "You want to stay until the Sovereign arrives, don't you?"

"It's an option, if Isin is willing. We're on his ship."

He studied her. "If I said no, would you plan to bring the *Starhawke* here as soon as it's available?"

"Yes."

Which meant *Phoenix* would be coming, too. There was zero chance Natasha would let Aurora take on the Sovereign without her. "Then I don't see much point in leaving."

Aurora gave him a wry smile, no doubt coming to the same conclusion. "Probably not."

One Hundred Thirty-Two

"This is beautiful."

Lelindia leaned into the circle of Jonarel's arms as her mom trailed her fingers over the leaves of the camninon tree. The gentle touch released the spicy scent into the air.

Her dad took an appreciative inhale. "Now that's a plant meant for baking," he declared, turning to Daymar. "I'd love to hear what dishes you use it for on Drakar."

"I would be happy to share them with you, though we do not have all the ingredients necessary for some of my birth clan's specialties." Her gaze met Lelindia's. "We can remedy that when you visit the Terfeli compound."

Anticipation bubbled up, making her giddy. She couldn't wait to see Daymar's childhood home, especially after the preview she'd been given while at the Kraed Embassy on Earth. The immersion room had replicated the setting, tantalizing her with glimpses of garden groves and grass-covered hills at the edge of a sparkling sea.

But first she planned to visit Azaana, to reconnect with the Suulh in preparation for Raehn's birth. She couldn't imagine a more perfect setting to bring her daughter into the world than the sonea laanaa on the tropical island, surrounded by the vibrant energy of the Suulh.

She was eager for her parents to meet them, especially Zelle, Paaw, and Maanee. She wanted her mom to have the opportunity to talk to them, since they'd all spent time with Lelindia's grandmother, Breaa, on Feylahn. Hearing the stories would be bittersweet, but it would give her mom a connection to the part of her life that had been ripped away by the Teeli.

She'd contact Aurora to discuss the logistics as soon as *Phoenix* returned and she'd welcomed Captain Montgomery onto the *Starhawke*.

Siginal slid his arm around his mate, gazing into her upturned face before turning to Lelindia. "We can take a shuttle to visit Clan Terfeli first, if you wish."

A smile danced over her lips. Two days ago, Siginal wouldn't have even considered such an offer. He would have insisted they spend time with Clan Clarek first.

But his behavior since the creevigan proved he was taking his mate's feelings into consideration and giving them priority.

Daymar's gaze met hers, a flash of joy that matched Lelindia's brightening the golden depths.

"We'll see how things go," Lelindia hedged. "I'd love to spend ample time at both."

Siginal nodded in approval. "The choice is yours."

Yep, big changes in his attitude.

Tehar appeared on the path. "*Phoenix* has returned. *Gypsy* will be arriving in the shuttle bay shortly."

Lelindia clasped Jonarel's hand in hers. "Let's go welcome our new guest."

Gypsy's familiar form sat comfortably in shuttle bay one, like a recurring guest who had a preferred seat at the table. But Nat wasn't the first one to appear. Instead, Cade, the Admiral, and a dark-haired woman who had to be Captain Montgomery rounded the shuttle's flank. Reynolds, Nat, and U-2 followed, U-2 almost glued to Nat's side.

"Lelindia!" Cade called out. "Happy belated birthday."

"Thanks!" she called back. "Welcome home."

The smile of contentment that creased his face confirmed he did, in fact, consider the *Starhawke* home. But the smile faded, his muscles tensing, as his gaze shifted behind her to Siginal and Daymar.

Cade and Daymar hadn't been in the same room since Academy days when he and Aurora had been dating. And the last time he'd been this close to Siginal, the friction between them had scraped like sandpaper.

Daymar stepped past her, opening her arms and drawing a very startled Cade into a warm hug. "It is good to see you again, Cade," she said loud enough they could all hear her.

Cade returned the hug tentatively, confusion evident in his expression. He kept Siginal in his line of sight as Jonarel's father hugged the Admiral. But his eyes widened to saucers as Daymar released him and Signal moved in. He backed up a step before Signal wrapped him in a bear hug.

"It is good to see you, Cade," Signal echoed Daymar's words.

Lelindia watched them closely, making sure Signal's hug wasn't inflicting any damage on his former adversary, but Cade's body didn't show any signs of trauma.

His expression, however, remained comically baffled as Signal released him. "Uh, thanks. You... too?" It came out more like a question than a statement.

Signal and Daymar turned to Montgomery, but neither moved to hug her. And with good reason. She was giving off strong *no hugging* vibes, her spine straight, her no-nonsense gaze direct.

"Signal, Daymar, Jonarel," the Admiral said smoothly, indicating each of them in turn, "it's my pleasure to introduce you to Captain Colleen Montgomery. Colleen, may I introduce Ambassador Signal Clarek, his mate, Daymar, and their son, Jonarel."

Montgomery shook hands with each of them. "I'm familiar with you by reputation, of course." Her gaze lingered on Jonarel. "It must have been a unique experience to be the only Kraed to attend the Academy and serve in the Fleet."

"It was," Jonarel agreed.

Montgomery's gaze moved to her, noting as Jonarel's arm slipped around her waist, his hand resting against the side of her rounded belly. She didn't seem surprised by the action, indicating her parents had talked about her and Jonarel while on *Phoenix*. "You must be Lelindia."

She accepted Montgomery's offered handshake. It was firm and respectful. "It's a pleasure to meet you."

"And you."

"How are you feeling, Colleen?" Lelindia's mom asked, moving next to Lelindia.

Montgomery's tough exterior softened a fraction. "Better than I have in years, thanks to you."

Her mom's friendly smile didn't match Montgomery's reserved demeanor. The dissonance made her curious about how Montgomery had behaved toward her parents while on *Phoenix*.

She'd have to ask her mom about it later. "Hey, Nat." The pilot had moved next to Cade, U-2 between them. "Glad to have you back."

"Thanks." Nat hooked her thumbs in the front pockets of her cargo pants as she studied Siginal and Daymar, who were gazing at her with curiosity, too.

"Siginal, Daymar, I'd like you to meet Natasha Orlov, owner and captain of *Phoenix*, and a dear friend of the crew."

Nat's cheeks turned a little pink. "That's a beauty of a ship you have there." She nodded in the direction of the *Rowkclarek*. "Can it camouflage like the *Starhawke?*"

Siginal's eyes lit up at the praise. "It can."

"Handy."

"Indeed."

A soft snort from Cade turned into a cough that he covered with his hand.

Lelindia fought her own smile. "Nat, can you stay for a while, or do you need to get back to *Phoenix*?"

Nat rocked on her heels. "I've got time."

She'd had a feeling that would be her answer.

After she introduced Reynolds to Daymar, she turned to her parents. "Would you be willing to show Captain Montgomery to her cabin so she can get settled in? She's next to you in G8."

Her dad smiled. "Absolutely. Come with us, Colleen. There's a lot to see on this ship."

"I'm going to stow my things on *Gladiator*." Reynolds followed the other three out through the hatch.

As it closed behind them, Nat let out a weighty sigh, her neck and shoulders relaxing.

Lelindia peered at her. "That sigh sounds like there's a story attached."

"There is." Nat's gaze flicked to U-2, who also somehow managed to look relieved.

"Then I suggest we gather in the lounge and enjoy pieces of my birthday cake while you tell it."

Ten minutes later they were all seated in the observation lounge, enjoying the chocolaty goodness while Nat, Cade, and the

Admiral recounted the issue they'd run into regarding Montgomery's hatred of A.I.

Lelindia frowned. "That's unfortunate, considering she'll be staying with us for the foreseeable future. I'm assuming that attitude would extend to Tehar, too?"

Siginal looked at her in alarm, his gaze darting to Nat.

Lelindia waved off his concern. "Nat already knows about Tehar. She chose to reveal herself when Nat met Unity for the first time."

His eyes widened even more.

"You're talking about Star?" Nat clarified.

Lelindia nodded. "Tehar is her Nirunoc name. Star is her ship name."

Nat nodded, her focus on Siginal, who looked ready to hyperventilate. "I understand how important her safety and the safety of her secret is to you. I would never betray the trust Star and Aurora placed in me."

Siginal moved his mouth like a fish, but nothing came out.

"We believe you," Daymar replied when Siginal remained at a loss. "Aurora chooses her friends with great care. So does our daughter. Their faith in you shows the kind of person you are."

Nat's cheeks flushed pink again. "Aurora saved my life. She and Pops..." Her gaze flitted to the Admiral and held. She swallowed audibly. "They're important to me."

"As you are to us," the Admiral replied.

Nat's blush deepened. She looked like she wanted to both hug the Admiral and crawl under the table to hide her embarrassment.

"What about me?" Cade batted his lashes at her.

Nat grinned, the emotional tension breaking just as Cade no doubt intended. "You're all right."

"All right?" He gasped in mock pain. "Damning me with faint praise."

Lelindia chuckled. "I see you two got along just fine during this mission."

Cade winked at Nat. "We did alright."

The Admiral smiled. "I think I missed out on some of the fun. You'll have to—"

Tehar appeared beside the table, her face drawn tight.

Lelindia's stomach did a somersault at her stricken expression. "What's wrong?"

"I just received an emergency message from Soileshun."

Her mind raced. The name sounded familiar, but...

"He's the Nirunoc at the Kraed Embassy," Tehar clarified.

Of course. She'd met him during her visit there. He was a member of Clan Terfeli, part of Daymar's and Remar's extended family.

"The Embassy is under attack by armed protestors." The look of near panic on Tehar's face ratcheted up the tension in the room. "They broke into the building, shouting threats about killing any Kraed they encountered. Remar has ordered a complete evacuation."

Her heart thumped like a bass drum. "They're evacuating the building?"

"They're evacuating from the planet."

One Hundred Thirty-Three

Aurora had only managed two hours of sleep, and those two hours had been filled with disturbing dreams of zombie-like Ecilam and a cloaked figure stalking her through a thick jungle. With each stumbling step her energy field had faded, her shield weakening the closer they got to grabbing her. She'd woken more exhausted than when she'd laid down, then spent another two hours staring into the semi-darkness as she ran through an endless loop of *what if* scenarios.

The Sovereign would definitely come when she lost contact with Tersinis. Her investment in Tersinis' suffering would ensure that. At the very least, she'd send ships to investigate and haul Tersinis back for questioning. Either way, it would give Aurora a chance to confront her enemy, whether it was here or after the Yruf tracked the Sovereign's ships back to the source.

If the *Starhawke* arrived before either of those things happened, so much the better. She'd be in a stronger position on the bridge of her ship than as a passenger on *Vengeance.*

But that left the question of what to do with *Vengeance* and *Phoenix.* Nat and Isin weren't going to sit out whatever confrontation was coming, but their ships couldn't camouflage like the *Starhawke* and Yruf ships, and *Phoenix* didn't have the kind of hull plating protection that *Gladiator* and *Vengeance* did.

The memory of *Phoenix's* hull bleeding debris into the void made her sick to her stomach. She couldn't go through that again, not when it could cost Nat her life. And if she was worrying about Nat during the confrontation, she wouldn't be able to focus on the Sovereign the way she needed to.

"Anybody else not sleeping?" Iolana whispered from the bunk above her.

A snort was Micah's response, while Celia turned her head, meeting Aurora's gaze.

"Guess that answers that question," Aurora commented, pushing the blanket aside and sitting up. Now that Iolana had pulled her out of her thoughts, she registered the emotional resonances of the three people in the cabin across from them, too. "Looks like a case of group insomnia."

"Yeah." Iolana dropped to the deck, smoothing her hair with her fingers. "What I wouldn't give for a surfboard and a wave to ride right now."

"I second that," Micah agreed, peering over the edge of his bunk at Celia. "Good morning."

Celia gazed back. "I don't think it's morning yet."

He snagged his comband from where he'd looped it around one of the metal posts and tapped the display. "It's two hours until dawn for our orbit, so technically it *is* morning." He hopped off his bunk, landing with a soft thump. "Birdie and I are used to early mornings, catching waves before work."

Remorse smacked Aurora in the solar plexus. She was the reason her brother wasn't living that life anymore. Iolana, too. If she hadn't sought her dad out to help her with controlling her physical reactions to the Necri and Suulh, they could both be enjoying that life right now.

"Knock it off, sis." Micah scowled at her.

"What?"

Snagging her hand, he pulled her to her feet and slung an arm around her shoulders. "You're feeling bad because Birdie and I can't surf on a starship."

She grimaced, but didn't contradict him.

"What you're forgetting is we're meeting aliens, exploring new planets, and helping to save the Union because we *are* on a starship."

"That's right," Iolana agreed. "I miss the waves, but this..." She gestured around them. "Is way more important. No regrets."

"You're sure?" Because she hated the idea that she'd unintentionally made their life path decisions for them.

Iolana chuckled. "Aren't you the empath? Couldn't you tell if we were lying to you?"

"Well... yes."

"Good. Then let's get moving. I call first in the bathroom."

Aurora's parents and Kai were already in the galley by the time the four of them arrived. The group worked in easy harmony, putting together a simple breakfast of oatmeal with nuts and cut-up berries.

"What's happening on the surface?" Aurora asked U-1 as she carried her bowl into the mess hall.

"Maceen and Helotis have gone through their first sequence of treatments for their injuries. Tersinis has refused to be treated until both her daughters are on the mend. Ahle has done what he can to stabilize her condition, but her unwillingness to sleep is inhibiting his efforts."

"Won't she eventually fall asleep from exhaustion?" Kai asked.

"Eventually, but the Ecilam don't require as much sleep as Humans. It could be another day before she's unable to remain conscious."

Micah nudged Aurora with his elbow. "Hey, sis, I think we've found someone who's more stubborn than you."

She stuck her tongue out at him. The happy sound of his laughter gave her an emotional lift. "How are the engineers com—" She cut off as Unity started bobbing up and down frantically.

"You need to get to the bridge. Now!"

Years of Fleet training had her out of her seat and into the corridor in a heartbeat, Celia right with her. They led the mad dash up the forward stairs and onto the bridge.

She skidded to a stop, whirling in a circle, searching the bridgescreen for what had prompted Unity's panic. And froze at the chaotic images playing like horror vids across the screen.

"...under attack," a frantic voice shouted over the roar of destruction.

"...breached our defenses!"

"...weapons aren't responding."

"...help us!" A woman's pained scream cut off abruptly.

Her gaze snagged on a set of brightly colored streamers flapping in the wind, their edges aglow with flame.

She recognized them, had seen them many times during shore leave while serving on the *Argo*. "Is that... Osiris?"

"Yes," Isin growled.

She hadn't even noticed him standing on the captain's platform.

Unity hovered beside her. "These are images from the planet's emergency distress signal. We're receiving them on the *Argo*."

Which meant this was happening in real time, right now. "Is the *Argo* close to Osiris?"

U-1 touched her shoulder, as if drawing comfort from her nearness. "No."

"How—" She had to clear her throat as dread squeezed her vocal cords. "How long until they get there?"

"Current estimate is seven hours, thirty-four minutes and eight seconds."

The grip on her throat almost cut off her air. "Who's attacking?"

The images changed to scattered orbital views of the starscape. Ships — a *lot* of ships — formed a battle line, bombarding the planet from above.

She recognized the design. These ships were bigger, more menacing, but the exterior matched the warship orbiting Tnaryt's Camp.

A glacial chill spread through her limbs and torso, turning her to ice.

Now they knew where the Sovereign had sent the rest of the Ecilam.

Captain's Log

Libra brings balance

I was more than halfway through the writing of this book before I realized Libra needed a point of view. That's hard for me to imagine now, seeing how the story turned out. But that's one of the quirks of discovery writing. Sometimes a piece drops into your lap when you least expect it.

The first time I'd written in her POV was for a short story titled GUARDIAN about the Ecilam attack on Stoneycroft. I included that story as a bonus feature in THE LEGACY OF TOMORROW. It was during the writing of that story and GUARDIAN MATE, the sci-fi romance where I explored how Libra and Brendan met, that Libra began to reveal herself to me — who she had been born to become, how her experiences had altered her trajectory, and the heartbreaking challenges she'd faced to keep her family safe from the Teeli. Bringing her in with a POV in this story allowed me to delve into her insights during Aurora's training and the emotional contradictions she struggled to reconcile during the confrontation with the Ecilam.

Her bravery in facing her past and her willingness to reevaluate her beliefs, especially regarding the Ecilam, earned her a place of honor on the cover.

Nat's mother

I've long wondered about Nat's history – what series of events left her an orphan who never knew her father and who had no ties to friends or her past. Nat's been avoiding telling me ever since the day we met, and I've respected her reticence.

Which is why I was floored when she suddenly opened up to Itorye. Nothing about that scene was planned, not Itorye's revelations about her upbringing, not Nat's decision to talk about her mom, and certainly not the tragic tale of her mom's death. Until Nat opened her mouth, I had no idea what she was going to say. Writing that scene, I was madly taking dictation, just keeping up with Nat as the words flowed. I'll admit a few tears flowed, too.

I've adored Nat from the first moment she took her place in the Starhawke Universe, but that moment, that vulnerability, made me love and cherish her even more.

Daymar's rage

I've had a single line in my notes ever since THE SIEGE OF ALLIANCE that asked, "Does Daymar ever get to see the recording of Lelindia and Jonarel's mating ceremony?" In this book, I finally learned the answer. But it wasn't until Lelindia and Daymar were standing in the corridor together, about to watch the recording, that I discovered something else. Daymar's experience of the past few months had been a LOT different from Siginal's.

Daymar's suppressed rage came out of nowhere, which made me turn my head and take another look at her and ask why. The answer scorched the page, the depths of her fury altering the narrative, revealing how much Signal had been denying the reality of how his actions had impacted her.

The scenes that followed practically wrote themselves. The creevigan was one of my favorites to write. It showed depths to Daymar and Siginal that I'd never plumbed before. Delving into Siginal's weaknesses as a mate and a leader, and pushing him to grow out of his comfort zone was a joy. I can't wait to see how their relationship will develop when Raehn finally makes her debut.

Montgomery's prejudice

Montgomery's reaction to Unity was another surprise I didn't see coming. I didn't have a plan for it, and wasn't sure how to deal with it when it happened. I'd had a picture in my head of who Montgomery was for a long time, one I refined during the writing of THE EXILE OF JUSTICE when I thought she was going to testify at the Admiral's trial. That scene ended up being cut, but it gave me a solid foundation for her character.

That vision of her remained strong when she first came on the scene at Hydra One. I loved Nat's description of her — crusty, strong-willed, and hard-nosed. She's tough but fair, firm but kind, a fighter who never quits, who's willing to lay down her life for her crew and the ideals of the Union. In a pitched battle, you want her on your side.

Which is what made her reaction to Unity so unexpected and in some ways, tough to write. She was the first person to not only distrust Unity, but hate them on a base level that no amount of logic could touch. It forced me to reevaluate my assumptions about her and her past, which also gave me insights into where her prejudices were coming from. I have no idea how she and Unity will learn to co-exist, but their interactions will keep me on my toes.

The future (and past) of A.I.

This deep into the series, you've no doubt figured out my attitude towards A.I. Ideologically, I think their potential is amazing. Star, Unity, and Alec would agree with me. But I have caveats regarding our current use of A.I., the two biggies being the energy consumption they require, which is astronomically supercharging our climate crisis, and their control by mega-corporations who care only about profits at the expense of everything and everyone else.

I could easily see this setup leading down the path Cade told Unity about, where A.I. gains sentience and decides to abandon us in favor of self-governance, plunging us into a dark age as we struggle to function without them. I can also see the climate crisis being exacerbated by A.I. dependence, pushing us toward an extinction-level event.

However, I'm an optimist by nature, which is why I describe my writing as hopeful sci-fi or hopepunk. Each of us can make a difference through the choices we make every day, every hour. Those choices accumulate, for good or evil, creation or destruction. It's our choice. To quote from one of my favorite movies, "Choose wisely."

Enjoy the journey!
Audrey

Bestselling science fiction author Audrey Sharpe grew up believing in the Force and dreaming of becoming captain of the *Enterprise*. She's still working out the logistics of FTL travel and transporters but writing science fiction creates her own private holodeck. Her award-winning first novel, *The Dark of Light*, launched the Starhawke Universe, which has expanded to more than a dozen books, including two sci-fi romances. Her books feature strong female characters, swoon-worthy aliens, and epic battles of good versus evil. When she's not off exploring the galaxy with Aurora and her crew, she lives in the Sonoran Desert, where she has an excellent view of the stars.

Discover a future of possibilities with Audrey in the Starhawke Universe. Visit her website and join the crew!

AUDREYSHARPE.COM